The Snake Eater
The Seventh Enemy
Close to the Bone

A Brady Coyne Omnibus

ALSO BY WILLIAM G. TAPPLY

THE BRADY COYNE NOVELS

Scar Tissue
Muscle Memory
Cutter's Run
Tight Lines
The Spotted Cats
Client Privilege
Dead Winter
A Void in Hearts
The Vulgar Boatman
Dead Meat
The Marine Corpse
Follow the Sharks
The Dutch Blue Error
Death at Charity's Point

NONFICTION

The Elements of Mystery Fiction
Sportsman's Legacy
Home Water
Opening Day and Other Neuroses
Those Hours Spent Outdoors

OTHER FICTION

Thicker Than Water (with Linda Barlow)

The Snake Eater
The Seventh Enemy
Close to the Bone

A BRADY COYNE OMNIBUS

William G. Tapply

St. Martin's Minotaur
New York

www.minotaurbooks.com

ISBN 0-312-26778-9

The Snake Eater was first published in the United States in 1993 by Otto Penzler Books, Macmillan Publishing Company.

The Seventh Enemy was first published in the United States in 1995 by Otto Penzler Books, Simon & Schuster Inc.

Close to the Bone was first published in the United States in 1996 by Thomas Dunne Books, an imprint of St. Martin's Press.

First St. Martin's Minotaur Edition: October 2000

10 9 8 7 6 5 4 3 2 1

THE SNAKE EATER

For Michael

ACKNOWLEDGMENTS

A writer feeds off the love and understanding of family and friends during the long self-absorbed process of novel-making. He is generally not good company. My kids, for some reason, seem to love me no matter how weird I get. My writing group keeps reminding me that it's supposed to be hard. Andy Gill, Elliot Schildkrout, Steve Cooper, Randy Paulsen, and Jon Kolb just pour me a Daniel's, deal another hand, tell trout stories, and, in a pinch, analyze my dreams.

For their indispensable help with this manuscript, I also want to thank Jane Rabe, Rick Boyer, Betsy Rapoport, Alcinda VanDeurson, Jed Mattes, and Michele Slung.

PROLOGUE

He should've taken a taxi.

That was his first thought after he completed his descent and began to shoulder through the bodies toward the front of the platform.

He held his briefcase flat against his crotch, like a shield. Women aren't the only ones who have to watch out for subway gropers. He'd learned that from personal experience.

As he wedged his way forward, the bodies closed in around him. Old, young, black, white, male, female. Not people. Just bodies. And as the bodies closed in, so did their heat. And their odors, all mingled, the stench of a hundred human bodies, smells of sex and anxiety and fear, farts and urine and sweat and booze and garlic all mixed in a disgusting stew of human stink.

He tried breathing through his mouth. The odors became tastes. He was afraid he might gag.

He tugged at the knot in his necktie, felt dribbles of

sweat begin to trickle down his sides, dampen the insides of his thighs, soak the back of his shirt under his linen jacket.

He pulled the briefcase tighter against him, grateful for the thin but comforting barrier.

The crush of bodies around him forced him up against a man who stood solid and unmovable in front of him. He was a head taller, this man, with a brown neck as thick as a telephone pole and a shaved brown scalp that glistened in the piss-colored light. Another body nudged him from behind, then settled against him. More bodies, bodies on both sides, bodies everywhere. They pressed his arms against his sides, holding him immobile with the heavy briefcase tight against his middle.

It was oddly silent there beneath the street. Some muffled human sounds. Breathing, grunting. No distinguishable voices. Distant mechanical sounds. Somewhere on the platform a radio. Rock music and static.

Why in hell hadn't he taken a taxi?

He felt the vibrations through the soles of his feet. As the tremoring grew, the crowd seemed to shake itself like a dog in a dream, muttering, twitching its separate parts to separate rhythms as it came awake, and then he heard the rumble, and it became a roar, and with it the metal-on-metal screech as the train approached the platform.

Thank God.

The bodies pressed tighter against him, forcing his face up against the damp shirt of the enormous man in front of him.

A hand snaked around from behind him, then an arm half encircled him. A forearm against his chest forced the top half of his body backward. And an odd pinprick low on his back, and then—

Oh, Jesus! A shaft of pain, sudden, searing, unbearable. He threw back his head, he opened his mouth, he knew he screamed. He heard nothing but the metallic squeal of brakes and the hiss and rumble of the engine. He screamed again and again as a red-hot arrow of indescribable pain burned toward his heart and bodies surged around him and the train roared and screeched.

That arm around his chest held him impaled on his pain. His knees buckled. His legs were suddenly cold, numb. He became detached from his body. He felt himself float above the crowd and drift there, separate now from the mob, looking down at them, looking down at himself and his pain.

But he saw only fog.

He had the urge to laugh. He instantly forgot why.

A gentle voice in his ear said, "Thank you. I'll take that." The briefcase. It was gone. His shield. Now his groin—

Another pain, quick and hard, rammed into the core of his soul, and with that ramrod of pain came the understanding of what that kind of pain meant.

The sudden urge to vomit. No strength for it. And then he felt himself spinning, spiraling.

The bottom half of his body began to melt. A snowman on a hot sidewalk. So that's how it felt to be dying.

To be dying.

Christ. Oh good Jesus Christ forever and ever world without end amen.

The book. The damn book.

It's true.

If he could just remain upright he wouldn't die. Nobody died standing up. That's true, isn't it? He tried to lift his hands, to grab the shoulder of the big man in front of him, something to hang on to, to keep him upright, to keep him alive. But his fingers were numb and his arms refused to move. He felt himself tilt sideways, settle momentarily against the man's broad, wet back, slip, slide, collapse.

Where are you, honey? Sweetheart? Are you there?

They were stepping around him, avoiding him. From somewhere far away he heard a woman's voice. "See? The bums are wearing neckties these days. Banker, lawyer, ha? High roller from Wall Street, ha? See? That's what's happening to them."

His mind formed the words "Help me." He thought he spoke those words. He couldn't hear his own voice. Couldn't hear anything. Just a hum, growing fainter.

Should've taken a taxi. . . .

1

It was the summer's first heat wave, and I was putting my pinstripe away for the weekend when Charlie McDevitt called.

"Coyne," I said. I wedged the phone against my shoulder and sat on the edge of my bed to tug at my pantlegs.

"Hey," he said.

"What's up?"

"Friend of mine needs a lawyer."

"I litigate, therefore I am," I said. "My motto."

"Ha," he said. "I know you. You take on new clients the way Red Auerbach signs rejects off the waiver wire."

"Rarely," I said. "You're right."

"Anyway, this one's criminal, not civil. But he needs you."

"Tell me." I dropped my pants in a heap on the floor. I lay back on my bed and lit a cigarette.

Charlie cleared his throat. "Guy name of Daniel

McCloud got picked up this afternoon in Wilson Falls, charged with possession, possession with intent, and trafficking."

"Where in hell is Wilson Falls?"

"Little nothing town out in the Connecticut Valley. More or less across the river from Northampton."

"They holding him?"

"Yes. Arraignment won't be till Monday."

"Was he?"

"What, trafficking?"

"Yes. Was he trafficking?"

"He grew marijuana in his backyard. The cops came with a warrant, ripped up his garden, filled several trash bags. Not to mention all the incriminating odds and ends they found in the house."

"Trafficking includes cultivation," I said. "Fifty pounds means trafficking. That's a felony worth two-and-a-half to fifteen. Must've been a major-league garden. What about priors?"

"One year suspended in '79 for possession. He also admitted to sufficient facts in '76. That's supposed to be sealed, of course, but . . ."

"But," I said, "the court sees it on his record anyway. Which makes this his third time up." I paused to stub out my cigarette, then said, "Sorry, pal. No deal. Friend or no friend, I'm not defending some drug dealer. I don't need that kind of business."

"He's no dealer, Brady. He grows it for himself. He's sick. It helps him. It's the only thing that helps him."

"Sure."

"Really," said Charlie. "Daniel doesn't deal. He needs you. This is a favor for me."

"He needs a good criminal lawyer, all right," I said. "So why me?"

"You'll like Daniel. And you're good."

"Christ, you know how much criminal work I've done lately?"

"I know what you *can* do, Brady. All those wills and divorces must drive you batshit after a while."

"That they do. So what's this Daniel McCloud to you?"

"He's just this quiet guy from Georgia who tried to get some money out of Uncle Sam, which is how I met him. He spent six years in the jungles of Indochina, got himself Agent Oranged, and not a penny for his misery. He runs a little bait-and-tackle shop on the banks of the Connecticut, likes to fish and hunt and hang out in the woods. Prison would kill him. Literally."

"And they nailed him growing fifty pounds of marijuana?"

"Looks that way."

"I don't know what the hell you expect me to do."

"You can start by getting him out on bail."

"Wilson Falls," I said, "is a long drive from Boston."

"So you'd better get an early start," said Charlie.

"Um," I said. "Tell me something."

"What's that?"

"This is one of your *pro bono* deals, right?"

"Nope."

"He can afford me?"

"I think so, yes."

"Be damned," I muttered.

A cop brought Daniel McCloud into the little conference room in the Wilson Falls police station on Saturday morning. He sat down at the scarred wooden table and looked at me without curiosity, gratitude, anger, or fear. Without, in fact, any expression whatsoever. Except, maybe, patience.

I held my hand to him. "Brady Coyne. I'm a lawyer."

He took my hand briefly. His handshake was neither robust nor enthusiastic, but I sensed great strength in it. He said nothing.

"Charlie McDevitt asked me to come," I said.

"Charlie." He nodded. "A good man."

"He didn't call me until about seven last night. This was the earliest I could make it."

He shrugged.

"I hope you weren't worried?"

"Worried?"

"You know . . ."

"I was waiting." He said it as if waiting and worrying were not activities that could be conducted simultaneously.

"Did you sleep okay?"

"Nay. I didn't sleep at all. I hardly ever do."

"I won't be able to get you out of here until Monday," I said. "They don't do arraignments on weekends."

"I know that," said Daniel. "That's why they waited until Friday afternoon to come for me. It's that farkin' Oakley."

"Oakley?"

"The cop who arrested me."

"What about him?"

Daniel jerked one shoulder in a shrug. "He didn't have to wait until Friday afternoon. You see?"

He spoke softly, and I thought I detected just the hint of a Scottish burr mingling into his southern drawl. His voice was almost musical.

I shrugged. "I'm not sure."

"He doesn't like me."

"Why not?"

He shook his head. "I don't know. Maybe it's that my woman is black. See, Mr. Coyne, Wilson Falls is a small town. Everybody knows everybody else. Who they live with. What they grow in their garden. How much they'd enjoy a weekend in jail. He could've arrested me anytime."

"Well, regardless of all that," I said, "the first thing we've got to do is get you out of here. Can you get your hands on some cash?"

"I have some resources." He smiled. He had, I noticed, terrible teeth. They were gray and stubbed and gapped. Several were missing. Later he would tell me, "You sometimes forget to floss regularly in the jungle."

"I'll try to get you out on personal recognizance," I told him. "I doubt if it will work. They'll want to go high. The courts are making examples of their drug cases these days. I'll need to know some things."

"I could use a smoke," Daniel said suddenly.

"Oh, I'm sorry." I put my pack of Winstons onto the table. "Help yourself."

He glanced down at the cigarettes, then looked up at me and shrugged.

"Oh, Christ," I said. "You can't smoke that stuff here."

"It's my medicine," he said, and that's when I first noticed that beneath the table that separated us his right leg was jiggling furiously. I looked hard into his face and saw a tiny muscle twitching and jumping at the corner of his eye. Behind his mask of calm, Daniel McCloud was, I realized, in agony.

"Charlie told me you encountered Agent Orange over there."

"Aye."

"That's how you met him?"

"Yes. We thought our government would want to take care of us."

"And it didn't work out."

"We got nowhere. Charlie tried to help. Good fella, Charlie."

"We?"

He shrugged. "Sweeney and I. Sweeney's one of my buddies. We were S.F. together, got burned together, and —"

"S.F.?" I blurted.

He smiled. "S.F. Special Forces."

"You were a Green Beret?"

He rolled his eyes. "We *wore* the farkin' hats. A green beret is a hat, and it's a book and a movie and a song. But it's not a man. We didn't even like 'em. Nobody put 'em on except when they had to. Anyway, Sweeney and I tried to get some medical help from the government. But we didn't have cancer, we weren't dead, or even, as far as they would admit, dying. We couldn't prove what we got was from the Orange. So we had no case."

"And marijuana helps you."

"Aye. It helps the itching and the pain. It's the only thing that helps."

"How do you feel now?"

"Right this minute?"

"Yes."

He exhaled deeply. "It's driving me crazy, Mr. Coyne."

"How much do you smoke?"

"I need six to eight sticks a day."

"My God!"

He shrugged. Daniel shrugged often, I was beginning to notice. It seemed to be his primary form of expression. When he shrugged, he gave his shoulders a tiny twitch and darted his eyes upward. It wasn't a very dramatic shrug. "It's the only thing that'll help," he said.

"What about the trafficking charge?" I said. "Do you sell it?"

He leaned across the table and gave me a hard look. "I smoke it. What do you think I am?"

"A drug dealer, of course."

"Never," he said quietly.

I shrugged. "Charlie told me you had money."

"Aye. I have some. That's not where I got it."

"If I'm going to represent you, I've got to know."

He peered at me, then nodded. "I don't sell it, Mr. Coyne."

"Do you share it? The grass?"

"Aye. With Sweeney. He needs it, too, same as me.

And sometimes Cammie. She's my woman. Just a stick now and then. She keeps me company with it."

Daniel McCloud did not fit my mental image of a Green Beret. He stood no more than five-eight, and he looked overweight in his baggy chino pants. His sandy hair was thin and uncombed, his face pockmarked, and his eyes were a washed-out blue. He wore steel-rimmed glasses. I guessed he was in his late forties, although he looked ten years older than that.

He looked like a lot of other country boys I have known who get old early in life.

He also looked like a man with a terrible disease who had spent a sleepless night in jail without his medicine.

"At the arraignment Monday," I said, "I'll have to argue for reasonable bail. I need to know some things."

He nodded.

"How long have you lived in Wilson Falls?"

"Almost twenty years."

"Own your own home?"

"Aye."

"And a business?"

"I've got a shop. I sell bait and tackle, bow-hunting stuff."

"You're a fisherman?"

He smiled. "Aye. I grew up in the outdoors."

"I love fishing myself. Fly-fishing, mostly. Fly-fishing for trout."

"I look at it a little different," he said. "I go after whatever is there, and I catch 'em any way I can. I like to improvise. Same way I hunt. Bow 'n' arrows, snares, slingshots.

It's how I was brought up." He closed his eyes for a moment. When he opened them, I saw in them for the first time a hint of feeling, something other than the pain, although I couldn't identify that feeling. Wistfulness, maybe. Or loneliness. "My daddy was a poacher down in Monroe, Georgia," he said softly. "He taught me the woods. He killed deer with bows and arrows and spears he made himself, so the wardens wouldn't hear him. They all knew he did it. But he never once got caught. That was the fun he got out of it. That was his sport. Outwitting the wardens. Fishing and hunting weren't sports for him. He was a Scotsman. Knew the value of things. My daddy took game and fish when he needed it to feed us. Never more, never less. He taught me how to survive in the woods. I knew all about survival before I ever got to Fort Bragg. How to eat whatever you could find, how to disguise your smell, how to be invisible, how to distinguish all the different sounds in the woods, what it means when there are no sounds. My daddy made me eat bugs when I was six. After bugs, any kind of meat's pretty good. Better when you can cook it, but good anytime." Daniel shrugged. "He used to tell me, 'Son,' he'd say, 'they make the farkin' law because they need general guidelines. They try to hit an average with it. But that don't mean it's right for a particular person. Maybe a deer a year per man is a good guideline. But it ain't right for us. You've got to figger what's right for you. That's your law.'"

He looked at me and smiled. He was, after his fashion, giving me his defense. I guessed this was a long speech for Daniel McCloud.

"Like growing your own marijuana," I said. "That's your law."

He shook his head. "God's law. Not mine. My daddy told me that if it don't hurt anybody else, and it helps you, then it's God's law you should do it. He never broke God's law. Shit, neither did I. I guess we both broke man's law some. Difference is, my daddy never got caught."

We talked a while longer. Daniel told me what I needed to know to handle his arraignment on Monday. I tried to explain how it would go. "We'll wait around for a long time. Eventually it'll be your turn. They'll read the charges against you. We'll argue about your bail. The judge will set it, and if you can make it you'll be released. Then you and I can start thinking about the probable-cause hearing."

I told him they'd bring him to the district court in Northampton on Monday morning and I'd meet him there. I told him it was a lousy deal that he had to spend the weekend in jail, that if he'd been arrested any day but Friday or Saturday he'd be arraigned and out on bail the next day. He repeated that he knew "that farkin' Oakley" had come for him on Friday afternoon on purpose, because he had it in for him and wanted him to suffer. I asked him if he was suffering. He nodded and said yes, as a matter of fact, he was suffering terribly, and he said it in such a way to make me understand that he was familiar with suffering and tried not to let it bother him. I asked him if I could bring him something. The only thing that would help, he said, would be a few sticks of cannabis.

I told him I didn't think I'd be able to do that for him.

When we stood up and shook hands, Daniel said, "Can you get me out of here?"

I hesitated. Bail would come high. But I nodded and said, "Sure."

The smile he gave me showed me what I hadn't seen before—that Daniel McCloud, survivor of the terrors of the Southeast Asia jungles, was scared.

2

I arrived at the Northampton District Court on Monday morning for the nine o'clock criminal session. I sat on one of the benches among the lawyers, witnesses, and accused citizens, feeling tired and headachy from getting up early and driving the two hours from Boston to Northampton—a long straight monotonous shot out the Mass Pike to Springfield, then a quick jog north on 91.

I wished I'd had the foresight to sneak a cup of coffee into the courtroom with me.

At the table in front of the bench the clerk shuffled a large stack of manila folders. A pair of probation officers whispered at their table.

About ten after nine a uniformed officer led six or eight bleary-eyed men into the prisoners' dock. Daniel was the last of them. He looked out of place among the others, young men all, the weekend collection of lockups. Sobriety test and Breathalyzer flunkees, I guessed.

I jerked my chin at Daniel. He nodded to me.

His leg, I observed, was jiggling madly.

Then a side door opened and the judge came in. One of the officers said, "All rise."

We all rose.

A voice from the back of the courtroom mumbled, "Hear ye, hear ye," told us the Honorable Anthony Ropek was presiding, and concluded, "God save the Commonwealth of Massachusetts."

The judge sat. The officer said, "Be seated." The rest of us sat. The clerk leaned against the bench and conferred with the judge for at least five minutes. High drama.

Then the clerk returned to his table and began reciting names. To each one, the probation officers responded. Usually one of them would say, "Terminate and discharge." A couple of times they said, "Request default warrant." They directed their words to the judge. The clerk, however, ran the show.

It was all routine court business, and it gave me a chance to size up Judge Anthony Ropek. He was small and gray and businesslike as, with an unintelligible word and small gesture, he repeatedly gave his official endorsements to the requests of the probation officers. He was an old-timer, I guessed, still in district court after all these years, which meant that he'd probably been passed over for superior court or federal seats enough times to know that he wasn't going anywhere else. This I took to be a positive omen for Daniel. Judge Ropek didn't strike me as a man with a motive to build a reputation at the expense of an ailing Vietnam vet who grew his own marijuana.

After the probation cases came the weekend motor

vehicle cases. All involved drunk driving. Most of them pleaded guilty, were fined, had their licenses revoked, and were enrolled in rehabilitation classes.

We heard a malicious destruction case. A mason with a long unpronounceable Italian name was accused of knocking down the brick walls he had constructed at a new condominium complex because the contractor had fired him halfway through the job. The prosecutor, a young female assistant district attorney, built her case entirely on the testimony of the contractor, corroborated by two witnesses, that the mason had cursed and uttered oblique threats when he was let go, and had thrust his arm from the window of his pickup truck and extended his middle finger as he drove away. Her implied argument, simply, was: Who else could have done it?

Nobody had seen him at the scene of the crime since the afternoon he was fired, the only point the defense attorney bothered to emphasize in his cross-examination of the witnesses.

When both sides rested, Judge Ropek said that he, for one, still retained reasonable doubt. Not guilty. It was the correct verdict.

The whole thing took less than an hour.

When the court recessed around eleven, twenty-five or thirty citizens had had their lives significantly altered by decisions rendered in the Northampton District Court. About a dozen couldn't drive automobiles for sixty days. Another dozen or so no longer needed to report to probation officers. A few would soon be arrested for probation violations. One Italian stonemason found himself relieved of both worry and a few thousand dollars in legal fees.

Daniel McCloud was still jiggling his leg and waiting.

I went outside for a cigarette. I wondered how Daniel had endured the weekend without what he called his medicine. I hoped his case would come up before the lunch recess.

I thought about what I had witnessed during the previous two hours. Justice. Routine, boring, repetitive justice had been dispensed evenhandedly by Judge Anthony Ropek. In the course of a week, justice would be meted out hundreds of times in this courtroom, as it would in dozens of other courtrooms across the state.

My law practice rarely requires me to perform the peculiar formalities of courtroom routines. Most of my work is done by telephone or in conference in a lawyer's office. Most of my practice is civil and probate, and you can judge the effectiveness of a civil or probate lawyer by his success in resolving issues before they find their way into a courtroom. It's the law of give-and-take, compromise, negotiation. It's my niche, and I'm pretty good at it.

Criminal law is different. The state, not a private citizen, is the adversary. The ground rules are more formalized, less flexible. Behind the state stand massive bureaucracies, enormous budgets, up-to-date technology. Behind the accused stands only a lone attorney, more often than not one who has been appointed by the state, and the presumption of innocence.

It usually turns out to be a pretty fair contest. The state bears the burden of proof. The presumption of innocence is a powerful ally.

On those relatively rare occasions when I find myself handling a criminal case, I inevitably recognize it as somehow more important. My client stands to lose not just some money, or his house, or custody of his children. Criminal clients go to prison when their lawyers screw up. Sometimes, because they are in fact guilty as charged, they go to prison even when their lawyers don't screw up. Under this system, remarkably few innocent people are imprisoned—although a remarkably large number of guilty people go free. Still, I, for one, never can avoid the feeling that I've screwed up whenever one of my clients goes to prison. Even when they're guilty, I always feel that I should have been able to get a "not guilty" verdict.

There's a big difference between "not guilty" and "innocent."

What would soon happen on that muggy Monday morning in July in the old Northampton courthouse, I knew, was the beginning of an intricate process that could land Daniel McCloud in M.C.I. Cedar Junction for fifteen years. What actually would happen would depend more than it should on me.

That Daniel did in fact grow marijuana in his garden, that he was therefore a guilty man by every definition except the one that counted—the due process of the law— did not affect my attitude toward his case. The presumption of innocence and the right to counsel—only those things were relevant.

If he'd been selling the stuff—not something the state needed to prove—I'd have felt differently about it. But, having agreed to take his case, I still would have done my best to get him off. That's the system, and it's not a bad one.

I flicked away my cigarette butt and went back into the courthouse. As I shouldered my way through the crowded lobby I felt a hand on my arm. I turned. It was the ADA who had unsuccessfully prosecuted the bricklayer. "You're Mr. McCloud's counsel?" she said.

I nodded. "Brady Coyne."

"Joan Redlich. Here." She handed me a sheet of paper.

"What's this?"

"The police report. You're entitled to it."

"Yes. Thanks. I'll want a copy of the warrant, too."

She smiled quickly. "You'll have it, Mr. Coyne."

She turned and headed into the courtroom. I followed her in and resumed my seat. I skimmed through the police report. It was written in the peculiarly stilted language policemen insist on using, on their theory, I assume, that it makes them sound highly educated.

To me, it always sounds like somebody trying to sound highly educated.

The report was signed by Sgt. Richard Oakley, Wilson Falls P.D.

Sergeant Oakley had written that the Wilson Falls police, acting upon a proper warrant, did on the afternoon of seven July confiscate an estimated fifty pounds or more of marijuana from the backyard garden of one Daniel McCloud, citizen of Wilson Falls. They did, pursuant to a search of the premises, also confiscate cigarette papers, a scale, a box of plastic bags, fifteen smoking pipes of various manufacture, and a cigarette rolling machine. They did consequently place the suspect, said Daniel McCloud, under arrest, recite to him his Miranda rights, handcuff him, and escort him to the jailhouse, where they did fingerprint and book him.

It was all pretty much the way Daniel had told it, except less eloquent.

A few minutes later the side door opened and Judge Ropek reentered. We all rose briefly, and then sat.

"Daniel McCloud," intoned the clerk.

Daniel stood, and the officer opened the swinging door to let him out of the dock. I went down front and Daniel met me there.

"You okay?" I whispered.

"No," he said. He glanced around, then muttered, "Bastard."

I followed his gaze. Standing stiffly against the side wall was a large uniformed policeman. He was staring at Daniel. He stood six-three or -four with the bulk to match. He had the bristly haircut and sunburned neck of a marine drill instructor. "Oakley?" I whispered to Daniel.

"Aye. Him."

"He's interested in his case," I said.

"He's interested in me," said Daniel.

The clerk read the charges. Possession of Class D marijuana, possession with intent to distribute, and trafficking.

The judge arched his eyebrows, then looked toward the prosecution table. "Trafficking, Ms. Redlich?"

Joan Redlich stood up and stepped toward the prosecutor's table. Her black hair was twisted up into a bun. I guessed it would fall halfway down her back when it was unpinned. She wore dark-rimmed tinted glasses low on her nose, a gray suit that disguised her figure, and low heels. She was slim and young and, in spite of her best efforts, pretty.

Female lawyers have told me that they dress for the judge. They have different wardrobes, different hairstyles, different cosmetics, which they adapt to the situation. Some judges—His Dirty Old Honors, the lawyers call them—like to see a little leg, a hint of cleavage, eye makeup. It disposes them favorably to the client's case. Others—especially female judges—resent it if the lawyers don't look as shapeless and sexless as they do in their black gowns.

Female lawyers resent the hell out of this kind of patent sexism. But they don't ignore it. It's an edge, if you read it right, they tell me.

Redlich tucked a stray strand of hair over her ear. She leaned toward the microphone that was wired to the tape recorder that preserved the proceedings and rendered obsolete the court stenographer. "Cultivation, Your Honor," she said. "He was growing it in his garden. The estimate is seventy pounds."

Ropek frowned, then nodded. I didn't like the looks of that frown. "Recommendation?"

She asked for a half-millon-dollar surety bond. Not unexpected. Since Reagan, all the courts have been trying to convert the drug cases that come before them into moral lessons.

"Mr. McCloud?" said the judge, looking from Daniel to me.

"Brady Coyne, Your Honor," I said into my microphone.

"Welcome, Mr. Coyne. Go ahead."

"I ask the court to release Mr. McCloud on personal recognizance, Your Honor. He has roots deep in the community. He's resided in Wilson Falls for the past twenty years. He owns property and runs a business there. He's a Vietnam veteran, Special Forces, and he's in poor health."

The judge peered at me for a moment, then nodded. He looked to the probation table. "Probation?" he said.

"One prior, Judge," said one of the officers. He stood and went to the bench, where he handed a folder to the judge. Judge Ropek glanced at it, then handed it back.

Then he looked at Daniel. "Two hundred thousand dollars surety bond," he said.

Daniel grabbed my arm. "I don't have that kind of money," he whispered.

"You need twenty thousand cash," I told him. "Can you raise it?"

He nodded. "Twenty grand. Okay. Yes."

We then argued about the date for the probable-cause hearing. Redlich asked for a month to give them time to process all the evidence. I asked for a week, citing the stress of waiting on Daniel's health. Judge Ropek set it for ten days hence, a small victory for the good guys.

Before the court officer took Daniel away, he gave me a phone number and told me to talk to Cammie Russell. She'd get the money.

And as I turned to head out of the courtroom, Joan Redlich handed me a copy of the search warrant. I thanked her and stuffed it into my attaché case along with the police report.

I called Cammie Russell from one of the pay phones

in the courthouse lobby. She had a soft voice with a hint of the Smoky Mountains in it. She said she'd be there in an hour. I told her I'd meet her outside the front door.

She actually arrived in about forty minutes. She was tall and slim in her white jeans and orange blouse. She had cocoa butter skin and black eyes. Her hair hung in a long, loose braid down the middle of her back. Her high cheekbones and small nose reminded me of a young Lena Horne. There was a Cherokee Indian somewhere in her ancestry. I guessed her age at twenty-five, but I figured she had looked the same way since she turned thirteen and would still look as good at fifty.

Then she smiled, and I amended my first impression. She looked *better* than a young Lena Horne.

She held her hand to me. "Cammie Russell," she said.

"Brady Coyne."

"How is Daniel?"

I shrugged. "I don't know how he usually is. I'd say confinement doesn't suit him."

"I can see you're a master of understatement, Mr. Coyne. He must be climbing the walls. Can we get him now?"

"If you brought enough money we can."

She held up the briefcase she was carrying and nodded.

An hour later Cammie Russell and I were eating ham-and-cheese sandwiches and sipping coffee on the deck behind Daniel's house in Wilson Falls. Daniel was slouched in a deck chair with his eyes closed, sucking steadily on a stick of cannabis. His leg no longer jiggled.

3

The deck across the back of Daniel's house looked out over a meadow that stretched toward a bluff above the Connecticut River. It had once been a tobacco farm, he told me, and he'd lived there since '73, when he retired from the Army. He rented a trailer and ran a bait and tackle shop for the ten years or so that it took him to realize that he'd never have to go back to the jungles. Finally he managed to accumulate some money, so he bought the land and the shop and built his house and, a few years later, Cammie's studio down next to the river.

Daniel's house featured angled cedar sheathing and glass and brick on the outside, and skylights and fireplaces and vaulted ceilings and massive beams on the inside. He told me he designed it himself, and he and some of his old army buddies did most of the work. It took them a couple of years to complete. The entire back was floor-to-ceiling glass that opened onto the big deck and overlooked the river.

The house was elegant and modern. It could have been a *Better Homes and Gardens* model. It contradicted every impression I had formed of Daniel McCloud.

After Daniel had sucked his second joint down to a quarter-inch nub, he stood up and said he needed a shower. He walked into the house.

"Is he stoned?" I said to Cammie.

She laughed. "He never gets stoned. It just eases his pain. It's the only thing that will." She was sitting up on the deck rail. "Daniel's death on drugs. That's why this business is so unfair. He saw a lot of men get killed over there because they were wasted and forgot to be afraid. It wasn't until he got back and tried every legal medicine they prescribed that he came to grass. Brian Sweeney put him on to it. The two of them have been trying to get help from the government. Mainly, they'd like to get the law to allow them to have marijuana legally."

"No way," I said.

She nodded. "'No farkin' way,' as Daniel would say. So he grows his own."

"Except they ripped up his garden," I said. "What'll he do?"

She shrugged. "He's got a little stashed away. Not much. I don't know how long it'll last him. I don't think he could make it without his medicine. In or out of prison."

"He can always buy it," I said.

Cammie's head jerked up. "Daniel?" She smiled. "You don't know Daniel. He would never—*never*—give money to a drug dealer."

"He's obviously a sick man."

"Wouldn't matter." She shrugged. "Can you get him off?"

"I don't know," I said. "There are plenty of mitigating circumstances in this case. But unless the prosecution screws it up, the facts will be hard to challenge. I mean, they don't have to prove he was selling it, and he *was* growing the stuff. So far the police appear to have gone by the book. If it goes to trial we'll probably have to give them a guilty plea. That'll be our only chance of keeping Daniel out of prison."

"If?"

"The next step is the probable-cause hearing," I said. "The prosecutor will have to demonstrate that she has enough evidence to justify a trial. If it gets to trial, I'll ask a friend of mine, a lawyer with a lot of experience at this sort of thing, to come aboard."

"You're not going to abandon him?" said Cammie.

I shook my head.

"Because," she continued, "I can tell he trusts you. He doesn't trust many people."

"I won't abandon him."

She cocked her head at me. "You were probably wondering about us."

I shrugged. "None of my business."

"Maybe it is," she said. "Maybe it relates to Daniel's case. Maybe you can use it. I mean, he really does hate drugs. What they do to people. Despises drug dealers. You should probably know, so you can judge. I doubt Daniel would tell you."

I nodded. "Okay."

She nodded and stared off toward the river. The Connecticut's a big broad river out there in the valley. It flows slow and deep through the old tobacco bottom land. It's not a trout stream, but bass and pike live there, and shad push up from the ocean every spring to spawn, and just looking at it gave me the urge to go fishing.

"He saved my life," said Cammie softly.

"Daniel?"

"Yes. I was this overachiever from a little mountain town outside of Knoxville. The youngest of eight. I had four sisters and three brothers, two of whom got killed in Vietnam. My momma sang choir in the Baptist church. So did I. One of my teachers got me into Smith College on a scholarship. I was going to be a great artist." She glanced at me and smiled softly. "I wasn't ready. I was homesick, I was over my head academically, I had no friends. I made some bad acquaintances." She shrugged. "Three months after I started my freshman year I was hooking in Springfield for coke money, living with a pimp, scared to death. Daniel found me and brought me here. I was eighteen. He got me straightened out. We lived in a trailer for a while. Eventually Daniel built me a studio and told me to just paint and cherish my life."

"What happened to the pimp?"

"I don't know." She shrugged. "This all happened years ago. I used to wake up from dreaming that he'd come for me. I haven't had that dream in a while."

"What about that policeman?"

"Oakley?"

I nodded.

"Well, he was the one who arrested Daniel, of course. Oakley's had it in for us from the start."

"How do you mean?"

Cammie gazed out at the river. "Small things," she said. "A ticket for parking in a handicapped zone, when the tire was barely touching the line. He stopped Daniel once in the middle of the afternoon, made him get out of the car and go through a bunch of drunk-driving exercises right beside the road, with all our neighbors driving by to watch. Oakley keeps showing up in the supermarket or the post office or the drugstore when I'm there, just kind of watching me with this spooky smile on his face. I'll turn around, and he'll be there, looking at me." She shrugged. "I don't know. It's no one thing. Maybe we're just paranoid about Oakley. It's a small town . . ."

"Are you afraid of him?"

Cammie closed her eyes for a moment. When she opened them, she turned to look at me and said, "Yes. I guess I am. Daniel's not afraid of him. But he worries about me. And now this . . ."

"The arrest."

She nodded.

We fell silent for a minute. Then I said, "Was Daniel growing marijuana when you met him?"

"Yes. He has this terrible raw, weeping rash on his back. From the Agent Orange. He doesn't talk about his pain, and when you're with him you'd never know how miserable he is."

"He seemed pretty miserable when I saw him in jail."

She nodded. "That's because he didn't have his medicine. It's worst at night. When he's sleeping he moans and thrashes around as if he was having one continuous nightmare." She looked up at me. "We don't sleep together. I mean, we're together, we . . . we're lovers, we make love . . . but he can't sleep with anybody else in the room, and I can't sleep with him anyway, because he's so restless. I sleep in my studio. It's down there." She gestured off to the left toward the river. I glimpsed the reflection of sun off glass through the trees. "It's got a bedroom, kitchen, living room, bath, and the whole top floor's a studio. Great light. I do watercolors, mostly, and— Oh, hi."

I turned. Daniel was standing there. He had shaved and changed his clothes.

Cammie smiled at me. "He's always doing that. Sneaking up on me." To him she said, "I suppose you were eavesdropping."

He twitched his shoulder. "I heard most of it."

"Okay?" she said.

Another shrug. "Brady's got to know."

"I've got a question," I said to Cammie.

"What?"

"Were you ever arrested?"

"Me?"

I nodded.

"Oh," she said. "I get it. If they knew I was a hooker, that I was a drug addict, it could go against Daniel."

"Unlikely," I said, "but it's possible."

She stared off toward the river for a moment, then said, "Twice. They pulled me in twice. Boomer got me off both times."

"Boomer?"

"Her pimp," said Daniel.

"There'll be a record of it, if it occurs to them to check," I said.

"It would be ironic as hell," said Cammie. "I mean, it was Daniel who got me out of that life."

"Well," I said, "one of the things Daniel has going for him is that he's a good citizen. But . . ."

"But living with me makes it look different," she finished.

I nodded. "If you look at it that way. Which is possibly the way the prosecution could try to make a jury look at it." I sighed. "Anyway, this is all a little premature. We've got the probable-cause hearing first, and we can try to make some good things happen there."

"Like what?" said Daniel.

"Like tainted evidence, improper warrant. Maybe all they got from your garden was tomato plants. If they ended up with less than fifty pounds of marijuana plants, they'll have to drop the trafficking charge, and that would be a very good thing."

Daniel smiled. "It was a big garden, and the crop was getting ripe. It was supposed to be my year's supply. That's probably why they waited until now to do it. So they got their fifty pounds."

"We'll see," I said. "For now, the ball's in their court."

"In that case," said Daniel, "let's go fishing."

I started to object that I had to get back to the office. But I caught myself. Hell, it was *my* office.

So I found a rumpled change of clothes in the trunk of my car, and Daniel and I strolled down to the river. We did it Daniel's way. No fly rods, delicate hand-tied flies, English reels, neoprene waders, bulging vests. We cut birch poles, captured some crickets for bait, and hauled a mess of panfish out of the sluggishly flowing Connecticut River. It was barefoot-boy-with-canepole fishing, and it harkened me back to the days when time was my most abundant resource and I squandered most of it aimlessly on the banks of muddy ponds.

We stopped and sat and smoked frequently, me my Winstons and Daniel his hand-rolled joints. We talked a little, gazed upon the river, and watched the birds. And we became friends.

When we had enough bluegills and perch for a meal, Daniel filleted them all with a wicked little blade that he kept sheathed against his calf.

Afterward, Daniel fried the panfish fillets, and he and Cammie and I ate them with steamed brown rice and sliced tomatoes and a bottle of what even I recognized as an excellent Chardonnay.

Later we sat out on the big deck behind Daniel's house to watch the sky grow dark. We sipped coffee and listened to Daniel's collection of blues tapes. Sonny Terry. John Lee Hooker. Brownie McGhee. Son House. Muddy Waters. Doc Reese. Mississippi John Hurt. Skip James. Lightnin' Hopkins. Howlin' Wolf. Jimmy Reed. Daniel and Cammie and I tapped our feet and made harmonica noises, and it was nearly midnight when the three of us walked around front to my car.

I told Daniel I'd see him in ten days for the probable-cause hearing.

"You've got to keep him out of prison," said Cammie.

"Our chances are excellent," I said.

Daniel shrugged. "They got my garden," he said. "Either way, I'm screwed."

I looked at him. "You can always buy some grass," I said.

"No," said Daniel. "I wouldn't do that. Sweeney might, but not me."

"I told you," said Cammie. "Daniel's death on drugs."

I called Charlie McDevitt the next morning from my office. "Daniel McCloud is quite amazing," I told him.

I heard Charlie chuckle. "I knew you'd like him."

"We went fishing, and it took me right back to when I was about eight," I said. "Him, too, I think. We were like a pair of kids. Except Daniel is about the most resourceful man in the woods that I've ever known."

"He survived six years in the jungle, you know," said Charlie.

"Well, he'd never survive prison. When I saw him in jail, he was like a caged animal, and I don't think it was just the fact that he didn't have his . . . his medicine. I mean, the marijuana eases his pain. But freedom nourishes him."

"He's a very complicated man," said Charlie. "Even though he doesn't like to show it."

"A little paranoid, though. He thinks it's personal with the cop who arrested him."

"Maybe it is," said Charlie. "Cops aren't immune from personal motives."

"Maybe so," I said. "Anyway, I like him a lot. He's very stoic. But it's pretty clear that he suffers a lot."

"I can imagine," said Charlie. "So what do you think? Have they got the goods on him?"

"It looks bad, truthfully. I'm not sure what I can do for him."

"You've gotta keep him out of prison, Brady," said Charlie. "It would kill him."

"What worries me," I said, "is that not having his medicine could kill him no matter where he is."

4

Ten days later, Daniel, Cammie Russell, and I were sitting in Judge Anthony Ropek's courtroom while he and his clerk worked their way through the morning's probation cases. Sergeant Oakley was there, too, standing stiffly in the back, staring in our direction.

It was a little after ten when the clerk intoned, "Daniel McCloud."

Daniel followed me through the gate to the defense table. Joan Redlich, the same ADA who had handled the arraignment for the state, moved to the prosecutor's table.

The judge peered down at her. "Is the Commonwealth ready?"

She glanced in our direction, then turned to the judge. She cleared her throat, leaned to the microphone, then said, "The Commonwealth moves to dismiss, Your Honor."

Judge Ropek frowned for an instant, then turned to me. "Mr. Coyne?"

"May I have a moment, Your Honor?"

He nodded. "Go ahead."

I hadn't expected the state to move for dismissal. It was more than I'd dared hope for. But I didn't have the luxury of exulting in our good luck. I needed to decide whether to move for a dismissal with prejudice. If prejudice was granted, it would prevent the state from ever reopening its case against Daniel. With a simple dismissal, they could try it again. The problem was, I'd have to convince Judge Ropek that there had actually been prejudice in Daniel's arrest. Daniel thought it had been personal with Sergeant Oakley. I doubted that I could convert Daniel's paranoia into an argument for prejudice that would convince the judge.

The other factor to consider was Joan Redlich's failure to request a continuance, which would have indicated simply that the state needed more time to prepare its case. She had asked for a dismissal, not a continuance. I guessed that they didn't have the evidence to prosecute the case.

I had no grounds for prejudice.

I looked up at Judge Ropek. "Thank you, Your Honor," I said. "No argument with the motion."

He looked back to Redlich and beckoned her with a crooked forefinger. "Approach," he growled.

She went up to the bench. I sidled up next to her.

"What the hell is going on?" said the judge to her in a harsh whisper.

"Apparently there's a problem with the evidence, Judge," she said.

"Apparently?"

She shrugged.

He looked at me. "You know anything about this?"

"No, Your Honor. But we'll take it."

"Don't blame you, Mr. Coyne." He shooed us away with the back of his hand.

We returned to our tables.

"Mr. McCloud, you are free to go," said Judge Ropek to Daniel. "The Commonwealth apologizes for your inconvenience."

Daniel blinked at him and nodded.

"Thank you, Your Honor," I said. I picked up my briefcase. "Come on," I said to Daniel.

I walked up the aisle and out of the courtroom. Daniel followed behind me. Cammie had grabbed his arm. We stopped in the lobby.

"What happened?" said Daniel.

I shrugged. "Somebody must've screwed up the evidence. You sure they didn't just get tomato plants or something?"

He smiled. "They got some damn good weed, Brady."

"Well," I said, "it's peculiar. But let's not complain. I only—"

I felt a hand on my arm. I turned and saw Joan Redlich. "Can I speak to you for a second, Mr. Coyne?" she said.

"Sure." I turned to Daniel and Cammie. "Be with you in a minute."

"We'll wait outside," said Daniel.

I turned to the ADA. "What's up?" I said.

"You tell me."

"Don't look at me," I said. "Surprised me as much as it did you."

She rolled her eyes. "Sure."

"Look," I said. "If you think I pulled a string, you're giving me more credit than I deserve."

She narrowed her eyes. "I figured, a fancy Boston lawyer . . ."

"You figured wrong. I'm not that fancy, and I thought you had a decent case, to tell you the truth." I smiled at her. "I was looking forward to it."

She did not smile. "Decent, yeah. I had a helluva good case. There were sixty-two pounds of marijuana plants in those trash bags they pulled out of that garden, according to the lab report. The warrant was okay and the search followed it perfectly. Look," she said. "I've got nothing against Mr. McCloud, okay? There's no evidence that he was dealing the stuff. I know he's sick. I mean, I've got plenty of bad guys to prosecute. I doubt if Daniel McCloud is a bad guy." She cocked her head and arched her eyebrows at me.

"He's actually a pretty good guy," I said.

"Regardless, there was no way we would've lost that trial. No matter how good you are."

"I'm pretty good. It would've been interesting."

"I don't think Daniel McCloud belongs in prison," she said. "I would have argued my ass off for a guilty verdict, Mr. Coyne. And I would've got it. And you probably would've requested a suspended sentence with a long probation, community service, and proper health care, and, between the two of us, I might not've objected too strenuously. The poor bastard deserves some help, and I think a lot of our vets've been getting screwed. But, dammit, I just don't like having the rug pulled out from under me, and I was wondering if you could help me out."

I held up both hands. "This discussion isn't really appropriate, Ms. Redlich," I said with a smile.

"Ah, come off it. We're just a couple of lawyers here."

"Well, as one lawyer to another, I haven't got the foggiest idea of what happened."

"You've got friends in high places, though, huh?"

I thought of Charlie. "Don't we all?"

"I busted my butt on this case, okay?" she said. "And they wait till yesterday to tell me to dump it?"

"Well," I said, "I don't blame you for being upset. But I can't help you. I don't know what happened."

"Would you tell me if you did?"

I nodded. "Maybe."

She peered quizzically at me for a moment, then shrugged. "Well, it was fun being your adversary, and if I didn't have a caseload that'd choke a hippo I'd get to the bottom of this. But, screw it. I do, so I guess I won't." She smiled and held her hand to me, and I grasped it.

"If it's any consolation," I said, "I think justice was done in there this morning."

She grinned crookedly. "Yeah. Whatever that means."

She turned and strode back into the courtroom and I went out into the summer heat.

I squinted into the sunlight as I tapped a Winston from my pack and lit it. Daniel and Cammie were sitting on a bench by the front entrance. I went over and sat with them.

"I could use a smoke," said Daniel, jerking his head at my cigarette.

"Not here you couldn't," I said.

"Just kidding."

"From now on, you've got to be careful," I told him.

"I can't live without my medicine," he said.

"I understand."

"What happened in there?" said Cammie.

"I don't know. The ADA didn't know, either. I gather her boss ordered her to dump the case."

"But why?"

"A small mystery that doesn't need to concern us. Daniel's free, all charges dropped for now. Let's be grateful."

"For now?" repeated Cammie.

"They could reopen the case."

"But it was dismissed."

"Without prejudice," I said. "Meaning there's no admission that they did anything wrong. But look. I don't think we have anything to worry about. This is one for the good guys."

"Do I get my weed back?" said Daniel.

I looked at him. He managed to withhold his grin for several seconds. I punched his shoulder. "The Wilson Falls P.D. is probably divvying it up right now," I said. "Maybe they divvied it up yesterday, and that's why the case got dropped."

"Wouldn't surprise me," he said.

We were strolling to the parking lot when Daniel suddenly stopped. I turned to follow his gaze. Sergeant Richard Oakley was leaning back against a Wilson Falls police cruiser. His arms were folded across his chest, and behind his reflector sunglasses he appeared to be staring at Cammie. He was grinning, baring his teeth.

She grabbed Daniel's arm. "Come on," she said.

Daniel remained there for another moment, glaring at the policeman. Then he shrugged, and we continued to my car.

"You can expect them to be watching you," I told Daniel as we drove back to his place. "They figured they had a good arrest. These things do not make policemen happy. You've got to be careful."

"Not them," he said. "Just him. Oakley. And anyway, he wasn't watching me. He was watching Cammie."

I stopped off at Daniel's house for coffee. Cammie offered to make lunch for me, but I told her I had to get back to the office. We sat at the table in Daniel's sun-drenched ultramodern kitchen. "I meant it about being careful," I said to him. "I don't know what happened in court today, but it's for sure that they'd love to try again."

Daniel shrugged. He had just stubbed out a joint. "I can't live without my medicine."

"So what are you going to do?"

"I don't know." He stood up. "Brady, I've got something for you. Wait here."

He walked out of the room. I lifted my eyebrows at Cammie. She shrugged.

He was back in a minute. He was carrying a box, the kind that holds a ream of typing paper. It was heavily taped along its seams. He put it on the table in front of me.

"What's this?" I said.

"My book."

"Daniel . . ." began Cammie.

"It's time, lass," he said. He sat down beside me. "You're a lawyer. You can handle it for me."

"You want it published?"

"Aye."

"You need an agent, not a lawyer, Daniel."

He shrugged. "Whatever."

"You want me to find an agent for you?"

"Yes."

I smiled. "Daniel, you understand—"

"That everybody and his sister has written a book they think is going to make them rich and famous. Yes, I know that. I'm not interested in getting rich or famous. That's not why I wrote it."

I nodded. I thought I understood. Daniel was haunted by mighty demons. His book was his exorcism.

"I'm using a pen name," he added. "This book isn't for me."

"What kind of book is it?"

He gave me an understated shrug. "A story, I guess."

"I mean, a novel? A memoir?"

"Just a story."

"Can I look at it?"

He peered at me for a moment, then shook his head. "No," he said. "It's all ready to send off. Can you just find someone to send it off to?"

"Sure," I said. "I'll see what I can do."

I got back to the office around two in the afternoon. Julie greeted me with a stack of messages. I clutched the box with Daniel's manuscript in it against my chest. "Don't pester me," I said. "I haven't had any lunch."

"Poor baby."

"Have you?"

She looked at me and rolled her eyes.

"I'm sorry," I said. "Of course you haven't. Let me make a quick call and then I'll run out for sandwiches."

I went into my office. Julie followed me. "How'd it go this morning?" she said.

"The prosecutor moved for dismissal."

Julie sat down. "No shit."

I sat, too. "No shit indeed."

"Why?"

I shrugged. "Beats me."

"Well, that's good, huh?"

"It certainly is. I mean, they would've presented their evidence and I would've moved for dismissal on the ground that their evidence was insufficient. I would've challenged the warrant, the reliability of their informants. All the usual things. But my motion would've been denied, and the judge would've found probable cause, and the ADA would've taken the case to the grand jury for an indictment. Which they would've gotten. And on to trial."

She gave me her stunning Irish smile. "You're a helluva lawyer, Brady Coyne. The prosecutor takes one look at you and figures it's a lost cause."

"Yeah," I said, "I guess that's what happened."

"Look," she said. "You want tuna?"

"I said I'd get them."

"Hey, you're the victorious attorney. I'll go out. You watch the phone."

"Tomato and lettuce with the tuna," I said. "On a bulky roll. Barbecued chips, dill pickle, ice-cold Pepsi."

"Don't press your luck, fella."

After Julie left I called Charlie, as I had promised him I would. When Shirley, his secretary, put me through, he said, "Well?"

"The Commonwealth moved to dismiss."

He was quiet for so long that I said, "Charlie? You there?"

"I'm here. What the hell happened?"

"Come off it," I said.

"What are you talking about?"

"I just don't understand why you made us go through the arraignment and then the hearing first. It would've been a helluva lot easier on all of us if—"

"Brady," said Charlie, "what the Christ are you talking about?"

"Don't give me your bullshit, old buddy. You pulled some strings. I'm calling to say thanks on Daniel McCloud's behalf."

"I didn't do anything."

"Hey, I understand that your overdeveloped concept of ethics prevents you from admitting it. But thanks anyway."

"Honest," he said. "I don't have that kind of pull with the Commonwealth. I don't work those streets. I'm just a D.O.J. drudge, one of Uncle Sam's soldiers, remember?"

"Listen, Charlie—"

"Brady, believe me, it wasn't me. I wish it was. If I'd thought there was anything I could do for you—for Daniel—I would've done it. But I didn't. You don't know what happened?"

"Maybe it *was* a fuckup with the evidence, then," I said.

"Probably. Those things happen."

"So I rescind my thanks."

"In which case," said Charlie, "I am absolved from having to say 'You're welcome.'"

"Daniel has written a book," I told Charlie.

"Daniel?"

"Yep. And I'm to find him an agent."

"What kind of book?"

"I don't know. He won't say."

Charlie chuckled. "Everybody's got a story these days, huh?"

5

Later that afternoon I left my office and strolled across the square to the Boston Public Library, where I copied out a dozen phone numbers from a writer's directory. Then I returned to the office and began calling New York literary agencies. They all wanted the same thing—a cover letter detailing the author's credentials and something they called a "chapter outline," which they explained was a brief narrative summary of the book's plot. Until they had a chance to review an outline, they all informed me, they wouldn't touch a manuscript from an anonymous and unpublished writer.

As far as I knew, Daniel had no credentials. And he had given me no outline.

I called him that night. "Credentials?" he said.

"Credits. Things that you've had published."

"Nay," he said. "I have no credentials. Unless you can count the demolition handbook I helped revise."

"I doubt if that would count."

"I was really a technical adviser on it anyway," he said.

"How about making an outline for me?"

"Just find someone who'll read the book, Brady."

"They don't seem interested in reading it."

"They'll be interested in this one."

"Daniel," I said, "do you know what the odds are on this book getting published?"

"I know all about long odds," he said quietly.

"The publishing world is a different kind of jungle," I said.

"Just find someone willing to read it. They'll take it."

I sighed. "Well, I'll keep trying. But no guarantees."

As I lay in bed that night, I thought I remembered having read in my alumni magazine that one of my Yale Law classmates had become a literary agent. Damned if I could remember his name, however.

It kept me awake half the night, which didn't help.

Charlie remembered. "Al Coleman," he said instantly when I called him the next morning. "Little guy with glasses. Looked like Woody Allen. Used to beat the shit out of me at handball. We kept in touch for a while after we got out of school. He went to work for Uncle right after Yale. Over at State, I think it was. Al was a pretty rigid guy. Couldn't take the bullshit, all the nuances and ambiguities that are more or less part of government work. Had this overdeveloped concept of the law, justice." He paused. "Not unlike you, in fact."

"Or you, for that matter," I said.

"I guess Yale bred that into us," said Charlie. "Anyway, Coleman quit after a few years, set up his own practice.

Again, kind of like you. A little of this, a little of that. Al and I lost touch, but I heard some kiss-and-tell writer hired him to defend a lawsuit, and he won it, so she retained him, and he ended up making a bundle representing her. Eventually he gave up his practice and set up an agency. As I recall, he specializes in ghostwritten celebrity biographies."

"Al Coleman," I mused. "Sounds familiar. Did I know him?"

"He came out to our place a few times," said Charlie, referring to the ramshackle house near the water that he and I rented while we were in New Haven. "You were with Gloria in those days, pretty oblivious to anybody else."

"Used to bring that tall blonde?" I said. "About six inches taller than him?"

"That's the guy. It figures you'd remember the lady."

"I remember her well. I wasn't that oblivious."

"Well, that's what Al Coleman does now. Represents writers." Charlie paused. "So you're really going to try to help Daniel, huh?"

"I promised him I would."

"I hear that getting an agent is about as hard as getting a publisher."

"I've heard that, too."

"Well, give Al Coleman a try. Sing the Whiffenpoof song to him. Maybe he'll give it a look."

"Yeah, I guess I will," I said. "I wonder what happened to the blonde?"

"She got old," said Charlie. "Like the rest of us."

I slipped over to the BPL at lunchtime. The directory

listed the Coleman Literary Agency on lower Fifth Avenue in New York City. The heart of the publishing district.

Back at my desk, I dialed their number. A sexy female voice answered.

"Al Coleman, please," I said.

"Who should I say is calling?"

"Brady Coyne. We're friends."

"One moment, sir."

I was treated to two minutes of Mozart while I waited on hold. Then she came back on and said, "Mr. Coyne, what was it you wanted?"

Fair enough, I thought. I hadn't remembered Al Coleman, and he didn't remember me. "Tell Al," I said, "that he used to come down to the house that Charlie McDevitt and I rented while we were all at Yale Law together. Tell him he used to bring a beautiful blonde with him. Tell him I have a manuscript that I want to give him first shot at. Because we're old friends."

"Oh," she said. She started to say something, then stopped herself. "Well, okay," she said instead. "Hang on a minute."

More Mozart. Then, "Hey, Brady. How've you been?"

"Cut the shit, Al," I said. "Charlie had to remind me of you, and you don't remember me."

He laughed. It was a good, genuine laugh. "I *do* remember Charlie. And that shack you guys rented. I remember you, too, except your name failed to ring a bell. I remember the vats of fish chowder you guys'd cook up and all the beer. I used to play handball with Charlie."

"He said you were good."

"Nah. Charlie was bad, that's all. You and Charlie used to claim that you made that chowder from fish you caught yourselves."

"True. We never told you what kind of fish they were, though."

"What, eels?"

"Among other unmentionables," I said.

He chuckled. "So you've written a book, huh?"

"Not me. One of my clients has written one, and he's asked me to find an agent for it. I thought of you."

"Tell me about it."

"I haven't read it."

"Send me an outline. I'll give it a look."

"No outline. He refuses to do one. Says the book speaks for itself. He's a funny guy. Very shy. Wants to use a pseudonym. He's a Vietnam vet, got himself doused with Agent Orange over there."

"Well, what've we got? A novel or what?"

"I don't know. A story, he calls it."

"Christ," he muttered. "How'm I supposed to take a book, you can't even tell me what kind of book it is?"

"I understand."

I heard Al sigh. "The market's real soft on Vietnam stuff just now, Brady."

"I don't even know if it's a Vietnam book. I was just hoping you'd look at it. I know you can't guarantee anything."

"You have any idea how many people are writing books these days?"

"Too many, I guess." I hesitated. "Listen," I said, "if

you could just glance at it, maybe tell me if it's worth anything. You know, if I should just tell Daniel to forget it."

He was silent for a long moment. Then he said, "I guess I could look at it. That's what the old school tie is all about, huh?"

"I appreciate it, Al," I said.

"Send it down."

"I will."

"It'll take me a few weeks to get back to you."

"Fine. Understood." I hesitated. "Hey, Al?"

"Yeah?"

"What ever happened to that blonde?"

"The one I used to bring to your parties?"

"That one."

"I married her."

"Yeah?"

"Yeah. She's the one who answers the phone here. You just talked to her. We've got four kids. What about you?"

"Me?"

"Yeah. You used to have a knockout brunette with you. I can almost remember her name."

"Gloria," I said.

"Right. What happened to her?"

"I married her."

"Oh."

"Yes. We have two boys. Divorced eleven years ago."

"Well, I'm sorry."

"Sometimes I am, too."

6

Al Coleman called me back two weeks later. "I really got my hands full here," he said. "I hardly ever take on a new client. I'm trying to avoid hiring anybody. It's just me and Bonnie. A two-person office, that's how I want it."

"Me, too," I said. "Maybe Yale bred that into us. The lone-wolf mentality. Does this mean—?"

"I handle everything myself," he interrupted. "Personal attention. My writers always know who they're dealing with. They appreciate it that way. I've got a few big name writers, and several good solid pros. They take all my time, keep me as busy as I want to be. It'd take something really special for me to bring another writer aboard, especially someone who's got no track record. Something like what you sent me, I just have a policy against even looking at stuff like that, and I'm afraid I'm pretty closed-minded about unproven writers. Do you understand?"

"Sure. That's fine. I appreciate your looking at it, anyway. So what did you—"

"I mean," Al went on quickly, "we do have to keep bringing new blood into the literary world and all that. Every bestselling author in history started with a first book. But a little mom-and-pop operation like mine, I just don't have the luxury of beating my brains out trying to sell something that's not going to make anybody any money. That's just how it's gotta be. Big agencies are different. They're always trying to sell promising new writers. It's like working *pro bono*. Every writer—your Hemingways and your Micheners and your Stephen Kings—they all started as unknowns. Agents and publishers know this. Nothing they like better than discovering the next Elmore Leonard. It's rare, first books making money. But good writers will make everybody money in the long run."

"So maybe you can recommend someone for me, Al. Someone who'll give this book a look. I mean, if it's got some potential."

"No. I can't."

"Well, sure, if it's not—"

"You said you didn't read it."

"No."

"You should read it."

"Well, when you send it back, maybe I will."

"You missed the point," said Al.

"The point?"

"Look," he said. "I'm not quite finished with it. But this thing is absolute dynamite. It's wild. An incredible yarn. A genuine page-turner, and not that badly written. It's a fucking powder keg, Brady. Bestseller material, handled right. This guy's got a fantastic imagination."

"You mean . . . ?"

"I mean I want it. Listen, I've got to finish it, and there are a few people I want to show it to. But as far as I'm concerned, you can tell your friend there that he can expect to be rich and famous real soon."

"I'm not sure he cares about rich, and I have a strong feeling he's dead set against famous."

"I think," said Al, "that we won't be able to avoid the rich part. Preserving his anonymity can probably be done. Still, eventually I'll need to talk with him."

"I'll see what he says."

"No disrespect, Brady, but you know you're superfluous here. The agent's the one who handles all the legal stuff, and I'd prefer to deal directly with the writer." He hesitated. "Or are you interested in a piece of the action?"

"I have no interest in the action," I said. "I'm just helping out a friend here."

"Whatever," he said. "I'll get back to you in a couple weeks. Meantime, ask—what'd you say his name was? Daniel?"

"Daniel, yes."

"Tell Daniel that he and I will have some work to do. I don't want to mess with his story, but there are some loose ends and rough spots. You might mention the rich and famous part to him, too."

I called Daniel as soon as I hung up from Al Coleman. I got his answering machine at the house, so I tried the shop. A male voice I didn't recognize said, "Yo?"

"Is Daniel there?"

"Hang on."

I heard him yell, "Hey, Daniel. Phone." There was a murmur of male voices in the background, a burst of laughter.

A minute later Daniel said, "McCloud."

"It's Brady."

"Yes?"

"Daniel, I've found an agent who's agreed to handle your book. He hasn't quite finished reading it, and he wants to show it to some other people. But he loves it."

"Yes. Fine."

"His name is Al Coleman. The Coleman Agency in New York."

"Okay."

"Listen," I said. "Do you understand?"

"Aye."

"It means you've got a helluva chance of getting it published."

"I understand that."

"You don't exactly sound elated."

"It's what I expected, Brady."

I paused for a moment. "Can you talk?"

"Not really."

"You've got a gang in the shop?"

"Aye."

"And you don't want them to know about the book, right?"

"Right."

"Well, that's a damn shame, because your most appropriate reaction right now should be to jump up onto your woodstove and dance a jig."

"Hold on, will you?" he said. Then I heard him say, "Hang this up when I tell you, Vinnie."

A minute later I heard a click, and Daniel said, "Okay, Vinnie. Hang it up." Then he said, "Brady, you there?"

"I'm here."

"I'm in the office now. Noisy out there."

"And you didn't want to be overheard."

"Aye. I want to tell you something."

"Go ahead."

"I don't want to dance a jig, lad. I don't want to celebrate. This book is not an ego thing. It's just a story that I wanted to tell. Do you get it?"

"Shit, Daniel, most people—"

"Most people who write books want to be writers, see their name on the jacket of a book, be on television."

I found myself nodding. "I hear you."

"Not me."

"Okay."

"You understand?"

"Yes, Daniel."

"Well, fine."

"What about meeting with Al Coleman?"

"No."

"But if he's going to represent you—"

"He'll do it through you. And I don't want you to tell him who I am."

"Right."

"Or the publisher, or the editor, or anybody else."

"Okay."

"That's your job, Brady. To make sure nobody knows."

"That's what I'll tell Al, then."

After I hung up with Daniel, I called Coleman back. "He won't meet with you," I said.

"Not good," he said.

"He's adamant."

"I'll have to live with it, then."

"Something else you should know, Al."

"Go ahead."

"I doubt if this guy intends to write another book. I mean, it's not that he burns to be a writer. I suspect he's got this one story in him, and now he's told it."

"You trying to discourage me?"

"No. Just being straight with you."

"Normally," he said, "that would be important information. In this case, I don't care."

"It's that good, huh?"

"I told you. This story's dynamite."

Julie buzzed me in my office after lunch on a Tuesday a couple of weeks later. "It's the Coleman Literary Agency," she said.

"Hot-damn," I replied. "I got it."

I pressed the blinking button on my phone console and said, "Al?"

"This is Bonnie," came the voice in the phone. "Please hold for Mr. Coleman."

"Hey, Bonnie?" I said quickly.

"Yes?"

"I remember you."

"I remember you, too, Mr. Coyne."

"You and Al used to come to our place. I should've made the connection before."

"It was a long time ago."

"I guess I just didn't expect that you and Al Coleman . . ."

"Would end up married."

"Well, yes."

"Because I'm taller than him."

"Well—"

"And he's not as handsome as, for example, you."

"I didn't—"

"Al Coleman, Mr. Coyne, was a terrific lover."

"Yeah?"

"Yeah. Still is. Here. I'll put him on."

I heard a click, then, "Brady?"

"Hi, Al."

"Brady, I'm sending back the manuscript."

"Huh?"

"I've decided not to handle it."

"But I thought—"

"Dynamite. I know. I said that. I thought it was a fucking novel." He paused. "Listen, Brady. I shouldn't've even called you. I should just send it back with the standard rejection form. But—listen. How well do you know this guy?"

"Daniel?"

"Yes. Is he really a friend of yours?"

"Well, yes. He's a client. Most of my clients are friends."

"Known him for a long time?"

"Not really. Look. What makes the difference?"

I heard Al clear his throat. "Brady, I probably shouldn't be telling you this. But I'd feel guilty if I didn't, okay?"

"For Christ sake, Al—"

"If I were you, I'd avoid this man like the plague."

"What?"

"Just give him back his manuscript, tell him it's unpublishable, and get the hell out of there. You don't want to be mixed up with this guy. He's a very scary man. He's dangerous."

"Come on, Al. I mean, shit, it's just a book. You—"

"You should trust me on this, Brady."

"Look, if you don't want the book . . ."

I heard him sigh. "I'll return the book. You read it. Then you can judge for yourself, okay? Hey, someone'll probably publish it. Good luck to you. But not me. I don't need it. I don't need the money that bad. I'm just not gonna get involved with a guy like that."

"Jesus Christ, Al—"

"Read the book, Brady. Then you'll see what I mean."

7

I swiveled around and stared out the window onto Copley Square. Al Coleman had loved Daniel's book, wanted it, thought it had bestseller potential. Then suddenly he hated it. He didn't say it was a bad book, boring, poorly written, any of the usual things that get books rejected. Instead, he talked about Daniel. A scary, dangerous man, he called him. What kind of reason is that to reject a book?

I knew Daniel. Not well, maybe, but a helluva lot better than Al Coleman. I suppose anyone who had survived the Vietnam jungle nightmare could be seen as scary. Daniel struck me as troubled, perhaps. Depressed, edgy, maybe a little paranoid. But he wasn't scary or dangerous.

And so what if he was? Lots of scary, sick, perverted people published popular books. It made no sense.

I'd make sure to read it when I got it back. Maybe then I'd understand Al's reaction.

I went back to the library and photocopied the entire

three-page listing of literary agents from a volume called *The Writer's Handbook*. I called every one of them, told them about Daniel's book, and found four who agreed to bypass the usual narrative outline preliminary and look at the manuscript, and who said they didn't mind what they called a "simultaneous submission." As soon as the manuscript came back I would make copies of it and send it to all four of them.

I told Daniel what had happened. He accepted that news with typical stoicism. He didn't ask why Al had changed his mind, and I was relieved that I didn't have to tell him. I told him I'd try to find another agent to handle it.

Two weeks passed from the day that Al Coleman had called to reject the book. The manuscript didn't arrive.

I called the Coleman Agency. A machine answered. I tried several times over the next two or three days. I would always get the machine with Bonnie's voice informing me that I should leave my name and number and my call would be promptly returned.

I did as instructed. My call wasn't returned at all.

This irritated the hell out of me. I decided I'd call Al Coleman at home. At dinnertime. Or late at night. I can't stand being ignored.

So I once again scurried over to the library and copied all of the Albert and Allen and Alan and Alfred and Alvin Colemans out of the Manhattan phone directory. There were twenty-three of them.

After supper that evening I began calling.

On my fourteenth try I got a machine with Bonnie's voice on it. I left a message there, too. I tried again at midnight, just before I went to bed. Again the machine answered. I didn't bother leaving a message this time.

I decided Al and Bonnie had gone on vacation.

A week later they were still on vacation.

And they were still on vacation five weeks later. It was the last week in September, and Al Coleman still hadn't returned Daniel McCloud's book to me.

When the phone beside my bed began jangling, I tried to reach for it. But I found that my arm, draped over Terri Fiori's hip, had gone to sleep and refused to awaken as fast as my head did.

"Someone's at the door," Terri mumbled.

"It's the telephone, hon."

"So get the phone already."

"I can't move my arm."

Terri moaned, turned, kissed my neck, reached across me, and picked up the phone. She had to slide the entire front of her body against the front of mine when she did it. It helped to wake me up. She held the receiver to my ear. She rubbed her smooth leg against mine and nuzzled my throat.

"Cut it out," I whispered.

She bit my numb shoulder.

"Hello?" I said into the phone.

"Brady?"

"Yes. Who's this?"

"It's Cammie Russell. Brady, something's happened."

I pushed myself up so that I was half sitting in the bed. "What's the matter?"

Terri pulled away from me and frowned.

"It's Daniel," said Cammie.

"What—?"

"He's . . . he wasn't in the house. I went to the shop. He's . . . they killed him."

"What?"

"He's dead. An arrow. Brady, I'm trying to keep it together here, but I don't know if . . ."

"Call the police and sit tight, Cammie. I'm on my way."

"No."

"No?"

"I can't call them."

"You've got to."

"No. I can't. It's—"

"Because of Oakley?"

"Yes."

"You think . . . ?"

"I'm not calling them, Brady."

I mouthed the word "coffee" to Terri. With the phone wedged between my shoulder and my ear, I fumbled on the bedside table for a cigarette. Terri kissed my belly and scurried bareass into the kitchen. I got a Winston lit and said into the phone, "Okay, Cammie. I'll be there in two hours. Stay in the house and lock the door. Don't answer the phone or let anybody in until I get there. Okay?"

"Okay."

"Are you all right?"

"I'm okay. But Daniel's dead. He's the only . . ."

"I'm on my way."

When I told Terri about it, she insisted on coming with me. She said that Cammie might appreciate having a woman there. I didn't argue with her. We filled a thermos with coffee and bought some crullers on the way to the turnpike entrance. I kept the needle on eighty all the way out the pike and was grateful that the state police had set no speed traps on that Sunday morning.

I pulled up in front of Daniel's house a few minutes before nine. Terri followed me up to the front door. I banged on it and yelled, "Cammie. It's Brady."

The door opened almost instantly. I suspected she had been at a window watching for me. "Thank you," she said. "I just . . ."

I put my arms around her and held her against me. Her body was limp and loose. Her head rested against my shoulder. I patted her back. "Are you all right?"

"Yes. I don't know. I keep thinking maybe I was wrong. Can we go see him?"

"Yes." I stepped back, then remembered Terri. "Cammie, this is my friend Terri Fiori."

Cammie nodded. "Hi." They shook hands.

We went down to the shop. I opened the door and went in. The two women followed behind me.

"Be careful not to touch anything," I said to them.

Daniel was sprawled on his back near the woodstove. He looked shrunken and pale and incredibly still, lying there on the floor in a lake of his own dark blood. The feathered end of an arrow protruded at an angle from his midsection. It had sliced through his T-shirt and entered his body just above his navel, then penetrated upward under his rib cage, neatly avoiding bone along the way. About a foot of arrow was visible. Since hunting arrows are usually thirty inches long, I figured a good foot and a half had sliced its way up through Daniel's diaphragm and into his chest cavity.

He had bled vastly from the entry wound. The front of his T-shirt was drenched, and a puddle the size and general shape of a bathtub surrounded his body. Broadheads are designed to maximize bleeding, and this one had done its job. An animal shot with a hunting arrow generally dies from blood loss, except when a lucky shot happens to nick its heart.

I guessed, in Daniel's case, that his assassin had got off a lucky shot. There was no way that arrow hadn't punctured his heart.

I squatted beside him, careful not to step in the congealed blood. His eyes were open and glazed and staring upward. He was obviously dead, but I pressed my fingers under his jaw anyway, seeking a pulse. There was none.

I got up, went to the phone beside the cash register, and dialed 911. I told the cop who answered that we had a dead body and gave him the address.

After I hung up, I turned to Cammie and Terri. They were standing by the doorway watching me. Terri had her arm around Cammie's shoulders.

"They'll be here in a minute," I told them. "Let's wait outside."

The three of us sat on the front steps of Daniel's shop. I smoked a cigarette. Cammie and Terri sat close to each other. Terri still had her arm around Cammie and was holding her hand. The September sun filtered through the big maples that overhung the building. Somewhere behind us a few crows argued.

"Any thoughts?" I said to Cammie.

"Oakley," she murmured after a moment.

"Come on," I said. "So he arrested Daniel. That doesn't mean—"

"I can't think of anyone else."

"Can you remember anything Daniel ever said that might make you think someone would want to murder him? Somebody other than Oakley, I mean?"

"No."

"When do you think it happened?"

"Sometime after midnight. We were together last night until about then. We started to watch *Saturday Night Live*, but I was tired so we shut it off after the first couple of skits. Daniel walked me back to my place, kissed me good-night, and I went right to bed. He mentioned he had a few things to clean up, that he'd be up for a while. Daniel would often go to the shop late at night. You know, to take inventory, work on his accounts, stack the shelves, look after the bait tanks. When he was working on his book, that's where he went. He didn't sleep much. He was always restless at night."

"But he didn't hint that he might be meeting somebody?"

She shook her head.

I looked hard at her. "He was running out of grass, wasn't he?"

She shrugged. "He still had some."

"But he knew he'd be needing more."

"It worried him, yes."

"Did he say anything about finding a source?"

She gazed away from me. "Not really."

"What do you mean?"

Her eyes returned to mine. "He was trying to cut back. To parcel out what he had left. He talked about having to do something. You know Daniel. He never complained. But he knew he couldn't live without his medicine. And he wouldn't buy it from a dealer."

"Nothing more specific than that?"

She shook her head. "No."

"And you didn't hear anything last night? A car, voices?"

"My studio's way out back. I was asleep."

At that moment we heard a siren's wail racing toward us. Then a police cruiser came careening into the parking area in front of the shop. Two uniformed cops emerged unhurriedly. Neither of them was Sergeant Oakley.

I stood up and went to meet them. "Brady Coyne," I said. "I made the call."

They both nodded. Neither offered his hand or his name. The younger of the two, a compact, dark-haired guy in his twenties, wandered over to where Cammie and Terri were sitting on the steps.

"What've we got?" said the other cop, a paunchy guy about fifteen years older.

"Daniel McCloud has been killed. With a hunting arrow. He's in there." I jerked my thumb backward, indicating his shop.

"McCloud, huh?" The cop shook his head. "Nice guy, McCloud. I usta buy bait from him." He looked over my shoulder toward Cammie and Terri. "The black one's his lady friend. Who's the other one?"

"She came with me."

"And you, Mr. Coyne?"

"I'm Daniel's lawyer. Cammie called me. She's the one who found his body. I drove up from Boston."

"Boston, huh? What's that, two hours on the pike?"

"I made it in an hour-forty."

"How come she didn't call us right away?"

I shrugged. "I guess she was pretty upset. Confused, you know?"

"She should've called right away."

"I know."

"She see anything?"

"She says no."

"And you?"

"I went in and looked at his body. He's dead."

"Shot with an arrow, huh?"

I nodded.

"Well," said the cop, "we'll just sit tight until the detectives get here and try not to mess up the crime scene."

At that moment I heard another siren, and a moment later an unmarked sedan pulled in beside the cruiser. It was followed shortly by an ambulance, then a state police cruiser, then another unmarked sedan.

For the next hour or so, state and local police, forensic experts, EMTs, photographers, and medical examiners swarmed around Daniel's place. Cammie, Terri, and I each had our own detective to question us. Mine was Lieutenant Dominick Fusco, a tall swarthy guy with thick, curly iron-gray hair. He told me he knew my friend Horowitz, a state cop from the Boston area.

I told Fusco that Daniel was both my client and my friend and I couldn't think of anybody—aside, possibly, from Sergeant Oakley of the Wilson Falls Police Department—who didn't like him. I said that I didn't think the bait and tackle business was likely to create murderous competition.

I also told him that Daniel used marijuana for medicine, and that his homegrown year's supply had been confiscated by the police in July, although the case against Daniel had been dismissed. Fusco said he knew all about that, and the implication was clear. They'd be checking out all the local drug sources closely.

Fusco told me that it looked as if Daniel's killer had ransacked the little office in back of the shop. He asked me if that suggested anything to me. I said robbery, obviously. He said there was still money in the cash register and it didn't look as if anything had been stolen from the shop.

If it wasn't robbery, then nothing suggested itself to me.

Otherwise, Fusco didn't tell me anything. And I didn't have much to tell him, either.

After a while the EMTs wheeled a stretcher out of the shop. A lumpy black bag was on the stretcher. It was loaded into the back of the ambulance, which then drove away. It didn't bother to sound its siren.

And, one by one, the various police cruisers and

sedans pulled away. Fusco was the last to leave. He had taken notes as we talked. I had given him both my office and home phone numbers.

He tucked his noteook into his jacket pocket. "We'll be in touch, Mr. Coyne," he said.

"Anything I can do, let me know."

"You can count on it."

He turned to go to his car. I said, "I've been thinking."

He stopped. "Yeah?"

"I don't think he was shot with a bow."

Fusco smiled. "No?"

"No. The angle of that arrow. Assuming he was standing up, to shoot him, you'd have to be lying on the floor."

"That's pretty elementary, Mr. Coyne."

I shrugged. "Guess so."

"They didn't shoot him," he said. "Somebody rammed that arrow into him."

"That's what I was thinking," I said. "He was standing there in front of him, or maybe beside him, and he grabbed that arrow with both hands and just shoved it in as hard as he could."

Fusco nodded. "Raises all kinds of questions, once you think of it that way, huh?"

"Yes," I said.

"Well," he said, "you have any further insights, or hypotheses, or questions, or anything, you be sure to let me know, okay?"

"You bet," I said.

8

We were still standing there, a few minutes after the last official vehicle had left, when a banged-up old Ford pickup chugged to a stop in the driveway.

"Oh, gee," muttered Cammie.

A vastly overweight black man climbed out the passenger side and a powerful-looking swarthy guy got out from behind the wheel. Cammie met them halfway. The three of them formed a huddle with their arms around each other's shoulders. They leaned forward so that their foreheads appeared to be touching. I could hear the low rumble of the black man's voice. It sounded as if he was praying.

After a few minutes, they straightened up. Cammie took each man by the arm and led the two of them back toward where Terri and I stood.

"Brady Coyne, Terri Fiori, this is Roscoe Pollard"— indicating the fat black man—"and Vinnie Colletti. Daniel's dear friends."

I stepped forward and shook hands with each of

them. Roscoe's eyes were large and dark and damp. "Hello, brother," he said softly in a deep bass voice.

Vinnie, who was shaped like a linebacker, said nothing when we shook. His eyes refused to meet mine.

Each of them nodded shyly at Terri.

"I called Vinnie and Roscoe right before you got here," Cammie said to me.

"You should've called sooner, sister," said Roscoe, who I took to be the spokesman for the two men. "We're only twenty minutes away. You shouldn't have been alone."

Cammie nodded. "I know. It was . . . I guess I wasn't thinking very clearly. I called Brady right away, he said he was coming, and . . ." She shrugged.

"You're Daniel's lawyer," said Roscoe to me. Up close, I saw that he was fat like a sumo wrestler. All that flesh was composed of great mounds of muscle.

"Yes," I said to him. "His lawyer."

"You got him out of jail."

I shrugged and nodded.

"Daniel talked about you. He liked you."

"I liked him, too."

He dipped his head in a kind of a bow. "Thank you for coming."

I nodded.

"We got here as fast as we could," he said to Cammie. "The, um, all the official vehicles were already here. We decided to wait till they left. No sense of confusing things."

Cammie smiled and nodded.

Roscoe turned to me. "Me and Vinnie live up the road a ways. Turner's Falls. We were with Daniel over there. We were family. We helped him build this." He waved at the shop and the house. "We hung around with him. Shooting the shit in the shop. Fishing, hunting, catching bait." He shook his head.

I understood that Roscoe and Vinnie had chosen to wait for the police to leave before they made their appearance. Their motives, I figured, were their own business.

"Let's go up to the house," said Cammie. "We'll have coffee."

The five of us went up to the house. Cammie, with her arms around the massive backs of the two big men, looked like a child between them.

We took coffee out onto the deck. Cammie sat staring dry-eyed off toward the river. It would take a while to sink in. Roscoe and Vinnie said little. Vinnie Colletti, in fact, had barely uttered a word since he arrived. Neither Terri nor I tried to disturb the somber mood. We all sat there with our own thoughts.

Sometime later we heard the sound of a motorcycle moving fast toward the house. Cammie jumped up without speaking and walked quickly around to the front.

Roscoe and Vinnie exchanged smiles. They remained on the deck.

Terri and I followed behind Cammie. As we got there, we saw a helmeted man skid a big Harley to a stop in the driveway. He leaped off his bike, took off his helmet, and held out his arms to Cammie. She ran to him and hugged herself against him. He held her for a long time. They swayed back and forth, and it was hard to tell who was comforting whom.

He was a tall, very thin man with a deeply creased face and a scraggly beard. He murmured into Cammie's ear. I noticed that Cammie was crying against his shoulder.

After several minutes the man lifted his head and noticed me and Terri. He whispered something to Cammie, who turned to look at us. Then she stepped out of his embrace, took his hand, and led him to us.

"Brady Coyne, Terri Fiori, this is Brian. Brian Sweeney."

Sweeney held out his hand to me and we shook. He dipped his head shyly and murmured, "Mr. Coyne." Then he turned to Terri and smiled. "Ma'am," he said.

"Brady is Daniel's lawyer," said Cammie. "And friend."

Sweeney nodded. "He's mentioned you," he said to me. He turned back to Cammie. "I came just as soon as I got your message. Sorry I wasn't quicker."

"Brian lives in Vermont," said Cammie. "He doesn't have a phone. You have to call the general store." She moved beside him and snaked her arm around his waist. "Brian is Daniel's best friend in the world."

"What in hell happened?" he said.

"Someone shoved a hunting arrow into his heart," I said.

"Jesus," Sweeney muttered. "They know who?"

"If they do they're not saying."

"An *arrow*?"

I nodded. "Yes. I saw it."

Up close, I could see that Sweeney was younger than I had at first thought. Early forties at the most, I guessed, about the same age as Roscoe and Vinnie. Barely twenty when he prowled the jungles of Indochina with Daniel. But already his hair was thinning and his skinny body was growing stooped and lines were etching themselves on his face. Under its ruddy sunbaked surface his skin seemed dull and sickly.

He stared solemnly at me. "This is hard to believe," he said. "I mean, *Daniel?* An *arrow?* Christ, there ain't *nobody*—" I saw his Adam's apple bob in his long throat, and then tears welled up in his eyes. "Ah, shit," he said. He turned to Cammie and pulled her against him. "Ah, damn, anyhow," he mumbled into her hair. "He was all we had," he said to her. "Both of us."

"Roscoe and Vinnie are here," Cammie told him.

"Good," said Sweeney.

The four of us went back to the house. Sweeney exchanged complicated ritualistic handshakes with Roscoe and Vinnie and then gave each of them a bear hug. The three of them wandered down to the end of the deck, where they stood close together, murmuring.

After a few minutes they came back. Tears glittered in Roscoe's eyes.

"You guys want sandwiches?" said Cammie.

"Good idea," said Sweeney.

Cammie and Terri went inside. I sat down with the other three men and lit a cigarette. Sweeney took a Sucrets box from his shirt pocket, flipped its lid, and removed a prerolled cigarette. He held the box to Roscoe and Vinnie. They both shook their heads.

Sweeney lit up, sucked in, and held it in his lungs.

Then he sighed. "We were all there together," he said to me, jerking his head at the other two men.

"Vietnam?"

He nodded.

"All of you stayed close."

They all nodded.

"It was Daniel," said Roscoe softly. "He kept us together. That's why we all ended up around here. To stick by Daniel."

"So who'd want to kill him?" I said.

The three of them shrugged.

"What about you?" said Sweeney to me. "Do you have any thoughts?"

"You mean, who killed Daniel?"

He nodded.

"Well, he was worried that he was running out of his medicine."

"Yeah," said Sweeney. "Me, too. Daniel kept both of us supplied."

"You—?"

He nodded. "I got Oranged, too. We talked about it after they ripped up his garden. But Daniel wouldn't deal with any supplier. I might," he added with a sly grin, "but not Daniel."

"The only other thing I can think of, then," I said, "is this local cop, this Sergeant Oakley, the one who arrested Daniel. Cammie suspects him, I think. But that seems pretty farfetched to me."

Sweeney shrugged. "Daniel was a lovable old bastard," he said.

I flashed back on Al Coleman's words. Coleman had called Daniel crazy and dangerous. "You sure of that?" I said.

The three of them all frowned at me. "What do you mean?" said Roscoe.

"Somebody didn't love him. Somebody killed him."

He shrugged. "Someone who didn't know him, then."

"A burglar, maybe."

"Nah," said Sweeney quickly. "No burglar would get the drop on him like that. Daniel was too quick and too careful for any burglar. Was anything stolen?"

"I don't think so. The office behind his shop was ransacked. But apparently nothing was taken."

Sweeney stared across the meadow. "I can do some checking around," he said. He glanced at Roscoe and Vinnie. "We all can."

"What are you thinking?"

He shrugged. "A man leads a team into the jungle . . ."

"You should share your thoughts with the police," I said. "You all should."

Sweeney turned to me. "I haven't got any thoughts," he said. "But I'm gonna check around anyway."

9

Lieutenant Fusco called me from Springfield a few days later. But I had no further insights for him. I realized that I hadn't known Daniel McCloud that well. I had represented him when he was arrested, and I had tried to find an agent for his book.

He was more than a client. Most of my clients are. I considered him a friend. But he was also a private man. He hadn't shared his demons with me, though I suspected that any man who had lived through the things he had lived through must be haunted. Cammie, more candidly than Daniel, had suggested as much.

Fusco had no insights, either, or at least none he chose to share with me. He did tell me that they had made no arrests, discovered no motive, identified no suspects. Cammie inventoried the shop for them, and they concluded that there had been no robbery. The office in the back had been messed up, but nothing appeared to be missing.

The medical examiner, Fusco told me, determined that Daniel had died almost instantly when the broadhead sliced through his heart. There was no evidence, either at the crime scene or on Daniel's body, of a struggle between him and his assailant. They had found no useful fingerprints or footprints or tire tracks, no stray human hairs or bits of skin, no scraps of fabric or lost buttons, no cigar ashes or cigarette butts. No witnesses. Nothing.

Terri and I took turns talking with Cammie on the phone each day during the week following Daniel's death. Roscoe Pollard and Vinnie Colletti, she told us, had left shortly after we did the day Daniel was killed. Brian Sweeney stayed a little longer, but then he, too, left. Daniel's army buddies, she said, were a lot like Daniel. They didn't like to stray far from home. But Sweeney, especially, was a comfort, and he called her every day, too, the way Terri and I did.

The state police had interrogated her repeatedly. She had to tell them her entire life story, and Daniel's, too, or what she knew of it. She gave them the names of everybody she could think of who knew Daniel—Roscoe Pollard and Vinnie Colletti and Brian Sweeney and his other "brothers" from Vietnam and the local guys who liked to hang around at the bait and tackle shop. She told me she thought they had arranged for a Vermont state police detective to talk with Sweeney, who was Daniel's best friend and had known him longer and better than anybody, including herself.

She had to tell them about how Daniel had rescued her from her Springfield pimp. That wasn't easy, she said.

She didn't like the way the cops glanced at each other out of the corners of their eyes or the exaggerated way they called her "Ma'am." But they had to know about Boomer.

She was okay, she told us. She said she guessed it still hadn't really hit her yet.

I figured the police regarded Cammie Russell as a suspect.

The following Saturday, just a week after the murder, Terri and I spent the day with Cammie. The three of us walked through the woods and along the river that Daniel had loved. Cammie and Terri seemed to like each other, which made sense to me, since I liked both of them. They whispered between themselves, and a couple of times Cammie laughed. Later, I grilled steaks for the three of us while Cammie and Terri tossed a big salad, and we ate out on the deck while Daniel's favorite Jimmy Reed tape played through the sliding screens. We had some wine and watched the sun sink over the river. Darkness settled into the woods and the night creatures came out. We put our heads back and looked at the stars. We switched to coffee.

"As soon as they release his body," said Cammie, "I'm going to give a party. I hope you both will come."

"Of course," I said.

"And then," she said to me, "I'll probably need to talk with a lawyer."

"Yes. I'll help all I can."

She reached over and squeezed my arm. "I know. You already have."

It was midnight. Terri yawned. We took the coffee mugs inside. "Thanks a lot for coming," said Cammie.

"We can stay with you," I said.

"I'm fine."

"Are you sure?"

She nodded.

I arched my eyebrows doubtfully.

She reached behind her back, then showed me the small automatic handgun that had materialized in her hand.

"Ah," I said. "You're armed."

"Daniel insisted."

"When?"

"Right from the beginning. I was afraid of Boomer coming for me. Daniel kept saying I shouldn't worry, but I wasn't very stable then. So he got this for me and showed me how to use it. I've never seen Boomer." She shrugged. "But I've just kept it."

"I thought Daniel hated guns."

"He didn't hate them. He just never felt he needed one. He thought I did."

"Do you have a license for it?"

Cammie shook her head. "Daniel said it was none of anybody's business. Anyway, he said it wouldn't be such a good idea. I do have a—I've been arrested. You have to get permits from the local police, you know."

"Oakley?" I said.

She smiled. "You know how he felt about Oakley."

"You could get in a lot of trouble, lugging that around."

"I don't lug it around. I just keep it on me when I'm around here alone, that's all. When Daniel was here, I kept it beside my bed. I feel better with it. For now. For a while."

She tucked her little weapon back into the holster at the small of her back.

Terri and I took the back roads home, through South Hadley, the self-proclaimed asparagus capital of the world, through Granby and Belchertown and Pelham and New Salem, heading north parallel to the Quabbin Reservoir, through the dark rural parts of Massachusetts. On Route 2 a few trucks whanged past us. Their backdrafts tugged at my steering wheel. Terri and I didn't talk much. I found some jazz on a Worcester radio station. They were playing a Miles Davis album. His trumpet had never sounded more blue.

"You've been awfully good to Cammie," I said to Terri.

"She's hurting a lot more than she shows."

"Does she talk to you about it?"

"Not really. She talks about Daniel. He was more like a father to her than . . ."

"I guess he saved her life."

"That's how Cammie sees it. He *was* her life. It's like she really doesn't have one now. But she's strong. I think she'll be okay."

I reached across the front seat and squeezed Terri's leg. "Well, you've obviously been good to her."

She laid her hand atop mine. "My nurse's training," she said.

As we approached the Acton turnoff, Terri said, "Brady, I think I want to sleep in my own bed tonight."

"Sure. Okay."

"Alone, I mean."

I shrugged.

"I'm sorry."

"No problem," I lied.

"I want to get Melissa first thing in the morning."

"I thought your mother had her for the weekend."

"It's what I want to do, okay?"

There was an edge to her voice that I had never heard before.

She kissed me hard and long at the door to her building, and I said, "Sure you don't want me to stay?"

"Not tonight."

I shrugged. "Okay."

"Do you understand?"

"No."

She put her arms around my neck and her cheek on my shoulder. "It's complicated."

"Try me."

"I really do want to get Melissa."

"Sure, but—"

"Okay. I want to be alone."

"You mean, you want to be apart from me."

"Yes."

"Okay. Fine."

"Try to understand, Brady. Cammie and I did a lot of talking. It's been a . . . an unsettling day."

"No problem."

"You don't understand, do you?"

"It doesn't matter."

She tipped her head back and looked into my face. "I'm sorry," she said. "I wish . . ."

"Don't worry about it," I said.

She tried to smile. It wasn't convincing.

She kissed me and pressed against me. I held her tight. After a long time she gently pulled away. "Tonight," she whispered, "I need to be alone. Just tonight. Okay?"

"You got it," I said.

She hugged me quickly, then fumbled in her purse for her keys. "Call me?"

"I will."

"Good night, Brady."

"'Night, Terri."

I walked back to the parking lot. When I got to my car, I turned to wave to Terri. But she had already gone inside.

10

I called Terri on Tuesday. "How's the weekend look?"
I said.

"Not that good. I—"

"Don't give me an excuse, hon. You don't have to."

She hesitated. "I'm sorry. You're right. I was going to
tell you I was all tied up with Melissa. It's true, but it's not
the point. I've been all tied up with Melissa plenty of times
and you've been a part of it. I don't want to get into lying or
making up excuses with you, Brady."

"You don't have to. I'm a big boy."

"My feelings for you haven't changed."

"But?"

"But . . . my feelings are making me nervous. I need
space."

"I guess," I said, "true love is when both people feel
the need for the same amount of space at the same time."

"I always thought it was when you stopped feeling
that you needed space."

"No," I said. "Everybody needs space."

I ended up spending the first day of my weekend space with my friend Doc Adams. We drank beer and played chess in his backyard in Concord, and toward the middle of the afternoon Doc mentioned a local pond that, he had heard, the state stocked with trout every September. Nobody seemed to fish there, Doc told me. Doc wasn't much for fly-fishing himself. He thought it a pretty yuppified sport, actually. He tried it a few times, and on one especially windy afternoon on the Deerfield River he drove a hook beyond the barb into his earlobe. I yanked it out for him—Doc never uttered a peep—and that was enough fly-fishing for him. But he loved to eat fresh-caught trout and he wondered if a man who claimed to be a good fly-fisherman might be able to harvest a meal from this secret pond of his.

Doc even volunteered to paddle the canoe and clean the fish afterward as well, should I get lucky.

The surface of the pond was littered with crimson and yellow maple leaves, which skittered around like toy sailboats ahead of a light puffy breeze. We saw lots of migrating birds—ducks in the coves and warblers in the pondside bushes—and I managed to catch a dozen or so fat ten-inch brook trout on gaudy little wet flies. We kept six and brought them back to Doc's house on Old Stone Mill Road. Doc sautéed them in butter with tarragon and shallots while his wife, Mary, and I drank wine and kibitzed. Mary asked about Terri. I told her that Terri was tied up with her daughter for the weekend. Mary cocked her head and looked at me sideways. I shrugged. She didn't pursue it.

The trout were delicious. Doc asserted that we could've caught twice as many using spinning gear. We argued our respective definitions of sport.

Mary said she knew a young sculptress, recently divorced. I told her I didn't think I was interested. She smiled and said she thought as much, but figured she should mention it.

Sunday morning I called the house in Wellesley. I wanted to say hello to Joey, my younger son. The answering machine took it. Gloria asked me to leave my name and number and the time of my call. I declined her invitation.

I tried Billy, my other son, at his dorm room at UMass. No answer.

So much for family ties.

I spent the afternoon rummaging distractedly through the weekend paperwork that Julie had stuffed into my briefcase. That evening around suppertime Cammie called. "Can you come to a party next Saturday afternoon?" she said.

"Yes. Wouldn't miss it."

"Dress casual."

"Gladly."

"They're releasing Daniel's body on Tuesday."

"Do they have any new evidence?"

"If they do, they're not sharing it with me."

"I'll give Lieutenant Fusco a call," I said, "see what he knows. I'll be there Saturday."

"Please bring Terri."

"I'll try."

After a hesitation, she said, "Is something the matter?"

"I don't know. A boy-girl thing, I guess."

She chuckled. "Tell her I'll be very sad if she doesn't come."

"I'll tell her exactly that."

And I did. I said, "Cammie will be very sad if you don't come."

"You don't need to do that, Brady," said Terri. "Of course I'll go with you. I hope *you'd* be sad if I didn't go."

"That's the truth. I missed you this weekend."

"Wow," she said softly.

"Wow?"

"That's about the most vulnerable thing you've ever said to me."

"I don't always say what I'm thinking."

"Maybe you should try it more often."

I pondered that bit of advice after I hung up with her. I concluded that, on the whole, it was dangerous advice.

I called State Police Lieutenant Dominick Fusco on Monday morning. He was unavailable. I requested he return my call. He didn't. I tried again Tuesday, and then on Wednesday. Finally, on Thursday afternoon, Julie buzzed me and said that Lieutenant Fusco was on the line.

I pressed the blinking button on my console and said, "Coyne."

"Fusco," he said. "What can you do for me?"

"I was just wondering how the Daniel McCloud investigation is going."

"That's what I figured. That's why I didn't call you right back."

"Well . . ."

"You haven't got anything for me, right?"

"Right."

"Mr. Coyne," said Fusco, "we don't normally feel obligated to share the progress of our investigations with citizens. If we did that, we'd have no time for investigating."

"Yeah, but—"

"Daniel McCloud's murder is not the only case on my agenda just now, Mr. Coyne. Here's how it works, okay? You got something for me, you make sure I know it. That's your duty as a citizen, lawyer or no lawyer. If I come up with something, I'll probably pursue the hell out of it. But it's possible I might not have the time or the inclination to share it with you. Get it?"

"This conversation we're having here is what you call effective public relations," I said. "Right?"

"My job," said Fusco, "ain't relating to the public. My job is arresting them when they break the law."

"Be nice, then, if you'd do your job."

I think Fusco and I hung up on each other simultaneously. Goes to show what happens when you say what you're thinking.

Terri and I had to park about a quarter of a mile from Daniel's house on Saturday afternoon. Daniel's friends had turned out in force. I hadn't realized he had that many friends. The roadside was lined with parked vehicles. Battered old pickups, mainly, with a few battered old sedans, most of them Fords and Chevvies. My BMW was one of the few unbattered vehicles in the bunch.

Terri and I walked to the house holding hands. We

wore jeans and flannel shirts and windbreakers and sneakers. Twins. Terri looked especially terrific in jeans. The way she squeezed my hand and bumped shoulders with me as we walked was terrific, too. It occurred to me that maybe she had satisfied her need for space for a while.

We weaved our way among the guests as we made our way toward the back of the house. I guessed there were close to a hundred people milling around Daniel's property holding plastic glasses or beer cans. I didn't recognize anybody, but several of them said, "Hey, how ya doin?" to me and Terri anyway. Rural good-neighborliness.

The bar was set up on the deck behind the house. That's where we found Cammie. When she saw us she smiled and came over. Brian Sweeney was with her. His hand was wrapped around a beer can, and the stub of a dead cigar was wedged into the corner of his mouth. Cammie had her arm tucked through his.

She exchanged quick kisses with Terri and gave me a big hug. Sweeney shook my hand and gave Terri a little courtly bow.

"Thanks for coming, you guys," said Cammie.

"Wouldn't have missed it," I said.

A man about Sweeney's age grabbed his arm. Sweeney whirled around, yelled, "Holy shit," and embraced him. They wandered away, their arms across each other's shoulders.

Cammie watched them for a moment, then turned back to us. She smiled. "Nothing tighter than army buddies," she said. She cocked her head at me. "Maybe later we can do some business?"

I nodded. "Of course."

Cammie turned to Terri, bent, and whispered something to her. Terri nodded. "Let me borrow her for a minute, okay?" said Cammie to me.

I shrugged. "Sure."

The two of them wandered away. Cammie had her hand on Terri's shoulder. I had the feeling they were discussing me.

So I found myself standing there on the deck. I was surrounded by people, but I was alone. I spotted Roscoe Pollard and Vinnie Colletti. Roscoe noticed me and waved. I waved back. I found several big washtubs full of ice and Budweiser. I went over and fished out two cans. I weaved through the people toward Cammie and Terri. The two women were leaning their elbows on the deck railing, staring off toward the river and talking softly, their heads close together. I pressed the cold beer can against Terri's neck. "Hey!" she squealed. She spun around and glared at me. I held up the Bud. "Oh," she said. "Thanks."

She took the can and turned back to her conversation with Cammie.

I shrugged and wandered off the deck and out into the yard. I started to head toward the knot of people that included Roscoe and Vinnie, then changed my mind. I felt like an outsider.

So I stood there. I sipped from my beer and lit a cigarette.

A hand squeezed my elbow. "You get the cold shoulder, there, Mr. Coyne?"

It was Sweeney. I smiled. "From the ladies?" I nodded. "Looks like it. And it's Brady, okay?"

"Yeah," he said. "Okay."

We found ourselves sauntering away from the crowd in the yard, headed more or less in the direction of the river. Sweeney, I guessed, like Daniel, was not comfortable in crowds.

"Listen," said Sweeney as we walked. "Daniel told me about how you kept him out of jail that time. It woulda killed him, you know?"

"I didn't really do much, truthfully," I said. "They dropped the charges before I could do anything."

"Well, he sure appreciated it."

He stopped walking to light a wooden match with his thumbnail. He ignited his cigar butt. "Hard to believe," he puffed.

"Daniel?"

He exhaled and nodded.

"That he's dead, you mean."

He shrugged. "Not so much that. I guess I never find death hard to believe anymore. How it happened, I mean."

"An ugly way to go."

He turned to face me. "There are uglier ways, Brady. Believe me. What I hear, that was pretty quick. What I mean is somebody getting the drop on him like that. I never saw Daniel with his defenses down."

"It's been a long time since you guys were in the jungle," I said.

"Don't matter. You never lose it." He removed the cigar from his mouth and took a long draft from his beer can. "You heard anything?"

I shook my head.

"No suspects, no evidence?"

"No," I said. "I talked to the state cop in charge a couple days ago. Lieutenant Fusco. Not very forthcoming. Doesn't seem to me they're getting anywhere. They questioned you, didn't they?"

"Me?" he said. "Yeah. State cops dropped by. Vermont cops. I'm living up there in the sticks. Kinda like Daniel. Little place in the woods. Catch some fish, shoot some deer." He smiled. "You don't get the jungle out of your system, you know? Anyways, they asked me about who might want to kill him. How the hell would I know?"

"You said you'd check around with the men from your team," I said.

He nodded. "I am. Most of 'em are here." He shook his head. "Hard to figure, though. I mean, somebody in command, sure, there'll be times when you want to kill the guy, if you know what I mean. But that's just the stress of it. Daniel brought us through."

"What about Roscoe and Vinnie?"

Sweeney turned his head and spat a flake of tobacco onto the ground. "Yeah," he said, "they were with us. Damn good soldiers. Good men, Roscoe and Vinnie."

"They're not . . . sick?"

"The Orange? Nope. They were the lucky ones."

"And they were close to Daniel, huh?"

"We all were close with each other. Daniel was our glue."

"He was a pretty lovable guy, from what I could see," I said.

Sweeney stopped and leaned back against the trunk of an oak tree. "Lovable," he repeated. He smiled. Sadly, I thought. "Well, he was, yes. But Daniel could fool you. You meet Daniel, you think he's this gentle teddy bear. Which he was. But in the jungle he was like some other kind of animal. I mean, a fucking predator, you know? He was completely comfortable, tuned in to every sound, every smell. He could tell you whether it was a monkey or a VC just by the sound of something moving a bush. And he could kill like no man I ever knew."

I nodded. "I guess that's how you survived."

"Were you over there, Brady?"

I shook my head.

He grinned. "Probably marching around in the streets, huh?"

I shrugged. "I did some of that, yes."

"I never hated Jane Fonda, myself," said Sweeney. "Figured most of you people just wanted us home. We wanted the same damn thing."

"That's how I felt about it."

"Old Daniel," said Sweeney, "he could be an animal in the jungle. But he wasn't an animal. He was a man." Sweeney chuckled softly. "The old Snake Eater."

"Snake Eater? Daniel?"

He nodded. "It was a term of honor. Actually, it's kind of a general name that's sometimes used for Special Forces guys. The Snake Eaters. Like Green Berets, except we all thought that was dumb. We never called ourselves Green Berets. But Daniel, that sonofabitch actually ate snakes. They taught us how to survive in the jungle, see? How to kill a snake and skin it and eat it raw. But Daniel, he already knew that. He did it when he was a kid. He'd eat any damn thing. Grubs and ants and leeches. I saw him do it. He kept tryin' to get us to do it, too. Ants I got so I could swallow. Never could get a leech down, though. No problem for Daniel. See, we were all *taught* how to eat all this stuff, but Daniel actually *did* it. He used to say, compared to the rest of it, raw snake was a 'farkin' delicacy.'"

I grinned. Sweeney had Daniel's blend of Scottish burr and Georgia farmboy down pat.

"So, anyway," he continued after a moment, "that's how come we called him Snake Eater. It's like, there are lots of godfathers. But only one you actually call Godfather. Listen, you want another beer?"

"After this conversation, I could use something."

Sweeney grinned. "Didn't mean to freak you out, there, Brady. I just—shit, I miss Daniel, that's all. Helps, talking about him."

I nodded.

"Hang on. I'll be right back."

He headed back to the house. I shaded my eyes and tried to spot Terri. I didn't see her.

Sweeney was back in a few minutes. He handed me a beer.

"Thanks," I said.

"We had to go through places where they had defoliated," he said. "We didn't know there was a problem."

"Agent Orange," I said.

He nodded. "Most of us got it. I guess Pollard and Colletti were about the only ones who didn't."

"How'd they manage to escape it?"

Sweeney shrugged. "Just lucky, I guess. Galinski died

of it. His widow got a little settlement from Uncle. Me and Daniel, we tried to get some help. Daniel's friend there . . ."

"Charlie McDevitt."

"Yeah. Charlie. He tried to help us."

"Charlie's a friend of mine. That's how I met Daniel."

"I know. When he was in jail. Anyway, Charlie tried to help us, but we got the runaround."

"Does smoking marijuana help you?" I said.

He cocked his head at me, then smiled. "Yeah. It's the only thing that helps. Daniel kept me supplied. Don't know what the fuck I'm gonna do now. Try growing my own, I guess."

A woman bumped up against Sweeney and grabbed onto his arm. "Hey, Bri'," she slurred. "How they hangin'?"

He looked at her, then smiled. He put his arm across her shoulders. "How you makin' out, Ronnie?"

"Jus' pissa."

She was probably in her forties. She was fat and graying, but she had youthful skin.

She was very drunk.

Sweened nudged her to look at me. "Ronnie Galinski," he said, "this is Brady Coyne. Daniel's lawyer."

She looked at me without interest, then turned back to Sweeney. "Don't know why the fuck I'm here," she said. "Wouldn'ta come, but Neddie woulda wanted me to. Neddie loved the bas'ard. Sumbitch got Neddie killed."

"It wasn't Daniel's fault," said Sweeney gently.

"That shit jus' ate him up, Bri'," she said. "His legs swole up and his skin fell off and his brain caught fire."

97

Sweeney put his arm around her. "I know, hon," he said softly. "I remember."

Sweeney glanced at me, then gently steered Ronnie Galinski away. He had his arm across her shoulders, and he was bending to her, talking to her.

Galinski. That, I recalled, was the name of the soldier who had died of Agent Orange poisoning. His widow was not, apparently, a Daniel McCloud fan.

I felt something soft brush the back of my neck. I turned around. Terri said, "Hi."

I touched her hair. "Having fun?"

"Weirdest wake I've every been to. Quite an assortment, huh?"

"Daniel's friends."

"One guy got my ear," she said. "One of Daniel's men. I wouldn't say he was exactly a friend. Tall, skinny man named Shaw. He was talking about how they all had to go through this defoliated part of the jungle, and they ended up with skin problems. It sounded as if he was blaming Daniel."

"I've been talking to Brian Sweeney. He seems to credit Daniel for getting them out of there alive."

Terri nodded. "Yeah, well this Shaw, he mainly blames Daniel for getting them in there in the first place."

A motive for murder, I thought. I did not share my thought with Terri.

We stood there together quietly for a while, watching the people and sipping our beers. It was not an uncomfortable silence between us. After a while, I said, "How's Cammie doing?"

"Good, I'd say. She seems to know everybody."

At that moment I became aware of a noise. It was a low, rising wail, and it came from the edge of the river at the far end of Daniel's property, and it took me a moment to identify it.

A bagpipe.

Gradually the hum of a hundred voices died and the wail of the pipes rose and moved into a long slow version of "Amazing Grace."

I felt a tightening in my throat and a burning in my eyes.

Bagpipes always do that to me.

Without speaking, Terri and I began to walk arm-in-arm toward the source of the music. I was aware that everybody else was following the music also, a silent mass of people moving toward the river as if hypnotized by those pipes.

The piper stood on the low bluff overlooking the Connecticut River. He was dressed in tartans and kilt. He was a big, rawboned guy, red-haired and red-faced. The crowd gathered at the bluff, a little aside from the piper. I glanced around. Nobody was smiling, nobody was talking.

He segued into "The Skye Boat Song." I heard Terri whispering beside me. "Speed bonny boat like a bird on the wing . . ."

The crowd moved and parted and Cammie and Brian Sweeney appeared, walking slowly. I noticed that they were barefoot. Sweeney's arm was around Cammie's waist. She carried a blue ceramic urn in both of her hands.

Daniel.

Behind the two of them strode seven other men, also barefoot, including Roscoe Pollard and Vinnie Colletti.

"That's Shaw," whispered Terri. "The bald one."

He was the last of the seven. The others shuffled along with their heads down. Shaw's head was up, and he appeared to be marching.

I looked around the crowd for Ronnie Galinski, but I didn't spot her. I guessed she might have passed out somewhere.

Cammie and Sweeney and the other seven filed down over the bluff to the river. The rest of us closed in behind them at the edge of the water.

The piper continued to play.

Cammie and Sweeney waded knee-deep into the water. The other seven gathered in a semicircle around them. They made cups of their hands as if they were at the altar rail receiving communion. Cammie moved from one to the other, pouring in a portion of Daniel's ashes.

The pipes rose, wailed, stopped.

It was very still there beside the river.

Sweeney held his cupped hands high in front of his face. The others imitated him. "So long, old Snake Eater," he said. I thought I could see tears glitter in his eyes.

They all let Daniel dribble through their fingers into the river.

The piper played "Danny Boy."

Cammie waded out of the river. Daniel's team followed behind her.

We all fell in behind them and moved slowly back to the yard behind Daniel's house. No one spoke.

The piper, still back on the bluff by the river, played "Going Home," the Dvorak tune. Terri wrapped her arms around my waist and cried against my chest. I rested my cheek on top of her head. I could have cried, too.

Bagpipes do that to me.

11

The guests began to shake hands and exchange hugs. The party was over. Terri and I were still standing there when Cammie came up behind me and grabbed my hand.

"Can I talk to you for a minute?" she said.

I turned to her. Her eyes were blazing. "What's the matter?"

"It's that shithead Oakley. Come see."

She led me down the driveway to the road where all the cars and pickups were parked. Every one of them had a white rectangle tucked under the windshield wiper.

I went to the nearest car, removed the ticket, and looked at it. Fifteen bucks for parking in a restricted zone. Sergeant Richard Oakley had signed it. I looked at Cammie and shrugged.

"What can we do?" she said.

"If it's illegal to park on this road, nothing."

"It's harassment," she said. "It's . . . it's perverted."

"Well," I said, scratching my head, "we could sure

make it awkward for our friend Oakley if everybody exer-
cised his right to appeal the ticket at a clerk magistrate's
hearing."

"We can't expect these people to do that. They have to
work. Some of them have driven a long way to be here."

I nodded. "Not much we can do, then. I've got a feeling that complaining to the police won't do much good."

"Yeah," she said. "That's probably just what Oakley
wants. I don't know what his problem is, but the hell with
him. I'll pay them myself. I don't want all these people
leaving with a bad taste in their mouth. Let's collect them."

Cammie and I went up and down the street, removing
all the tickets. There were fifty-three of them. Oakley had
made out half of them. A cop named Wentzel did the other
half. It would cost Cammie over $750 to pay them all.

We went back to the house. "Don't tell anybody,"
she said.

"Okay."

The shadows lengthened and a chill crept into the air.
The people began to drift to their cars. Cammie and Brian
Sweeney stood at the edge of the driveway, shaking hands
and thanking everybody for coming. Terri and I fell in line.

When we got to Cammie, she said to me, "Would you
guys mind waiting? I'd like to talk to you for a minute."

"Sure. Okay."

Terri and I went back to the deck. I fished around the
bottom of one of the washtubs, up to my elbow in half-
melted ice, and found two cans of Budweiser. I gave one to
Terri. We sat in deck chairs with our feet up on the railing
and stared off toward Daniel's river.

"He's probably in Holyoke by now," I said.

She nodded.

"He'll cross the line into Connecticut by dawn."

"Brady . . ." Terri reached over and held on to my hand.

"He should reach the ocean sometime on Monday."

"That bagpiper," she said.

I nodded and sipped my beer.

After that we didn't talk. We continued to hold hands.

After a while Cammie came back and sat down beside us. She sighed deeply. "What'd you think?" she said.

"It was memorable," I said. "Perfect. Was the piper your idea?"

"Brian's," she said. "Having the rest of Daniel's team do the ashes was his idea, too. I think Daniel would've liked it."

"Me, too," I said. "Did Roscoe and Vinnie and Brian all leave?"

She nodded. "They're not very sociable. All of those guys are like that. They're just different from other people."

"I wanted to ask them something," I said.

"What?"

I hesitated. Then I said, "I guess a lot of the men got Agent Orange poisoning over there. The way Daniel did."

Cammie nodded. "Brian did. One man died of it. There were others."

"Well, it occurred to me . . ."

"You think they blame Daniel?"

"That Shaw does," said Terri.

Cammie narrowed her eyes and peered at me. "So you think . . ."

I shrugged. "There was a woman here who seemed to hate Daniel. Her husband died from the Agent Orange. Galinski."

"She was pretty drunk," said Cammie.

"I'm just trying to figure out who'd want to kill him."

Cammie nodded. "Me, too. But his army buddies? After all they went through together?"

I nodded. "I know."

We stared into the darkness for a while. I thought of all the Vietnam vets I knew. Several of them had tried to tell me about the horror they carried around in their heads. I knew that those of us who hadn't been here could never understand.

"Look," said Cammie after several minutes. "I hate to impose on you . . ."

"No problem," I said. "If you can put your hands on Daniel's papers, I'll try to sort it out for you."

"I don't exactly know what he had," she said. "Or even where he kept it. I guess we should check his office."

"At the shop?"

She nodded.

The three of us walked around the house to the shop. Cammie unlocked the door and we stepped inside. I found the light switch. It looked exactly as it had the morning we found Daniel's body there, minus the body. The large oval bloodstain was still there, black and dull. The blurry outline of a man's body was visible in the middle of it.

I heard Terri exhale quickly.

"I guess I should get in here and clean up sometime," said Cammie. "But I just . . ."

Terri put her arm around Cammie's shoulder.

We stepped gingerly around the bloodstain to the door that led to Daniel's office. It stood ajar. I pushed it open.

It was a small square room, ten by ten, no bigger. One small window. There was a desk and a file cabinet and a swivel chair. An old Underwood typewriter sat on the desk. The drawers of the desk and the cabinet hung open. Papers were scattered over the floor. It had been torn apart, all right, just as the police had said.

"Let's see what we've got," I said.

The three of us got down on our knees and gathered the papers together. They were all business records—bills, accounts, inventories, catalogs, tax records. I sorted through them and made a pile of the stuff that I might need to probate Daniel's estate.

"Is there anything missing?" I said to Cammie after we finished.

She shrugged. "I couldn't tell you. I never came in here. I didn't know anything about his business. Just that I assumed he lost money at it. This," she said, waving her hand around the little room, "was his little sanctuary. It's where he came when he was writing his book."

"He never showed it to you, huh?"

"He was very secretive about that book. He worked on it for, I don't know, three or four years. He'd sneak down here and wouldn't tell me why for the longest time. I'd tell him, I'd say, 'You meeting some girl or something?' And he'd give me that old smile and say, 'Nay, lass. No girl.' But he wouldn't say what it was. Daniel was a secretive man anyway, but I kept bugging him, and finally he admitted he was trying to write a book. I asked him what it was about. He told me not to ask. He made it clear. It was none of my business. So I didn't ask. I just knew that it was important to him and he didn't want anybody to know about it. I think it would be neat if Daniel's book got published."

I nodded. I realized that Daniel's murder had driven thoughts of his book from my mind. "I'll check with Al Coleman again, see what the holdup is. He said he was sending it right back, and that was over a month ago. There are plenty of other agents. But meanwhile, there's got to be insurance records, a will, deeds, things like that that I'll need. None of that stuff's here."

Cammie snapped her fingers. "He kept a strongbox in his bedroom closet. That's probably what you want."

We locked up the shop and went back to the house. A couple of minutes later Cammie placed a cheap metal box on the kitchen table. It wasn't locked. Inside I found several manila envelopes. Daniel had carefully labeled each of them with a black felt-tip pen. "Deed." "Will." "Automobile." "Medical." "Business." "Tax." "Insurance."

None, I noticed, was labeled "Book."

I decided to take the whole box with me. I could look through all of it later.

Then Cammie switched on the floodlights that lit up the yard, and Terri and I helped her fill plastic trash bags with beer cans and plastic glasses. There were hundreds of them — in the house, on the deck, in the gardens, all over the lawn, under the shrubbery. I told Terri that Daniel's yard after the party was our world in microcosm. She told me I was unnecessarily cynical. I said I didn't think so.

Cammie insisted that Terri and I stay for supper. We

made ham-and-Swiss-cheese-and-tomato sandwiches on whole wheat and washed them down with more beer. We had coffee on the deck.

"What are you going to do?" Terri said to Cammie as we studied the night sky.

"I don't know. Nothing for a while. Paint."

"Going to stay here?"

"For now." She shrugged.

"Will you be okay?"

She smiled. "I've got my friends," she said.

Terri asked me to spend the night with her in Acton. I accepted. She slept pressed tight against my back with her arm draped over my hip, and I lay awake for a long time with her soft breath on the back of my neck, and I knew that just then neither of us was feeling any need for space.

I also knew that that would change. It always did.

Sunday evening I emptied the manila envelopes from Daniel's strongbox onto my kitchen table and began to sort through their contents. He had everything well organized. It would be easy.

He had bequeathed the house and the studio to Cammie. The shop and its contents went jointly to Brian Sweeney, Roscoe Pollard, and Vinnie Colletti.

The last envelope I opened was the one labeled "Insurance." It contained policies on his car and his buildings, plus a modest army policy on his life. The beneficiary was Cammie.

Inside the big insurance envelope was a smaller envelope. I opened it and spilled its contents onto the table.

Photographs. Six of them. Plus two index cards.

The photos were five-by-seven black-and-white head-and-shoulder shots. Six men. On the back of each was printed a name and address. The printing did not match Daniel's.

Each of the two index cards had a name and address printed on it in Daniel's hand.

I looked at the photographs. All of them were creased and smudged and dog-eared, as if somebody had carried them around in his hip pocket for a while. I recognized none of the faces. None of the names meant anything to me.

Friends of Daniel? Distant cousins? War buddies? Agent Orange victims? Debtors or creditors?

Enemies?

I couldn't recall seeing any of the faces at Daniel's funeral party. The photos showed six adult white males, all in some stage of middle age. None was particularly distinctive.

I read the addresses. The two on the index cards were in western Massachusetts, as were two on the backs of photos. Two were in Rhode Island, one in New Hampshire, and one in New York.

I sat there at my table, puffing a cigarette and gazing out onto the dark harbor.

On Monday I called Cammie and read the eight names and addresses to her. None of them was familiar to her. None of them was anybody who had been invited to the party. As far as she could recall, Daniel had never mentioned any of them to her.

"Well," I said, "they were somebody to Daniel. They were in with his insurance papers."

"Insurance?"

"Which may or may not mean a damn thing."

"What are you going to do?"

"I don't know. Talk to these people, I guess."

"You think . . . ?"

"That I've got a list of possible murderers? One of them did it? Maybe."

"Wow," she breathed.

"So I'll check them out."

"Maybe Brian or Roscoe or Vinnie might recognize them. They've known Daniel a lot longer than me."

"Sure," I said. "These could be names from the war. I'll give those guys a call."

"Hang on," she said. "I'll get their numbers."

She came back onto the line a minute later. She read Brian Sweeney's contact telephone number in Vermont to me. Pollard and Colletti shared the same phone in Turner's Falls, Massachusetts. "Let me know what you find out," she said.

"You can count on it."

"You better be careful, Brady."

"Believe me," I said, "I know how to be careful. Discreet and careful. That's me."

12

The number Cammie had given me for Brian Sweeney was, I remembered, a general store in East Corinth, Vermont. Most likely *the* general store. Gas pumps out front, spinning rods and aluminum lawn chairs and pyramids of maple syrup cans in the window, a wheel of Vermont cheddar and a cracker barrel next to the wood stove, ammunition and knives under the glass counter, cases of beer and sacks of dried beans and bait tanks out back. On the map, East Corinth appeared to be little more than an intersection on the back road from Bradford to Barre, which weren't exactly major metropolitan areas themselves.

"General stow-ah," said the guy who answered the phone when I called Monday morning. "Ed he-ah."

Ed sounded like one of those disillusioned New Jersey dentists who chuck it all and flee to northern New England to pursue their dream of the simple honest country life and end up finding it complicated by leaky roofs, dried-up wells, mud seasons, blackflies, endless winters, suspicious natives, and hard-hearted bankers. More disillusionment.

Generally after a few years they end up practicing rural dentistry.

"I'm trying to get ahold of Brian Sweeney," I told Ed.

"Ain't he-ah just now," said Ed. "Generally comes by lat-ah in the afternoon. I can give him your name."

Ed, I decided, had a poor ear for the significant differences between the Down East Maine inflections—which Hollywood television productions never get right anyway—and those of small-town Vermont.

"My name is Brady Coyne," I said. I spelled it for Ed, and gave him both my office and home numbers. "I'm in Boston. Tell Sweeney to call collect. I'll be at one place or the other."

"Brian'll be by lat-ah," repeated Ed. "He'll want to tell me about the hunting. It's bird season up here now. Pa'tridge, woodcock. Brian's got himself a pair of nice Springers. Hunts all day, don't quit till he's got his limit." Ed tried out a country-boy chuckle. "Heh-heh. Sometimes he don't quit even then."

I managed to disengage myself from Ed only after he told me about how all the male teachers and students played hookey from the regional high school during the first week of the deer season, and how he opened the store at four a.m. that week to sell buckshot and deer urine scent and coffee and sandwiches. I suspected Ed valued the hunters' company as much as their business.

I tried the Turner's Falls number for Roscoe Pollard and Vinnie Colletti. No answer.

I spent the rest of the morning telephone sparring with other lawyers on behalf of clients, and it wasn't until noontime when I found a minute to call Al Coleman in New York. I expected to hear Bonnie's voice on their office answering machine, and I was prepared to leave a strongly worded message. "Where's that damn manuscript?" Something to that effect.

Instead Bonnie answered in person. "The Coleman Literary Agency," she said.

"Oh, hi," I said. "It's Brady Coyne. I didn't expect you to answer."

"I'm back. Just for the week, I hope. Trying to get everything cleaned out. I've gotten all your messages. I would've eventually returned your call."

"Cleaned out?"

There was a long pause before she said, "You don't know, do you?"

"Know what?"

I heard her expel a long breath. "About Al."

"What's going on?"

"Al died."

"Oh, shit. What happened?"

She sighed again. I suspected she had been asked that question many times and didn't enjoy answering it. "It was about a month ago. He . . . they said he got mugged."

"Mugged?"

"They found his body in the subway station. He was stabbed. He bled to death. He lay there a long time before somebody figured out that he wasn't a derelict in an Irish linen sports jacket passed out in a pool of blood."

"God!" I managed to mumble.

"New York," said Bonnie Coleman. "I hate this goddam city."

"Look," I said. "You don't have to—"

"It's okay, Mr. Coyne. His clients have to know. I'm
turning everything over to Keating and Keating. They're
very good. A big Park Avenue agency. It's been a little complicated. See, I'll continue to get the commissions on Al's
old accounts, but—you don't need to hear this."

"No, it's all right. I'm not really a client. He had a
manuscript."

"Yes, I remember."

"Al had decided not to handle it. He was going to
return it—"

"You haven't got it yet?" she said.

"Well, there's no hurry, really. But when you can . . ."

"I don't think I have it."

"Has it been sent? Did it get lost in the mail?"

"I don't know." She paused for a moment. "I don't
remember sending it. I—it's been a tough month, Mr.
Coyne."

"I'm sorry."

"Yeah." She didn't sound as if she believed me. She
must have heard a lot of insincere "I'm sorry"s lately.

"I mean it," I said. "I'm very sorry."

"Okay. Thanks."

"And I'm sorry to be pestering you."

"I assume Al mailed your manuscript to you."

"I haven't got it."

"Wouldn't be the first time the postal service screwed

up. I'll check around. There's still lots of junk here. I'm still finding stuff in the back of the file cabinets. Christ, he kept most of his deals and agreements in his head. I mean, he'd write himself notes, but damned if anybody except him could understand them. You know what I mean? He'd send a proposal to six publishers, and what he'd write down would be the first names of the editors. Then he'd shove the notes under his blotter. I mean, *he* knew what he was doing, but it's been a bear, trying to straighten it all out without him."

"I was just hoping to get that manuscript back."

"What was the title of it?"

"I don't know."

"Well, but . . ."

"And I don't know the author's name, either."

"How . . . ?"

"He used a pseudonym. I don't know what that was. I sent it to Al sealed, just the way the writer gave it to me."

"Well, I'll look for it. I'll see what I can do."

"Thanks," I said. I hesitated. "Bonnie, about Al . . ."

"It's happening all over this city. Which is no consolation. It's a jungle. The police just throw up their hands. A nice quiet little man gets senselessly, randomly murdered, and we're supposed to understand that it's the chance you take, living in this wonderful city. I can't wait to get out of here."

"When did you say it happened?"

"A month ago."

I mentally calculated. It was just about a month earlier when Al Coleman told me that he had decided not to handle Daniel's book. He said he was going to mail Daniel's manuscript back to me. When it didn't arrive, I had tried calling. That's when I began to get answering machine messages.

Al hadn't returned my calls because he couldn't. And Bonnie had other things on her mind.

He died, I figured, before he had the chance to mail back Daniel's manuscript.

"Bonnie," I said, "that manuscript is probably lying around somewhere."

"Probably," she said. "When I find it, I'll ship it along."

"Thanks. Look, if there's anything I can do . . ."

"I've got a good lawyer, Mr. Coyne."

"I mean, as a friend."

"I don't even know you."

"Al and I went to school together."

She laughed softly. "And neither of you remembered each other."

"True," I said. "Still . . ."

"I'm sorry," she said. "I sound rude. I don't mean to be. I've got Al's old friends coming out of the woodwork at me. Most of them want to console me by screwing me. I'm just kinda fed up with guys offering to help, you know?"

"That's not what I meant," I said.

"No, I suppose it's not."

"I guess there really isn't much I could do."

"No, probably not," she said. "I appreciate the thought, though. I'll look for that book."

"Okay. Thanks."

After I hung up from Bonnie Coleman, I swiveled around to stare out my office window down onto Copley Square. The noontime crowds were beginning to swarm over the concrete plaza that separates the public library from Trinity Church. The fountains were turned off, and without them the plaza is pretty stark. But during good weather, secretaries and accountants and sales clerks and stockbrokers mingle there at lunchtime, eating sandwiches from waxed paper on the benches. The men loosen their ties and the women hitch their skirts up over their knees and tilt their faces up to the sun.

On this October Monday they had a crispy autumn day for it. There wouldn't be many more of them.

Somebody murdered Daniel McCloud.

Somebody murdered Al Coleman, too.

Daniel's manuscript was missing.

It seemed to me unlikely that those were unrelated events.

The phone rang just as Julie was pulling the dust cover over her computer terminal for the day. She moved to answer it, but I waved her away. "Go," I said. "I got it."

She hesitated, her hand poised over the console, then smiled and took it back. I reached over and picked up the phone.

"Brady Coyne," I said.

"I have a collect call from Brian Sweeney. Will you accept it?"

"Sure."

"Go ahead," said the operator.

"Brady?" came Sweeney's voice.

"Hey, thanks for calling." Julie kissed my cheek and wiggled her fingers at me. I wiggled mine at her. She left. "Cammie gave me this number," I said to Sweeney.

"I ain't got a phone in my place. I like it that way."

"Sorry to bother you."

"No problem. What's up?"

"Hang on a second. I want to read something to you." I fumbled in my jacket pocket and took out the piece of paper on which I had written the eight names and addresses from Daniel's "insurance" file. "Okay. Got it. Some names. I was wondering if any of them rang any bells with you."

"Names?"

"From Daniel's files. Six of them have photographs that go with them. Cammie didn't recognize any of them. We thought maybe you would. Figured they were friends, acquaintances of Daniel."

"Or enemies, huh?" said Sweeney.

"Yes. Or enemies."

"Okay. Go ahead."

I read them to Sweeney over the phone. When I finished, he said, "Read them again, willya?"

I read the eight names again.

"Nope," he said after a minute.

"You don't know any of these people?"

"Never heard of them."

"Well, okay."

"Sorry."

"Thanks, anyway."

"I didn't know many of Daniel's friends. Just guys from the army."

"And these aren't army names?"

"No. At least, not from when Daniel and I were together. Which was most of it."

"Damn," I said.

"Wish I could help you out."

"Oh, well." I stuffed the paper back into my jacket pocket. "How was the hunting?"

"Daniel wouldn't have approved."

"Why not?"

"I used a shotgun."

"Got some, though, huh?"

"Sure. I always do."

After I hung up with Sweeney I tried the Turner's Falls number again. Roscoe answered. "Yo," he said.

"It's Brady Coyne."

"Who?"

"Daniel McCloud's lawyer."

"Oh, sure. Sorry. What's up?"

"I've got some names. Wondering if they ring any bells with you."

"What kind of names?"

"I found them in Daniel's insurance papers."

"Insurance?"

"Eight names. Six of them have photographs with them."

"So?"

"I don't know. Can I read them to you?"

"Sure. Go ahead."

I did.

"Nope," said Roscoe.

"You don't recognize any of them?"

"No."

"Are you sure?"

"I'm sure, man."

"Brian didn't, either."

"If he didn't know them," said Roscoe, "it's not likely I would. Sweeney and Daniel were tight."

"Is Vinnie there?"

"No."

"Well, would you mind asking him for me?"

"Asking him what?"

"If he recognizes any of the names?"

"Why not? You better read 'em again. If I don't write 'em down, I'll forget."

I read them again, spelling the names.

"Okay," said Roscoe.

"Have him call me." I gave him my phone numbers, office and home.

"If anybody'd know, it'd be Sweeney," said Roscoe.

"He was Daniel's closest friend, huh?"

"As close as the Snake Eater'd let anybody get."

I called Cammie from my apartment that evening. She answered with a cheerful "Hello." I heard music in the background. I recognized a Tom Petty song.

"It's Brady," I said.

"Oh, hi. What's up?"

"Well, for one thing, neither Brian nor Roscoe ever

heard of any of those names. For another, Al Coleman, the guy I sent Daniel's book to, was murdered in New York City and the manuscript is nowhere to be found. Otherwise, nothing's up."

"Murdered? The agent?"

"Yes. Mugged is the verdict. A small statistic. Stabbed to death in a subway station."

"You think . . . ?"

"Quite a coincidence, I think."

"Him and Daniel, you mean."

"Yes."

"Oh, boy."

"Anyway," I said, "I just wanted to let you know. I guess I was hoping maybe you'd thought about those names."

"I thought about them, but I'm coming up blank," she said. "So now what do we do?"

"Maybe I'll try to look up one of these people, see what they've got to say."

"Is that a good idea?"

"Why not?"

"I don't know. Can't do any harm, I guess. The book, though," she said. "I feel bad about that."

"Me, too."

"I've been thinking about it. Now that Daniel's gone, maybe we could get it published with his real name on it."

"I'd like to do that," I said. "I'd like to read it."

"It's missing, though, huh?"

"Al Coleman's wife is trying to find it. But Daniel must have had another copy."

"I can look around." She hesitated.

"He . . . what did you say? He got mugged?"

"Yes. Knifed in a subway station."

"Jesus," said Cammie softly. "What a world."

13

We lingered over coffee while Melissa told us tales of the fifth grade. At recess a boy named David had snatched her Red Sox cap off her head and thrown it up into a playground tree. Another boy, "Old Ross," had shinnied up to retrieve it for her.

"I think David likes me more than Old Ross," she said, looking from Terri to me for affirmation.

"They both like you," said Terri.

"Old David likes you more," I said.

"He's a wicked tease," said Melissa.

"That's how you can tell."

"Which one do you like?" said Terri.

"Oh, Mom. You know."

"Last week it was Kevin."

"Well, it still is. I'm not *fickle,* you know."

Terri darted a glance at me. A *meaningful* glance, although its precise meaning was lost on me.

Melissa abruptly fell asleep in the backseat on the way home from the restaurant to Terri's apartment in Acton.

I carried her up and laid her on her bed. Terri touched the back of my neck, smiled, and mouthed the words "thank you," then bent to undress her. I retreated into the living room. I flicked on Terri's television, but as usual her reception was poor. I turned it off and found some classical music on her radio.

Terri came out in a few minutes. "Drink?"

"Sure. Thanks."

She disappeared into the kitchen. I slouched on her lumpy sofa. I heard her rap the ice-cube tray against the counter. She came back with two short glasses filled with ice and bourbon. She slumped beside me and handed one of the glasses to me.

I held it to her. "Cheers, then."

She touched my glass with hers. "Sure. Cheers."

We sipped. We sat not quite touching. It was Mendelssohn. The *Italian* Symphony. Lush. Romantic. I hummed the theme. Terri poked at the ice cubes in her drink with her forefinger.

"Out with it, woman," I said.

She turned to face me. "Out with what?"

"Whatever it is that Melissa's presence has allowed you to avoid saying to me all evening. That's been on your mind for a month."

She shrugged. "Who said anything's on my mind?"

"Well?"

She nodded. "If I could put it into words I would."

"Don't worry about being articulate. Please try."

She shrugged. "Aw, Brady . . ."

"The thrill is gone, huh?"

She put her hand on my leg. "No," she said. "If the thrill was gone it would be easy. The thrill is still there, and it's been a long thrilling time now, and ..." Her hand fell away. She shook her head.

"Scary, huh?"

"Not exactly scary. It's ... uncomfortable for me. It almost hurts. It doesn't fit into my life. It warps everything. It rubs against edges of myself that I didn't know I had."

"Don't you go using that L word on me," I said.

She frowned at me. I smiled, to let her know I was attempting levity. There were times when levity was uncalled for. I usually managed to find those times.

"Damn you," she whispered.

I touched her hair. "Hey," I said. "I'm sorry."

She tilted her head away from my hand. "Don't," she said.

"Try to tell me about it."

"I can't," she said. "It's me, not you."

"The old S word, then."

"Sex? Hardly."

"Space," I said.

She shrugged and nodded. "It's not much of a life," she said, laying her head back on the sofa and addressing the ceiling, "but it's mine, and it works, and it's the only one I know."

"And I've screwed it up."

"No, you haven't. Not yet. And I don't want you to. It just seems inevitable that sooner or later it's got to—I don't know, change, evolve into something else. Something not as good."

"It doesn't have to change."

"Sure," she said. "You'd be happy just to go on and on this way, seeing each other a couple of times a week, sleeping together on the weekend, otherwise just going our own separate ways. And what happens? Where does it go? Nothing stays the same, Brady."

"You're not alluding to the M word, are you?"

"Oh, Christ," she muttered. She laughed quietly. "Look," she said, turning to face me. "If we end it right now, it will always be what it is. It'll always be a thrill. I know you. You'll never get married again. And don't worry, because I don't think I ever will, either. I mean, neither of us has the guts to utter the dreaded L word, never mind the forbidden M word. The way I see it, we've got two choices. We can just bumble along until we get sick of each other and start to despise each other, or we can keep it the way it is by not letting it go anywhere else."

I rolled my eyes. "Makes perfect sense."

"I'm serious. And you don't need to be sarcastic."

I shook my head. "Dames," I said.

She smiled and crept her hand onto the inside of my thigh. She touched my neck, then leaned toward me. The kiss itself was soft and tentative. But Terri's hand moved certainly. "Still a thrill, huh?" she mumbled, her mouth on my throat.

Her fingers went to my belt buckle. I moved to help her, but she pushed my hands aside. "Let me," she said.

We lay together on the sofa long after the *Italian Symphony* ended, Terri's head on my shoulder, our legs entwined.

"We can remember it this way," she whispered.

"I'll miss you."

"Me, too."

"Seems kinda dumb," I said.

"Listen to your head."

"This is all about Daniel, isn't it?"

"I don't know, Brady. All I can tell you is, it's about me. Please don't try to make me explain it."

"You are one complicated broad."

"We all are," she said.

I shuffled through the six photos and two index cards and picked one of the cards. The name on it was William Johnson. It sounded like an alias. He lived at a Summer Street address in Springfield. I dialed information and asked for his phone number.

"I have no William Johnson at that address, sir," said the operator.

"Maybe he has an unlisted number."

"No, sir. Not at that address."

She ended up giving me seven William Johnsons who had phones in Springfield. Between no answers, busy signals, and answering machines, it took me the rest of Monday and most of Monday evening to connect with all seven of them. None of them would admit he had ever lived on Summer Street or heard of Daniel McCloud. Two of them said that Summer Street was in a part of town they wouldn't be caught dead in.

One of those seven William Johnsons, I figured, was

lying. But I had no idea which one, and I didn't know how to pursue it.

The names Daniel had written on the index cards were:

William Johnson
287 Summer St.
Springfield, Mass.

Carmine Repucci
66 Farrow Dr.
Chicopee, Mass.

Chicopee is more or less a suburb of Springfield. The fact that the two index cards carried addresses so close to each other seemed as if it must be significant.

The six photographs, which showed ordinary-looking men of indeterminate middle age, bore this information on the backs:

Boris Kekko
11 Broad St.
Amherst, Mass.

James Whitlaw
422 Hillside Ave.
Pawtucket, R.I.

Mitchell Evans
9 Windsor Dr.
Saratoga Springs, N.Y.

Michael DiSimione
1146 W. Central St.
Providence, R.I.

Bertram Wanzer
2 Hubbard St.
Holyoke, Mass.

Jean Beaulieu
245 River Dr.
Manchester, N.H.

On Tuesday morning I delivered a cup of coffee to Julie and told her to hold my calls until further notice.

"What's that supposed to mean?" she said. "Further notice?"

"I've got to make some phone calls. I don't know how long it'll take. Maybe an hour. Maybe the rest of the morning."

"Trying to scare up a date for the weekend, huh?"

"That's not really funny."

She arched her eyebrows. "Are we having girl problems?"

I smiled, shrugged, and said, "We'll survive."

She narrowed her eyes. Trying to decide whether to tease me or offer sympathy, I guessed. "You'll grow up," she said, which wasn't exactly teasing but certainly wasn't the least bit sympathetic.

"Let's hope not," I said. I pivoted around and strode

to my office. At the door I said, "Until further notice. Remember."

"Poor baby," she said. Teasing, I decided.

I spread the six photos and two index cards over my desk, studied the photos for a few minutes, then turned them over. I observed again that the names and addresses on their backs did not appear to have been written in Daniel's hand, while those on the two index cards did.

I lit a cigarette and reached for the phone.

There was no listing for Carmine Repucci. So much for the two guys on the index cards.

The information operator found no Kekko with a telephone in Amherst.

There were several Whitlaws in Pawtucket, Rhode Island, two named James. One lived at 422 Hillside Avenue.

A woman answered the phone with a cheery "Hello?"

"I'd like to speak to James Whitlaw, please," I said.

"I'm sorry." The cheeriness in her voice had disappeared.

"He's not in?"

"Who is this?"

"My name is Brady Coyne. I'm an attorney, and—"

"Please," she said.

"Pardon me?"

"Mr. Coyne, what is it?"

"I just need to speak to Mr. Whitlaw. I think he has some information for me."

She sighed. "You can't speak to my husband."

"But—"

"Somebody's either playing a dirty trick on both of us, or else you've been misinformed. James died eight years ago."

"Oh" was all I could think of to say.

"What did you really want, Mr. Coyne?"

"I'm sorry," I said. "I'm embarrassed."

"Can I help you?"

"I don't know. Does the name Daniel McCloud mean anything to you?"

She hesitated, then said, "No. I don't think so."

"A friend of your . . . of Mr. Whitlaw?"

"Could be. I don't know. I don't know anybody named Daniel McCloud."

"Can I ask you a question?"

She sighed. "I guess so."

"How did your husband die?"

"He drove his car into a bridge abutment. It exploded. They said he was drunk."

"Oh, gee . . ."

"It was a long time ago, Mr. Coyne."

"Would you mind if I ran a few other names by you?"

"What kind of names?"

"Just to see if you recognize any of them. People your husband might've known or mentioned to you."

"I suppose so."

I read the other seven names and, as an afterthought, added Al Coleman.

"No," she said. "Uh. They don't ring any bells."

"Well, then, I'm sorry to bother you," I said. "Thank you for your time."

"It's okay."

There were half a dozen phone listings for Evans in Saratoga Springs. None lived on Windsor Drive or had the first name of Mitchell.

An entire DiSimione clan lived in Providence, but none lived at 1146 West Central. I jotted down the numbers of the five Michaels, thinking I'd try them later if nothing better turned up.

A man's voice answered Bertram Wanzer's phone in Holyoke. Bingo, I thought. Finally.

"Is this Bertram Wanzer?" I said.

"This is Robert."

"Is Bertram there?"

"No," he said, "the bastard is not here."

"Could I leave a message for him?"

"Look," he said, "what do you want, anyway?"

"I'm a lawyer," I said. "I need his help on a case."

"Well, good luck."

"Can you tell me how I can reach Bertram Wanzer, please?"

"No, I can't."

"Do you mind—?"

"Look, friend. Old Bert walked out on my mother six years ago, okay? No good-bye, no note, nothing. He just fucking left her, not to be heard from since. It took her three years to realize the sonofabitch wasn't coming back. So she divorced him. That's it. He's dead, as far as we're concerned. So when you talk to him, tell him we're doing just fine without him. Better than ever, okay?"

"But you don't know how I can reach him."

"I told you—"

"Yes. I'm sorry. Listen, I didn't know any of this, obviously. Maybe you can help me."

"I doubt it."

"You're Bertram Wanzer's son?"

"His stepson. I don't like to admit it."

"How old were you when he . . . left?"

"Seventeen."

"Do you remember his ever mentioning a man named Daniel McCloud."

"I don't remember much of anything about him. No. No McCloud."

"Are you sure? It's very important."

"I'm sure."

"Is your mother there?"

"She's working."

"Would you mind leaving a message for her? Ask her about Daniel McCloud. If it rings a bell have her call me. Will you?"

He sighed. "Give me your number."

I left my office and home numbers with Robert Wanzer, less than hopeful that I'd ever hear from Bertram's former wife. I scribbled a reminder for myself to try her in the evening.

There were several Johns but no Jean Beaulieu on River Drive or anywhere else in Manchester, New Hampshire. I took down all the numbers for John. I should, I knew, try them all.

But I had lost my enthusiasm for this research. I knew how private investigators did it. They just kept calling.

They'd visit all the William Johnsons in Springfield, all the Michael DiSimiones in Providence. They'd drop in on Mrs. Whitlaw and the former Mrs. Bertram Wanzer, ingratiate themselves, get them talking. Doggedly, mindlessly, they'd keep at it until something turned up.

Private detecting was more painfully tedious, even, than practicing law.

I lit a cigarette and swiveled around to look out my office window.

Eight names from Daniel's insurance file.

I'd taken my best cuts. I had struck out.

I tried Lieutenant Fusco's number. A female cop told me that Fusco wasn't available. I told her to tell him that I had some names that might interest him in regard to the McCloud investigation. She said she'd have him get back to me.

I hung up and buzzed Julie.

"Hi, there" came her voice over the console.

"This is your further notice," I said.

"Goodie. Wanna do some law?"

"Not especially."

"I'll be right in."

Charlie McDevitt and I had lunch at Marie's two days later, which was the first Thursday in November. When the coffee came, Charlie leaned across the table and said, "Well?"

"Well, what?"

"Well, what do you want?"

"Who said I wanted something? Any reason a man can't buy his old roomie lunch?"

"You don't just buy me lunch. We do each other favors and repay them with lunch. Or else we buy the lunch first, thereby creating an obligation. That's how you and I do it."

I lit a cigarette. "A sympathetic ear, maybe."

He cocked his head and smiled. "The beauteous Terri Fiori, huh?"

"She decided to break it off. Before the thrill was gone."

"You're the one who usually does that," said Charlie.

I nodded. "I guess that's true."

"So it must've been easier this time, her doing it."

"Easier, I guess. But it hurt more."

"You ought to settle down, Brady."

"Think so?"

He looked at me. "No, I guess not."

"She did it nicer than I ever could have."

"Give yourself credit," said Charlie. "I bet you made it easy for her."

I shrugged. Charlie and I did not exchange locker-room talk.

"So you're sad. That's good. You'll remember it fondly."

"Boy," I said, "I sure as hell will."

Our waitress refilled our coffee cups.

"You want advice?" said Charlie.

"No, thanks."

"Didn't think so."

"I've been trying to get ahold of Lieutenant Fusco," I said after a minute. "The state cop in charge of Daniel's murder."

"And?"

"He won't talk to me, won't return my calls."

"Why should he?"

I shrugged. "I'm trying to help. I want to know what's happening."

"Hey, Brady," said Charlie.

"Yeah?"

"Forget it."

"Who says?"

"Me. Your friend."

"I said I didn't want advice."

"On matters of the heart, I don't have any useful advice. On stuff like this I do. Whether you want to hear it or not. Forget it. Go practice your law. Last time I looked, you were getting rusty."

"I don't think so," I said.

He sighed, then smiled at me. "Okay. I tried. What can I do?"

"I'd sure like to know who rammed a broadhead into Daniel McCloud's heart."

"Me, too. The cops'll do that for us."

"I got the feeling they won't. I got the feeling they aren't even trying."

"Just because they aren't confiding in you?"

"Partly, I guess. But I'm getting these vibes."

"Yeah. Vibes are good."

"I mean it," I said. "Something's going on."

"Fine. So I repeat. What can I do?"

"I've got some names."

"Names?"

"Cammie gave me Daniel's records. I'm handling the probate for her. Anyway, we found an envelope in with his insurance stuff. It contained six photographs and two index cards. Eight names and addresses."

"Insurance?"

I nodded.

Charlie stared at me for a moment. "And you think one of 'em killed Daniel?"

I shrugged. "There's more. Daniel had written this book, and I sent it to Al Coleman. Remember?"

He nodded.

"Listen, Charlie. At first Al loved Daniel's book. Then a couple of weeks later he called to tell me that he'd changed his mind and was sending the book back. Said he didn't want to deal with Daniel. Sounded almost like he was afraid of him or something. Anyway, the manuscript didn't arrive, so I tried calling to find out where it was. Kept getting their answering machine. Finally last week I got ahold of Al's wife. Bonnie, the girl he used to bring to our place in New Haven. She told me Al got mugged. They found him dead in a subway station."

"Shit." Charlie shook his head slowly.

"This had to've happened sometime shortly after he called me to reject Daniel's book."

"So?"

I shrugged. "Coincidence?"

"Most things are, Brady. What are you getting at?"

"I don't know. I just want to know who killed Daniel, and why. That's all."

"And you think this book . . . ?"

"I don't know what to think. I keep remembering how Daniel's trafficking charges got mysteriously dropped.

That's when he gave me the book. Next thing we know, he and Al Coleman are dead. Now I've got these names . . ."

Charlie stared at me for a minute, then sighed. "Okay. Give me those names. I'll run 'em through the big mainframe, see what I can find out for you."

I nodded. "Good. You've earned your lunch."

I had copied the names onto a sheet of legal-size yellow paper, along with notes from my telephone efforts. I took it from my jacket pocket, unfolded it, and smoothed it out in front of Charlie.

"This Whitlaw died in an auto accident eight years ago," I said. "I talked to his wife. That's the phone number. It's for sure that he didn't kill Daniel. And this Wanzer in Holyoke, he skipped out on his family six years ago, never to be heard from. The rest must've moved or something, because I got no phone numbers for them."

Charlie picked up the paper, folded it, and stuck it into his pocket. "Let's see what we can find out," he said.

"I'm looking for the connection to Daniel."

"Well, hell, I know that."

"This lunch here, it's your payment."

He nodded. "I'll do it," he said. "It doesn't change anything, though."

"What?"

"The advice is golden. You should forget it, Brady."

"I'll consider it."

"Bullshit you will," said Charlie.

14

I called State Police Lieutenant Horowitz at 1010 Commonwealth Avenue that afternoon. He answered his phone with a weary "Yeah. Horowitz."

"It's Brady Coyne. How you doing?"

"Fantastic. But listen. Hearing your voice is still special, you know?"

"I just thought I'd brighten up your day."

I heard him blow a bubble and pop it into the receiver. "So whaddya want?"

"You think the only reason I'd call you is because I want something?"

"Yeah."

"If you wanted something and thought I could help, would you call me?"

"Bet your ass. You owe me."

"Feel free."

"I already do. So what is it?"

"A colleague of yours name of Fusco. Lieutenant Dominick Fusco. Springfield."

"Sure. I know him."

"He's investigating a homicide. The victim was a client of mine."

Horowitz sighed. "So?"

"He won't answer my calls. I want to know how the investigation is going."

"He's probably too busy. You know, investigating homicides."

"I had something I wanted to tell him. Left a message for him to get back to me. He hasn't. He's avoiding me."

"Hard to blame him. If I had as much sense as him, I'd avoid you, too."

"So will you?"

"Will I what, Coyne?"

"Will you find out what the story is? The victim's name was Daniel McCloud."

"Like do they have suspects, have they made an arrest?"

"Yes. Like that."

"Do I get lunch out of this?"

"Absolutely."

"Even if Fusco's got nothing?"

"I just want to know. And I do have some information for him."

He exploded his bubble gum. "I'll get back to you."

He hung up as I was saying "Thanks."

Gloria was perched atop a barstool when I walked into Skeeter's Infield after closing the office for the weekend

Friday afternoon. She was wearing a little black skirt that had ridden halfway up her thighs. She still had great legs.

The rest of her looked equally terrific. Maybe there were a few tiny crinkles at the corners of her eyes and a few strands of gray mixed in with her glossy brown hair that hadn't been there when she took my photograph outside a courtroom in New Haven more than twenty years earlier.

But two kids—now young men—and one divorce later, Gloria Coyne still had it.

I slid onto the stool beside her.

"Hi," I said.

"Hi, yourself." She tilted her cheek for me to kiss, which I did, chastely.

"Been good?"

"You mean my behavior or my health?"

"Either," I said. "Both."

"My health is excellent."

"Otherwise no comment, huh?"

She grinned.

"What are you drinking?"

"White wine, please."

"You used to like gin-and-tonics with a maraschino cherry in the bottom."

She shrugged. "I mostly just have a glass of wine nowadays."

"How about a gin-and-tonic? For old time's sake."

"White wine is fine, Brady. You go ahead and have your Jack Daniel's."

"You used to drink lots of gin. And you'd get all . . ."

"Amorous," she said.

I smiled.

"That's probably why I've just been sticking to white wine lately," she replied.

Skeeter came over and held out his hand. "Hey, Mr. Coyne. How ya doin'?"

I took his hand. "Pretty good, Skeets. You?"

"No complaints. Except for the Sox."

"They need someone who can get from first to third on a single," I said.

"And someone else who can come in from the bullpen and throw strikes. What ever happened to Dick Radatz? What're you folks drinking?"

"Blackjack on the rocks. Lady'll have a glass of white wine."

"No, I think I'll have a gin-and-tonic," said Gloria. "With a maraschino cherry in it."

Skeeter nodded and went to make our drinks. I turned to Gloria. "Thanks for coming."

She shrugged. "It sounded important."

"How are the boys?"

She frowned. "Fine, I guess. They're pretty much men, you know."

"Heard from Billy?"

"Not lately."

"Me neither."

She put her hand on my arm. "You didn't ask me to meet you so we could pool our ignorance about William and Joseph, Brady. What is it?"

"I don't know." I paused to light a cigarette. "I just don't understand women, I guess."

"This is not a revelation to me."

"I know."

"You're looking for insight."

"Yes. After all these years, I suppose I still am."

"Girl trouble, huh?"

I shrugged.

"And you want my advice?"

I looked up at her. "I got dumped."

She grinned. "Welcome to the real world."

Skeeter brought our drinks. I lifted my glass, and Gloria touched it with her gin-and-tonic. "To the real world," I toasted.

Gloria sipped her gin and tonic and smiled.

"Remember Terri?" I said.

"Pretty lady. The boys liked her a lot. Too young for you."

I shrugged. "She didn't think so. Neither did I, actually. Now, maybe, I'm not so sure. Anyway, I had this friend, nice quiet guy living a peaceful country life, with a lady friend who loved him, and he was, um, murdered, and—"

"Murdered," said Gloria. "Aw, Brady."

I nodded. "A tragic, inexplicable thing. Terri has talked a lot with Cammie—Daniel's woman friend—since it happened."

"And then she dumped you."

"Yes. I guess that's what you'd call it. That's the chronology of it. And I just can't help thinking there's a cause-effect relationship between the two events. Daniel getting murdered and Terri ending it with me."

She smiled and shook her head.

"What's funny?" I said.

"You. Men. Your egos."

"Oh. I see."

"Think about it."

I thought about it. "So you're saying . . ."

"You've always been the one to do it," she said. "Starting with me. Right?"

I shrugged.

"So it's happened to you, that's all. Long overdue. Admit it. It's just . . . you. Don't try to make anything more out of it. I know. You'd rather there was some explanation. Something that would allow you to escape with your dignity, or pride, or masculine ego, or whatever it is. The lady dumped you, Brady. She beat you to it. Simple as that."

I sipped my drink. "You're enjoying this, aren't you?" I said.

Gloria shrugged. Then she smiled. "Yes."

After a minute, I said, "It hurts, though, you know?"

She touched my hand. "Believe me, I know."

We finished our drinks. I asked Gloria to have dinner with me, but she said she had a date. I walked her out to her car and held the door for her while she slid in. Her skirt slid way up and she didn't bother tugging it down. I bent in and kissed her cheek. "Thanks for the wisdom," I said.

"Hey," she said, "that's what ex-wives are for."

15

Saturday night. Late. I wondered what Terri was doing. I thought of calling her. I was afraid there'd be no answer at her apartment, though. So I didn't. In keeping with my mood, John Coltrane's sax was blowing "Blue Train" on the stereo. I was at the table by the glass sliders sipping Sleepytime tea and trying to work my way through some back issues of the *Yale Law Review* when the phone rang.

Terri, I thought.

Wishful thinking, I knew.

"It's Cammie," she said when I answered.

"Nice to hear your voice. Everything all right?"

She let out a long breath.

"Hey, are you okay?"

She uttered a sound in her throat. A moan or a sob.

"Cammie, what is it?"

"Oh, shit," she mumbled. "Brady, can you help me?"

"Of course. What's the matter?"

"I almost shot a cop."

"What?"

"It was just a few minutes ago. I had just gone to bed. I heard noises outside. I went to the window. I saw somebody skulking around with a flashlight. I put on a robe and grabbed my gun and I went out onto the porch. He . . . he was right there. He shone his light in my face and I started to point my gun at him and he said he was the police."

"Oakley?"

"Yeah. Him. I never saw his face. But I recognized his voice. He said he was just checking to make sure everything was all right. He said he was concerned for my safety. Because of Daniel, I guess is what he meant. He . . ." Her voice trailed off.

"Maybe he was just doing his job."

"Bullshit." Her voice was harsh. "It's just what Daniel said. Brady, he saw that I had a gun. He'll figure out it's not licensed. I will not give up my gun."

"Maybe you should. What if you had shot him?"

"Are they supposed to come prowling around at night like that?"

"No. Not without telling you first."

"And shining the light like that on me. I know the bastard was . . . looking at me."

"Did he say anything?"

"Just what I told you. I told him to just leave me alone, I was fine. He called me ma'am, polite as pie, tipped his hat, even. Sarcastic, see? Brady, isn't there anything we can do? In court, or something? This has been going on too long. It's not fair."

"I don't know, Cammie. He hasn't really done anything illegal."

"He's been harassing me—us, me and Daniel—since day one. Isn't that enough?"

"Cammie, I'd love to help you—"

"Yeah, but . . ."

"No. Listen. I'll talk to his chief. See if we can straighten it out that way."

"Will you?"

"Sure. Monday. Okay?"

"Thank you."

"In the meantime, keep your doors locked."

"Doors locked and gun handy," she said.

"For Christ sake, be careful."

"Exactly."

I had been to the Wilson Falls police station once before, when I visited Daniel during his weekend in jail. It occupied one wing of the town hall, a no-nonsense square brick building across the village green from the Congregational church.

Chief Francis Padula kept me waiting for fifteen minutes. I sat by myself on a wooden bench and smoked two cigarettes under the watchful eye of the desk sergeant. He didn't even offer me coffee. I knew there had to be a pot of cop coffee somewhere around there.

Finally the chief appeared from a corridor and said, "Mr. Coyne?"

I stubbed out my cigarette and stood up.

He came toward me. He was a compact man in his late thirties with a small mouth and closely cropped hair. He wore a starched white shirt with French cuffs and a blue-and-gray striped necktie snugged tight to his throat. He extended his hand to me without smiling. "Francis Padula," he said.

I took his hand. "Thanks for seeing me."

"Come this way." He turned and I followed him into his office.

He sat behind his desk. I took the straight-backed wooden chair across from him. He folded his hands on the blotter and said, "You were Daniel McCloud's attorney."

I nodded.

"Damn shame," he said.

"Yes."

"I can't talk about the case."

"That's not why I'm here."

He leaned forward and arched his eyebrows. "So what is it?" His eyes were fixed on mine. They were dark brown, almost black. The exact same shade as Terri's, I realized.

"It's about Officer Oakley."

He leaned back. "What about Officer Oakley, Mr. Coyne?"

"I'd rather not file a complaint."

"I'd rather you didn't. Maybe you better explain."

So I did. I related Cammie Russell's complaints to the chief—her perception that Oakley had been harassing her and Daniel for years, how he had arrested Daniel, ticketed the cars of all the guests at the funeral party, and frightened Cammie the previous Saturday night by prowling around the property. Padula studied the ceiling as I talked. I couldn't read his expression. Bored patience or thoughtful concern. One or the other.

When I was done, he said, "I'm not sure I understand your problem."

"You add it all up," I said, "and it's pretty obvious. I mean, ticketing all those cars, for example, while there's a funeral going on."

"All those cars were parked illegally. It's what I instruct my officers to do. Ticket illegally parked vehicles."

"Still. Under the circumstances, it was uncalled for."

"That arrest last summer," he said, "was classic. Perfect police work. I think you know that. You don't think Officer Oakley acted on his own on that one, do you?"

I shrugged.

"Look, Mr. Coyne. Wilson Falls is a small town. I have a small force. When police work needs to be done, there are only a few policemen to do it. Sergeant Oakley is one of them. Any citizen who runs into a police officer here, they're very likely to run into Richard Oakley. Something like that marijuana bust, several of my officers were involved. Oakley was one of them. That's all. It was a good bust."

"So why did the prosecution dismiss it?"

He leaned forward. His eyes bored into mine. He opened his mouth to say something, then closed it. "Ancient history," he said.

"What about the other night? You just can't do that. Skulking around, scaring a citizen like that. It's harassment. I want it to stop."

He shook his head. "Come off it, Mr. Coyne. It's not harassment."

"Maybe a judge should decide that."

He smiled thinly. "And she would have to testify. I'm sure her character is impeccable."

"Look—"

"You know how it works, Mr. Coyne."

"Somebody should've told her that there'd be an officer coming around, at least."

Padula nodded. "That's my responsibility."

"I just want Oakley to leave her alone. Rightly or wrongly, he upsets her. It seems simple enough."

"It's fairly routine to keep an eye on a woman who lives alone after a murder has occurred."

"Sure," I said. "It's good responsible police work. Fine. But it doesn't need to be Oakley. So maybe he hasn't done anything wrong. Maybe it's all in her head. But he spooks her. It doesn't seem necessary. Cammie Russell just wants him to steer clear of her."

"I'll consider what you've told me." He stared at me for a moment. "There's some things you don't know, Mr. Coyne."

"There are lots of things I don't know."

He shrugged.

"Something you should tell me?" I said.

He hesitated, then said, "No. It doesn't matter. I'll speak to Sergeant Oakley." He stood up.

I was dismissed. I reached across his desk to shake hands with him. "Thanks," I said.

He came around the desk as I turned for the door. "Mr. Coyne."

"Yes?"

"Richard Oakley's a good cop."

"Sure."

"He did not murder Daniel McCloud."

"Goodness," I said. "I should hope not."

Fifteen minutes later I pulled into the gravel turnaround in front of Daniel's shop. A cardboard sign hung in the window. CLOSED. I shaded my eyes and peered in. It still looked exactly as it did on the morning I saw Daniel's body in there. I couldn't tell if the bloodstain had been cleaned up.

I walked up the path to the house. I wanted to tell Cammie that I had talked to Oakley's chief. I also needed a mug of coffee.

I rang the bell and waited for her to come to the door. It was one of those gray mid-November New England days when the air is cold and moist and a brittle breeze brings the promise of the season's first snowfall. I shivered and hugged myself in my insubstantial sports jacket. After a minute I tiptoed up to peer through the high window on the door. I saw no lights inside, no sign of life.

I followed the path around the house and continued across the back lawn to Cammie's studio.

There was no bell beside the door. I knocked and called, "Cammie. It's Brady."

I waited. From inside I could hear music, too blurred and faint to identify.

After a minute or two I knocked again. When there was no response, I tried the doorknob. I had told her to keep it locked. But it turned and the door swung open. I stepped inside. "Cammie?" I called.

The woodstove in the middle of the open living room/dining room/kitchen area radiated heat.

Sarah Vaughan was singing "Lover Man."

I didn't see Cammie.

An empty coffee mug sat on the table. A few dirty dishes were piled on the counter beside the sink. The music was coming from the studio upstairs.

"Hey," I called, louder than before. "Cammie? You here?"

I stood there uncertainly, rubbing my hands together beside the woodstove, looking around.

After a few moments I went to the spiral stairway that led up to her studio. As I climbed them the music grew louder.

I stopped at the top step. Skylights and four walls of glass bathed the room in diffuse but bright natural light. I squinted into it for a moment.

Cammie stood at the far end with her back to me. Beyond her through the glass stretched the pewter ribbon of the Connecticut River, winding its way through the umbers and ochers of the late autumn countryside. She was working at an easel. I heard her humming to Sarah Vaughan's music.

She wore cutoff jeans. Her long slender legs were spread wide, as if she were balancing herself on a ship's deck. Her feet were bare. So was her back.

I hesitated at the top of the stairs. It occurred to me to turn quietly and go back down the stairs. Cammie was deep into her work.

She was also virtually naked.

But I did not retreat. I stayed, staring, rooted by the sight of her—the slim perfect line of her legs, the smooth vee of her back tapering into the narrow waistband of her shorts, the pale curve of a breast under her arm, the long black braid bisecting her brown back, the orange ribbon knotted around it.

So I stood there stupidly and watched her, and after a minute she turned slowly around. She held a paintbrush in her right hand, and she had another one clenched between her teeth.

She reached up with her free hand and took the brush from her mouth.

"Hi, Brady," she said quietly.

I nodded. "Hi."

Her breasts were small, perfectly formed. The button on her shorts was open and her fly was half unzipped.

Her eyes glittered and her face shone with her tears.

Sarah Vaughan still sang.

"Cammie, I'm sorry, I—"

She held up her hand. "Don't," she said. She dropped her brushes into a water jar.

She walked toward me. I didn't move.

"Sarah always makes me cry," she said. She came close, reached up her hand, touched my cheek, moved it around to the back of my neck. I felt her other hand slither inside my jacket, move over my shirt against my chest. Her eyes were level with mine. Her mouth was inches from mine. My arms hung at my sides.

Tears continued to overflow her eyes and roll down her cheeks. She took her hand from my neck and peeled off my jacket. Her fingers went to my tie, loosened it, dropped it onto the floor.

"Cammie—"

"Shh," she said. She tilted toward me and kissed me softly on the mouth. She unbuttoned my collar.

I reached up, touched her hands, then gripped her wrists. "No, Cammie," I said gently.

"It's okay." She tried to smile.

"No. It's not." I let go of her wrists and put my arms around her. "It's not okay," I said into her hair. I held her tight.

She burrowed her face against my shoulder. "It's Terri, isn't it?" she mumbled.

"Yes. And Daniel." I hugged her against me. "And us. It's us, too."

We had coffee on the sofa downstairs. Cammie had pulled on a paint-stained T-shirt. Outside, tiny snowflakes had begun to angle down from the leaden sky.

Cammie had replaced Sarah Vaughan with Muddy Waters. He was singing "Sugar Sweet."

"Terri talked to me a lot," said Cammie. "About you. After Daniel died. She likes you a lot."

I nodded. "I know."

"She's pretty confused."

"Aren't we all?"

"Speak for yourself," she said.

"I was."

"Give her time, Brady."

"I think she's made up her mind."

"Minds," said Cammie, "are for changing."

I shrugged. "Terri's very strong-minded."

She nodded. "You're right. Maybe it's better this way anyway."

"That's what I've been thinking."

"I don't know which is worse. Knowing she's there but gone or . . ."

I knew what she was thinking. Or knowing the person you love is dead.

"I talked to your local police chief," I said.

"About Oakley?"

"Yes. I think you'll be okay now."

"Really?"

"This Chief Padula. I think I trust him."

She nodded. "Thank you." She stared out the window for a minute. "What about Daniel's book?"

"I don't know. It hasn't turned up. I guess Al Coleman must've put it someplace. But he's dead, so . . ."

"I've looked all around the house," said Cammie. "Daniel must have kept a copy somewhere."

"No luck, huh?"

She shook her head. "He never talked about it, never shared it. Whatever he was writing, it was a private thing. I never expected him to want to have it published. I figured he was just trying to sort out his feelings. Catharsis—his therapy. When he gave it to you, I was jealous. I mean, he was sharing whatever it was with the world, but not me. I tried teasing him. I even pretended to be angry. But he refused to say anything about it. And after he died, I felt guilty. Do you understand?"

"For giving him a hard time."

She shrugged. "That, yeah. But more for trying to violate his privacy. I mean, if he wanted to keep it from me, he must have had his reasons, and that should have been good enough for me. I'd say, 'Come on, old Snake Eater, gimme a look.' And he'd get that gentle faraway look of his, and he'd say, 'Nay, lass. It's not for your sweet eyes.'" She turned to face me. The tears had begun to well up again. "Ah, shit."

I hugged her. She cried against my chest.

"It's not fair," said Cammie. "I guess that guy—that stranger—and Daniel were the only two people in the world who got to read it. And now it's gone."

"And so," I said, "are both of them."

Cammie heated up some homemade chowder and we watched it snow while we ate. She held me tightly at the door, but she didn't cry.

"Will you come back?" she said.

"Sure," I said.

She tilted back and looked at me. "Thank you."

"For what?"

"For . . . being my friend."

"I'll be back," I said. "I promise."

She kissed me on the cheek.

"And you've got to make me a promise," I said.

"What?"

"Keep your door locked."

She smiled. "I left it open for you."

"How . . . ?"

156

"I knew you'd stop in. At least I hoped you would." She shrugged. "I don't know what else I was hoping. Forgive me. I'm glad we didn't—"

I touched her lips with my finger. "Nothing to forgive," I said.

The snow wet my face as I walked back to my car, and after I got started it made slush on my windshield. It was melting on the pavement, but it had begun to stick to the dead leaves in the oak trees along the roadside.

I expected it would turn to rain as I headed east.

A mile down the road from Daniel's house the cruiser materialized in my rearview mirror. He switched on the blue flashers and his high beams at the same time as he hit the siren. I pulled onto the shoulder and turned off the ignition. He stopped behind me.

I lit a cigarette. Through my rearview mirror I watched him step slowly from the cruiser and saunter toward me. It was Oakley. He paused to peer at my rear license plate. I rolled down the window. Tiny pellets of snow blew in and melted against my cheek. He came up to the side of my car and stood just behind my left shoulder so I couldn't see his face.

"License and registration," he said.

I found the registration in the glove compartment. I slid my license from my wallet. I handed the documents to him. I didn't ask him why he pulled me over. He didn't offer to tell me. He went back to his cruiser. I smoked my cigarette and waited.

He was back five minutes later. He bent down to the open window, braced himself with his hand on the windowframe, and said, "You were going too fast. Roads're wet and slippery. You've gotta go careful, conditions like this. I could have cited you. I'm doing you a favor."

Oakley looked older up close. His short dark hair was liberally flecked with gray, and the skin around his eyes was puffy and cross-hatched. He was forty-five, give or take a few years.

He wore a wedding band on the ring finger of his left hand. For some reason, that surprised me. The only Richard Oakley I knew was the one Daniel and Cammie had described for me. It didn't seem likely that anybody could love that Oakley.

He also had some letters tattooed on the back of his hand. They were crude and blurred, and they were upside down to me. But I made them out.

"Semper Fi," they read.

Oakley had been a marine.

He thrust my papers through the window. "Slow down, okay?"

I took the papers. "Sure," I said. "Thanks."

He hesitated as if he wanted to say something else. Then he stepped away from my car. "You can go," he said. "Just drive carefully."

"Yes. Okay."

I pulled away. In my rearview mirror I could see Sergeant Richard Oakley standing there beside the road, watching me go.

16

Government Center occupies several city blocks between Cambridge and Congress streets, on the back side of Beacon Hill. It was erected on the corpse of Scollay Square back in the sixties, and there are still some of us who mourn the demolition. Gone is the Old Howard, where a kid could pay two bits to hear a bald man tell dirty jokes and then watch a fat lady strip down to pasties and a G-string. Gone, too, the Blue Parrot, where a teenaged boy could buy a beer, no questions asked, get propositioned by a forty-year-old hooker, and be invited to step into an alley for a fistfight with a sailor, all in the same evening.

Now it's all massive concrete-and-glass buildings and brick plazas. Progress.

Charlie McDevitt's office is high in the J.F.K. Federal Building. I got there around four on Wednesday afternoon. Charlie had called that morning and said he didn't want to talk about it on the phone.

When Shirley, his secretary, saw me walk into the

reception area, she beamed at me. I went over and kissed her cheek. She stood up and hugged me against her great pillowy bosom. "Ah, Mr. Coyne. 'Tis good to see ye."

"You're looking terrific, sweetheart," I said.

Which was true. She had snow-white hair permed into an elaborate do, smooth pink skin, and a healthy abundance of flesh. The prototypical grandma.

"Will ye be takin' him fishin', Mr. Coyne?" she said.

"No, alas," I said. "Fishing season's about ended for the year."

"Maybe come winter some of that silly ice fishing, then."

I nodded. "Maybe."

"Ye should. Himself's needin' some distracting."

"I'll see what I can do."

"Well, go on right in, then. He's expecting you."

I pushed open the door. Charlie was at his desk talking into his phone. He raised his eyebrows when he saw me and jerked his head at the empty chair by his desk. I sat. He rummaged in his bottom drawer and came up with a half-full pint of Early Times. He set it on his desk. I reached over to the sideboard and snagged two water glasses. I poured two fingers into each and slid one of them to Charlie's waiting hand.

Charlie said, "Yeah, okay, get back to me, then," and hung up the phone. He let out a long sigh. "Hey," he said to me.

"Hey, yourself."

He picked up his glass, gestured toward me with it, and took a sip. I did the same.

He rummaged among the papers on his desk top and found a sheet of computer paper. He unfolded it in front of him. "Those names," he said, looking up at me.

I nodded.

"You were hoping to locate them."

"Yes."

"Well," he said, "I located six of them. But it's not going to help you."

"Why not?"

He shrugged. "They're all dead."

I lit a cigarette. "Dead, huh?"

"Yup."

"And the other two?"

He shook his head. "Couldn't locate them."

"Meaning what?"

"Meaning they seem to have disappeared themselves."

"Disappeared?"

"Vanished. Run away. Who the hell knows?"

"Dead, maybe."

Charlie nodded. "Maybe."

I swallowed some Early Times. It burned all the way down. "So what do you think?"

"About the connection with Daniel McCloud, you mean?"

I nodded.

Charlie shrugged. "Well, he's dead, now, too."

"And if these guys are dead—"

"It means they didn't kill Daniel," said Charlie.

"Let's have a look," I said.

He turned the printout around for me. "Mostly FBI

file stuff," he said. "I got a little from the IRS and we even had some data in our own files. I couldn't print it out for you, of course. I'd have twelve G-men with submachine guns pointing at me in about a minute if I did that. But I made some notes and put 'em together for you. What you've got there is a summary. Best I could do. I wasn't sure what you wanted."

I skimmed through it, then went back to the top and read Charlie's notes slowly.

William Johnson. Seven arrests. All drug related. One conviction, served six months at Massachusetts Correctional/Billerica in 1981. His frozen body was found behind a condemned warehouse in Springfield in the winter of 1984. He had been stabbed nine times in the chest and abdomen. He died from the blood loss, not the cold. Assailant unknown.

Carmine Repucci. Small-time thief originally from East Boston. Spent time in prison on three separate occasions, including nine months in Billerica in 1981. His last address was in Chicopee. Found dead in his rented room the day after Christmas of 1987, shot four times in the face and chest. No arrests for his murder.

I glanced up at Charlie. "These first two," I said. "Johnson and Repucci?"

He nodded. "Both crooks. Murdered."

"Daniel had their names on index cards. All the others had photos."

Charlie shrugged. "Yeah? So?"

I shook my head. "I don't know."

"None of the others were murdered," said Charlie.

Boris Kekko. Master's degree candidate in international relations at the University of Massachusetts, Amherst campus. Died of a broken neck in March of 1985 from a fall into an elevator shaft at one of the UMass high-rise dormitories. Charlie had noted in parentheses, "Elevator surfing??" I remembered that game. The kids would get themselves beered up, then jam open the doors and ride up and down on top of the elevator. Sometimes they stepped or fell into the open shaft. Sometimes they fell off the elevator. I remembered Boris Kekko's photograph. He had an open, Slavic face. Balding. Middle-aged. Not a kid.

James Whitlaw. Sales rep for a small computer firm. In August of 1985 Whitlaw drove his Honda Civic into a bridge abutment near Narragansett Bay. The medical examiner's report indicated he had been legally intoxicated. Whitlaw was the one whose wife I had reached.

Mitchell Evans. Professor of comparative government at Skidmore College in Saratoga Springs, New York. Disappeared between semesters in January 1986.

Michael DiSimione, one of the Providence DiSimiones, the crack cocaine lords of New England. Arrested many times, never indicted. Had agreed to testify before a Senate committee in return for immunity and admission in the Federal Witness Protection Program when, in October of 1986, he apparently changed his mind and shot himself behind his right ear in a New York City hotel room.

Bertram Wanzer. Software engineer for a now defunct electronics firm in Holyoke. Disappeared sometime in the summer of 1987, divorced by his abandoned wife three years later. I had talked with his stepson Robert.

Jean Beaulieu, independent trucker, accidentally

drowned in the Merrimack River south of Manchester, New Hampshire, on July 4, 1989 when intoxicated.

I looked up at Charlie. "Jesus," I said.

He shrugged.

"What do you make of it?"

"I don't know," he said. "Six of 'em are dead."

"Maybe all eight," I said.

He nodded. "Could well be."

"And now Daniel."

"He'd make number nine," said Charlie.

"And you might add Al Coleman to the list." I lit a cigarette and stared out Charlie's office window. "Except for their all being dead—or at least six of them, not counting Daniel and Coleman—what's the connection?"

"You tell me."

"Let's play with it."

"Well," he said, "they're all males."

I nodded impatiently. "Yeah, okay. Something else, though."

"I can't see it," said Charlie. "Except they were all on Daniel's list."

"Which means they *are* connected. Daniel knew what it was."

Charlie swiveled his head to look at me. "His book?"

I nodded. "That'd be my guess. He was researching something, and found it. Whatever it was, these names are the key." I shook my head. "If they were all murdered, or all crooks, or all in the same business, or something, it might start to make sense."

"Or if they were all born in the same hospital, or went to the same school. They knew each other. Were friends."

"Or enemies."

"Or had the same enemy."

"They all fucked the same woman," I said.

"Christ, Coyne," said Charlie. "Maybe they were all veterans. In the army together."

"Not with Daniel they weren't," I said. "Brian Sweeney already checked that out." I snapped my fingers. "Agent Orange victims, maybe. Like Daniel."

"Maybe they were all those things," said Charlie. "Or some combination. Into something together. There's gotta be a connection."

I stared down at the printout. "Well," I said, "I don't see it here."

"I can dig a little more."

"Yeah?"

He shrugged. "Why not?"

"You want me to buy you lunch or something?"

He waved his hand impatiently. "I'm as curious as you are. Daniel was my friend, too."

"His book," I said. "Wish I could lay my hands on it. He knew something."

"Bet your ass he did."

"And he got murdered," I said. "And so did Al Coleman."

"Seems like more than coincidence, doesn't it?" said Charlie.

17

After a microwaved TV dinner that evening—chicken, green beans, mashed potatoes, and gravy—I unfolded Charlie's printout onto my dining-room table. I took turns reading the dim dot-matrix printing and staring out the sliding glass doors at the dark harbor six floors below my apartment building.

There were a few lights blinking down there on the cold black water.

Not many lights flickered in my cold black brain. At least, none that helped me to see who killed Daniel McCloud.

I saw some isolated connections on the list. The two guys on index cards, the names without photographs, William Johnson and Carmine Repucci, were the only two who had been murdered. Both had spent time at M.C.I./Billerica in 1981, both were small-time hoodlums, both ended up living in the Springfield area. Most likely they knew each other.

There was a student and a professor. International relations and comparative government were both specialties in political science.

There was a computer sales rep and a software engineer. Same industry.

There was one suicide, but it was possible that Jean Beaulieu, the trucker who drowned, made two.

Two had disappeared. It was logical to hypothesize that they, like the others on the list, were dead.

None of the deaths was by natural causes. Not counting the two disappearances, there were one suicide, two murders, and three accidents.

A clever killer can make his work look like a suicide or an accident. If he succeeds in hiding a dead body, he can make it look like a disappearance.

All eight could have been murders.

What had Daniel learned?

Did his name belong on that list? Number nine? That's where it belonged chronologically.

Or make it ten. Al Coleman probably belonged on the list, too.

Say that. Say ten connected deaths. Say all were murders.

Say there were ten murders by a single killer.

Then whoever murdered the eight also murdered Daniel and Al.

Solve one crime. That solves them all. Including Daniel's.

Clouds scudded across the full moon outside my window, momentarily giving me a peek at it before they moved in front of it again. The Beaver Moon, I recalled idly. Where the hell did it get a name like that? I could get out the *Old Farmer's Almanac* and look it up.

If I had Daniel's book, I believed I could look up the answer to the question I really cared about: Who murdered him?

Charlie called me the next afternoon. "Something weird's going on," he said without preliminary.

"Tell me."

"I was about to." He hesitated. "I can't punch up those names on my computer anymore."

"What do you mean?"

"Shit, Brady, wasn't I clear? I came in this morning and tried to get back into those files. They're not there. Ours, FBI, IRS. Gone. They were there a couple days ago. Now they're not."

"So—?"

"So how the hell do I know? These computers are screwed up half the time. Still, it's weird."

"Charlie . . ."

"Look," he said. "Before, I was just pretty much humoring you, trying to satisfy your curiosity. Because we're friends and I admire your . . . whatever, your tenacity, your singleness of purpose, even if your purposes sometimes elude me. And I guess I figured maybe we both owed it to Daniel. Now I'm curious myself. So you don't even have to tell me. I'm going to see if I can find out what's going on here. I'll be in touch."

Charlie hung up without saying good-bye.

• • •

I stayed at the office after Julie closed up shop, and I reached the former Mrs. James Whitlaw in Pawtucket around six. She answered with a breathless "Yes?"

"Mrs. Whitlaw?"

"Yes. Goodness. I ran for the phone. Who is this?"

"It's Brady Coyne calling again."

"Who?"

"I called you a while ago. I was looking for your husband."

She was silent for a moment. Then she said, "I'm sorry . . . ?"

"I'm a lawyer. You told me about Mr. Whitlaw's death."

"Oh. Yes, I remember."

"Would you mind answering a couple of questions for me?"

"Look, Mr. Coyne—"

"It's very important."

"Does this have anything to do with his . . . the accident?"

"In a way, yes, it does."

"Because I never believed it, you know."

"Believed what?"

"That he was drunk when he crashed."

"No?"

"No. Oh, James might have a beer now and then. But he was not a drinker. And he was a very careful person. Not wild. Not at all. He was actually . . . most people thought of him as rather boring. Actually, he was. Boring. But he was steady and he was a good man. He always used his seat belt, and he just wouldn't get into a car and drive if he'd had more than one beer."

"So you think . . . ?"

She laughed quickly and without humor. "I don't think anything anymore. It doesn't really matter, does it?"

"Maybe it does, Mrs. Whitlaw." I glanced down at the pad of yellow legal paper where I had scratched some reminders. "May I ask you a few questions?"

"I don't see any harm in it, I guess."

"Did your husband attend college?"

"Yes. The University of Connecticut."

"What did he major in?"

"Business administration. He started for his master's but didn't finish."

"Was he in the service?"

"Oh, yes. The lottery took him from graduate school."

"Was he in Vietnam?"

"Yes. He was wounded."

"Wounded?"

"A mine. He lost three toes. He walked with a limp. He was quite self-conscious about it."

"Did he ever encounter Agent Orange over there?"

"No, I don't think so."

"Was he by chance in the Special Forces?"

"Huh?"

"The Green Berets?"

"Oh. No. He was a marine lieutenant. All that was a long time before I met him, Mr. Coyne. He told me all these things. We were only married for two years when he . . ."

"Yes," I said. "I'm sorry."

"He told me all about his life. He had had a hard life. We were very happy, the time we had."

I cleared my throat. "I'd like to read some names to you, see if you recognize any of them."

"You mentioned other names to me when we talked before, didn't you?"

"I guess I did. Can I do it again?"

"Well, okay. I'm not sure I was really paying attention before."

I read the other seven names to her. I added Daniel's name onto the end.

"Hmm," she said. "I don't know."

"Want me to read them again?"

"Yes."

I did.

"No. Some of the last names. Evans, Johnson. But not with the same first names."

"These might've been men your husband knew, names he could've mentioned to you."

"It was a long time ago."

"People he might've known in the war."

"He didn't like to talk about the war."

"Sure." I hesitated. "I have a different question."

"All right."

"Mrs. Whitlaw, was your husband ever in trouble with the law?"

She paused. "I don't see . . ."

"It's important," I said.

"I don't know. I didn't know him for very long." She stopped. "Who are you, anyway?"

"I told you. My name is—"

"I don't think I should talk to you anymore."

"Mrs. Whitlaw—"

She hung up on me.

The other connection I had made was with Robert Wanzer, Bertram's stepson. Wanzer was the software engineer who had abandoned his wife. She had eventually divorced him in absentia. Young Robert, I recalled, was still angry.

He answered the phone with a grumbly "H'lo?"

"Is this Robert Wanzer?" I said.

"Yuh."

"This is Brady Coyne again. I spoke to you last week."

"You were looking for my stepfather."

"Right. You explained what happened. I wonder if you'd mind answering a couple of questions for me."

"I'd mind," he said. And he hung up.

I held the dead phone against my ear for a moment, then put it back onto its cradle. I figured I could learn something from the folks who made a living soliciting over the telephone. I was two for two in getting hung up on. Not a winning percentage.

I gave Robert Wanzer the time it took me to smoke a cigarette, then called again.

"H'lo?" he said.

"Your stepfather did not abandon your mother," I said quietly.

"Who the hell *are* you, anyway?"

"I told you—"

"Yeah, right. So what are you talking about?"

"I believe he was murdered."

There was a long silence.

"Mr. Wanzer, are you there?"

"I'm here," he said. "You better explain yourself."

"It's too complicated to explain," I said. "You'll have to trust me."

"Why should I?"

"What've you got to lose?"

"Hm," he said. "Right. Good point. What do you want to know?"

"I have some questions about Bertram Wanzer."

"You don't think he ran off?"

"No."

"Why?"

"If you'll answer my questions, maybe I'll be able to answer yours better. Okay?"

"Go ahead."

I asked him the same questions I had asked Mrs. Whitlaw. I learned that Bertram Wanzer had earned a bachelor's and master's at MIT in math. He had never been in the service. He had been arrested several times in the sixties and early seventies for demonstrating against the war and in favor of civil rights. He settled down, got a job, married. Then, without warning, he disappeared.

"This is what he told us," said Robert. "This all happened before my mom met him. I was a kid when he came along. He adopted me. He was like a father. I called him Dad. They were good years. The best of my life. My mom's, too. Then . . ."

"Mr. Wanzer," I said, "I'd like to read some names to you, see if they ring any bells with you."

"What kind of bells?"

"People your stepfather might've been associated with. Friends of his. Business acquaintances. Just names he might've mentioned."

"I was only seventeen when . . ."

"Let's try."

"Okay."

I read the seven other names plus Daniel's.

"Sorry," he said.

"Are you sure?"

"I'm sure I don't remember any of them. He might've mentioned them or something, but I don't remember it."

"Would you mind copying them down and running them past your mother?"

"I guess that'd be okay."

I read them to him, spelling them. Then I gave him my phone numbers, office and home.

"Let me know," I said. "Anytime."

"Sure."

"Even if she comes up blank."

"I'll call you," he said. "Can I tell her that my stepfather was murdered?"

"I'm not positive he was," I said. "But I think so. If you think it'll make her feel better . . ."

"It will," he said. "Guaranteed."

18

I tried to call Charlie the next morning, but Shirley told me that he was out of the office. I asked her to have him call me.

I tried Horowitz. He was out, too. So I spent the morning practicing law. Julie told me that I needed the practice.

Charlie called around noon. "Let's have lunch," he said.

"Good. I got some thoughts."

"Me, too. Meet you at Marie's in an hour."

He was at our usual corner table when I got there. I took the chair across from him and said, "What're you drinking?"

"Tap water."

"Looks good."

Our waitress, a BU undergraduate named Rita, came over and said, "Hi, Mr. Coyne. Want a drink?"

"I'll have the same as my uncle."

"It's one of our specialties," she said.

When she left, I said, "Listen, I got some hypotheses. Want to hear them?"

Charlie nodded. "Go ahead."

"I talked to the widow Whitlaw and Bertram Wanzer's son last night. Looking for commonalities. Wanzer got arrested a few times for civil rights and antiwar stuff, and when I asked Mrs. Whitlaw if old James had ever had a problem with the law she hung up on me, which answered that question. Then there was that DiSimione in Providence, who was a candidate for the Witness Protection Program. A big-time hood, obviously. Add to that the two small-timers who got murdered in Springfield, Johnson and Repucci, and we've got all five in trouble with legal problems of one sort or another. That's five for five that we know of. We also know Daniel got arrested on that marijuana thing, so if the other three on the list . . ."

I let my voice trail off. Charlie was rotating his water glass between the palms of his hands, staring down into it as if he'd noticed bugs swimming there.

"Hey, Charlie?"

He looked up. "I've been listening, Brady."

"What d'you think?"

He shrugged. "Anything else?"

I flapped my hands. "Shit. I thought that was interesting enough. Okay. The other thing is a possible connection to Vietnam. We know about Daniel. This Whitlaw—he was a marine, not SF, but he got some toes blown off over there. Wanzer evidently stayed home. But he was an active protester. Check this thought: Daniel was bitter about his getting Oranged, Whitlaw, maybe, was equally pissed at losing some digits, and Wanzer opposed the war anyway. If the others—Charlie, what the hell is the matter today?"

He wasn't looking at me. It was hard to tell if he had even been listening. He slouched across from me playing with his glass and staring down at the table.

His head came up. "Brady, I gotta tell you something."

I shrugged. "Go for it."

At that moment Rita delivered my glass of water. "Ready to order?" she said.

"I'll try the cannelloni," I said.

"Just a bowl of minestrone," said Charlie.

"Wine?"

"No," said Charlie. "Thank you."

Rita smiled and left. Charlie gazed off in the direction she had taken. I sensed that he wasn't really focusing on how gracefully Rita's slim hips rolled in her tight jeans.

He turned to face me. "Neighbor of mine, guy named Lewis, Jimmy Lewis, he's got this beagle. It's just a pet, his kids' dog, really. They call him Snoopy. Anyways, my neighbors on the other side are this middle-aged couple named Tomchik. Quiet folks. No kids. But they've got a pet rabbit called Daisy, one of those expensive breeds with long fur and big floppy ears. Daisy is like their kid, okay? You know how childless couples can be with their pets. I mean, they keep this bunny in a cage out back, but they like to bring her into the house, feed her table scraps, take her for a ride in the car, even. Okay, the other evening Jimmy

Lewis comes over. He's looking kinda upset. I give him a drink, ask him what's up. He says he wants to talk to me. I say sure, go ahead. Seems that the other day Snoopy the beagle comes marching into the house and he's got Daisy the rabbit in his mouth. Old Daisy's stone-dead, all covered with dirt and dog drool and whatnot. Jimmy's visibly upset, telling me this. He says, 'So what would you have done, huh?' I shrug. I figure he's about to tell me what he did and he just wants me to tell him he did the right thing."

Charlie paused to sip his water. I took that opportunity to say, "Um, Charlie? Is there a point to this? Because we've got some important things to discuss here."

He waved his hand. "Bear with me. Jimmy says he knelt down and told Snoopy 'good dog' and patted his head and took Daisy's corpse from his mouth. He says to me, 'Shit, Charlie. The Tomchiks loved that stupid bunny. How in hell am I gonna tell 'em that my dog killed Daisy, huh? They'll hate me forever.' So Jimmy takes Daisy to the kitchen sink and washes all the mud and shit off her, then brushes her and fluffs her with a hair drier."

"A hare drier?" I said.

Charlie shrugged. "Sure. Pun optional. Anyway, after it gets dark he sneaks into the Tomchiks' backyard with Daisy under his arm. He sticks her into her cage, latches it, and skulks back home. He's telling me this, and he says, 'See, Charlie, I figure they'll assume old Daisy had a stroke or something, died peacefully, looking all clean and pretty the way they keep her. No harm done, right?' And I nod to him. Sounds good to me."

"You going somewhere with this?" I said.

"Almost there," said Charlie. "Jimmy says a couple days later he runs into Mrs. Tomchik at the market. They exchange greetings, the way neighbors do, how've you been, your yard's looking nice, stuff like that, and Mrs. Tomchik gives Jimmy this mournful look and says to him, 'I guess you didn't hear.' And Jimmy says innocently, 'Hear what?' And she says, 'We had a death in the family.' And Jimmy's saying, 'Oh, shit,' to himself, because he knows how much those people loved that dumb rabbit. And she says, 'Yes. Poor Daisy has passed on.' And Jimmy says, 'My sincere condolences. I hope it was painless.' And she says, 'Yes. We think Daisy must've had a heart attack. But the strangest thing happened.' 'What's that?' says Jimmy. 'Well,' says the woman, 'we buried her, of course. And then somebody dug her up and cleaned her off and put her back into her cage.'"

Charlie folded his hands on the table and peered at me.

"You're trying to tell me something," I said.

He nodded.

"It's pretty oblique."

He shrugged.

"Okay," I said. "I get it. But I don't understand. Yesterday you were hot to figure out what happened to Daniel McCloud, and now you're saying we should leave dead rabbits where they're buried, or something to that general effect."

"Something," said Charlie, "to that precise effect. Listen," he said, leaning toward me and grabbing my wrist, "as your best and most trusted friend, who profoundly hopes we'll slip into our golden years together, you and I, casting Pale Morning Duns at rising brown trout in Rocky Mountain rivers and slicing golf balls into sand traps on all the great courses in the world, I'm saying to you: Forget it. Okay? Leave it be. Daniel's dead. Irrevocably dead. Nothing anybody can do about it. It's a shame, but it happens. One way or the other, it always happens."

I pulled my wrist out of his grasp. "What the hell is the matter with you?" I said.

"Come on, Brady. I mean it. You keep doing this, and it's time you outgrew it."

"Doing what?"

He waved the back of his hand around in the air. "This," he said. "This . . . amateur detective work. This poking your nose into places it doesn't belong."

"Don't you care what happened to Daniel?"

Charlie shrugged. "I wish he was still alive, if that's what you mean."

"What about whoever murdered him? Don't you want to see him fry?"

He shook his head slowly. "Justice, you mean. You want justice."

"Yeah. Justice."

"Brady, what is it? Really? Why do you keep glomming onto these things like a big old snapping turtle with a stick in its mouth, shaking your head around and refusing to let go? And don't give me that justice crap. Anybody who went to law school knows better."

I sighed. I shook a Winston from my pack and lit it up. "You're asking a serious question?"

Charlie nodded. "A serious question. Yes."

"Shit," I said. "We've talked about this before. You know me. I just like knowing things. Or maybe I should say, I don't like not knowing. Call it a character defect, if you want. I can't help it. I'm impatient with the mysterious ways of nature or life or God or whatever you want to call it. Some great Catholic theologian once said, 'Whatever is, is to be adored.' Well, I think that's bullshit. 'Whatever is, is to be *understood*.' That's my motto. That's what this is all about, being alive and human. Trying to figure things out. Wanting to know things that you don't know. Listen. You're always giving me this line, Charlie. Fine. I expect it. But you never really mean it. Tell the truth. I think you kinda like it when I go banging around trying to understand things. Right? You usually try to help me. Now you're different. Now I got the feeling here that you really do mean it. What's up?"

"Teilhard de Chardin," said Charlie. "The theologian. Whatever is, is to be adored. God's way. Go with the flow. Comforting wisdom, that."

"It doesn't comfort me."

Charlie shrugged. So did I.

Rita brought our food. Charlie hunched over his soup. I attacked my cannelloni. We didn't talk. Charlie slurped about half of his soup, then put down his spoon and pushed the bowl away.

"You all right?" I said.

He shrugged.

"Hey. Marie makes the best minestrone in the city."

"My stomach's been a little off lately."

I nodded. "That explains it, then."

"What?"

"Your gloom. All these negative emanations zipping out of your skull. Whaddya say, Charlie. Let's figure this sucker out, huh?"

"No, Brady. Please. Forget it."

"Come on, old buddy. You perform some computer tricks, and I'll do some pinching and tickling, and we'll see who squeals and giggles. Whaddya say?"

He shook his head. "I'm serious, Brady."

I stared at him. He lifted his gaze to meet mine. "You really are, aren't you?" I said.

He nodded. "Yes. Back off. Do what I tell you."

"Well, fuck it, then," I said.

"You'll back off?"

"Shit, no. I'll just have to do it without you."

19

I walked back to Copley Square from Marie's in Kenmore with the collar of my jacket turned up against the November chill. But I was more chilled by Charlie than by the weather. He was always telling me to grow up and mind my own business. But he never really meant it. Charlie, as a prosecutor for the Justice Department, had plenty of opportunity to nose around in crime and mystery. It was his business, and he enjoyed it, and he understood why I sometimes found myself trying to figure out who had cheated, robbed, extorted, and occasionally even murdered my clients or their friends and relations.

We always joked about it. Lawyers do that. If law school doesn't make you cynical, the practice of law quickly does.

Lawyers rarely admit they're committed to justice. They never admit it to each other. We talk mostly about billable hours, sometimes about winning. Among ourselves, we call the law a business and ourselves businessmen.

But most of the lawyers I know still nurture the vestige of what got them into law in the first place. The quest for an abstraction. Justice.

Ever since the day I met him at Yale, Charlie McDevitt had always dreamed of a seat on the Supreme Court. With Charlie, it was never prestige. It was the ultimate opportunity to make justice.

Now something in him had changed, and it worried me.

But it didn't change my mind.

When I got back to the office I called Horowitz at the state police barracks. When he answered the phone I said, "You get ahold of Lieutenant Fusco yet?"

"Ah, shit," he said. "I told you I was gonna do that, didn't I?"

"You promised."

"What was the question?"

"The Daniel McCloud murder in Wilson Falls."

"Right." He popped his bubble gum. "Okay. I seem to recall there was a lunch in this for me."

"There was, yes."

"Where?"

"You name it."

"I will."

"Couple of things, while you're talking with Fusco," I said.

"I wouldn't push too hard, Coyne."

"I called him a while ago. Had some names I thought he might want to check out."

"Names?"

"Maybe connected to the McCloud murder."

"And?"

"And he never called me back. I'm just trying to cooperate."

"Hm," said Horowitz doubtfully.

"Anyway," I said, "along the same line, there's something specific you can mention to him when you talk to him. Okay?"

"Go ahead."

"Just a couple of old crimes out near Springfield that Fusco might know something about. Got a pencil?"

"I've got a pencil, for Christ's sake," he growled.

"Okay. One, William Johnson, murdered in 1984. Two, Carmine Repucci, murdered in 1987."

"So what's the question?"

"Mainly, if and how the two of them might be connected. They were both small-timers, spent time in Billerica. I'd like to know if they were there at the same time, maybe cellmates. Were they partners when they got out? I'd like to know if they were in Vietnam, or in the service at all, and if so, when and where. I want to know if anyone's been prosecuted for their murders, or suspected but not prosecuted, or what."

"What you want to know," said Horowitz, "is how either of these two guys might be connected to your McCloud. Right?"

"What I really want to know," I said, "is if the same person killed all three of them."

"This'll be one helluva lunch you're gonna owe me, Coyne. But, yeah, lemme see what I can find out."

"When?"

"When what?"

"When are you going to see what you can find out?"

"I can't do it while I'm talking to you, can I?"

"Nope."

After I hung up with Horowitz I began to rummage among the neat stacks of paper that Julie had assembled on my desk, and before I knew it she was poking her head into my office and telling me she was leaving. I wished her a pleasant weekend and returned to my paperwork. She stood in the doorway for a minute beaming at my diligence, and I wondered if she had talked to Charlie. Julie would like it if she thought I had overcome my childish obsession with unbillable hours.

At five-thirty Horowitz called. "Meet me at Hilary's in fifteen minutes," he said.

"You mean please?"

"No. Meet me."

"Okay."

After I hung up I reorganized the stacks of paper on my desk. There was a new stack now. Stuff I had done. It wasn't very tall. But I was proud of it.

I switched on the answering machine, got my jacket, locked up, and left. J. C. Hilary's is across the square from my office building. Horowitz had chosen it for my convenience, which wasn't characteristic. And when I thought about it, I realized it was uncharacteristic of him to meet me at all. Usually he'd tell me what he'd learned over the telephone.

He must've learned something.

I found a booth and ordered a bourbon old-fashioned. I sipped at it and smoked cigarettes and watched the Friday evening bar crowd tell loud stories and flirt with waitresses, and I was halfway through my second drink before I saw Horowitz shoulder his way toward me. He was three-quarters of an hour late.

He slid into the booth across from me. "Traffic," he muttered.

"I thought cops were never bothered by traffic. Flick on the siren and the flashers and everyone pulls over to let you by."

"Shit," he said. "Flick on the siren and the flashers and everyone ignores you. I need a beer."

He looked around and caught the eye of the waitress. She nodded to him and in a minute or two she came over. "Sir?"

"Gimme a light beer."

"We've got Coors, Mich, Bud, Miller."

Horowitz waved his hand. "Michelob, I guess."

He stuck his forefinger into his mouth and removed a wad of chewing gum. He put it into the ashtray. He looked up at me from under his shaggy black eyebrows. "Coyne," he said, "I got instructions for you."

I rolled my eyes. "Goodie."

"Leave cop work to the cops."

"This from Fusco?"

He leaned toward me. "This is from me. All you do is annoy people. You take up their time. You get in the way. You do more harm than good. You—"

"I've heard it," I said quickly. "You're trying to tell me

that Fusco doesn't have anything, that they're making no progress on the McCloud case."

He shrugged. "That's true, but—"

"And everyone's embarrassed at their incompetence and they don't want the civilians to know it."

"Listen," he said. "There's things you don't know."

"Hey," I said. "A revelation."

"Dammit, Coyne. I'm talking to you as a friend here."

"That's a first."

He stared a me for a moment, then lowered his eyes and shook his head slowly back and forth. "I mean it," he muttered.

"About being my friend?"

"No. About putting down your fucking lance and leaving the windmills to us."

The waitress brought his beer and said to me, "Another, sir?"

"No," I said. "I've got to stay sharp so I can figure out what my friend here is trying to tell me that he won't say."

She frowned, then shrugged.

After she left, Horowitz said, "Okay, Coyne. I'm gonna be straight with you."

"Another first."

"The McCloud case is on the back burner."

"You mean they've buried it."

He shrugged.

"Why?"

"Can't tell you."

"Do you know?"

"I got an idea."

"This Fusco's doing?"

"No."

"Somebody higher than Fusco, then."

"Look," said Horowitz, "I shouldn't have told you that much, okay? Except I am trying to impress upon you the importance of your backing off."

"As a friend."

"Sure," he said. "As a friend. Okay?"

"I don't get it."

"You don't have to get it, Coyne. You're not supposed to get it. You're just supposed to do it. Go argue alimony, or whatever it is you do."

"And leave cop business to the cops."

"Yes."

"Except they're not doing it."

He blew out a long sigh. "Call it a warning. Call it advice. Call it whatever you want. Just tell me you hear me."

"I hear you," I said.

He sighed deeply. "Good."

"I will take it into account."

"You pigheaded son of a bitch," he said.

"What about Johnson and Repucci?" I said. "Learn anything about them for me?"

"If I tell you will you get the McCloud bug out of your ass?"

I stared up at the ceiling, pretending to ponder. "Okay," I said. "It's a deal."

"Mean it?"

"Sure." It was a lie, but it didn't bother me.

He stared at me for a moment. "Okay," he said.

"Johnson and Repucci both did time at Billerica in 1981. Their sentences overlapped by about three months, and they were in the same cellblock, so they undoubtedly knew each other. Johnson got out first and turned up in Springfield. Repucci grew up in Eastie, and that's where he got arrested. When he got out, he went to Chicopee, which, as you know, is right next to Springfield. Whether him and Johnson worked together or not I couldn't tell you. Logical assumption, though. They were both fringies, well known by the police, pulled in several times, but never charged with anything. When Johnson got offed, they questioned Repucci about it, but nothing came of it. They never made any arrests on Johnson's murder. Guess they assumed it was a territory thing. Drugs, hookers, protection. One less asshole on the streets. You know how it works."

Horowitz shrugged. I nodded.

"Anyways, Repucci got it a few years later. Same deal. The assholes want to knock each other off, saves us all a problem."

"So neither murder was solved," I said.

"Right," said Horowitz. "No arrests, even."

"You check on their war records?"

"Neither of 'em was ever in the service."

"They don't sound like the kind of gentlemen who'd march for peace."

He shrugged. "They weren't arrested for it. That's all I can tell you." He picked up his beer and took a small sip.

"That's it?" I said.

"That's all."

I fumbled in my jacket pocket and found the printout

Charlie had given me. I unfolded it and put it in front of Horowitz. He glanced down at it, then looked up at me. "What's this?"

"Some names."

"Christ," he said. "I can see that."

"Johnson and Repucci are on this list. This is what I wanted to tell Fusco about. There's some connection among all of them. Plus Daniel McCloud."

Horowitz picked up the printout and, without looking at it, refolded it and handed it back to me. "I told you already," he said. "And you promised."

"You won't check them out for me?"

"Absolutely not. And don't you, either."

I tucked the printout into my pocket. "Right," I said. "I promised."

20

The shrill of the telephone beside my bed popped my eyes open. Seven o'clock. My brain reluctantly ground into gear, and the vise around my temples reminded me of two more bourbon old-fashioneds at Hilary's after Horowitz left, then a steak, then stopping at Skeeter's on the way home where I watched the basketball game and argued with a guy who didn't think Bob Cousy could even break into the starting five for Holy Cross in the new era of basketball.

I'd had a few beers at Skeeter's. The Celtics won, and I believed I won my argument, too, and so I'd celebrated with a mug of coffee laced with Jack Daniel's.

Skeeter had made sure I wasn't driving before he gave it to me.

And throughout the evening, on the level beneath the basketball and the booze and the fellowship of the bar, the question festered in my brain: Why had first Charlie and then Horowitz, two trusted friends, both been so humorlessly earnest in warning me off the Daniel McCloud case? Both of them had indulged me plenty of times in the past, no questions asked, no judgments rendered.

And now, at seven a.m., too damn early on a Saturday morning, my phone was ringing. What now?

I got it off the hook and against my ear. "Yuh?"

"Hey, Pop. You awake?"

I groaned. "I am now." Joey. My younger.

"Well, say hi to Terri for me."

"Huh?"

"Terri. Listen. Feel around. She's the one beside you."

"There's nobody here but me."

"Yeah?"

"Yeah."

"Something wrong?"

"Nothing's wrong. She's not here. We're not together these days."

"Hm. Too bad. Well, listen. You wanna go climb a mountain?"

"Are you speaking figuratively or literally?"

"Literally. Me and Debbie're gonna climb Monadnock today and we were wondering if you and Terri'd like to join us. Or you and some other lady. Or just you, if that's how it is."

"Monadnock's not a climb," I said. "It's a stroll up a long hill."

"I know a trail up the back side. I mean, you don't need ropes, but there are some rocks. Okay, so it's not a climb. It's not a stroll, either. Call it a hike."

My head was killing me. The last thing on earth I felt

like doing was climbing a mountain. Which was a very good reason to do it. "Okay," I said. "Climbing Monadnock will give my life some metaphorical significance."

"Whatever that's supposed to mean. Hang on. Debbie wants to say hello."

I took the opportunity to light a cigarette. It did not help my head.

"Hey, Brady?"

Debbie was a junior in high school, a year behind Joey. They'd been together for a year and a half—longer than I'd lasted with Terri, and longer, in fact, than any exclusive relationship I'd managed to sustain with any woman during the decade since Gloria and I were divorced. I wasn't sure how that was significant, but I believed it was. When Joey introduced me to Debbie, she'd called me Mr. Coyne. About the third time the two of them came to my apartment to eat chili and play cards, Debbie had started calling me Brady. I liked it better than Mr. Coyne.

"Hi, kiddo."

"You gonna come with us I hope?"

"Sure."

"Bringing Terri?"

"Nope. She dumped me."

"Aw. That sucks. Want me to fix you up with a friend of mine?"

"What, some high-school junior?"

"No. An older woman." Debbie giggled. "A senior."

"Tempting. But not today, honey. Don't tell Joey, but I'm a wee bit overhung this morning."

"Mountain air'll cure that. Well, see you soon, then. Here's Joe."

"We'll come get you in an hour," he said. "I got the lunches and everything. Don't forget to bring some extra layers and foul-weather gear. This is November. Mountaintops get chilly."

"For Chrissake, son. *You're* the kid, remember?"

"Gets confusing sometimes, doesn't it, Pop?"

"Not to me," I growled.

It wasn't until after I hung up that I wondered how it happened that Debbie and Joey were together at seven on a Saturday morning. And Terri and I weren't.

The sun shone brilliantly in a transparent November sky. The air carried a chilly bite. It was a perfect day to climb a mountain, figuratively as well as literally. Within fifteen minutes the mountain breeze blew my head clear. It felt good to stretch the hamstrings. Joey's trail offered its challenges. It was erratically marked by an occasional splash of white paint on a rock or tree trunk, and we strayed from it a few times. In several places we had to clamber over rocks. Joey went first, then Debbie. He helped her from above and I had the pleasure of boosting her up from underneath. Then they both reached down to haul me up.

When we got to the top Joey unpacked his knapsack and we ate the salami and extra-sharp cheddar sandwiches Debbie had made. Southern New Hampshire lay spread out around us in its muted November colors, and from up there you couldn't see the shopping malls and high-tech office complexes and condominium developments that had invaded the once-rural landscape. Just trees and meadows, hills and distant mountains, meandering country roadways and rivers, the way it had always been. A man or an automobile would have been a speck, impossible to identify. That was the perspective from the mountaintop. From that distance, the details were indistinct. The big picture came into focus.

It was important, I realized, to climb atop a mountain once in a while.

I mentioned these thoughts to Joey and Debbie as we sat there munching our sandwiches. Debbie nodded. Joey told me I should quit with the metaphors.

He was probably right.

We sat up there drinking coffee with our backs against a rock, sheltered from the hard persistent wind, until clouds obliterated the sun. Joey cocked his head at the sky. "We better head back," he said.

Billy, my older boy, is irresponsible and lazy, a dreamer and risk-taker, sometimes a hell-raiser. He'd switched his major about six times at UMass already, and he'd just begun his junior year. Lately, he was talking of quitting altogether and heading west to become a fly-fishing guide, a career I sometimes aspired to myself. He always seemed to have three or four simultaneous girlfriends, who all knew and liked each other and adored Billy.

Joey's the practical one. He got his homework done ahead of time, mowed his mother's lawn—sometimes without even being reminded—and had, as well as I could tell, remained faithful to Debbie for what amounted to a significant chunk of his young postpubescent life. He kept his room reasonably neat and won prizes at science fairs and sent thank-you notes. He always finished what he started.

It was as if I had been divided in half and a whole man was constructed from each contradictory part.

I loved them both equally and without reservation.

So it was Joey who had to remind his father that we ought to get back down the mountain ahead of the storm. Billy would have wanted to experience a November blizzard on a mountaintop.

The snow came quickly on a hard northeast wind, catching us exposed before we had descended into the tree-line. It blew at an acute angle, tiny hard pellets of frozen mist. The three of us hastily donned all the layers we had brought with us and plowed downhill. The rocks grew slippery. Joey again went first, and then the two of us helped Debbie down, and once she lost her footing and if I hadn't been gripping her wrist she would have fallen. When we reached the tree line, the trail leveled off a little and the snow became rain, and the three of us turtled our necks into our jackets and slogged through the dripping woods.

The descent seemed to take much longer than the climb. I mentioned this to Joey. He accused me of looking for metaphors again.

We stopped at a coffee shop in Jaffrey for hamburgers and hot tea, and it was after eight in the evening when Joey and Debbie dropped me off. I invited them up, but there was a party in Wellesley that required their presence. I thanked them for inviting me along. They shrugged as if there was nothing strange about a couple of high-school kids wanting a parent to join them for a Saturday outing.

I figured I must have done something right.

I began shucking layers the moment I closed the door to my apartment behind me, and I left a soggy trail of clothes all the way to the bathroom. I got the shower steaming and stood under it until the final vestiges of chill were driven from my bones.

I slipped on a sweatshirt and jeans, made myself a watered-down Jack Daniel's, and it was only when I went into the living room to catch the third period of the Bruins game that I noticed the red light of my answering machine winking at me. Blink-blink, pause. Blink-blink, pause. Two messages.

And that reminded me of Daniel McCloud, and the eight names he had posthumously left for me, and the warnings from Charlie and Horowitz, and Cammie and Oakley, and all the rest of it, and it occurred to me that I had, for one day on Mount Monadnock, not thought about any of it.

I depressed the button on the machine.

"Brady, it's Terri" came the familiar voice. "It's, um, about three Saturday afternoon. I was just—I don't know why I called, actually." She laughed quickly. "Melissa's at Mother's, and it's pretty gloomy outside. I had WBUR on and they were playing Mendelssohn and I was remembering how we . . . Ah, I'm sorry. I guess I just wanted to hear your voice, for some reason. Anyway, hope all's well with

you, Brady Coyne." There was a long pause. "Well, 'bye,"
she said softly before the machine clicked.

Then came another voice. "Mr. Coyne? This is
Bonnie Coleman. Al's wife, remember? It's around five
Saturday. Will you give me a call, please?" She left a num-
ber with an 802 area code. Vermont.

I hastily jotted down the number while my machine
rewound itself.

Daniel's book, I thought. She'd found Daniel's book.

What was she doing in Vermont?

I lit a cigarette, then pecked out the number she had
given me. A man answered. His voice was cultured, elderly,
cautious. "Yes?" he said.

"May I speak with Bonnie Coleman please?"

"Who shall I say is calling?"

"My name is Brady Coyne. I'm returning Bonnie's
call."

"One moment, sir."

I puffed my Winston and took a sip from my glass of
Jack Daniel's. The ice had melted in it.

"Mr. Coyne?"

"Hi, Bonnie. Let's make it Brady."

"Thanks for getting back to me," she said. "I, uh, have
some information I'd like to share with you."

"Great. Let's have it."

"It really doesn't lend itself to the telephone.
Something I'd like to show you."

"Have you found the book?"

She hesitated. "Not exactly. Look, I'm staying with the
Colemans for a while."

"Al's parents?"

"Yes. We're leaning on each other."

"So let's get together, then."

"Good. How's tomorrow?"

"That would work. Where are you?"

"Dorset. Know where it is?"

"Sure. North of Manchester, which is the home of Orvis and the Fly-fishing Museum, on the banks of the fabled and overrated Battenkill River."

"It's a beautiful river."

"It's the trout fishing that's overrated. Where shall we meet?"

She described a coffee shop on the Ethan Allen Highway, known to Vermonters as Historic Route 7A, just north of Manchester Center. We agreed to meet there at noon. I inferred that either she didn't want Al's bereaved parents to see her with another man so soon after their son's death or she wanted to insulate them from the information she had for me.

In either case I found myself intrigued.

Maybe it was a breakthrough. Maybe finally I'd learn something that would connect the dots—the missing manuscript, the list of eight mysterious names, Daniel's murder, as well as Al's, and the strange protective reactions of Charlie and Horowitz to my inquiries.

I tried to conjure up Bonnie Coleman's image from our days in New Haven. I remembered blond hair, a flirtatious smile, long slender legs. But that was more than twenty years ago.

She'd undoubtedly aged. Hadn't we all?

21

I sprawled on the sofa and flicked on the Bruins game. It was tied at two-all midway through the third period and remained that way through the five-minute overtime. Everything was happening between the blue lines. The puck bounced and dribbled from team to team, the players kept trying to knock each other down, and they all seemed less interested in winning than in preventing defeat. Another insight into the human condition. I'd had a productive day at such insights, although any useful applications for them had so far eluded me.

When the game mercifully ended, I clicked off the set and dialed Daniel McCloud's number. Cammie answered with a cautious "Hello?"

"It's Brady."

"Oh, gee. How are you?" I heard Bonnie Raitt in the background.

"I'm fine," I said. "I was just wondering—"

"Brady, can you hold on for a sec? I can't hear you

very well." She put the phone down, and when she came back on a minute or two later I no longer could hear the music. "You still there?"

"I'm here."

"That's better. What's up?"

"I was mainly just wondering if our friend Sergeant Oakley is behaving himself."

"Oh, yes. Since you did whatever you did, I haven't seen him."

"That's good," I said. "Cammie, remember those names?"

"Names?"

"Daniel's photos."

"Oh. Yes, I guess so."

"Have you thought about them?"

"Truthfully, no. I mean, I didn't recognize any of them. They didn't mean anything to me. Just names. You know?"

"Listen. I'm going to read them to you again. I've learned a few things about them. I want you to write them down, think about them some more, maybe rummage around among Daniel's stuff, see if you can come up with anything."

"Do you think this is going to get us anywhere?"

"I don't know. It's all I can think of. Fusco—the state cop—he's apparently given up on the case. Charlie McDevitt and my friend Horowitz are practically ordering me to stop poking around in it. So I can't think of anything else to do."

"You want me to write them down?"

"Yes."

"Hang on. Lemme get a pencil and paper."

A minute or so later she came back on the phone and said, "Okay. Read 'em to me."

I read the eight names to Cammie. I told her what I had learned about each of them. How they all had either died or disappeared. Murder, suicide, accident. Dates. Connections. I went slowly, and several times Cammie asked me to repeat what I had said. When I finished, I said, "And I'm willing to bet that Daniel and Al Coleman—he's the one I sent the manuscript to—that they belong on that list, too."

"Jesus, Brady."

"Any bells chiming for you, Cammie?"

She let out a long breath. "Afraid not."

"You sure?"

She hesitated. "Brady, what are you trying to say?"

"Nothing. I guess I had hoped that with the information that goes along with the names, maybe something would click for you."

"You sound as if you had an idea. A suspicion or something."

"No," I said. "I hoped you did."

"I'm sorry." A pause. "Hey, Brady?"

"Yes?"

"Why don't you come visit me tomorrow? I'll cook something, we can take a walk down by the river."

"It's tempting, Cammie. But I can't. I'm going to meet the widow of Daniel's agent. She might have some information for me."

She laughed softly. "You're incredible."

"Me?"

"You have all these people trying to scare you off the case, and it only makes you poke deeper."

"Somebody's got to."

"And it might as well be you, huh?"

"It might as well," I said.

"Well, will you come see me sometime?"

"Yes. Soon. I promise."

I stared up into the darkness of my bedroom hearing a Tennessee mountain stream in Cammie's soft chuckle and remembering how she looked standing by her easel silhouetted against the floor-to-ceiling glass in her studio, a paintbrush clenched in her mouth, her honey-colored back smooth and bare, her legs long and sleek, how she turned and came to me, the firm slope of her stomach, the high lifting curve of her breasts, and it became a dream, and in the dream I did not grasp her wrists to stop her from undressing me, and when I was completely undressed and she was, too, Cammie had somehow become Terri and I abruptly woke up.

Terri.

I hadn't returned her call.

I drifted back to sleep thinking about it.

I was halfway down the elevator before I realized I was clutching my briefcase. I cursed Julie. Every afternoon she stuffs the thing full of paperwork—my homework, she calls it. She's gotten me into the habit of lugging it back and forth to the office. The habit of opening it every evening has thus far mercifully eluded me. Usually I drop it inside the doorway of my apartment when I get home and pick it up the next morning on my way out.

So now, on a Sunday morning on my way to Vermont, I was carrying my briefcase for my meeting with Bonnie Coleman.

I tossed it onto the backseat of my car and headed out.

The sky was high and pale and the air was brittle on Sunday morning. Calendar winter was still a month away. But in the shaded spots along Route 2, hoarfrost whitened the ground like snow and skim ice glittered in the puddles from Saturday's rain.

I turned north on Interstate 91, then west on Route 9 in Brattleboro, heading across the narrow southernmost width of Vermont. I ascended, then descended the Green Mountain spine, found Route 7A just north of Bennington, and pulled into the peastone lot in front of Dave's Cafe north of Manchester a few minutes before noon.

There were half a dozen cars already parked there. One of them was a burgundy Honda Accord with New York plates.

I went inside. To the left of the lobby was a small bar, apparently closed. To the right lay a dining room. A sign by the entryway said, "Please Seat Yourself." I went in. Some mounted brown trout and deer antlers and framed Currier and Ives prints hung from the knotty pine walls. High-backed booths lined the front and side by the windows.

Tables were scattered across the floor. None of the tables was occupied. Everyone wanted a window view of the highway.

I stood there for a moment. Then I saw a hand and a glimpse of blond hair. I went over and said, "Bonnie?"

She nodded. "I thought that was you. Thanks for coming."

I never would have recognized her on the street, but knowing who she was, I remembered her. Aside from three parallel vertical creases between her eyebrows and a barely noticeable thickening of the flesh on her throat, she still looked pretty much as I remembered her at twenty, although I knew she was at least twice that.

I slid into the booth across from her.

She smiled at me. Her eyes were the same color as the Vermont sky. "I remember you," she said. "You and your friend Charlie. You guys were wild."

I nodded. "We still are."

"I bet. Want some coffee?" She gestured to an earthenware urn and two matching mugs that sat on the table.

"Coffee would be great."

Bonnie poured the two mugs full.

I picked up the one she pushed toward me and sipped. "How are you doing?" I said.

She shrugged. "I'm doing okay. It's hard, but I'm getting there. Al's parents are like big solid slabs of Vermont granite. They've been great. I lean on them and they hold me up. We weren't especially close when—when Al was alive. The kids aren't handling it that well." She shook her head. "It takes time, I guess."

I nodded. "I'm really sorry. Anything I can do . . ."

"Thanks. Time. That's all."

Bonnie talked about New Haven, how she'd met Al when he was a law student and she an undergraduate at Yale, the parties at the place Charlie and I rented on the ocean, how Al started as a State Department attorney, their early married life in Georgetown, how Al became disillusioned, quit, set up a practice in New York and evenually became a literary agent, the famous writers whose passes she had rebuffed.

She waved her hand in the air and smiled. "Hell," she said. "You didn't come all the way up here to listen to my life story." She reached down to the seat beside her and brought up a spiral-bound notebook. She placed it on the table.

"Al's?" I said.

She nodded. "He was pretty haphazard about things. A lousy record keeper. He kept track of his appointments in his head. Otherwise, it was my job. Keeping track of things. Or else we would've gone broke. After he died, I spent more than a month going through all the little scraps of paper he left scattered around, just trying to make sure all the loose ends got tied up before I turned the business over to Keating. Anyway," she said, tapping the notebook with her forefinger, "I found this."

"What's in it?"

"More notes. When he got a manuscript he liked, he'd sometimes want to suggest some changes. He liked to play editor, and he was pretty good at it from what the writers used to tell me. You know, cut a scene here, change the ending there, tighten up a plot line, sharpen a character. He'd usually call up the writer and they'd talk about it. A few of them would even listen to him. Most of them would argue with him. But he kept doing it, because he wanted his books to be good. Anyway, there's a couple of pages in here I wanted to show you, and you'll see why we couldn't really discuss it over the phone."

She picked up the notebook and flipped through it, then turned it around so that it lay open and facing me on the table. She leaned over and twisted her head so that we both could read it.

At the top of the page a black felt-tipped pen had printed the words *SNAKE EATER*, and under that, "BC anony.—Daniel??" I looked up at Bonnie. "The man who wrote the book was called Snake Eater by some of his war buddies," I told her. "This BC would mean me. Brady Coyne. The author was anonymous. His first name was Daniel. I must've mentioned that to Al."

She nodded. "My guess was that this might be your book. This was the only set of notes I couldn't account for."

I glanced through the scratches and scribbles on the page. Much of it was illegible. There were sketches and squiggles, some recognizable such as a bird and a woman's breast and a snake and a palm tree and a man smoking a cigar, others just abstract designs, as if Al's black felt-tip kept doodling randomly as he read. A Freudian could find vast significance in all of it, probably. But I couldn't. Here and there I was able to decipher some of his hieroglyphics, although figuring out what they meant wasn't so easy.

I looked up at Bonnie. "He had awful penmanship."

She smiled. "I think he did it on purpose."

"These are the only ones I can make out." I moved my finger from place to place on the two pages, stopping where the letters made sense to me:

— *ed for gramm & spel*

— *ch w BC re au 2 talk*

— *needs prol*

— *ch w PV* This was underlined three times, and beside it, in green pen, Al had scratched: *Fr 1:00 Rock Cent*

— *PV — Sun* This was the last notation on the second page. It was written in pencil.

I flipped forward through the notebook, but the rest of the pages were blank.

"I know it's not much," said Bonnie.

"Can you make sense of any of it?"

She pointed to *ed for gramm & spel*. "This means edit for grammar and spelling," she said. "Al was a stickler for removing as many objections as possible before he'd show anything to an editor. And this BC must be you again."

"Check with me regarding the author. Al told me he wanted to talk with the author. I told him that Daniel wouldn't do it." I moved my finger. "And here. It must mean he thought it needed a prologue."

Bonnie nodded.

"What about PV?" I said. "It's mentioned twice. Mean anything to you?"

She shook her head. "I thought it might be somebody's initials. An editor or publisher or something. But I know all the publishing people Al dealt with, and there's no house and no editor with the initials PV. I checked our

Rolodex. There are a couple of V names who are writers, but none with the first initial of P. There's also a television guy, someone Al liked to talk to about movie rights. Vance. But it's Jack. There's no PV that I know of."

"Rock Cent?" I said, touching the marks Al had made.

"Rockefeller Center is my guess," said Bonnie. "Al liked to go there to meet with editors, have lunch, watch the girls in little skirts twirl around on their skates, do business." She frowned. "Maybe this refers to some other book, nothing to do with this one. PV could be an author's initials. Or even some kind of abbreviation of a title."

"It could be the pen name Daniel—the author—used," I said.

"But Al didn't know who he was. How could he have an appointment to meet him?"

I shrugged. "Good point."

"And here," she said, twisting her head around so that it was close to mine, "PV again. And Sun must mean Sunday. Another . . ."

Her voice trailed away and she slouched back in the booth. I frowned at her. Tears had welled up in her eyes. "Bonnie?" I said.

She shook her head. "Sorry."

"What is it?"

"Nothing. I'm sorry. Sunday, that's all. Al died—got killed—on a Sunday." She tried to smile. "Oh, I'm doing just fine, I am. Shit." She rummaged in her pocketbook and found a tissue. She dabbed her eyes and blew her nose. "Dammit," she muttered.

"I know this is hard," I said.

She sipped her coffee and made a face. She looked at her watch. "Look," she said, "I've got to get back to the kids."

"Sure. Would you mind if I photocopied these two pages? I'd like to have them to study."

"There's one of those twenty-four-hour places down the road. They've got a copier."

I put a five-dollar bill on the table and we left. I followed Bonnie a mile or so south on 7A. We stopped at a convenience store that doubled as a video rental. I photocopied the two pages from Al Coleman's notebook. It cost me twenty cents.

Outside, Bonnie and I shook hands. "Sorry about the tears," she said.

"You're entitled."

"Thought I was done with all that."

"I don't suppose one ever is."

She smiled, then held out her hand. I took it. "Thanks," she said.

She climbed into her Honda and I watched her drive away.

I slid the two sheets of photocopied paper into my briefcase and headed home. And all the way back to Boston I pondered who—or what—PV could be.

22

I got back to my apartment around four in the afternoon. We were approaching the shortest day of the year, and already the sun had sunk low behind the city's buildings. In my childhood, Sunday afternoons in the wintertime were always my most depressing times, and little has changed since then.

I tucked my car into its reserved spot in the basement garage, retrieved my briefcase from the backseat, and took the elevator up to the sixth floor.

The instant I opened the door I knew something was wrong.

I have an eccentric concept of order, I readily confess. Shoes, T-shirts, bath towels, magazines, fly rods—everything finds its place in my apartment. They usually happen to be places that most people wouldn't consider appropriate. But I know where things are, and if they're not there I know where to look.

I do not, however, keep my private papers scattered

across the living-room rug. I do not keep my desk drawers upside down on the kitchen table or the cushions of my sofa in a heap in the corner or my canned goods and refrigerator contents strewn around the kitchen floor.

My place had been pillaged.

I wandered around the living room, staring at the mess. Whether it had been a thorough job or a hasty one I couldn't tell. Nor could I determine if any papers were missing. My TV was there, and my stereo, and the two Aden Ripley watercolors still hung on the wall. The canned goods and pots and pans had been swept out of the cabinets in the kitchen. The freezer door hung open and melting ice dripped into a big puddle on the floor.

I went back into the living room, shoved the cushions back where they belonged on the sofa, and sat down. I lit a cigarette. My hands, I noticed, were steady.

I remembered Daniel's office the day he was killed. It had been trashed, too.

I smoked the cigarette down to the filter, crushed it out, and stood up. I went into my bedroom. I groped, then found the wall switch. When the light went on, I saw the arrow sticking into my mattress.

It was a mate to the one that had protruded from Daniel McCloud's chest—the same design on the aluminum shaft, the same colored fletching. But instead of slicing up through Daniel's abdomen into his heart, this one had been rammed into my bed—in just about the place my chest would have been had I been sleeping there. It had sliced through the blanket and two layers of sheets and penetrated deep into the mattress.

I have been accused on more than one occasion of not being sensitive or intelligent enough to take a hint.

It's a bum rap. I'm pretty good at understanding hints when I hear them. I just tend to ignore them, which is different.

Anyway, this wasn't a hint.

It was a warning, and a blatant one, and it was the same one that Charlie McDevitt and Horowitz had issued to me.

Only this one was impossible to ignore.

Sticking razor-sharp hunting broadheads into mattresses wasn't Charlie's style, or Horowitz's, either. It was exactly the style of a man who would shove an arrow into a man's abdomen, however.

I sat on the edge of my bed. I gripped the arrow and tried to twist it out. It came reluctantly. "Son of a *bitch*," I muttered. I yanked it from the mattress, then pulled it through the sheets and blanket, and when I got it free big tufts of mattress stuffing clung to the barbed broadhead. It left behind a jagged three-cornered hole in my mattress, just as it would have in my chest.

I carried the arrow out into the kitchen. I poured two fingers of sour mash into a glass, paused, then splashed in some more. I lit another cigarette.

Anger makes me glacially calm and focused. Fear gives me the shakes. I knew I was angry. Getting burglarized made me angry. But I noticed my hands. They were trembling.

I was angry *and* afraid.

A murderer had been in my apartment. I was entitled.

How the hell had he gotten in? It wasn't the most constructive question I could think of. But it was the one that my anger and my fear conspired to raise first.

Part of my hefty monthly rent check goes to paying the security guard who sits in the lobby of the building. He has a bank of closed-circuit television monitors in front of him that he's supposed to watch continually, but that must get a little boring, since he has his own portable television set tuned to more interesting channels. Nobody bothers complaining. Harbor Towers is a quiet building, inhabited mostly by retired old folks who spend the cold half of the year in Florida, plus a few separated or divorced single people like me who appreciate privacy. Nothing much ever happens in my building, and although the guards wear revolvers on their hips, none of the many we've had over the years has ever had an occasion to remove one from its holster.

For a visitor to gain entrance into the building, he must buzz the guard, who will then scrutinize the appropriate closed-circuit monitor and pick up the intercom phone. The visitor will give his name and the number of the unit he is visiting. The guard will ring the unit. The resident will okay his guest, who will then be buzzed in. The visitor will sign into the book, noting his or her name, the number of the unit visited, and the time. All visitors must sign out, too.

Residents, of course, have their own keys.

Most of us who live there park our cars in the basement garage and take the elevator directly up, bypassing the guard. But without our plastic parking card, which we must insert into a slot to make the barrier go up, we can't drive into the garage.

There are four fire doors that open into the building plus a service entrance in the back. They can only be opened from the outside with a passkey. A closed-circuit camera is trained on each of them.

If I wanted to invade a building such as mine, I would walk into the garage, ducking under the barrier and sticking close to the wall so that the closed-circuit camera would miss me. I'd have to take my chances getting onto the elevator, since there's a camera trained on it, too. If I kept my back to the camera, it's unlikely a guard would set off an alarm if he happened to notice me. He'd assume I was a resident even if he were watching that monitor instead of a ball game. Even more foolproof, I'd lurk in the shadows until some residents drove in. Then I'd walk onto the elevator with them. They'd assume I was one of the many residents they had never met. The guard would assume I was their guest. And an hour later my face would be forgotten by all of them.

Of course, if I had a passkey, or was adept at picking locks, I could get in through a fire door and then enter someone's apartment where I could, if that's what turned me on, strew papers around and shove arrows into mattresses.

I called Tony, the weekend guy, through the building intercom.

"Yo," he answered.

"It's Brady Coyne, 6E," I said.

"Hey, Mr. Coyne." Tony was a cheerful guy, a retired

shoe salesman who'd only been on the job for a couple of months. His main responsibility was to be there sitting on his fanny. He liked to watch soap operas and sitcoms, and I figured he barely earned the five bucks or so he was paid per hour.

"What's your shift these days, Tony?" I asked.

"Noon to eight, same as it's been."

"So you've been there since noon today?"

"Yep. Why? Problem?"

"Did anybody come looking for me?"

He hesitated. "You okay, Mr. Coyne?"

"I'm fine."

"You sound a little—I don't know—shaky."

"I'm okay. Was there anybody for me?"

"Um. Hm. Nope. Nobody. Expecting someone?"

"No, not really," I said. "Did anybody come looking for anybody who wasn't home? Or did you notice anything suspicious at all today?"

"Nah. Quiet day. Sunday, you know?"

"Any deliveries?"

"Nope. Sunday. You sure you're okay?"

"Yes, dammit." I took a breath. "I'm sorry, Tony. Listen, did you catch anything from the garage?"

"Whaddya mean?"

"I don't know. I'm just wondering if you saw anyone you didn't recognize today, someone who might've come around and then left, or buzzed me but found me out or something."

"Jeez, no, Mr. Coyne. Nothin' like that. Quiet. It's Sunday."

"Who was on before you?"

"That was Lyle. He had four to noon."

"Take a look in the book, see what's there after nine this morning."

"Like what?"

"Guests. Anybody who might've signed in."

"Okay. Hang on." There was a minute or two of silence, then Tony said, "Nothin' here, Mr. Coyne. Sunday morning, people go out. No guests at all. You know, half the tenants are away anyhow."

"Sure. Did Lyle make any notations?"

"Huh? What kind of notations?"

"I don't know. That he saw anything unusual."

"I guess he would've called in an alarm if he did, huh? That's what we're supposed to do. Anything at all, just buzz the police. He would've noted it if he'd done that. Nothing here. Quiet day. Sunday."

"Right," I said. "Sunday. Listen, has anybody reported losing their keys?"

"Keys?"

"House keys."

"Jeez, no. I heard nothing like that from anybody."

"Okay." I hesitated. "Well, thanks anyway, Tony. If you think of something, give me a buzz, will you?"

"Sure. You bet. Hey, Mr. Coyne. Really. Somethin' wrong?"

"No. No problem. Thanks."

"You bet."

I took my drink and my souvenir hunting arrow to the glass sliders and stared out into the November night. I fondled the arrow and sipped my drink. My hands were no longer trembling. All I saw outside was darkness. I went back to the phone and dialed Charlie's number at home. When he answered, I said, "How'd you feel if someone got a key to your place, sauntered in, trashed it, and stuck an arrow into your bed?"

"What the hell are you talking about?"

"When I got home this afternoon I found the place turned upside down. There was an arrow up to its hilt in my mattress. It looks identical to the one that was sticking in Daniel. I've been trying to sort out my feelings. Anger and fear, mingled together. Lots of fear, I think."

"For Chrissake, Brady—"

"I'm sorry," I said quickly. I took a deep breath. "I'm not accusing you of anything."

"It kinda sounded like it."

"Well, I'm not. I just need to talk to somebody. Look. This thing has freaked me out, Charlie."

"An arrow sticking into your bed? I don't blame you."

"I was away most of the day. When I got back it was there. Right where I would've been if I'd been asleep."

"A warning, you figure, huh?"

"Of course. What else? The sonofabitch was *here*. First you warned me, then Horowitz warned me, now this."

"Horowitz? The state cop?"

"Yes. He told me what you told me."

"About Daniel?"

"Yes."

"To back off?"

"Yes. In the strongest possible terms. Like you did."

"Well, you don't think Horowitz broke into your place, trashed it, and jammed some arrow into your bed, do you?"

"Of course not."

"Or me?"

"Shit, no, Charlie. I didn't intend that at all. I just don't know what to think. I know what I'm *supposed* to think. I'm supposed to think I better stop trying to figure out who killed Daniel."

"You should, you know."

"Yeah, well, maybe you're right."

"Well, good. It's about time you got some sense." Charlie let out a long breath. "Did they take anything?"

"I don't know. I don't think so. Maybe it was all just to make an impression. Rip up the place, stick an arrow into the bed where I could've been. Just a message."

"A pretty blatant message, at that," he said.

"Charlie, I don't know what to do. Jesus . . ."

"You could have been lying in that bed, Brady."

"Don't think for one minute that hasn't occurred to me."

"Next time, then."

"I know. Thanks for the sympathy."

"That why you called? For sympathy?"

"I don't know why I called. You're acting weird lately."

"*Me?* Me weird? Check the mirror, Coyne."

"I did. I saw this guy who just had the wee-wee scared out of him."

"That's better than seeing someone with an arrow in him."

"He's also pretty mad, this guy in the mirror," I said.

"Listen to the scared part, Brady. That's the part that makes sense."

"I know."

"Look," he said. "I don't know anything about this, and yes, I'm concerned. I'm frightened, too, okay? I don't want to lose you, buddy, and I'm glad you called me. But exactly what do you want?"

I laughed quickly. "I don't know. Not advice, because you already gave me that, and it's sounding more and more sensible all the time. Not sympathy, because that's useless. Your friendship doesn't need confirming. Maybe I hoped you'd have some insights, but I suppose I didn't really think you would. I guess I just wanted to vent."

"Vent away."

"I already did."

"Lemme think about it," said Charlie.

"Okay."

"I'm a little confused myself," he said.

"Those names disappearing from your computer's memory."

"Yeah. That's strange." He hesitated, then said, "Hey, Brady?"

"What?"

"You called the cops, didn't you?"

"Why?"

"Jesus! To tell them about the burglary, the arrow in your bed."

"And what would the cops do?"

Charlie hesitated; then he chuckled. "They'll ask you

if anybody is hurt. You'll say no. And about four hours later they'll arrive, glance around, ask if anything's missing, drop some cigar ashes onto your carpet, and you'll end up feeling as if you're the criminal. That's if they show up at all."

"Exactly. I talked to the security guy. That's as much as the cops would do. He didn't know anything."

"You should still call them. Report the crime. Be a good citizen."

"Yeah, well, I probably won't."

"Listen," he said.

"I know what you're going to say."

"I'm gonna say it anyway. Please. Stop. Cease and desist. Trust me on this."

"I trust you, Charlie."

"So what're you gonna do?"

"I don't know. Sleep on the sofa, I guess."

And after I cleaned up my apartment and made sure the chain was secured and the deadbolt thrown, that's what I did, although I didn't do much actual sleeping. Mostly I stared up into the darkness. I keep a .38 in the safe in my office. I decided to remove it the next day and bring it home with me.

Otherwise, I didn't come up with any helpful ideas.

I dozed off, then abruptly awoke. It could have been ten minutes later. Or several hours. I didn't check the time. I thought I had heard something. I lay there in the darkness, trying not to move. I felt a vise around my chest. My breaths came quickly. I darted my eyes around the shadowy corners of my living room. I heard nothing, saw nothing.

My heart was tripping along like a snare drum.

I switched on the lights and padded barefoot through all my rooms, wishing I had my .38 in my hand.

Nobody was there but me.

I retrieved my briefcase from the floor by the door and opened it. I found the envelope with the photos and index cards, and the printout Charlie had given me, and the two photocopied pages from Al Coleman's notebook. I brought them to the sofa and looked at them. I didn't know what I expected to find. I picked up the photos and fanned them out like a poker hand. I studied the six black-and-white faces as if they might speak to me. Six ordinary-looking American men gazed blankly back at me. They said nothing. I put them down and took up the index cards. William Johnson. Carmine Repucci. Two minor-league crooks who ended up violently murdered, the way most of them do. No faces. Just two names.

After a while I became sleepy. Those eight names and a faceless man with an arrow in his hand all swirled through my brain as I drifted off for the second time that night, and when I awakened the sun was streaming into my living room, and if I'd had dreams of arrows being rammed into me, I'd blissfully forgotten them.

23

I dialed Cammie's number standing up while sipping my second cup of coffee, and Daniel's voice startled me for an instant before I realized it was his answering machine.

"I'm not here. Say who you are and I'll get back to you" was all he said.

After the beep, I said, "You should get the message on the machine changed, Cammie. It's Brady. About nine Monday morning. Please call me at the office right away." I left the number, hung up, grabbed my jacket, and headed out.

Julie was on the phone and Rita Nathanson was waiting for me. I smiled at both of them, and neither smiled back. Rita's appointment was at nine. I was half an hour late.

"Sorry I'm late," I said. "Come on in, Rita."

Rita's ex-husband had stopped sending child-support checks from Boise, Idaho, where he had retreated upon their separation. When she called me the previous week, I told her that it would take a while but I'd handle it. She insisted on a meeting. I knew what she wanted. She wanted to cuss the bastard out to a sympathetic ear. That's one of the things I offer my clients. A sympathetic ear. Maybe not a sympathetic soul, but at least an ear.

It's billable time, and a good deal for all concerned. I charge a little less for an hour of ear-lending than do most of my psychoanalyst friends. When my clients run out of useful cusses, I'm generally able to supplement their repertoire.

For that half hour with Rita, I almost forgot Daniel and Al Coleman and my ransacked apartment and that arrow sticking out of my mattress.

After Rita left, Julie stormed my portal. She was intolerant of my haphazard office hours, especially when we had a busy week facing us. I pretended to be properly chagrined, and finally I made her smile. Then she sat down and laid out the week's schedule of appointments, conferences, and court appearances for me. I murmured during her pauses, and after a few minutes, she stopped and said, "Brady, what's eating you?"

I shook my head. "It's too complicated to explain. I'm okay."

"You're . . . different. This isn't woman problems. Something wrong with one of the boys?"

"No. It's nothing. Go ahead."

She shrugged and finished giving me my instructions. I paid closer attention. And after she left, I tried to focus on all the projects she had left with me. It was slow going.

Cammie called a little before noon. When Julie put her through, I said, "Hi, Cammie."

"Gee, hi. I just came up from the studio and saw the machine blinking. I gotta get a phone down there, I guess. What's up?"

"We need to talk."

"Boy, sounds ominous."

I tried to laugh. "Not ominous. Some things have happened, but mainly I want you to look at these photos. I've given you the names, but you haven't seen the faces." I hesitated. "And I've got some thoughts I want to share with you."

"Sure. Okay. When?"

"The sooner the better. How's tonight?"

"Tonight's good. What time?"

"I'll come right from the office. I'll try to get away by five. I can hit the pike and be there in two hours. Say seven?"

"I'll cook something for us, then."

"Don't do anything special." I paused. "See if Brian and Roscoe and Vinnie can be there, too. They can help. We can all put our heads together."

"Sure. Okay."

I failed to take into account five o'clock outbound traffic on the Mass Pike, and it was after seven-thirty when I pulled up in front of Daniel's house in Wilson Falls.

I grabbed my briefcase from the backseat, climbed the front steps, and rang the bell. Cammie pulled the door open. She was wearing a short black skirt over black tights and a bulky orange sweater and a tentative smile.

She grabbed my hand and led me to the living room. Brian Sweeney was sitting on the sofa. He had a drink in his hand and the stub of a cigar in his mouth. He stood up and we shook hands.

"How ya been?" he said.

"I'm okay. You?"

He shrugged.

"Drink?" said Cammie.

"Sure."

"Bourbon, right?"

I nodded. I sat on the sofa beside Sweeney while Cammie went into the kitchen. "Are Roscoe and Vinnie coming?" I said.

"I guess not," he said. "Cammie said she tried to call them. Nobody home."

Cammie came back with my drink. "I tried several times," she said. "I guess they're away. If you want, I'll try again after we eat."

"Good idea," I said.

"I'm going to broil some fish," she said. "It'll take about fifteen minutes. Everything else is ready. I thought we could have a drink first."

"Fine," I said.

Cammie looked at me over the rim of her glass. "Do you want to talk now or later, Brady?"

"Later, I think. Maybe Roscoe and Vinnie can make it."

"All right."

I told Cammie and Sweeney about climbing Mount Monadnock with my son and his girlfriend, and all of us carefully avoided mentioning Daniel or the circumstances of his death or Sergeant Oakley or anything unpleasant. When we finished our drinks Cammie got up and brought me and Sweeney refills then she went into the kitchen.

"You got it figured out, Brady?" said Sweeney.

"No," I said. "I've got some new questions, that's all. And I've got these photos I wanted you guys to see."

"What kind of questions?"

"Let's hold it till we've eaten. I want Cammie in on it, too."

The broiled swordfish was garnished with sprigs of fresh parsley. The little golf ball red-skinned potatoes had been boiled, then drenched in butter. Green beans and slivered almonds, avocado salad, a smooth white wine.

Sweeney and I cleared the dishes from the table. Cammie tried Roscoe and Vinnie again, and again got no answer.

We took coffee back into the living room. Cammie and Brian sat beside each other on the sofa. I took the chair across from them. I had my briefcase on my lap.

"Okay, Brady," said Cammie. "Now. What's up?"

I reached into my briefcase and took out the envelope with the photos in it. I laid them on the coffee table so Cammie and Brian could see them.

"These are what you found in Daniel's papers, huh?" said Sweeney.

"Yes. Recognize any of them?"

He picked them up one by one, looked at them closely, turned each of them over to read the name and address, then handed them to Cammie, who did the same thing. When they were both done they looked at me. "Nothing," said Brian.

"Me, neither," said Cammie. She frowned at me. "You said there were eight photos . . ."

"Six photos. There were two index cards with names and addresses on them in with the photos. The names were William Johnson and Carmine Repucci."

Cammie and Brian both shrugged.

I leaned across the coffee table and touched Cammie's hand. "What was Boomer's name?" I said.

She frowned. "Boomer?" She shook her head. "I don't know. Everybody called him Boomer."

"When you were . . . with him, with Boomer—you never heard the names William Johnson or Carmine Repucci, then?"

"No. I—" Her hand went to her mouth and her eyes widened.

"What is it?"

"Pooch," she whispered.

"Huh?"

"Pooch. Repucci." She turned to Brian. "Those two names . . ."

"You knew Repucci?" I said.

She turned back to face me. "If Pooch was Repucci, then Boomer was . . ."

"William Johnson," I finished for her.

"I don't get it," said Brian.

"They were both murdered," I said. "I think Daniel killed them both."

Cammie stared at me for a minute, then nodded. "Yes," she said. "Yes, that fits."

"Tell me," I said.

Her dark eyes stared into mine for a moment. Then she sighed and nodded. "Okay. There's not much to tell. Brian's heard most of it. Boomer picked me up one night in Springfield. I was just at rock bottom, Brady. I didn't know who I was, where I came from, what I was doing, how I got there. I was in a bar, trying to hustle coke money. He took me home, gave me a couple of lines, made love to me. Told me he loved me, he wanted to take care of me. It's what I thought I needed. I had lost my soul. He filled in the empty place. He *became* my soul, do you see? And he had a supply. He gave me everything I needed. After a while he put me out on the streets. I had to work for it. Pooch was a friend of his, his supplier, I think. I was frightened of Pooch. I thought I loved Boomer. But what did I know? I was a junkie. A cokehead. I didn't know either of their real names. They just called each other 'Boomer' and 'Pooch.' I didn't care what their names were. Anyway, Daniel came along. He found me on the street and brought me here and straightened me out. Then *he* became my soul. It was different. He *did* love me. I lived in fear of Boomer for years. He had always made it clear that if I tried to get away he'd cut my face. But I never saw him. It was several years later when I saw Pooch. After Daniel saved me, after I got off the coke, after I started painting and loving Daniel, after I had finally stopped being afraid of Boomer. I saw Pooch sitting in a car in the parking lot outside the Star Market in Wilson Falls. Parked right next to my car. I was petrified. I dropped my groceries on the ground and just got out of there. I had to get back to Daniel. Pooch, he—he just smiled at me. Sitting there in his car smiling at me through the tinted window, and I thought if I just get back to Daniel everything will be okay."

"Did Repucci ever bother you after that?"

"No. I never saw him again."

"Because Daniel killed him."

She shrugged, then nodded. "I guess so. It makes sense now." She stared at me for a moment. "Daniel killed them for me. Boomer and Pooch . . . I never knew their real names."

"So if he killed those two," said Sweeney. "You think . . . ?"

I nodded. "It fits."

Cammie shook her head. "You think he killed those others, too?" She frowned. "But why? Who were they, anyway? Jesus, Brady. Who killed Daniel, then?"

"At first I thought it was in the book," I said. "It was a book about those eight men in Daniel's insurance file. Somebody killed them, and in the book Daniel named the killer, so that man killed Daniel, too, and ransacked his office looking for the book. The book was the evidence. And the same man killed Al Coleman, because he had the book, and he'd read it, so he knew. That's what I thought at first. Then it occurred to me that William Johnson was your Boomer. His profile fit what you told me about him. He and Repucci were together in prison, both ended up in Springfield, where Daniel found you. You and Daniel both had good reason to kill them. Truthfully, my first thought was that you did it. But that would mean you'd killed all eight of them, and Daniel and Al Coleman, too, and I didn't believe that. That left Daniel. Now, if Daniel himself was the killer of Johnson and Repucci and the other six, these here"—I touched the six photographs on the coffee table—"then we've got another killer to think about. Somebody who, for some reason, didn't want Daniel to publish his confession. So this other person killed Daniel and he killed Al to make sure the secret in that book would never get out."

Cammie was frowning at me. "What secret?" she said. "Who'd want to keep it a secret besides Daniel?"

"I'm not sure."

"I'm confused," said Sweeney.

I nodded. "It's complicated. I need your help in sorting it out."

The two of them slumped back on the sofa. "Wow," whispered Cammie.

"Wow is right," said Sweeney. "Listen, do you want more coffee?"

"Sure," I said.

Cammie started to get up, but Sweeney touched her arm. "Sit tight," he said. "I'll get it." He stood up and went to the kitchen.

"I wish Roscoe and Vinnie were here," said Cammie. "Daniel was closer to Brian, but he saw Roscoe and Vinnie about every day. They might be able to help."

"We'll catch up to them," I said.

Cammie reached over and put her hand on my arm. "Something's bothering you, Brady."

I shrugged and nodded.

"What is it?"

"I had an uninvited visitor yesterday."

"A what?"

"I was away for most of the day. When I got back, my place had been ransacked. And I found an arrow sticking into my mattress."

"An arrow?"

"Yes. The mate to the one that killed Daniel."

Her fingernails dug into my arm. "Oh, God. Who—?"

Sweeney came back into the room. At first I didn't notice it. Then he raised his arm and I saw what he was holding. It wasn't a coffeepot. It was an autoloading shotgun with the barrel cut back to about twelve inches. He waved it at me. "Whyn't you sit over there beside her," he said.

"I'll be damned," I said.

"Just do it, Brady."

I got up and sat beside Cammie. Sweeney took the chair.

Cammie was staring at him. "Brian, what are you . . . ?"

"It was him," I said to her. "He killed Daniel."

"How . . . ?"

"When you think about it, it's simple," I said. "Who else could get that close to Daniel, catch him with his guard down? Either Roscoe or Vinnie, or both of them together. Or Brian."

She frowned at me, then turned to Sweeney. "Brian?" she whispered.

"It's a long story," he said. "You don't need to know."

She stared hard at him. "If I'd known this . . ."

Sweeney shrugged. "Better that you didn't know."

"You son of a bitch," she whispered.

"Listen," he said. "Both of you. Let me tell you a story. Our team was in the jungle, and some of the snake eaters were scouting a village, and the rest of us were hiding by an old cart path, and along came a couple of dogs, and behind them was this old grandmother and two little boys. The dogs sniffed us out where we were hiding, and they started yapping and the grandmother and the kids saw us, so Daniel says we've gotta kill them all or they'll go back and there'll be VC all over the place. So—"

"I don't want to hear this," said Cammie quickly.

Sweeney held up the hand that wasn't holding the shotgun. "Listen to the story, darlin'," he said. "You'll learn something. So I killed them. Daniel ordered me to do it. I told him I couldn't do it, and he took out his forty-five and pressed it against my ear and ordered me to do it. So I did. I was nineteen years old. I got up and went to those people and gave them candy bars and cut their throats. Then I killed the dogs, too." Sweeney shrugged. "Something like that changes a man."

"So you hated him for that," she said.

"Huh?" he said.

"You hated Daniel. Enough to kill him."

He shrugged and smiled at both of us, and when he did he reminded me of Daniel, the way he used to shrug, with a quick roll of his eyes and a twitch of his shoulders. "He made me see a part of myself I didn't like," he said. "I couldn't forgive him for that. But hate?" He frowned, weighing the accuracy of the word. Then he shook his head. "No. I loved him. I owe him my life. We all do. He was our leader. Our father. He made us do things that we didn't want to do. But we understood. We had to do them to survive. He made us grow up. He showed us things in ourselves that we didn't know were there, that we didn't want to know were there. Oh, some of the men hated him, I know. But they were too afraid of him to admit it. And even they loved him, too. Like you love a father you also fear and think you hate."

"But you killed him," I said.

He shrugged. "Daniel taught me how. He taught me that I could."

"Tell me about Al Coleman," I said.

"Nothing to tell. Something that had to be done."

"Because he had the book."

"He had the book. And he knew."

"About you?"

"No," said Sweeney. "About Daniel."

24

Sweeney picked up my briefcase and set it on the coffee table. "What other goodies you got in here?"

I reached for it. "I'll show you."

"That's okay." He grinned. "You just relax."

He opened the briefcase and reached in. He removed the computer printouts that Charlie had given me, and the photocopied pages from Al's notebook. He spread them out on the coffee table and glanced at them without entirely taking his attention from me and Cammie sitting across from him.

"You've been busy," he said.

I shrugged.

He reached into the briefcase again. His hand came out with my .38 in it. "My, my," he said. He held it up and peered at it. "All loaded and everything." He squinted at me. "You knew what was going to happen tonight, huh?"

"No," I said. "I didn't know what was going to happen. I just figured something would. I didn't know whether it would be you or Roscoe or Vinnie or even Cammie. Or maybe none of you. Maybe I was way off base." I shrugged. "Somebody broke into my apartment yesterday. I kind of figured whoever it was would make it a point to be here tonight. Whoever it was really wanted these photographs."

Sweeney held the shotgun steady with his right hand. It was pointing at my chest. With his left hand he put the photos and papers and my .38 back into the briefcase. He snapped it shut and dropped it onto the floor beside him. "It's getting stuffy in here," he said. "Let's go outside, get some fresh air."

Cammie frowned, then said, "I can open a window."

"He's not really making a suggestion," I said.

She looked at me and nodded. She started to stand up.

"Wait," said Sweeney. "Put your hands behind your necks. Both of you."

"Jesus," said Cammie.

I laced my fingers behind my neck. "Do it," I said to her.

She did. Then we both stood up. Sweeney stood, too. "Okay," he said. "Let's go get some air."

We went out onto the deck. Sweeney stayed about five paces behind us with his ugly sawed-off autoloading shotgun leveled on us at his waist. When we descended the steps onto the lawn, he said, "Okay. Why don't you put your arms around each other? Like you were lovers out for a stroll."

"Brian," began Cammie. But she stopped. I put my arm across her back and rested my hand on her hip. I felt her shiver against the chill November air. Her arm went around my waist. That way, it would be impossible for either of us to make a sudden move at Sweeney.

He directed us along a path through the woods. The sky was clear and bright with the moon, and we had no problem following the path. Through the trees off to our left I could see moonlight glimmer on the river, and I recognized the place where Daniel and I had fished. But we didn't angle toward the river there. We kept moving, and the path narrowed so that Cammie and I had to fend off branches as we walked hip to hip.

Suddenly Sweeney whispered, "Stop!"

We stopped, and Cammie said, "What—?"

"Shut up!" he hissed.

We stood there, not moving. I moved my hand up and down Cammie's side, hoping to comfort her, and I could feel the tenseness in her muscles. She pressed her arm against my hand and held it tight against her.

I tried to hear what Sweeney had heard. A soft breeze hissed through the trees and made crinkly noises among the brittle oak leaves that still clung stubbornly to their branches. A dog barked far across the river.

Otherwise I heard nothing.

After a minute or two, Sweeney said, "Okay. Let's go."

We continued to push through the forest. Cammie and I walked arm-in-arm. We used our free outside forearms to deflect the brush that grew close to the path. Sweeney remained five or six steps behind us, far enough back so that the saplings would not whip against him after we passed, but close enough to hear us if Cammie and I tried to whisper and certainly close enough to spray both of us easily with buckshot if we tried a sudden move.

Sweeney, I realized, had done this before. He'd crept along narrow jungle paths at night with all his senses raw and alert. He'd probably moved prisoners who he knew would kill him if they could. And none of them ever had. He'd been trained to kill, and he had killed. He'd learned how to survive, and he'd done it. He'd killed and survived as a profession. Even after he left the jungles of Indochina.

He'd killed Daniel. And I had cried when the bag-pipes played "Going Home" and Daniel's ashes sifted through Brian Sweeney's fingers, and partly, at least, I had cried because I could see how he had loved the man he called the Snake Eater.

He would kill me and Cammie, too. It was easy for him. After he'd killed a Vietnamese grandmother and two little peasant boys and their dogs, he had learned he could kill anybody.

After we'd been walking for about fifteen minutes, Sweeney said, "Go left here."

We pushed through the undergrowth where there was no path, descended a long slope, and found ourselves on the banks of the Connecticut. The river was broad and slow-moving there. Far across the way I could see a few orange pinpricks of light, and I imagined people in their homes watching television, brushing their teeth, making love in their bedrooms.

Cammie and I stood there on the half-frozen mud beside the water, still holding each other by the waist. The slow eddying currents lapped softly against the rocks. Sweeney stood behind us.

"Okay," I said. "Now what?"

"Wade in."

"Are you—?"

"Do it," he said quietly.

"Can I ask a question first?" I said.

"No."

"But there's a couple things—"

"No," he said. "Wade in."

"This is pretty good," I said. "You kill us in the water, and we float downstream for a while, and the police will never be able to figure out where we were shot, and after our bodies have been in the cold water for a while they'll have a helluva time trying to determine the time of our death, and by the time they find our bodies you'll be back in Vermont, and if anyone thinks to question you, you'll swear that's where you've been right along, and nobody will be able to say different."

"Just walk into the water," said Sweeney. "Slowly."

"Come on," I said to Cammie, urging her with my hand against the side of her waist.

We stepped in. For just an instant I felt nothing. Then the frigid water penetrated my shoes and my feet instantly went numb. I could feel the slow currents tug at my pantlegs. With my arm around her waist I helped Cammie keep beside me. I patted her hip, trying to comfort her, to tell her that it was okay, that I had a plan. When we had waded in up to our waists I would signal her with my fingers, alerting her, then I'd yell, "Now!" and I'd push her away from me and dive quickly to the side in the opposite direction from her, and maybe Sweeney would choose to shoot at me instead of her, and maybe he'd even panic and hesitate too long and miss both of us, and we could swim a long way under water, out toward the middle of the river beyond the short range of Sweeney's sawed-off shotgun. We could swim and float far downriver. It was a chance. We could get away. One of us might, anyway. Cammie, probably. It would be me he'd go for first. If I could dive deep enough quickly enough, the pellets would not penetrate the water with enough force to kill me.

When we were in up to our knees, Sweeney said, "Okay. Stop there."

Too shallow, I thought. He knew what I'd been thinking. If we tried to dive in knee-deep water, he'd get one of us at least.

"Turn around."

Cammie and I had to release each other to turn to face him.

He stood about ten feet from us, only a few feet from the brushy banks of the river. The water came to his ankles. He was holding that wicked weapon in his right hand. The stubby barrel was braced across his left forearm. It didn't waver. The black hole of the bore stared at my chest. He'd go for me first. Cammie might still have a chance.

I put my arm around Cammie's back. She let her arms dangle at her sides.

"I got nothing against you," Sweeney said. "Either of you."

"Why don't you just do me," I said. "No purpose in killing her. She didn't do anything. She doesn't know anything."

Sweeney laughed softly. "Neither do you," he said.

Keep him talking, I thought. As long as he's talking to us, he won't shoot us.

"You're right," I said. "I don't understand any of it. So

Daniel killed those guys. So what? What's it to you? You killed Daniel? Why? It makes no sense."

"It doesn't have to make sense to you."

"Let her go, Brian."

"I wish I could. But—"

The gunshot exploded suddenly, and I reacted to it like a sprinter to the starter's gun. I shoved Cammie away from me and dived sideways, and I didn't feel anything except the frigid water, a quick paralysis in my chest, and I pushed under water as hard and as deep as I could. I heard another explosion, muffled down there with my ears in the water, and at first I was exhilarated that he had missed me, and then I realized that he must have gone for her first, and part of my mind tried to tell me to turn back, to try to help her, to go for Sweeney. But I kept swimming toward the middle of the river, as deep under water as I could go. There was nothing I could do for Cammie. If he'd missed her somehow, she'd make it. If he got her, there was no reason to go back to Sweeney except to let him kill me, too.

I stayed under until I grew faint and my lungs burned. I forced myself to surface slowly. I rolled over so that my face pointed up, and I allowed just my nose and mouth to break through the skin of the water. I gasped deeply for air, and my breath sounded harsh in my ears. I found that my toes reached bottom. Cautiously I stood with just the top half of my head out of water and turned toward the shore.

A flashlight was playing across the water's surface, moving toward me. Quickly I ducked under. I could see it pass over my head. After it swung by, I lifted up again.

I heard Sweeney call this time. "It's all right," he was

calling, in a voice that wasn't his own. "He's dead. You can come in."

I'm not dead, I thought. Don't go to him, Cammie. It's not all right.

"Come on in here," he yelled. "You're gonna freeze."

Then I recognized the voice. It wasn't Sweeney.

It was Oakley.

25

I stood there up to my ears in the Connecticut River, and I found that the adrenaline that had flooded through me was gone. I began to shake uncontrollably against the frigid water, and maybe in a delayed reaction against the fear, too.

Oakley was talking conversationally from the bank of the river, and his voice carried clearly across the river's surface. "He's dead, Miss Russell. Mr. Coyne, it's okay. You can come back. I'm not going to hurt you. Come on. You'll freeze out there."

His flashlight continued to move across the water, and when it approached me I instinctively ducked under until it had passed. Then I bobbed up again.

Oakley said, "I'm a policeman. You folks are safe now. Come in. You've got to get warm."

From somewhere off to my left came Cammie's voice. "Brady? Are you all right?"

"I'm fine," I said. "Let's go in."

The flashlight swung to me, went past, stopped, came back. It held me in its glare, and for a moment I thought Oakley intended to shoot me after all. "Move the light," I said.

It swung away, and I watched it find Cammie. She was wading to shore thirty or forty yards downriver from me.

When I got to shore Cammie was huddled inside a bulky black-and-red checked wool jacket that I assumed was Oakley's, and Oakley was standing there, holding the flashlight pointed down so that its beam reflected off the water and lit up the area. He was wearing a shoulder holster over his sweater. The handle of a revolver protruded from it.

Brian Sweeney lay facedown in six inches of water a few feet from the muddy bank of the river.

"Miss Russell, Mr. Coyne, you folks better get back to the house and find some dry clothes or you'll catch pneumonia. Call the station for me and tell them that I'll be here with the body. Okay?"

"Okay," I said.

"Wait there until they come, then maybe one of you can bring them here. We'll talk all about it later."

I put my arm around Cammie's shoulders and we trudged back through the woods to Daniel's house. We walked as fast as we could in our wet clothes, and as long as we were moving and the blood was circulating I didn't feel the chill.

As soon as we got into the living room we stripped off our clothes. Cammie padded naked to the bathroom and came back with a pair of big bath towels. We rubbed each other's bodies with them, and after a minute or two of that Cammie put her arms around me and pressed herself against me, and I held her while she sobbed.

After a while I felt her body relax. She tilted up and kissed my jaw. "I'll find some clothes for you," she said.

I wrapped the towel around my waist and went to the phone. I dialed 911 and told them to come to Daniel's house, that Sergeant Oakley was here with a dead body.

When Cammie came back, she was wearing jeans and a sweatshirt and had a bundle of clothes in her arms. Daniel's sweatshirt fit fine except the arms were too short. His pants were loose at my waist and the cuffs came halfway up my calves.

We went into the kitchen. Cammie poured some Wild Turkey into a pair of glasses. We stood there leaning against the counter with our own thoughts, not talking, just sipping and staring out into the night until the police arrived behind the wailing of their sirens.

Cammie and I went out onto the front porch to meet them. There were four or five cars and an ambulance. Police Chief Francis Padula stepped from the passenger side of a squad car and came to the steps. "Where is he?" he said.

"I'll show you," I said.

I led a parade through the woods to the river where Oakley was waiting with Sweeney's body. Besides the chief there were two uniformed policemen, one detective, two EMTs, a photographer, and a medical examiner. After I showed them to the place, one of the uniformed cops walked me back to the house. Cammie was seated on the sofa in the living room. A detective had pulled up a chair in front of her, and they were talking quietly. They looked up when the cop and I entered. Cammie tried to smile at me and failed. The detective said, "Take him into the other room." Then they resumed their conversation.

The cop and I went out into the kitchen. I poured a little more bourbon into my glass and sat with it at the table. The cop remained standing. He was guarding me. I ignored him.

After a while the detective came in and nodded at the policeman, who left, presumably to go stand watch over Cammie.

The detective sat across from me. "Nichols," he said, and he held his hand to me. I shook it.

"Tell me," he said.

"It's much too complicated to try to tell more than once."

"Let's start with an easy one. Who's the dead guy?"

"His name is Brian Sweeney. He was a friend of Cammie Russell's."

"Oakley killed him?"

"Yes."

"You see it?"

"Not exactly."

"Explain."

"Look," I said. "Really. Am I going to have to do this again?"

"Probably."

"For the DA?"

"Among others. Yes."

"I don't understand much of it," I said.

"Just what you know, Mr. Coyne. What you saw. I just want you to tell me what happened tonight. Your speculations you can hang on to for now. Okay?"

"Okay." So I told Detective Nichols that I had come to visit Cammie and Sweeney, that she had cooked dinner for us, and that afterward, while we were in the living room, Sweeney had gone into another room and come back with his gun. He forced us to walk down to the river and then wade in, and I assumed he was going to shoot us, but Oakley got him first.

I could see the questions in Nichols's face. But he didn't ask them. "Okay" was all he said.

When Chief Padula came back an hour or so later, I told him the same story, and he just said we'd have to make a deposition the next morning, and I realized that the Wilson Falls police were mainly concerned with the fact that one of their officers had killed a man, and they needed to know whether it was justifiable.

All the other questions would be asked eventually, I assumed.

The cars pulled away one by one, as the various jobs were completed. Finally the only ones left were Padula and Oakley.

"If you wouldn't mind putting on some coffee, Miss," said the chief, "Richard and I would like to talk to you."

Cammie eyed Oakley warily, then went into the kitchen. The rest of us followed her. She put together the coffee, and all four of us sat at the table listening to the pot burble. We didn't talk. When the coffee was ready, Cammie got up and poured four mugs full.

Oakley looked at Cammie. "Francis says I gotta tell you this. That I owe it to you."

She shrugged, avoiding his eyes.

Oakley glanced at Padula, who nodded quickly to him.

"I guess you think I've been harassing you," said Oakley. "That I've been out to get you or something." He paused, staring at Cammie, as if he wanted her to say something. When she didn't look up at him, he said, "Okay. Maybe I owe you an apology. So I'm sorry. I am. I never meant it that way. But I want you to understand."

She glanced up at him, then looked back down into her coffee.

"I had—I have a daughter," said Oakley. "About your age. What're you, twenty-four, twenty-five?"

"Twenty-nine," mumbled Cammie.

He nodded quickly. "Janie's her name. She was a sweet, nice girl. National Honor Society. Played field hockey. Organized a Students Against Drunk Driving club at the high school. Never a problem. Her mother and I split when she was about twelve, and she handled it. Loved us both, never acted out. Not like a lot of kids. When I got remarried, she and my new wife hit it off fine. Anyway, the summer after she graduated, I lost her. She was all set to go to college. Westfield State. She planned to be a PE major, wanted to coach and teach. And then she was gone. I mean, she disappeared. Her mother didn't know where she was. Me neither. And I'm a cop." Oakley stopped and rubbed the palm of his hand across his forehead. "Look," he said. "I won't drag this out. She turned up in Boston. She was living with this bastard—this guy. She was hooking for him, getting money for him so he could buy drugs for the two of them. He was an older guy, a Vietnam vet, a burnt-out crazy bastard who carried knives and guns. A Boston cop found her for me, told me where she hung out, a bar in Dorchester, for Chrissake, and she was living with this guy, and I went there ready to kill the son of a bitch, and I was gonna bring Janie home. Something happened. I don't know. They were gone. Disappeared." He shrugged. "That was seven years ago. I don't know where she is. I still don't know."

Oakley looked up. Cammie had been staring at him while he talked. He gave her a quick smile. "I know this isn't your problem, Miss," he said. "And maybe I made it your problem, and if I did I am really sorry. See, she was . . . I can't tell you about the big empty place that's always there inside of me, and how loving my little girl is a lot like hating her for what she did to herself. I hated that guy, that was easy. But I hated her, too. It's as if she was two people, one of them my beautiful little girl and the other one somebody different who ruined her. She did it to herself. I blamed her for that." He shook his head. "This probably doesn't make any sense. See, when you showed up with McCloud, and then I found out about you, what you'd been into, it was like you were the bad half of my Janie, and he was that bastard who ruined her, and . . ."

He looked at Chief Padula, who stared back at him without expression. Oakley shook his head. "Fuck it," he mumbled. "I'm sorry, that's all. I just couldn't stand it, seeing you with him and his drugs and knowing that he had ruined you just the same way that other screwed-up Vietnam vet had ruined my girl. I wanted to save you. I tried to keep an eye on you, to protect you. Maybe it didn't look that way. When I arrested him, that was a good bust. It wasn't just me. But in my head I was doing it for you. To get him away from you. For your own good."

He stared down at the tabletop for a moment. Then he blew out a loud breath and glanced up. His eyes moved from Cammie to me to Padula, then returned to Cammie. "Look," he said quietly. "I got nothing against vets. I did a tour in country myself. But it works two ways, you know? I mean, it messed up a lot of guys. I don't really blame them. But a lot of them never got better. I just figured McCloud was one of them. Like the guy Janie . . ."

He shrugged.

"I wanted to put him away somewhere where he couldn't ruin you anymore. I guess cops aren't supposed to think that way. But I did. I admit it. Anyway, something happened. He got off. I blamed you for that, Mr. Coyne." He glanced at me. "If it wasn't for you, McCloud would've gone to prison and she would've been okay." He turned to Cammie. "And I hated you, God help me. But I loved you, too, and I wanted to protect you. Does this make any sense to you?"

"No," whispered Cammie.

"You had it wrong," I said. "Daniel McCloud saved Cammie. He wasn't the one who ruined her. He rescued her from it."

Oakley stared hard at me. "I don't buy that shit," he

said softly. He took a deep breath and let it out slowly. "The cops all knew what she'd been into," he said. "And I knew what he was after. McCloud, I mean. I could see. I knew. He was old enough to be her father, and he grew enough dope in that garden to keep the whole town stoned. There were times when I wanted to kill them both. And sometimes I just wanted to grab her and take her away. What I mainly did, though, was I watched over her. I figured I could protect her. I was just . . . I kept seeing Janie . . ."

Oakley slumped back in his chair, shaking his head. "I'm sorry," he mumbled. "That's all. I'm just sorry."

I looked at Chief Francis Padula. "You knew all this?"

He shrugged. "He didn't do any harm. He followed the book. I understood. I thought he was right. About Miss Russell and McCloud, I mean."

"He was wrong," said Cammie. "It was Daniel who kept me going."

"Well, it's a good thing Sergeant Oakley was here tonight," said Padula quietly.

26

It was after one in the morning when Oakley and Chief Padula finally left. Cammie and I poured the dregs from the coffeepot into our mugs and topped it off with Wild Turkey. We went into the living room. Cammie put on one of Daniel's Jimmy Reed tapes. We sat close together on the sofa and sipped and hummed.

Once she said, "Thinking of him?"

"Daniel?"

"Yes."

"I was, as a matter of fact."

"I don't understand much of it," she said.

I shrugged. "Me neither, really."

After a while Cammie squirmed against me and rested her cheek on my chest. My arm went around her shoulders. We dozed until the tape ended.

Cammie yawned and stood up. "Ready for bed?"

"Yeah," I said. "Time to hit the road."

"That's really dumb. We've got to give our depositions

at nine in the morning. By the time you get home, you'll have to turn around and come back."

"Good point," I said. "I'll take the sofa."

"You don't have to sleep on the sofa, Brady."

"The sofa will be fine."

She looked at me for a moment, then smiled. "Okay. I'll get some blankets for you."

We were sipping coffee in the kitchen. The early-morning sun was streaming through the windows. When the phone rang, Cammie picked it up.

She said, "Hello?" and then listened for two or three minutes without saying anything. Then she said, "He's here. I'll tell him," and hung up.

She turned to me. "That was Chief Padula. He says they don't need our depositions."

"That's impossible."

She shrugged. "It's what he said."

"Did he say why?"

"Nope."

"Will he want them sometime later, is that it?"

"That's not what he said. He said they wouldn't be needing them, everything was under control, and thanks for all the help."

"You sure you understood properly?"

"Dammit, Brady," said Cammie softly.

I went over to her and hugged her. "I'm sorry," I said. I kissed her hair. "It makes sense, I guess. They got Daniel's case dismissed. Then they quashed the investigation of his murder. This fits. Are you going to be all right?"

I felt her nod against my chest.

"I better go, then," I said.

"I know."

"Let's keep in touch."

"Right," she said. "Give me a call sometime."

"I will," I said.

"Or just drop in. Anytime. I'll be here."

"Sure."

She tilted up her face. I kissed her forehead, found my briefcase, and headed back to the city.

At seven-fifteen Thursday morning Charlie called me. "You awake?" he said.

"Still on my first caffeine injection. Go slow with me."

"Nine o'clock. My office."

"I can't."

"You've got to."

"Is this . . . ?"

"You gotta be there, Brady."

It was the tone of his voice, not his words, that convinced me. "Okay. I may be a few minutes late."

"Brady, hang on a minute," said Charlie. "Man here wants to speak to you."

I waited, then a soft, cultured voice said, "Mr. Coyne?"

"Yes."

"My name is Philip Varney. I'm delighted that we'll be meeting."

I said nothing.

"You, um, you have in your possession, I believe, some government property that we'd like returned."

255

"Six photographs."

"Exactly. Thank you. I look forward to seeing you."

Philip Varney. PV. From Al Coleman's notes.

I got to my office a few minutes after eight-thirty. Julie wouldn't be in for another half hour. I loaded up the coffee machine and left a note on her desk. "Unscheduled meeting. Should be back by ten. Kisses, BLC."

I went into my sanctum and emptied the contents of my briefcase onto my desk. The envelope with the photographs and index cards. The printout Charlie had given me. Al Coleman's photocopied notes. My .38. I put all of it into my office safe. Then I gathered up the assorted manila folders, loose papers, and fly-fishing catalogs from my desktop and stuffed my briefcase full.

I took the briefcase out to the reception area and sat at Julie's desk to wait for the coffee machine to finish its job. When it did I poured myself a mugful and sipped it with a Winston.

It was five minutes of nine when I picked up my briefcase, locked up, and headed over to Government Center. It would be a twenty-minute walk.

"This is Phil Varney," said Charlie when Shirley ushered me into his office.

He was a gangly guy with dark-rimmed glasses and sparse graying hair brushed straight back from his high shiny forehead. His jacket hung over a chair and his necktie was pulled loose and his cuffs were rolled up past his bony wrists. He looked as if he'd been at work for a long time already this morning. He was leaning against the wall tapping the bowl of a cold pipe in the palm of his hand. He came to me with his hand extended. "Pleasure, Mr. Coyne," he said.

I shook his hand and nodded.

"Have a seat," he said.

"I'll stand," I said. "I've only got a minute."

"Let's all sit," said Charlie.

I shrugged and sat down. Charlie and Varney sat, too.

"FBI?" I said to Varney. "CIA? DEA? What?"

He glanced at Charlie, who said, "Don't ask, Brady. Just listen. Okay?"

"Sure. Okay."

Varney cleared his throat. "You did bring our property with you?"

I patted my briefcase.

He smiled. "Well, good. Why don't you just give it to me and we can all get back to work."

"Sure," I said. "I've just got a couple of questions first."

"Brady . . ." began Charlie.

"I know," I said. "What I don't know won't hurt me." I looked at Varney. "Okay? Can I ask you a couple of things?"

He stopped tapping his palm with his empty pipe and pointed the stem at me. "Charlie's right," he said quietly.

I propped my briefcase up on my lap. "It's only fair."

Varney shrugged. I would have sworn he was going to

say, "It's your funeral." What he actually said was "What do you want to know?"

Varney began to stuff the bowl of his pipe from a leather pouch. I lit a Winston. "I know that Daniel McCloud killed eight people," I said. "I know two of them were small-time criminals, and I know his motive for those was personal. I also know that Brian Sweeney, Daniel's best friend, killed him and Al Coleman. My first question, Mr. Varney. Daniel was killed because he'd written a book about the eight killings, and Coleman was killed because he'd read the book and he wouldn't give it to you. Right?"

Varney took his time firing up his pipe. In a moment Charlie's office was filled with pipe smoke. It was the kind of smoke that reminded me of summer campfires beside a trout river and October bonfires, a good rich masculine smoke.

Those perfumed tobaccos make me gag.

Varney gazed at me through the smoke. "Right," he said.

"And you sent Sweeney after me because I had the photographs."

He nodded. "Not to kill you, Mr. Coyne. You didn't know enough to warrant killing. Just to get our property back."

"He broke into my place. Didn't find it. Shoved an arrow into my bed."

"Sweeney had an unfortunate flair for the dramatic sometimes. But he was very good."

"He was going to kill me, and Cammie Russell, too."

Varney shrugged. "Our people are highly trained. They're expected to use their judgment."

"Improvise," I said. "Do whatever's necessary."

"We try to avoid killing whenever possible," said Varney.

"Incriminating, those photographs. Assignments. Daniel's assignments. He was supposed to destroy those photos, wasn't he?"

Varney turned to Charlie. Charlie said, "Brady, shit. Leave it, will you?"

"I can't," I said.

Varney stared at me for a moment. Then he said, "You're right, Mr. Coyne. Daniel McCloud assassinated those six men. He did it well, and he was well paid for it. We assumed he had destroyed the photographs per his instructions."

"A highly trained Special Forces soldier with skills adaptable to the home front," I said.

Varney puffed his pipe and nodded.

"Wet work."

Varney glanced at Charlie, then turned and smiled at me. "If you wish," he said.

"Why'd he do it?" I said.

"Well, of course, the local police quickly identified him as the prime suspect in the William Johnson killing. It was sloppy. Performed with more passion than finesse. So, in a nutshell, we made a deal with him."

"You got him off the hook for Boomer. In return, he was to provide services for you."

Varney spread his hands. "Yes. Exactly. Now you know."

"You paid him well."

"Handsomely."

"You got the marijuana charges dismissed."

"It was the least we could do."

"He killed Carmine Repucci, too."

"That was his, not ours. We let him have it. Sort of a bonus."

"And later you sent Sweeney to kill him."

"Mr. Coyne," said Varney, "I trust I don't even need to remind you that if a single word of this conversation should ever be heard outside these office doors—"

"You'd deny it," I said. "I know how the government works, and you're right. You don't need to remind me. Pretty damn effective, denial. And without the photographs or Daniel's manuscript, who'd believe such a wild story? It would be stupid and fruitless for me to say anything about this."

He smiled and nodded. "We understand each other, then."

"Good," I said. "Tell me about Sweeney."

"Not much to tell. McCloud had suggested him to us, and we approached him. He was more than willing. Very proficient in his own right, Sweeney. Did some very good work for us. And then he was the obvious candidate for the McCloud job."

"And the Al Coleman job, too."

"Yes, Mr. Coyne. And the Coleman job, too."

"Because he knew too much. Right?"

Varney's pipe had gone out. He puffed at it without effect. He frowned at it, then laid it on Charlie's desk. "I think that's enough, Mr. Coyne."

"One more thing," I said.

He shook his head. "Enough, okay?"

"Who were those six men?" I persisted. "The men in the photographs."

Varney sighed. "You could probably guess."

I shrugged. "Government enemies. Men beyond the reach of the courts. Like that?"

"That's it, Mr. Coyne," he said. "End of discussion."

"Yeah, okay," I nodded. "I do have one more question." I turned to Charlie, who had been sitting there quietly staring out of his window. "Charlie," I said.

He turned to look at me.

"You knew all this?"

"Me?" He smiled. "Shit, no. Oh, I suspected something other than an electronic snafu when I lost those names off the computer. That's why I tried so hard to ram it through your concrete skull that you should back off. Otherwise?" He shrugged.

I turned to Varney and lifted my eyebrows. He nodded. "Charlie knew nothing of this."

"Then why are we here?"

"Here? You mean in this office?"

"Yes."

"Would you have met me anywhere else, Mr. Coyne?" said Varney.

"Probably not."

"I worry about you," said Charlie.

"I know," I said. "I'm glad."

"Well, then," said Varney. "Those photographs?"

"Sure," I said. I unsnapped my briefcase and dug into it. I rummaged around, then looked up at him. "Damn," I said.

"What?" said Varney.

"I thought they were here." I dumped out my briefcase onto Charlie's desk and pretended to look through all the papers. Then I snapped my fingers. "I remember now," I said.

"God damn it, Coyne," said Varney.

I shrugged. "Sorry. I'll have to get them for you."

"Damn right you will. Let's go."

"No. Not now. I've got to be in court today. Meet me at Locke-Ober's at five-thirty. I'll have the photos with me."

"You better—"

I held up my hand. "Anyone who can arrange the murders of ten men doesn't need to threaten me. I'll be at Locke's bar at five-thirty, Mr. Varney."

He looked at me for a moment; then he smiled. "That'll be fine, Mr. Coyne." He held out his hand.

I shook it. "I'll see you then."

Charlie walked me out of his office, leaving Varney behind. "I hope the hell you know what you're doing," he whispered to me.

"Hey," I said. "I forgot the photographs."

He squeezed my arm. Hard. "Sure you did."

27

I got back to my office around ten-thirty. Julie looked up at me. "You said ten," she said.

"You know me."

She smiled in spite of herself. "Coffee?"

"I'll get it." I went to the machine and poured two mugs full. I gave one to Julie, then took the chair across from her desk. I lit a cigarette. "What've we got today?"

"It's all on your desk, Brady. I had to rearrange some things. You're pretty packed in from eleven on."

"Cancel everything."

"Oh, no, you don't. You can't—"

"Julie," I said, "I'll make it up to you. But you've got to do your thing. Tell them whatever you've got to tell them. Reschedule everything."

She frowned at me. "This isn't fishing, is it?"

"No."

"Something more important."

"Than fishing?" I pretended to dwell on that question. "I'm not sure I'd go that far. But it's pretty damn important."

I reached The Honorable Chester Y. Popowski in his chambers at the East Cambridge courthouse at five of eleven. Pops always takes a recess at quarter of eleven—out of deference to his aging prostate, he says—and his secretaries all know me well enough to put me through to him.

Pops sits on the Superior Court bench. He's been there for several years. We were classmates and friends at Yale. Now he's one of my clients. "Hey, Brady," he said into the phone.

"You finish taking your leak?"

"Blessedly, yes. What's up?"

"What time do you expect to go into recess this afternoon?"

"Oh, the usual. Four, four-fifteen, at the latest. Wanna buy me a drink?"

"I do want to do that. And I will, as payment for the favor you're going to do for me. But not today."

"What's today?"

"I just want your signature."

"Sounds mysterious."

"It is. And it will remain so. I'll be there at four-fifteen."

"I'll be here."

•   •   •

"Call Zerk for me," I said to Julie. "If he's not in, have him get back to me. Make sure it's understood that this is very important."

She snapped me a quick salute. "Aye, aye, sir."

Julie knows when not to ask questions.

I spent the next two hours at my typewriter, getting it all down.

My phone rang a couple of minutes after one.

"I've got Zerk for you," said Julie.

"Good," I said. I pressed the blinking button on the console. "Zerk, I need a favor," I said.

Several years earlier, when Julie was out on maternity leave, Xerxes Garrett clerked for me in return for my tutelage on his law boards. He passed and set up a practice in North Cambridge that has evolved into the mirror image of my practice. My clients tend to be wealthy, and therefore elderly and white. Zerk's are mostly poor, young, and black.

He's the best criminal defense lawyer I know. If he wanted to, he could become very rich very fast. So far he's resisted it, for which I admire him enormously.

He's also one of my trusted friends, for which I am grateful.

"Darlene say you been phoning me, man," he said. "Something about urgent."

"More like important," I said. "You in court this afternoon?"

"That's where I'm at right now. Another three minutes and I go try to keep Ellen Whiting's boy Artie out of prison. He not a bad boy, she says."

"You're at East Cambridge?"

"I practically live here."

"Meet me in Judge Popowski's chambers at four-fifteen, can you?"

"I'll be there."

"Bring your notary seal with you."

"Heavy paperwork, huh?"

"Yes. Heavy paperwork."

Julie went out for sandwiches. I chose that time to use the photocopier. I didn't want to risk her seeing a thing. By the time she came back with our tuna on onion rolls, I had the two manila envelopes stashed in my briefcase.

Pops and Zerk were both there when I arrived. They were munching carrot sticks from a plastic bag on top of Pops's desk. When I went in and took the chair beside Zerk, Pops shoved the bag at me. I held up my hand and lit a cigarette instead.

"This'll only take a minute," I said.

"And you're not going to tell us what it's all about," said Pops.

"Right. You don't want to know." I rummaged in my briefcase and removed the envelope that contained the originals.

I had typed three single-spaced pages. At the bottom of each I had left two lines. One for my signature and one for a witness. I spread the three sheets of dense typing on Pops's desk. "I'm now going to affix my signature to each of these pages," I said to the two of them. "After each one, Pops will sign to attest. Then Zerk will notarize our signatures."

My two friends both nodded.

"You won't read these pages," I said.

"We ain't so dumb," said Zerk.

I nodded. "A fountain pen would give it the right flair," I said to Pops.

He handed me the one he always wears in his shirt pocket.

I wrote my signature on the bottom of each page. Pops signed as witness. Zerk squeezed his notary public seal beside the signatures. Then I put the three sheets of paper back into the big envelope, along with the smaller envelope that held the six photographs and two index cards, the computer printouts from Charlie, and the two photocopies from Al Coleman's notebooks.

"Tape," I said to Pops.

He rummaged in the drawer of his desk and handed me a roll of cellophane tape. I taped up the envelope.

"Pen again," I said.

Pops handed his pen to me.

I wrote across the envelope: "In the event of my demise, convey all contents unopened to Mickey Gillis at the *Boston Globe.*" I signed my name under it.

I handed the envelope to Zerk. He looked at it, then looked up at me. He showed it to Pops.

"Demise," said Zerk, grinning. "Shee-it!"

"A technical term," I said.

"Mickey Gillis," he said. "That reporter who's got the hots for you."

"That one," I said. "Not exactly hots. More like luke-warms."

"This for when you get offed."

"This for *if* I get offed."

"You want me to keep it for you, man?"

"Keep it secure, Zerk. Tell no one you've got it. Tell no one you met with me today. You, either," I said to Pops.

They both shrugged.

"Well, thanks." I stood up. "Drinks for both of you. Next week sometime." I shook hands with each of them and turned to leave.

"Wait," said Zerk. "I'll go down with you."

"No. I'll go down alone."

Zerk turned to Pops. "Heavy paperwork," he said, weighing the envelope in his two hands and nodding solemnly.

Phil Varney was perched on a barstool just inside the entrance to Locke's. I climbed onto the empty one beside him and placed my briefcase on the bar. Varney glanced at it, then at his watch. "You're right on time, Mr. Coyne," he said.

"I wouldn't have missed it," I said. I caught the bartender's eye. "Daniel's, rocks," I told him.

We didn't say anything until my drink was delivered. Then Varney held his glass at me. "To the satisfactory completion of our business," he said.

I clicked his glass and sipped my drink.

"Well," he said, "let's have it, then."

I removed the manila envelope from my briefcase and handed it to him. He opened it and removed all the papers. He glanced through them, frowned up at me, shuffled through the papers again. Then he carefully put his glass down on the bar and said softly, "What the fuck is this, Coyne?"

"Pretty self-evident, isn't it?"

"Photocopies? All photocopies? And this . . . this fucking document?" He waved the copies of the three pages I had typed and signed and Pops had witnessed and Zerk had notarized. The copies, of course, had no signatures on them. "What the Christ is this?"

"You can read it at your leisure," I said. "I think I got it all down. Not, of course, in the same detail as Daniel McCloud's manuscript. But enough, I think. I signed the originals, and my signatures have been witnessed and notarized. The photographs—you see I've photocopied them for you, just to verify for you that I have them—they're with the document, as is an assortment of corroborating stuff, copies of which you have there. The originals of everything are in a safe place, where they will remain."

I took another sip of my drink, then lit a cigarette.

"Unless something happens to you," said Varney in a low voice.

"Oh, right," I said. "In that case, the newspapers get everything."

"You're playing a dangerous game, Coyne."

"The way I see it, this is less dangerous than all the alternatives I could think of. Look at it this way. It protects both of us. It's in your interest to make sure nothing happens to me. And it's in my interest to make sure nobody hears a word about any of this." I tapped my fingers on the papers on the bar. "Tit for tat. Good deal all around, huh?"

Varney stared at me for a long moment. Then he smiled. "I guess we understand each other."

"I hope so."

"We're not that different, you and I," he said.

"I'm not flattered."

He shrugged and smiled again. "We think the same way." He gathered up the papers and slid them into the envelope. "One thing still puzzles me," he said.

"What's that?"

"Sweeney couldn't come up with any copies of McCloud's book."

"Not for lack of trying," I said, remembering how the little office in back of Daniel's shop had been tossed.

"Now that we've got this—this stalemate between us, I was wondering . . ."

"I don't think there is a copy," I said. "Sweeney got the original for you. There's nothing among Daniel's things. I don't have one. Al Coleman's wife doesn't have one."

"Let us both hope nobody has one," he said.

"Which reminds me," I said. "If anything should happen to Cammie Russell or Bonnie Coleman, the deal changes."

"And if a copy of that manuscript turns up in the wrong hands, Mr. Coyne, the deal's emphatically off."

"I think we both understand the deal, then," I said.

He nodded. "We do. And it's a good deal all around. You want another drink?"

"I wouldn't mind."

28

On the last Sunday in January I drove out to Wilson Falls. Cammie and I held hands and walked along the shoreline of the Connecticut. The muddy banks were frozen solid. The bays and edges of the river were iced over, but out in the middle open water marked the main channel.

Snow had fallen, melted, and fallen again through the halting progression of the New England winter. The landscape was all white, daubed here and there in ocher, sepia, burnt sienna. Tree skeletons poked up through the snow, stark black, and splashes of dark green marked groves of evergreens. Chickadees and nuthatches flitted among the leafless bushes.

It was one of those transparent winter days when the sun shines so bright and ricochets so hard off the ice and water and snow that it seems to slice through the air, and even wearing sunglasses I had to squint the pain out of my eyes. The sun carried no warmth. Just light. Cammie and I wore ski parkas and wool hats and gloves. We walked slowly, picking our way over the logjams and boulders along the rim of the river. Cammie talked about Daniel. She missed him, but she was healing. She didn't ask me any difficult questions, for which I was grateful. It saved me the trouble of lying to her.

I pointed out the place where Daniel first took me fishing. It seemed like a very long time ago. A little farther along, we stopped for a moment at the spot where Sergeant Richard Oakley shot Brian Sweeney.

Both places looked different under the ice.

We walked until the shadows grew long and the sun began to settle behind the low hills across the river. Then we turned back.

Cammie made hot chocolate. We played our favorite Jimmy Reed tape. Outside, darkness fell fast. We sat in rocking chairs by the woodstove, sipping our cocoa and staring at our stockinged feet.

"Have you talked with Terri?" said Cammie.

"Not for a long time. I think as soon as we decide we can be friends without being lovers, we will talk."

"It's good to be friends."

"Yes."

"Better, sometimes."

"Yes." I reached my hand to her.

She grasped it and squeezed it and held on. We continued to study our feet. "I've decided to leave, Brady."

I sipped my cocoa and said nothing.

"Vinnie and Roscoe are taking over Daniel's shop. With Brian gone, it's theirs free and clear. They want to buy all this from me." She waved her free hand around. "We're working out the details."

"What will you do?"

She gave my hand a squeeze and then let go. "I'm going home," she said. "I've got some money now. I'll buy my mother a proper house, build myself a little studio. I want to paint the mountains. In the mornings, with that wonderful early light, there's a mist that comes off them. I think I can capture that."

"It sounds good, Cammie."

"Now, without Daniel, that's where I should be. It's where I belong."

I found myself nodding. I turned to look at Cammie. She was smiling softly at me, and I could see the question in her eyes.

Where do *you* belong? they were asking.

But Cammie did not ask me that question.

I was glad she didn't, because I couldn't have answered it.

THE SEVENTH ENEMY

For Sarah

◎ ACKNOWLEDGMENTS ◎

I am grateful to my candid and perceptive critics Rick Boyer, Vicki Stiefel, and Otto Penzler, who helped me beat this story into submission.

I owe thanks as well to many unwitting consultants, who, in a variety of social, public, and private settings over the years, have engaged me in enthusiastic debate and discussion on the subject of gun control. I have concluded that the issue is far more complicated than it seems.

O n May 5, 1994, Congress-
man Douglas Applegate (D–Ohio) voted "aye," and by the margin
of that single vote the United States House of Representatives
passed a bill banning the manufacture and sale of nineteen spec-
ified semiautomatic assault guns.

The battle to control paramilitary weapons such as the Uzi
and the AK-47 had been waged for years in American govern-
ments at all levels. Before Congressman Applegate voted "aye,"
the gun lobby had won every skirmish.

My own education in the politics of gun control came two
years before the passage of the House bill. It began on a quiet
Sunday evening in May when my boyhood chum Wally Kinnick

called me from Logan Airport, and I have to believe that the events that ensued in Massachusetts in 1992 helped to inform the debate in the United States Congress in 1994 and contributed to Douglas Applegate's historic "aye" vote.

Brady L. Coyne
Boston, Massachusetts
December 1994

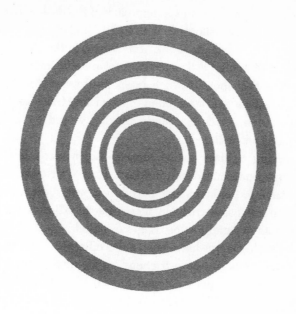

MAN WITH ASSAULT GUN SLAYS WIFE AT LIBRARY
by
Alexandria Shaw
Globe Staff

Harlow—The silence of the public library in this little central Massachusetts community was shattered by gunshots on Wednesday afternoon. Maureen Burton, 32, a part-time librarian, was pronounced dead at the scene. Two others are in intensive care at the University of Massachusetts Medical Center.

According to eyewitnesses, David Burton, 37, an unemployed electrician and the estranged husband of the librarian, entered the building at approximately 3:45 in the afternoon carrying an AK-47, commonly known as a "paramilitary assault weapon." Witnesses report that Burton approached the desk where Mrs. Burton was seated, shouted, "I've had it!" and opened fire.

At least three bullets struck Mrs. Burton in the chest, killing her instantly. Police estimate that twelve to fifteen shots were fired altogether, some of which struck two bystanders.

Burton's body was later found in his pickup truck on the outskirts of town, dead of a single gunshot wound to the head, apparently self-inflicted.

According to state police records, the incident in Harlow marks the fourteenth death in Massachusetts this year directly attributable to semiautomatic assault weapons such as the AK-47, which are characterized by their capacity to fire a large number of shots as rapidly as the trigger is pulled.

Six of those victims have been police officers.

Massachusetts has no restrictions on the purchase or ownership of assault weapons beyond those that apply to target or sporting weapons. "If you have an FID [Firearms Identification Card] you can walk into a gun shop and buy an Uzi," says State Police Lieutenant Victor McClelland. "It's as easy as that."

Neighbors of the Burtons report that the couple were often heard arguing and had not been living together for over a year. Mr. Burton, they say, had recently been despondent over losing his job.

"Maureen had no children of her own," Geri Hatcher, sister of the victim, told the Globe, "which was one of the reasons she loved to work at the library after school. David refused to have children, and they argued about it a lot. That's why she left him. She planned to get divorced. I guess he couldn't stand it."

The names of the other two victims have not been released.

I was sitting out on the steel balcony that clings to the side of my apartment building and savoring the evening air, which was warm for early May. It was an excellent evening for balcony sitting, and I had left thoughts of newspaper reading and television watching inside. A skyful of stars overhead and a harborful of ship lights six stories below me mirrored each other. At Logan across the Inner Harbor a steady stream of airplane lights landed and took off, and I could see the streetlights from East Boston and, way off to my left, headlights moving across the Mystic River Bridge. Harbor smells wafted up, seaweed and dead fish and salt air and gasoline fumes diluted and mingled by the easterly breeze—not at all unpleasant.

285

I had tilted my aluminum lawn chair back on its hind legs. My heels rested on the railing of the balcony and a glass of Jack Daniel's rested on my belly, and when the phone began to ring I contemplated letting the machine get it.

I knew it wasn't Terri. It had been six months. Since Terri, I often found myself watching the harbor lights with a glass of Daniel's.

But it could have been one of my boys. They often call on Sunday evenings, Billy from U Mass needing money, or Joey from his mother's home in Wellesley just wanting to chat with his dad.

So I unfolded myself and padded stocking-footed into the kitchen.

"Brady Coyne," I said into the phone.

"Hey, guy."

"Wally," I said. "What hostile wilderness outpost are you calling me from this time?"

"About as hostile as you can get. Logan Airport."

"Just passing through?"

"Actually, I could use a lift," he said. "I've been waiting here for an hour. The guy who was supposed to meet me didn't show up."

"Need a place to crash for the night?"

"If you don't mind, it looks like I do."

"Hey," I said, "that's what lawyers are for. Cab service. Emergency accommodations. Sharing their booze. What terminal are you at?"

"Northwest. I'll wait at the curb."

"I can practically see you from here," I said. "I'll be there in fifteen minutes."

There's always somebody from our childhood who becomes famous, about whom we say, "I knew him—or her—when we were kids. You'd never have predicted it." It's the skinny girl in seventh-grade geography class who always kept her lips clamped tight over her mouthful of braces, and who ten years later smiles dazzlingly from the cover of *Cosmopolitan*. Or the stumbling overweight grammar school boy who goes on to play linebacker for Notre Dame, or the computer nerd who gets elected to Congress.

Most of us knew a kid who became an author or athlete or politician or actor or criminal, and we feel a kind of pride of ownership, as if we were the first to recognize his talent.

Wally Kinnick was that kid from my youth.

Nobody would ever have predicted fame for Wally. He was a quiet, unambitious teenager, a modest student with a very short list of activities on his college applications. He preferred hunting and fishing to playing sports or running for Student Council. Hell, he wanted to become a forest ranger. A more anonymous career I couldn't imagine.

After high school, I lost track of Wally for a while. When he popped up again he was famous. Outdoorsmen knew him as an expert. To environmentalists he was an ally.

Politicians considered him a nuisance.

It started with an innocuous local Saturday morning cable television program out of Minneapolis. At first it was called simply "Outdoors," a derivative good-old-boy hunting and fishing show featuring Wally and his guest celebrity of the week. But as Wally refined his television personality and style, he became "Walt" and his show became "Walt Kinnick's Outdoors." ESPN picked it up and sent him on hunting and fishing excursions to remote corners of the globe. He used the show as a forum for taking dead aim at the enemies of wildlife and their habitat.

Nobody could figure out whether Walt Kinnick was a liberal or conservative, Democrat or Republican. He defied labels. He sought the truth. He cut through the bullshit. He stepped on toes. Indiscriminantly.

Walt Kinnick's name and face and voice became as well known—though certainly not as beloved—as that of Julia Child.

By the early 1990s, Walt Kinnick had become the Ralph Nader of the environment. He submitted to questioning by Larry King, traded jokes with Letterman, testified before blue-ribbon commissions, wrote magazine articles. He even endorsed an insect repellent on television commercials.

He made enemies. He got sued. I was his Boston lawyer. He had other lawyers in other cities.

He had a cabin in the Berkshires in western Massachusetts near the Vermont border, a retreat where he went to fish and hunt and escape the rigors of public life. He'd invited me out several times, but our schedules never seemed to mesh.

Like most of my clients, Wally was also a friend. Otherwise I wouldn't have been so willing to go pick him up at the airport at eleven o'clock on a Sunday evening in May.

When I got to the Northwest terminal, I spotted him instantly in the crowd that was clustered by the curb. He was wearing a sportcoat and necktie, his idea of a disguise. On television he always wore a flannel shirt and jeans with a sheath knife at his hip. But Wally Kinnick stood about six-three and sported a bushy black beard, and he would have been hard to miss regardless of what he was wearing.

I parked in the no-stopping zone, got out of my car, and walked up to him. I grabbed his shoulder.

He whirled around. "Oh, Brady," he said. "Thank God. Let's get the hell out of here. I hate airports."

He was bending for the overnight bag that sat beside him on the pavement when a man appeared behind him. He touched Wally's shoulder and said, "Walt Kinnick? Is that you?"

Wally turned. "McNiff?"

"God," said the man, "I'm sorry I'm late. My kid had the car this afternoon and left the tank empty and I had to drive all over Clinton to find a gas station that was open on a Sunday night and there was a detour on Route 2 . . ." He flapped his hands in a gesture of helplessness.

"Sure," shrugged Wally. "It's okay. Oh, I'm sorry," he said quickly. "Brady Coyne, Gene McNiff."

I shook hands with McNiff. He was a beefy guy with thinning red hair and small close-set eyes.

"Gene's the president of SAFE," said Wally.

"SAFE?"

"Second Amendment For Ever," said McNiff. "We're sort of the New England arm of the NRA. Walt's here to testify for us."

"We need the Second Amendment to keep us safe," said Wally. "SAFE, get it?"

I smiled. "Cute."

"Brady's my lawyer," said Wally.

McNiff arched his eyebrows. "Lawyer, huh?" He nodded. "Well, it's always good to have a lawyer, I guess. You'll be there tomorrow, then, Brady?"

"Oh, sure," I said, wondering what the hell he was talking about. "Absolutely. Wouldn't miss it."

"Good, good," he said. He turned to Wally. "Look, I'm really sorry I was so late. You must be pooped. So shall we . . .?"

Wally glanced at me, then turned to McNiff. "I figured we'd gotten our signals crossed, Gene. So I called Brady. He invited me for the night. You don't mind, do you?"

McNiff frowned. He clearly minded. But all he said was, "Sure. No problem. Really sorry I kept you waiting. I should've at least tried to call or something."

"That's okay," said Wally. "Brady and I have some work to do anyway, so it worked out fine. Just too bad you had to come all the way in here."

McNiff shook his head. "My own damned fault."

Wally reached for his hand and shook it. "See you in the morning, then, Gene."

McNiff forced a smile. "Right. See you there. Um, I'll meet you in the rotunda a little before ten. Okay?"

Wally nodded. "Sure. I'll be there."

McNiff turned and trudged away. Wally and I got into my car. He said, "Boy, that's a relief."

"Why?"

"I was supposed to spend the night with him. Dreaded the thought of it. All the local SAFE guys'll be waiting there in his living room, all primed to tell me about the big buck they nailed last year and how much they hate liberals. They'll want to stay up all night drinking Budweiser and shooting the shit with the big television personality. So now McNiff comes home without me, he's a bum. I'm sorry for him, but I'm thrilled for me. I know

289

it's part of the job, but I really hate that shit."

"You told him you and I had some work to do."

"Nah. Not really. A little peace and quiet's all I want."

"You mind telling me what you're doing in Boston?"

"There's a bill up before a subcommittee of the state Senate. SAFE flew me in to testify."

"What kind of bill?"

"Assault-weapon control. The hearing's tomorrow morning. I'll go and do my thing, then head out to Fenwick for a glorious week at the cabin, reading old Travis McGee novels, sipping Rebel Yell, chopping wood, and casting dry flies on the Deerfield."

"You're testifying against this bill, I assume."

"Hell," said Wally, "SAFE doesn't pay expenses for someone to testify in *favor* of gun control, you know."

"How can you testify against controlling assault weapons?"

I heard him chuckle from the seat beside me. "It's complicated."

"This is something you want to do?"

"Telling people what I believe in?" he said. "Yeah, I kinda like it, to tell you the truth. The upside of being a public figure is you can say what you think and people actually listen to you. Sometimes you get to believe you can make a difference. The downside is they take you so damn seriously that you have to be very careful about what you say."

"You don't want my advice on this, I gather."

"I never ignore your advice, Brady."

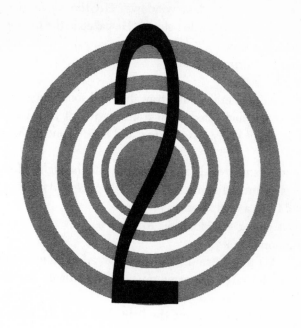

Wally and I had always done our business in my office or over a slab of prime rib at Durgin Park. He'd never been to my apartment. When we walked in, he looked around, smiled, and said, "Pretty nice."

I tried to see my place the way he did. To me it was comfortable. I have an understanding with my apartment. I give it plenty of freedom to express itself, and it doesn't impose too many obligations on me. The furniture can sit wherever it likes. I can leave magazines and neckties on it, and it doesn't complain. Fly rods hide in closets and newspapers find sanctuary under the sofa. I let my shoes go where they want. It's their home, too.

I expect, to Wally, it looked messy.

291

He dropped his overnight bag onto the floor and went over to the floor-to-ceiling glass windows. He slid them open and stepped out onto my little balcony. He gazed at the harbor. "This ain't bad," he said.

"Slug of bourbon?" I said.

"Ice. No water."

I broke open an ice-cube tray, dumped some cubes into two short glasses, and filled them from my jug of Jack Daniel's. I went to where Wally was standing and handed one of the glasses to him.

We stood side by side and stared out into the night. After a few minutes he turned to me and said, "You once told me that you'd wanted to be a civil liberties lawyer."

"I was young and idealistic. And naive."

"No money in it?"

"It wasn't that," I said. "I mainly wanted to be my own boss. So I took the cases that came my way. Not a damn one of them involved the Bill of Rights."

He nodded. We watched the lights of a big LNG tanker inch across the dark horizon. After a few moments, Wally said, "So what's your take on the Second Amendment?"

"What do you mean?"

"The right to bear arms. Is it absolute?"

"Well, the Supreme Court has said many times that no right is absolute. The individual's rights are limited by the rights of society. You know, you can't yell 'Fire!' in a crowded theater, even though the First Amendment says you've got the right to free speech. I'm not up-to-date on Second Amendment cases, but I do know that there are federal and state laws regulating handgun sales that have withstood court challenges."

"But the Second Amendment seems to be based on the rights of society, not the individual," he said. "It's not so much that I have the right to bear an arm as that we all have the right to protect ourselves and each other."

"'A well-regulated militia, being necessary to the security of a free state,'" I quoted, pleased with myself. "Yes. Except the idea of a militia is pretty antiquated."

"Damn complicated," Wally mumbled.

"The nature of the law," I said. "It's why we have lawyers."

I casually flipped my cigarette butt over the railing and watched it spark its way down to the water below. When I glanced at Wally, he was grinning at me. Wally preaches the importance of keeping our environment pristine. We should pick up trash, not dump it. I agree with him. And I had just thrown a cigarette into the ocean.

"Look," I said, "it's the filthiest, most polluted harbor in the world."

Wally shrugged. "I wonder how it got that way."

"Yeah," I mumbled. "Valid point." We stared into the night for a while. Then I said, "I thought those things were already regulated."

"What things?"

"Assault guns."

"You're thinking of automatic weapons. You know, the kind where you hold down the trigger and they keep firing. This bill is about semiautomatics. They shoot a bullet each time you pull the trigger."

"That's what they mean by paramilitary, then?"

He nodded. "They're modeled after military weapons. Your Uzi, your AK-47. Assault guns've got large magazines, but they're not fully automatic."

"A lot of sporting guns are semiautomatic, aren't they?"

"Sure," said Wally. "Shotguns, hunting rifles."

"So what's the difference?"

"Functionally, the only difference is the size of the magazine. Except, of course, your assault gun *looks*—well, it *looks*—like a military weapon. And they're pretty easy to modify into fully automatic." Wally turned and smiled at me. "You're not that bad at cross-examination, Brady, you know that?"

"I was just interested," I said. "Sorry."

"No, don't be. Talking about it helps me clarify it."

"So this *is* a consultation."

He turned to me and smiled. "You gonna put me on the clock?"

"I guess I should. Julie would be pleased. Want another drink?"

He shook his head. "Mind if I use your phone?"

"You don't have to ask." I flapped my hand at the wall phone in the kitchen. "Help yourself."

He went into the kitchen, took the phone off the hook, and sat at the table. He pecked out a number from memory. I turned my back to him, sipped my drink, and watched the clouds slide across the sky. I wasn't trying to listen, but I couldn't help hearing.

"Hey, it's me," said Wally into the phone. "Here, in Boston. . . . With my lawyer. . . . Just one night, then to the cabin. Gonna be able to make it? . . . Yeah, good. Terrific. I'll meet you at your place tomorrow, then. . . ." His voice softened. "Yeah, me, too. Um, how's? . . . Oh, shit. Well, look. Keep all the doors locked and don't be afraid to call the cops. . . . I know, but you should still do it. . . . Christ, babe, don't do that. I'll see you tomorrow, okay? It'll wait. . . ." He chuckled softly. "Right. You, too. Bye."

I heard him hang up. He came into the living room and slumped onto the sofa. I went over and took the chair across from him. We both put our feet up on the newspapers that were piled on the coffee table.

"That's a friend of mine," he said. "She's having problems with her husband."

"You fooling around with married ladies?"

"She's in the middle of a messy divorce. The guy's not handling it with much class."

"You didn't answer my question."

"I'm not fooling around with her," he said. "I'm serious about her."

"Sounds like a good situation to stay out of."

"My lawyer's advice?"

"Your friend's advice."

He shrugged. "You can't always pick 'em. You'd like Diana. She and I are gonna spend the week at the cabin. Hey, why don't you join us?"

"Sure," I said. "Just what you want. A threesome."

"No, really," he said. "We've got a spare bedroom. Diana would love it. So would I."

I shook my head. "I can't spare a week."

"A few days, at least. How about it? The Deerfield should be prime."

"Boy," I said, "I haven't had any trout fishing to speak of all spring. I could maybe take Thursday and Friday."

"Done!" said Wally.

"I gotta check with Julie."

"Assert yourself."

"It's not easy with Julie. But I'll try."

We sipped our drinks, chatted aimlessly, then began to yawn. I pulled out the sofa for Wally, found a blanket and pillow for him, and got ready for bed. When I went back to the living room, he was sitting at the kitchen table reading through a stack of papers and making notes on a legal-sized yellow pad. A pair of rimless reading glasses roosted on the tip of his nose.

"What's that?" I said.

"A copy of the bill I'm supposed to testify on tomorrow and some of the SAFE propaganda. I haven't had a chance to look it over."

"You probably ought to before you talk about it," I said. "Lawyer's advice."

"And that," said Wally, "is why I pay you those outrageous fees."

Whether it was the booze, or visions of Deerfield brown trout eating my dry flies, or just seeing Wally again, I don't know, but I lay awake for a long time. It all must have affected Wally the same way, because even as I finally drifted off to sleep I could still hear him pacing around in my living room mumbling to himself.

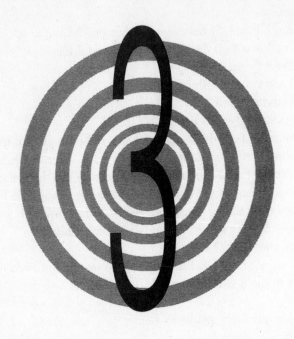

When I stumbled into the kitchen the next morning, Wally was slouched in the same chair at the table, scratching on his yellow legal pad. I poured two mugfuls of coffee and slid one beside his elbow. "You been sitting there all night?" I said.

He took off his reading glasses, laid them on the table, and pinched the bridge of his nose. Then he reached for his coffee and took a sip. "I slept for a while."

"This must be important," I persisted, gesturing at what looked like an entire pad's worth of balled-up sheets of yellow paper scattered on the floor behind him.

Wally leaned back and rolled his shoulders. "Actually it's just a little subcommittee hearing, one of those deals where you slip in and slip out and nobody listens to what you say because they've already got their minds made up, but the law requires a public hearing. So they set it up for Monday morning before the press rolls out of bed and everybody just wants to get it over with."

"Then why. . . ?" I gestured at the litter of paper balls on the floor.

"I just like to do things right," said Wally with a shrug. "It's a character flaw."

I waited until nine to call Julie. "Brady L. Coyne, Attorney," she said. "Good morning."

"It's me."

"Where are you?"

"Home. I'm gonna be late."

"How late?"

"Couple, three hours."

"No, you're not. Mrs. Mudgett has a ten o'clock."

"Call her. Reschedule."

"Aha." I could visualize Julie squinting suspiciously. "Who is it? The Hungarian or the Italian?"

"I'm not with a woman, Julie. I'm with a client, and we should be done sometime before noon."

"Don't try to bullshit me, Brady Coyne," said Julie.

"No. Listen—"

"I know you," she said. "You don't set up meetings with clients. Especially on Monday mornings. You avoid meeting with clients. You hate meeting with clients. I'm the one who sets up meetings. Then I have to keep kicking your butt to make you show up for them. Look. If you're hung over, or if you're calling from some fishing place in New Hampshire, or if you've got your legs all tangled up with some woman and just can't summon up the strength of character to kick off the blankets, okay, fine. I mean, not fine, but at least I know you're telling the truth."

"It's Wally Kinnick. He flew in unexpectedly last night. He's got a problem. I'm his lawyer. My job is to help my clients with their problems. So—"

"Ha!" she said. "I know the kinds of problems you and Mr. Kinnick discuss. Like how to catch big trout on those little bitty flies you use."

"No, listen," I said. "This is lawyer stuff. We're here at my place, and we've been conferring, and we've got more work to do, and I'll be there by noon. And don't give me any more shit about it or I'll fire you."

"Ha!" she said. "You'd go broke in a week."

"I know. I won't fire you. I'll give you a raise. Call Mrs. Mudgett and reschedule her. Oh, and, um, you better clear my calendar for Thursday and Friday."

"Fishing, right?"

"Well, yeah, but—"

"Boy," sighed Julie. "To think, I could've been an emergency room nurse, run the control tower at O'Hare, something easy on the nerves."

"Thanks, kiddo," I said. "Love ya." I made kissing noises into the phone.

After I hung up, Wally said, "From this end it sounded like you were taking a bunch of shit from a wife."

"Worse. A secretary."

Wally grinned. "That Julie's a piece of work."

His testimony before the Senate Subcommittee on Public Safety was scheduled for ten. It was a gorgeous May morning, so we decided to walk over from my apartment on the harbor. I carried my briefcase and Wally lugged his overnight bag. We talked about fishing and baseball and micro-breweries and girls we knew when we were in high school. We did not discuss gun control.

We got to the Common at about nine forty-five and took the diagonal pathway that led to the State House. Halfway across, Wally stopped and said, "Oh-oh."

"What's the matter?"

"Look."

I looked. The golden dome atop the State House gleamed in the morning sunlight. On the sidewalk in front a mass of people were milling around in a slow circle. I saw that many of them were carrying placards.

Several of them, in fact, were dressed in cartoonish animal costumes. I saw a Bambi, a couple of Smokey-the-Bears, and several person-sized rabbits.

They were chanting. At first I couldn't distinguish what they were saying. Then it became clearer.

"Kinnick's a killer."

That was the chant: "Kinnick's a killer."

I turned to Wally with raised eyebrows.

"Animal rights activists," he said. "For some reason, they don't like hunters."

"Ah," I said. "The good folks who splash red paint on fur coats. Does this happen often?"

He nodded. "Yep. Some places you expect it. Washington, of course. Denver, New York, San Francisco. Dallas, on the other hand, or Cheyenne or Billings? Never. Boston, or, best of all, Cambridge? Definitely."

"I love their costumes," I said.

Wally shrugged. "Part of their schtick. Come on. Let's go."

We climbed the steps that took us from the Common up to Beacon Street. The demonstrators patrolled the sidewalk across the street. From where Wally and I stood I could read the signs they carried.

LET'S MAKE HUNTERS THE NEXT ENDANGERED SPECIES, read one.

A Smokey look-alike carried a placard that said, SUPPORT YOUR RIGHT TO ARM BEARS.

HUNTERS MAIM WITH NO SHAME. A big rabbit held that one.

PEOPLE FOR THE ETHICAL TREATMENT OF ANIMALS. An uncostumed pregnant woman.

KILLERS JOIN SAFE.

FUND FOR ANIMALS.

STOP THE WAR ON WILDLIFE.

HUNTING: THE SPORT OF COWARDS.

ANIMAL LIBERATION.

COMMITTEE TO ABOLISH SPORT HUNTING.

OPEN SEASON ON KINNICK.

KINNICK'S A MURDERER.

REMEMBER BAMBI.

There were thirty or forty demonstrators, I guessed, an equal mix of men and women, various ages, costumed and not, moving slowly back and forth, chanting "Kinnick's a killer" and waving their placards. A policeman stood off to the side watching them.

"I didn't realize you were so popular," I said to Wally.

He grinned. "Like it or not, I've become the nation's most visible hunter."

"I would've said you were an outdoorsman, a conservationist."

"Sure," he said. "Me, too. But to some people, if you hunt, that's what you are. A hunter. None of the rest matters. You're a murderer, and it doesn't matter what else you do, what else you stand for."

"How'd they know you'd be here?"

"Gene McNiff probably told the media that I was testifying. That's McNiff's main thing. Politics, lobbying, public opinion. He speaks to any group that'll listen. Watchdogs the six New England legislatures. Prints his newsletter. Keeps gun issues alive in the media. That's SAFE's whole purpose. If they didn't do these things, they believe the Second Amendment would be doomed." He touched my arm. "Well, shall we?"

"Lead on," I said.

We crossed the street and approached the milling crowd of demonstrators. "Excuse us," said Wally. "Please let us through."

Some of them paused and stepped back to let us pass. We began to edge through the crowd. Then someone shouted, "That's him! The big guy with the beard! That's the killer!"

Others echoed the cry. "That's Kinnick! That's him!"

"Come on, folks," said Wally. "Get a life, huh?"

They closed in around us. The chant rose up, loud, frenzied voices. "Kinnick's a killer. Kinnick's a killer." Their bodies bumped ours. They were yelling into our ears. I felt an elbow ram into my ribs. Something thudded against the back of my shoulder. I felt a hand grab my arm and yank me. I stumbled forward.

Wally was tugging me up the steps and the crowd was behind us. "Wait, now," said Wally. "Be cool."

We stopped at the first landing on the stairway, flanked by the statues of Horace Mann and Daniel Webster on the State House lawn. I turned to look back. The demonstrators, people and ersatz animals, were all staring up at us, waving their placards and yelling. I could read the passionate hysteria of their conviction in their faces. Their chant was out of sync now, so that their words mingled into an undifferentiated swirl of hate-filled noise.

One tenderhearted animal lover in a rabbit costume was giving us the paw.

The policeman hadn't moved. The expression of resigned cynicism on his face hadn't changed.

"Jesus," I said.

"True believers," said Wally. "Goes to show what happens to people with too much time on their hands."

"Are they here for the hearing?"

"Naw. They don't care about assault weapons. They care about animals. They're here for me."

"They're kinda scary."

"All true believers are."

We continued up the long flight of steps and entered into the lobby of the State House. It was packed with tourists on this Monday morning. A teacher was addressing a knot of elementary school children in front of a glass-covered display case. I wondered if she was explaining the example of democracy at work that Wally and I had just experienced outside.

Wally and I wove our way among the people into the second lobby, which was equally mobbed. More school children. Tourists. A busload of senior citizens. Harried tour guides and teachers. We passed through into the third round room, this one directly under the golden dome. It was an oasis of relative quiet.

Old murals encircled the arched ceiling. Historic flags were illuminated behind glass cases.

We stood there for a moment before Gene McNiff appeared. He grabbed Wally's hand, shook it, and said, "You guys okay?"

"Fine," said Wally.

"Speak for yourself," I said.

"Did they hurt you?" said McNiff to me.

"I'm fine."

"If they did, we can sue their assess. Right, Mr. Coyne? You're a lawyer. I'd love to be able to sue those animal nuts."

"They seemed pretty harmless," I said.

"Don't count on it," said McNiff. He turned to Wally. "Right?"

Wally shrugged. "They've got friends in high places, they've got money, and they've got one of those deceptively convincing arguments. I never underestimate them." He grinned. "They're something like SAFE."

McNiff glanced at Wally and frowned. "Well," he said with a shrug, "they're not our concern today. The Second Amendment. That's today's agenda. Let's go."

Wally and I followed McNiff to a flight of stairs that descended into the bowels of the State House. We turned down a corridor and came to a door marked "Hearing Room." Someone had written "S-162" in black felt-tip on a piece of typing paper and taped it onto the door. McNiff pulled it open and we stepped inside.

We found ourselves standing at the rear of a narrow rectangular room. In front was a long table behind which sat four men and two women with microphones in front of them. A smaller table in front of the committee had one chair and one microphone. A uniformed policeman sat there facing the committee, mumbling into the microphone. I couldn't distinguish his words above the drone of voices in the acoustically primitive room, because behind the witness were rows of folding chairs—a hundred, minimum, I guessed—and it looked as if every one of those chairs was occupied. The narrow aisle down the side of the room was blocked with standees. This was a public hearing, and, at ten o'clock on this Monday morning in May, the public had turned out for it.

I scanned the audience. I saw only a few women in it. Ninety-percent men. Some were wearing business suits, but most of them wore shirts open at the neck, working clothes, blue jeans, boots. None of them had on an animal suit. It was a predominantly blue-collar crowd, and their unspoken message was clear: We are the voters, the masses, the majority that refuses to be silent. We hold the power to fill or to vacate legislative seats. We are watching you.

Many of them, I noticed, were glancing around at Wally and mumbling out of the sides of their mouths to the people around them. They seemed to be ignoring the policeman who was testifying up front.

Wally, Gene McNiff, and I stood at the side of the room leaning our backs against the wall.

"Who are all these people?" I said to McNiff.

"Ours," he said.

"SAFE?"

"Yep." He smiled. "We turn 'em out. The sacred right to bear arms is under attack everywhere. We've got to be vigilant."

True believers, I thought. Paranoia rampant.

"Why don't you try to find a seat, Mr. Coyne?" said McNiff. "Walt, we've got to get up front with the witnesses."

He led Wally toward the front of the room. I spotted an empty seat. I edged my way down the aisle and squeezed in between two flannel-shirted men.

A minute later the guy on my left thrust a clipboard into my hands. It held several mimeographed sheets of paper. Each sheet had "S-162" and the date printed across the top and columns marked "name," "address," "pro," and "con." I flipped through them. The "pro" column had been checked by none of those who had signed the sheet. The "con" column was solid with checkmarks.

I scratched my name and address. I checked neither pro nor con. I hadn't read the bill. Then I passed the clipboard back to the man on my left. I noticed that he looked at it, checking me out.

The policeman finished his testimony and was dismissed. Another witness was called. He wore glasses and a three-piece suit. He took the witness seat and laid a slender attaché case on the table in front of him. He opened it and slid a few sheets of paper from it. I heard him clear his throat into his microphone, and for a moment the low din in the hearing room subsided. "My name is Earl Clements," he said. "I'm a professor at the New England School of Law. My field is constitutional law, my specialty the Bill of Rights."

Around me, the men in the audience, SAFE members all, resumed their talking and chuckling, paying no further attention to the professor up front. I guessed that they'd heard him before. They weren't there to become informed anyway. They were there simply—to be there.

The amplification system in that room was as primitive as the acoustics, and the noise continued as the law professor began to speak, so I only caught snatches of the beginning of his statement.

". . . well-regulated Militia . . . security . . . shall not be infringed. . . . intended as an individual, not collective, right. . . . Significant that it comes second only to free speech. . . . Militia historically means the citizens at large, not the organized armed force of the state. . . . Federalist 29 . . . Hamilton refers to the militia as a check against the potential despotism of a standing army, which the Founding Fathers feared, with good reason. . . . in Federalist 46 Hamilton emphasized the 'advantage of being armed' . . . a 'barrier against the enterprises of despotic ambition.'"

As he spoke, his voice became clearer and more confident, and as it did, he seemed to win the attention of those seated in the audience. The noise subsided enough for me to hear the testimony more clearly.

Professor Clements cited several Supreme Court decisions which, he argued, tended to be misinterpreted by those who promoted gun control.

From my seat I could observe the six committee members up front. One of them was fiddling with his wristwatch. Another seemed to be studying some papers on the table in front of him. The two female senators, seated side by side, were whispering to each other. The other two members were staring blankly at the professor.

305

He concluded by quoting the familiar aphorism of John Philpot Curran: "'The condition upon which God hath given liberty to man is eternal vigilance; which condition if he break, servitude is at once the consequence of his crime and the punishment of his guilt.'" The professor looked up at the committee. "I urge you to reject this bill. It contradicts the spirit of liberty and both the intent and the words of the Constitution. Thank you for hearing me today."

After a pause, a few of the men in the audience clapped. The scattered applause died quickly.

The chairman of the committee said, "Any questions for Professor Clements?"

None of the committee members had any questions.

"Well, thank you, then, sir," said the chairman. "Please leave us a copy of your statement." He waited while the professor stood up, handed him the papers from which he had been reading, and left the room. Then the chairman said, "Our next witness is Walter Kinnick."

As Wally moved to the witness chair, somebody from the back of the room shouted, "You tell 'em, Walt." Several people applauded.

Wally removed a sheet of yellow paper from his jacket pocket and unfolded it onto the table in front of him. He looked up at the committee. The chairman smiled at him and nodded, and I saw Wally return the nod. The room grew quiet. Wally cleared his throat into the microphone. Then he began to read.

"My name is Walter Kinnick," he said slowly, in that familiar television voice. "I grew up in Massachusetts. Although my primary residence is now in Minnesota, I also own a place in the western part of the Commonwealth. It's a retreat, and I come here frequently to hunt and fish. I have been a hunter all my life, and I own several guns. I'm the host of a weekly television program that promotes hunting, fishing, camping, conservation, and outdoor recreation in general. I speak today strictly as a Massachusetts property owner and taxpayer, a private citizen, a concerned citizen."

Wally paused to glance up at the six senators. They wore the same blank expressions they'd showed during the previous testimony. Boredom. They already knew what he was going to say. The public hearing was pro forma, something that the law required but which they didn't expect to inform them.

"I have studied this proposed legislation, S-162," Wally continued. "I have studied it from the standpoint of a sportsman, a gun owner, one who enjoys recreation with firearms. I have looked for its flaws." He hesitated, cleared his throat, again peered at the committee people. He waited until each of them was looking at him. Then he said, "I find no flaw in this legislation. I think it's time that responsible gun owners acknowledged the right of the state to regulate and limit the distribution of certain weapons whose only purpose is to abet the commission of crimes and kill other people. This is good legislation. It's clear, specific, limited. I'm for it. I urge you to pass it. Thank you."

The room was dead silent for a moment. Then a murmur arose from the audience. I looked around at the rows of men who had come to show their numbers. They were whispering among themselves, frowning, shaking their heads. I could read their lips. What did he say? Did I hear that right? Was that Kinnick?

The chairman cocked his head and stared at Wally for a moment, his eyebrows arched in an expression of surprise. "Well," he said. "Thank you, Mr. Kinnick." Then he glanced at the five other committee members and said, "Any questions for Mr. Kinnick?"

One of the women said, "Ah, Mr. Kinnick, you mean you're in favor of this bill, then, is that right?"

"Yes."

"You think assault weapons should be regulated?"

"I think they could be regulated in the manner set down in this legislation without violating any basic rights. Yes."

"Do you belong to the NRA, sir?"

"I speak as a private citizen," said Wally, sidestepping the question.

"Do you own an assault weapon?" she persisted.

"If I did, and if this bill were passed, I would obey the law," said Wally, avoiding that one, too.

"Your testimony comes as a surprise, Mr. Kinnick," she said. "Are there many gun owners who feel the way you do?"

"I have no idea, Senator," said Wally.

She smiled, then shrugged. "No more questions," she said to the chairman.

"Anybody else?" he said.

When none of the other senators ventured a question, the chairman said, "Mr. Kinnick, we thank you for your testimony. You're excused. Please leave a written copy of your statement with me for the record."

I stood up, intending to follow Wally out of the hearing room. But a crowd blocked my way as many members of the audience rose from their seats and headed toward the door. Anger and confusion registered on their faces and in their voices, and they bumped and pushed against each other, jamming the narrow aisle. So I settled back into my seat to wait for them to pass.

Above the angry undercurrent came the amplified voice of the chairman calling the next witness. I didn't catch his name or see where he came from, but a moment later a small, bespectacled man in a brown suit took the seat where a few minutes earlier Wally Kinnick had been sitting.

The man chose to wait for the noise in the room to subside

before he began speaking. It took several minutes, because the people in the audience weren't paying any attention to him. He sat there patiently, waiting them out, while the committee chairman banged his gavel.

Finally the witness cleared his throat and said, "My name is Wilson Bailey and I live in Harlow, which is a small town west of Worcester that you may not have heard of. I teach chemistry in the regional high school there. I'm no expert on guns or law enforcement or anything, so I want to thank the chairman for the opportunity to tell you my story here today. I hope it will help you decide to vote in favor of this bill."

As he spoke, I leaned forward to see Wilson Bailey more clearly. He had no written statement or notes in front of him. He gazed from one committee member to the other as he talked. His voice was soft and confident. If he had memorized his speech, he had done it well. He made it appear that he was speaking directly from his heart.

"Two years ago last April," Bailey continued, "my wife and daughter were checking out books at the Harlow Public Library. It was a Wednesday, a rainy spring afternoon just after school had let out for the day. My wife was thirty-four years old. We had learned only a week earlier that she was pregnant with our second child. Her name was Loretta, and we had been married for nine years. She taught Sunday school. Elaine, my little girl, was seven. A first-grader. She loved to read and draw pictures of rainbows and trees that looked like lollipops and people with big smiles on their faces. She was planning to try out for Little League when she was old enough. She had a pet hamster named Bobo. She was afraid of frogs. We were planning to go to Disney World in June, right after school got out. We already had our airplane tickets."

Bailey paused and cleared his throat into the microphone. The sound of it echoed in the room. Many of the SAFE members from the audience had left after Wally's testimony. Those who remained were silent, listening.

"I learned afterward that the librarian who was at the desk that day had, a week earlier, gone to court for a restraining order on her husband. He beat her and she was afraid of him. Just at the time when my little Elaine was checking out her books at the desk, the librarian's husband appeared. He was, apparently, very drunk and very angry. He had in his hand an Avtomat Kalashnikov semiautomatic rifle. An AK-47. He held it at his hip and began shooting. I don't know what the magazine of an AK-47 holds. But he emptied it in the library. He killed his wife and he killed Elaine and he killed Loretta and he killed our unborn child, and then he went outside and climbed into his pickup truck and drove down to the river and killed himself."

Bailey stopped, met the eyes of each of the subcommittee members in turn. "Senators," he said, "I suppose that man might have murdered his wife with a knife or a clothesline or a conventional firearm. Perhaps no legislation could have prevented that. But this man owned an AK-47. He kept it behind the seat in his truck. It was available to him any time he wanted to use it. As a result Loretta Bailey, aged thirty-four, and Elaine Bailey, aged seven, and her unborn sibling are senselessly dead, and my life is worse than death. It shouldn't have happened. I don't want to hear that it's the price we must pay for liberty. Nobody construes the Constitution to permit such things. I know the Second Amendment For Ever people and the NRA would have you believe that. But they are wrong. I know their votes and their money have defeated legislation such as this one in the past. That's why Loretta and Elaine died. Senators, please. The job of the government is to protect its citizens. To ensure domestic tranquillity. And don't pretend that the certainty of severe punishment would have deterred this man from bringing his AK-47 into that library. It's very clear that if he did not have that weapon handy in his truck at the time when he got drunk and his fury at his wife took control of him, Loretta and Elaine Bailey and another Bailey child would be alive today. This legislation you are considering could save the life of a pregnant woman or an innocent child who only wants to check a Curious George story out of the library. If it saves one life, it's good legislation. I urge you—I beseech you—to support it."

Wilson Bailey slumped back in his chair. The room was silent. Even the SAFE members in the audience were obviously moved by the man's story. For a long moment, nobody spoke.

311

Then the chairman cleared his throat and said, "Uh, thank you, sir, for your testimony." He glanced at the other committee members. "Any questions?"

They all shook their heads.

"Well, if you have a copy of your statement, Mr. Bailey, please leave it with me."

"I have no statement, Mr. Chairman," he said. "It's my story, and I don't need to write it down. But with your permission, I'd like to leave a photograph of Loretta and Elaine Bailey with you."

Bailey stood up, handed a photograph to the chairman, and left through the door that Wally had taken. I edged out into the aisle and followed behind him.

The corridor outside the hearing room was a chaos of shouting voices, elbowing bodies, and flashing cameras. It took me a moment to realize that Wally stood at the center of it. I wedged my way among the bodies until I was close to him. He was speaking with several reporters.

". . . not a constitutional lawyer," he was saying. "I don't pretend to know what the Founding Fathers had in mind."

"But aren't you afraid," said a female reporter, "that by disagreeing with the NRA you will alienate your allies?"

"I'm afraid of plenty of things, miss," said Wally. "But that's not one of them. The NRA holds the Second Amendment sacred. I guess right now I'd just refer you to the amendment that comes right before it, which is also a pretty good one. I have an opinion, and I stated it, and thank God we live in a country where a man can do that."

"The Second Amendment For Ever organization invited you here, is that correct?" asked a different reporter.

"SAFE arranged for me to testify, yes."

"Did they know what you were going to say?"

"I say what I believe. Nobody tells me what to say."

"But did they understand that you would testify in favor of this bill?"

Wally smiled at the reporter. "Don't be silly," he said.

Another reporter wedged forward. "Mr. Kinnick, are you concerned that your television show will lose its supporters because of your testimony today?"

Wally shrugged. "No. I don't worry about things like that."

"Do you intend to campaign for gun-control legislation?"

"I testified today in favor of this one particular bill. If I learn of other pieces of legislation that I have an opinion about, and if I am given the opportunity to testify, I will. On gun control or any other issue. It's what they call democracy."

Wally glanced in my direction. "Ah, Brady," he said. "Let's get out of here." To the reporters he said, "That's all, folks. I've got an appointment with my lawyer."

The reporters all began to yell at once.

"Wait."

"Mr. Kinnick, one more question."

"But, Walt, what about—"

But Wally had shouldered his way past them. I caught up with him, and we moved quickly down the corridor and up the stairs. Several of the reporters were following behind us, shouting questions. Wally didn't stop, and neither did I, until we reached the top of the steps outside the building.

Down at the foot of the wide stairway, the animal people were still marching with their signs. Wally leaned back against a pillar and looked down at them. "Jesus," he mumbled.

Three or four reporters came puffing up to us. Wally straightened up and turned to face them. "Okay, you guys. Enough. Give me a break."

"Just one more—"

"No more questions," he said.

The reporters backed off but remained there, as if they were waiting for something else to happen.

I fished out a cigarette and lit it. "Quite a performance," I said to Wally.

"Nah," he said, shaking his head. "It wasn't any performance."

"You shocked the hell out of them."

"I guess I shocked the hell out of me, too." He smiled wryly at me.

"Those SAFE guys are kinda pissed."

Wally nodded. "Guess I don't blame them. But if they think I was being frivolous, they're dead wrong. It would've been a helluva lot easier to say what everybody expected me to say, believe

313

me." He shrugged. "I was awake most of the night, thinking about it. I came to Boston intending to speak against this bill. I still don't like gun control. I've testified on the issue plenty of times. I've never supported any kind of gun control before. I believe that weapons are neutral, and you've got to deal with the people who misuse them. That's the NRA line, the SAFE line, and in general I buy it. I just think that if we're going to have any credibility in this climate of opinion today, we've got to show that we're reasonable and thoughtful, that we're willing to compromise a little. This bill won't hurt anybody. Probably won't help anybody, either. We can give on this one without really giving anything away. I figure just maybe I can crack the stereotype. You know, that gun owners and hunters are all single-minded idiots, or reactionary fascists, or sadistic murderers, or even just irresponsible citizens. Give 'em something to think about. Can't hurt." He touched my shoulder and smiled. "Sorry. Guess this thing's got me a little wound up."

I shrugged. "It was great theater."

"It wasn't supposed to be theater, Brady. I just keep struggling with the fact that I've gotta go on living with myself."

"I was proud of you."

"You ain't got much company today."

"You ready to get going?" I said.

He gazed down again at the animal demonstrators, who were still chanting, "Kinnick's a killer." He nodded. "In a minute. They sound like they're running out of steam."

So we stood there. I smoked and Wally rested his back against the brick pillar, and the reporters eyed us, and the people in animal costumes marched and chanted at the foot of the stairway.

I had just taken the last drag on my cigarette when Wilson Bailey emerged from the building. He blinked in the May sunshine. The reporters, who had missed his testimony in order to quiz Wally, ignored him. Bailey spotted Wally and came up to him. He held out his hand. "Mr. Kinnick," he said. "I'm Wilson Bailey. I testified right after you."

Wally shook his hand. "Good to meet you," he said without enthusiasm.

A couple of reporters, I noticed, were edging closer. One of them snapped a photo of Wally and Bailey shaking hands.

"We were on the same side," said Bailey. "I liked what you said."

Wally shrugged. "Thanks."

Bailey's head bobbed up and down with his enthusiasm. "Well, sir, it was great, and I thank you." He turned to the reporters. "Did you folks hear my testimony?" he said to them.

They stared at him and shrugged.

"Please," said Bailey. He fumbled in his jacket pocket and came up with a sheaf of photographs. "My wife and daughter. I'd like you to know what I had to say today."

He handed out the photos. The reporters closed around him.

"Good chance to get out of here," mumbled Wally.

"That man had quite a story to tell," I said. "His wife and daughter were killed by an AK-47."

"They were killed by a person," said Wally.

I shrugged. "I stand corrected."

We were halfway down the steps when a voice called, "Hey, Kinnick! Wait!"

We stopped and turned around. Gene McNiff was hurrying toward us. His eyes blazed and his mouth was an angry slash across his red face.

"Who the fuck do you think you are?" he snarled at Wally.

"A United States citizen, I guess," said Wally mildly.

"I arrange this whole thing," growled McNiff, "agree to take care of your expenses, and you—you fucking betray me. You killed us in there. I hope you know that every member of the NRA in the country will hear about this. You're dead meat, Kinnick. Trust me."

"Don't worry about the expense money, Gene," said Wally with a smile. "I appreciate all you've done."

"Well, I ain't done with you," said McNiff.

Wally touched my elbow. "Come on, Brady. Let's go get some coffee."

We started down the stairs. Behind us, McNiff yelled, "This ain't the end of it, Kinnick."

"He's going to be in trouble for bringing me here," said Wally. "That's what he's upset about."

"I don't blame him."

"Me, neither." He shrugged. "Tough."

The demonstrators spotted us. "There he is," several of them shouted, and they all turned to look at us.

"Excuse us," said Wally. "Come on, now, folks. Some of us have things to do today. Let us through." We moved directly toward them, and they parted to let us pass. They mumbled slogans at us, but they seemed to have lost their energy, or their enthusiasm, for it.

"That," I told him after we had crossed Beacon Street, "was quite a morning. In one fell swoop you made enemies of both the animal rights crowd and the NRA."

"Well," he said, "if you're still my friend, I'm happy. I could use a cup of coffee."

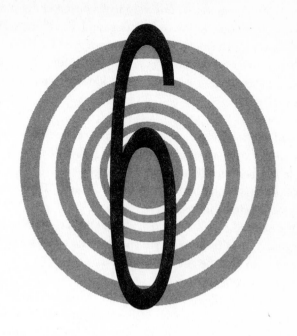

"Well," I said, "we can go down to Charles Street or cut over to Newbury. Plenty of little European-type cafés where we can get a cup of raspberry-chocolate–flavored coffee and a croissant."

"Or?"

"The Parker House in the other direction. Best coffee in town."

"Or?"

"Well, there's a Dunkin' Donuts right over there on Tremont Street."

"Dunkin' for me," said Wally.

I smiled. "Somehow I knew you'd say that."

We strolled down Park Street to Tremont, crossed over, and

went into the Dunkin' Donuts. Five or six people were perched on stools at the counter. There were half a dozen tables, none of which was occupied. We got coffee and doughnuts at the counter—toasted coconut for me, honey-dipped for Wally—and took them to one of the tables near the rear of the small place.

I lit a cigarette and sipped. "What kind of trouble are you really in?" I said.

"Trouble?"

"Testifying that way. Everybody's afraid of the NRA."

He took a bite out of his doughnut. "I guess I'd be in more trouble if I didn't testify the way I believed."

"You surprised the hell out of them," I said. "The chairman had quite a twinkle in his eye."

Wally nodded. "He's a friend of mine. Diana's, actually. Pretty good guy. A trout fisherman. He sponsored a clean water bill a year or so ago that she got involved in."

"So now what happens?"

"To me?" He smiled. "Now I take the T over to Diana's place in Cambridge, climb into her Cherokee, and we tool out to Fenwick, and at three o'clock this afternoon we'll be casting dry flies on the Deerfield River. And you'll join us later, huh?"

"I can probably break away Thursday."

"You'll make it a long weekend, at least, I hope. It should be—" Wally stopped, glanced over my shoulder to the front of the shop, and said, "Oh, oh."

I turned around. Three men had entered. They stood inside the doorway. They were staring in our direction.

"Friends of yours?" I said to Wally.

"SAFE boys. I remember the fat one."

I watched them as they sidled up to the counter. They gave their order, then turned to stare at me and Wally. One of them was, indeed, fat, although he was also tall, an over-the-hill offensive tackle with a pockmarked face and a pale untrimmed beard. The second man was equally tall, rail-thin, with bushy black eyebrows and dark hair clipped to a buzz. Right out of *Deliverance*. Both of them appeared to be in their late thirties. The third man was younger, twenty or so. He wore a ponytail and an earring. His cheeks were pink.

318

All three of them wore blue jeans and flannel shirts. The SAFE uniform.

They paid for their coffee and headed our way. "Don't say anything," whispered Wally.

They came directly to our table. The fat guy slammed against it with his hip. Wally's coffee mug tipped and spilled.

"Oh, sir, I'm terribly sorry," said the fat man, his voice dripping with mock politeness. "Please, let me help you."

He grabbed a napkin and began to smack Wally's chest with it. Wally grabbed both of the man's wrists and held them immobile. He smiled mildly up into the fat guy's face. "Thanks, anyway," he said quietly. "Apology accepted. I'm fine."

The fat man wrenched his hands free and stood there dangling his arms and glaring down at Wally.

The dark-haired man stepped forward. He put his coffee mug in front of Wally. "Here, sir. Take mine." Then he hit it with the back of his hand so that its entire contents spilled onto the table and flowed into Wally's lap. "Oh, how careless of me," said the dark guy.

I found my fists clenched. I started to stand up, but Wally frowned at me. I sat down.

"Take it easy, boys," he said quietly. "You've made your point."

"Fuckin' traitor," said the young guy. "Who the fuck do you think you are?"

"I *know* who I am," said Wally.

The kid grabbed a handful of Wally's jacket. "You better watch your ass," he said.

"And you better let go," said Wally softly.

The kid yanked at Wally's jacket and the next thing I knew he was staggering backward holding his stomach. He ended up sitting on the floor gasping for air.

Then Wally stood up and so did I. The other two, the fat guy and the dark-haired guy, held their ground. Their arms hung at their sides as if they were gunfighters ready to draw. Their eyes were narrowed and their mouths worked soundlessly at finding words to express their feelings.

"Does Gene McNiff know you're here?" said Wally to them.

"McNiff's an asshole," mumbled the fat man.

"Hasta be, bringing you here," said the other one.

"You want to start a brawl in a public place, it's not going to help your cause any," Wally said. "Why don't you boys go home and think about it?"

"You get the message?" said the dark guy.

"I would infer that you aren't happy."

"'I would infer,'" mimicked the fat guy. "Fuckin' big shot."

"Your ass is grass, man," said the other one.

The young guy had regained his breath. He got to his feet. "I want a piece of him," he said.

The fat guy put his hand on his shoulder. "Not now, Dougie." He turned to me. "You, too, Mr. Lawyer. We know you."

I dipped my head. "My pleasure."

By now the waitress had come out from behind the counter. She was young and pretty in her soiled white uniform. "I've called the police," she said.

"Shit," said the fat guy. "Let's get out of here."

He turned and walked away. The other two followed behind him. The young guy, Dougie, turned at the doorway. "This ain't done with," he said. Then they all left.

The waitress smiled at us. "Are you all right?"

"No problem," said Wally. "Little misunderstanding."

"Let me get you more coffee."

"Thank you."

She went back behind the counter. Wally and I sat down. She returned a moment later with two cups of coffee and a big wad of napkins. "I probably *should've* called the police," she said.

Wally was dabbing at the coffee stains on the front of his shirt and pants. He grinned at her. "You didn't?"

She shook her head. "You looked like you could handle it."

Wally touched her arm. "You did just right. Thanks."

She shrugged. "Stuff like this happens here now and then. We're open late. Guys come in, drunk, mad at the world. I can get a cop in about thirty seconds if I need one." She gestured at the coffee. "This is on the house."

She went back to the counter. Wally sipped his coffee. I lit a cigarette. "You handled yourself rather well," I said. "I'm glad you were here."

"Hell," he said, "if I hadn't been here you wouldn't have had a problem."

"Good point."

At that moment a woman appeared at our table. "Alex Shaw, Boston *Globe*," she said. "I saw what just happened. Can we talk?"

Wally glanced at me, then said to the woman, "My friend and I are just having a quiet cup of coffee, miss."

"It didn't look that quiet to me."

"There's no story," said Wally. "Just a misunderstanding among friends."

Alex Shaw pulled out a chair, sat down, and hitched it up to our table. Her reddish-brown hair was cut chin length, and it framed her face like a pair of parentheses. She wore big round eyeglasses, which kept slipping down her nose. "I know better," she said, poking at her glasses. "You're Walt Kinnick, and I just heard you testify, and those three guys are members of SAFE and they threatened you. They believe you betrayed them."

Wally didn't say anything.

"I followed you here," she persisted, "hoping for an interview."

"An interview," said Wally. He turned to me. "She followed us here, Brady." To her he said. "This is Mr. Brady Coyne. He's my lawyer. He advises me on things. Brady," he said, turning to me again, "I thought back there after the hearing I told all of those journalists I didn't want to answer any questions."

"That you did," I said.

"And just now I think I said that there was no story."

"You are correct, sir," I said in my best Ed McMahon imitation.

"Implying, I thought, that I just wanted to sit here and relax and sip this delicious coffee with you in privacy."

"As a lawyer," I said, "I would interpret it precisely that way."

"Because I said all I have to say at the hearing."

"You said it concisely and clearly," I said.

"And I have a certain mistrust of journalists."

"Not without reason, sir," I said.

"Journalism," said Wally, "being nothing more than the ability to meet the challenge of filling space."

321

"As Rebecca West so shrewdly observed," I said. "Journalism also being the profession that justifies its own existence by the great Darwinian principle of the survival of the vulgarest."

"Oscar Wilde," said Alex Shaw, who was grinning. "Are you guys having fun?"

"My lawyer advises me to refrain from comment on my statement at the hearing," said Wally.

"What about what just happened here?"

Wally glanced at me, then said, "Nothing happened here, Miz Shaw."

"Looked to me like you were both victims of an assault. I heard what they said to you. They threatened you. Do you take their threats seriously? I mean, these are guys who love guns. Are you frightened?"

Wally caught my eye and gave me a small headshake. Neither of us said anything.

"I'd like to hear your side of the story," she persisted.

"If you heard my testimony, you got it all," said Wally.

"I mean on what just happened here."

"Nothing happened," said Wally.

"It was pretty obvious where they were coming from."

Wally shrugged. "We'd just like to drink our coffee, if you don't mind."

She stood up. "Okay. Maybe you'll give me an interview this afternoon?"

"Sorry. I'm leaving momentarily. After I drink my coffee."

She turned to me. "Mr. Coyne, how about you?"

I shook my head. "I've got to get to the office."

She nodded. "Too bad. Guess I'll have to do the best I can with the story without your input."

"Fill up that space," said Wally.

She stood there for a moment, frowned at Wally, then peered at me through her big glasses. "Lawyers," she said, "are the only persons in whom ignorance of the law is not punished."

"Jeremy Bentham?" I said.

"You are correct, sir," she said, and hers wasn't a bad Ed McMahon imitation, either. She grinned wickedly, then turned and left.

We watched her go. She was wearing a short narrow skirt, and Wally said, "Admirable legs, Coyne."

"Jesus, Wally. You can't say things like that."

"Why not? It's true."

"Doesn't matter. It's offensive."

"Oh," said Wally, touching his fingertips daintily to his mouth. "How insensitive of me. I've offended you."

"Not me, asshole."

"Who, then?"

"The vast majority of women who don't happen to have admirable legs, I guess. You're supposed to admire their brains."

"Oh, sure. How porcine of me."

I smiled. "Well, you're right about her legs, of course."

"That one has admirable brains, too, I suspect."

"Dangerous combination," I said, "admirable legs *and* brains."

He nodded, sipped his coffee, then sighed. "I really don't need this kind of publicity, Brady. I can see it. WALT KINNICK IN COFFEE SHOP BRAWL. Or KINNICK ASSAULTS SAFE MEMBER."

"Maybe you should've given her an interview," I said.

He shrugged. "I just want to go fishing."

Wally wrote out the telephone number and sketched a map to his cabin in Fenwick on a Dunkin' Donuts napkin. It looked complicated. Fenwick was way out in the northwest corner of the state. Numbered highway to paved road to gravel road to a maze of dirt roads. The cabin was up in the hills at the end of a pair of ruts. Significant landmarks along the route included a wooden bridge, a lightning-struck oak tree, a stone wall, and a spring-fed brook.

I told him I'd get there sometime Thursday morning. He said he and Diana would be expecting me. He told me that the Fife Brook Dam usually drops the water around two in the afternoon that time of year, and that's when the fishing gets good. So I should be sure to get there by noon to give us time to have some lunch and get geared up. It would be about a three-hour drive from Boston.

We finished our coffee. Wally left a five-dollar tip on the table, which was more than we'd paid for our coffee and doughnuts. Then we walked out onto Tremont Street.

We shook hands outside the Park Street T station. Wally descended into the underground and I set off down Beacon Street. I cut across to Newbury at Clarendon so I could peek into the shop windows and art gallerys along the way, and it was a few minutes before noon when I walked into my office.

Julie was hunched over a stack of papers. She glanced up at me, said, "Hi," and returned her attention to the papers.

"Hi, yourself," I said. I frowned at her. "You're not mad?"

"Mad?"

"Having to handle everything yourself this morning? Not having the exquisite pleasure of my company?"

"Hey, it's your office, you're the lawyer." She sat up and arched her back. "I'm just the secretary. You pay me a salary. I make my money whether you're here or not. What do I care that Mrs. Mudgett is looking for a new attorney to handle her divorce, that Mr. Carstairs of the ABA called long distance the way you told him to, or—"

"Oh, shit," I said. "I forgot about Carstairs."

"—or Mr. McDevitt canceled your lunch plans. What do I care? I did my job."

"I had to meet with Wally Kinnick. I told you that. He was testifying at the State House."

"What's the case?"

"There's this bill on assault weapons, and—"

"What's our case, I mean?"

I shrugged. "There's no case. He just wanted his lawyer there."

"Moral support, huh?"

"Well, legal support, too, you might say."

Julie sniffed. "Well," she said, "you better get back to

Carstairs, and you better try to soothe Mrs. Mudgett's savage breast. She wants legal support, too, you know. And I know you'll call Mr. McDevitt."

I snapped her a salute and went into my office, where I lit a cigarette and called Phil Carstairs. He wanted me to give a speech in Houston. I declined. Charlie McDevitt was at lunch, so I flirted with Shirley, his grandmotherly secretary, for a few minutes. Then I called Mrs. Mudgett, managed to appease her, and rescheduled.

I persuaded Julie to hang out the Gone Fishin' sign and sweet-talked her out of the office. We headed for Marie's in Kenmore Square. It was lunchtime already. We had both put in a hard morning.

I stayed at the office until nearly seven that evening, in an abortive effort to convince myself that I was a responsible and hard-driving attorney. I stopped for a burger and beer at Skeeter's on the way home, watched a little of the Monday night baseball game with my coffee, and it was after nine when I got back to my apartment.

The red light on my answering machine was winking at me. I pressed the replay button as I wrenched off my necktie. The machine whirred, clicked, and then Wally's voice said, "Hey, Brady. It's Wally, up here in Fenwick. Give me a call." He left his number.

I went into the bedroom and shucked off my office clothes. I pulled on my apartment sweat pants and T-shirt, lay down on my bed, and dialed Wally's number. It rang three times, and then his answering-machine voice said, "Sorry. I guess I'm not here. Leave your number and I'll get back to you."

I waited for the beep, then said, "It's Brady, returning your call. I'm home. I hope everything's—"

There was a click, and then a woman's cautious voice said, "Hello? Brady?"

"Yes, hi."

"Hang on for a sec. Let me turn off the machine. There.

Sorry. Walter's been letting the machine take his calls."

"Anything wrong?"

"I'll let him tell you," she said. "But listen. Walter says you're going to come out and do some fishing with us."

"I'd like to, if the invitation still stands."

"Oh, absolutely. We'd both love it. I'm looking forward to meeting you. The fishing's been lovely. Listen, I'll put him on."

A moment later Wally said, "Nice little caddis hatch this afternoon, Coyne. We had a couple hours of glorious dry-fly fishing. You missed it."

"I don't need that from you," I said. "What's this about not answering your phone?"

I heard him blow out a big breath. "Those boys don't waste any time."

"Who? SAFE?"

"You got it. Kinnick's betrayed the cause, and they're threatening to boycott our sponsors. The producers are getting jumpy. My damn phone's been ringing off the hook."

"So what're you going to do?"

"Do? Shit. I'm going to let my machine answer the phone while I go fishing, that's what. You expect me to retract?"

"No," I said. "I certainly wouldn't expect that. But what's going to happen?"

"Oh, it'll die down. I'm not worried. Pain in the ass, that's all."

"Is that why you called?"

"Nah. I don't need a lawyer for this. I just called to tell you about the fishing. You are coming, aren't you?"

"If you still want me to."

"We both do."

"Thursday, then."

I beat Julie to the office on Tuesday morning, and when she walked in at precisely nine o'clock, as she always did, the coffee was ready. I poured a mugful for her and took it to her desk. She reached into her big shoulder bag and pulled out a newspaper. "Did you see this?" she said, waving it at me.

"Nope."

She opened it onto her desk. "Take a look."

A small headline at the bottom left of the front page read, ASSAULT WEAPON BILL HEARD BY SENATE SUBCOMMITTEE.

A box in the middle of the text read, "News Analysis, p. 6."

I skimmed the front-page article. It summarized the intent of the bill and highlighted the testimony of some of the witnesses. It continued on page six. I opened the paper to that page. There was a photograph of the animal rights protestors. Their signs were clearly legible, and in their Bambi and Smokey and Bugs Bunny costumes they looked silly. The State House loomed in the background. The caption read, "Animal Rights Groups Picket Senate Appearance of Walt Kinnick."

Another photograph, this one smaller, showed Walt shaking hands with Wilson Bailey, the poor guy from Harlow whose wife and child had been killed in the library. I was standing there behind Wally's shoulder. The caption read, "Walt Kinnick Congratulated by Admirer After Assault-Weapon Testimony."

An article entitled "Assault Weapons Explosive Issue—News Analysis" began on that page. Its author was Alexandria Shaw, the reporter who had witnessed the confrontation in Dunkin' Donuts.

> Emotions ran high as the Senate Subcommittee on Public Safety heard testimony on S-162, a bill which will, if passed, severely restrict the ownership and distribution of certain paramilitary guns labeled "assault weapons" in the Commonwealth.
>
> Assault weapons are defined in the bill as all semiautomatic rifles and shotguns with large magazines (a semiautomatic weapon fires a shot as fast as the trigger can be pulled). The Uzi and the AK-47 are among the twelve weapons specifically designated for control in the bill.
>
> Representatives of the Police Chiefs Association of Massachusetts testified in favor of the legislation, citing the danger to policemen from criminals armed with the semiautomatic weapons.
>
> Second Amendment For Ever (SAFE), a branch of

the National Rifle Association (NRA) and staunch opponents of all forms of gun control, presented testimony citing the Second Amendment (the right to bear arms) and argued that stiffer penalties, not gun control, are the appropriate remedy for assault-weapon–related crimes.

Perhaps most controversial of all was the testimony of Walt Kinnick, the popular host of the ESPN television series "Walt Kinnick's Outdoors." Kinnick has been an outspoken advocate of outdoor sports, including hunting. Kinnick testified in favor of the regulation of assault weapons, surprising both the subcommittee and the observers in the hearing room, who were predominantly members of SAFE.

It is believed that Kinnick's appearance before the subcommittee was arranged by SAFE. It is certain that the nature of his testimony took the pro-gun organization by surprise.

Gene McNiff, president and executive director of SAFE, refused to comment on Kinnick's testimony.

"It surprised me, I admit it," said Senator Marlon Swift (R–Marshfield), the chairman of the subcommittee. "Coming from someone like Walt Kinnick, it's really something to think about."

Angry words were exchanged between Kinnick and McNiff outside the State House. Later, Kinnick and his attorney, Brady L. Coyne of Boston, were accosted by SAFE members in the Dunkin' Donuts on Tremont Street. Neither Kinnick nor Coyne would comment on the incident.

It is clear that the Massachusetts gun lobby, which has generally had its way with the legislature in recent years, was dealt a severe blow this morning by Walt Kinnick's unexpected testimony. The Subcommittee on Public Safety is expected to report on S-162 by the end of the month.

I looked up at Julie. She was grinning. "You're famous," she said. "Nice picture, too."

329

I shrugged. "I didn't realize it was such a big deal."

"Check the editorial," she said.

I leafed through the paper and found the page. The lead editorial was titled, "Time to Get Tough on Guns." It read:

> The Second Amendment For Ever supporters have had it their way too long. Stubborn, single-minded, hopelessly out of touch with prevailing opinion, SAFE has opposed any and all efforts to regulate the ownership and distribution of guns, including paramilitary assault weapons, in the six New England states.
>
> Backed by powerful allies and a well-stocked war chest, SAFE has intimidated advocates of even the most modest efforts to control gun-related crime. Legislators have bowed and scraped before the SAFE bombast. Time after time we have seen gun-control legislation die in subcommittee, shot down by the high-caliber SAFE arsenal.
>
> Yesterday, the courageous testimony of Walt Kinnick punctured the SAFE bubble, and it will never be the same again. The nation's most famous hunter, and himself a gun owner, Kinnick issued an appeal that rings true to all who would listen.
>
> Very simply, the time has come for hunters and gun owners to be reasonable, Kinnick told the subcommittee. We agree.
>
> We don't argue with the right of sportsmen to possess their shotguns and hunting rifles. But assault weapons have only one function: to kill people. They do not belong in the hands of private citizens. It's time for SAFE to join the rest of us at the brink of the twenty-first century. SAFE must take to heart the testimony of its most respected spokesman, Walt Kinnick. Be reasonable, compromise, or cease to exist.

For someone who just wanted to get away and do some quiet trout fishing, Wally had made quite a splash. If Gene McNiff had been upset after the hearing, I wondered how he felt now.

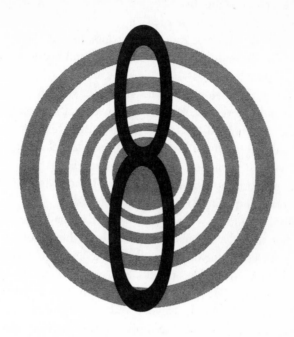

I spent most of Tuesday morning on the telephone, and Julie and I had chicken salad sandwiches at my desk for lunch. Sometime in the middle of the afternoon, while I was trying to outline the article I had promised Phil Carstairs out of my guilt for refusing to make a speech to the ABA in Houston, my intercom buzzed. I picked up the phone and said, "Yeah?"

"Brady," said Julie, "there's a Miz Shaw here to see you."

"Who?"

"She's a reporter for the *Globe*."

Julie wanted me to talk to her. Otherwise she wouldn't have buzzed me. I generally do what Julie wants.

"I'm right in the middle of something," I told her. "Why

331

don't you give her an appointment?"

"She's on deadline, Brady."

I sighed. "Okay. Send her in."

There was a discreet knock on my door, then it opened. Julie held it for Alexandria Shaw. I stood up behind my desk. "Come on in," I said.

"Thanks for seeing me," she said. She wore a pale green blouse and tailored black pants. Her wide-set blue-green eyes peered from behind the oversized round glasses that perched crookedly on the tip of her nose. She took the chair beside my desk without invitation. She poked her glasses up onto the bridge of her nose with her forefinger. "I know you're busy. I'll try to make it quick. Do you mind if I record it?"

Before I could answer she had removed a small tape recorder from her shoulder bag and plunked it onto the top of my desk. When she leaned forward to fiddle with it, her short auburn hair fell like wings around her cheeks. She switched on the recorder and said into it, "Tuesday, May nineteenth, four forty-five P.M. I'm talking with Brady Coyne, Walt Kinnick's lawyer." She snapped it off, rewound it, and played it back. It sounded fine. She dug into her bag again and came up with a notebook and a pen. "Okay," she said, "a couple questions."

I held up both hands. "Hey, slow down," I said. "Do you want coffee or something?"

"I don't know about you," she said, "but I gotta get this story in by seven. Fill the space, you know? Survival of the vulgarest." She grinned quickly. "So if you don't mind, let's get to it."

I smiled. "I don't really have anything to say."

"About that incident at the Dunkin' Donuts yesterday—"

"No comment," I said quickly.

"Are you a member of SAFE?"

"Me?"

She grinned. "I guess that answers my question."

"Who cares, anyhow?"

"Hey," she said. "I gotta fill the space, remember?"

"Well," I said, "I am a member of the ABA and Trout Unlimited and the Sierra Club. But I don't belong to SAFE. Or the NRA. Or lots of other worthy organizations."

332

"You think they're worthy?"

"Who, SAFE?" I shrugged. "I don't know much about them."

"Do you sympathize with them?"

"Excuse me," I said, "but really. Who cares about me?"

"You're Walt Kinnick's lawyer."

I shrugged.

"Right?" she said.

"Yes."

"Are you defending him in any litigation?"

"Come on. No comment. You know better. Really."

"Did you advise him on his testimony yesterday?"

I smiled. "You obviously don't know Wally."

"You're his boyhood friend, right?"

She had done her homework. "Yes. We went to high school together."

"And you and he were threatened yesterday at Dunkin' Donuts."

I shook my head. "No comment, okay?"

She jabbed her finger at her eyeglasses. "Mr. Coyne," she said, "I don't know what your opinion is of SAFE, but there's a major story here and I want it."

"I already told you I don't know anything about SAFE."

"Sure you do. They're mobilizing against Walt Kinnick, did you know that?"

"What have you heard?"

"They've got the NRA working with them, and they're trying to mount a boycott against the sponsors of his show. They're investigating him. They've got lots of resources. Any skeletons, they'll find them. If they can discredit him, they will. Seems obvious, if you're his lawyer you're going to be involved in this."

Skeletons. Like the fact that Wally was shacking up with a woman who was still technically married. "How do you know these things?" I said to Alexandria Shaw.

She smiled. "It's my job."

"And if they find some of these—skeletons?"

She shrugged. "It's the job of the newspaper to print it. And," she added, glancing sharply up at me, "I assume it will be your job to protect him."

333

"So you want . . ."

"Balance," she said.

"Well, I just don't see how I can help you. I don't know about any skeletons in Walt Kinnick's closets, and if I did, I'd hardly tell you about them. As his friend, and especially as his lawyer, I am not the one to help you. I'm sorry. I shouldn't have seen you."

"I'm just trying to get the whole story, Mr. Coyne. SAFE has been very forthcoming with the media."

"Organizations can do that. It's trickier for individuals."

"When the individuals are public figures," she said, "like Walt Kinnick, they're fair game." She tilted her head and grinned at me. "Hunting metaphor, huh? Fair game?" She shrugged. "Now you're on their list. Walt Kinnick and you. If you're not for them, you're against them. A turncoat is the worst kind of enemy. Right? Those people are told how to think by their leadership, and that's how they've been instructed to think, so—"

"What do you mean, their list?"

"SAFE publishes a list of their so-called enemies in their newsletter. Prominent people who oppose their party line. The word is that you and Walt Kinnick will be high on their next list. How do you feel about that?"

"Flattered. Humble. Unworthy."

She smiled quickly. "Come on, Mr. Coyne. Any comment?"

I shrugged. "I appreciate the warning, Ms. Shaw."

"It wasn't a warning. Just some information that'll be in my story tomorrow. I wish you'd give me a hand with the rest of it."

"Sorry. I can't."

She stared at me for a moment, then nodded. She reached into her bag and came out with a business card. She put it onto my desk. "If you change your mind, hear anything else . . ."

"Right," I said. "Sure."

"Oh, one more thing."

"Yes?"

"How can I reach Walt Kinnick?"

I shook my head. "Sorry. Can't tell you. Privileged information."

She smiled. "Didn't think so." She snapped off the tape recorder and stuffed it into her bag. Her notebook followed it.

She stood up and held out her hand to me. "Thanks," she said.

Her grip was firm. She actually shook my hand. "I'm afraid I wasn't much help," I said.

"Everything helps," she said. "You'd be surprised."

I spent Wednesday doggedly trying to clear enough odds and ends off my desk to appease my conscience so that I wouldn't feel compelled to lug my briefcase to Fenwick. Julie, of course, would pack it up for me, as she did every day, and I'd dutifully take it home with me when I left the office. I'd prop it against the inside of the door to my apartment, the way I always did, so I wouldn't forget to take it back to the office with me.

But I wasn't going to bring the damn thing on my fishing trip. Briefcases and fly rods don't belong in the same car together.

So I skipped lunch and stayed at the office until nearly eight and felt wonderfully masochistic and virtuous. I was a man who had earned a few days of trout fishing.

That evening I assembled my gear, not an easy task since I found it scattered all around my apartment. My fly rods were in their aluminum tubes in the back of my bedroom closet. My waders lay rumpled in the corner of the living room. I found my reels on the bottom shelf of the linen closet. I discovered fly boxes on my desk, in the kitchen cabinet with the canned soup, in the drawer of my bedside table.

I nearly abandoned the search for my favorite fishing hat, the stained and faded Red Sox cap that my friend Eddie Donagan, the one-time Sox pitcher, had given me. It was studded with bedraggled flies, each of which had caught me a memorable fish, and I needed it for luck. I finally found it in the last place I expected—hanging on a hook in the front closet.

When I got all the stuff assembled, it looked as if I had enough equipment for a two-month African safari. When I got it packed in my car there certainly wouldn't be any room for a clunky old briefcase.

I showered, brushed my teeth, and climbed into bed. I started to turn off the light, then changed my mind. I picked up the phone on the bedside table and pecked out the familiar Wellesley number.

It rang five times before Gloria mumbled, "H'lo?"

"Sorry. You sleeping?"

"Oh. Brady. No."

"Busy?"

"Not really."

"I'm sorry. Didn't mean to interrupt anything."

"I said I wasn't busy."

"You said, 'Not really.'"

"That means no."

"Well, but you said, 'Not really.' What did you mean, 'Not really,' if you didn't mean you really were busy?"

"Brady, dammit, do you always have to cross-examine me? You don't have to play lawyer with me. If I was busy, I would've said I was busy. Okay?"

I sighed. "Okay."

I heard Gloria sigh, too. "Shit, anyway," she said.

"I'm sorry."

"Yeah. Fine."

"Everything okay?"

"Except for Perry Mason phone calls, fine."

"Well, good."

"That why you called? To find out if I was busy?"

"Well, no." I cleared my throat. "I'm going to be away for a few days. Thought you should know."

"Why?"

"Well, I've got a chance to go fishing with—"

"No. I mean, why did you think I should know?"

"Oh." I hesitated. "The truth is, I guess it feels better, thinking that there's someone who should know when I go somewhere. I mean, everybody should have somebody who knows when they're going away. Does that make any sense?"

"No," said Gloria. But I heard her chuckle. She knew me. She understood.

"Somebody who—cares," I said.

"I'm not stupid, you know," she said softly. "You're looking for someone to play wife for you."

"No, I just—"

"I'm not your wife, Brady. I was your wife. When I was your wife, it was appropriate, your telling me when you were going somewhere. Which you used to do a great deal, if you remember. I don't recall that you ever actually asked. You told me. Then you went."

"I asked," I said. "I always asked."

"Yeah. You'd say, 'I'm off to Canada with Charlie Saturday, remember?' Some question."

"I didn't—"

"Or you'd say, 'You don't mind if Doc Adams and I spend the weekend out on the Beaver River, do you?' Like that. Asking."

"It's the Beaverkill. Lovely trout river."

"Whatever." Gloria laughed softly. "Brady, if you want to tell me when you're going somewhere, that's fine. If you want me to be a telephone wife now and then, I can handle it. Go fishing. I don't care. Have fun. Don't fall in. Whatever you want out of it. Okay?"

I lit a cigarette. I took a deep drag, let it dribble out. "I don't know why I called," I said.

"Me neither," she said. "When Terri was on the scene you didn't call that much."

"I guess not."

"I'm not your girlfriend, you know."

"I know."

"So why are you calling me?"

"I don't know. I mean, family . . ."

"You made your choices, Brady."

"Billy's at school, Joey's in his own world. You . . ."

"I'm divorced. So are you. We're divorced from each other, as a matter of fact."

"I don't like the idea of being out of touch."

"That's the choice you made."

"Yeah."

"You can't have it both ways."

"I guess not."

"That was always your problem," she said. "Wanting it both ways."

"It was more complicated than that."

"Not really."

"Yeah," I said. "Maybe you're right."

"Look," she said. "If it'll make you feel better, leave a number with me."

"Just in case something . . ."

"Right," she said.

I read Wally's phone number to her.

She repeated it. "This is Walt Kinnick?" she said.

"Yes."

"I've been reading about him in the paper. You, too, actually."

"Yeah, well we're just going to do some fishing."

She hesitated a minute. "Are you okay?"

"Sure. Fine."

"I don't know," she said. "It sounds . . ."

"Nothing to worry about."

"I didn't say I was worried." She paused. "Maybe a little concerned."

"Yeah?"

"Um."

"Thanks," I said.

"Sure," said Gloria. "It's what we ex-wives are for."

"And that," I said, "is why every man needs one."

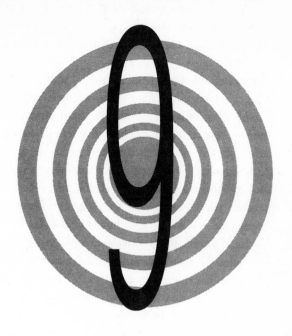

I was on the road a little before seven. I beat the westbound commuters onto Storrow Drive, angled onto Route 2 by the Alewife T station, and had clear sailing. Morning fog hovered over the swampy places alongside the highway. It would burn off by mid-morning. It promised to be a perfect May day in New England.

Sixty miles or so west of Boston Route 2 narrows from a divided superhighway to a twisting two-laner. Here it is called the Mohawk Trail. It dips and wiggles through towns like Erving, which prospers on its paper mill and its waste treatment plant, and Farley and Wendell Depot and Miller's Falls, which don't appear to prosper at all.

On an October Saturday, the Mohawk Trail is crammed with leaf peepers, most of them out-of-staters. Caravans of automobiles pull onto the narrow shoulder so that gaudy vistas of crimson maples and bronze oaks and bright yellow aspens can be recorded on Kodacolor.

It's pretty as hell. Photographs rarely do it justice.

Personally, I'd rather meditate upon a single scarlet maple leaf, preferably one that is floating on a trout stream past my waders, than on several billion of them all washed together over hillsides that stretch on for a hundred miles. I agree with Thoreau: All of Nature's mysteries are revealed on a single leaf.

Actually, I'm a leaf peeper myself in May, and when the trail began its acute northwest ascent into the Berkshire foothills west of Greenfield, I found myself marveling at the thousands of pale shades of green and yellow and pink in the new May leaves that walled the roadside and formed a canopy overhead. Even the bark on the new saplings rioted with color—the gold of the willows, the black of the alders, white birch, gray aspen. The maples exploded with their crimson springtime blossoms. The wild cherry blooms were white.

Nature's colors are more understated and subtle in May than they are in October. In May they're fresh, young, natural, full of vigor and confidence. October foliage is the desperate makeup of old age, trying too hard to recapture the beauty that has irreversibly passed.

May's my favorite month.

The fact that the best trout fishing New England offers comes in May could have something to do with it.

I pulled to the side of the road where it picked up the Deerfield River just west of Shelburne Falls. I consulted the map Wally had drawn for me on the back of the Dunkin' Donuts napkin. Nine miles past the old inn in Fenwick, according to Wally's sketch, an unmarked gravel road angled off the paved road to the right. The gravel road forked exactly two-point-two miles past a wooden bridge. The left fork followed the river. I was to go right. A lightning-struck oak tree stood at the point of the fork.

The right fork began as gravel but, after two hundred yards, turned to dirt. It twisted up into the hills. Wally had indicated several other roads branching off it. At exactly one-point-nine miles from the dead tree I was to follow the ruts to the left. A brook paralleled the wrong road. A stone wall and an old cellar hole marked the correct one. From there, a one-mile ascent would take me to Wally's cabin. That's where the road ended. Wally had drawn a picture of his place. Smoke twisted from its chimney.

I suspected Wally liked his cabin because no one could find it without one of his maps.

I found the unmarked gravel road. I recognized the fork by the dead oak. From there it got confusing. The road was narrow and rocky. The previous night's rain puddled in the ruts. What on Wally's map appeared to be small tributaries off a central roadway were, in fact, branches of equally untraveled dirt roads. It would've driven Robert Frost crazy. I drove slowly, glancing frequently at the Dunkin' Donuts napkin. Finally the ruts narrowed and brush began to scrape against both sides of my car.

I stopped. This felt wrong. I looked again at the map. It didn't help.

I stepped out and leaned against the side of my car. I didn't know where the hell I was. But, I decided, wherever it was, it was a perfectly fine place to be on a May morning. I was in the woods. All around me birds were whistling and cooing and flirting with each other. From somewhere above the canopy of new leaves came the squeal of a circling hawk. He was hunting, not flirting. A gray squirrel cussed me from the trunk of a beech tree. Off to my right I heard a brook burbling its way downhill over its boulder-strewn watercourse.

Maybe in one sense I was lost. But I knew exactly where I was.

The road was too narrow for turning the car around, so I had to back down to where it branched. I got out and walked up the left tine of the fork, where I found the stone wall and the cellar hole. According to Wally's map, I was no longer lost.

So I stood there and told myself what a cunning woodsman I was, and after a minute or two I noticed the smell of woodsmoke. I climbed into my car and chugged in second gear to Wally's cabin.

It was made from weathered logs. A roofed porch spanned the entire front. Rocking chairs were strategically placed to encourage the loafer to prop his heels up on the railing and sip bourbon at sunset and watch the bats fly and the deer creep into the clearing. Big picture windows bracketed the front door. Smoke did indeed wisp from the chimney.

It was more than a cabin and less than a house. From the outside, it looked spacious and inviting.

I parked beside a mud-splattered black Cherokee, shut off the ignition, and stepped out. My BMW was mud-splattered, too.

Before I had taken two steps toward the cabin, a liver-and-white Springer spaniel came bounding to me. I scootched down to scratch his ears, and he rolled onto his side and squirmed and whined.

Suddenly there came a shrill whistle, the kind that basketball coaches make by jamming two fingers into the corners of their mouth. I never learned to whistle that way.

A woman's voice yelled, "Corky!"

Instantly the Springer scrambled to his feet, trotted back to the porch, and flopped down beside the woman who was standing there waving at me. Her blond hair was pulled back into a careless ponytail. She was wearing a white T-shirt and faded blue jeans and bare feet. She was slim and tall. She looked about sixteen. She was smiling at me.

"Hey, Brady," she called.

I waved back at her. "Diana. Hi."

I went to the porch. Up close, I saw that she was closer to thirty-six than sixteen. Tiny lines webbed the corners of her dark eyes and bracketed her mouth and lent character to her face. She looked even better up close.

The legend on her T-shirt read, "I FISH THEREFORE I AM."

She was holding out her hand. I took it. Her grip was firm. "You made it," she said.

"Only took one wrong turn."

"That's par. I hope you're ready to go fishing. Time for one cup of coffee. Let's get your stuff."

We headed back to my car. Corky scrambled up and heeled behind her.

"Where's Wally?"

She jerked her head backward in the direction of the cabin. "On the phone."

"Problems?"

"He doesn't seem particularly concerned. He'll be out in a minute."

We unloaded my stuff and lugged it to the cabin. As we stepped onto the porch the front door opened and Wally stood there. He grinned and held up one hand like an Indian. "Howdy."

"Hiya," I said.

He held the door for me and Diana. It opened into a brightly lighted space that encompassed the kitchen, dining area, and living room. A huge fieldstone fireplace took up the entire side wall. Brass-bottomed cookware and sprigs of dried herbs hung from the kitchen beams and framed wildlife prints hung on the raw cedar walls.

"You're in here," said Diana. She pushed open a door with her foot. It was a small bedroom. One queen-sized bed, a dresser, bedside table, chair. The single window looked out back into the woods. "Bathroom's through there," she added, indicating a doorway.

We dumped my stuff on the bed, then went back into the living room. Wally handed me a mug of coffee. "We oughta be on the river in an hour," he said. "Drink up."

"Let the poor man relax," said Diana.

"How can I relax?" I said. "I want to go fishing."

I sat on the sofa in front of the fireplace, where embers were burning down to ash. Wally sat beside me and Diana took a rocking chair. Corky flopped onto the bare wood floor beside her. She reached down absentmindedly to scratch his ears.

"Who was it this time?" she said.

Wally waved his hand dismissively. "One of the assistant producers."

343

"Is this serious?" I said.

He shrugged. "The word's gotten around. Kinnick has betrayed the cause. I guess SAFE's got the NRA boys calling the station from all over the country. But, shit, we've always had stuff like that. Today the NRA, tomorrow People for the Ethical Treatment of Animals or the congressman from New Jersey. I don't know, I just seem to piss people off. The producers complain and worry and create disastrous scenarios, but I think they actually kinda like it when I offend. Controversy. That's the ratings game, I guess. They like to say, bad reviews are one helluva lot better than no reviews. No, he was just wondering what I said in Boston that got the switchboard all lit up. I told him, just like I've been telling everyone else. He said it sounded okay to him."

"You seen a newspaper recently?" I said.

"Absolutely not. Newspapers are not allowed in this place. Or televisions, either. We get some ink?"

"The *Globe* thinks you're a hero."

"Sure. They would." He stretched elaborately. "Ready to go?"

I gulped the dregs of my coffee and stood up. "I'm ready."

"Me, too," said Diana. The instant she stood, Corky scrambled to his feet and scurried to the front door. He whined and pushed at it with his nose. "Okay, okay," she said to the dog. "You can come."

Corky turned and sat, resting his haunches back against the door. I'd have sworn that dog was smiling.

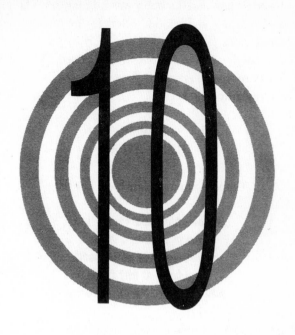

The four of us piled into Diana's Cherokee—she drove and Wally sat beside her in front, while Corky and I shared the backseat. After twenty minutes—and at least that many forks in the dirt roads—we pulled onto the grassy parking area on the banks of the Deerfield just downriver from the hydroelectric dam. Only one other car was there, a late model green Volvo wagon with Vermont plates and a Trout Unlimited sticker on the back window.

When I stepped out I could hear the river gurgling down in the gorge beyond the screen of trees. Here and there through the leaves I caught the glint of sunlight on water. I was familiar enough with the sounds of the Deerfield to know that the dam had reduced its flow and the water was running low. The sun was warm and mayflies and caddis flitted in the air—perfect fly-fishing conditions.

I glanced at the sign tacked onto a fat oak tree, identical to the signs that were spaced every fifty feet along the river.

In bold red letters, it read:

**WARNING
RISING WATERS**

Then, in more sedate black lettering:

**Be constantly alert for a quick
rise in the river. Water
upstream may be released
suddenly at any time.
*New England Power Company***

I smiled to myself. On two occasions in the years I had fished the Deerfield I had failed to be "constantly alert." Twice I had been lifted from my feet and swept downstream on the crest of the rising water.

The first time it happened I was trying to make a long cast to a large trout. Charlie McDevitt fished me out.

The second time, two men with guns were chasing me and a boy named E. J. Donagan. That time a bullet grazed my buttock, and it was E.J. who saved me.

I had no desire to try it again.

Another sign on an adjacent tree, also one of many, read:

CATCH AND
RELEASE
AREA
ARTIFICIAL
LURES ONLY
NO FISH OR BAIT IN
POSSESSION

A guy from North Adams named Al Les had worked mightily to persuade the state to set aside these several miles of beautiful trout water for no-kill fishing. The trout here were bigger and more abundant than elsewhere in the river, the logical result of their being allowed to continue their lives after being caught by a fisherman. If your idea of good fishing did not require you to bring home trophies, this was the place.

More than fifty years ago Lee Wulff said, "A good gamefish is too valuable to be caught only once." Thanks to people like Wally Kinnick and Al Les, Wulff's wisdom has been gradually catching on, and those of us who love fishing for its own sake have been the beneficiaries.

The three of us pulled on our waders and rigged up our rods, while Corky sniffed the shrubbery and lifted his leg in the prime spots.

Wally was ready first. "I'm heading down," he said.

"We'll be right along," said Diana.

After Wally disappeared down the steep path, Diana smiled at me. "He's like a kid when he's going fishing. I love his passion for it."

"I knew him when he was a kid," I said. "Nice to see he hasn't changed."

She was tying a fly onto her leader tippet. She squinted at it, clamping the tip of her tongue in her teeth. She was, I thought, very beautiful in her floppy man's felt hat and bulging fishing vest and baggy chest-high waders.

We started down the path, me first, Diana behind me, and Corky at her heel. It was narrow and descended abruptly, so that I had to grip saplings to keep from slipping. Halfway down, I came upon Wally. He was crouched there in the pathway, peering through the trees down at the river.

Without turning around, he held up one hand and hissed, "Shh."

I stopped right behind him.

"Look," he whispered, pointing down at the river.

I peeked through the foliage. A fishermen was standing knee-deep in the water. His rod was bent. He was bringing a fish to his net. It looked like a large one.

347

"Hey," I said. "A good—"

"Shh!"

The angler had stepped directly out of the Orvis catalog. His vest was festooned with glittering fishing tools and gadgets, and his neoprene waders looked new and custom-fitted. His slender split-bamboo rod was bent in a graceful arc. He netted the fish and then knelt in the water to remove the fly from its jaw. He was turned away from me so that through the foliage I couldn't clearly see what he was doing.

Suddenly Wally muttered, "Bastard!"

"What?" I said.

"The son of a bitch killed the fish. He slipped it into the back of his vest."

"You sure?"

"Damn right I'm sure."

"But it's—"

"Of course. They're all supposed to be released. He's a fuck-ing poacher."

We hunkered there in the path for another minute or two. Then Wally said, "Let's go."

We scrambled the rest of the way down the slope and found ourselves standing on the cobbled bank of the river where, in high water, we'd be up to our knees in surging currents. Big boulders along the edges were still wet from where, not too much earlier in the morning, they had been underwater.

The fisherman had resumed casting. Wally called, "Hey! How're they biting?"

The angler turned, hesitated, then smiled. "Oh, hi. They've just started to rise."

"Catch any?" said Wally.

He shrugged. "A couple."

Wally waded toward him. Diana and I followed along a few steps behind. Corky sat on the bank.

The fisherman stopped casting. He cocked his head, squinting at Wally. "Hey," he said. "I know you."

Wally smiled at him.

"Walt Kinnick, right? Damn! I watch your show all the time. I heard you had a place near here. Jesus, what a treat!"

He held out his hand to Wally, who took it.

"You know," said the guy, "I'm a real fan of yours. A couple years ago I drove all the way down from Brattleboro to hear you speak at the Boston Fly Casters club."

Wally nodded and said, "That's a nice-looking fly rod."

The angler grinned. "Neighbor of mine in Vermont custom made it for me. I love it. Guess I ought to. Cost me fourteen hundred bucks." He held it out to Wally. "Give it a try."

Wally handed his own rod back to Diana and took the man's split-bamboo fly rod. He examined the workmanship, nodding his approval. He waved it in the air a few times. "Sweet," he said. "I bet it casts like a dream." Wally glanced at the man. "Come here often?"

"Couple times a week. It's only an hour or so from home, and it's better than any of the rivers in my own state."

"It's been terrific since they made it catch and release, huh?" The guy nodded.

"I hear," said Wally, "that sometimes guys'll sneak in with bait, catch a bunch and kill them. It's a shame that the wardens don't patrol it better." He waved the man's rod in the air, admiring its flex. "The way I figure it," he continued, "we've got to more or less patrol it for ourselves." Wally turned around to Diana and me and showed us the fly rod. "This is a beautiful piece of work, Brady," he said. "Damn shame that this guy doesn't deserve it."

The fisherman was frowning now. "Just a minute, there—" he said.

Wally turned back to him. "I saw you kill that trout," he said quietly.

"What—?"

"How long did it take the guy in Vermont to make this rod for you?"

The guy frowned. "Almost two years from the time I ordered it. But I—"

Wally gripped the rod with both hands. "It took five years to grow that trout you killed," he said softly.

"I don't know what you're talking about," the guy muttered.

Wally held the man's rod up at eye level and began to bend it. "Hey—!"

349

It cracked halfway up the butt section. Wally twisted the two broken parts until the splintered halves separated. He handed the mangled rod back to the wide-eyed fisherman. "That's the price for killing that fish," he said.

The guy dumbly took his rod. He stared at it for a moment. Then he looked up at Wally. He was shaking his head slowly back and forth. "You broke my rod," he finally said.

Wally nodded.

"You *bastard*. You broke my rod. Who the *hell* do you think you are?"

Wally shrugged. "Try obeying the rules, friend," he said. He turned his back on the guy. To Diana and me he said, "Let's head upstream where the water's not polluted."

The three of us began to wade away. The man with the broken rod yelled, "God *damn* it, Kinnick. That's fourteen hundred bucks. I'll sue you, you son of a bitch."

"This is my lawyer," said Wally, gesturing to me. "Talk to him."

I turned to face the man. "Brady Coyne," I said, dipping my head cordially. "My number's in the Boston book."

The guy glared at me but said nothing.

We headed upstream. "That was a little extreme, don't you think?" I said.

Wally shrugged. "Bastard deserved it."

"It's obvious you're not interested in a lawyer's advice."

"Nope."

"You can't just run around breaking people's fly rods, for God's sake."

"I know," he said. "It's a terrible habit of mine."

Diana smiled. "Walter's a real diplomat. He makes enemies wherever he goes."

"Yeah, just what he needs," I said. "More enemies."

"Judge a man by his enemies," said Wally. "I'm going fishing."

He waded in and began casting. Downstream from where we stood, the fisherman with the broken fly rod was standing there knee-deep in the Deerfield River staring at us. As I watched, he trudged out of the water and disappeared up the path toward the parking lot.

Diana and I continued to pick our way upstream through the

calf-deep water over the slippery rocks. We hooked elbows with each other for our mutual balance. Corky followed along on the bank. "He's a very impetuous man," said Diana. "You must know that. It makes him lovable and impossible, all at the same time."

"It's actually kind of admirable, in an Old Testament sort of way."

"Yeah, but he scares me sometimes."

"We grew up together, you know," I said. "We used to fish and hunt when we were kids. We haunted a place on the other side of town we called the Swamp. Several hundred acres of forest and wetland. Full of game. Rabbits, squirrels, grouse, pheasants. We hunted every Saturday during the season and hardly ever managed to kill anything. A pretty little brook with native trout ran through it. Wally and I loved the Swamp. It was our playground. When the other kids were on the baseball diamond or the football field, Wally and I played in the Swamp. Anyway, we went there one April to fish and we began to find these surveyor's stakes in the ground. You know the kind, with orange paint on top and lot numbers written on them. Wally went absolutely berserk. Screaming and cussing at the top of his lungs. Started to race through the woods ripping up those stakes and heaving them as far as he could. I tried to tell him that he couldn't do things like that, but he paid no attention to me, and after a few minutes I got into the spirit of it myself. I think we ended up finding about fifty of those surveyor's stakes. We yanked every one of them out of the ground, and I've got to admit, it felt good." I shrugged. "Of course, it didn't do any good. Within a year the bulldozers were there, and a year after that they had that pretty little brook flowing through a concrete culvert and roads were cut through the woods and foundations were all poured and I guess there wasn't a grouse or a rabbit left."

Diana looked at me and smiled. "And he's been metaphorically ripping up surveyor's stakes ever since. He's managed to make a career of it."

"Like I said. It's admirable. Of course," I added, "as his lawyer, I'd advise against it. But he never consults me."

Diana and I picked out likely stretches of river to fish, and soon I was lost in the rhythms of fly casting. Little cream-colored

351

caddis flies were dancing over the surface of the water, and here and there trout swirled and splashed at them. I had to change flies a few times before I found one that the fish liked. I missed a couple of strikes, and then I managed to hook one, a fat rainbow of about fourteen inches. He jumped clear of the water three or four times before I was able to bring him to my side. I slipped my hand down the leader and twisted the barbless hook from his mouth. He finned in the water beside my leg for a moment before he darted away.

The river bubbled musically. Birds chirped in the trees. The May sunshine warmed my arms and face. I caught a few trout. Now and then I heard Wally grunt or Diana squeal, and when I glanced at them, their rods were bent. After three or four hours—my sense of time completely deserts me when I'm fishing—the insects disappeared from the water and the trout stopped rising. I waded to the bank, sat on a boulder, and lit a cigarette. Corky bounded over and sat beside me. I scratched his ears.

A few minutes later Wally and Diana reeled in and came over to join me. They sat beside each other on a large flat rock. Diana tilted up her face and nuzzled Wally's beard. "How you doin', big guy?" she said softly.

He smiled quickly. "I'm still pissed."

"Some day you're going to break the wrong guy's rod, you know."

He shrugged. "If the guy's been killing fish illegally, it'll be the right rod."

"You know what I mean," she said.

He hugged her against his side and looked at me. "Remember the Swamp, Brady?"

I nodded. "I was telling Diana about those surveyor's stakes."

"I'm *still* pissed about that," he said.

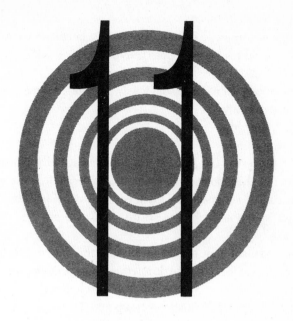

Back at the cabin, Diana took Corky out for a walk and I went into my bedroom to change out of my fishing clothes. When I walked into the living room, Wally said, "Listen to this."

He was standing by his answering machine. He pressed the button. It whirred for a moment, then a recorded voice said, "Walter Kinnick, you have betrayed the Second Amendment For Ever and you deserve to die a just and ironic death."

The machine clanked and rewound itself.

"Jesus, Wally," I said. "Have you had any other calls like that?"

He shrugged. "A few yesterday. They upset Diana. I figure they're just venting their frustrations. Harmless."

"This guy didn't sound harmless," I said. "Play it again."

Wally did.

"Recognize the voice?" I said.

Wally shook his head.

"'Just and ironic,'" I said. "Interesting language for a death threat. I wouldn't have expected anything quite so literate."

"Yeah," said Wally. "The guy's a poet."

"Somebody from SAFE, obviously," I said. "Taking exception to your testimony."

"Well, fuck him."

"Sure," I said.

"Not to worry," he said. "When someone actually plans to kill somebody, they don't call them to announce it. Anonymous phone calls?" He dismissed them with a wave of his hand. "Just another variation on heavy breathing. Come on. I'm starved. Let's eat."

Wally grilled giant steaks on his hibachi, I tossed the salad, and Diana was forbidden to do anything except kibitz, which she did, wittily. Then we sat on the front porch eating and sipping beer and watching the shadows creep into the meadow. Bats and swallows swooped and darted at moths and mosquitoes, and after the shadows had deepened from gray to purple a doe and her spindly-legged fawn tiptoed into the opening.

Once from inside the cabin we heard the phone ringing. "Let the machine get it," said Wally when Diana started to get up.

She shrugged and sat down.

I punched my palm. "Damn it," I said. "You should've saved that tape."

"Why?"

"That message you had. You should've saved it."

"What for?"

I shrugged. "I don't know."

He smiled. "Me neither. Anyway, too late now. It's been recorded over."

"What kind of message this time?" said Diana.

"Just another nut, honey," he said.

"I think it's scary."

He reached over and squeezed her hand.

We sat out there in the darkness for a while longer. Finally

Wally stretched, groaned, and stood up. "Gotta make a few calls," he said. He bent over, lifted Diana's hair, and kissed the back of her neck. "I'll meet you in the sack," he said to her. Then he went inside.

Diana and I sat in the darkness for a few minutes. Then she said, "Do you play cribbage?"

"I was the champion of Raven Lake Lodge up in Maine a few years ago. Wrested the title from a couple of very crafty Penobscot Indian guides. I'm probably too good for you."

"Let's find out."

She went inside. I lit a cigarette. A few minutes later the porch light went on and Diana shouldered open the screen door. She was carrying a tray which bore a cribbage board, a deck of cards, and two mugs of coffee.

We played cribbage and sipped coffee while the moths swirled around the porch light and the night birds called in the darkness. Once Diana paused in the middle of shuffling the deck and said, "Brady?"

"Um?"

"Those phone calls?"

I nodded.

"It's scary."

"I know," I said. "But Wally's probably right. Some people get off on phone calls. They're cowards."

"Mm," she said doubtfully.

A little later she suddenly began giggling.

"What is it?" I said.

"That man? Whose rod Walter broke? Did you see his face?"

"I think Wally's right," I said. "He deserved it."

She beat me three games to two. She got all the good cards.

As my penalty for losing, I went in to refill our mugs. Wally was seated at the kitchen table with the telephone wedged against his ear. He rolled his eyes at me.

I brought coffee out to Diana. "Doesn't he ever stop working?" I said.

"He pretends to. When we come out here, he always swears he's going to forget it. But every time I turn around, he's on the phone."

355

We sipped our coffee in comfortable silence for a couple of minutes. Then she leaned toward me and touched my arm. "You were probably wondering about us," she said. "Me and Walter, I mean."

I shrugged. "None of my business whatsoever."

"I want to tell you. Maybe you can give me some advice."

"Legal or personal?"

"Either," she said. "Both."

"As long as you don't value it too highly," I said. "Anybody can give advice."

"You're a friend. That makes it worth something."

"Thank you," I said.

"It's kind of a cliché," said Diana quietly, "now that I think of it. My husband works for a public relations firm, and one of their clients is this bank president or something who wanted to get onto Walter's show. Anyhow, there was some kind of reception at the Bostonian Hotel, and Howard had to go because his client was going. And Walter was there. Now, I had one of those marriages—well, Howard and I had been married for about six years, just drifting along. Nothing bad, but nothing much good, either. And when I met Walter—well, something happened. I just thought he was the sexiest, most down-to-earth guy I'd ever known. I mean, I talked to him for about three minutes and I just wanted him to wrap his arms around me and never let go." She shrugged. "I loved him instantly. I never believed that happened. But it does. It did."

"And Wally?" I said.

"He was charming. We talked. I couldn't take my eyes off him. I just wanted to grab him." She smiled. "I made the mistake of letting him know how I felt. I mean, looking back on it, it was something out of a romance novel. I don't even remember what I said, but it seemed outrageously bold at the time. Walter smiled at me, picked up my left hand, looked at my wedding ring in a meaningful way, dropped my hand, and without a word he turned around and walked away from me. That same night I told Howard I was leaving him. Which I did. Not for Walter. It had been coming for a long time. Meeting Walter, it just—it made me confront it. So I got my own place in Cambridge and filed for divorce. See, that response I had to Walter, it made me realize the

356

truth about my marriage. Regardless of Walter, I just knew that the marriage had to end. It wasn't really that I left Howard West for Walter Kinnick. I just—I guess I left Howard for me. Anyway, I wrote Walter a long letter. I didn't really expect to hear from him. I mean, I'd met him just that once, and I had no reason to believe that he'd even remember me. But eventually he wrote back to me. It was just a short polite note, really. He answers all his fan mail, and that's all my letter was to him." She smiled. "But I wrote back to him, and he answered that one, too. We did that for nearly a year. Finally we got together, and . . . " She shrugged.

"I thought Wally told me you weren't divorced," I said.

She nodded. "Right. I'm not. Howard's still fighting it. He did not take it well." She laughed ironically. "There's an understatement for you. Howard went bananas is what happened. See, Brady, I've got nothing against Howard. I just don't want to be married to him. But somehow his entire self-image is at stake here. It's not that he loves me or needs me or can't live without me. Not *me*. I honestly don't think it's me he really cares about. It's the *idea* of me. He feels that if he loses me he's a failure. He just can't believe that somebody wouldn't want to be married to him." She paused, gazed up at the sky, took a deep breath, and whooshed it out. When she looked at me again, her eyes had brimmed with tears. "It's so *damn* frustrating. I thought we could be friends. You know, I figured we'd tell each other it was a pretty good six years and get on with our lives. Just to show you how naive I was, I even thought Howard would be happy for me, that I'd found someone I really loved."

"It hardly ever works that way," I said.

"You do divorces, right?"

"I do them. I also had one of my own."

"So you know what I mean. It's been three years. He calls me. Talks and talks. He yells, he cajoles, he cries, he begs, he threatens, he—"

"Threatens?" I said.

She laughed quickly. "Wrong word. He never leaves death-threat messages on my answering machine, if that's what you mean. Oh, he'd like me to believe that he's going to kill himself or something, that he can't live without me. Psychological threats like

357

that. Just trying to make me feel guilty. I know him. He likes everything in its proper place. He hates surprises. This—I guess it surprised him. It's out of place. He doesn't know where it fits. It makes
him a little crazy. I never saw that part of him before. It makes *me*
crazy sometimes. I mean, it's unnerving, seeing something new in
somebody after you've been married to him for six years."

"But he hasn't threatened you," I said.

She smiled. "No. Not physically, or financially, or anything.
Not Howard. Oh, there are all those phone calls. When I'm not
home, he'll fill the entire tape on my answering machine.
Promising to change and in the same sentence threatening to
jump off a bridge. It's all crazy. I've had my number changed,
had it unlisted, but Howard's got connections. He finds it out.
And sometimes he comes to my apartment building, banging on
the door, yelling up from the street. He sat on my front steps all
night a couple times when Walter was there. The only time I can
relax is when I'm here or on a trip with Walter."

"He doesn't belong to SAFE, does he?"

"Howard?" She laughed. "As far as I know, he's never touched
a gun."

"It still sounds pretty frightening," I said.

She shook her head. "Howard West doesn't frighten me. He
makes me furious, and he drives me nuts sometimes. But I'm not
afraid of him. He's—well, actually, he's probably like the guys
who are leaving those messages. He's a coward."

"I don't know," I said. "I keep reading about these stalkers . . ."

She laughed. "He's not like that at all. I know Howard West."

"He doesn't know about this place?"

"Whew!" she said. "I hope not."

"It takes time."

"I know," she said.

"You've got a good lawyer?"

She nodded.

"I wasn't looking for business," I said quickly.

She patted my hand. "I didn't think you were."

I was wide awake at six-fifteen the next morning. Back in the city, I tend to sleep late, probably because nothing there seems worth getting up for. Give me a taste of clean country air and a day on a trout river, and sleeping seems like a waste of time.

I pulled on my jeans and a T-shirt and stumbled into the kitchen. Diana was seated at the table sipping coffee and reading a magazine. She looked up and smiled at me. "Coffee?"

"You bet. I'll get it."

I went to the coffee machine and poured myself a mugful. I took it to the table and sat down across from her.

"Sleep well?" she said.

"Like a bear in January. Where's Wally?"

359

She jerked her head in the direction of the front door. "Walking with Corky. He hardly slept last night. He shrugs all this stuff off, but it eats at him. His producers, apparently, really are giving him a hard time. I guess some of their sponsors are getting fidgety."

"Boy," I said, "they don't waste any time."

"What's going on, Brady? These past few days . . ."

I shrugged. "The gun lobby is pretty upset. They figured Wally for a solid ally, which makes him the worst kind of traitor in their eyes. They've threatened to mobilize some kind of boycott of his TV sponsors."

"Can they do that?"

"I don't know," I said. "It'll probably all go away. The NRA, along with its local arms like SAFE, is one of the best-funded and most sophisticated pressure groups in the country. They've always been very successful. If that bill should become law, it would be like them to blame it on Wally. That's probably what's got him worried."

Diana smiled down into her coffee mug. "Walter never really worries. He sees things as challenges, not worries. About all he's told me about this assault weapon business is that he's satisfied he did the right thing, and if his sponsors drop him they'd be doing the wrong thing. I've gotten the impression that his producer would like him to make some kind of retraction on television, or at least say something that would fudge the issue. He would never do anything like that. So," she said with a smile, "he's walking in the woods. Going to church, he calls it." She looked up at me. "How do you like your eggs?"

"Over easy," I said. "But you don't—"

At that instant from somewhere outdoors came the sharp crack that I instantly recognized as a rifle shot. There was a pause, and then several more in quick succession.

Diana and I sat there for a moment looking at each other. Then she whispered, "Oh, Jesus."

She leaped up from the table, and I did too. We ran outside. I followed Diana around to the side of the house.

"Walter!" she screamed.

There was no answer.

She yelled again and again, and then Corky came bounding out of the bushes. He was wagging his tail, happy to see her. He rolled onto his back beside her, squirming in anticipation of having his belly scratched.

Diana scooched down beside him. "Where's Walter? Come on, Corky. Let's find Walter."

Corky scrambled to his feet and looked at her, and I would swear he understood exactly what she was saying. He turned and headed back into the woods. Then he stopped and looked at us, as if to say, "You guys coming, or what?"

We followed him through the thick undergrowth for about a hundred yards. Then we heard Wally moan.

"Walter!" Diana yelled.

We found him sitting on the ground, hunched over, hugging himself with his knees drawn up tight to his chest. Diana ran to him and knelt down beside him. "Honey?" she said.

Wally looked up at her. His face was wet with pespiration. "I'm okay," he mumbled.

"Let me see," I said. I squatted beside him. "Let's try to lie down," I told him.

Diana and I helped him onto his back. He groaned and squeezed his eyes shut. His breath came in quick shallow gasps.

A dark wet blotch was spreading across the front of his shirt. It looked like he'd gotten it in the stomach.

Diana leaned close to his face. "Honey?" she whispered.

"Hey, babe," he mumbled.

She looked at me. "What do we do?"

"Get a blanket. Call an ambulance."

She ran back to the house.

I wiped his face with my handkerchief. "How's it feel?" I said to him.

"Hurts like hell," he mumbled through clenched teeth.

I carefully unbuttoned his shirt and opened it. The bullet had struck him just above and to the left of his navel. It made a neat black hole from which blood was seeping steadily, and I didn't see how it could have missed vital organs on its way through him.

I helped Wally roll onto his side. The exit wound in his back was bigger and uglier and had bled profusely, judging by the black puddle that had already soaked into the leaves under him. I took off my own shirt, balled it up, and held it tight against the ragged hole in his back. "Hang on, old buddy," I told him.

Diana returned with a blanket, which we spread over Wally. She cradled his head on her lap. "The ambulance is on its way, honey," she said.

He opened his eyes and tried to smile. "They got me," he said.

"Who?" I said. "Did you see them?"

His eyes closed again. "Oh, shit," he moaned. He gagged, turned his head to the side, and vomited weakly.

Diana wiped his mouth and beard with the corner of the blanket. "Oh, baby," she whispered. "Don't die, baby."

I bent close to him. "Wally, did you see who shot you?"

"Gotta rip up all those fuckin' stakes, Brady," he mumbled. "Gotta save the Swamp."

His head lolled to the side. His eyelids drooped and his eyes rolled up and his mouth hung open slackly. Diana whispered, "Oh . . ."

I pressed my fingers against the side of his throat. It took me a moment to find the flutter of his pulse. It felt like the panicky beating of an insect's wings.

I looked up at Diana. Her eyes were wide.

"He passed out," I said. "He's lost blood. He's in shock. How soon before that ambulance will get here?"

She shook her head back and forth rapidly. "I don't know. I gave them directions. They seemed to know where we are. They said they were on their way." She bent down and kissed Wally's damp forehead. "Hang on, big fella," she whispered. She laid her cheek against his bushy black beard.

Far in the distance I heard the wail of a siren. I remembered all the wrong turns one could take, how even with Wally's map I had gotten lost trying to find his cabin. I recalled the ruts and mud of the roads. Wally could die while the ambulance wandered through the woods getting stuck in potholes.

I told Diana to hold the makeshift compress against the wound in Wally's back. Then I jogged back to the cabin and started down the dirt road.

It seemed forever, but it was probably only a couple of minutes later when the white van appeared. I waved my arm for it to follow me, then trotted back to the cabin. It pulled up on the lawn. Three EMTs in white jackets leaped out. "What've we got?" one of them said.

"Gunshot wound in the stomach. This way."

I led them into the woods to the place where Diana was kneeling beside Wally.

Within a minute or two they had him bandaged and on a stretcher and were carrying him through the woods back to the ambulance, one EMT on each end and the third holding up a bottle with a tube snaking down to Wally's arm. A plastic oxygen mask was strapped over his nose and mouth. They loaded him into the back. Two of the EMTs climbed in with him. The third slammed the door shut behind them and slid in behind the wheel. Then the vehicle spewed dirt from its rear tires and disappeared down the muddy road.

I stood there staring down the roadway. After a few minutes I heard the wail of the siren. It faded, then died.

Diana was beside me hugging my arm. "It was all so sudden," she said quietly.

"Where'd they take him, do you know?"

"North Adams. There's a hospital there. I'm going."

"I think we should wait. The police will be here."

"The hell with them," she said. "I'm going to be with Walter."

"You're right. The hell with them. Let's go."

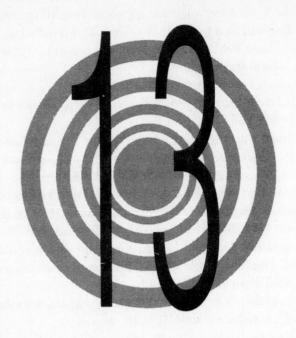

I drove and Diana huddled against the door, and we didn't talk at all during the half-hour or so that it took us to drive down out of the hills to the hospital in North Adams. I figured we were both thinking the same thing.

Wally would be dead when we got there.

We jogged from the parking lot to the main entrance of the hospital. Inside, a young woman sat behind a counter chewing gum. She smiled and lifted her eyebrows when Diana and I approached her. I said to her, "Walter Kinnick."

She turned to face her computer terminal with her fingers poised over the keyboard. "Can you spell it?"

"He would've just got here. In an ambulance."

"Emergency?"

"Yes."

She pointed toward an elevator bank. "First floor. Go left and follow the signs."

"Thanks," I said.

Everybody in the emergency room seemed to be occupied with emergencies, but I finally got the attention of a gray-haired nurse.

"Walter Kinnick," I said to her. "He just came in by ambulance."

"I'm not—"

"Gunshot wound," I said.

She nodded and smiled quickly. She had a pumpkin-shaped face and a gap between her front teeth. She reminded me of Ernest Borgnine. "We didn't have his name," she said. She seemed much friendlier than most of the characters Ernest Borgnine played. "He's in surgery." She gestured off to her left. "You can wait in there. I'll make sure the doctor knows you're here."

"Is he okay?" said Diana.

The nurse shrugged. "I don't know, miss. I'm sorry. You'll have to wait."

A television was mounted on a wall bracket in the waiting room. A mid-morning soap opera was playing loudly on it. There were ten or a dozen other people in there, also waiting. Most of them were staring vacantly at the TV show.

Diana and I sat down. She let out a long breath. I put my arm around her shoulders. "All we can do is wait," I said.

"I'm very frightened," she said.

"I know. Me, too."

I found a six-month-old copy of *Sports Illustrated*. I paged through it from back to front, looking at the pictures, then put it down, glanced around, and spotted a coffeepot. I got up and poured two Styrofoam cupfuls. I handed one to Diana, who looked at me and nodded.

The coffee had the consistency of maple syrup.

I flipped through an old *New Yorker*, pausing at the cartoons, which didn't seem that funny.

365

We had been sitting there for an hour or so, me glancing through magazines and Diana staring up at the television, when a voice said, "Ah, excuse me?" I glanced up. He was a nondescript guy, receding hairline, plastic-rimmed glasses, middle-aged paunch, wearing baggy corduroy pants and a short-sleeved blue shirt.

"Yes?" I said.

"You're with the gunshot wound?"

"Yes. Is he—?"

"I'm the sheriff," he said. He held his hand out to me. "Mason."

"Brady Coyne," I said, shaking his hand. "This is Diana West."

Mason glanced at Diana and nodded. "Ma'am," he mumbled.

"How is he, do you know?" said Diana.

Mason shrugged. "No idea, miss," he said. "They tell me gunshot wound, I gotta come see what's up. They didn't say he was—" He cleared his throat. "Anyways, I need to know what happened. You can start by giving me his name."

"Walter Kinnick," I said. "He—"

The sheriff nodded quickly. "Okay. Sure. I know who he is. He's got the Palmer place up there in Fenwick, right?"

"Yes," said Diana.

Maybe they didn't have cable in that part of Massachusetts. Still, Mason must have known that Wally was a television personality. But I figured that, like most rural folks, he made it a point to be staunchly unimpressed with wealth or fame. Wealthy and famous people keep getting lost in the woods. They don't know how to change flat tires. They wear impractical clothes.

To the locals, Wally wasn't the television guy. Wally was the guy who bought the Palmer place up in Fenwick, and probably paid more for it than he should have, and just used it for vacations now and then. A city boy. An outsider.

Mason squatted down in front of us. "That where it happened?"

Diana nodded. "Outside. In the woods."

"Tell me about it."

"Wally was out walking with the dog," I said. "We were inside. We heard shots. When we got out there, he was on the ground. He was hit in the stomach."

"You see or hear anything besides the gunshots?"

"I don't—"

"Anybody? Somebody running? Voices? Noises in the woods? A vehicle? The sound of a vehicle starting up?"

I shook my head.

"No," said Diana.

"How many shots?"

"Three or four," said Diana. "Real close together."

"Actually," I said, "I think there was one shot, then a pause, then three or four after that."

Mason shrugged. "Who called it in?"

"I did," said Diana.

"When you heard the shots?"

"We ran outside. Corky—that's my dog—he led us to him. Walter was on the ground in the woods. When we realized he had been shot, I went back and called."

"But you didn't actually see anything."

"No," she said.

"Mr. Coyne?"

I shook my head.

"Was Mr. Kinnick conscious?"

"Yes. He passed out before the ambulance arrived."

"Did he say anything?"

"He said, 'They got me.'"

"Is that all?"

I nodded. "I asked him what he meant, who got him, but he didn't say. He mumbled some things that made no sense. Then he passed out."

"What things that made no sense?"

"I don't exactly remember. References to things he and I did as boys. We grew up together. It seemed to me he was hallucinating."

"But maybe he saw who did it."

I shrugged.

Mason was still squatting down in front of us. He shifted his weight, then glanced from Diana to me. "And you two?"

I frowned. "What?"

"How are you related? To Kinnick, to each other."

"I'm his lawyer," I said. "Diana's his . . ."

367

"Friend," she said.

"And what were you doing there?" he said to me.

"At the cabin? A little vacation. We were fishing."

"The three of you."

I nodded. "The three of us."

"The Deerfield, huh?"

"Yes."

He nodded. "I hear it's been fishing good. So what do you figure happened?"

"Somebody hid in the woods and tried to assassinate him," I said. "It's pretty obvious."

Mason smiled. "Who'd want to go do something like that?"

"Somebody who belongs to the Second Amendment For Ever," I said. "See, Wally testified in favor of a gun-control bill last Monday. SAFE brought him in to testify against it, but he ended up supporting it." I shrugged.

Mason scratched his chin. "That's quite a theory, Mr. Coyne."

"He's been getting anonymous phone calls. I heard one of them on his answering machine yesterday. Said he was a traitor to SAFE. It was a death threat."

"Really?"

"Yes. And Gene McNiff threatened him right after he testified and then a gang of SAFE guys followed me and Wally to the Dunkin' Donuts on Tremont Street and attacked Wally, and . . ." I let out a deep breath. "Jesus. It's obvious."

Mason put his hand on my arm. "Calm down, there, Mr. Coyne. Just relax."

"Look," I said, "if it's *not* one of the guys who threatened him on the phone, it's quite a coincidence, don't you think? The way I understand it, every gun-totin' member of SAFE figures Walt Kinnick's their biggest enemy in the world, and one of them figures he's going to serve the cause, so he calls up Wally and tells him he deserves to die for his treachery, and next thing you know Wally's been shot in the gut with a gun."

"Coincidence?" Mason rubbed his chin with the palm of his hand. "Yeah, I guess it could be at that. That's more'n likely what it is. A big coincidence. Fact is, coincidence explains most things. Listen, I ain't saying it *wasn't* some nutcake done it. But you're

368

forgetting the most obvious thing, and you should never forget the obvious thing."

"What's the obvious thing?" I said.

Mason looked at me over the tops of his glasses. "Hunting accident, Mr. Coyne."

"Oh, for Christ sake."

He shrugged. "Don't be too quick to jump to conclusions, there," he said. "Listen. It's turkey season, right this very minute. This part of the state, we get a lot of gunshot wounds in turkey season. Last couple years, no fatalities, thank God. But accidents, you know? Those ridges up there by the Palmer place are prime for gobblers, and everybody around here knows it. The boys get out there way before dawn, hunker against a tree trunk in their camouflage jumpsuits with their tight-choked twelve gauges, and they work on their calls and they wait, and when they see one they let loose. Even if they don't see one, after a while they sometimes *think* they see one. Pretty nerve-racking, turkey hunting. You sit and you sit, morning after morning, just waiting. Imagination starts workin' on you. Little movement in the bushes?" Mason flapped his hand. "A charge of number-four shot hits a twig, it deflects, and the head of a gobbler's just about belt-high on a man . . ." He shrugged as if it was self-evident.

"They sounded like rifle shots to me," I said.

"You were inside when you heard them?"

I nodded.

"They came from out in the woods, right?"

"Yes. But a rifle sounds a lot different from a shotgun."

"It's illegal to hunt turkeys with a rifle, Mr. Coyne."

"Yes," I said. "That's my point."

"Sure." He smiled. "Good point."

"Well," I said, "I assume you intend to investigate it."

He nodded. "Why, sure. Have to investigate a gunshot accident. Law requires it. Accidents happen. But we can't have folks running away when they shoot somebody. It's like a hit and run. We don't put up with that."

"A hit and run?" said Diana.

"Same idea, miss."

She shook her head. "Hardly," she mumbled.

369

"You're planning to talk to Wally, aren't you?" I said.

Mason shrugged and said nothing. I caught his meaning. He'd talk to Wally if Wally didn't die.

"Somebody tried to kill him," said Diana quietly.

"Maybe so, miss," said Mason. "We'll go up to the Palmer place and have us a look, all right. And we'll inquire around, see who might've been hunting those ridges this morning. Maybe one of 'em'll admit to firing those shots. Maybe one of the boys saw something. Any vehicle parked by the roadside, they'd notice. Don't you worry. Let's just hope Mr. Kinnick comes out of it okay."

He stood up and arched his back with a small groan. "You folks take care, now," he said. "Maybe we'll talk again. Meantime, we'll all be prayin' for Mr. Kinnick."

Diana looked up at him. "Thank you," she said.

He started to walk away, then stopped and said, "He didn't happen to save that tape, did he?"

"Tape?" I said.

"On the answering machine. The threatening message."

I shook my head. "No."

Mason shrugged, then left the room.

Diana sighed heavily. "What do you think, Brady?"

"I think he really believes it was a hunting accident. I guess gunshot wounds are pretty common in these parts. So Sheriff Mason's had a lot of experience with men being dragged out of the woods bleeding with bullets in them. The big crime, from his point of view, isn't the shooting. It's that the shooter ran away. He thinks we're paranoid because probably everybody gets paranoid if they or their friends get shot."

"But the phone calls. . . ?"

"This is the country, Diana. It's not Cambridge. Everyone out here hunts and owns guns. Most of them probably belong to SAFE. Maybe Mason himself is a member. He wouldn't believe that anybody from SAFE would do this. He's got his mind made up, and I don't think he's likely to pursue a sophisticated investigation. Far as he's concerned, it was a hunting accident."

"What about the state police, or the FBI, or something?"

I touched her arm. "It's the sheriff's case," I said. "Those others won't be involved in it."

What I meant was that they wouldn't be involved if Wally recovered. If he died, it would become a homicide case. Then everybody would be involved.

I decided not to explain that to Diana just then.

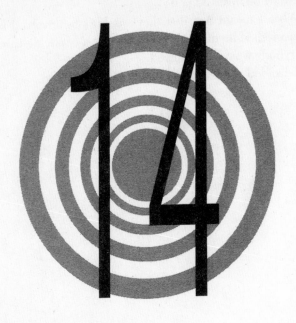

After another hour or so I got up and went back to the emergency admitting area. I found the same gray-haired nurse seated at a computer monitor. "Excuse me . . ." I began.

She looked up at me and shook her head. "He's still in surgery," she said. "I'll be sure you know when there's any news."

"He's been in there a long time."

She shrugged. It meant he hadn't died yet.

Diana had been slumped in her chair with her eyes closed since Sheriff Mason had left. When I returned to the waiting room, I touched her arm and said, "How about something to eat?"

She opened her eyes and looked at me. "No. I feel like I'm going to throw up as it is."

"They told me he's still in surgery."

Her eyes closed. "He's going to die."

I didn't say anything.

Sometime after three o'clock in the afternoon the gray-haired nurse appeared in the waiting room. A young doctor wearing hospital greens stood beside her. She caught my eye, turned to the doctor and spoke to him, then left. The doctor approached me and Diana. We both stood up.

"We can talk better outside," he said, jerking his head in the direction of the corridor. Diana and I followed him.

I guessed he wasn't yet thirty, but deep creases had already etched themselves into his forehead. His eyes were bloodshot. He needed a shave. "You're with Mr. Kinnick," he said.

"Yes. Is he—?"

"I'm Dr. Frankel. We've got him patched up. He's . . . stable."

Diana slumped against me. I put my arm around her.

"Stable?" I said.

The doctor sighed. "I won't try to fool you. It was messy. It nicked his liver and intestine. He lost a lot of blood. But it could have been a lot worse. His vital signs are good. We got him cleaned out and sewn up. He's a strong, healthy man."

"Will he be okay?" asked Diana.

"The worry is always infection with something like this," he said. "We've got him on antibiotics. I think he'll be fine."

"Thank God," she whispered. "Can we see him?"

"Come back tomorrow, miss," he said. "He's in ICU, and he's heavily sedated. You've got to go and give the desk some information." He touched her shoulder and smiled wearily. "Okay?"

"I'd just like to see him."

"You're his wife?"

"No. His—friend."

He nodded. "Talk to the nurse at the desk. Maybe she'll sneak you in for a peek."

We followed the doctor back into the admitting area. Diana answered some questions for the gray-haired nurse at the computer, then the nurse came out from behind her counter.

"You want to come, Brady?" said Diana.

I shook my head. "I'll wait for you here."

I had no desire to see Wally lying unconscious on a hospital bed with plastic tubes coming out of his nose and legs and arms and penis, with monitors ticking his heartbeat and measuring his blood pressure. Seeing him that way wouldn't do Wally any good, or me, either.

Diana was back in ten minutes. Her face was streaked with tears. "He looks so—so shrunken," she said.

I put my arm around her shoulders. "Let's go home," I said.

She nodded. "Yes. I've got to feed Corky."

I found a head of lettuce in the refrigerator. I tore it into a big wooden bowl, added half a jar of ripe olives, dumped a can of tuna fish onto it, and drenched it with Italian dressing. I tossed it with wooden salad forks until the tuna was all shredded and sticking to the lettuce. Then I took it out onto the porch and placed it ceremoniously on the table beside Diana.

She had been sitting there gazing out over the meadow since we returned from the hospital. Corky was lying beside her, and she was absentmindedly scratching his ears. I had poured her a glass of Zinfandel. It sat untouched beside her.

She looked up at me and tried a smile. It worked for just a moment. "Oh, nice," she said.

"I'll be right back." I went inside, found two salad bowls, forks, napkins, and my own wineglass. I carried everything out to the porch and filled Diana's bowl with lettuce, tuna, and olives.

I handed it to her. "Eat," I said. "This is my speciality. I call it Brady's Special Italian Salad Minus the Anchovies, Sweet Peppers, Tomatoes, and Bermuda Onion. We could also use a big loaf of hot garlic bread, actually. But I'll be offended if you don't love it."

She took a small bite. "It's great. I do. I love it." She put her fork down.

"Eat it. You haven't eaten since breakfast. You've got to eat."

"I'm really not that hungry, Brady. But this is delicious."

374

"It's not going to help Wally, you getting sick."

"I know. You're right." She picked up her fork and took another bite. She chewed thoughtfully, then looked at me. "Brady, remember the man whose rod Walter broke?"

"It was only yesterday, Diana."

She smiled softly. "Yes. It seems like a long time ago."

"You think he's the one who shot Wally?"

She shrugged. "He was pretty mad."

"I'll mention it to Mason when I see him. He was driving a green Volvo wagon with Vermont plates. Maybe somebody noticed a Volvo somewhere near here this morning." I hesitated for a moment, then said, "There was something else we didn't mention to the sheriff."

She looked up at me.

"Your husband," I said gently.

Diana frowned, then shook her head. "Howard isn't the type at all."

"You heard some of those threatening messages."

She nodded. "None of them was Howard."

"Wally played one for me when you were out with Corky yesterday. After we got back from fishing."

"I didn't hear that one," she said. "Too bad he didn't save it. I would certainly recognize Howard's voice on an answering machine."

"Too late for that."

"Well, you can mention Howard to that sheriff if you think you should. But it wasn't him. No way."

"Yeah," I said. "It's pretty obvious who it was."

"Turkey hunters," she said, and we both smiled.

The sun had fallen behind the mountains and shadows blanketed the meadow. Diana and I sat there picking at our salads and gazing into those shadows. Suddenly she sat forward and whispered, "Look!"

My first thought was that she had spotted a man with a gun.

Then I saw the shape, and then three other shapes, and I realized that four wild turkeys had tiptoed into Wally's meadow. I had never seen a wild turkey before. Just paintings of Pilgrims with blunderbusses and photographs in *Field & Stream*. Ben Franklin believed the turkey, not the bald eagle, should have been the national bird. When I was growing up in the Commonwealth, there were no wild turkeys. The Massachusetts Division of Fisheries and Wildlife began to reintroduce them into the state in the 1970s, and the birds had, from all I'd read, done well. They reproduced and eventually established themselves securely enough that they could be hunted.

Turkeys are the wariest of all wild creatures, the most worthy quarry for a human hunter.

It's a lot easier to stalk a man than a turkey.

These four were all hens. Gobblers travel alone, at least in the spring mating season when they're staking out their territory and trying to lure in hens that they can seduce.

I've always been fascinated with nature's various rituals of love and lust. Many of them are at once ceremonious and comical, violent and tender. Males strut, sing, and fight each other. Females flirt and blush and play hard-to-get and wait for the biggest toughest guy in the neighborhood to assert his dominance. It reminds me that people are creatures of nature, too, although a lot of us don't like to admit it.

As we watched the four hen turkeys, they abruptly ducked their absurd heads and scuttled back into the woods.

It was hard to imagine how a hunter could mistake a six-foot-three-inch man with a black beard for a turkey.

I turned to Diana. "That was—"

I stopped. Her head was bowed. She was crying.

I touched her shoulder. "What is it?"

"I feel like it's my fault," she said softly. "It's my punishment for trying to be happy. Sometimes I think—I don't deserve it. I don't deserve Walter, I don't deserve—anything. Sometimes when we're together I'm just happy all over, and it scares me. It makes me think that something's going to happen, because you can't just be happy. It never lasts. Something always happens."

I nodded. Diana was right. Something always happens. "I don't know about you," I said, "but I could sure use a hug."

She turned to me and tried to smile. "I could use one, too."

She stood up, and I did, too. She leaned against me. I put both of my arms around her. She snuffled, then began to shudder. She sobbed loudly. I stood there holding her for a long time, while the shadows darkened in the meadow.

15

A knock on my bedroom door woke me up. "Come in," I mumbled.

Diana pushed open the door. "Are you decent?"

"Many people don't think so," I said.

She laughed and put a mug of steaming coffee on the table beside my bed. "I'm going to the hospital," she said.

"What time is it?"

"Seven. I'm leaving now. If you want to come . . ."

"I think I should hang around in case the sheriff shows up. Maybe later."

She bent down and kissed my forehead. "Thank you, Brady

Coyne. I'm awfully glad you're here. I don't know what I would've done . . ."

"I'll come along later. If there's any news, call me."

She looked solemnly at me and nodded.

After I drank my coffee, showered, and dressed, I whistled for Corky and we went outside. Dark clouds hung over the mountains. I could smell rain in the air. I pushed through the dense woods until I came to the little clearing where we had found Wally. I knelt down and found some dark splotches on the leaves where he had bled. I looked around. Surrounding the clearing was thick undergrowth. A mixture of birch saplings and alders and hemlocks and knee-high weeds separated the clearing from the forest. An assassin could hide himself nicely in that undergrowth. I supposed it was also the kind of place a turkey hunter might hide.

I stood up and pushed my way through the close-growing vegetation and began to look around. I didn't know what I expected to see—a footprint, a cigarette butt, anything—but I kept my eyes on the ground and tried to do it in an orderly way, studying every square foot. Corky snorted and snuffled here and there, hunting like a Springer spaniel is supposed to.

The woods were damp and dark and quiet, the way it gets when all the wild creatures know a storm is coming.

After what seemed like a long time I was aware that it had begun to rain. I heard the drops pattering softly on the leafy canopy over my head.

Soon the natural umbrella overhead would become saturated, and then the rain would begin to dribble down. But for now I was dry. I continued my search. I found ferns and mushrooms, clusters of tiny blue flowers, wild strawberries just breaking into blossom, a single pink lady slipper. But no footprints. No sign of an assassin.

Corky hadn't caught any interesting scents, either.

I had turned to go back to the cabin when something caught my eye, a dull metallic glitter. I knelt down. It was a rifle cartridge, an empty bronze-colored cylinder, half hidden under the leaves. I picked it up and held it in my palm. It was about an inch long, with a narrowed-down neck. The legend .223 REM was engraved on its round end.

I looked back in the direction of the clearing where Wally had fallen. It was about a hundred feet away. There was a small opening in the thick growth, no more than a foot in diameter, and about waist-high on a tall man. Through it I could see the place where Wally would have been standing.

I imagined a man kneeling here, training his rifle on that opening, patient, figuring that sooner or later his quarry would appear. This was where the assassin had waited.

I prowled the area on hands and knees. The canopy over my head had become saturated. Rain came dripping down onto me, and I soon became drenched. I found no boot prints or cigar butts or matchbooks or driver's licenses. But I did find two more spent cartridges in the leaves, identical to the first one. These I picked up on the end of a twig and wrapped in my handkerchief. Maybe the shooter had left his fingerprints on them.

I knew I should turn the cartridges over to Sheriff Mason. I also knew I wouldn't do that. He'd smudge them and drop them into his pocket, and that would be the end of them. As long as Wally lived, it was simply a local incident. The man in charge had decided it was a hunting accident. He had neither the resources nor the inclination to consider other scenarios.

When I got back to Boston I'd call Horowitz. He'd know what to do.

I had changed into dry clothes and poured myself a fresh mug of coffee when the obvious thought hit me.

Any assassin who wanted to kill Wally probably wouldn't reject an opportunity to kill me.

And he probably wouldn't pass up the chance to take a shot at Diana, either. A crackpot with a rifle would undoubtedly subscribe to the theory of guilt by association.

She and I had spent the previous evening lounging on the porch watching the darkness seep into the meadow. It had been stupid.

I didn't want to spend any more time in Wally's cabin. I didn't want Diana to, either.

She called me a little after noon. "He was awake for a little while," she said. "Groggy, pretty out of it. But he recognized me. He has no idea what happened."

"Did you talk to the doctor?"

"Briefly. He seemed pleased. Walter had a fever in the night, but it's come down. He says that infection is still the main concern."

"Diana, listen," I said. "I want Wally transferred to Mass General as soon as possible. I'm going to make a few calls. Okay?"

"But—"

"The best medical care in the world is at Mass General. Anyway, I want him near us. And we're not staying here."

"You can go home, Brady. I'll be fine. I'm staying."

"No, you're not. It's not safe."

She was quiet for a minute. "You really don't think it was an accident, do you?"

"Of course it wasn't an accident."

"So you think. . . ?"

"You and I are going to find a motel tonight. Tomorrow we go home. Wait for me there. What do you need me to bring?"

"Brady—"

"We're going to do it my way, Diana."

"Just bring Corky, then."

I caught Doc Adams at his home in Concord. I explained to him what had happened. Doc knows every medical person in eastern Massachusetts and has an affiliation with Mass General. He said he'd handle the whole thing.

He called me back at four o'clock. "It's all arranged," he said. "There's a room waiting for him. They'll bring him by ambulance tomorrow morning."

"I appreciate it."

"I've seen Kinnick's show," said Doc. "He's my kind of guy."

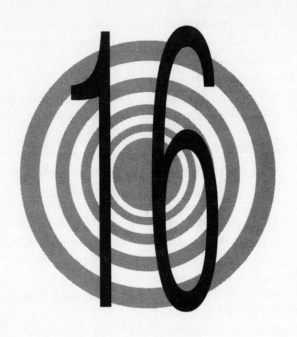

I finally summoned up the nerve to peek in on Wally Sunday morning, just an hour before they were going to load him into the ambulance for his trip to Mass General. They'd cranked his bed into a half-sitting position. He bristled with tubes, just as I'd imagined. Some of them were introducing fluids into him, and others were evacuating them.

I sat down in the chair beside his bed and squeezed his shoulder. "How you feeling?" I said.

"Just pisser." One of the tubes snaked up through his nostril and down his throat. When he talked, it came out as a soft croak.

"Has the sheriff been in to see you?"

Wally rolled his eyes. I guessed it would hurt too much to shrug his shoulders. "Dunno. Been sleeping."

"Did you see anything?"

"Huh?"

"When you were shot."

"Nothing." He closed his eyes for a moment.

"Pain?" I said.

"Comes and goes."

"Who did it, Wally? What do you think?"

"Not SAFE. They're not that stupid."

"Who else, then?"

"Dunno."

I leaned close to him. "You have a suspicion?"

He sighed. "None. Sleepy."

Diana and I waited in Wally's room until they wheeled him out to the ambulance that would take him to Boston. Then she and Corky and I drove back to the cabin. We cleaned up and packed and loaded our cars. Then she climbed into her Cherokee and I got into my BMW, and I followed her down the hill.

When we got to the gravel road, Diana bore left to head back to Cambridge. I impulsively took a right. Saturday's rain had stopped sometime overnight. It was a sparkling Sunday afternoon in May, and I was reluctant to leave the woods and the clean air and the river.

I followed the dirt road that paralleled the Deerfield, crossed the narrow bridge, and pulled into the grassy area where Wally and Diana and I had parked a couple of days earlier. This time there were eight or ten cars there. None of them was a green Volvo wagon with Vermont plates and a Trout Unlimited sticker on the back window.

I didn't bother rigging up. I clambered down the steep path and found a boulder on the water's edge to sit on. From that vantage I could see three anglers casting flies. The one closest to me was a woman. She cast with fluid grace, and it relaxed me to sit and bathe my face in the sunshine and watch her. She was casting to a fish that was rising in a tricky location where the current eddied behind a rock. She changed flies a couple of times, shifted her position, and then I saw a little spurt of water engulf her fly. Her rod arced, and a minute later she knelt by the riverbank and unhooked what looked like a rainbow of fifteen or sixteen inches. She released it gently, stood, and noticed me. She grinned and waved and I waved back to her. Then she waded back into the river.

I sat there for a few minutes longer, then climbed the path to my car. I had found what I'd come here for—that "momentary stay against confusion" that Frost wrote about. Trout rivers—even when I don't fish in them—do that for me.

I got into my car, followed the dirt roads to Route 2, and turned left. I was headed east, back to the city. I kept it below the speed limit. I was in no hurry to get home. Tomorrow I'd have to go to the office. It always amazed me how a few days in jeans and moccasins blunted whatever enthusiasm I had for the practice of law.

Up ahead on the right I saw a sign that read GUNS. Why not? I thought. I pulled into the peastone parking area. Only two other vehicles were there, a blue Ford pickup and an old Buick sedan.

It was a low-slung square dark-shingled building. Hand-printed signs in the window advertised AMMO, BAIT, TACKLE, AND GUNS NEW AND USED.

I climbed the steps and went in. A bell jangled when the door opened. A beagle was sleeping on an old sweatshirt beside a cold woodstove in the corner. He opened his eyes, looked me over, decided I wasn't a rabbit, and closed them again. Two men were leaning toward each other over a glass-topped display case. The one behind it, I figured, ran the place. The other was a customer, or perhaps just a friend in for a chat.

On the wall behind the glass case stood a rack of guns. There must have been forty or fifty of them standing there on their butts. Guns of every description—double-barreled shotguns, pumps, autoloaders, bolt-action rifles, rifles with scopes.

The glass case under the two guys' elbows contained boxes of ammunition and an assortment of handguns.

I glanced around the rest of the place. Against the back wall stood the bait tanks. There was a free-standing rack of spinning and bait-casting rods. Rotating display racks held lures affixed to cardboard, vials of scent, spools of monofilament, hooks, bobbers, swivels, lead weights. There were knives and hunting bows, bowsights and broadheads, canteens and tents and sleeping bags, camouflage suits and boots.

It reminded me of an old-time Five and Ten, with a theme.

I prowled around while the two men talked at the counter. I took a small Buck knife from a shelf, slid it from its sheath, and tested it against the ball of my thumb. I'm a sucker for good knives. I collect them the way some people collect paintings. In fact, a well-made knife to me is beautiful, a work of art. I only actually use two or three of my knives. But I do like to own them.

I continued browsing until the customer left the store. Then I went up to the counter.

"How ya doin'?" he said. He had a bristly black mustache and watery blue eyes. Late thirties, early forties.

"I'd rather be fishing," I said.

He nodded. "Ain't that the truth."

I put the knife on the counter. He picked it up. "Want this one?"

I nodded. "It fills out my collection."

"Buck makes a good knife." He hit some keys on his old-fashioned cash register. "Forty-two bucks. Plus two-ten for the governor."

"Fine," I said. I jerked my head in the direction of the rack of guns. "What kind of rifle would you use for turkeys?" I said.

"Rifle?" He smiled. "No kind, that's what. Get yourself arrested, hunting turkey with a rifle. You want a tight-bored twelve-gauge autoloader for turkey. One of those Remingtons with the thirty-inch barrels, they'll send out a nice tight pattern of number fours. You want to shoot your turkey in the head, which ain't much bigger'n silver dollar. You wanna kill a turkey, you need all the help you can get. Shotgun's the thing for gobblers."

"You wouldn't use a rifle?"

"Not in Massachusetts, unless you want to break the law. Some guys go after turkeys with a bow. Helluva sport, bow and arrow hunting for turkey. You plannin' on goin' after a turkey?"

"I never did it. Sounds like fun." I fumbled in my pockets and brought out one of the empty cartridges I'd found in the woods, the one I'd already handled. I had sealed the other two in a plastic bag, hoping there were fingerprints on them.

I handed the cartridge to the guy. "You wouldn't use one of these for turkey, then, huh?"

He squinted at it for a moment, then handed it back to me. "Very common varmint load, the .223 Remington. Put a good scope on a .223 and it'd probably work real fine on a gobbler. Except, like I say, it's illegal."

"So I'd want a shotgun," I said.

He nodded. "You need camouflage, turkey call, maybe a spread of decoys. I got all that stuff. Also a video that'll teach you how to call. You've gotta know how to call 'em in. Kinda late to get started, actually. Spring season's about over now."

I nodded. "Maybe next year I'll try it." I took out my wallet and handed him my Mastercard. "I'll take this nice Buck knife, anyway."

He ran the card through his machine and gave me the slip to sign.

I peered up at the rack of guns behind him. "How's the market for assault guns these days?" I said.

"A little slow. I've sold maybe three or four this spring."

"If a man wanted to get himself, say, an Uzi . . ."

He shrugged. "No problem. I haven't got one in stock, but I could order it for you. I get 'em on trade-in now and then, too."

"As easy as that?"

He smiled. "So far, that's all there is to it. You want to buy a gun, if I've got what you're after here, you give me money, show me your FID card, and I give you the gun."

"That's it?"

"Yup. That's it."

"Any gun?"

"Any gun you want. If I ain't got it in stock, I can order it for you. Whatever you want."

"Even a military weapon?"

"You bet. Except for full automatic, of course."

"There's no waiting period or anything?"

"Thank God, not yet. Matter of time, I suppose, the way things are going." He cocked his head at me. "You lookin' for an Uzi?"

"Nope. Not today. This knife will do me for today."

He dropped the knife into a bag, and I took it, thanked him, and headed for the door. A table just inside the entrance held a coffee machine and a stack of papers. I picked one up. The SAFE logo was blazoned across the top—a flintlock musket poking through the A in SAFE, and under it the slogan: "The right of the people to keep and bear arms shall not be infringed."

"Can I take one of these?" I said to the guy behind the counter.

"Help yourself. They're free. Just got 'em in Wednesday."

I waved and went out to my car.

When I slid behind the wheel I looked at the four-page newsletter. The front page was taken up by a two-column article with the title, "Another Attack on Gun Owners."

It was written by Gene McNiff, SAFE executive director. I skimmed it. It gave an acutely biased summary of each witness's testimony on the assault-weapon bill, and concluded with a dire warning about the impact the legislation would have, if passed, on the liberties of the American people.

Walt Kinnick's statement before the subcommittee was characterized as a "cynical betrayal."

The second page, and the first column on page three, contained a series of short pieces reporting events at New England rod-and-gun clubs.

The right-hand column on the third page was called "Know Your Enemy."

It was a list, and the words "Brady Coyne" jumped from the middle of it and smacked me in the face.

"The following people," read the lead-in to the list, "want to take your guns away from you. Let them hear from you. Let them know how you feel. Let them know that all of us decent law-abiding gun owners are not going to lay back while they rip up our Constitution."

There were ten of us, complete with our mailing addresses and phone numbers. Walt Kinnick was number one. Second was Marlon Swift (R–Marshfield), the state senator who had chaired the subcommittee before which Wally had testified. Then came the governor of Connecticut, followed by both United States senators from Massachusetts and the congressman from Rhode Island's Second District.

Then, in seventh place, Brady Coyne. Me. Enemy number seven.

Seeing my name there in print made me shiver. I was an actual enemy. I was on a list. Name, phone number, address.

Wally was at the top of the list, and he had nearly been assassinated. Somebody had let Wally know how how he felt. The list, giving his phone number, came out on Wednesday, just two days after the hearing. That's when he began getting phone calls.

SAFE obviously didn't take their enemies lightly.

They shot them.

One week earlier I had never even heard of the Second Amendment For Ever organization. Now my friend had been shot in the stomach, and I was their seventh-ranked enemy.

I wasn't sure I had the courage to be a worthy enemy.

Then I thought, Hell, if they wanted an enemy that badly, they could have me. Like Boston Blackie from the early television days, I was willing to be an enemy of those who made me an enemy.

Blackie had been a friend to those who had no friends, and that suited me, too. Walt Kinnick seemed to be losing a lot of friends.

I glanced at the rest of the names that filled out the list of ten. Eighth was a United States senator from Vermont. Number nine was a congresswoman from Maine. Gun-control advocates, I assumed.

Number ten was Wilson Bailey, the poor guy whose wife and

child had been mowed down in a small-town library near Worcester by an angry man with an assault gun. Wilson Bailey had struck me as an eminently worthy enemy, a man with plenty of courage and conviction. Wilson Bailey might need a friend, too.

As I started up the car and pulled out of the parking area, I thought of the guy behind the counter of the gun shop. Either he hadn't read my name off my credit card, or he hadn't committed the SAFE list to memory. I doubted he'd have been so friendly if he'd realized I was such an important threat to his livelihood, even if I did buy a nice Buck knife from him.

I got all my gear put away and took a short glass of ice cubes and bourbon out onto my balcony to think about it all. A moon sliver hung like a thin slice of honeydew melon over the horizon. I lit a cigarette and sipped from my glass. It was very clear to me that some fanatical member of SAFE had tried to kill Wally. The newsletter had given Wally's phone number and post office box number in Fenwick. The SAFE vigilante had called the number and left his message. A few inquiries of the local shopkeepers and gas station attendants would have directed him to "the Palmer place," Wally's cabin.

Probably it was seeing my own name on that list that led me

to my next conclusion. Or maybe it was irrational. But it seemed eminently likely to me that the same crazy man who shot Wally might have gotten it into his skewed brain to work his way down the list, picking off enemies one by one, to the greater glory of God, Country, and the Second Amendment For Ever.

I'd be number seven, if he got that far.

State Senator Marlon Swift was number two. If my logic was sound, he would be next.

There had been two messages on my machine when I got back from my adventures in the Berkshires. The first was from Doc Adams, Sunday afternoon, advising me that Wally was safely ensconced in a private room at Mass General Hospital. Doc had dropped in on Wally and found him sleeping.

Charlie McDevitt had called, asking for a report on the trout fishing.

There were no anonymous death threats.

Not yet, I thought. It wasn't my turn.

I watched the moon rise for the length of time it took me to finish my drink. Then I went inside. I found the SAFE newsletter, sat at the kitchen table, and punched out the phone number for Senator Marlon Swift's home in Marshfield.

A woman answered. I asked for the senator.

"Who's calling, please?" she said. Her voice was pleasant, neutral, efficient, as if she was used to having strangers call on Sunday evenings and knew how to handle them.

"My name is Brady Coyne," I said. "I'm Walt Kinnick's attorney."

"Who?"

"Walt Kinnick," I said. "He testified before Senator Swift's subcommittee on Monday. If it's not convenient . . ."

"I'll see if he can come to the phone," she said.

A minute later a cautious voice said, "Yes?"

"Senator Swift," I said, "it's Brady Coyne. I'm Walt Kinnick's lawyer."

"Sure," he said. "What can I do for you?"

"Have you seen the latest SAFE newsletter?"

He chuckled. "Yes. Walt Kinnick has supplanted me as their

number-one enemy. Damned disappointing. My constituents want me to be at the top of that list. Gun control is a big issue in my district."

"Did you know that Wally was shot?"

There was a long pause. Then he said, "What did you say?"

"Walt Kinnick was shot. It happened Friday up at his cabin in Fenwick. He's—"

"Is he all right?"

"Yes, I guess he's going to be okay. They transferred him to Mass General this afternoon."

"What do you mean, shot?"

"He was in the woods. They got him in the stomach."

"And you think . . ."

"Senator, Wally was number one on that list. You're number two."

He laughed quickly. "And you, if I recall, Mr. Coyne, are also on the list."

"Yes. I'm seven."

"So you're calling—"

"To warn you, I guess."

"You think there's some nut working his way down the list, is that it? First Kinnick, second me?"

"I don't know. Yes. That occurred to me."

"Mr. Coyne," said Swift, "you'd probably be surprised to know that Gene McNiff and I are good friends."

"As a matter of fact, yes, that surprises me."

"We've worked together on several pieces of legislation. As the chairman of the Subcommmttee on Public Safety, I need the support and advice of men like McNiff."

"But—"

"We disagree on gun control. But we agree on many things."

"I see."

"You're not into politics much, huh?"

"I've read my Machiavelli."

"Well, if you've read old Niccolò carefully, you would understand that Gene McNiff and I are both politicians. He understands my position. I understand his. We respect each other.

He's damn good at what he does." Swift hesitated. "So am I. That's why I keep getting reelected."

"If I remember correctly," I said, "Machiavelli said that it's better to be feared than loved. Maybe SAFE has taken that piece of wisdom to heart."

"Machiavelli also said that politicians should know how to play both the lion and the fox. Gene McNiff's very foxy. No fox would send an assassin after his enemies."

"Well," I said, "I just thought I'd let you know. Wally had a couple of threatening phone calls before they shot him."

"Phone calls, huh?"

"Yes. I heard one of them. The caller said Wally was an enemy of SAFE and deserved to die."

"And you think one of these callers shot him, is that it?"

"It seems pretty obvious. I mean, the sheriff out there thinks it was a hunting accident, but—"

"If you intended to shoot somebody, would you call them first?"

"I don't know what I'd do if I was that crazy. Sure. Maybe I would."

"I've been on the SAFE list for years," said Swift. "No one has taken a shot at me yet."

"You're not concerned, then?"

"Nope. Damned sorry about Walt. But I suspect that sheriff's probably right."

"Well, I'm sorry to bother you, then," I said. "Just figured you might want to know."

"Look, Mr. Coyne. I appreciate the call, and I'm glad it's not a death threat." He chuckled softly. "But listen. Number seven's pretty far down the list, so I don't think you need to be too concerned. They'll catch up with him before he gets that far."

I hung up, feeling vaguely foolish.

Maybe it *was* a hunting accident.

Nah. No way.

I poured one more finger of Jack Daniel's over the half-melted ice cubes in my glass, then pecked out the Wellesley number.

"Hello?" Gloria's voice sounded sleepy.

393

"Wake you up?"

"Oh, Brady. No. I was reading."

"Just to let you know that I'm back."

"You didn't have to." She yawned. "I wasn't worried about you. I mean, you didn't fall in, did you?"

"No."

"Catch lots of fish?"

"A few."

"Well," she said, "that's nice."

"The boys okay?"

"I guess."

"You?"

"I'm fine, Brady. Thank you. Shit."

"What?"

I heard her sigh. "I guess I don't know why you called."

"I just wanted to hear a friendly voice."

"Well, I'm sorry to disappoint you." She hesitated. "I *am* sorry. I would just think, after ten—what is it, almost twelve?—after twelve years . . ."

"We can still be friends," I said.

"We *are* friends. I'm glad you're back safe and sound. Welcome home. I'm sorry I'm grouchy."

"It's fine. Your grouchiness. It's comforting."

She laughed. "Good night, Brady."

"Good night, Gloria."

I hung up and went to bed.

Julie, as expected, had a big backlog of phone calls for me to return, conferences to schedule, and papers to go over. I did all the phone business and took a halfhearted swipe at the papers, and it wasn't until mid-afternoon when I finally got the chance to call state police headquarters at 1010 Commonwealth Avenue.

I asked for Lieutenant Horowitz, expecting I'd have to leave a message for him. But he picked up the phone and growled, "Yeah. Horowitz."

"Coyne," I said.

"I'm busy. We're even. No favors."

"You already know that Walt Kinnick was shot over the weekend, then."

"*What?*"

"Walt Kinnick was—"

"I heard you. Kinnick's the television guy, right? His name's
been in the papers. What happened?"

"You haven't heard."

"For Christ sake, Coyne. If I knew, I wouldn't be asking,
would I?"

"I suppose not."

"So tell me."

I told him.

Horowitz was quiet for a moment after I finished. Then he
mumbled, "It's not our jurisdiction. Local cops. Unless they invite
us in." Another pause, then, "Lemme see what I can find out."

"Sheriff Mason was the one I talked to," I said.

"Mason, huh?"

"From Fenwick, I assume. That's where the cabin is."

"I can figure it out, Coyne."

"I found three spent rifle cartridges in the woods."

"At the scene of the crime, huh?"

"Yes."

"And you gave them to the sheriff, right?"

"No."

"Why the hell not? You trying to obstruct justice, Coyne?"

"Mason thinks it was a hunting accident."

"And you don't, of course."

"No. That's why I'm calling you."

"Thanks a shitload. What the hell do you want me to do?"

"I don't know. Do you want these cartridges or not?"

"It's not my jurisdiction, I told you."

"I know. They're .223 Remington. Varmint load."

He chuckled. "Varmint, eh?"

"Yes. I talked with a guy at a gun shop."

"You at your office now?"

"Yes."

"Got those cartridges with you?"

"Yes."

"I'll have somebody pick them up."

"I'll be here till six or so."

"Okay."

He hung up without saying good-bye. Horowitz wasn't big on formalities.

I stared at the stack of remaining paperwork on my desk. It failed to inspire me. I looked up the number for the Boston legislative office of the senior senator from Massachusetts. A chipper young woman answered. "Senator Kennedy's office. May I help you?"

"I don't suppose I could talk to the senator," I said.

"He's in Washington, sir. If you could tell me what it's about . . ."

"Well, it's sort of personal. Not political or legislative or anything like that."

"The senator's office checks in with us every day," she said. "If you want to leave a message, I'll see that they get it."

"Well, okay," I said. I cleared my throat. "Perhaps the senator is aware that he's number four on the enemies' list of the Second Amendment For Ever. That's the New England gun lobby. I just wanted to alert him to the fact that the man listed number one has been shot, and—"

"Can I have your name and phone number, sir?"

"Sure." I gave them to her.

"Thank you. As you were saying?"

"Well, Walt Kinnick—that's SAFE's enemy number one—he was shot over the weekend. Not killed, but badly hurt. And I just figured that the senator should be, um, aware of it."

"An assassination attempt? Is that what you're saying?"

"I guess so. Yes."

"I'll see that the senator's office gets the message, Mr. Coyne. Thank you."

I called the junior senator's office and conveyed the same message to the enthusiastic young man who answered. He, too, thanked me.

The rest of my fellow enemies, except for Wilson Bailey way down at number ten, were out-of-state politicians. I decided I'd done my good deed for the day and didn't call them.

I sighed and reached for my stack of paperwork.

I was moving semicolons around on a will when Julie buzzed me. "Alexandria Shaw on line one," she said.

"Who?"

"The reporter, Brady."

"Oh, right. Okay." I poked the blinking red button on my telephone console and said, "Brady Coyne."

"Mr. Coyne, it's Alex Shaw from the *Globe*."

"Sure. Hi."

"I'd like another interview. Can we set something up?"

"Boy, I don't know. I've been away, and—"

"I heard about Walt Kinnick. I know he's in Mass General. I know you were there when it happened."

"You must be a helluva reporter," I said. "There's at least one state police lieutenant who didn't know that."

"I am," she said. "I'm a terrific reporter. Look. I think there's an important story here, Mr. Coyne."

I hesitated for a moment, then said, "I do, too."

"I'll buy you a drink."

"One?"

"Sure. Then you can buy me one."

"Fair enough," I said. "Where and when?"

"You know Papa Razzi on Dartmouth Street?"

"Italian, right?"

She laughed. "Good for you. Six-thirty okay?"

"Six-thirty's fine. And Ms. Shaw?"

"Yes?"

"Don't expect too much from me."

"I understand. You're a lawyer. I never expect much from lawyers, Mr. Coyne."

I dictated some letters to Julie. The state trooper arrived right after she left at five. I gave him the plastic bag containing the three spent rifle cartridges I had found in the woods near Wally's cabin and told him that I had not handled two of them so they might get fingerprints off them.

He nodded quickly and said, "Thank you, sir," by which I figured he meant, "We know our job, dummy."

After he left I tried to call Charlie, but he had already left the office.

No one answered at Doc Adams's house.

I stirred legal papers around on top of my desk. After the events of the weekend, practicing law felt frivolous and make-believe. It felt—well, it felt like *practicing,* and I had trouble concentrating on it. I alternated glancing at my watch and swiveling my chair around to gaze out the window behind my desk. The slanting late afternoon sun glowed against the brick buildings and reflected gold on the glass, and I mourned another precious day in May that had been sacrificed to the ungrateful gods of Earning a Living.

On the Deerfield, trout would be eating insects off the surface of the water.

Wally Kinnick lay in a hospital bed, bristling with plastic tubes.

I was willing to bet that somebody, somewhere, was plotting another assassination.

At six-twenty I switched on the answering machine, locked up, and strolled over to Dartmouth Street. I tried to remember what Alexandria Shaw looked like. All I could remember was big round glasses perched low on her nose and her habit of poking at them with her forefinger.

And her legs. She had good legs. I knew better than to remark on them. But I remembered them.

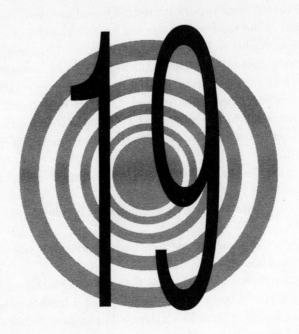

Very good legs, in fact. Smooth, tanned, shapely legs.

The Monday after-work crowd was sparse at Papa Razzi's Trattoria, and I spotted Alexandria Shaw's legs astride a barstool. She was wearing a blue and green print dress. It had ridden up several inches above her knees. She was holding a cigarette in one hand and a whiskey sour glass in the other.

I took the empty stool beside her. "This wasn't taken, I hope," I said.

She turned and smiled at me. "Saving it for you. Had to fight off about a hundred hunky guys." She put her cigarette into an ashtray and held her hand out to me. "Thanks for coming."

I took her hand. "I rarely turn down a free drink," I said. She wasn't wearing her big round glasses. Her eyes were the same blue-green color as her dress. They were widely spaced and tilted slightly upward at the corners. She had high, pronounced cheek-bones.

She smiled. "You're staring at me."

"I almost didn't recognize you," I said. "You're not wearing your glasses."

"The magic of contact lenses."

"I didn't know you were beautiful."

She shrugged. "Beauty usually gets in the way."

I pondered that one. With me, apparently, she did not expect her beauty to get in the way.

The bartender came over and took a cursory swipe in front of me with his rag. "Sir?"

"Bourbon old-fashioned, on the rocks. And another sour for the lady."

"I want to hear all about your adventures," she said.

I remembered my strained Sunday night phone conversation with Gloria. Gloria hadn't wanted to hear anything about my adventures.

Alex Shaw is a reporter, I reminded myself. Not an ex-wife.

"I imagine you do," I said.

She smiled.

"I'm not sure I trust you," I said.

"You're a lawyer, Mr. Coyne. You're not expected to trust any-body. I'll bet you can take care of yourself."

"And you're a reporter, undoubtedly skilled at dealing with people who think they can take care of themselves."

She smiled in an obvious burlesque of seductiveness, lifting her chin and drooping her eyelids. Then she laughed and crossed her eyes. "You're an eyewitness to a murder attempt," she said. "I've already got the facts of the story. But I want . . ." She shook her head. "There's a *real* story here. I don't know if you can help or not."

Our drinks arrived. We clicked glasses. We sipped. She took out a cigarette. I held my Zippo for her. She steadied my hand with hers, dipped her cigarette into the flame, and looked up at me through the smoke she exhaled. I had the sense that Alex

401

Shaw was accustomed to getting men to tell her things, regardless of how well they thought they could take care of themselves.

I snapped the lighter shut and dropped it onto the bar. "What are you trying to do?"

"Interview a source."

"Why didn't you wear your glasses?"

She shrugged.

"You're not going to, um, try to seduce me into saying something I don't want to say, are you?"

"Seduce? Oh, my."

I smiled.

"Make it Alex, okay?"

"Sure. And I'm Mr. Coyne. Fair?"

She rolled her eyes. "Fair."

"Tell me, Alex," I said. "What's your angle?"

"Angle, Mr. Coyne, sir?"

"On gun control. On the Second Amendment For Ever. Are you trying to make a case?"

"A case?" She snorted. "Lawyers make cases. Reporters make stories. I want to know what happens, and why it happens, and who's responsible for it happening, and where it happens, and when. That's it. The story. Gun control? I could give a shit. Honestly. I'm reporter, not a columnist. SAFE? Hey, if they make stories, I love 'em."

"Fill up your space."

"Right," she said. "Survival of the vulgarest."

"Well, you're probably wasting your time with me."

"I seriously doubt it," she said. "Look. Can't we just relax, have a couple drinks, and talk? Like friends? How could that be a waste of time?"

"I don't know anything," I said.

"In that case, you certainly can relax."

I sipped my drink. "I didn't really see anything," I said. "I was inside when I heard the shots. So I—"

"How many shots?"

"I'm not sure. Four or five, maybe. There was one, then a pause, then several in rapid succession. Anyway, I ran outside and we found Wally on the ground in the woods. He'd been hit in the stomach. It looked bad. There was a lot of blood. I really thought he was going to die. Diana ran back in and—"

"Diana?"

"I didn't say that."

"Who's Diana?"

"Goddess of the hunt. Nobody. Forget it."

She shrugged. "Okay. Continue."

"That's it, really. The ambulance came, they took Wally to the hospital in North Adams. He made it through the surgery and now he's in Mass General. It looks like he's going to be okay."

"You didn't see who did it?"

"No."

"Did Kinnick?"

"I don't know."

"What did the police say?"

"To me? Nothing. The sheriff interviewed us. He was clearly going through the motions. He wanted it to be a hunting accident. It's spring turkey season. Popular sport in the Berkshires."

"Who's the sheriff?"

"Guy named Mason. Fenwick, that's the town."

"Hunting accident, you said?"

I shrugged.

"You don't believe that, do you?"

"No."

"Why?"

"They hunt turkeys with shotguns. Wally was shot with a rifle."

"Really?"

"Yes. I found some empty cartridges."

"Do you have them?"

I shook my head. "I turned them over to the authorities."

"That sheriff?"

"No. The state police."

"But they don't have jurisdiction."

"No. Not unless . . ."

"Unless Kinnick dies," she finished.

"Right."

"So what *do* you believe, Mr. Coyne, sir?"

I spread my hands. "It seems obvious."

"Somebody from SAFE, huh?"

"It could be," I said. "That's what I think, but I guess it could be anybody. Someone like Wally, a public figure and all—who knows what nutcakes out there think he's a bad guy?"

"You're both on that enemies' list of theirs."

I touched her wrist. "Look," I said. "You've already got your story. I haven't told you anything you don't already know, or suspect. Am I right?"

"You haven't told me anything. Right."

"I mean, that business about the rifle cartridges . . ."

"What rifle cartridges?" She smiled.

"Exactly," I said. "So when you write your story, there's no reason why I should appear in it."

Her free hand touched mine where it lay on her wrist. She leaned toward me. "Listen, Mr. Coyne. If I've got the chance to interview the victim of an assassination attempt before he's assassinated, it would make one helluva story. Don't you agree?"

I took back my hand and used it to pick up my drink. "One helluva story, indeed," I said. I took a sip. "Maybe you wondered why I agreed to meet with you."

She smiled. "You wanted to see what I looked like without my glasses."

"Actually, I didn't know you were ever without them," I said. "No, I just decided that if it *was* some whacko from SAFE . . ."

"A big newspaper story might get the organization to crack down on its membership."

I nodded. "Something like that, I guess. And it would alert any potential, um, targets."

She tilted her head and gazed at me solemnly. "There seems to be one target who's already alert. Maybe even a little frightened."

"He might not actually admit it," I said. "But it could be true. And you might as well make it Brady, I guess."

She smiled.

"And if you want to talk some more," I said, "maybe we ought to get a table and have some dinner."

"I've got a better idea," she said. "I live just around the corner, on Marlborough Street. Why don't I make something for us?"

"Yeah?"

"Sure."

"You really know how to treat a source," I said.

Her apartment was halfway down the Berkeley-Clarendon block, on the third floor. Tall windows admitted the sun's soft setting afterglow into her living room. Both side walls were lined with floor-to-ceiling bookshelves. There was a big sofa with a patch-work quilt rumpled on top of it, a pair of ummatched leather chairs, a coffee table piled with newspapers and mugs and ash-trays. In the corner stood a scarred cherry dining table with a typewriter and stacks of books on it.

Terri Fiori and Sylvie Szabo, my former loves, both kept messy apartments, I remembered. Hell, I kept a messy apart-ment. And Alexandria Shaw's place was messy.

Gloria, my ex-wife, kept a decidedly unmessy home.

There was probably something significant in that.

A stereo system had its own table by the front windows. Alex flicked it on. Somebody was playing the saxophone. It could have been Stan Getz.

She took my hand and led me into the kitchen. She waved at a cabinet. "Booze," she said. "Help yourself. I want to liberate myself from panty hose."

I found a bottle of Old Grand-Dad, a glass, and a tray of ice cubes in a freezer that needed defrosting. I made a drink and took it back to the living room so I could study her library.

It was a random collection, randomly organized. I found noth-ing on the subject of fly fishing. The closest thing was a paper-back entitled *Breeding Tropical Fish*. I took it to the front window and stood there looking at the pictures and sipping my drink.

Her cold hand on the back of my neck made me jump. I turned around. She had changed into a white T-shirt advertising the Walk for Hunger and black sweat pants. Her feet were bare.

She reached up and tugged at my necktie. "If you don't get comfortable I'll feel obliged to wrestle my panty hose and bra back on," she said.

I took off my tie and jacket and handed them to her. She tossed them onto the sofa.

She tiptoed up and kissed my chin. "That's better." She turned and went into the kitchen, trailing behind her the scent of soap. "Hope you like pasta," she called back over her shoulder.

A red candle burning in an old wine bottle. Fresh plum tomatoes and onion slivers, boiled down into a sauce, poured over linguini, and sprinkled with grated Parmesan cheese and dill. Sliced cucumber with a few drops of vinegar and fresh basil. Two bottles of chianti.

The dill gave the pasta an eccentric flavor. I liked it.

Alex Shaw was thirty-seven, never married. "Sequentially monogamous," was how she put it. Her relationships tended to end when the man of the moment wanted to move in with her, or wanted her to give up her own place to live with him. "That's how I know it's not going to work permanently," she told me after we had taken the second bottle of chianti to the sofa. "I figure, if giving up my space doesn't feel right, then there's no future in the relationship."

"And now?"

She smiled. "That's *not* why I called you."

"Nobody?"

She shook her head.

"Me neither," I said.

She looked at me for a moment. "You've been divorced for twelve years," she said softly. "Two boys. William, a junior at U Mass. Joseph, senior at Wellesley High. Ex-wife, Gloria, professional photographer. One-man law office, catering to prominent wealthy Bostonians. Mostly family law and probate. Avid trout fisherman. You once shot and killed a man."

"He was—"

"He was a criminal. You were not charged."

"Alex—"

She burrowed her head against my shoulder. "I'm a good reporter, Mr. Coyne, sir," she mumbled into my chest.

I stroked her hair. "I'm still not sure I trust you," I said.

"Does that mean you won't kiss me?"

"It means that's all I'll do."

And I did.

And as difficult as it was, that was all I did.

After the noontime recess on Tuesday, I took a cab from the courthouse in East Cambridge over to Mass General. Wally had a private room with a view of an air shaft. A vase of spring flowers sat on the table beside his bed. A television on an adjustable shelf flashed silent color pictures overhead.

His bed was cranked up under his knees and behind his head, folding him into the shape of an N. A plastic tube was trickling clear fluid into the back of his hand. His eyes were closed.

I poked his shoulder. "Hey, are you awake?" I whispered.

He opened his eyes, blinked once, and focused on me. "What time is it?" he croaked.

"Noon."

"Day?"

"Tuesday."

"City?"

"Boston."

"Correct." He grinned. "You win another spin at the wheel."

"So how're you feeling," I said, "aside from that chronic pain in the ass?"

He hunched his shoulders and rotated his head. He winced, then smiled quickly at me. "They wake you up every three hours to shove things into your orifices and then they ask you how it feels. With a thermometer in your mouth, all you can do is mumble, which is what they want to hear, because they don't like to know that your worst problem is all the gadgets they're sticking into you. All I want is a good night's sleep. I try to sneak in naps between interruptions. Mainly, I feel tired, Coyne. Other than that, I just feel stupid."

"Huh?"

"I can't keep track of things. I can't tell whether I'm awake or asleep. I have dreams."

"Drugs, huh?"

"I guess." He yawned. "You just missed Diana, I think."

"You think?"

"She was here. Or else I dreamed it. Or else it was yesterday." He grinned through his beard. "A certain part of it I dreamed, I'm pretty sure, because I don't think I really jumped her. I'm not used to being tethered to a bed."

I pulled a wooden chair up next to him, turned it around, and straddled it. I rested my forearms on the back. "What do you remember about it?" I said.

"It?"

"Your . . . accident."

"The last thing I remember is kissing Diana and taking Corky into the woods. He got to chase a rabbit, and we flushed a grouse." He shrugged.

"You don't recall hearing anything or seeing anything."

"No."

"When we found you, you said, 'They got me.'"

"They?"

"That's what you said."

He shrugged. "I don't remember seeing anything."

"Are you sure?"

He turned his head and glowered at me. "Jesus, Coyne."

"I'm sorry, Wally."

"Enough of the fucking interrogation."

"Okay. I just hoped maybe we could figure it out. You do know what happened."

"Sure. I got bushwhacked."

"Have you thought about it?"

He grinned crookedly. "In what the nurses quaintly call my 'moments of lucidity,' it's about all I do think about."

"Somebody tried to kill you, you know."

"Sure. I know." He cocked his head at me. "Have you and I already discussed this?"

I nodded. "Sort of. Back when you were in North Adams. You were heavily sedated."

"What'd I say?"

"You said, as I recall, that you were sleepy."

"I didn't mention anybody then?"

"No. The sheriff out there is calling it a hunting accident, you know."

He smiled. "A hunting accident."

"Yes. He thinks a turkey hunter let off some wild shots in the woods that you got in the way of."

"Sure," he said. "That's probably what happened."

"You don't believe that."

"Of course not." He reached up, grimaced, and adjusted the pillow behind his neck. "I don't believe much of anything, Brady. But here's what I think. I think if *anybody* was hit by a stray bullet, the first thing he'd do would be to try to figure out all the people who'd have a motive to murder him. And he'd sure as hell come up with a few names, and then he'd feel better about it, because, when you think about it, accidents are a helluva lot scarier than murders."

"In this case," I said, "I personally would prefer it if what happened to you was an accident."

He grinned. "Sure. Because if it was, it'd mean nobody would be after you."

"You know about the SAFE enemies' list, then."

He jerked his head at the vase of flowers. "Gene McNiff sent them. A copy of the newsletter came with them."

"By way of reinforcing the threat?"

Wally smiled. "Nah. By way of telling me it wasn't them."

"What do you think?"

"I don't think McNiff had anything to do with it."

"But somebody else from SAFE?"

He tried to shift his position in the bed. The effort caused him to bite his bottom lip.

"Pain?" I said.

He nodded. "Listen," he said. "I don't like the idea of an accident. I mean, random things just—happen. People invented a wrathful God to account for randomness, because the most arbitrary, vengeful God of man's imagination is easier to accept as a cause than—than no cause at all. We want logic, motive, cause and effect, purpose. Without purpose, life is chaotic and meaningless. Nobody likes to think that bullets fly randomly around the woods hitting people who happen to be in the way. It's a hell of a lot more comforting to believe in rational explanations than in randomness. Having an enemy out gunning for you—at least it makes a kind of sense. If things just happen randomly, that means they're out of our control and the world's crazy. Nobody likes that."

"Thank you Sören Kierkegaard." I smiled at him. "You *have* been doing some thinking."

"It's the best thing to do with a moment of lucidity."

"So you don't *want* it to've been an accident. Does that mean you *believe* you have an enemy who wants to kill you?"

Wally chuckled. "That's not especially comforting, either, is it?"

"You were shot with a rifle, not a shotgun, you know."

"It felt like a bazooka."

"It was a rifle. I found some empty cartridges not far from where you were hit. They were .223 Remington."

"Varmint load," he muttered. "Were they fresh?"

I shrugged. "I don't know."

He shook his head. "I just don't think SAFE was behind this."

"You think it *was* a hunting accident?"

"I kinda believe in randomness," he said, "even if I don't like it."

"But you said, 'They got me.' I assumed you meant SAFE."

He shrugged. "I don't know what I was thinking. I don't remember seeing anything."

"What about their enemies' list? You're number one. Hey, I made seventh place myself. Seems to me some whacko out there sees that, figures he's going to answer the call."

He frowned at me. "Work his way down the list, you mean? Is that what you think?"

I shrugged.

"You were thinking of those phone calls," he said.

"Sure. That one I heard. He sounded pretty serious."

"He'd have to bump off a couple of United States senators to get to you, you know."

"I know. I was thinking he might skip over the hard targets. Paranoid, huh?"

Wally reached over and squeezed my arm. "Shit, Brady. I'm sorry I dragged you into this."

"Yeah. Me, too."

"Jesus, though," he said. "It'd be incredibly stupid for SAFE to send out a hit man to shoot their enemies."

"Of course it would. I doubt that they voted on it in executive session, took nominations, elected an assassin. I just figure there's one warped mind out there somewhere . . ."

"I don't know." Wally squeezed his eyes shut and sighed. "I'm sorry I can't shed more light on this, Brady. All this thinking's hurting my head. This moment of relative lucidity is deserting me."

"Okay." I stood up, then leaned over and gripped his shoulder. "I'll be back."

"Good. We can do more philosophy."

"I'll see what I can find out."

"Track down that turkey shooter."

I got back to the office around one-thirty. Julie was on the phone. I poured myself some coffee and sat on the edge of her desk to sip it. When she hung up, she said, "Where've you been?"

"I visited Wally after court."

"How is he?"

"He seemed pretty good. We had a long philosophical discussion. He's out of ICU, so I guess that means he's coming along."

"Want me to have some flowers sent over?"

"I don't think Wally's the flowers type. I'll bring him a book next time I see him."

I spent most of the afternoon on the phone, with frequent visits to the coffee urn, and it was nearly five when Julie poked her

413

head in. "Lieutenant Horowitz has arrived and I am departing," she said.

"Horowitz is here?"

"Yes. And I'm out of here."

I blew her a kiss. "Send him in."

He was wearing a green blazer with gold buttons over a pale blue button-down shirt, chino pants, loafers. No tie. He was working on a wad of bubble gum, as usual.

He didn't offer to shake hands. Horowitz wastes little time on ceremonies. He went over to the sofa and sat down.

"You want some coffee?" I said.

"Julie offered me some. I declined. Can't chew gum and drink coffee at the same time."

"Nasty habit, that gum."

"So you keep telling me."

"You'll get yourself a case of TMJ."

"Yeah." He grinned. "I keep trying cigarettes. But I'm hooked on the gum."

I sat across from him. "What's up?"

"Nothing, basically. Which bothers me. I talked to a friend of mine at the headquarters in Springfield. Like I told you, it's not a state police case. They got a report from the local cops, who're calling it a hunting accident. No suspects. Presumably they're investigating it. The local guy, this sheriff . . ."

"Mason," I said.

Horowitz shrugged. "He interviewed the witnesses, which were you and the lady and the victim, and none of you saw anything, and he went up and looked around the crime scene, which had already been rained on by the time he got there and where he didn't see anything, and when you cut through all the bullshit in those reports, he got nothing."

"You came all the way over here to tell me this?" I said.

"I *didn't* come all the way over here. I had some business downtown. So I was already over here, figured I'd drop in. You know, out of deep and abiding friendship, all that shit. Listen, Coyne. This stinks, as you know. There's thousands of guys out there who confuse their guns with their peckers and who've most likely decided that Walt Kinnick is trying to emasculate them. It doesn't take a particularly vivid imagination to build scenarios."

"That's what I've been doing," I said. "Building scenarios."

"You don't buy the hunting accident theory, either, huh?"

"Of course not. It's stupid."

"Figure it this way," said Horowitz. "Our guy sneaks up on the cabin like he used to sneak up on VC villages and never quite got it out of his system. Turkeys are okay, but the rush just isn't the same, right? I mean, Kinnick is the first certified enemy he's had in twenty-five years. So he scouts it out, learns Kinnick's habits, knows he goes for a walk first thing in the morning. Same basic route every day. We're all creatures of habit. So our assassin lays in wait, and . . ." He shrugged.

"That's more or less how I see it," I said. "It's pretty obvious it wasn't any accident. The question is, who's the shooter?"

Horowitz rubbed his chin with the palm of his hand. "Those cartridges you gave me?"

"Yeah?"

"Proves it was no turkey hunter. They use shotguns."

I nodded. "I knew that."

"You were thinking an Uzi or something?"

I shrugged. "An assault gun of some kind. Yes, that occurred to me."

"Not an Uzi. An Uzi takes 9 millimeter. The .223 Remington is a 5.56 millimeter load. The 5.56 works in an FNC Paratrooper, a Valmet, a Beretta AR-70, a Galil Model 223 AR, a Steyr AUG-SA, though. There's some others."

"Are those what they sound like they are?"

He nodded. "Semiautomatic paramilitary weapons. Assault guns. But before you get all excited, keep in mind that the .223 is a common varmint load. Winchester and Remington, among others, make rifles chambered for the .223. They probably hunt varmints up in those hills, but they don't use varmint rifles for turkey hunting."

"Whatever kind of gun it was," I said, "it was no accident. Find any fingerprints on those cartridges?"

He shook his head. "A few smudges. Nothing useful."

I shrugged. "Too bad."

"These shots," said Horowitz. "They came close together? Like about as fast as a person could pull the trigger?"

I nodded. "There was one shot, then a pause, then several. Yes, about as fast as you could pull the trigger. Like a semiautomatic."

"All the lab could tell us," he said, "was that the same gun fired those three cartridges. They can't tell us anything about the gun. Of course, if they had the gun, they could match it with the marks of the firing pin and the ejectors on those cartridges." He pushed himself to his feet. "Well, anyhow, it's all academic," he said. "Unless the local cops want to invite the state cops in, it's their case. Of course, if Kinnick should die . . ."

"Then it would be your case."

"Right. Then it would be a homicide. We've got plenty of cases already. Probably not worth it, having him die."

"Probably not," I said.

I was watching the ball game that evening when my intercom buzzed. "What's up, Tony?" I said into it.

"There's a couple of people here who want to see you, Mr. Coyne."

"Who are they?"

I heard a murmur of voices. Then Tony said, "They told me to tell you it's government business."

"Shit," I said. "The IRS this time of night?"

"I don't think they're IRS, Mr. Coyne."

"Well, in that case I guess you can send them up."

"They're on their way."

A couple of minutes later there was a discreet knock on my door. I padded stocking-footed to it and opened up. A man and a woman stood there. He wore a conservative gray business suit with a blue tie. She wore a green pants suit. She appeared to be in her mid-thirties. He was a few years younger. They had grim faces, trim bodies, and short haircuts. They could have been big sister and little brother, and I thought for just a moment that they were handing out copies of *The Watchtower*.

"Special Agent Krensky," said the woman. "This is Agent Tilson."

She held up a leather folder and let it fall open. I squinted at it. The words "Secret Service" jumped out at me.

"You sure you've got the right apartment?" I said.

"You're Brady Coyne?"

I nodded.

"May we come in?" she said.

"Sure."

I stepped aside. They hesitated, so I turned and walked back into my living room. They closed the door and followed behind me.

"Want some coffee or something?"

"No, thank you," said Agent Krensky.

"Have a seat." I gestured at the sofa.

"That's all right, thanks."

So the three of us stood there in the middle of my living room. I reached over and turned off the volume on the television. The Sox had a one-run lead in the eighth, and I figured I could at least keep an eye on the action.

"So what can I do for you?" I said.

"We take all assassination threats very seriously," she said.

"Oh well—"

"You *are* the Brady Coyne who called Senator Kennedy's office on Monday?"

"Yes."

"And you did leave a message threatening him with an assassination attempt."

"Yes. Well, no, not exactly. You see—"

They were both staring at me.

"Oh, Jesus," I said. I began to laugh. Neither Agent Krensky nor Agent Tilson so much as smiled. I took a deep breath. "Look. I didn't threaten the senator. I *warned* him. I called Senator Kerry's office, too. They're on an enemies' list, and the person at the top of that list has already been shot. So I was trying to be a good citizen."

"You didn't threaten the senator?" This was Agent Tilson, speaking for the first time.

417

"Shit, no. What did that girl tell you, anyway?"

The two of them exchanged glances that defied interpretation. Then Krensky said, "What's this enemies' list?"

"Hang on. I'll show you." I went over to my rolltop desk. Tilson followed right behind me. I rummaged among the papers until I found the SAFE newsletter. I handed it to Tilson.

He turned it over to Krensky, who frowned at it and then arched her eyebrows at me. "You better explain," she said.

So I explained about SAFE and Wally's testimony, the confrontation in Dunkin' Donuts and the phone calls Wally had received. I told them about how Wally got shot in the stomach and how he was doing okay at Mass General. I told them that, personally, I found it a bit unnerving to be on that enemies' list, and I figured that the senator might want to know that he was on it, too.

Agents Krensky and Tilson shrugged at each other. "How about that coffee, Mr. Coyne?" said Krensky. "Is it already brewed?"

I poured three mugs of coffee, and we sat in the living room sipping it. "Didn't figure you for an assassin," said Tilson. "Nothing in your files."

"You've got files on me?"

He smiled. "Why, sure."

"But you know the senator's history," added Krensky. "And that of his family. The word 'assassination' sends up a red flag, as you can imagine."

"That girl I talked to must've garbled my message."

She shrugged. "If it's any comfort to you, Mr. Coyne, you should know that the senator's name is on many enemies' lists. SAFE is only one of them. We've investigated the organization very thoroughly, of course. They are under constant surveillance. There is absolutely no hint of subversion or conspiracy or any illegal activity whatsoever."

"Plenty of paranoia, though," I said. "Hell, they publish a list of enemies and distribute it to guys with guns. What do they expect? It doesn't need to be the organization. It could be an individual. A vigilante. Some nutcake acting on his own."

She nodded. "We take these things very seriously, I assure

418

you. This—um, this incident with Mr. Kinnick—we'll certainly see that it's followed up." She paused to sip her coffee. "I expect that Mr. Kinnick does have his enemies. Perhaps one of them learned that he is on the SAFE list and figured that suspicion would fall on them."

"I thought of that," I said.

"I assume the local police are investigating."

"Yeah, the sheriff out there in Fenwick is all over the case." She smiled.

"You should talk with Lieutenant Horowitz. He's with the state police. Friend of mine."

"Sure," she said.

"Look, if you think I'm overreacting—"

"No," she said. "You're not. And neither are we. You should always react. Ninety-nine percent of the time there's nothing to it. But if you react quickly and alertly at that one-hundredth time you can prevent a tragedy."

While Krensky talked, Tilson casually picked up his mug and began wandering around my apartment. Somehow I didn't think he was studying my decor or admiring my profoundly untidy housekeeping habits. No, he was taking inventory, applying his training, drawing inferences about my character and stability from what he saw, comparing all the pieces of evidence with the classic assassin profiles he'd studied.

And it suddenly occurred to me that these Secret Service agents were trained to mistrust people, and they knew exactly how to handle people whom they mistrusted. Chat with them. Be friendly. Sip coffee with them. Make them drop their guard. Get them talking. See what they reveal.

It gave me a small insight into paranoia.

"You believe me, don't you?" I said.

"About what, Mr. Coyne?" said Krensky.

"That I wasn't threatening the senator."

"You weren't, were you?"

"Of course not."

"Why shouldn't we believe you?"

"You *should* believe me. My friend was nearly killed."

She smiled. "Of course," she said. Then she plunked her mug

down onto the coffee table. As if that was a cue, Tilson came back and put his mug down, too. Krensky stood up. So did I. We walked to the door.

Krensky turned and held out her hand. "We're sorry to disturb your evening, Mr. Coyne."

"That's okay. It's good to know you folks are on the ball."

I shook Tilson's hand, too.

"We'll keep in touch," he said.

For some reason, that struck me as ominous.

I spread open the Wednesday *Globe* on my desk and found Alex
Shaw's story on page twelve.

The headline read, KINNICK SHOOTING CALLED HUNTING ACCI-
DENT.

> Local police in the western Massachusetts community
> of Fenwick have no suspects in the shooting that left
> Walt Kinnick, the famous sportsman and television per-
> sonality, hospitalized with a gunshot wound.
>
> Kinnick was shot in the abdomen early Friday morn-
> ing at his Berkshire retreat. Visiting with him at the time
> were his attorney, Brady L. Coyne of Boston, and his

friend Diana West, of Cambridge. Neither witness could be reached for comment.

"It's spring turkey season," said Sheriff Vinton Mason in a prepared statement. "Kinnick's cabin is right in the middle of some good turkey country. Our office is attempting to determine who was hunting in that area on Friday."

Ironically, four days prior to the incident Kinnick testified on Beacon Hill in favor of legislation that would restrict the ownership and use of certain paramilitary firearms known as "assault weapons." Kinnick's testimony opposed that of the Second Amendment For Ever (SAFE) pro-gun lobby, with whom Kinnick was thought to be allied. Subsequently, the bimonthly SAFE newsletter ranked Kinnick number one on its list of "enemies."

Kinnick is the host of the cable television program "Walt Kinnick's Outdoors" and a prominent environmental activist.

I smiled after I read it. Alex's use of the word "ironically" was inspired. Otherwise, her piece was a model of journalistic objectivity. Just the facts.

And yet she had managed to plant the implication that Sheriff Mason was either a dumb hick law officer or a clever obfuscator, that Diana and I had seen something, and that SAFE had powerful motives to kill Wally.

Or maybe I was giving Alex too much credit. It was just a small news item on page twelve. It gave the who, what, where, and when of it without editorializing about the why.

No. That "ironically" made all the difference.

Besides, I knew that Alex lusted to learn the "why" of the story.

She lusted, I recalled, quite literally. It had been a sensational kiss.

She called me in the middle of the morning. "Did you see it?" she said.

"Yes. Loved that 'ironically.'"

She laughed. "I rather liked it myself. My boss is bullshit that he didn't catch it. Listen. I'm on the fly, but I've got a proposition."

"Okay. Shoot."

"Jesus, Brady, don't say that."

"Sorry."

"I've set up an interview with Gene McNiff—you know, SAFE's executive director?—for tomorrow afternoon. I'd love some company."

"Moral support, you mean."

"No," she said. "Your company. I don't need moral support, or any other kind. I'm supposed to meet him at the SAFE headquarters in Clinton at four."

"I don't know, Alex. I'm a big enemy of theirs. I would think my presence could make for a rather hostile interview."

She chuckled. "I thought of that. It wouldn't hurt."

"I thought you just wanted company."

"I do. It's a pretty drive out there in the spring. Lots of apple orchards. Maybe they'll be in blossom now. Tell you what. I'll buy you dinner afterward."

"Four o'clock, huh?"

"I'll pick you up around three."

"Okay."

"Good. See you tomorrow, then."

"Hey, Alex?"

"Yeah?"

"Thanks."

"For what?"

"For how you handled the story."

"I couldn't very well not mention you or Ms. West at all. I corroborated everything, of course."

"I understand."

"I left out those cartridges you found. But that's because nobody at State Police headquarters would talk to me and corroborate it."

"Which," I said, "comes as no surprise to this reporter."

"And," she added, "I did omit the fact that you're on their enemies' list. That's what you mean."

"Yes. I don't need that."

"The last thing I want, Mr. Coyne, sir, is people shooting at you. I've got other things in mind for you."

"Yeah," I said. "So do I."

"Tomorrow at three, then."

In the middle of the afternoon, Julie buzzed me. "Brady," she said, "Senator Swift's office is on line three."

"Okay," I said.

"Hey!" she said quickly.

"Yes?"

"What's this all about?"

"Well, shit, I don't know. Let me talk to him, okay?"

"You don't have to bite my head off."

"I'm sorry," I said.

"You'll keep me informed?"

"Of course. You're the boss, remember?"

I punched the blinking button on the console and said, "Brady Coyne."

"Mr. Coyne," came a male voice, "this is Senator Swift's office."

"Yes?"

"The senator wonders if you'd be able to meet with him."

"Why?"

"He'd rather discuss that with you himself, Mr. Coyne. If at all possible, he'd like to get together with you at the Commonwealth Club at six this evening. Does that work for you?"

"The Commonwealth Club . . ."

"It's on Berkeley Street, sir. Just around the corner from—"

"I know where it is," I said.

"Six o'clock, then?"

"Sure."

The Commonwealth Club is one of those exclusive anachronisms that continue to thrive in Boston: a private men's club, membership rigidly restricted. WASPs only. Republican WASPs. Wealthy Republican WASPs, preferably those whose fathers and grandfathers were also wealthy Republican WASPs.

Because my clientele is skewed to the wealthy, it also tends to be skewed to Republican WASPs with inherited money. I've been inside several anachronisms like the Commonwealth Club. I'd rather have a beer at Skeeter's, but business is sometimes business.

Senator Marlon Swift and I did share membership in a different, even more exclusive, club: the SAFE Top Ten Enemies' club. It gave me a fraternal feeling for the senator. So I would endure the oppressive leather furniture polished by generations of wealthy Republican WASP backsides, the mahogany woodwork stained dark from a century of Cuban cigar smoke, the dusty martinis and the baked finnan haddie served by murmuring old butlers in full livery, and all the dour old bankers and brokers reading their *Wall Street Journals* at the Commonwealth Club to meet with Brother Swift.

When I told Julie I had an audience with Senator Swift at the Commonwealth Club, she arched her eyebrows and said, "Well, la-dee-da."

That's about how I felt about it.

I'd agreed to meet the senator at six, but I waited until six-fifteen to lock up the office for the ten-minute stroll over to the Commonwealth Club. It's not my habit to be late for appointments. Julie thinks it's important to keep people waiting, on the theory, probably sound, that it puts them at a psychological disadvantage. I sometimes defer to her judgment, but I don't agree with it. It's a game. I don't like to think of my law practice as a game.

But in the case of my engagement with Senator Marlon Swift, I wanted him to be there when I arrived, because I didn't feel like having to wait for him. I didn't know if he subscribed to the same theory Julie did. In my experience, the more important a man

426

thinks he is, the more likely he is to play the keep-'em-waiting game.

Politicians generally think they're pretty important.

A small brass plate over the doorbell read "The Commonwealth Club." Elegantly understated. I pressed the buzzer. A shriveled-up little man with sharp blue eyes pulled open the door a moment later. He was wearing a tuxedo that hung a little loosely on him. He appeared to be at least eighty years old. "Sir?" he said, looking me up and down.

"Brady Coyne," I said. "Senator Swift is expecting me."

"Of course."

He stood aside for me. I walked into the foyer, which was as big as my entire apartment. White Italian marble, dark wood wainscoting, textured wallpaper, massive oil portraits, brass sconces, and a crystal chandelier.

I looked around appreciatively. "Pretty nice," I said to the old guy.

His eyes twinkled, but all he said was, "Yes, sir. Right this way, please."

I figured the butler lived in a triple-decker in Southie and had been taking the T over here to his job every day for the past fifty years. If he answered the door, he sure as hell wasn't a member. Probably an Irish Democrat. I wanted to ask him about himself, but he had already begun to lead me through the foyer and into the spacious sitting area.

Leather furniture, dark woodwork, subdued lighting, exactly as I had imagined. Some of the chairs were occupied with men smoking and drinking and studying newspapers. Television sets glowed silently here and there, tuned to a cable channel that flashed Dow Jones numbers. What conversation I heard was soft and conspiratorial.

On the back wall a large window with tiny panes overlooked a small courtyard. Senator Marlon Swift sat in a leather chair gazing out at the tidy gardens.

"Senator?" said the butler.

He looked up, saw me, and pushed himself to his feet. "Mr. Coyne," he said, extending his hand. "Thank you for coming on such short notice. What will you drink?"

427

I shook his hand. I was tempted to ask for a Bud, no glass necessary, but decided I had no reason to offend. "Jack Daniel's on the rocks, please," I said.

The old butler made a tiny bow and left. The senator gestured to the chair opposite his. I sat, and he did, too.

"Another beautiful spring day," he said.

I smiled and nodded.

"Sox are off to a good start this year."

"Yes," I said.

"How's Walt doing?"

"He seems to be out of danger. It was touch and go for a while."

He nodded. "Good. Nice guy, Walt. I've fished with him, you know. His friend Ms. West worked with me on some legislation a while back. His testimony last week was courageous. Didn't really surprise me, though. Walt's a straight shooter." Swift glanced at me and grinned. "Poor figure of speech, I guess."

I smiled and waited.

He shifted uncomfortably in his chair. He was, I guessed, about my age. He didn't look particularly senatorial. His sandy hair was thinning on top, and he wore dark-rimmed glasses. He was a little shorter than me, on the thin side. "Um, Brady," he began. "Can I call you Brady?"

"Sure."

He grinned shyly. "My friends call me Chip."

"Okay."

"This is difficult," he said.

I shrugged and waited.

"I live in Marshfield, and—oh, thank you, Albert."

The old butler set my drink on the table beside me. I looked up at him. "Thanks," I said.

"Sir?" he said to Swift.

"Not now, thanks."

After Albert had slid away, the senator leaned back in his chair and stared out the window. Without looking at me, he said, "You and I have some mutual friends, Brady. They speak highly of you. They say you're a man of your word. You can be trusted."

I said nothing.

"Discreet," he said. "That's the word they all use. 'Brady Coyne is discreet,' they tell me."

"I'm also a pretty good lawyer."

"Um." He turned his head. "They say that, too. Brady, I want to share something with you."

"And you want me to give you my word that I won't tell anybody what you're going to tell me."

"Yes. Exactly."

"You're not my client, Senator. Privilege is not operative."

"I know. Your word is good enough."

"I think I know what you're going to tell me," I said. "You're putting me on the spot."

He shrugged. "I understand that. My choice is not to tell you. I just figure that you're the one person who can use what I have to say—"

"Without involving you," I finished.

"That's it."

"Okay." I nodded. "You've got my word."

He held his hand out to me and I shook it. Then he returned his gaze to the courtyard outside the window. "I commute from Marshfield," he said quietly. "I own a real estate office down there. My brother runs it. My, um, my Senate duties occupy me. But I drive up and back every day, because I love the peacefulness of the country." He shrugged. "It's not exactly rural, but the air smells of salt and you can see the stars at night. I have several acres that abut conservation land, and every evening, regardless of what time I get home, I change into my running togs and take my two setters out for a slow jog through the fields and woods." He smiled, still looking out at the courtyard. "I don't pretend that it really keeps me in shape. But it cleans out my head."

"Senator—"

"Chip," he said. "Please. Anyway, it was after sundown before I got out with the dogs last night, and we had nearly finished our run, when . . ."

He turned and looked at me, and I saw the fear in his eyes.

"They tried to shoot you," I said.

"Christ, yes," he said. "I was in the Army, Brady. I know a gunshot when I hear it, and my reflexes took over. I fell to the ground and flattened myself out. It was only an instant, and then it was over. There were several rapid shots. I heard them zipping through the trees over my head. Then I heard someone running through the woods. I lay there a long time after I couldn't hear him anymore."

"Did you call the police?"

"Hell, no."

"Don't you think you should have?"

He nodded. "Of course I should have. But I didn't. And I won't. That's why I'm telling you. I'm not sure I can explain it to you."

"You really don't have to explain anything to me, Chip. But if somebody took a potshot at you . . ."

"I know. You're on that list, too."

I shrugged.

He smiled. "Politics is a complicated business, Brady. I have nothing to gain, and much to lose, if this—this assassination attempt were to become known."

"I don't understand."

"Like I said. It's complicated. My subcommittee reported favorably on that assault-weapon bill. Mine was the deciding vote. My record on gun control remains unblemished."

"You support it?"

"Yes. Always. My constituents support gun control. So, therefore, do I. I'm in a powerful position. Chairman of the Senate Subcommittee on Public Safety." He shrugged. "SAFE is more powerful than me, though. As I mentioned to you on the phone the other night, I work with them. Their influence is very important to many of the public safety issues that come before my subcommittee. On the subject of gun control, however, I've been at odds with them for years. They always get their way."

"I still don't see—"

"I had a phone call on my machine yesterday when I got home."

"Just one?"

He shook his head. "I've had plenty of phone calls in my career. Many of them hostile. But yesterday's was—it was different."

"What did he say?"

"Well, it was a death threat. He mentioned SAFE. But it wasn't so much the content of it. It was the tone and the syntax."

"Calm," I said. "Cool. Intelligent. Articulate. Not what you'd expect from a gun-crazy fanatic."

"Why, yes," he said. He arched his eyebrows and peered at me for a moment. Then he smiled and nodded. "Exactly. Cool and articulate. Which made it sound—more frightening."

"I hope you saved the tape."

The senator rolled his eyes. "I'm afraid not."

"Walt Kinnick had a message like the one you describe the night before he was shot," I said. "He didn't save that one, either."

He nodded. "We both blew it. Too bad. Anyway, I don't want any publicity on this. I'm telling you because—well, you were thoughtful enough to call and warn me, and you already know what's going on, and you might be able to use the information. And you've given me your word. I've got plenty of enemies, Brady. I guess every politician does. As far as I'm concerned, SAFE is just one of them. Listen. There isn't a politician alive— even an insignificant state senator—who doesn't think about assassination. It's a disease. A communicable disease. The virus is spread through the newspapers, on television. I'm not just concerned about myself—though God knows I'm frightened. Two United States senators, others, are on that list."

"I'm on that list," I said.

"Exactly."

"That's why you wanted to see me?"

"Yes. To tell you that it would appear your fears are well founded. Walt Kinnick, now me. Number one, then number two. To warn you to be careful."

"You should have told the police."

He shrugged. "Maybe. It was a judgment call. If the police know, the newspapers will pick it up thse way they did with the Kinnick thing. With no witnesses, no suspect, no evidence at all . . ."

"Your image, huh?" I said.

"Yes, I suppose so. My image. The war hero. The man who stands up to powerful special interests such as SAFE. The man with the balls to say no. The man of courage and conviction. The

431

man who—figuratively, of course—dares his enemies to take their best shot. That's my image." He smiled. "It's not necessarily *me*, mind you. But I've got an election coming up next fall. The polls are okay. I don't want to upset them."

"Appearances," I said. "Machiavelli. You don't actually need to be brave. But it must appear that you are."

He nodded. "Yes. That's politics. Do you understand?"

I shrugged. "It doesn't really matter if I understand. Personally, I'd just as soon see that our shooter gets nailed. The sooner the better."

"I know. That's why I feel I must apologize to you. I'd like to see him nailed, too. I didn't like lying there with my face in the dirt. It did not conjure up pleasant memories."

"But your image . . ."

"Yes. No politician wants to come across as frightened, or panicky, or overreacting, or vulnerable. All of which," he said with a small smile, "happen to describe me perfectly right now." He waved his hand. "Anyway, I went out to the woods this morning to look around." He reached into his pocket. "I found these."

He opened his fist. It held two empty brass rifle cartridges. "Take them," he said. He spilled them into my hand. "I don't want them."

I looked at them. They were .223 Remington. They looked identical to the three I had found near Wally's cabin. "How did you—?"

"Prudence," he said, "is one of those important qualities that Machiavelli mentions. I have friends at Ten-Ten Commonwealth Avenue, Brady. After I talked to you on the phone, I inquired about the Kinnick shooting. My contact at Ten-Ten told me you had dug up some evidence." He shrugged. "Now you have some more evidence. Please. Do not tell anybody where they came from."

"Christ, I'm supposed to lie to the state cops?"

He waved his hands. "Or do nothing, if you prefer. It would be helpful, I think, to know for certain that we're dealing with the same man with the same gun. But my name must be kept out of it. I have your word on it."

I shrugged. "Yes. You do."

"Thanks." He glanced around the room. "Want another drink?"

"No, I guess not." I leaned toward him. "Look, Chip," I said. "Do us both a favor, huh?"

"What's that?"

"Talk to Lieutenant Horowitz."

He gave his head a small shake.

"Horowitz is discreet," I said, "and maybe you can convince him that the state cops should be involved in this thing. Right now it's just a hillbilly sheriff out in Fenwick."

"I don't know," said Swift. "I'd like to help you out, but . . ."

"Help us all out," I said. "He missed you last night. He might try again."

"Yeah," he said. "I thought of that."

The senator invited me to have dinner with him at the Commonwealth Club. Poached salmon. I declined. I told him I'd made other plans for dinner.

My plan—which I had made at the precise moment that Albert admitted me into the club—was to stroll over to Skeeter's Infield down the alley off State Street, climb onto a barstool, yank off my necktie, roll up my shirtsleeves, and have one of Skeeter's big burgers and a couple of draft beers. The Sox would be on the tube and I could argue speed versus power with a banker or a broker or an electrician or an auto mechanic who had seen Ted Williams launch one into the bleachers and who would remember Billy Klaus and Al Zarilla.

I like poached salmon. But I couldn't wait to get out of the Commonwealth Club.

It was after eleven when I got back to my apartment. I undressed my way to my bedroom. I pulled on a pair of sweat pants and a T-shirt, then went into the living room. I eyed my answering machine cautiously. A steady red eye stared back at me. No messages.

It felt like a stay of execution.

I made myself a mug of Sleepytime in the microwave and took it to the table. I found the SAFE newsletter and sat there with it, sipping my herb tea and trying to read between the lines.

Walt Kinnick was alive, but he was lucky. All but one shot missed him. But that one bullet could have hit him an inch to one side or the other, ripped open a big artery and minced a vital organ or two, and he'd have been dead in three minutes.

Senator Swift had not been hit at all. He had his Army-tuned reflexes to thank for his life, and now he was too scared to talk to the police.

Maybe our assassin was a lousy shot. I found scant consolation in that possibility.

Horowitz wasn't at his desk when I called the next morning. It was nearly noontime when he got back to me.

"What now?" he said.

"I got a couple more empty rifle cartridges for you. They're .223 Remington."

"Our shooter again?"

"Yes, I'd say so."

"Where'd you get 'em?"

"I can't tell you."

"What the fuck do you mean, you can't tell me? I'm a cop, for Christ sake."

"I'm a lawyer, for Christ sake."

"Well, why don't you take your cartridges and pretend they're suppositories for your hemorrhoids, then, Coyne. I ain't got time for games. You trying to pull some kind of privilege shit on me?"

"Yes." I took a deep breath. "No. Listen. I gave my word. If I hadn't, I wouldn't have gotten the cartridges."

"You think you've got evidence about a felony?"

"Yes. I know I do."

He was silent for a moment, except for the sounds of gum chewing. I waited for him.

"Okay," he said. "What *can* you tell me?"

"These cartridges were fired at a different place and at a different time from those that came from the woods in Fenwick."

"And at a different person, huh?"

I said nothing.

"If the lab tells us they were fired by the same gun, you know what that means, Coyne?"

"It means you guys would have jurisdiction on the case."

"Correction," he said. "It means we *could* have jurisdiction. We need more than some fucking cartridges."

"I know. You need evidence of where they came from and that they are linked to attempted assassinations."

"That's right, Mr. Lawyer. And without that evidence—say, in the form of reliable testimony—hell, I could get by with hearsay testimony—we can't do squat."

"I gave my word."

"So it's your ass, Coyne."

"I know. I'd feel better if you guys were on the case. But at least you could take a look at these cartridges."

He sighed. "Fine. Okay. Someone'll be over." And he hung up.

A young female state police detective arrived less than an hour later. I handed her the two empty cartridges. I made sure that I had smudged Senator Swift's fingerprints on them.

I tossed the last of the day's paperwork into the Out box a minute before three. Alex Shaw would be over, and I was eager to get out of the office. So when my console buzzed, I assumed that Julie would tell me Alex had arrived. But she said, "You got a call on line two, Brady."

"Shit," I said. "Who is it?"

"It's your wife."

"My *ex*-wife, Julie. Gloria's my ex-wife."

"I know that," she said sweetly.

I depressed the button and said into the phone, "Hi, hon."

"Brady," she said, "why didn't you tell me?"

"Tell you what?"

"I saw that article in the *Globe*. It said you witnessed a shooting. Is that true?"

"Well, more or less. I—"

"So you called me Sunday night and never even mentioned it?"

"You didn't seem exactly—"

"Brady, I *do* care about you, you know."

"Sometimes I don't know that," I said. "Sometimes I can't tell."

She was silent for a moment. I lit a cigarette.

"I know," she finally said. "I teased you about checking in and out with me. You've got to understand, though. You seem much more conscientious about doing that now than you ever did when we were married. It makes me angry. Does that make any sense to you?"

"As much as anything makes sense, I guess."

"Then when I have to read in the paper that you—you might've been killed, *that* makes me angry, too."

"I wasn't really in any danger, Gloria. They were after Wally."

"What makes me angry is that I had to read it in the paper. Brady, I worry. It's my nature. I imagine bad things. I worry about William and Joseph all the time. And I try to imagine what would become of them if . . ."

"If something happened to me?"

"Yes."

"They'd be fine, Gloria. They're strong young men."

"Or me."

437

"Huh?"

"What would become of me?" she said. "I mean, if something . . ."

"To quote you, we're divorced, remember?"

"Does that mean we're no longer—connected?"

"I never thought it meant that," I said. "No."

"That I can't still care about you?"

"No."

"Then why didn't you tell me?"

"I didn't think you cared."

"Really?" she said. "You really didn't think I cared?"

"Actually," I said, "I thought you did care. I was going to tell you when I called. I *wanted* to tell you. To talk to you about it. But when we started talking . . ."

"I was bitchy."

"Yes."

"But you know me," she said. "You know that doesn't mean anything."

I sighed. "Gloria, listen."

"What?"

"I know you, yes. I guess I understand your—your moods. Just like you understand mine. But if you recall, we don't like them. Each other's moods. They upset us, make us angry. They make us not want to communicate with each other. It's the way we've always been. It's why we're divorced."

"Which we should be," she said.

"Sure."

"It still . . ."

"It's over, anyway," I said. "It happened. Wally got shot, but he's going to be fine, and I'm fine. Okay?"

There was a hesitation. "Okay." Her voice was small and strangled. "Fine."

"Are you crying?"

"Of course I'm not crying. Why should I cry?"

"It sounded as if you were crying," I said.

"I'm *not* crying. You think—"

"I'm sorry," I said.

"You make me so angry, sometimes."

"I know," I said. "I don't mean to. It's how we are."

"We didn't used to be that way."

"No. It's too bad. I don't have any wisdom on it."

She laughed softly. "There's a first."

"What?"

"You admitting you don't have wisdom on something."

"You—us—you're much too complex for my simple brain, hon."

"Anyway," she said after a moment, "you're okay, huh?"

"Yes. Thanks. I'm okay."

"Well, good. Next time . . ."

"I hope there won't be a next time."

"Me, too," she said quietly.

Julie tapped on my door and stepped into my office just an instant after I hung up with Gloria. "The light went off," she said. "I know you're off the phone."

I sighed and nodded. "I'm off the phone."

"Are you all right?"

"Fine."

"She really cares about you, you know."

"Who?"

"Gloria."

I nodded. Julie believed in marriage. Hers with Edward appeared to be working well. She was happy. She wanted the same happiness for me. Julie believed that my divorce from Gloria was a mere aberration, a pothole in the highway toward marital bliss.

Julie figured that eventually Gloria and I would recognize the error of our ways and reunite.

Actually, Julie believed that the errors were in *my* ways. She believed that Gloria would take me back instantly, and I had learned that there was no sense in trying to explain to her that things were much more complicated than that.

"You love her, don't you?" she would say.

And I would admit that yes, in certain peculiar ways, I loved Gloria.

"And she loves you?"

I would nod and shrug.

"So?"

And I would say, "Well, you never know what might happen," because that was the only thing I could say that would get Julie off the subject. But it also convinced her that she was right, and that Gloria and I shared a destiny.

"So," she said, standing in front of my desk with her fists placed on her slim and shapely hips, "did you get things worked out?"

"With Gloria?"

"Yes."

I nodded. "Yes. Everything's fine."

"Well, good. She was upset."

"I know. Things are fine now."

Julie sat in the chair across from me. "There's somebody here to see you."

"Why didn't you say so?"

"Brady," she said, "I felt so bad. I mean, there you are, talking with Gloria on the phone, and she's all upset and needing you, and right there in our office is this gorgeous woman who you have a date with."

"That's Alexandria Shaw."

"I *know* who she is."

"She's a reporter, Julie."

"So? Everybody's got to be something, no matter how—how *predatory* they are."

I smiled. "The last time she was here, you insisted I see her. You said she had a job to do and I should help her."

"The last time she was here," said Julie, "she wasn't gorgeous. She had these big goofy glasses down on the end of her nose, and if you don't think I understand what's going on when she comes in here in her tight pants and perfect cheekbones and no glasses . . ."

She sputtered to a stop. I smiled.

"You're such an old letch," she mumbled.

"You're worried about Alex's virtue?"

"No." She allowed herself to smile. "Yours."

I reached across the desk and gripped Julie's hand. "Gloria and I really are divorced," I said.

"Yeah, well that's just stupid."

"Go tell Alex I'll be out in one minute, will you?"

Julie nodded. She stood up and started for the door. Then she turned to face me. "I hope you were nice to her," she said.

"Gloria?"

"Yes."

I nodded. "I think I was, yes."

Julie was hunched over the keyboard. Alex Shaw sat across from her with her knees pressed together and her briefcase on her lap.

The two women were studiously ignoring each other.

"Hi," I said to Alex.

She looked up without smiling, then stood and moved toward the door.

"See you tomorrow," I said to Julie.

She glanced up at me, nodded once, then bent back to the keyboard.

Alex drove a small Toyota sedan. She had double-parked in front of my building. We climbed in. She started up. A Bonnie Raitt tape was playing. Alex hummed tunelessly as she cut expertly through the city streets. Soon we were on Route 2, heading west toward Clinton.

We didn't talk.

When we turned onto Route 62 in Concord, I finally said, "What's the matter?"

"Nothing."

"You haven't spoken to me since we left my office. Something's the matter."

She shrugged.

When we got to Maynard, I said, "Stop the car, please."

Alex turned to me. "Why?"

"Please. Pull over."

She did. She turned to look at me. "What's this all about?"

"I want to get out."

"Huh?"

441

"I don't need this."

"This what?"

"This silence. I'll catch a cab back to the office."

"It's not you," she said.

"Who, then?"

"Me, I guess."

"You better tell me about it."

"Actually," she said, "it's your secretary."

"Was she rude to you?"

"Oh no. Friendly as all getout. Tells me you'll be ready in a minute, but you're on a very important phone call. Your wife. 'He's on the phone with his wife,' she says. Like I'm supposed to understand this is a major priority for you. Now, I know she means ex-wife. But she says wife, and even though I know what she's trying to do, I'm still thinking, what's he doing talking with his ex-wife and keeping me waiting when he knows I've gotta be in Clinton by four, and your secretary keeps chatting away, telling me what a terrific father you are and how devoted you are to your family—she calls it family, see, implying, that it's not just your sons but her, too—your wife—and by the time you come out I'm—aggravated. Aggravated with your secretary for fucking with my head, angry with myself for letting my head be fucked with so easy, and mainly angry at you, because . . ."

"Because?"

"Because, God damn it, I'm a woman and I'm entitled to be angry with a guy if I want."

"Aha!" I said. "My first insight of the day."

She smiled. "Insight, huh?"

"Yes. I know men are no smarter or more competent or anything than women. But I've always maintained that we're different."

"Well, jeez. Of course we're different." She reached over and put her hand on my leg. "Thank God," she said.

"Most women," I said, "seem to think it's an insult to make note of differences between the genders."

"We're different, all right."

"I wish I understood it better."

"Don't try," said Alex. "Just enjoy it." She drummed her fingers on the steering wheel, then said, "Well?"

"Well what?"

"Are you gonna get out?"

"Guess not," I said. "It's an expensive cab ride back to Boston from here." I reached over and touched her hair. "I'm sorry about Julie."

"That's okay," said Alex. "She's a woman. I understand."

She pulled away from the curb. A minute or so later we passed a car that had pulled to the side of the road. I turned to look at it. It was a blue Ford Escort. A classically nondescript vehicle.

"What's the matter?" said Alex.

"That car back there."

"That little Ford?"

"Yes."

"What about it?"

"I think it was behind us on Storrow Drive."

"There must be a million of those cars on the road."

"I know," I said. "That's what bothers me."

Ten minutes later we picked up Route 117, a country road that wound past meadows and newly planted cornfields and apple orchards. The apple trees had already dropped their blossoms and were bursting with shiny pale green leaves. I turned and looked out the back widow. There was no blue Ford Escort in sight.

"I tried to reach Senator Swift," said Alex.

"Senator Swift, huh?"

"I wanted an interview." She glanced sideways at me. "He's next on the list, you know."

"Um," I said.

"I got the brushoff."

"Figures."

"Yeah, I guess. Still, if he gets assassinated, I'll really be upset."

"Hell, so will I."

"I mean," she said, "what a story."

And a few minutes later she said, "I wonder why he wouldn't see me?"

"Who?"

"Chip Swift. I've interviewed him plenty of times. Politicians usually fall all over themselves for reporters. Publicity is their nourishment."

"He's probably just busy."

"Maybe." She was silent for a moment. "Still, I wonder . . ."

I didn't ask her what she wondered. I had the uncomfortable feeling that she knew I had met with the senator at the Commonwealth Club, and somehow she had managed to make me feel guilty that I wouldn't tell her all about it.

Women can do that.

SAFE headquarters occupied the first floor of a converted
Victorian house on Route 110 in Clinton, not far from the
Wachusett Reservoir. The upper two floors appeared to be apart-
ments.

We pulled into the dirt parking area and got out. As we did a
blue Escort cruised past. I couldn't see the driver's face.

"Did you see that?" I said to Alex.

"That car?"

I nodded.

"You think it's the same one?"

"I don't know. If it is . . ."

She squeezed my arm. "Brady," she said.

445

I shrugged. "Paranoia. Forget it."

We climbed onto the porch. A sign over the doorbell instructed us to RING AND COME IN. So we did.

We walked into the first room off the narrow hallway. It was dominated by a long conference table which was piled with magazines and newspapers and file folders. Two men in T-shirts and jeans were standing by the window drinking Cokes from cans and talking. They stopped their conversation when they saw us. Both of them looked familiar. One of them was tall and gaunt, with close-cropped black hair and gray stubby teeth. The other one was twentyish, with an earring and a blond ponytail and a red face. I couldn't recall his name, though I knew I'd heard it. I had met both of them in the Dunkin' Donuts on Tremont Street.

The younger one hesitated for just an instant, then smiled at us. "How ya doin'?"

Alex and I smiled back. "Just fine," I said.

"Kin I help you?"

"I'm here to see Mr. McNiff," said Alex. "I'm Alexandria Shaw from the *Globe*. I have an appointment."

"Hang on a sec. I'll get him for you."

He disappeared into an inner room. The other guy brushed past us and went out toward the front door without saying anything.

Alex nudged me with her elbow. "Those two guys . . ."

"Right. Dunkin' Donuts."

"Do you think they recognized you?" she said.

"Sure."

"But—"

At that moment Gene McNiff came into the room. His short-sleeved shirt hung untucked over his stomach. If he was surprised to see me with Alex, he didn't show it. "Miz Shaw, welcome," he said, holding out his hand to Alex. She took it. Then he looked at me. "And Mr. Coyne. Hello."

"Hello," I said. We shook hands, too.

"Let's go into my office where we can talk," said McNiff. "Want a Coke or something?"

Alex and I both declined. We followed him through the doorway into a cluttered office. Several metal file cabinets and bookcases stood against the wall. There was a big oak desk with two telephones and several messy stacks of papers. A table held a computer and printer, a copier, and a fax machine. Four unmatched chairs sat randomly on the floor.

The guy with the ponytail was there, too. "Dougie," said McNiff to him, "did you meet Miz Shaw and Mr. Coyne?" To us he said, "This is Douglas, my oldest son. He does a lot of work for SAFE. Sort of my right-hand man."

Dougie nodded to us and gave me a lopsided smile. "I guess we already met, actually. No hard feelings, huh?"

"No problem," I said.

"Well," said McNiff, "we've got some things to discuss, so . . ."

Dougie hesitated for a moment, then left the room.

McNiff gestured at the empty chairs. "Sit, please."

Alex and I sat.

"So," said McNiff after he had settled himself behind his desk, "how is he?" He was looking at me.

"Who?"

"Walt. How's he coming along?"

"He's okay," I said. "It was touch and go for a while."

"Damn shame. Accidents like this shouldn't happen. It only takes one or two irresponsible people to make all gun owners look bad. You know," he said, cocking an eye at Alex, "SAFE has been lobbying for better safety training programs for years. I take every hunting accident personally."

She smiled and nodded. "Mr. McNiff—"

"Gene," he said. "Call me Gene."

"Sure." She cleared her throat. "Mind if I tape this?"

He waved his hand. "Not at all."

She took her little portable tape recorder out of her briefcase, tested it, then put it onto McNiff's desk between them. Then she flipped open her notebook. "Okay," she said. "Now, can we—?"

"Miz Shaw," said McNiff quickly, "I'd like to tell you some things you might not know. Would that be all right?"

"Sure. Fine."

"I'll give you some of our pamphlets, and I hope you'll read them. I mean, I know why you're here." He glanced at me and smiled. "I'm not sure why *you're* here, Mr. Coyne." He dismissed me with a wave of his hand and looked back at Alex. "Anyway, I know your reputation. You're a fair reporter. That's why I welcomed this chance to talk to you. See, SAFE has this unfortunate image, and it stems from our unrelenting battle on behalf of the Second Amendment. But we do a lot more than just fight against the unconstitutional abridgement of the right to bear arms. We teach young people gun safety. We hold special classes all over New England for women who want to learn how to defend themselves. These programs are very popular, Miss Shaw. Women are feeling that they've been the victims of violent crime for too long. They're upset—as we are—about the lack of protection they get from the police and the courts. So they are learning how to defend themselves." He paused and leaned toward us. "And that is precisely what the Second Amendment is all about. It's what SAFE is all about."

McNiff paused, then leaned back and folded his hands on his desk. I had the impression that he had given this speech more than once.

He smiled at Alex. "I hope I'm not boring you."

"Not at all, Mr. McNiff. Please continue."

He shrugged. "We lobby not just for the right to own firearms, but also for tougher penalties for gun-related crimes. See, we know that if the right to own guns is curtailed, then law-abiding citizens will do what the law requires. But criminals don't obey laws. The politicians can disarm the good citizens. But they can't disarm criminals." McNiff shrugged. "End of lecture." He picked up a handful of pamphlets and gave them to Alex. "I hope you'll read them, Miz Shaw. It will help you to understand."

She took them and put them into her briefcase. "Mr. McNiff," she said, "four days after dramatically testifying in favor of gun control, Walt Kinnick was shot. You were seen publicly threatening him. Your newsletter named him the number-one enemy of your organization. It came out two days before the shooting. I'm sure it's obvious to you how that looks."

McNiff nodded. "I'd have to be an imbecile not to see how it looks. It looks like an attempted assassination. But I guarantee that no member of SAFE shot Walt Kinnick." He hesitated. "*I certainly didn't.*"

"I didn't mean—"

"Listen," he said. "I publish a newsletter every two weeks. A regular feature is our enemies' list. There's *always* a number-one enemy. Before Walt Kinnick, none of our enemies had ever been shot at. Not one. Ever. And believe me, we've had some pretty big enemies." He leaned forward on his desk and stared hard at Alex. "Look. Our members come from all walks of life. We've got policemen, salesmen, mechanics, schoolteachers, housewives. Lawyers and newspaper reporters, too. You name it. Some of them are highly educated. Some are dropouts. Some are smart, and some, probably, aren't so smart. But they all share our belief in the Second Amendment. And they all know that assassinating our enemies with guns is the worst possible thing for our cause. It's absolutely unthinkable that any SAFE member would do this."

Alex was scribbling in her notebook. She looked up at McNiff. "But you do advocate harassing your enemies with boycotts and so forth. You do publish their phone numbers and addresses." Alex glanced at me, then said, "Walt Kinnick received some threatening phone calls the day before the shooting. The callers mentioned SAFE."

"Sure," said McNiff. "Anybody would. Good way to deflect suspicion, huh?" He shrugged. "We advocate legal, nonviolent activities that help us make our point and demonstrate our influence. Sure we do. All organizations do those kinds of things to promote their cause. We also try to get our friends elected and our enemies defeated. We play by the rules. We believe in the Constitution. Sometimes our members make phone calls. Nothing illegal about that. Maybe some of them are angry. But we don't go around shooting people who disagree with us."

"Walt Kinnick was expected to testify against gun control. Instead, he testified for it. You have been quoted as calling him a traitor."

McNiff nodded quickly. "Yes. He was. That's why he's our number-one enemy. But that doesn't mean we want him to be shot."

"But doesn't that make him different from all your other enemies?"

449

"We've been betrayed before," said McNiff with a shrug. "Politicians betray our cause all the time."

"Don't you think it was sort of inevitable that sooner or later some nut with a gun would try to serve the cause by shooting an enemy?" said Alex.

"I think," said McNiff slowly, "that the least likely nut to do that would be a member of SAFE. Every one of our members knows that the irresponsible or criminal use of firearms is our worst enemy. Hey, it's obvious someone shot Kinnick. Whether it was an accident or not, I don't know. But I'll tell you this. Maybe it was an attempted assassination. But it wasn't any member of SAFE."

"What are you doing about it?" she said.

"Doing?"

"How are you addressing what happened to Kinnick?"

McNiff spread his hands. "I'm not. There's nothing to address."

"But—"

"I assume the police are addressing it. I hope they catch whoever did it, and I hope they prosecute him and punish him. But it's none of our business. SAFE has nothing to do with what happened to Walt Kinnick. We're always upset when accidents and crimes with guns occur. But accidents or irresponsible behavior or criminal acts do not change our views about guns, any more than drunk-driving accidents change anybody's mind about automobiles."

Alex was frowning into her notebook. "There are other enemies on your list," she said.

McNiff looked at me and smiled. "Yes. There are always ten enemies. Every two weeks, ten enemies. Most of them are perennials. Now and then we have some new ones."

"Like Walt Kinnick," she said.

He nodded. "And Brady Coyne."

"Why is Mr. Coyne on your list?" she said.

"He obviously helped convince Kinnick to reverse his position on gun control. Kinnick came to town prepared to testify against that bill. After meeting with his lawyer, he testified for it." He looked at me. "You must be a very convincing man. A

450

convincing man who opposes the Second Amendment is an enemy of SAFE."

"If you think I convinced Wally to change his mind, you don't know him very well," I said.

"Good lawyers make a living convincing people to change their minds," said McNiff.

I shrugged. "I'm not that good."

Alex glanced at me and gave me a little nod. She was inviting me to plead my case more fully. I realized that was why she had invited me to join her on this interview.

"I have no public position on gun control," I said to McNiff.

"Only through Kinnick," he said.

"I never even heard of SAFE before I picked up Wally at the airport that night."

"I bet you had opinions on gun control, though," said McNiff.

"I have opinions on lots of things. Now and then I even express them. That's the First Amendment. Comes right before the Second."

McNiff smiled.

"If it matters to you, I wouldn't have considered myself your enemy."

"Not me," said McNiff. "SAFE."

"Whatever. I generally see too many gray areas in complicated issues to make anybody a worthwhile enemy."

"If you're not for us," he said, "you've gotta be against us."

"No, I don't," I said. "I can just not give a shit one way or the other, like most people."

He shrugged. "There'll be another newsletter in a week or so. I'll be making a new enemies' list. Maybe you won't make it this time."

"I'm only an enemy," I said, "of those who make me an enemy."

"And a friend to those who have no friends," said McNiff with a grin. "I remember Boston Blackie, too."

"What about those others?" said Alex to McNiff.

"Which others?"

"On your list."

"The others have been there before. Politicians. Our biggest enemies are politicians who don't think for themselves, who take polls before they decide what they believe. Fortunately, we have lots of friends in government, too."

"Those who vote your position," said Alex. "People who do think for themselves."

McNiff shrugged. "Politics is politics."

She glanced at her notebook. "What about Wilson Bailey?"

"What about him?"

"He's not a politician."

"No. He's been on our list before. He's made a career out of testifying against us. It's a tragic thing, what happened to his family. But his is a tired old argument. Unfortunately, it has a lot of emotional punch. So far he hasn't hurt us."

Alex and McNiff talked for another fifteen minutes or so. Nothing new was said. Finally Alex glanced at her watch and said, "I've taken enough of your time, Mr. McNiff." She shut off her tape recorder and stowed it and her notebook in her briefcase.

He walked us out to the porch and held out his hand to Alex. "I hope you'll look at those pamphlets I gave you," he said.

"Sure. I will."

He turned to me. "Mr. Coyne, please convey to Walt my wishes for a speedy recovery."

I nodded. "Okay."

"And I hope you're enjoying your brief appearance on our list."

I smiled. "Oh, it's a lot of fun," I said. "I always wanted to make somebody's enemies' list."

He touched my arm. "We're *not* after you, you know."

"It's comforting to hear you say that."

We got into Alex's car. I lit a cigarette. "Thanks," I said.

"Huh?"

"For giving me a chance to tell McNiff my side."

"I think he heard you."

"We'll see if it gets me expunged from his list."

"I hope it does," she said. "Even if it costs me a helluva story."

"I hope it does, too."

"He's good, isn't he?" she said.

"Yes. Very convincing, I thought. Get anything useful?"

She shrugged. "Everything's useful. I'll get a story out of it.

"'SAFE Leader Denies Group's Responsibility for Kinnick Shooting,'" I said.

"Something like that. What'd you think?"

"I think Gene McNiff knows nothing about what happened to Walt. I think he's upset about it. Not necessarily because of Walt. Because it looks bad for SAFE."

"I agree," she said. She started up the car. "Hungry?"

"Getting there. I could use a drink."

"Me, too. Know anything around here?"

"There's a place in Acton, if you like Italian."

"I like Italian. Lead on."

We followed the pretty winding country roads to 2A in Acton and pulled up behind the restaurant a little after six. Inside we were greeted by the owner, who served as his own maître d'. He gave us a courtly bow. "Good to see you, Mr. Coyne," he said. To Alex he said, "And nice to see you again, too, miss."

He led us to a secluded little table in the corner, gave us the wine list, and left.

"What was that all about?" said Alex.

"What?"

"He said it was good to see me again. I've never been here in my life."

"You picked that up, huh?"

"Oh yes. We reporters are quick that way."

"I never told you about Terri."

"Want to?"

I shrugged. "We ate here a lot. She lives right down the street. This was our table."

"Do I look like her or something?"

"Well, aside from the fact that her hair's long and black and yours is short and kind of auburn, and her eyes are practically black and yours are greenish-blue—yes. I mean, you're both very beautiful. I can see why our host is confused. Another man blinded by beauty."

Alex smiled. "What happened?" she said.

I lit a cigarette and exhaled slowly. "She dumped me."

"Why?"

"I'm still working on that one."

Alex put her hand onto mine. "In my experience," she said, "I've found it's a lot easier to be the dumpee than the dumper."

454

"Yeah," I said. "Easier. But it hurts more."

She leaned forward. I met her halfway. She kissed me on the chin, then the cheek, then the mouth. We held that one for a moment. Then she pulled back. "It still hurts, huh?"

"A little."

"It's good to see."

"What?"

"That you hurt. I mean, that you *can* hurt. That you admit it."

I reached across the table, touched her jaw, and gently steered her mouth close enough that I could kiss it again. "I'm feeling a tiny bit better," I said.

"Maybe we can work out a rehabilitation program for you," she said. Then she turned her head, looked up, and grinned.

A young waitress was standing beside us, smiling. "Wine," I said. "A good first step on any recovery program. Let's have some wine."

When we left the restaurant, it was nearly ten. There were only a dozen or so cars left in the parking lot. One of them, parked by itself at the dark end of the row, was a blue Ford Escort. When we climbed into Alex's car, I gestured at the Escort and said, "Drive around that way."

She frowned for an instant, then nodded. She backed out of the space, then swung around past the Escort. Her headlights briefly lit the other car's interior. Nobody was sitting in it.

She continued out the driveway. "Just another blue Escort," she said.

"Driver slides down so we don't see him," I said.

She reached over and touched my leg. "It must be scary," she said softly.

"Yeah, it kinda is. There's a little shopping mall just over the hill. Why don't you pull in there and douse your lights."

"Sure." She hit the accelerator, zipped over the hill, darted into the lot in front of an all-night convenience store, and switched off her headlights.

We watched the road. A couple of minutes later a blue Escort rolled past us, beat the yellow traffic light, and continued east on 2A toward Boston. We watched until its taillights disappeared.

I sighed. "Millions of Escorts on the road."

"Yeah," said Alex, "but now you've got me paranoid, too."

"Hey," I said, "you're not on any enemies' list. You just hang around with the wrong people. Let's go home."

Alex pulled up in front of my apartment building a little before eleven. "Nightcap?" I said.

"Oh, Christ," she grunted.

"What?"

"'Nightcap.' That's beneath you. You mean, do I want to go up with you and make out on your sofa. Right?"

"'Make out'? I haven't heard anyone say that that since I was sixteen."

"Isn't that what you mean?"

"Something like that, I guess." I smiled. "Something *exactly* like that. Yes."

"And if things progress nicely, maybe you can persuade me to spend the night."

"I didn't—"

"Well, I'm warning you," she said. "I have to get up early, and I'm very grouchy in the morning."

"I can live with that," I said. "Let's have that nightcap."

I woke up abruptly. Alex was sitting astride my hips shaking my shoulders. In the dim light from the hallway, I saw that she had put my old Yale T-shirt back on again. "Hey," she said. "Wake up for a minute."

"Was I snoring?"

"No. Listen. I want to know something."

"What time is it?"

"Three-ten."

"Jesus, Alex."

"If you knew more about this, would you tell me?"

"About what?"

"The Kinnick thing."

457

"No."

"No what?"

"No, I wouldn't necessarily tell you."

She rolled off me and lay on her back beside me with her hands under her head. I turned onto my side. She rolled over to meet me, and I slid my arm around her. My hand snaked under the T-shirt and traced the curves and angles of her back, down over her smooth rump, than back up again. "There might be things I couldn't tell you," I said into her hair.

"Lawyer stuff."

"Kinda."

"I understand."

"Well, good."

She was silent for a moment. Her fingers moved on my back. Then she said, "But do you?"

"Do I what?"

"Know something? Have some facts?"

"Yes."

"That you can't tell me."

"Right."

"Like who's following you around in a blue Ford Escort?"

"No," I said. "I don't know who's doing that. Assuming I'm not imagining it. Which I probably am."

"You think you're paranoid," she said.

"I don't know. Do you?"

"It depends."

"If somebody really is following me for purposes of finding a propitious moment to shoot me, and it scares me, is that paranoia?"

"I don't think so. I think that's just sensible." She burrowed her face against my shoulder. "What about ideas?" she mumbled. "Hypotheses, scenarios? Do you have ideas you aren't sharing with me, too?"

"Not really."

"What does that mean?"

"It means I haven't come close to figuring it out, but I'm thinking about it."

"But you don't want to share your thinking with me."

"Right."

"Why?"

"Because it's tied into what I know. I can't separate them. You should understand this."

"I do," she murmured. "I was just wondering."

I hugged her against me. The T-shirt had ridden way up over her hips. "Let's go back to sleep, then."

Her hand crept onto my thigh. "Fat chance," she said.

◎

"Your coffee's on the table."

I opened my eyes. Alex was sitting on the bed, fully dressed. Her hip pressed against mine, separated by the blanket that covered me. I reached up to touch her face. Her hair was damp. She bent down and kissed me quickly on the forehead. "I'm out of here," she said.

"What time is it?"

"A little after seven."

"What's your hurry?"

"I got a story to write."

"'Veteran News Hound Seduces Vulnerable Attorney,'" I said. "That's the one."

I reached up, hooked my arm around her neck, and pulled her down to me. I nuzzled her throat.

"Oh, shit," she mumbled. "Again?"

◎

A half-hour later she was sitting on the side of the bed pulling on her pants and I was propped up in bed sipping lukewarm coffee. "I think I'm going to try to reach Wilson Bailey today," she said.

"Poignant human interest story," I said, drawing circles on her bare back with my forefinger.

"That's not the story I'm after. That's an old story that I should've written when it happened but didn't. Now the man is the number-ten SAFE enemy."

"I forgot. You're collecting interviews with potential assassi-

459

nation victims." She was hunching herself into her bra. "I give you a lot of credit," I went on. "You really throw yourself into your work."

"Mr. Bailey," she said, "might be more forthcoming if I sit on him in the middle of the night."

"Worth a try."

She stood up and buttoned her blouse. Then she smiled. "I'll call you later."

"I've heard that one before."

"I will." She waved and headed for the door. "Have a good day."

"Come give me a kiss."

"No way, buster," she said. "You saw what happened last time I did that."

My bathroom mirror was still foggy. Alex had written "Hi" in the condensation with her finger. I was relieved to note that she did not dot the "i" with a little heart or a happy face.

While I showered, I thought about being followed by a nameless assassin in a blue Escort and wondered again if I were imagining it. Alex had reminded me that Wilson Bailey was number ten on the list. And from there my mind took a convoluted route to the realization that if I did get shot, there was nobody who knew what I knew who could warn Wilson Bailey that he was a logical target, too.

So before I left for the office I found my copy of the SAFE newsletter and dialed Bailey's number in Harlow, Massachusetts. It rang four times before I heard the click of an answering machine. A cheerful female voice said, "Hi. You've reached the Bailey household. I guess no one's home right now. Please leave a message and we'll get back to you."

It was, I guessed, the voice of Bailey's dead wife. She had been gunned down in the public library. But her voice still lived on an answering machine tape. Wilson Bailey, I imagined, could not bring himself to eradicate this last surviving vestige of her.

She had used the pronoun "we." There was no longer a "we" at Wilson Bailey's house.

I had to clear my throat before I spoke to his machine. "Mr. Bailey," I said, "this is Brady Coyne. I saw your testimony before the Senate Subcommittee on Public Safety last week. I have some important things I'd like to discuss with you. Please call me." I left my home and office numbers.

Then I went to work.

◎

Julie buzzed me in the middle of the morning. "It's Lieutenant Horowitz again," she said. "Line one."

Got it," I said. I pressed the button and said, "Hey."

"Where'd you get those cartridges, Coyne?" he said.

"I can't tell you. I already told you that. What'd you find out?"

"Why the fuck should I tell you what I found out if you won't tell me where you got them?"

"Because I might be able to figure something out, and then I could tell you and you could capture a vicious criminal and you'd be a hero."

"Gee whiz," he said. "Golly. You'd let me take all the credit?"

"Sure. You need it more than I do."

"They were shot from the same gun," he said. "I bet you knew that."

"I suspected it. Can you say anything about the gun?"

"Can you say anything about how they came into your possession?"

"No."

"God damn it, Coyne."

"Somebody took some shots at somebody and left those cartridges behind. That's all I can tell you."

"Who? Where? When?"

"I can't tell you."

"Because you gave your fucking word."

"That's it."

"Well, the fingerprints on those cartridges were all smudged and I can't tell you anything about the gun, and if I could, I wouldn't, and fuck you very much," he said, and he hung up.

Around noon Julie buzzed me again. "It's her," she said.

461

"Her?"

She chuckled. "Her with the cheekbones. Line one."

"Thanks, kid." I switched over and said, "Hi."

"Hi," said Alex. "How are you?"

"I didn't sleep that well last night."

"Me neither, actually. But I feel just fine."

"Did you get your story written?"

"Yep. Funny thing. As I thought about it and listened to the interview, I became more and more convinced that McNiff was straight with me."

"I thought so, too."

"My story doesn't have much to do with the Kinnick shooting. It's just about SAFE. What they do, what they believe. Those pamphlets are pretty convincing."

"So you buy their line?"

"Hey," she said. "I'm a reporter, remember? I tell the story, that's all. SAFE's in the news. What they stand for is newsworthy. Whether I buy it or not is irrelevant. Wanna do lunch?"

"Can't. I've gotta be in court at one. How about later?"

"I've got an editorial meeting that'll drag on till eight or nine. We generally order up pizzas."

"You could come over for a nightcap afterward."

"Hoo, boy. Another nightcap, huh?"

"Sure. A nightcap."

"I might not get there before ten."

"That's okay."

After court that afternoon I took a cab over to Mass General. I didn't notice any blue Ford Escorts following us, which only convinced me that he had either changed vehicles or was lurking back there somewhere in the traffic.

Wally was wearing a bathrobe and sitting in a chair. He was not attached to any plastic tubes.

Diana was sitting cross-legged on his bed.

"Hi, folks," I said. I shook Wally's hand and Diana and I exchanged pecks on the cheek. I sat beside Diana. "How's it feeling?" I said to Wally.

"Better and better." He glanced sideways at Diana and said,

"About ready for strenuous exercise. How about you? Been fishing?"

"Not since the Deerfield."

"Well shit, man. The month of May's passing you by." He smiled. "I was just telling Diana. I had a visit from a friend of yours today."

"Friend of mine?"

"Yeah. State cop named Horowitz. Said you've been bugging him about me. He complained a lot. He respects the hell out of you."

I nodded. "I respect him, too. Crabby son of a bitch. What'd he have to say?"

"He didn't say much of anything. Asked me some questions. Just, basically, what I remembered. Which isn't much of anything. Wanted to know if I could think of anybody who'd want to shoot me. I mean, aside from the SAFE connection."

"What'd you tell him?"

Wally shrugged. "I mentioned the animal rights crazies. I mean, they're at least as fanatical as the SAFE guys. They've been convicted of burning down medical laboratories and issuing death threats to scientists who use animals in their research. Otherwise, I guess I've probably stepped on a hundred sets of toes over the years. Anybody who builds dams on salmon rivers, clear-cuts forests, dumps poisons into trout streams, votes the wrong way. I can think of a dozen politicians and CEOs who'd probably like to see me in an urn."

"Did you mention Howard?" said Diana.

Wally turned and looked at her. "Yes, honey," he said. "I had to."

She nodded, then turned her head to stare out at the air shaft.

"What about poachers with expensive bamboo fly rods?" I said.

"I forgot that one."

I smiled. "I'm sure Horowitz found the interview helpful."

"I don't know. He just sat there chomping on his gum."

"It's not even a state police case," I said.

"I know. It's officially a hunting accident. Your friend Horowitz doesn't seem to buy it."

"Neither do I," I said.

He cocked an eye at me. "You seem pretty emphatic about that."

I nodded. "I am."

"Do you know something?"

"Not much."

"Well, shit, man. What?"

"I can't tell you."

"You playing lawyer with me, Brady?"

"Not really."

"Somebody else get shot at?"

I shrugged. "Maybe something like that."

"A listed enemy?"

I nodded.

"Christ," mumbled Wally, and I knew he was thinking that I was a listed SAFE enemy, too, and it was his fault.

"Don't worry about it," I said. "I talked with Gene McNiff yesterday and got everything straightened out."

"Sure," said Wally. "Good." He sounded dubious.

I stayed for about an hour. The three of us talked mostly about fishing. Wally planned to recuperate back at his cabin once they released him from the hospital. Diana was going to stay with him. Neither of them seemed worried about returning to the place where the shooting had occurred.

His producers had assured him that they would adjust their filming schedules to accommodate him. They had even started renegotiating his contract with his agent. Walt Kinnick had become an even more marketable commodity since the shooting. The sponsors were lining up. The SAFE threat of a boycott had not, apparently, scared anybody away.

When I stood up to leave, Wally said, "Brady, do me a favor."

"Sure."

"Take Diana out to dinner."

"You trust me with this beautiful woman?"

"Course not," he said. "But I trust her."

"You do?" she said.

"Absolutely."

She grinned at me. "I can't stand it."

"How's tomorrow?" I said to her.

She nodded. "Terrific."

"Where?"

"Do you know Giannino's?"

"Behind the Charles Hotel?"

"Yes. We can eat out on the patio. It's nice outdoors this time of year, and they have good Italian food there. If you don't mind coming to Cambridge."

"Sounds fine. Seven?"

"Perfect. I'll meet you there."

"Thanks," said Wally.

"It'll be my pleasure," I said.

I decided to stop at Skeeter's on the way home for a giant burger and a glass of beer. It was one of those May evenings when even in the city the air smelled clean and fresh, and it wasn't until I turned off Cambridge Street onto Court Street that I became aware of my tail.

He had been lounging by the entrance to the hospital, and when I stepped outside after my visit with Wally and squinted into the slanting late afternoon sunshine, he had looked away from me a little too quickly. I noticed it, but it didn't register. I might have noticed a blue Escort, but I wasn't looking for an undistinguished thirtyish man wearing khaki pants and a brown sports jacket.

But when I turned off Cambridge onto Court Street I glimpsed that same man sauntering along in the same direction on the opposite side of Cambridge Street. I kept walking, and from the corner of my eye I saw him cross Cambridge and head down Court Street. He stayed behind me and on the other side of the street.

When I got to Congress Street, I stood on the corner waiting for the light. I glanced back up the street, but couldn't spot the guy in the brown sports coat. The light changed, I crossed Congress to State, and continued along until I came to Skeeter's alley. When I turned in there I had another chance to look behind me. My tail, if that's what he was, had disappeared.

I went inside and hitched myself onto a barstool. The TV over the bar was playing "Wheel of Fortune" with the sound turned off.

"Hey, Mr. Coyne," said Skeeter. "By yourself tonight?"

I had once met Gloria at Skeeter's, and he had been completely charmed by her. "Yes, I think so," I said, remembering my tail. "How about a draft Sam and a burger?"

"Medium rare, right?"

"The burger, not the beer."

Skeeter poured my beer and slid it in front of me. I lit a cigarette and took a sip, and as I did I glanced in the mirror over the bar. A man in a brown sports coat came in, looked casually around without letting his eyes linger on me, then took a seat in a booth near the door.

I stared openly at him through the mirror. He picked up a menu, studied it, then lounged back and looked up at the television. He was as nondescript as a blue Ford Escort—thinning brown hair cut neither short nor long, medium build, blue Oxford shirt open at the neck. Just an average working stiff happy that another day at the office had ended.

I finished my cigarette, stubbed it out, picked up my half-empty draft of beer, and took it to his booth. "Mind if I join you?" I said.

He turned his head, shrugged, and gestured to the seat across from him. Then he resumed looking at the television. "That Vanna White," he said, still staring at the screen. "Some nice-lookin' broad, huh?"

"A little on the thin side," I said.

"She'd look good to you, if you see my old lady. How do you get waited on in this place?"

"You've got to order at the bar. It's just Skeeter. No waitresses."

"What're you having?"

"Skeeter's burgers are the best in town."

"Burger and a beer," he said. "Sounds good."

"Why are you following me?" I said.

"It's my job." He continued watching the television.

"You're not that good at it," I said. "I saw you in the Escort last night. I picked you up about halfway over here from the hospital."

"Actually, that was another guy in the Escort. But I did follow you from your apartment to your office this morning. Then to the courthouse, then the hospital, then here. You didn't catch on to me until you come out of the hospital? That's not bad, huh?"

"I don't get it," I said.

He swiveled his head around and smiled at me. "It doesn't matter whether you get it or not, Mr. Coyne. And it doesn't matter whether you know we're watching you or not, either."

I sat back in the booth and laughed. "Oh, shit," I said. "You're not an assassin, are you?"

"Not on this assignment I'm not."

"Secret Service, right?"

"Bingo," he said. "You win a night with Vanna."

"Are you protecting me?"

He rolled his eyes. "Not hardly."

"Oh," I said. "I get it. You're making sure I don't assassinate somebody."

"Or conspire with somebody," he said. "Like Gene McNiff."

"Is that what you think I was doing out there yesterday?"

"Me?" He laughed. "I don't think, Mr. Coyne. I keep track of you and report it to the lady who does the thinking."

"Agent Krensky."

"Her own self. My boss."

"Will you report this conversation to her?"

"Sure. That's my job."

"What will you tell her?"

"I'll tell her you and I shared a burger at Skeeter's Infield from seven-oh-nine until whenever, then I tailed you home."

"Would you mind telling her that I'm no assassin and she's wasting a lot of taxpayer's money?"

"I'll tell her," he said. "But she don't listen to me."

We ended up eating together at his booth and watching the first few innings of the Red Sox game. He didn't tail me home. He strolled along with me. We ended up talking baseball. He was a

Cubs fan and his name was Malloy. That's all he would tell me.

I couldn't decide whether to be relieved or annoyed that the Secret Service was following me around.

I kicked off my shoes inside the door, dropped my jacket and tie onto a kitchen chair, and sat on my bed to divest myself of the rest of my lawyer duds. I pulled on a pair of jeans and a T-shirt, then went into the living room.

My answering maching was winking at me. Wink-wink, pause. Two messages. I pressed the button. The machine whirred, clicked, and then came Alex's voice. "I'm running a little late over here," she said. "It's gonna be closer to eleven. Assume that's still okay. I'm pooped. Can't understand why. I might want to skip the nightcap and go straight for the nightshirt. I'm on the fly. Bye."

The machine clicked. Then a voice that I had heard once before on an answering machine tape said, "Brady Coyne, you have betrayed the Second Amendment For Ever and you deserve to die a just and ironic death."

The machine rewound itself. Its red eye stared unblinking at me. I stared back at it.

29

I'd heard that message before. It was the same one Wally got the night before he was shot. The same precise syntax. I remembered the word "ironic" in Wally's message, and I recalled that Alex had used the word "ironically" in her article. People who understand irony always impress me. Gene McNiff had said that all kinds of people belonged to SAFE.

Still, the man who left me this message didn't fit my image of a typical SAFE redneck bent on shooting his enemies.

I replayed the tape. Alex sounded warm and sexy. It occurred to me to tell her not to come over. I didn't want her to be in the way if something was going to happen. But I didn't think anybody would try to shoot me in my bed behind a brick wall six stories above the Boston Harbor. About the only way to accomplish that would be from a helicopter.

Besides, I knew I'd appreciate having someone to hold on to.

My answering machine was old. I figured the heads needed cleaning or something, because the fidelity was too poor to attempt to identify the speaker by his voice. He might've even attempted to disguise it, I couldn't tell. It could have been anybody. If it was a voice I'd heard before, I couldn't determine it by this brief recorded message.

I removed the tape and replaced it with a new one.

I poured myself a finger of Jack Daniel's and stood by the open sliders. The moon shimmered on the corrugated water of the harbor six stories down. Somewhere out there a bell-buoy clanged quietly, and the air smelled of old seaweed.

I tried to figure out what to do. Or not do. Call Horowitz? And what would he do? Tell me to stay in my apartment, probably. And for how long? Until they caught the shooter? And what if they never caught him? The peculiarity of American law enforcement is that it cannot act until a crime has been committed. Horowitz couldn't do a damn thing to prevent me from getting shot.

If Agent Malloy continued to tail me, he probably wouldn't be able to prevent an assassination, either. But he'd be in a good position to catch the shooter. That offered me a little consolation. Very little.

I couldn't decide what to do. In the end, I did nothing.

I was glad Alex was coming over.

I finished my drink and picked up the clothes and magazines and fishing gear that were strewn around my apartment. I didn't want her to think I was a slob.

I was sitting out on the balcony sipping another shot of Daniel's when the intercom sounded. I buzzed Alex up, and when she came in I hugged her hard for a long time.

"What's wrong?" she said.

"I'm just really glad to see you."

She pressed herself against me, then tilted her head back and grinned. "I'll say you are."

I didn't tell her about sharing a burger with Agent Malloy, and

471

I didn't mention the telephone message. It didn't seem quite that ominous anymore. Besides, she wanted to get into her nightshirt.

So did I.

◎

I felt her mouth on the back of my neck. I hugged my pillow. "I'm out of here," she said.

I rolled onto my back. Alex was standing beside the bed smiling down at me. I lifted my hand to her, and she backed away. "Oh no you don't," she said. "I gotta get to work."

"What time is it?"

"Seven-thirty. I'm late."

"It's Saturday," I said.

"I work on Saturdays. You want some coffee?"

"I don't work on Saturdays," I said. "I sleep on Saturdays. No coffee."

"Call me?" she said.

"I will."

I heard the door click shut behind her. I lay there with my eyes closed, feeling vaguely edgy and depressed. Then, with a jolt, I remembered the phone call. Somewhere out there a man had threatened my life. I thought about it. He had bushwhacked Wally in the woods in the early morning and Senator Swift in the woods at night. Perhaps he'd wait to nail me in the woods, too. If I stayed in the city I'd be all right.

At least I hoped so. The thought consoled me enough to allow me to drift back to sleep.

I woke up around nine. Ah, Saturday. I love Saturdays. I pulled on a pair of jeans, wandered into the kitchen, poured a mugful of coffee, and took it out onto the balcony. I sat there sipping and smoking and tilting my face up to the sun. I thought about a faceless man who thought I was his enemy, and I decided not to let him ruin my day. So I turned my thoughts to all of the good things I could do with a beautiful Saturday in May. Most of those things involved rivers and trout.

Then I remembered that I had agreed to meet Diana in Cambridge for dinner, and that spoiled my trout-fishing reverie.

Fishing for me is, among other important things, an escape from time. Having to leave a river because my watch tells me to takes a lot of the fun out of it.

Anyhow, I decided it might not be such a good idea to go fishing on this day. An out-of-the-way trout river would make an excellent location for an assassination. I wasn't going to cower behind my apartment door for the rest of my life. But there was no sense in doing something foolhardy.

I retrieved the *Globe* from outside my door, refilled my mug, and went back out onto the balcony. I read the lead paragraphs of each of the front-page stories, folded the paper back to the Friday-night box scores, found the chess problem and solved it, then paged through the whole paper, back to front.

Alex's piece was buried in the middle of the Metro section. I noticed it because it was accompanied by a stock photo of Gene McNiff. GUARDIAN OF THE SECOND AMENDMENT was the headline. I read it through and smiled. I figured her editor, alerted by the "ironically" that Alex had slipped into her previous piece, had wielded his blue pencil with a vengeance this time.

It was a puff piece. The Second Amendment For Ever organization had earned the grudging respect of political insiders by their success in stonewalling antigun legislation. They had some sound constitutional and sociological arguments to support their position, which Alex summarized nonjudgmentally. SAFE also supported get-tough anticrime legislation, ran hunter-safety programs, conducted self-defense seminars. Gene McNiff was a real estate attorney who received a tiny stipend from SAFE for his service as the group's executive director.

Alex had made McNiff sound thoughtful, dedicated, sincere, tolerant, sane.

Her article did not mention Walt Kinnick.

I wondered what her first draft had looked like before her editor took his swipe at it.

Lots of lawyers work on weekends. Big high-powered firms expect it, especially from the young associates. Partners feel

473

obliged to work weekends, too, in order to set an example for the associates.

But not me. One of the main advantages of working in a one-man law office is not having to impress anyone or set an example for anybody. I only have to impress myself, and I'm easily impressed.

I know I don't set a very good example.

I respect the law. I give my clients their money's worth. But the law is not my life. I rank family and friends and fishing and the Red Sox above my law practice.

Julie, even after all the years we've been together, doesn't respect my personal hierarchy of values. She keeps telling me that my business should come first—or maybe second, after family—which, of course, is one of her functions. I need her to question my priorities, because if she didn't, it wouldn't get done.

Julie's my conscience, and as I loafed around my apartment her voice kept nagging at me from inside my head. "Get to work," it said. "Catch up."

In the end I did what I do about three Saturdays a year. I went to the office.

It felt good to stroll leisurely across the Common and up Boylston Street to Copley Square in jeans and sneakers and a polo shirt, and although I failed to spot him, I suspected that Agent Malloy or one of his counterparts was somewhere behind me, and that felt good, too. I liked unlocking the office at noon-time and making a vat of coffee and leaving the answering machine on. A few uninterrupted hours and I could get a lot done. That would shut up Julie's voice in my head.

Then I might enjoy a truly carefree Sunday.

Except I kept thinking about being number seven on the SAFE list, and how, after Senator Swift, the only enemies above me were out of the state. And I remembered that calm, cultured voice on my answering machine telling me that I deserved a just and ironic death. It's hard to be carefree when you figure you're the next target of an assassin.

I still managed to plow through a large stack of papers.

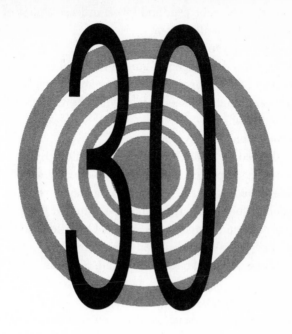

30

I locked up around five, went home, showered and changed, and took the T to Harvard Square. I was at the bar inside Giannino's at ten of seven, sipping a glass of Samuel Adams, Boston's own beer. I had seen nobody who looked like a Secret Service agent all day.

I told the hostess that I was expecting somebody, and when she arrived we'd like a table out on the patio.

Diana got there fifteen minutes later. She climbed aboard the barstool next to mine and kissed my cheek. "Hi," she said.

"Hi."

"I just came from the hospital. Sorry if I'm late."

"You're not. I was early. How's Wally?"

"All grabby and talking dirty. I'd say he's on the mend."

The bartender came over and Diana ordered a glass of white wine. I asked for another Sam.

"And how are you?" I said.

She smiled and shrugged. "I guess I'm all right. I mean, sometimes when I don't expect it I suddenly remember hearing those shots, running out and seeing him lying there. He's safe now, don't you think?"

"As safe as anybody ever is, I guess."

She slapped my arm. "You are such a comfort, Brady Coyne."

The hostess appeared. "Your table's ready now, sir," she said.

She escorted us outside, described the day's specials in delicious detail, and left menus with us. We studied them, debated the offerings, and watched the mix of Cambridge folks prowl around the patio. We had placed our orders and started to talk about fishing when Diana suddenly said, "Oh, shit."

"What?"

"You've got to excuse me for a minute."

She got up and strode across the open area to one of the outdoor bars. I saw her stop beside a man who was seated there. He was a lanky guy with thinning brown hair and pale skin. He was wearing a sports jacket, a tie pulled loose at the collar, chino pants, and a hangdog expression.

They held a brief but animated conversation. It looked pretty one-sided. Diana jabbed with her forefinger and shook her fist at him. He folded his arms and looked down at his lap. After a few minutes, Diana put her hands on her hips, and the man slowly climbed off the barstool and ambled away. Then she came back and sat across from me.

She tried to smile, shook her head, and let out a short laugh. "Sorry about that," she said.

I shrugged and said nothing.

"That was Howard."

I nodded. "That's what I figured."

"He followed me here."

"Why?"

"That's what I asked him."

"And?"

"He loves me. He wants me to come home. He forgives me. He's worried about me."

"Worried?"

She nodded quickly. "I hang around with dangerous people."

"Wally."

"Yeah. And you." She sighed heavily. "Shit, anyway."

I touched her arm. "What are you going to do about it?"

"Do? What are my choices?"

"I don't know. The usual, I guess."

"Restraining order, you mean."

"That's one."

She shook her head. "I just can't. It's not as if he wants to hurt me."

"Has this ruined our evening?" I said.

She smiled. "Hell, no."

Our salads arrived. We ate them. Diana said, "I guess I mainly feel sorry for him."

"Sounds to me as if that's his objective. To make you pity him."

"I guess it is."

She had a spicy chicken dish. I had scallops and mushrooms in a cream sauce. We didn't talk much.

Afterward we wandered around the Square. We browsed through bookstores. I looked for old first-edition fishing books at bargain prices. I found a few books, but there were no bargain prices on books in Harvard Square.

We watched a street performer juggle five basketballs.

A girl with bare feet and a braid down to her waist sang and played acoustic guitar in front of the Coop. She sounded exactly like Joan Baez, and I asked her if she knew "It's All Over Now, Baby Blue," the Dylan song. She sang it beautifully, and I dropped a five-dollar bill into her guitar case.

Diana and I had a beer at Grendel's. We didn't talk about Wally's shooting or Howard or SAFE. She told me about trips she'd taken with Wally, steelhead fishing in Oregon and British Columbia, a two-week river float in Alaska, tarpon fishing in the Keys and Belize. I countered with tales of the trout that live in the spring creeks of Montana's Paradise Valley.

I didn't tell her about the phone message I'd received the previous evening or the fear that gnawed on the margins of my consciousness. Being with her comforted me. Our assassin only went after his enemies when they were alone in the woods.

Diana's condo was on one of the little side streets that connect Broadway with Cambridge Street, a fifteen-minute walk from the square. We cut through the Harvard Yard. It was deserted, which I found strange for a Saturday night until I remembered that nowadays the ever-shrinking college academic year ends sometime around the first week of May.

Her tree-lined street was quiet. Old houses stood shoulder to shoulder, separated from each other only by the width of a driveway. Cars were parked solid on both sides.

We stood on the porch. Diana fumbled in her purse for her keys, found them, and unlocked the door. "I'll put on some coffee," she said.

"Thanks, no," I said.

She turned to me and put her hand on my arm. "Hey," she said softly.

"It's okay," I said. "No misunderstanding. It was a nice evening."

"You sure?"

I nodded. "Thanks anyway."

She tiptoed up and kissed my cheek. "Well, thanks. It was fun. I'm glad to have you as a friend."

"Me, too," I said.

She opened the door and went inside. She turned and smiled. "Good night, Brady," she said.

"Night, Diana."

The door closed. I heard three locks engage. I went down the steps to the sidewalk. I touched my cheek where Diana had kissed it. I decided when I got back to the square I'd call Alex from a pay phone. I could take the subway to her place on Marlborough Street, or she could meet me at my place. Either way—

No sound registered. If there was the click of a safety being released, or a shoe scuffling on concrete, or a harsh breath being exhaled, I don't remember hearing it. But something made me flinch an instant before the shot cracked from across the street at the same instant that glass exploded beside me, and I lurched sideways and stumbled onto the pavement and pressed myself flat between two parked cars. Several shots boomed in the night air, one after the other, so close together they sounded like a single extended explosion, and I huddled there, wedged under the front bumper of a car with my arms around my head.

It was over as abruptly as it started, and the street was quiet. I lay there, reluctant to move. I listened, but heard nothing. No clatter of running feet, no squeal of tires. Just the hum of the evening and the whisper of the spring breeze in the trees.

I crawled out and knelt behind the car that had probably saved my life. Cautiously I peered over the hood. I saw nothing.

"Brady?" Diana was standing on the porch. "Brady!" she yelled.

"I'm okay." I stood up.

"What—?"

"He missed."

"Oh, Jesus!"

She came down the steps to me. I put my arms around her. She was trembling, and I felt myself beginning to shake, too. She hugged me hard, and I held on to her. After a minute we went to the steps and sat down. I fumbled out a cigarette and got it lit.

"Diana," I said, "I'm sorry."

"Huh?"

"I'm sorry. He could've . . ."

"He wasn't after me," she said. "If he was, he wouldn't've waited till I went inside. He was after you. He must've followed us."

"Unless he knew where you lived."

"But if he was after you . . ."

"You're right," I said. "He must have followed us."

"What do we do?"

"We don't sit out here," I said. "We go inside. You make some coffee. I call the police."

By the time I got the 911 operator I heard sirens in the distance. When I told her that there had been gunshots, she said they'd already had two calls on it and a cruiser was on its way. I gave her Diana's address. She said she'd radio it to the cruiser.

479

A few minutes later there came a knock at the door. Diana answered it and led two uniformed Cambridge police officers into the kitchen. One looked like a high school freshman and the other was about my age. The older one took out a pen, flipped open a notebook, and asked what happened. I told him. He took a lot of notes.

Was I sure it was gunshots I'd heard, not fireworks or a car backfiring?

I was sure. One of them had broken a car window, if he'd care to check outside.

And did I think the shots were aimed specifically at me?

I believed they were.

Why?

I told him about the SAFE enemies' list, and Wally, and the identical phone calls we'd both received. I did not mention Senator Marlon Swift, or the fact that I'd been under Secret Service surveillance, or that I had apparently been abandoned by Agent Malloy.

Was there anybody else I could think of who'd want to shoot me?

I tried to make a joke of it. I mentioned Gloria.

The cop looked up and frowned at me.

I told him I was kidding.

He said he supposed they'd go outside and look around.

I suggested that he should contact Lieutenant Horowitz at 1010 Commonwealth Avenue.

The cop looked at me sharply.

I told him Horowitz was a friend of mine.

He shrugged and asked how he could get ahold of me in case they needed to talk to me again.

I gave him my card.

The two cops left.

Diana and I sipped coffee at her kitchen table. "Are you all right?" she said.

"Yes. How about you?"

She shrugged.

We sat in silence for a few minutes. Then she said, "I was thinking . . .

"Howard?"

She looked at me and nodded. "First Walter, now you. You were with me."

"Where does he live?"

"Out in Westwood."

"Why don't you call him?"

"What will I say?"

"It's about a forty-five-minute drive from here. If he's there . . ."

She nodded. She stood up and picked up the kitchen phone. She pecked out a number from memory, then shifted with the telephone wedged against her ear and gazed at the ceiling. After a long minute she hung up. She looked at me. "No answer," she said.

I shrugged. "All it means is that he's not home."

Tears brimmed in her eyes. "I just can't believe it."

"It doesn't mean anything," I said. "It just means he's not home."

I finished my coffee. Diana walked me to the door. "I'm sorry," she said.

"You didn't do anything wrong," I said. I kissed her forehead. "Wally once mentioned to me that you knew Senator Swift."

"Chip Swift? Sure. I worked with him on a bill he was sponsoring. It was pretty exciting, actually. At the time, it helped me get my mind off Howard. We got the bill passed and Chip had a big party for all of us who had worked on it at his place down in Marshfield." She looked up at me and frowned. "Why? Why are you asking about Chip?"

I touched her arm and smiled quickly. "Nothing, really. I just wondered."

I took a cab back to my apartment. Alex had left a message on my machine. She said, "Oh well. Guess you've got a date tonight. Too bad."

I poured myself two fingers of Daniel's, no ice, and took it out onto my balcony.

Wally had been shot once, not fatally. He could have been

killed, but all the other shots had missed him. A wounded man lying on the ground would make an unmissable target for an assassin bent on murder.

Marlon Swift hadn't been hit at all.

Neither had I.

Whoever had fired at me had stood somewhere across the street, no more than fifty feet from me. He had shot the window out of a car, missing me by several feet. He was either the world's worst marksman, or his intention was not to kill me. And if it wasn't murder—then what was it?

No answers came to me out there in the night air.

Maybe my turn had come and gone. He hadn't tried to finish off Wally. As far as I knew, he hadn't taken another crack at Chip Swift. Maybe no murders would happen. Maybe this man with the gun was just working his way down the SAFE list trying to scare the shit out of his enemies.

In that case, the shooter had achieved his goal. He *had* scared the shit out of me.

I went inside and called Horowitz's number. He wasn't there. I asked to be patched through to him and was told he was unavailable, would I like to leave a message. "Tell Lieutenant Horowitz that Brady Coyne called," I said. "Tell him that the guy who shot Walt Kinnick took a crack at me and missed."

I disconnected, then called Alex. It rang several times before her muffled voice said, "H'lo?"

"It's me. You were sleeping."

I heard her yawn. "Yup. You okay?"

"Sure. I'm fine."

"Miss me?"

"Yes."

"Tomorrow, 'kay?"

"I'll talk to you tomorrow," I said. "Sleep tight."

"You, too, sweetie."

My dreams were jumbled and vivid and continuous. When I
awakened on Sunday morning, though, I could only remember
one of them. I was wrestling in the woods with Bobby Farraday.
It was night and the ground was muddy and a flock of crows
perched on the low limbs above us. The crows didn't make any
noises. They had their heads cocked down and they watched us
with their shiny black eyes. Bobby seemed much stronger than
me, and I didn't fight back. I just lay there and let him twist my
arms and legs. It didn't hurt me at all. I kept wanting to ask him
why he was trying to hurt me, but I couldn't seem to speak.
Bobby didn't say anything at all in my dream.

Bobby Farraday was a kid I'd known in grammar school. We

hadn't been friends. He was a frail, somber boy, frequently absent. When the rest of us frolicked on the playground during recess, Bobby would sit and watch us with his round sad eyes. He died of leukemia sometime in the summer after fourth grade. I hadn't had a conscious thought of Bobby Farraday for more than thirty years.

Sunday was a brilliant May day. It would be wasted if I didn't take myself fishing. But the Bobby Farraday dream lingered. It was a death dream, of course. One might logically expect to have a death dream or two after hearing a volley of gunshots whiz overhead on a quiet Cambridge street.

And somewhere on the fringe of my consciousness, I was aware that there were other, deeper levels to my dream. I struggled to decipher it. But try as I would, its meaning eluded me. It made me feel edgy and vaguely depressed, and it dampened my enthusiasm for fishing.

Horowitz called a little before eleven. "What the hell happened last night?" he said.

I told him.

"I got a call from the Cambridge cops," he said. "They called it an alleged shooting."

"It wasn't alleged," I said. "It happened. There were two witnesses."

"The only thing they came up with was a broken windshield on an old Chevrolet."

"No empty cartridges?"

"Nope." He paused, and I heard his bubble gum snap. "Listen, Coyne," he said. "Your name has been popping up around here lately."

"What do you mean?"

"For one thing, this goddam Secret Service agent was asking questions."

"They were following me," I said. "Not doing a particularly good job of it, either."

Horowitz laughed. "Yeah, I heard you made one of 'em. Of

course, they'd been on your tail for a few days by then. They dropped you."

"I figured they did. Otherwise they would have witnessed an assassination attempt."

"On you," he said. "Right. Anyway, I also got a call from a certain state senator, and—"

"What state senator?"

"I think you know, Coyne."

"Swift?"

"None other. He told me all about it, on account of you told him I could be trusted, which I can, though I don't like playing these fucking games. Both Swift and this female agent tell me you suggested they give me a jingle. Then this thing last night."

And?"

"And nothing, if you mean do we know who's taking potshots at SAFE enemies. Far as I know he took a whack at numbers one and two and then moved on to number seven which, as you know, is you. Doesn't look like he wants to tangle with big-name politicians. You got any ideas?"

I hesitated for a moment, then said, "Well, I can give you the name of someone with a motive to shoot at Walt Kinnick, and maybe at me."

"But no motive to shoot a state senator, huh?"

I hesitated. "Maybe him, too."

"Who is it?"

"His name is Howard West. He's the estranged husband of Walt's lady friend."

"A stalker type, huh?"

"Maybe. Yes."

"Okay," said Horowitz, "that would certainly explain Kinnick. But why would he shoot at you and Swift?"

"He saw me and Diana having dinner together. And Diana used to work with the senator and went to a party at his house. If West is really crazy jealous . . ."

"Hm," said Horowitz. "That's a motive, I guess. What about means and opportunity?"

"I don't know. He was in Cambridge last night. He saw me and the lady together."

"Where's this guy live, do you know?"

"Westwood. But—"

"But what?"

"But I guess I still think SAFE is behind it."

"Yeah," said Horowitz. "Probably. Still, I guess we ought to check this Howard West out."

"What about protecting other people on that list?"

"On the basis of what?"

"Three of them have been shot at already."

"Yeah," he said. "Be nice if we could protect everybody. Unfortunately, it doesn't work that way. You're not having any other useful thoughts, are you?"

"Yeah," I said, "I'm having thoughts."

"Well?"

"They're pretty vague," I said. I didn't think Horowitz would place much credence in my dreams. "I haven't figured out if they're useful or not yet. When I do I'll let you know."

"Make it snappy, Coyne. One of these days this nut might kill somebody."

"That," I said, "is certainly one of the thoughts I've been having."

After I hung up with Horowitz, I retrieved the SAFE newsletter with its enemies' list from the rolltop desk in the corner of my living room. After Wally and Senator Swift, enemies number three through six—the Connecticut governor and the two United States senators from Massachusetts and the Congressman from Rhode Island—had apparently been skipped. Brady Coyne, the seventh enemy, had been next.

Eight was the senator from Vermont, and nine was a United States congresswoman from Maine. If Horowitz was right, the next target of the assassin would be Wilson Bailey, enemy number ten.

I didn't want to underestimate this shooter. He *had* shot Wally, and it almost killed him. Senator Swift had saved himself by his reflexes. I had been plain lucky, although, as I remembered it, I must have heard or sensed something, because I had flinched and ducked behind a car an instant before the first shot was fired. Otherwise, maybe I'd have been killed.

That's what my Bobby Farraday dream was all about.

I dialed Wilson Bailey's number. His answering machine picked it up. "Hi," came the woman's cheery voice. "You've reached the Bailey household. I guess no one's home right now. Please leave a message and we'll get back to you."

I swallowed hard before I responded to the dead Mrs. Bailey's invitation. "Mr. Bailey, it's Brady Coyne again," I said. "If you're there please call me right back. It's very important." I left my phone number.

I skimmed through the Sunday *Globe* while I waited for Bailey to return my call. There was a long piece by Alex comparing safety procedures and evacuation contingencies at the Seabrook and Plymouth nuclear power stations. It was strong, frightening journalism. I told myself I should call and congratulate her. But I didn't want to tie up the phone in case Wilson Bailey tried to reach me.

I remembered the man's testimony. His wife and daughter and unborn child had been murdered in an utterly random act of violence in a small-town library. I tried to imagine being Wilson Bailey, the horror of it. I found it unthinkable.

Two o'clock came and went. No call from Bailey.

I found a map and located the town of Harlow, where Bailey lived. It was near the Ware River, a decent trout stream in the middle of the state that I fished occasionally. It looked as if it would take about an hour and a half to drive from Boston to Harlow.

I went to the phone and dialed Alex's number. Her answering machine invited me to leave a message. "Good article," I said. "You're a helluva reporter, lady. I'm going fishing. I'll call if I don't get in too late. I'm feeling a bit hug-deprived."

I gathered together my fishing gear. I found myself wanting very much to talk to Wilson Bailey. After that, maybe I'd feel more like trying to catch a trout.

I pondered my Bobby Farraday dream all the way out to Harlow. The more I thought about it, the more ominous it seemed. I knew enough about dream interpretation to understand why I'd had that dream. But that didn't help me to figure it out.

The SAFE enemies' list told me that Wilson Bailey lived at 78 Aldrich Street. The kid at the 7-Eleven store in Harlow had never heard of Aldrich Street. But he had a town map, and together we located it. I bought a can of Pepsi, thanked the kid, and followed the directions I had written down from the map.

Harlow appeared to be a typical old New England mill town whose mill had long since been closed down and which now survived as a bedroom community halfway between Springfield and Worcester. It was a reasonable commute to either city, and as I navigated the streets I saw considerable evidence that optimistic real estate developers had targeted Harlow during the boom of the seventies and abandoned it in the collapse of the eighties. There were many building lots that had been cleared but not built on and unoccupied homes with piles of raw dirt and For Sale signs in front.

The dwellings on Aldrich Street were small and neat and of the same vintage, all cut from the same half-dozen architectural plans. They were set back from the road among tall pines on large lots. I drove slowly, checking the mailboxes out front for street numbers. Kids pedaled their bikes in the street and played basketball in the driveways. Men rode mowers back and forth across their front lawns. Young matrons wearing cotton gloves and T-shirts and shorts knelt on the edges of flower gardens.

It was a pleasant residential street, the kind of place where the neighbors got together for barbecues on summer Saturday evenings, and the kids swam in each other's pools, and the grown-ups pitched horseshoes and played volleyball. A nice street for raising a young family.

Aldrich Street was a dead end. Number 78 was the last house on the right. Number 76 next door had a For Sale sign out front. The house appeared empty. On the dead-end side of Bailey's house lay undeveloped woodland.

A Plymouth station wagon was parked in his driveway. His lawn had been mowed within the past few days. The gardens were neatly edged and mulched. The foundation plantings of azaleas and rhododendrons rioted in full pink and red bloom.

I parked behind the wagon, got out, and slammed the door. I walked up to the front door and rang the bell. I heard it jingle inside. I waited, then rang it again. A minute or two later a fat old golden retriever came sauntering around from the back of the house. He sat at the foot of the steps and looked up at me.

I descended the steps and scooched down beside him. I scratched his ears. "Do you live here, boy?" I said to him. "Is your master out back?"

489

He cocked his head at me as if he understood what I was saying. I stood up, and the dog stood, too. He started around the side of the house. I followed him.

It was a typical suburban backyard, with a swing set and a small above-ground pool and a metal toolshed and a flagstone patio with a gas barbecue grill and a picnic table and some folding aluminum lawn furniture.

I squinted into the afternoon sun and saw Wilson Bailey sleeping on a chaise on the patio. He was wearing sneakers and chino pants and a white polo shirt. The dog went over and lay down beside him. I followed him.

"Mr. Bailey. . . ?" I began. But I stopped. Because I saw the dark puddle under the chaise and I knew Wilson Bailey would not answer me.

He was lying on his back. His eyes stared up at the sky. His mouth was agape and a trail of crusted blood ran from the corner of his mouth and made a dark stain on the front of his shirt. The back of his head had been blown away. The weapon lay on his chest. It was short and ugly. Bailey's right thumb was curled inside the trigger guard.

His left arm was folded over the gun and across his chest. He was clutching something in his left hand. I bent to look at it. It was a photograph of a plain round-faced young woman and a very pretty little girl.

I wedged two fingers up under his jawbone. His skin was the same temperature as the air. I felt no pulse.

I backed away from him and sat heavily on a lawn chair. The dog came over and laid his chin on my leg. I stroked his nose for a moment, then lit a cigarette. I stared at Wilson Bailey lying rigidly on the chaise while I smoked the Winston down to the filter. Then I stood up and went to the back door. It was unlocked. I went into Wilson Bailey's kitchen and dialed 911.

I sat on the front steps to wait. The dog waited with me. Within a couple of minutes I heard the sirens, and then two cruisers skidded to a stop in front of the house. I waved toward the backyard, and two of the cops jogged in that direction. One stayed out front to talk to the kids on their bikes and the neighbors who began to gather there. The other cop came to the front steps where I was waiting.

"You called it in?" he said.

I nodded.

"The detectives are on their way." He turned his back on me, folded his arms, and stood there watching the street.

A rescue wagon arrived a minute later, and then another cruiser, and then a couple of unmarked vehicles. I continued to sit on the front steps patting the dog and smoking, and the cop stood there ignoring me.

The uniformed cops kept the curious neighbors in the street and off the front lawn. They draped yellow crime scene ribbon all the way around the yard. Official people kept moving back and forth from the back of the house to their vehicles parked in front. Distorted voices crackled from police radios. After a while a graying man in a green plaid sport coat came along and said something to the uniformed cop who was guarding me. The cop sauntered away and the guy in the sport coat sat beside me on the steps. "You're the one who called it in?" he said.

I nodded.

"Lieutenant Morrison, state police." He held his hand out to me.

We shook. "Brady Coyne. I'm a lawyer."

"Mr. Bailey's lawyer?"

"No." I shook my head. "It's a long story."

"You better tell me."

So I did. I began with Wally Kinnick's testimony before the state Senate subcommittee where Wilson Bailey had also testified, the SAFE enemies' list, Wally's getting shot, my conversation with Senator Swift, the Saturday night gunshots on the Cambridge street. All of it. Except I didn't tell him about my Bobby Farraday dream. It was beginning to make sense to me, but I didn't think it would to the lieutenant.

"So you came out here to warn Mr. Bailey?" said Morrison.

I shrugged. "Warn him. Or ask him why he was doing it. I wanted to talk to him. I thought I understood what he'd been living with. It seemed like a better reason than most to try to shoot people."

"It looks like he shot himself."

I nodded. "I know."

"Stuck the muzzle in his mouth and pulled the trigger."

I nodded again.

"How do you figure it?"

"Me?" I said.

"Yes."

I shrugged. "I guess he felt he just had to do something."

"So he was number ten on that list, huh?" he said.

"Yes," I said. "It was his turn."

Morrison nodded.

After a minute, I said, "That gun . . ."

"It's a Valmet," said the lieutenant. "Pretty common assault weapon. Made in Finland. Semiautomatic. Modeled after an automatic military weapon they make. Fifteen-round magazine."

"What's the caliber?"

"It's 5.56 millimeter."

"That's .223," I said.

He looked at me and shrugged.

"You should talk to Lieutenant Horowitz in Boston," I said.

"Horowitz has been on this case?"

"Sort of."

Morrison was silent for a moment. Then he said, "We got a little problem here, Mr. Coyne."

I looked at him.

"No note," he said.

I remembered that Bailey had spoken without notes at the subcommittee hearing. When asked to hand in his written statement, he had instead given the committee members a photograph of his wife and daughter. "That photograph he had in his hand," I said.

"Yeah?"

"I think that was his suicide note, Lieutenant. I think he believed that photograph says it all."

He smiled quickly. "Yeah, I guess maybe it does at that, doesn't it?"

Lieutenant Morrison sat with me for a while longer. We didn't talk anymore. I figured he was just keeping track of me. Or maybe I was some kind of suspect. I didn't really care.

A rescue wagon drove across the lawn and around the side of the house. A few minutes later it returned and disappeared down Aldrich Street. It didn't bother to sound its siren.

Gradually the onlookers in the street went back to mowing their lawns and playing basketball in their driveways and pedaling their bikes and weeding their gardens.

I rode with Lieutenant Morrison in the backseat of a state police cruiser to headquarters in Springfield. Another cop followed behind us in my car. I gave my deposition to a tape recorder, telling my story and answering the lieutenant's questions.

It was after dark when I got home. There was one message on my answering machine. Alex's voice said, "I'm glad you had a chance to go fishing. Nice day for it. Call me when you get in, if it's not too late, huh?"

I went out and sat on my balcony and decided I didn't want to talk to anybody.

◎

When I got to the office Monday morning, I said to Julie, "Hold my calls, kid. And cancel anything on the calendar. I don't want to be disturbed."

She opened her mouth, gave me a quick hard look, then closed it. She nodded. "Okay, boss."

I fiddled around with paperwork all day. There was plenty of it. But my mind kept wandering, and I frequently found myself swiveled around in my chair with my back to my desk, staring out the window at the concrete and glass of Copley Square.

My console didn't buzz and my phone didn't ring all day.

At five o'clock Julie tapped on my door, then opened it. Without speaking, she came to my desk and laid a sheet of paper onto it. "Your calls," she said. "You'll notice that Alexandria Shaw called several times. You should call her back."

"I thought you didn't like her."

"I do like her. And I wish you'd call her. Maybe you'll tell her what you're not telling me."

"Okay," I said. "I'll call her, then."

"Good." She turned and went to the door.

"Good night," I said to her.

She stopped and frowned at me. "Good night, Brady."

"I'll tell you about it when I'm ready."

She nodded. "I know you will."

I stared at the phone for the length of time it took me to smoke a cigarette. Then I tried Alex at home. Her machine answered again. I hung up without leaving a message, then called her number at the *Globe*. She answered with a brusque, "Alex Shaw."

"Hi," I said.

"Oh, geez. How are you?"

"I'm okay."

There was a pause. Then she said, "No, you're not. I can hear it in your voice."

"You're right," I said. "I'm not. I want to talk to you about it. But not now."

"Want me to come over tonight?"

"I don't think so. I wouldn't be very good company. Give me a couple days, okay?"

"Okay," she said. "Whatever you say."

"Are you upset?"

"Should I be?"

"No. I do want to see you. I've just got to sort out some things."

"Call me when you're ready, then, all right?"

"I will," I said.

I fooled around with paperwork the next day, too. No calls, no visitors. When Julie gave me my messages that afternoon, I saw that one was from Wally. "Getting discharged tomorrow," it said.

So I walked from the office over to Mass General. Wally was dressed in jeans and a flannel shirt and sitting in a chair. Diana was sprawled on the bed. When she saw me she scrambled up and hugged me. "Are you okay?" she said.

"Sure, I guess so. Why not?"

"I called several times. Your secretary wouldn't put me through. After what happened Saturday night, and then you found that poor man . . ."

"Your friend Horowitz was in," said Wally. "He told me all about it."

"I bet he had some questions for you, too."

Wally smiled. "Why, sure. But he did smuggle in a quart of Wild Turkey."

"I suppose it's all gone by now," I said.

"Not quite. We probably ought to find a way to get rid of it. It'd be risky to try to smuggle it out again."

495

So Diana slipped out of the room and came back a couple of minutes later with three water glasses and a pitcher of ice. We closed the door and Wally retrieved the bottle from his duffel bag and we toasted each other's good health.

He and Diana were headed straight to the cabin in Fenwick the next day. They planned to unplug the telephone so they could fish and read and eat and sit in the sun and make love without interruption, and from the way they kept looking at each other, it wasn't hard to deduce which activity held the highest position on their order of priorities.

They planned to stay for at least two weeks. They hoped I'd join them.

I shrugged. I was behind on my office work. Maybe I could get away for a weekend.

They didn't press me, but they made it clear they were sincere.

We toasted the trout of the Deerfield River.

Wally said that Gene McNiff had called. The assault-gun bill, which had passed Senator Swift's subcommittee by a single vote, had been buried in committee and was officially dead for the current legislative term. McNiff told Wally that as far as he was concerned, there were no hard feelings.

We toasted Gene McNiff.

Horowitz had said that the state police lab confirmed that Wilson Bailey's Valmet was the same gun that had shot Wally and missed Senator Swift. So we toasted Horowitz.

Wally's doctors had given him a clean bill of health, and we toasted that, too.

When I left the hospital a couple of hours later, I felt peppier than I had for a while.

But by the time I walked into my empty apartment, the effects of the Wild Turkey toasts and Diana's and Wally's happiness had worn off.

I sat on my balcony and stared down at the dark harbor and thought about Wilson Bailey and Bobby Farraday. Then I went to bed.

◎

I got to the office before Julie on Wednesday. When she arrived, I brought her a mug of coffee. "No calls," I said.

"Brady, you can't—"

"Just one more day. Okay?"

She shrugged. "Whatever you say."

Sometime in the middle of the afternoon she knocked and then came into my office. "Listen," she said.

"Julie, please."

"Alexandria Shaw is here to see you."

"Tell her I'll call her later."

"I think you should see her now."

I looked up at her. "Why?"

"She's very upset."

"Shit," I mumbled.

Julie smiled. "Brady, as adorable as you are, I've got the distinct impression that Miz Shaw is not feeling lovelorn."

"What did she say?"

"She needs to talk to you. She says it's a professional matter."

I sighed. "Fine. Okay. Send her in."

Alex was wearing her big round glasses. Behind them, her eyes were red and swollen. I stood up and went to her. She allowed me to hug her. But she did not return my hug. She rested her forehead against my chest for a moment, then stepped back. "I've got something I want you to hear," she said.

"Okay. Say it."

She shook her head. "Not me. It's a tape. Can we sit?"

I gestured to the sofa. She sat down, and I sat beside her. She fumbled in her briefcase and came up with her little tape recorder and a cassette. "It came in the mail this morning," she said. "I've listened to it once." She inserted the cassette, then switched on the machine.

"Miz Shaw," came the recorded voice, which I recognized as the same voice that had left a message on my answering machine, "by the time you get this I will be dead. So you might consider this my suicide note. I have much to say, and I think it will be easier just to talk this way than to try to write it all down. I suppose you'll have to turn this over to the police, and that's okay. But I hope you can use what I've got to tell you. I've tried every other

497

way I know to get this story in front of the public where it belongs, and so far I've failed."

His voice was soft. But it was firm and conveyed strength and conviction. "Oh, this is Wilson Bailey, and it's Saturday evening. I've just returned from Cambridge where I shot my Valmet in the general direction of Mr. Brady Coyne. A few nights ago I did the same thing to Senator Marlon Swift down in Marshfield. I know this isn't coming out very logically. I hope you'll bear with me."

He cleared his throat. "See, Miz Shaw, you wrote the story about the massacre in the Harlow public library two years ago. Maybe you don't even remember it. I know that every day you have a different story to write, and I imagine that yesterday's news is something newspaper people quickly forget. But in your story you mentioned the fact that two bystanders were wounded by a man with an assault weapon. The man killed his wife, the librarian. That was your story. But my wife Loretta and my daughter Elaine were those two anonymous bystanders who were rushed to the hospital. Elaine died that night. They tried to operate on Loretta, but she didn't make it. Neither did the baby she was carrying.

"I kept looking at the *Globe*, waiting for your story about Loretta and Elaine. I thought that was a much more important story than the one about that man killing his wife. I still do. I mean, the story is very obvious. That horrible weapon was the criminal, not that crazy man who shot it. He intended to kill his wife, okay. That was his crime. But it was the gun, that AK-47, not the man, that killed my family. Don't you see? So I waited for that story, and it never came. The true criminal, that gun, that AK-47, was never accused or indicted or convicted of the crime. Loretta and Elaine—they just—they just died, Miz Shaw. Like it was an accident or a disease or something. Just one of those things that happens all the time."

There came the low hum of recorded silence from the tape. Alex reached quickly for the machine and turned it off. I looked at her. Her cheeks were wet with tears. "He's right," she said. "I never followed up that story. I intended to, but I didn't. Other stories came along, newer news. I didn't think of them as people. They were—they were just stories."

498

"Do you think it would have made a difference?" I said.

She shrugged. "I don't know. Yes. Yes, I guess I do."

I put my arm around her. She rested her head on my shoulder for a moment. Then she cleared her throat, sat forward, and clicked the tape recorder on.

The hum of silence continued for a few seconds. Then Bailey's voice said, "Excuse me, Miz Shaw. I'm trying to think clearly here. I want you to understand."

There was more silence. Then, "Since that afternoon two years ago I have devoted the poor miserable remnants of my life to one thing. Getting rid of those evil weapons. I have written letters to newspapers and magazines. Very few of them have been printed. And when they are, they are edited so that they don't say what I intended. I have harassed legislators with letters and phone calls. Mostly they avoid me. I have tried to testify both in Washington and on Beacon Hill. A couple of times I have been heard. But my testimony—my story, the story of Loretta and Elaine—has been ignored. Ignored by the politicians, Miz Shaw, and ignored by the press. At first I didn't understand. It's all so obvious to me. But then I began to see. It's all about money and votes, and I don't have either. Groups like the Second Amendment For Ever, they have the money and the votes. They get heard. They get their stories in the newspapers. Like today's *Globe*, Miz Shaw. A nice story about SAFE, and I suppose you couldn't very well accuse them of shooting at Mr. Kinnick or Senator Swift, although, of course, they *are* responsible for it. But what about Loretta and Elaine? Where's their story?

"When I testified two weeks ago, what were the stories? They were all about the courageous Walt Kinnick, risking his career as a friend of guns to speak in favor of a very modest gun-control bill. You heard him. What does he know? To Kinnick and to the politicians and to all the others, it's a political issue, an abstraction. They say what they think will serve them, and then they're done with it. When I heard Kinnick, my first thought was: Aha. An ally. But then I realized. He's just another politician. Shallow, uncommitted, cynical, opportunistic. He'll say whatever serves him, reap the publicity rewards, and then go fishing. It's not an issue for men like him, not a cause. It's just an opportunity to advance himself.

Men like Kinnick, they're as bad as the politicians. No. They're worse. We expect cynicism from politicians. We expect more from the Walt Kinnicks of the world. I was naive. Men like Kinnick don't care whether the legislation passes. They only care about what they can get out of it. They test the wind, they take their public opinion polls, and then they decide what they believe. We expect that of politicians. You'd hope for more from someone like Walt Kinnick. So he comes out for the bill. Big deal. The bill meant nothing to him. Just a chance to get his name in the paper. What about Loretta and Elaine, Miz Shaw? Were you there to hear me, or were you one of those who rushed out to interview Walt Kinnick and marvel at his courage? I tried. I did my best. I thought my story would—would make a difference."

Bailey's long sigh hissed in the tape recorder. There was silence for a moment. Then, "It took me a while to figure it out, Miz Shaw. The enemy was not the press, not the government. It was the money and votes of SAFE. It was SAFE that was telling you what to write, telling the politicians how to vote. And after my testimony that day, when I stood out there on the State House steps, I heard Mr. McNiff threaten Mr. Kinnick. And then I knew what I had to do. I knew that SAFE and all their cynical self-serving arguments had to be discredited. It was obvious, once I saw it. And then I read your stories about how they distributed lists of their enemies. What did they expect men with guns to do about their enemies? If you, Miz Shaw, if the press and the politicians believed that SAFE was murdering their enemies—if they were using those evil guns to do it—then you and the politicians and everybody else could no longer ignore them. The entire anti-gun-control argument would be exposed for what it is—a license for killing innocent people.

"I thought about it for a long time, Miz Shaw. I realized that Elaine's and Loretta's deaths were just the beginning. More deaths were needed. And a few days later the names of those victims were given to me on the SAFE list of enemies. Mr. Walt Kinnick was to be first."

Bailey actually chuckled. "Miz Shaw, you would be amazed at something. You understand, I owned no firearms. But several years ago I tried to purchase some Mace for Loretta, because I

500

was concerned for her safety in this awful violent world of ours. And I was told that I couldn't make this purchase without a Firearms Identification Number. An FID, they call it. So I went to the Harlow police station, and in due course I got a card for me and one for Loretta, because she had to have her own if she wanted to carry Mace legally. Loretta and I, we always obeyed the law. So anyway, after I saw the SAFE newsletter, I took my FID card to a gun shop near here and I picked out this weapon. It's very evil-looking. The man told me it was called a Valmet, and he assured me it was an assault gun. He showed me how to use it and he sold me ammunition and I bought that gun. Miz Shaw, I just bought it. It was no different from buying a book or a quart of milk. I walked into the shop with my FID card and my Visa card and I walked out with that wicked gun and a box of ammunition." He paused. "I see I'm close to the end here. I'm going to turn over the tape."

Alex reached forward, ejected the tape, turned it over, and reinserted it into the machine.

"Wait a minute," I said to her.

She hesitated, then sat back on the sofa.

"Come here," I said. "Please."

She turned to me. I held her against me with my face in her hair.

Her arms dangled at her sides, and after a minute she pulled back and poked at her glasses. "Let's listen to the rest of it," she said.

She hit the play button. "Okay," said Bailey's voice. "I bought that Valmet. Probably just the way that David Burton bought the AK-47 that killed Loretta and Elaine. And I drove to Fenwick and found where Walt Kinnick lived, and while they were off fishing I called and left a message for him, pretending I was someone from SAFE. I walked up there that night, and in the morning I waited in the woods outside his cabin until he came out. I wanted to kill him. He was a cynic and an opportunist, and I guess, after two years of getting nowhere with men like him, I hated him. I thought I had to kill him. He was the number-one enemy. If he was assassinated with an assault gun, they couldn't very well ignore the evil influence of SAFE any longer. The

501

influence that made it so easy for me to walk into that shop and buy that gun. Isn't that ironic? Miz Shaw, the hardest thing I've ever done was to aim that gun at Mr. Kinnick. And I pulled the trigger, and he fell, and I thought, Oh, my God, what have I done? And I kept pulling the trigger, but I wasn't aiming, because, you see, I was crying. Crying for Mr. Kinnick, who I thought I had killed, and crying for Loretta and Elaine and all the other victims of these evil weapons.

"But," he continued after a pause, "my mistake was that I didn't kill him. You wrote one piece in the paper. But you failed to implicate SAFE, Miz Shaw, and you said nothing about the weapon that shot him. So I went after Senator Swift. But I didn't have any hate left in me. I couldn't shoot him. I couldn't make myself point that gun at him. I thought maybe if I shot into the air it would be enough. But nothing. Not a word in the newspaper. The next people on that list were out of state. So it was to be the lawyer, that Mr. Coyne, who I would kill. Hate had nothing to do with it. I had to kill somebody, I realized that. Otherwise there was no news. But I couldn't do it, Miz Shaw. I couldn't make myself aim at him."

I reached for Alex's hand and gripped it hard. She gave my hand a quick squeeze. I glanced at her. Behind her glasses she was crying.

Wilson Bailey laughed quietly. "See, Miz Shaw? There has to be a killing. Who's left? Now you know. It's not SAFE that's shooting at people on their list. But if you think about it, it's still their fault. I have this weapon right here, and I walked into a store and bought it because no one has had the courage to stand up to SAFE and tell them it's wrong. Please, Miz Shaw. I *could* have killed Walt Kinnick and Senator Swift and Brady Coyne. You see that, don't you? And I *can* kill myself."

The tape hissed quietly for a long moment. Then Bailey said, "I was there, Miz Shaw. I was in the library. I saw it all. I saw that man walk in. I saw the gun. I saw him raise it to his hip. Loretta and Elaine were there. I saw that gun jump in his hands when he fired. I saw Elaine, little sweet Elaine, lifted off her feet when those bullets hit her. I saw Loretta start to reach toward her before the bullets slammed her backward. I still see these things.

502

Every minute of my life since that day I see these pictures, over and over again in my head. Miz Shaw, I have thought about this for a long time. There's still one question I cannot answer. It's this: Why in God's name wasn't I standing at the desk with Elaine and Loretta? Why did I have to keep living?"

The tape hissed. Alex reached toward the machine and switched it off.

We sat there, staring at it, not speaking.

"What are you going to do?" I said finally.

She shrugged. "I've got to give it to my editor. I wanted you to hear it first."

"I was the one who found his body," I said.

"I know," she said. "We got the police report. You figured it out, huh?"

"Not really. Certainly not all that." I gestured at her tape recorder. "I tried to call Bailey. To warn him. He didn't answer. It was his wife's voice on his answering machine. It said, 'We're not here.' That 'we,' it got to me, I guess, because there was no 'we.' The woman who had made that recording *was* dead, and he had never changed it. It was just him, all alone, living in the same house with his ghosts. That got me imagining what it must be like to be him, to live with what he'd had to live with. And I got this—it was just a vague indistinct feeling. A discomfort. After I got shot at Saturday night, I was frightened, of course. That night I had a dream, and he was in it, although I didn't recognize him. See, my subconscious was playing with it, making connections that my conscious mind refused to recognize. I tried to reach him again Sunday morning. Still no answer. So I went out there to meet him, and I wasn't sure why. I wanted to know him. I thought it was to warn him. But I think on another level I knew he was the one doing the shooting. Except it was all out there on the fuzzy fringes of my consciousness where I couldn't quite focus."

"So you followed your intuition."

I shrugged. "Something like that, I guess."

"It must have been awful for you."

"Yes, it was. I'm sorry I put you off. It wasn't fair of me."

"I understand."

503

"I couldn't talk to anybody. It's how I am sometimes."

She touched my arm. "It's all right, Brady."

"I think a hug would've helped more than anything."

She poked at her glasses. "All you had to do was ask."

"Can I have one now?"

She smiled softly. "Sure," she said.

I stood up. She took off her glasses and put them on the table beside the tape recorder. Then she pressed herself against me and wrapped her arms around my waist and laid her cheek against my chest. I held her tight with my face buried in her hair. After a minute she tried to lean back to look at me, or maybe to kiss me, but I held her against me. I didn't want her to see that my eyes were a little watery.

"Um, Miz Shaw?" I said, when I felt I could trust my voice.

"Mm?"

"How would you like to spend a weekend in a cozy cabin in the woods with me and two of my very best friends? We'll keep the phone unplugged, and we can do a little fishing and reading and sitting in the sun and . . ."

"And what?" she mumbled into my chest.

"And . . . and be together."

Her arms tightened around me. "I'd like that very much, Mr. Coyne, sir," she whispered.

CLOSE TO THE BONE

for Vicki

who's on every page
with thanks
and love

Justice, though due to the accused, is due to the accuser also.

—Benjamin Cardozo

I went to the woods because I wished to live deliberately, to front only the essential facts of life, and see if I could not learn what it had to teach, and not, when I came to die, discover that I had not lived. I did not wish to live what was not life, living is so dear; nor did I wish to practise resignation, unless it was quite necessary. I wanted to live deep and suck out all the marrow of life, to live so sturdily and Spartanlike as to put to rout all that was not life, to cut a broad swath and shave close, to drive life into a corner, and reduce it to its lowest terms, and, if it proved to be mean, why then to get the whole and genuine meanness of it, and publish its meanness to the world; or if it were sublime, to know it by experience, and be able to give a true account of it in my next excursion.

—Henry David Thoreau

ACKNOWLEDGMENTS

I am indebted to Vicki Stiefel, Rick Boyer, Jed Mattes, and Elisabeth Story for their perceptive help on this yarn. My heartfelt thanks.

1

Julie keeps telling me I'll never be a proper lawyer if I keep driving out to the suburbs to meet my clients at their homes whenever they request it. The clients, she maintains, are supposed to come to the lawyer's office in the city. They should make appointments, preferably weeks ahead of time because, according to Julie, any lawyer who can see a client at a moment's notice can't be very busy, and if he's not very busy he can't be much good, and if he's not much good then clients will not be inclined to make appointments with him in the first place. When it's done properly, says Julie, the clients who appear in their lawyer's office at their appointed time should be kept waiting while the lawyer accrues billable hours with another client, who has also been kept waiting.

Julie is probably a better legal secretary than I am a lawyer. I know that if I listened to her I'd accrue more billable hours, which is how Julie measures the success of a law practice.

So when Roger Falconer called on a gray Tuesday afternoon in November and said he needed to confer with me immediately, I said, "I've got an opening at four-thirty, Roger," as Julie had trained me to do.

My heart wasn't in it, of course. Roger Falconer, I knew, simply didn't sit in the waiting rooms of lawyers or doctors—or governors or senators or the CEOs of multinational corporations, either.

Hell, Roger Falconer had *been* the CEO of a multinational corporation before he retired. Back in the sixties and early seventies he had also been the state attorney general and the Republican candidate for governor and, apparently encouraged by losing that one, for United States senator. He lost that election, too, but, as he liked to point out, what could a Republican expect in Massachusetts, the only state that failed to cast its electoral votes for Nixon in 1972?

In fact, a lot of people who courted Roger's influence or money, or both, still called him "Senator," and he didn't bother to correct them.

I called him Roger. He didn't try to correct me, either.

"Four-thirty, huh?" he said. "Your last appointment of the day?"

"Uh huh." I knew what was coming, and I was helpless to avoid it.

"You should be able to be here by five-thirty, then," he said.

I sighed. "Sure, Roger. I guess I can be there around five-thirty. What's up?"

"A matter of utmost gravity, I'm afraid. I'd rather not discuss it over the phone, Brady."

When I slipped into my trench coat and headed out of the office a few minutes after four-thirty, Julie arched her eyebrows from behind her computer monitor.

"I'm off to see Roger Falconer," I said. "I've got to be there at five-thirty, and I don't need any shit about which of us is the mountain and which is Mahomet. It's a matter of utmost gravity."

"I didn't say anything," she said.

"Yeah, but I know what you're thinking."

She flashed her pretty blue-eyed Irish smile. "Utmost gravity? Did you actually say that?"

"Roger's words."

"Hey," she said with an elaborate shrug. "It's your law practice. If you want to go traipsing around the countryside at the summons of doddering old political has-beens, why should I care?"

"You should care, of course. That's your job. And I'm glad I've got you to do it."

"I don't see why the old poop can't come to the office like everyone else."

"Well, he won't. If I didn't go to him, he'd just get himself another lawyer." I bent and kissed her cheek. "I'll fill you in tomorrow."

It took over an hour to negotiate the rush-hour traffic from Copley Square, out Storrow Drive onto Route 2 and thence to Lincoln. I turned onto Route 126—Thoreau had called it "the Walden road"—and drove past the pond and the acres of fields and forests that the Lincoln town fathers and mothers have preserved from development so that folks like Roger Falconer can live thoroughly insulated from the riffraff.

Roger's long driveway wound through the dark oak and pine woods, past the tennis court and the swimming pool and the putting green, and ended in a turnaround in front of his big, square Federal-period colonial. Floodlights mounted under the eaves lit the flower gardens and the lawn, now mostly frost-killed and brown and littered with dead leaves. Orange lights glowed from every window.

A little white two-seater Mercedes convertible was parked behind a gunmetal gray Range Rover. I pulled in at the end of the line and got out of my car. A northeast wind hissed through the pine trees and rattled the clumps of dried leaves in the oaks. It felt damp and chilly on my face. It would bring freezing rain or wet snow. In November it could go either way. I climbed the front steps and rang the bell. A minute later the door swung open and a youngish woman I didn't recognize greeted me with a frown.

She wore a dark blue wool dress with a high neck and a low hem, just a touch of eye shadow and lip gloss, and no jewelry except for a diamond the size of a Brazil nut on her left hand, the hand that was holding a can of Coke. A slim blonde, pretty in a cool, brittle, elegantly fashionable way, early thirties, I guessed. "You are . . . ?" she said.

"Brady Coyne," I said. "I have an appointment with Roger. And you?"

"Pardon?"

"We haven't met," I said.

"I'm sorry." She tried on a smile that didn't quite make it up to her eyes. "Brenda Falconer. I'm the Senator's daughter-in-law." She lifted her Coke and took a quick, nervous sip.

"Glen's wife?" I said.

"Yes." She smiled again, and it worked better this time. "That, too." She extended her hand and allowed me to touch it for a moment. Then she turned. "They're in the library," she said over her shoulder. "This way."

I followed her down the wide center hallway and through a living room full of clunky old antique furniture and decorated with dark portraits of clunky old men. We stopped outside the open doorway to Roger's library, which was a room as big as my entire apartment. At the far end a brace of golden retrievers—Abe and Ike, named after Roger's political heroes—slept on the hearth by a blazing fieldstone fireplace. The walls were lined floor to ceiling with old leather-bound volumes. Rolltop desks and oak tables and leather sofas and armchairs were scattered about, and seated in two of the armchairs were Roger Falconer and his son, Glen. They were studying the fire, apparently ignoring each other.

Brenda cleared her throat and the two men looked up. "Ah, Brady," said Roger. "Come, sit. Brenda, dear, get Brady a drink."

"I can get my own drink," I said to her.

She shook her head. "It's okay. Really. What would you like?"

"I'll have what you're having," I said to her. "Thanks."

She left the room and I went over to where Roger and Glen were sitting. Empty highball glasses rested on the table between them. Roger didn't bother rising as we shook hands. He was almost completely bald now, and I knew he was closing in on eighty, but he still could've passed for the man who had run for the Senate back in the early seventies. His pale eyes glittered with enthusiasm and conspiracy, and his grip was strong. "You remember Glen?" he said.

"Sure." I held out my hand to the younger man. "How are you?"

"Not that good, actually," Glen said. He stood to shake hands with me. He was several inches taller than my six feet, and his face was longer and more angular than his father's. His sandy hair had receded perceptibly since the last time I had seen him, which had been a few years earlier.

After we sat down, Glen leaned toward me. "Look—"

"Brady," interrupted Roger, "we have a problem."

"I figured," I said. "A matter of utmost gravity, I think you called it. Sounds like a problem to me."

"A week and a half ago," he said, "Glen had an automobile accident. He, um, there was a collision with another vehicle."

"Who hit whom?" I said, addressing my question to Glen.

But it was Roger who answered. "He hit them."

"Them?"

"There were two passengers in the other car," said Roger. "A woman and her four-year-old boy."

He paused, gazing at me with his eyebrows arched behind his steel-rimmed glasses, waiting for me to figure it out. I did, but I said nothing.

There was a discreet rap at the door, and then Brenda came in. She handed me a glass of Coke rattling with ice cubes. I looked up at her. "Thanks," I said.

She nodded. "You're welcome." She stood there, looking from Roger to Glen.

"Thank you, my dear," said Roger with a nod, dismissing her.

Her eyes flickered and met mine for a moment before she turned and left the room. The door latched softly behind her.

"Your wife isn't included in this matter, huh?" I said to Glen.

"Family business," said Roger, who apparently did not consider wives to be members of his family.

I shrugged and took a sip of Coke.

"The woman was seriously injured in the collision," Roger said. He cleared his throat. "She died this morning."

"Right," I said. "And Glen was drunk."

Roger nodded.

"And they're going to charge him."

"Yes. Vehicular homicide, DUI."

"What about the little boy?"

"He was in a car seat. He's okay."

"Lucky," I said.

Roger nodded. "I guess so."

"I don't do these kinds of cases," I said.

"I know," said Roger. "But you're my lawyer."

"Did you take a Breathalyzer?" I said to Glen.

He nodded. "I flunked. My license was suspended."

"But you weren't charged?"

"No. Not then." He glanced at his father.

"I took care of it," said Roger. "But now, with the woman, ah, failing to survive . . . "

"You can't take care of this," I said.

Roger shook his head. "We need a good lawyer."

"You need a miracle."

Glen leaned toward me. "Listen, Brady—"

"Shut up," said Roger conversationally. "Brady's right, and if it weren't our family's name that the newspapers will be plastering all over the front page, I'd leave you out there twisting in the wind." He turned to me. "Do you know any miracle workers?"

"Yes, as a matter of fact."

"Who?"

"I'll talk to him."

"I'd rather—"

"Do you want me to handle it, Roger?"

"I do."

"Good. I will handle it." I drained my Coke and stood up. "That's it, then. I'll be in touch with you."

Roger looked up at me. "Brady," he said, "it's—"

"I know. A matter of utmost gravity. I'll call you tomorrow."

He pushed himself out of his chair. Glen started to stand, but Roger said, "I'll see Brady out," and Glen sat down again.

I held out my hand to Glen. "Good luck," I said.

He shrugged and we shook. "Thanks."

Roger followed me back through the living room to the front

door. I didn't see Brenda. I put my coat on and opened the door. "He doesn't seem that contrite," I said.

"My son is an alcoholic," said Roger, as if that explained everything.

"It's hard to be sympathetic."

Roger nodded. "He's looking at prison time, isn't he?"

"Sounds like it."

"How much?"

"Not enough," I said.

2

Alexandria Shaw was waiting for me when I got to my apartment a little after seven-thirty. Her feet were bare and she was wearing a pair of my sweatpants and one of my raggedy old Yale T-shirts, and she was curled in the corner of the sofa prodding at her scalp with the business end of a pencil and frowning through her big round glasses at a yellow legal pad. My old black-and-white television was tuned to *Jeopardy,* but Alex didn't seem to be watching it.

I went over and kissed the back of her neck. "I didn't have a chance to call," I said. "I was hoping you'd be here."

"Gimme a minute, sweetie," she mumbled.

"Working on a story?"

"Mmm."

I threw my trench coat over the back of a chair, followed my nose into the kitchen, and lifted the lid off the pot that was simmering on the stove. I took a sniff, then went back into the living room. "Lentils, huh?" I said.

She looked up, poked her glasses up onto the bridge of her nose with her forefinger, and smiled. "Lentils are very good for you."

"You don't mind if I add some hot sausages, do you?"

"Hot sausages taste good," she said. "An unbeatable combination, lentils and sausages. Something that tastes good to neutralize something that's good for you. I brought garlic bread and salad stuff, too, if you want to throw it together."

In the refrigerator there were half a dozen Italian sausages that I had grilled a couple of days earlier. I cut them into bite-sized chunks and added them to Alex's lentil soup. I tossed a green salad in a wooden bowl and put the loaf of garlic bread into the oven and set it for "warm." Then I poured two fingers of Rebel Yell over a glass of ice cubes. I took the glass into the bedroom, where I climbed out of my suit and into a pair of jeans and a flannel shirt.

When I returned to the living room, Alex was sipping from a bottle of Samuel Adams lager and watching the television. I paused in the doorway and gazed at her sprawled on my sofa, dressed in my baggy old sweatpants, with a pencil stuck over her ear and her glasses slipped down toward the end of her nose. She looked incredibly sexy.

I'd met her in May. Within a few weeks we were exchanging "sleepovers," and on Labor Day weekend we'd exchanged house keys. During my entire ten years of divorced bachelorhood, I'd never done anything like that.

Oh, we kept our separate apartments—hers on Marlborough Street in Back Bay and mine in the high-rise overlooking Boston Harbor. We did not quite concede that we were living together. But that's about what it amounted to.

It should have felt strange and stressful to a man who'd been alone for a decade and had conscientiously avoided making any commitments to a woman in that time. But it didn't. With Alex, it felt natural and logical.

"Macedonia," she called out suddenly.

"*What is* Macedonia," I corrected. "You've got to give the question."

She nodded without taking her eyes from the television, and a moment later she said, "Carthage! *What is* Carthage, I mean."

I slumped onto the sofa beside her. She leaned her cheek toward me and I gave her a loud, wet kiss.

"Mmm," she said. "Nice."

"How're you doing?"

"I've gotten practically all of them right so far."

"Good. That's not what I meant."

"Oh. Like, how was my day?"

"Like that, yes."

"Turn that thing off, will you?"

"Gladly." I reached over and snapped off the television. Then I slumped back on the sofa.

Alex wiggled against me and laid her cheek on my shoulder. "Wanna start again?"

"Sure," I said. I turned, touched her hair, and kissed her softly on the lips. "How was your day?" I said.

"Good. Fine." She nuzzled my throat. "Had an interview with the governor. If you think stories about the implications of Massachusetts converting to a graduated state income tax are exciting, I had a helluva day."

"If anyone can make those stories exciting, you can," I said.

"Yes, I can," she said. "How're you?"

I blew out a long sigh. "It was okay until the end. Sometimes I feel like a goddamn glorified butler for all the self-important old farts who are my clients. I had to drive all the way out to Lincoln at four-thirty for a conversation that would've taken ten minutes on the telephone because Roger Falconer doesn't make office visits and thinks his business is too fucking grave to conduct on the telephone. 'A matter of the utmost gravity.' That's what he called it. So instead of getting home at five-thirty, it's, what, nearly eight?"

"Almost eight, yes," she said softly. "I thought you liked your clients."

I nodded. "Oh, I do. I don't accept clients I don't like. But some of them can be pretty damn self-important. Sometimes it gets to me. Whatever happened to the guy who was going to argue civil liberties cases before the Supreme Court?"

"Your career took a different turn, Brady. You do what you do, and you're very good at it, and you're your own boss, and it makes you a lot of money. There are worse things."

I sipped from my drink. "There are better things, too. I mean,

Billy's out there in Idaho, a ski instructor in the winter and a trout-fishing guide in the summer and a bartender in his spare time. I'd like to do that."

"Your son is a twenty-one-year-old college dropout," she said. "You're not."

"No," I said. "Not even close. There are times I wish I was, though. I'd like to drop out and head for the Rockies, even if I'm not twenty-one."

Her hand squeezed my leg. "Would you bring me with you?"

"Out West?"

"Yes. Would you come?"

"You bet."

"Why not do it? Let's do it, Brady."

I sighed. This was one of Alex's favorite conversational topics. "Sure."

"What's stopping you?" she persisted. "Billy's off on his own, Joey's got that scholarship to Stanford. You've fulfilled all your obligations. It's time to live your own life."

"My clients—"

"Can't get along without you. I know." She snuggled against me. "I'd do it. I really would."

"You would, huh?"

"Sure. We could buy a little ranch. We'd have horses."

"And dogs."

"Yes," she said. "Dogs. And cats, too, and maybe a goat. And a meadow for some cows, and beyond it a view of the mountains—"

"Don't forget the trout stream running through the meadow."

"Right. So I could watch you catch trout while I sat in the hot tub."

"And afterwards I'd join you in the hot tub, and we could watch the sun set and drink beer."

"Mmm," she said. "Nice. Really nice."

"Could we really do that?"

"Sure," she mumbled. "Why not?"

"What about your career?"

"You mean," she said, "what about *your* career?" She blew out a sigh. "Or maybe you mean, what about our relationship? If we did that, you'd never get rid of me."

"I don't want to get rid of you." I nuzzled the back of her neck.

She looked up at me. "No?"

"No. It was nice coming home, sniffing the aroma of lentil soup, and finding you here."

"It happens a lot that way."

"And it's always nice."

"Well," she said, "I'd go out West with you. I would. Then I guess I'd be there every day, and maybe you wouldn't like that so much. You'd get sick of lentil soup."

"I *would* like it. Especially if you let me put hot sausages in it."

"But it won't happen," she said. "I understand."

I laid my head on the back of the sofa and gazed up at the ceiling. "Sometimes I think I'm turning into an old fart myself," I said.

"You're more like a middle-aged fart," she said.

"I mean," I persisted, "you're right. What's stopping me? The boys have grown wings and flown away. I've had a little career, made some money. My clients don't need me. There are certainly plenty of lawyers who can do what I do. I hate living in the city. I hate feeling I've got to jump when I get a summons from people like Roger Falconer. I could be a bartender."

"You'd make a lovely bartender," Alex said.

"Or a trout guide. I could do that."

"I bet you'd like that," she said.

I sighed. "It's fun to think about."

She sat up, turned, and frowned at me. "You're stuck, sweetie. You should try to get unstuck. Life is too short."

"I know." I pushed myself to my feet. "Let's eat."

After supper Alex and I pulled on sweatshirts and sat out on the balcony overlooking the harbor. A misty rain swirled in the wind, and whitecaps glittered in the city lights, but we were protected from most of it by the building and the balcony above us. We sipped coffee and I smoked a cigarette.

"I heard about Glen Falconer's accident," she said.

Alex is a reporter for the *Globe,* and she knows that I must protect the confidentiality of my clients. Some aspects of my business I cannot discuss with anybody, but especially not with a reporter, even if she's the woman who has a key to my apartment and makes lentil soup for me. So she never asks me questions. Some of the information she gets in her job as a reporter is confidential, too, so I don't ask her questions, either. Sometimes our conversations are elliptical, and sometimes we have to search for topics we can both talk about freely.

Sometimes we can talk elliptically and still help each other do our jobs.

"What'd you hear?" I asked her.

"He flunked the Breathalyzer. He was driving a big car and he collided with a little Honda. Two people were hurt."

"One of them died this morning," I said.

"I didn't know," she said. "Shit, I hate it when that happens."

"Me, too." We were quiet for a couple of minutes, then I said, "What else did you hear?"

"He either rolled through a stop sign or failed to look before he entered an intersection. The Honda had the right of way. He sideswiped her. She swerved into a parked car. Her chest hit the steering column."

"No seat belt?"

"I guess not. The other passenger was a child in a car seat. Not injured. So they're charging him, huh?"

"You'll probably read about it in tomorrow's *Globe,*" I said.

"Falconer's a big name in Boston."

"Roger's is."

"Glen's got lots of his daddy's money," she said. "Ergo, his is a big name, too. This isn't his first, you know."

I nodded. Glen's license had been suspended once before for DUI when he was nailed for speeding on Route 95. He had taken the class required by the Commonwealth for convicted drunk drivers, got his license back, and then apparently resumed his old ways.

"In Sweden, I think it is," I said, "one conviction and you lose your license for life."

"Sensible people, the Swedes." She reached for my hand and squeezed it. Out on the harbor a big oil tanker was inching through the chop. "I'm getting chilly," she whispered. "Almost ready for bed?"

"Definitely."

"You're not defending him, are you?"

I laughed. "Not me, babe. Glen needs a magician, not some paper pusher."

"You're not a paper pusher, Brady. You're a fine attorney."

"Hey," I said. "I am one helluva paper pusher. You want some paper pushed, see Brady Coyne. Don't knock paper pushing."

She squeezed my thigh. "I'm sorry. You are indeed a superior paper pusher, and a noble profession it is. So who're you getting to defend Glen Falconer?"

"Paul Cizek, if I can persuade him to take the case."

"Ah," she said. "The Houdini of the criminal courts."

"Paul's the closest thing to a magician I know," I said. I stood up and held both of my hands down to Alex. "Come on. I've got a magic trick I'd like to show you."

3

The next morning I left a message with Paul Cizek's secretary at Tarlin and Overton. He called me back a little before noon. "How's the mighty fisherman?" he said when Julie connected us.

"Alas," I said, "yet another season hath ended and I did not wet nearly enough lines to satisfy my lust. And you and I never did spend time together on the water."

"Too bad, too," he said. "I found stripers and blues in every creek and estuary and tidal flat on the north shore. I found them in the rips and in the surf and against the rocks and—"

"And you caught them on eels and sandworms and herring and bunker."

"Do I detect scorn in your tone, Coyne?"

"Scorn? No. I know you fish with nothing but bait. It's a pretty low-down way to do it, but you—"

"I'm a pretty low-down guy," said Paul, "not to handicap myself with flimsy fly rods and elegant little handcrafted confections of hair and feather that have no smell to them. *Chacun à son qout,* if you ask me. The fishing was pretty damn good, and you missed it. Now the boat's in the garage and my gear is stowed away for another dreary New England winter."

"Next year," I said.

527

"Yeah. You keep saying that."

"Just call me. I'll come."

"You willing to arise before the sun and witness the dawn of a new day from the deck of *Olivia* with me?"

"Absolutely. And how is Olivia?"

"You mean the boat or the wife?"

"The wife. I know you take good care of the boat."

"Olivia's good. Asks after you all the time. Keeps saying we should get together. Wants to meet your Alex. Olivia's been kicking some serious water-polluting ass. Her little group's got three civil suits and two criminal cases pending. She's really into it, and I admire the hell out of her. Some weeks we hardly see each other. She's off watchdogging local zoning- and planning-board hearings, testifying before legislative subcommittees, making speeches, harassing lawmakers, organizing fund-raisers, and I—"

"You, I understand, are kicking some serious butt yourself, Paul."

I heard him sigh. "I've won a few cases."

"What I hear, you've won some impossible cases."

"The presumption of innocence is a powerful ally, Brady."

"And the assembled might of the state's district attorneys makes a powerful adversary. No kidding, you've pulled some out of a hat."

"Yeah, I guess." He was silent for a moment. Then he said, "So what's up?"

"I've got a case for you."

"Tell me about it."

"You know who Roger Falconer is."

"Sure. Everybody knows Falconer. What'd he do?"

"Nothing. Or at least nothing that anyone's going to indict him for. It's his son."

"Glen's his name, right?"

"Yes. He's about to be charged with vehicular homicide."

"DUI?"

"You got it."

"Did he do it?"

"He was driving the car, all right. They got him on the Breathalyzer. The woman died yesterday."

"Aw, shit," he said.

"So what do you say?"

"I gotta check a few things. I'll get back to you this afternoon."

Paul called back around three and told me that Tarlin and Overton was inclined to accept the Falconer case, but before he made a firm commitment he wanted to meet with Glen. We agreed to assemble in my office at seven that evening.

I asked Julie to call and set it up. "Roger'll probably want to be in on it and try to talk you into holding the conference out in Lincoln. That's unacceptable. If Roger insists on joining us, fine. But it's got to be here. I want Glen in my office at seven, or else he'll have to do his own shopping for a lawyer."

Julie grinned. "I can do that."

"I know," I said. "You do it better than I do."

"You don't do it at all."

"That's because it's your job," I said.

She buzzed me five minutes later. "All set," she said. "The old man grumbled and wanted to talk to you. I told him you were tied up. They'll be here at seven."

"Both of them?"

"That is my inference, yes."

"Sure," I said. "Roger'll want a firsthand look at Paul. I don't think he lets Glen blow his own nose without telling him which hand to use."

"He lets his son drive drunk, though, huh?" said Julie.

"Driving drunk," I said, "is evidently the way Glen asserts his independence."

Glen Falconer arrived about a quarter of seven and, as expected, Roger was with him. Julie escorted them both into my office and offered coffee, which we all accepted.

Roger and Glen sat beside each other on the sofa. I took the armchair across from them. "Paul Cizek will be here shortly," I said. "He's the miracle worker I mentioned."

"Cizek?" said Roger.

I nodded. "He's with Tarlin and Overton in Cambridge. He sort of specializes in *Mission Impossible* criminal cases. Which is what this one looks like."

Roger leaned forward. "What kind of name is Cizek?"

"Huh?"

"I said—"

"I heard what you said, Roger," I said. "I just didn't believe it."

"We don't want some sleazy—"

"Gotcha," I said quickly. I stood up, went to my desk, and buzzed Julie.

"I'm brewing some fresh coffee," she said over the intercom. "It'll be a few minutes."

"See if you can reach Paul Cizek," I said to her. "Tell him to forget it."

"Wait," said Glen.

"Hang on," I said to Julie. I looked at Glen. "Your father doesn't want a lawyer with a *Z* and a *K* in his last name defending you."

"You don't understand," said Roger.

"Of course I understand," I said. "I understand perfectly. It's really not that complicated."

"I didn't say—"

"You said enough."

Glen glanced at his father, then said, "I don't care what the man's name is. I need somebody good. I don't care if he's sleazy, as long as he's good."

"What's it going to be, gentlemen?" I said.

"Why don't you tell us about him," said Roger.

"Here's what you need to know," I said. "You asked me to get Glen a lawyer. I have done that. Paul Cizek happens to be a good friend of mine. I'm his family lawyer, just like I'm yours, although that's not relevant here. More to the point, Paul's simply the best lawyer in Boston for Glen's case, in my professional opinion. You have retained me because you are willing to pay me money to hear my professional opinion on the legal matters that present themselves to you. My opinion on legal matters is arguably more acute than yours, or else you would not have retained me. Ergo, your choices are to accept or to reject my opinion. Which is your choice, Senator?"

Roger stared at me for a moment, then smiled. "You never call me 'Senator,' " he said.

"Only when you piss me off, and even then rarely to your face."

"I guess I do piss people off sometimes. Sometimes I do it on purpose. Sometimes it just happens. I like it best when people tell me up front that they're pissed at me. That's why I like you." He sighed. "I'm sorry, Brady. I value your opinion. It's more reliable than mine. Your opinion is worth money to me."

"So?"

"So maybe we need a lawyer with unusual consonants in his last name."

"Julie?" I said to the intercom.

"I'm listening," she said.

"Cancel the call to Paul."

"Aye, aye, Captain."

I went back and sat across from Glen and Roger. "I would've kicked you both right the hell out of here if you'd started that discussion in front of Paul," I said to Roger.

"Times keep changing, Brady," he said. "I'm an old man. I have trouble keeping up."

"You have trouble keeping your prejudices to yourself, and you've got to try harder." I turned to Glen. "Paul Cizek is a helluva good lawyer, and he's on a roll lately. About a year ago he defended a guy accused of molesting the children at a day-care place in Arlington—"

"Jesus," said Glen. "I remember that one. It was all over the news. Guy name of Benson."

"Actually it was Benton," I said. "Victor Benton."

"Right," said Glen. "Benton."

"Never heard of him," said Roger.

"He made films," Glen said. "Kiddie porn. Little kids, they were, grammar school. He made them undress at rest time, told them to— to do things to each other. Sometimes he did things with them. He got it on his camcorder, made tapes, sold them in Canada. That's what he was accused of, anyway. They thought they had the guy absolutely nailed." Glen turned to me. "This Cizek, he's the one who got Benton off?"

"Paul negotiated a plea bargain," I said. "Now the guy's doing community service and seeing a shrink. As long as he stays out of the day-care business and away from little kids, he's a free man."

"He would've lasted about a week in prison," said Glen.

"Not many lawyers could've gotten Victor Benton off," I said. I looked directly at Roger. "Paul has done some work for the Russo family, too."

Roger's eyebrows went up. "Russo," he said. "They're—"

"Mafia," said Glen. "I remember a recent case. A hit man, wasn't it? It was all over the television. Was that Cizek, too?"

"That was Paul Cizek," I said.

"He got the man off," said Glen. "The DA thought he had an airtight case. But they ended up with a hung jury."

"Paul Cizek is very good at what he does," I said.

"I want this guy," said Glen.

Roger had been sitting there frowning. "Child molesters and Mafia hit men?" he said softly. "This is the man to defend a Falconer?"

"No, Roger," I said. "This is the man to defend a drunk driver by any name. Listen. He's not defending you, and he's not defending your family name. He's defending Glen, who got loaded, not for the first time, and climbed into his car and drove it into another car and killed a woman. Paul might not be able to win the case. But if anybody can, it's Paul Cizek. That's my opinion. Okay?"

"Sure, Brady." He shrugged. "Okay."

Julie brought in a tray with a carafe of coffee, three mugs, sugar, and milk. She placed it on the low table beside me and said, "Anything else?"

"That's great," I said. "When Paul gets here, just bring him in."

Julie turned and left the room. Glen followed her with his eyes.

I filled the three mugs with coffee, sipped from mine, and lit a cigarette. "Just so you don't embarrass me in front of Paul with more irrelevancies," I said to Roger, "there are some other things you probably should know. Paul did not go to Harvard or Yale or Princeton. Not BC or BU, even. His old man was an immigrant Polish cobbler in Medford who was disabled by a stroke when Paul was fifteen and didn't die for another five years. His mother was a checkout clerk at K Mart and cleaned office buildings at night to put food on the table for Paul and his four siblings. Paul commuted to UMass Boston, then got his law degree from Suffolk, part-time. It took him about ten years to get through college and law school. He earned his way by waiting tables and tending bar at Italian restaurants in the North End, and probably met a lot of future clients in the process. The Middlesex County DA hired him for about fifteen grand a year to handle a caseload that would overwhelm an entire State Street firm. Within two years Paul Cizek was prosecuting homicides and getting convictions at an astounding rate. All the fancy downtown firms courted him, but he went to Tarlin and Overton in Cambridge because they wanted to keep him in front of juries, where he belonged. He's been with them almost five years. Paul's about forty now. He's got a nice house in Lynnfield and a Boston Whaler and a wife who went to Wellesley, who's a lawyer herself." I paused. "Let's see. Anything else I should tell you before he gets here?"

"He sounds like our man," said Roger.

"I hope you won't be startled by his appearance," I said.

He shook his head and shrugged.

I smiled. "But you probably will be."

I figured Roger had Paul Cizek pegged as a fat, big-nosed, toothpick-chewing caricature of a sleazy defense lawyer, a swarthy, foreign-looking man in a shiny suit with red suspenders and a flowery necktie and pointy shoes. In fact, Paul had fair skin, blond hair, ice-blue eyes, and the chiseled features of Butch Cassidy—or maybe it was the Sundance Kid. The Newman character.

When Julie escorted Paul into my office, Roger, to his credit, didn't blink. Paul was wearing chino pants and a cableknit sweater under an expensive tweed jacket. He shook hands graciously all around, declined Julie's offer of coffee, then said, "I'll need to talk to Glen for a few minutes."

I touched Roger's arm. "He means alone," I said.

Roger looked up. "Huh? Oh, sure."

Roger and I went out to my reception area, and about ten minutes later Paul and Glen came out.

"Okay," said Paul to me.

"You'll take the case?"

He shrugged. "I like challenges."

4

Thanksgiving, Christmas, New Year's Eve. Celebrations of family and tradition and peace and love and hope.

In the decade since Gloria and I had split, I had been finding the entire season disorienting and depressing and lonely, and I always greeted the arrival of the new year with relief because it marked the end of the holidays.

This year Alex made it different. At her insistence, we cooked a Thanksgiving turkey with stuffing and squash and sweet potatoes and giblet gravy and cranberry sauce and mince pie, and my old friends Charlie and Sarah McDevitt came over to share it with us. Then Alex bought a tree for my apartment, and we decorated it with homemade strings of popcorn and cranberries. On Christmas Eve we ate chili and drank eggnog and sang along to the entire *Messiah* and talked to my sons on the telephone and made love, and on New Year's Eve we drank champagne and watched the ball descend over Times Square on television, and the next day I realized that I'd made it through the whole time without once feeling disoriented or lonely or depressed.

It was a revelation.

★   ★   ★

I was staring out my office window at a cloudless January sky and dreaming of trout rivers and mayflies when Julie buzzed me. "Mr. Cizek, line two," she said.

I hit the button and said, "I was just counting the weeks until I might go fishing. I ran out of fingers."

"Try not to think about it," he said. "Better yet, let me buy you a beer."

"That might help. When?"

"Tonight? Say around six?"

"None too soon. Name the place."

"Skeeter's."

"I'll be there."

I had talked to Paul a couple of times after the November meeting in my office, when he agreed to take Glen Falconer's case. I'd filled him in on Glen's legal and personal history and given him a few tips on dealing with Roger, whom he had instantly pegged as an obtrusive pain in the ass. The week after Thanksgiving a Middlesex County grand jury handed down an indictment, as expected, and Glen Falconer's trial was scheduled to begin the first week of February.

When the indictment came in, the *Globe* ran Alex's story on the bottom left of page five, without a photo. She had been assigned to cover the trial and kept me updated on the case. Her boss had not at first seemed especially intrigued with the human-interest appeal of the Falconer story. Alex and I both suspected that the tentacles of Roger's influence had wiggled into the *Globe*'s editorial offices. But gradually the juicy details of the Falconer family history and the tragedy of the fatal automobile collision found their way into her stories.

Glen had been ignored and emotionally abused as a child, while his high-profile father bought and sold in the marketplace of influence and power and tyrannized his wife and son. No wonder Paul became an alcoholic ne'er-do-well as an adult.

Otherwise, the plight of the Falconer family had not occupied me. I had other things on my mind, trivial questions such as, What's it all about? and Who cares anyway?

Alex kept saying we should both quit our jobs, load all our stuff

536

into a truck, and head for Montana. I kept wondering why I always tried to change the subject.

On one especially dismal winter day shortly after the arrival of the new year, I was having lunch at Marie's with Charlie McDevitt. I mentioned how I'd been finding myself preoccupied with how I might squeeze maximum enjoyment from my remaining years of mortality. "I feel like I'm coasting through life," I told Charlie. "I need a plan. Some days I just want to chuck it all and go live in a cabin out West with Alex."

"You want to give God a big chuckle?" said Charlie.

"Huh?"

"Just tell Him you've got plans," he said.

I left the office around five-thirty. The city was dark and bone-chilling cold. The wind off the water funneled between the buildings and knifed into my body. I walked briskly, hunched into my topcoat, up Boylston, past the Public Gardens, diagonally across the Common, left on Tremont, and then down Court Street to the alley off State Street to Skeeter's Infield.

I walked in, rubbed the cold out of my palms, and looked around. The bar was crowded and the early sports news was playing on the two big television sets at the ends. Skeeter was hustling behind the bar. When he saw me he lifted his chin in greeting.

Paul wasn't at the bar. I spotted him in the last booth. A short man in a camel-hair topcoat and felt hat was standing in the aisle, bent over with both hands on Paul's table. The man seemed to be talking intently. Paul was looking down into a glass of beer.

I went over to the booth. Paul glanced up, frowned for an instant, then said, "Oh, Brady. You're a little early."

I nodded. "Sorry. I walked fast. It's too damn cold out there to dawdle."

He smiled. "Don't be sorry. Have a seat."

The man who'd been talking to Paul straightened up, and I slipped into the booth across from Paul.

"Mr. Coyne," said Paul, tipping his head in the direction of the man in the camel-hair coat, "Mr. Vaccaro."

Mr. Vaccaro mumbled, "Hiya," without offering his hand, so I didn't offer mine.

"Mr. Vaccaro was just leaving," said Paul.

"Yeah," the man said to Paul. "We'll talk, though, huh, Mr. C.?"

"I'll think about what you've told me," said Paul. "Okay?"

"Sure. Sorry. I'm on my way. I just—we gotta talk sometime, you know what I mean?"

"I know what you mean, Eddie."

The man stood there for a moment, then shrugged, turned, and left.

Paul lifted his glass of dark beer and took a sip. "Nippy out there tonight," he said.

"Radiational cooling, they call it," I said. "Makes you wonder if this is the year spring will never come. Was that a client?"

"*Former* client." Paul looked toward the bar and lifted his hand, and a minute later Skeeter came over and placed a bottle of Sam Adams in front of me. "Howya doin' tonight, Mr. Coyne?" he said.

"Cold of limb and cold of heart," I said.

"Ain't it the way, though." He pointed at Paul's glass. "You okay, Mr. Cizek?"

Paul gave him a wave. "Fine for now, Skeets."

After Skeeter went back to his post behind the bar, I lit a cigarette and said, "So what's up, Paul? It's been a while."

"If my fucked-up sense of ethics didn't forbid it," he said, "I'd dump this damn Falconer case."

"Roger bothering you?"

He ran his fingers through his hair. "Not anymore. I fired the old bastard a month ago."

"You fired him?"

"Yep. He raised the bail, and that was fine, but I guess he figured that entitled him to plan the defense."

"I suspect he's not pleased with the kind of ink he's been getting," I said mildly.

"I'm just trying to win a case," said Paul. "If he cares more for his own image than whether his son spends the next ten years at MCI Concord, we should just plead guilty and take what they give us. I don't even ask my clients for their advice on how to run a trial, never mind their relatives. I guess Roger's not used to not being consulted. He second-guessed every move I made, and as polite as I tried to be to him, I finally just had it up to here. Told him I didn't want to see him ever again. Told him the next time he showed up with Glen, I was outta there. Surprised he didn't go running to you. I think you're the only person he listens to."

I shrugged. "He knows what I would've told him."

Paul sipped his beer. "I don't like Glen, either. He's got this attitude like it's a big nuisance, him being put on trial, and who the hell did that woman think she was, out there with her baby getting in the way, while he was exercising his God-given right as an American citizen to get shitfaced and barrel around in his car. I mean, yeah, I've gotta try to shift the blame. That's basic strategy. But I'd feel a lot better if the guy showed a little remorse. Bottom line, he killed a woman."

"Sorry I got you involved," I said. "I just figured you were the best man for the job."

He waved his hand dismissively. "I probably am," he said. "Anyway, it's not the old Senator, and it's not Glen, and it's not really even this case, and I don't know why I'm crying on your shoulder." He let out a deep breath and looked up at me. "Except I guess I don't feel like crying on Olivia's shoulder anymore."

"Uh-oh."

"Nah, it's not what you're thinking. She's okay. It's just me. Listen. I remember you telling me that once upon a time you wanted to be a civil liberties lawyer."

I smiled. "That was a long time ago. Law school and youthful idealism. A deadly combination."

He nodded. "Sure. And now you've got a practice that's the envy of every lawyer in the city."

"I haven't had a civil liberties case in my entire career, Paul. It's always been a regret. And somehow I doubt that you envy my practice."

"In lots of ways I do," he said. "I mean, you've got to coddle people like Roger Falconer, and that's no fun. But look at what I do."

"You perform miracles, Paul. That Benton case—"

"Yeah, exactly. I performed a miracle, and now that goddamn sodomist is walking the streets."

"Sodomist? With children? Jesus." I shook my head. "I knew about the pornographic videotapes. But I never heard anything about sodomy."

"It never came out in the trial." Paul nodded. "I managed to get the whole sodomy thing suppressed. You know. Tainted evidence, shoddy investigation, impeachable witnesses. Typical." He shrugged. "See what I mean? That's what I do. I put child sodomists back on the streets."

I sipped my beer and gazed at him. "I get it," I said. "You're afraid you're going to win this case and Glen Falconer will be free to get drunk and smash his car into somebody else."

"Sure. Absolutely. And he will, too. But that ain't exactly it, either." He leaned across the table. "I loved prosecuting, Brady. Prosecuting was straightforward and unambiguous, you know? Every single son of a bitch I went after had done something bad. My job was to prove it, to make the case, to convince the jury. When I succeeded, I knew I had made justice happen."

"And you practically always succeeded," I said. "Listen, old buddy. You're doing justice now, too, and you know it."

"Sure," he growled. "The right to counsel, the presumption of innocence, all that shit. But you know and I know that just because the law presumes somebody's innocent doesn't make him innocent. It's all just a fucking game, Brady. You go to trial to win the game, not to do justice. You play the media, you pick your best jury, you work on the judge. You wait for the prosecution to fuck up, or, even better, you sucker 'em into fucking up, and then you cram it down their throats. That's how it goes. If they don't fuck up, I lose. But they practically always fuck up somewhere along the line. Listen, how d'you think I felt when that foreman looked at Eddie Vaccaro standing there beside me and said, 'The jury cannot agree on a verdict,' huh?"

"Vaccaro," I said. "The guy who was just here?"

"Yeah, him."

"Jesus," I said. "I didn't make the connection. He's a hit man. I don't think I ever met a hit man before."

"You're not missing anything, Brady." Paul lifted his beer glass halfway to his mouth, then put it down. "Eddie Vaccaro shoots people for a living. The first bullet through the eyeball, then one behind the ear. That's his signature. By all rights, he should be doing life in Cedar Junction now. Instead the DA has pretty much given up going for a retrial. So Eddie Vaccaro's a free man. Back doing what he does best, I presume. Shooting people in the eye. Thanks to me."

"The thrill of victory," I said.

"Bullshit. I felt like I'd murdered that guy in the restaurant myself, just like bargaining Victor Benton down to community service made me feel like it was me who'd been sodomizing little kids. All the time I'm interrogating witnesses on the stand and challenging evidence and manipulating procedure, I'm thinking, Man, I wish I was prosecuting these miserable pricks instead of defending them. I wish I was putting them away rather than getting them off."

"Somebody—"

"Oh, yeah," he said quickly. "Somebody's got to do it. It's their right to counsel. Sure. You know, there are times I wish I wasn't so damn good at it. There are times it almost makes me cry to see an inept, inexperienced, overworked prosecutor up there trying to get my client convicted. I'm practically screaming to myself, 'No, you dumb schmuck. Don't put that witness up there. I'm gonna have to destroy that witness.' You know what I mean?"

I nodded.

He took a sip of beer. "God help me, Brady, sometimes I find myself rooting for the other side. There are times I almost wish I'd lose."

"Maybe you should go back to prosecuting."

"Yup, I think of that. Olivia and I could sell the house and sell the boat and sell her new Saab and sell most of our furniture and go back to the little apartment on Memorial Drive. Maybe after ten or fifteen years I could run for DA and stick my thumb into the political pie and make television statements and never have to go into a courtroom again until I lost an election."

I smiled and nodded. "Alex and I are talking about moving out West."

"Really?"

I shrugged. "I doubt it'll ever happen. But thinking about it sometimes makes it seem real, and that makes me feel better for a little while. It's an option. It makes me feel that there's a way out if it ever gets intolerable."

Paul looked up. Skeeter was standing by our booth. " 'Scuse me, men," he said, "but I wondered if you wanted a burger tonight? Or a refill?"

I glanced at Paul, and he nodded. "Burgers, Skeets," I said. "You know how we like 'em. And I'm ready for coffee."

"Coffee for me, too," said Paul.

Skeeter grinned and ambled away.

"I don't feel that way," said Paul after a minute. "I don't feel like I've got any options. Tarlin and Overton pays me a shitload of money, which they should considering how much I make for them. I like my house and I like my boat and I like my wife. I just . . . "

He shook his head, and I said, "You just what?"

He smiled quickly. "I guess I just don't like myself very much. Brady, God help me, I want to lose this case. I want Glen Falconer to spend ten years in prison. I want six big guys with tattoos all over their fat hairy bellies to ream his butt in the showers. And I want that sanctimonious old shit to spend the rest of his miserable life regretting the way he raised his son, and I want your Alex to drag the Falconer name through all the puke and slime she can find. That's what I want."

"If you feel that way, you should quit the case."

"The thing is," he said, "I can win. I expect to win. And I don't have it in me not to do my best to win."

"So that makes you the best lawyer for the case."

He nodded. "That's the problem."

"Just as I promised Glen."

"Sure. And all my vows and training forbid me from quitting just because I don't like the Falconers and don't like defending them. Nope. I've gotta see it through."

"I guess I don't know what to say, Paul."

"I didn't expect you to say anything, old buddy. I just expected you to listen and pretend to understand. Which you did."

"I didn't pretend," I said.

Skeeter brought our burgers, big, thick, juicy hunks of ground sirloin and half-melted slabs of cheddar between slices of toasted garlic bread. Between mouthfuls Paul told me he and Olivia were hoping to get away for two weeks after the Falconer trial. Someplace warm and distant from fax machines and cellular telephones, where there might be fish to catch and piña coladas to sip by the pool and where, they thought, they might try to make a baby.

"It's always fun to try, anyhow," he said, and by the time we had wiped all the burger juice off our chins and finished our coffee, Paul was waving his arms and drawing diagrams on the placemat and explaining to me how he expected the state to focus on Glen's Breathalyzer results, and how he knew he could raise enough reasonable doubt to deep-six the prosecution's entire case.

We huddled in our topcoats outside Skeeter's. "I'm parked in the garage," Paul said. "Want a lift?"

"I'll walk," I said. "Penance for Skeeter's burger."

He held out his hand and I took it. "Thanks," he said.

"What for? You paid."

"I feel better. You got me back on track."

"I didn't say anything, Paul."

He grinned. "Just talking with somebody who's as fucked up as me helps."

"I guess you came to the right man, then."

5

When I was a kid, we celebrated our national holidays—Columbus Day, Armistice Day, George Washington's Birthday—on the days when they actually occurred. As soon as the new calendars were printed I thumbed through them to see if I was going to get gypped out of a no-school day because one of the holidays fell on a Saturday that year. I didn't like it when it happened that way. But it never occurred to me to think of it as unfair. Holidays came when they did and, like most things, you took 'em when you got 'em.

Somewhere along the line they decided to homogenize and regularize our holidays. No longer do we celebrate the signing of the armistice that ended the Great War on November 11 (the eleventh hour of the eleventh day of the eleventh month, I recall my third-grade teacher, Mrs. Shattuck, telling us). Now we're supposed to call it "Veteran's Day." And now kids are excused from school on Mondays, regardless of when October 12 or February 22 happen to fall. Instead of commemorating Washington's birthday, we celebrate something called "Presidents' Day," honoring not only the father of our country but also Franklin Pierce and Warren G. Harding and Gerald Ford.

I've questioned a lot of school-age kids, and I have yet to find one who can tell me the historical significance of November 11. A lot of them are even cynical about the fact that George Washington never told a lie. I asked my son Billy about it once, back when he was in junior high, and he said, "Oh, nobody believes that cherry tree story. It's a myth. Everybody tells lies, Pop."

I don't know what they're teaching kids nowadays.

The word *verdict* derives from the Latin roots meaning "to tell the truth." So it was appropriate that on the morning of February 22, the birthday of the man who, I still like to think, always told the truth (but a Thursday this year and therefore not Presidents' Day), Alex called me from a pay phone at the Middlesex County Courthouse, where she had been following the Falconer trial. "They expect the jury to bring back their verdict this afternoon," she said. "Why don't you meet me for lunch and then join me in the courtroom for the show?"

"Lunch sounds good," I said, "but why should I want to watch them announce the verdict? It's not as if I haven't been inside courtrooms."

"I just figured, Glen Falconer's really your client, and Paul Cizek is your friend. The Senator's been in the front row the whole time, you know, mostly glaring at Cizek and trying to make eye contact with Glen. I suspect he'd appreciate your show of support."

"What's the buzz?" I asked.

"Hard to judge. Cizek destroyed the Breathalyzer witness, and he made some points with the crime scene evidence. He scored on the fact that the victim was not wearing a seat belt, too, and raised some very reasonable doubt, some are saying, about whether the woman was driving safely herself. He's created some sympathy for Glen, too, mostly at the expense of Roger. Abusive father and husband creates mentally disordered wife and neurotic, alcoholic son. I don't think anybody doubts Falconer was drunk and ran into her, though. It'll be interesting. Cizek's been a tiger, and there's no doubt that the jurors love him."

"What do you think?" I asked her.

"I think he's absolutely adorable."

"I meant," I said, "how do you think it'll turn out? The verdict?"

"I'm just a reporter, honey. I'm not supposed to speculate."

545

During the course of the trial, which had lasted into a third week, Alex had kept me updated. I had tried to root for Paul to win and for Glen Falconer, who was, after all, the son of one of my important clients, to be exonerated. But something in me kept hoping that Glen would get nailed. I hate drunk drivers, and I hate seeing people elude justice because they happen to have more money and influence than other folks.

"It'll probably be a circus, huh?" I said to Alex.

"Probably. Everybody loves a circus."

"Pretty girls in spangled leotards?"

"Oh, yes. The place is packed with them. I've got mine on."

"Okay. Lunch it is. I'll have Julie clear my afternoon. The usual place?"

"I'll see you there at noon."

There's a little bar and grill around the corner from the courthouse in east Cambridge where we lawyers and reporters and other regulars go for lunch. It was mobbed. Alex and I ate BLTs and drank coffee at the bar and could barely converse over the din. Everybody seemed to be arguing about the Falconer case. I inferred that many drinks and a lot of dollars were being wagered on the verdict.

Shortly after Alex and I squeezed onto benches near the front of the courtroom, Paul and Glen came in and sat at the defendant's table. I saw Roger's bald head in the first row directly behind them.

Alex pointed toward the prosecution table. "See that man?" she said. "The guy with the beard in the front row?"

I followed her finger. "Who's he?"

"The husband of the victim. He's been giving interviews to anybody who'll listen to him. You've probably seen him on the news."

"You know I hardly ever watch the news."

She squeezed my hand. "Right. And you don't read newspapers much, either."

"Just your stuff."

"Of course. For its literary qualities. Anyway, keep an eye on him. His name is Thomas Gall, and if you ask him, he'll tell you that the credibility of the entire American system of justice rests on the outcome of this case."

"Meaning what?"

She shrugged. "He just says that the jury had better find Falconer guilty."

"Sounds like a threat."

"Actually," said Alex, "it sounds like a man who is devastated over the random loss of his wife to a drunk driver."

"I can relate to that," I said.

"Sure," she said. "Everybody can."

A little after two o'clock the jury filed in. Paul and Glen stood and faced them.

"Have you reached a verdict?" said the judge.

The foreman, actually a forewoman with gray hair wearing a severe black dress, stood and said, "We have, Your Honor."

A moment later the words "not guilty" were drowned in a cacophony of groans, cheers, shouts, and cries. Down front I saw Glen grab Paul's arm and pump his hand. Roger had both arms raised in a victory salute. Reporters were crowding the aisles and pushing toward the doors. The repeated banging of the judge's gavel had no perceptible effect on the chaos.

I felt Alex's fingernails dig into my wrist. "Look," she said.

She was pointing at Thomas Gall. He was a thick-necked, black-bearded man wearing a corduroy sport jacket over a blue oxford shirt without a necktie, and he was shouldering through the crowd in the direction of the defense table. His teeth were bared and his eyes were narrowed and he was shaking his right fist in the air. I saw his mouth moving, and then his words rose above the general din of the courtroom.

"This ain't done with, you murderin' son of a bitch," he yelled, raising his arm above the crowd and jabbing his forefinger toward Glen. "You neither, you creep." This was directed at Paul Cizek. And then Gall turned dramatically, lifted his arm, and pointed at the judge. "Or you," he growled, and, taking in the jury with a sweep of his hand, "or you, neither, all of you."

Alex mumbled, "Meet me outside," and slipped into the aisle. I saw her working her way toward Gall, but a pair of uniformed police officers got to him first. They pinned his arms by his sides and half-carried him out a side door.

I waited in my seat, and after a while the hubbub died down. I stood up and went to the front of the courtroom. I didn't spot Alex, but Glen and Paul were seated at the defense table. Paul was leaning forward, talking intently, and Glen was sitting back, his arms folded across his chest. He was staring up at the ceiling, nodding now and then. Roger was standing with both hands gripping the barrier rail, watching them.

Brenda, Glen's wife, sat on the front-row bench a few spaces away from Roger. Her blond hair was twisted into some kind of a fancy bun on the back of her head, and she wore a pale blue business suit over a silky white blouse with a frilly collar. She held her hands folded quietly in her lap, and she seemed to be studying the decor of the courtroom. I leaned down to her and said, "Congratulations."

She looked up, frowned for just an instant of nonrecognition, then smiled quickly. "Oh, hello."

"Brady Coyne," I said. "We—"

"Yes, I remember."

"You must be pleased with the verdict," I said stupidly.

"Sure." She shrugged. "I guess so."

I frowned, and she cocked her head and met my eyes levelly for a moment. Hers, I noticed, were greenish blue, the same color as her suit.

"It must've been hard for you," I said. "Sitting through all this."

"Hard?"

I shrugged. "Not knowing how it would turn out."

"Mr. Coyne," she said with a smile, "everything always turns out right for the Falconer men." She held my eyes for a moment and then returned her gaze to the front wall of the courtroom.

I stood there for a moment, but it was clear that my conversation with Brenda had ended. I turned to Roger and touched his arm. "So what do you think?" I said.

He turned. "Oh, Brady. What brings you here?"

"Loyalty."

He smiled thinly. "Right. Good of you."

"I understand Paul Cizek has performed some miracles these past couple of weeks."

"Your Paul Cizek is a crude, disrespectful man who allowed the newspapers to turn this into a circus. He refused to communicate with me and I should have fired him."

"Except you weren't his client."

He shook his head. "No. Glen was his client. But I'm paying. When I'm paying, I expect to participate."

I shrugged. "Just as well you didn't fire him. He got the job done, I'd say."

"Yes, he did. By dragging in the family's private affairs, resurrecting the memory of Glen's absent mother and his father's deficient parenting and his entire neglectful upbringing. He had that jury feeling sorrier for my poor, misguided son than they did for the dead woman."

"I heard he was pretty good with the prosecution witnesses, too," I said.

Roger nodded. "Yes, there was that. We won, and I'm glad. And after the party, we'll never have to deal with Mr. Cizek again, and I'm glad about that as well."

"Planning a big celebration, are you?"

He turned to me, and once again Roger Falconer's famous senatorial smile spread across his face. "A small celebration, Brady. And you must come."

I shrugged. "Well . . . "

"I insist. You deserve much of the credit for our, um, victory."

I nodded. There was no tactful way I could get out of it. "Sure. I'll be there."

"And bring your little friend with you."

"My little friend?"

"Miss Shaw, the reporter. She *is* your friend, isn't she?"

"Yes, I suppose that's one of the things she is to me."

"Just tell her no interviews in my home."

"Oh, Alex is a cultured and respectful person, Senator. She knows how to behave."

He touched my shoulder. "I'm sorry, Brady. I forget my manners sometimes. It's been a difficult time."

"Well, it's over, and if you haven't thanked Paul Cizek you are certainly forgetting your manners."

He gave me his smile again. "Of course. He did a magnificent job." He reached for my hand and shook it. "Tomorrow evening, eight o'clock."

"I wouldn't miss it," I lied.

6

Floodlights glittered on the newest layer of February snow, and more was filtering down softly. The gunmetal gray Range Rover and the little white Mercedes two-seater were pulled up directly by the front porch of the Falconer house in Lincoln, precisely where they'd been the last time I'd been there.

A dozen or fifteen vehicles were parked in an area that had been cleared by a snowplow next to the circular driveway. I pulled into an empty space and turned off the engine.

Alex touched the back of my neck. "Let's have a cigarette before we go in."

"Are we nervous?"

"We are not nervous," she said. "We are simply not looking forward to this."

"None of us is. We shall pay our respects, or whatever you call it, and we shall depart as quickly as possible."

We lit cigarettes. Alex is one of those oddly nonaddictive people who can smoke a cigarette now and then and enjoy it enormously, without ever getting hooked. She laid her cheek on my shoulder. The windows inside my car began to fog over. "We could just stay here and make out," she murmured.

"Your clothing will become all disheveled, and your lipstick will get smeared, and what will your mother say?"

"Valid point. We mustn't make out. Maybe just grope a little."

We smoked in silence for a few minutes. "What's bothering you?" I said.

"I just hate these things."

"This has nothing to do with the editorial in today's *Globe,* then."

"The one criticizing the prosecution of the Falconer case? The one calling for a new look at the Commonwealth's record in convicting drunk drivers? The one that practically declared Glen Falconer a public enemy?"

"That's the one I had in mind," I said.

"Why should that make me wish I were home with you wearing sweats and playing Trivial Pursuit and drinking beer on a snowy Friday in February rather than all high-heeled and panty-hosed at a party full of people I don't know and don't even want to know?"

"Because it was you who wrote the editorial?"

"That was the paper's editorial, Brady. It was unsigned, because it was the opinion of the editorial staff."

"But you wrote it."

I heard her chuckle beside me in the darkness of the front seat of the car. "So what'd you think of it?"

"Awfully convincing, hon. Don't worry about it. Nobody in there will know you wrote it."

"Somehow I think Roger Falconer knows everything."

"Well, he's too cultured to say anything. Besides, even Roger Falconer can see the truth in what you said."

Alex stubbed her cigarette out in the ashtray, and I followed suit.

"Gimme a kiss," she said.

I did. It lasted a good long time.

Finally she turned on the dome light and squinted into the rearview mirror. She touched up her lipstick, then said, "Lemme see your face."

I turned to her and she dabbed at my mouth with a tissue. Then she planted a very gentle kiss on the tip of my nose.

"Okay," she said. "Let's get this over with."

Roger greeted us at the door. I was relieved to see that he was wearing a Harris tweed jacket over a dark green turtleneck. Black tie wouldn't have surprised me, and I was still in my office pinstripe.

He gripped my hand. "Brady, damn good of you to come," he said. I guessed he had been using the identical greeting for everybody who had arrived at his door that evening. Nevertheless, Roger made it sound personal and sincere. Sounding personal and sincere regardless of how he actually felt was one of the many talents that had made Roger Falconer a big-time politician and successful businessman.

"Good of you to invite us," I replied. I doubted if I sounded as sincere as Roger. I turned to Alex. "Alex, this is Roger Falconer. Roger, you know Alexandria Shaw?"

He took her extended hand in both of his. "Ah, yes. I've enjoyed your work, Miss Shaw. You're a fine writer. Your coverage of my son's trial has been most, um, objective."

Alex dipped her head and smiled. "Thank you, Mr. Falconer."

Roger took our coats and led us into the living room. A bar had been set up along one wall, and on the opposite side of the room was a long table holding hors d'oeuvres. A couple dozen people stood in clumps. "Help yourself to drinks," said Roger. "Brady, may I borrow Miss Shaw for a moment? There's somebody I'd like her to meet."

Alex rolled her eyes at me, gave her head a tiny shake, and mouthed the word "please."

"Sure, Roger," I said, ignoring her.

As Roger steered her away, she turned and stuck out her tongue at me.

I made my way to the bar. A college-aged girl wearing a white shirt and a black skirt stood behind it. "Like a drink, sir?"

"A Coke, please. I'm the designated driver."

She cocked her head at me, then grinned. She poured some Coke over a glass of ice cubes, and as she leaned across the table to hand it to me, she whispered, "I think it's disgusting, don't you?"

I gazed around the room. Just about everybody was holding a wine or highball glass or a beer bottle. After consuming free booze at the party celebrating Glen Falconer's exoneration from a vehicular homicide DUI charge, they would all climb into their cars and drive over the twisting, snow-slicked back roads of Lincoln.

"I don't know about disgusting," I said to the girl. "But it's pretty damn ironic."

"I lost two friends in high school," she said.

I nodded. "I used to lie awake every night when one of my sons was out in a car. Now they're away from home, and I only lie awake sometimes."

She hugged herself. "It's good money."

"I don't blame you," I said.

I felt a tug on my sleeve. I turned and found myself mashed in a strong embrace. A big wet kiss landed directly on my mouth.

"Oh," I said when she pulled back from me to give me a look at her. "Mary. What're you doing here?"

"I heard you'd be here, you sexy man." She grabbed my arm in both of hers. "Frankly," she whispered, "I am delighted to see a familiar face. Doc said we had to come, and I told him he could go right ahead, but he insisted I come too, and now he's off pontificating about impactions or occlusions or something. Probably to a bevy of beautiful young women. Gee, it's good to see you."

"How do you guys know the Falconers?"

"Oh, you know," she said. "Dr. Charles Adams, the oral surgeon for the wealthy and influential. Kinda like you're the lawyer for all of them."

"A lot of Doc's patients are my clients, it's true. So how's he doing? I haven't seen him for a while."

"Oh, he's full of wanderlust as usual. He wants to buy another motorcycle. I keep waiting for him to grow up."

"Don't hold your breath," I said.

I felt a hand on my elbow. "Excuse me, Brady."

I turned. Paul Cizek stood beside me.

I grabbed his hand and shook it. "Hey, congratulations," I said.

He nodded. "Sure. Thanks." To Mary he said, "Will you excuse me? I need to talk to Brady."

She shrugged. "That's okay."

"Have you two met?" I said.

Mary smiled at Paul. "I've seen you on television. I'm Mary Adams."

They shook hands. Then Paul and I excused ourselves. He gripped my arm and guided me into Roger's library. Nobody was there except the goldens, Abe and Ike, who were snoring and snuffling, each on his own leather sofa. The lights were low and a fire crackled in the fireplace. We sat in the same armchairs that Roger and Glen had been sitting in when I had been summoned to Lincoln back in November.

"What's up?" I said.

"I gotta talk to somebody."

"You want a lawyer or a shrink?"

"I don't know. Both, maybe."

"There's a top-notch oral surgeon here," I said. Then I looked at him. His knee was jiggling and frown lines creased his forehead. I touched his arm. "I'm sorry, Paul," I said. "You *are* upset. What is it?"

"I don't know. I got this big empty sucking feeling in my belly. It's been there for awhile. It keeps getting bigger and emptier."

"You feel bad about the Falconer trial, huh?"

"That, yeah. It was like winning a ten-to-nothing baseball game, you know? You wish they'd get a few runs, make it close, at least. The prosecution did a lousy job, Brady. Hell, it was a game I should've lost, and the terrible thing is, I wish I did." He flapped his hands. "And then . . ."

His voice trailed away and he stared into the fireplace.

"Then what?" I said.

He turned to me and shrugged. "Olivia and I are a little shaky. More and more she's throwing all her frustration and energy into her work, and I guess I am, too." He hunched his shoulders and squeezed his hands between his knees. "It's all falling apart. I don't know what to do."

"Didn't you tell me you and Olivia were going to get away for a couple weeks after the trial? Head for some tropical place and relax? Make a baby, I thought you said."

"Yeah, well, we like to play with that fantasy sometimes. But she's decided she's got too much going on and can't leave right now."

"You don't need a lawyer, pal," I said.

"You think I do need a shrink, huh?"

"I don't know. Maybe you just need a little down time. Big cases take a lot out of you, and there's always that letdown when they're over. The agony of victory and all."

He looked up at me and smiled. "Postpartum blues."

"I wouldn't know about that."

"You were there yesterday, weren't you?" he said.

"I heard the jury give their verdict, sure. I wanted to shake your hand, but you disappeared with Glen."

"I had to get him out of there. That guy—"

"Gall? The husband of the victim? I heard him."

"He freaked Glen out of his wits."

"What about you?"

"Me?" Paul nodded. "Yeah, he kinda freaked me out, too. I mean, he didn't really scare me, but the poor bastard had to sit there and watch the case against the guy who killed his wife go swirling down the drain. Honestly, I felt bad for him. I can't blame him for being totally pissed. The hell of it is, it feels like it's my fault."

"People think a trial is supposed to reveal the truth," I said.

"It's just a lawyer contest," he said, "and I'm getting sick of it."

I sighed. "I don't know what to tell you, Paul."

"There's nothing to say. Thanks for listening."

"Let me get some names for you."

"Names?"

"Somebody to talk to."

He stared at me for a minute, then said, "Yeah. Okay." He stood up. "I've gotta get out of here."

"Did you bring Olivia?"

He shook his head. "She had some meeting or something." He shrugged. "We don't do much together anymore."

"I would've liked to see her."

"Some other time, I guess."

Paul and I walked out into the party. He turned and shook my hand. "We'll have to get together. Do some fishing."

"I'd like that," I said. "I'll be in touch with you."

Paul weaved his way through the crowd toward the front door. I looked around for Alex. Instead I saw Doc Adams coming toward me. "They let the hoi polloi into this affair, huh?" he said.

"Apparently," I said. "You're here."

He narrowed his eyes. "You got lipstick on your mouth."

"Your wife attacked me a little while ago. She seems sex starved."

"Must be, to go after an ugly son of a bitch like you. So what's new?"

"Actually," I said, "maybe you can help me. I could use a referral to a good psychiatrist."

"Midlife angst, counselor?"

"Well, yeah, sure. But it's not for me."

"Of course it isn't."

"Well, it's not. Can you get me a few names?"

"Can do," said Doc. "What about lunch? I'm at Mass General on Wednesdays and Thursdays."

"Sounds good. Give me a call." I scanned the room. "I'm ready to get out of here. Have you seen Alex around?"

He grinned. "Why, sure. I was holding her in thrall with a tale of a miraculous mandible reconstruction I performed last week. Young housewife whose husband smashed her face with his fist."

"Jesus," I said. "What a world."

"Amen," said Doc.

At that moment Alex appeared. "Hi," she said to me.

"Hi yourself."

"You got lipstick all over you. It's not mine."

"It was this guy's wife. She attacked me."

Alex put her arm around my waist. "I don't blame her."

Doc smiled at us. "Hard to believe," he said. "You give her a perfect opening and she doesn't insult you."

"Not in public," I said.

"And she's not jealous."

"Nope. She trusts me."

Doc grinned. "She'll get over it."

Alex squeezed my arm. "About ready to go, handsome?"

"Yes. Definitely. Have you seen Glen? I really ought to say hi to him."

"I haven't seen him," she said.

"I heard he refused to attend," said Doc. "I was talking to his wife."

I grinned. "You hit on all the women here?"

"Only the pretty ones. All she'd say was that Glen wasn't feeling well, which sounded to me like he was either in the bag or seriously hungover."

"In that case," I said to Alex, "we're out of here."

I had lunch with Doc Adams the following Thursday. He gave me a list of four psychiatrists. "They've got good reputations for helping men through depression and midlife anxieties," Doc said. "They're friends of mine. They're pretty booked, but they said they'd be willing to take on a new patient on my referral."

"Contrary to popular belief," I said, "you are a kind and thoughtful man."

"Jesus," he said. "Don't tell anybody. It'd ruin my reputation."

I called Paul Cizek's office that afternoon and left a message asking him to call me. A week passed and I called again. All his secretary would tell me was that he wasn't in his office. I repeated my message, adding that I had some names for him.

He didn't return that call, either. I tried him again a few weeks later, suggesting lunch, and again a month or so after that.

He never returned any of my phone calls. Winter turned into spring and the leaves began to pop out and the days lengthened and I stopped trying to reach Paul Cizek. I thought I understood. He didn't want my help and regretted exposing his fears and weaknesses to me. When he wanted to get together, he'd let me know.

7

When I got home from the office on the first Friday in June, the sliding glass doors that gave me my view of the harbor were wide open and a damp east wind was whipping the curtains around.

I found Alex slouched on her spine in one of the aluminum chairs on the balcony. She'd taken off her shoes, and she had her legs stretched out in front of her with her heels propped on the railing. Her skirt was bunched up around her hips so that the wind could blow on her bare legs. She held a bottle of Samuel Adams on her chest, and she was staring out at the thunderheads that were building on the horizon in the fading daylight.

I bent and kissed her forehead. It tasted damp and salty. "You're gonna get wet," I said. "It's raining."

"It's not raining yet," she said, still gazing out at the roiling sky. The dark clouds were tinged with orange. "The wind is picking up water from the top of the ocean and blowing it around. It's refreshing. It feels tingly on my skin."

"You don't want to change your clothes? That's an expensive silk skirt you're ruining."

She took a long swig from her beer bottle, placed it on the concrete floor beside her, and returned her gaze to the sky. "I'm cool. I'm extremely cool. I'm wicked cool."

I noticed that there was a six-pack of Sam Adams on the floor beside her left elbow. Two unopened bottles were left in the cardboard container. "How long've you been here?" I said.

"I don't know. Ten minutes. A few hours. I forget. I've been watching the clouds. They're pretty awesome, don't you think? It's like there's this big guy out there at the edge of the ocean, and he's blowing up all these big black balloons. I can feel his wet breath on my legs when he blows. It feels good. And those balloons are getting bigger and bigger and they're filling up the sky, and I'm waiting for the sky to get so crowded with those big black clouds that they'll all explode." She held up her hands, then spread them wide apart. "Boom!"

"Let me change my clothes," I said. "I'll sit with you and watch the big guy blow up the balloons."

"Let's get naked." She stood, unsnapped her skirt, balled it up, and threw it over the rail. It opened in the wind, flapped like a big drunken bird, and sailed away. Then she turned to me and stripped off my jacket.

"No, wait," I said. "That's an expensive suit." I grabbed it from her and threw it into the living room behind me.

She yanked my necktie off and tossed it over the balcony. "Now do me," she said, and I unbuttoned her blouse while she worked on the buttons of my shirt, and both shirt and blouse went out into the storm. She wanted to sacrifice my pants to the guy who blew up the black balloons, but I snatched them from her and threw them inside, and then we were standing there, Alex in her pink bra and matching panties and me in my boxers, holding each other while the wind blew cold and wet on our skin. She trembled in my arms, and when I teased her chin up with the knuckle of my forefinger, I saw that she was crying.

I kissed both of her eyes. "What's the matter, honey?" I said.

"I guess I had too many beers."

"Okay. That's okay. You're entitled. Why did you have too many beers?"

She ducked her head against my chest and mumbled something.

I bent to her ear. "I couldn't hear you."

She tilted up her face and looked at me. "I got it."

"You got what?"

"The contract. Sally called today. My agent. They sent her a contract."

"Hey," I said. "Slow down. What agent? What contract are you talking about?"

She slumped back into the chair. "I was going to tell you. But I was afraid it would be bad luck to talk about it. To want it. And I didn't know if I wanted it or not, anyway." She shivered. "I still don't."

I put my arm around her. "A contract for what, hon?"

"A book." She shivered. "They're giving me money to write a book."

I stood up and held my hands out to her. "Come on. Let's go inside, make some coffee, get some clothes on. I want to hear all about it."

Fifteen minutes later we were sipping hot coffee at the table. We'd changed into sweats, and on the other side of the sliding glass doors, the sky was full of dark clouds and it had begun to rain.

"Now," I said. "Tell me about your book."

Alex smiled quickly. "Remember that series I did on abused wives?"

I nodded. "Sure. There was Pulitzer talk, as I recall."

"Well, they want me to do a book on it. A different book. The publisher liked my slant. It looks at the dynamics that produce these abusive relationships."

"You mean how women drive men to it?"

She looked sharply at me, and I quickly held up my hand. "Joke, kid."

She nodded. "I know when you're joking. You're not always funny. It's about how mothers raise their boys to beat their wives, and how fathers raise their daughters to seek out abusive men to marry, and how abusers and victims seem to seek out and marry each other, and . . . " She shrugged. "Anyway," she said, "I got the contract. Sally called today."

"And that's why you drank more beers than usual and threw away your clothes."

"Yup. I'm gonna be a real writer. I'm sorry, Brady."

"Sorry? Why? This is wonderful news."

"I'm sorry I didn't tell you about it before."

I reached across the table and put my hand over hers. "That doesn't matter. Congratulations. It's an appropriate occasion to drink a lot of beers and discard your clothing."

She was shaking her head. "What if I can't do it? What if I spend the money they give me and I can't write anything? What if the paper dumps me and won't take me back?" Tears welled up in her eyes. "What if . . . "

I squeezed her hand. "I'm proud of you. You're going to write a wonderful book. You're a hard worker and a terrific writer. Publishers don't invest money in people who can't do the job."

"They don't know me like I do," she said.

When we finished our coffee, I took her hand and led her to the shower. We stripped off clothes and stood under the steaming water. Alex cried and pressed against me, and I held her tight until she whispered, "I'm okay now." I lathered her up all over and twirled her slowly under the hot spray. "Now your turn," she said, and she washed me. We toweled each other dry and then she took my hand and led me to the bedroom.

We made love. We dozed.

Sometime in the evening I awakened. Alex had her arm thrown across my chest and she was breathing softly on my cheek. I slipped away from her, pulled on a pair of jeans and a T-shirt, went into the kitchen, and dumped two cans of Progresso minestrone into a saucepan.

While it heated I smoked a cigarette and stared out the sliding door at the storm that raged over the harbor. Raindrops as big as acorns splattered against the glass. Six stories down, frothy white combers rolled across the black water. Now and then lightning lit up the sky.

I felt Alex press herself against my back. "I love a big storm," she whispered.

"It reminds us who's boss."

"Yes. It puts things into perspective."

"I've got some soup heating on the stove."

She snaked her hand under my T-shirt and rubbed my chest. "So what if I can't do the dumb book," she said.

"You can do it."

"I think I can."

"We should be celebrating," I said.

"We already did."

"That was it?"

She chuckled. "No. That was just the prologue. Let's have some soup. Then we can celebrate some more."

Later we lay in the dark staring up at the ceiling. "I'm sorry for acting like a female hysteric," Alex murmured.

"I think that's a redundancy."

"What is?"

" 'Female hysteric.' The word *hysteria* comes from the Greek word for 'uterus.' Originally, at least, they thought only females were susceptible to hysteria."

"Because they had a uterus," said Alex.

"Because they were female, which was more or less defined as having a uterus."

"Males didn't have hysteria."

"No," I said. "Being deprived of uteruses and all. When males had those symptoms, they figured there was really something wrong with them."

"The doctors giving those diagnoses being predominantly male."

"Exclusively male back then, I believe," I said.

She rolled onto her side and kissed my shoulder. "I'll have to move," she said softly. "I'll need a quiet place. In the country, probably. Maine, maybe, or Vermont. Someplace cheaper. I'll have to get a leave from the paper, and I'll have to live on the advance for two years, and anyway, I *want* to move. But . . . "

"I understand," I said.

"Do you? It'll be someplace not—not so near to you."

"We'll work it out."

"I've been thinking," she said.

"What have you been thinking?"

"You could come with me. It wouldn't be Montana, but . . . "

"It's something to think about," I said quietly.

We lay there in silence for a few minutes. Then Alex said, "Brady?"

"What, hon?"

"You're more important to me than a book, you know?"

I didn't say anything.

"Hey?"

"Mmm?"

"Did I say something wrong?"

I hugged her against me. "Sometimes you think too much," I said.

"I want you to be happy."

"Me, too," I said. "I want both of us to be happy."

When both of my sons fled the East Coast for Western time zones, I stopped being frightened when the phone awakened me in the middle of the night. Billy liked to tell me about the trout he was catching in Idaho. Rubbing it in, I called it, but I was always happy to hear from him, even if it did interrupt my sleep. Joey called less often and less spontaneously than his brother, but as smart as he was, he always seemed surprised when I reminded him that eleven o'clock in the evening in California was 2:00 A.M. in Boston.

So when the telephone shrilled in the dark that night, it didn't jar me upright in bed the way it used to when the boys were still teenagers living with Gloria and my first waking thought was of automobile accidents.

I fumbled for the phone, got it after the second ring, and held it to my ear. "H'lo?"

"Brady?" It was neither of my sons. Billy calls me Pop and Joey calls me Dad, and both of them generally call me collect. Anyway, this voice was female.

"Yes, this is Brady," I mumbled.

"It's Olivia."

"Oh . . . ?"

"Olivia Cizek. You were the first person I thought of to call. I'm sorry to wake you up."

"It's okay." I bunched my pillow behind me and pushed myself into a semi-sitting position. Beside me Alex twitched and groaned. "What's the matter?" I said softly into the phone.

"It's very strange. It's . . . "

"Olivia, are you okay?"

"I don't know. I—the Coast Guard just called. They found Paul's boat."

"What do you mean?"

I heard her exhale a loud breath. "His boat. It was drifting somewhere out around the Merrimack River. They towed it in, and then they called me, and—"

"Where's Paul?"

"I don't know." She hesitated, then said, "Oh. You probably don't know, do you?"

"Know what?"

I heard her take a breath. "Paul and I separated a couple months ago, Brady."

"I didn't know," I said. "I'm sorry."

"He's been living up there. On Plum Island. Since we—we split. Up there in that—he calls it a shack. They called here for him. They got the numbers off the boat and this was the address, but—"

"Olivia, listen," I said. "We've had a big storm tonight. Paul's boat broke away from its moorings, that's all. Call him and tell him what happened. He's pretty lucky they found it in this storm. It could've been sunk or gone halfway to Labrador."

"I tried calling him. There was no answer." She paused. "You don't get it," she said.

"What do you mean?"

"He doesn't keep his boat moored. He trailers it. Do you understand?"

Alex mumbled something and rolled toward me. I reached for her and pulled her against me.

"Brady?" said Olivia.

"I understand," I said quietly. If Paul trailered his boat, he did not keep it moored at any marina. He kept it in his garage or driveway. Paul's boat would be in the water only if Paul was on it.

"I told them something happened," said Olivia. "He went out in that storm."

"I'm sure there's an explanation."

"I gave them your name," she said. "Was that all right?"

"Sure, Olivia. Anything I can do to help . . . "

"You *are* our lawyer."

"Yes, I am."

"So now what? Now what'm I supposed to do?"

"What did the Coast Guard tell you?"

"They said someone would be in touch. I guess they're . . . they're looking . . . "

"There's nothing else you can do," I said. "I'm sorry. It's hard. But all you can do is wait."

"He never wore a life jacket," she said. "He loved to go out alone at night. Especially when it was stormy. He said that a storm would churn up the bait, get the fish excited. It's so dumb."

"Hang in there, Olivia. Call me when—"

"When they find his body."

"Anytime. Call me when you hear anything. Or even if you don't. Whatever I can do to help, call me."

"Thank you," she said in a small voice. "Thank you, Brady."

I hung up the phone. Alex mumbled, "Everything okay?"

"No," I said. "Paul Cizek took his boat out this evening. The Coast Guard towed it in. Paul wasn't on it."

I lay there for awhile with Alex's cheek on my shoulder and her leg hooked over both of mine, but I couldn't get back to sleep. So I slid out from under her, pulled on my jeans and a clean T-shirt, and padded into the kitchen. I plugged in the coffee and leaned against the counter until it finished perking. Then I poured myself a mugful and took it out onto the balcony.

The storm had swept the air clean, and the sky was turning pink out on the eastern horizon. I didn't need a wristwatch to tell me that it was close to 5:00 A.M., because at that time of June the sun rises a little after five, and when I'm on my balcony I can see it happen.

Olivia Cizek, I figured, had called around four.

I imagined her sitting somewhere in her house sipping coffee and staring out the window waiting for the phone to ring. She and Paul had separated. But being separated wouldn't stop her from caring.

I remembered the last time I'd seen Paul. It had been at Glen Falconer's victory party. He'd asked for my help, and I'd tried to give it to him. But as far as I knew, he hadn't accepted it. Maybe I could have tried harder.

No. I'd done what I could. I was not responsible for his leaving Olivia.

The sun cracked the horizon on schedule, a sudden flare of light in the clear morning air. "Daybreak," it's called, and the word applies literally when it happens over the ocean.

It took only a few minutes for the earth to rotate far enough to reveal the entire circumference of the sun. The color quickly burned out of the sky, leaving it pale blue and cloudless. It promised to be a perfect Saturday in June.

Ideally I would spend a perfect June Saturday at a trout river. Mayflies of various species hatch from April through October on New England rivers, but their name is no coincidence. They hatch most prolifically in May and June—big, smoke-winged Hendricksons; March Browns and Gray Foxes, which look like miniature sailboats on the water with their barred wings unfurled; little yellow sulphurs and big yellow Light Cahills; and green drakes, which are really more cream-colored than green and look as big as sparrows when they lift off a river.

Mayflies are among Mother Nature's most graceful and beautiful creations, and I think I'd believe that even if trout didn't gluttonize on them when they ride on a stream's currents to dry their wings.

But trout do gluttonize on mayflies, and when they do, they can be fooled into eating an imitation made of feathers and fur and hair wound onto a small fishhook, provided, like the real thing, it drifts freely and naturally on the surface of the stream.

Selecting the best imitation to tie onto the end of my leader, casting it so that it drifts directly over a feeding trout, and doing it so cleverly that the trout confuses that fur-and-feather concoction with a real mayfly and pokes his nose out of the water to eat it— that is the appeal of trout fishing in June.

I figured I wouldn't do any fishing on this particular Saturday in June, keeping my nonfishing record for the season intact. Paul Cizek had gone overboard during the storm. Olivia would need me.

I was smoking a cigarette, working on my second mug of coffee, and watching the gulls cruise over the harbor when Alex kissed the back of my neck.

"Good morning, sweetie," she said.

I turned my head so she could kiss my cheek. Then I kissed hers. "Hi," I said. "Coffee's all brewed."

She showed me the mug she was holding. "Are you okay?"

"I'm pretty worried about Paul."

"Tell me about it. I was kind of out of it when the phone rang."

She sat in the aluminum chair beside me and held onto my hand while I talked. When I told her that Paul and Olivia had separated, she squeezed my hand a little harder.

"You think he went overboard during the storm," she said when I finished.

"I guess there are a lot of explanations for finding his boat out there without him on it," I said. "But that's the one that makes the most sense."

"If he went overboard—"

"He probably drowned. He never wore a life jacket. I'm trying not to create scenarios. There's nothing I can do about it. I'm just trying to wait and see what happens."

"His wife will call you again?"

"I expect so. If she doesn't, I'll call her."

"You were hoping to go fishing," she said.

"Yes. I was going to call Charlie and see if he wanted to go. If he didn't, I'd probably have gone alone. I haven't been all year. I've pretty much lost my heart for it now."

She lifted her mug, drained it, then stood up. "I've got to get to the office," she said. "Will you be okay?"

"Sure. It's Olivia I'm worried about."

Olivia called a little after eight. "They want to talk to me," she said.

"Who?"

"The Newburyport police."

"When?"

"As soon as I can get there."

"If you want," I said, "I can be in Newburyport in an hour."

"Oh, yes, thank you," she said softly. "I could really use your support." She was silent for a moment, then she said, "Brady?"

"Yes?"

"What do you think they want?"

"I guess they're just trying to figure out what might've happened."

"If they found him—his . . . his body—they would've told me, wouldn't they?"

"Yes, I think they would."

"So . . . "

"Try not to jump to conclusions, Olivia. Let's take it a step at a time. How well do you know Newburyport?"

"I've been there. Not well, I guess."

"When you turn off the highway onto Route 113 you'll see a Friendly's ice cream place on your left. I'll meet you there. We'll have a cup of coffee, then we can go talk to the police together. Okay?"

"Yes. Okay."

I hung up the phone and headed for the shower. The police wanted to question Olivia Cizek because they always want to question the spouse when someone dies mysteriously or violently.

The police were already assuming Paul Cizek had died.

Olivia may not have realized it, but she needed a lawyer.

I found her sitting at a booth staring into a cup of coffee. It didn't look as if she'd slept much.

I slid in across from her. "Good to see you again, Olivia."

She looked up and smiled quickly. "Thank you for coming," she said. She had pale gray eyes, almost silver, and a sprinkling of freckles across the bridge of her nose, and when she smiled the tiny lines at the corners of her eyes and her mouth crinkled.

I reached across the table and squeezed her hand. "It's a tough time for you. I'm your lawyer. And your friend."

"I'm a lawyer, too, you know."

I nodded.

"They think I might've done something," she said.

A waitress appeared at the table. "Just coffee, please," I said. "Bring the lady a refill." When she left, I said to Olivia, "You know how it works. You're the spouse. But I doubt if the police are pursuing any theories right now. They're investigating. They want all the information they can get. It's logical for them to talk to you, that's all."

"But you think you should be with me."

"Yes."

"To protect me."

"To protect your rights, yes. But mainly because I figured you could use a friend right now."

"I sure can. That's why I called you." She smiled quickly. "And I guess I understand that if that friend is also a lawyer, so much the better."

"So tell me about last night."

"What do you mean?"

"What you did."

She frowned, then said, "Oh. Like, do I have an alibi?"

I shrugged. "Yes."

"I had a meeting up in Salem until about seven-thirty or eight. Then I went home."

"Directly home?"

"Yes. Directly home."

"Then what?"

"Then nothing. I went home, heated a frozen chicken pie in the microwave, ate it while I watched the news on CNN, and went to bed. I read for a while and then went to sleep."

"Any phone calls?"

She frowned for a moment, then shook her head. "No. No calls. Nobody to verify where I was. That's what you're getting at, isn't it?"

"The police might ask," I said.

The waitress brought our coffees. Olivia stirred milk into hers.

"I don't have any alibi, Brady," she said. "After I left the meeting I went straight home. I had no visitors. I didn't talk to anybody on the phone until I got that call from the Coast Guard. I could've gone up to Newburyport and dumped Paul off his boat. There's nobody to say I didn't. Except me. And if you don't believe me—"

I gripped her wrist. "Stop," I said softly. "Cut it out. The police might ask these questions, and I want to know the answers before they do. No one's accusing you of anything." I let go of her wrist and took a sip of coffee. "It would help me to know what happened to the two of you."

She shrugged and looked down into her cup.

"You were separated," I said. "Paul moved out. What happened?"

She lifted her cup to her mouth and held it there for a moment. Then she put it down. "We just drifted apart, I guess."

"That's no answer, Olivia."

She looked at me, then nodded. "No. It's really not. It's true, but it's not really what happened. See, as soon as Paul took the job with Tarlin and Overton, he changed. Before, when he was prosecuting, he was a wild man. Just bubbling with energy and enthusiasm and—and righteous zeal. Oh, he loved to nail the bad guys. He was making justice happen, he liked to say. He really believed in it. He was like a kid. It was like electricity just crackled out of him. We had so much fun. I loved it. I thought he was the sexiest man. You know?"

I nodded. "I know what you mean," I said. "I knew Paul back then, too."

She took a quick sip of her coffee. "I mean, sometimes he'd work fourteen or sixteen hours a day. And when he got home he'd be absolutely wired. He'd keep me up half the night talking about his cases. We didn't see that much of each other. But when we were together, it was intense. I had my own career." She smiled. "Our life was full and complicated and exciting."

She bowed her head for a moment. When she looked up, she was no longer smiling. "Everything changed when he took that job. He still worked long hours, and he was making about ten times as much money. We bought a nice house and he got a new boat and everything, and we tried to pretend things were great. We were moving up in the world, right? But when he'd come home, he'd plop himself in front of the TV. Or during the fishing season he'd just change his clothes and hitch the trailer to his car and take off.

He didn't talk much about his work. When he did, all he'd say was that he was keeping bad guys out of prison. He didn't really complain about it, at least not at first. It took me a while to realize that he was trying to protect me. He didn't want to make me unhappy or to make me feel like he was suffering on account of me. But I knew he didn't believe in what he was doing. And he kept getting worse. He kept winning cases, and they'd reward him by giving him nastier people to defend. I mean, he had that child molester, and he had that Mafia man, and then he got that drunk driver—"

"I talked him into that one."

She shrugged. "It didn't matter. If it hadn't been that man, it'd've been someone else. The point is, gradually we just stopped talking. I finally started telling him he should quit and go back to work for the DA. He'd just smile. I tried to talk him into getting help. He was depressed, and I was worried about him."

"Did you ever think—?"

"He'd kill himself?" she said. "Is that what you think happened last night?"

"He's seemed awfully depressed to me last time I saw him."

She shook her head. "I don't know. He had his fishing. During the season, he seemed okay. Getting out on his boat alone at night always seemed to make him happy."

"He'd been worse lately, though?"

She smiled. "He never left me before."

I nodded.

"It was his idea, Brady. I didn't stop loving him or wanting to be with him. But he felt it was the only thing left to do. I don't know, maybe he thought it was just the only way left that would protect me. I never felt he didn't love me. But he was tortured, and he knew I was miserable. Even the fishing didn't help him anymore. He was desperate. I think part of it was that he put a lot of pressure on himself, trying to be admirable for me. He figured if he despised himself, I must despise him, too. I didn't. I loved him. But if we got divorced, he could stop worrying about how I felt about him. Does that make any sense?"

I shrugged. "I guess so. As much as anything makes sense." I took a sip of coffee, then said, "Did you ever go out on the boat with him?"

She frowned. "What . . . ? Oh. You mean, did I know how to operate it? Did I know his routines?"

"Yes."

"Could I have gone out with him last night, you mean."

I nodded.

"I could have. I mean, I've got nobody to say I didn't. But I didn't. But, yes, I went out with him a few times, especially . . . before. Before he changed jobs. It was sort of fun, but I knew he really liked it best when he was by himself. I could drive a boat, yes, and I could stun an eel and rig it on a line, and I knew how to read the currents and the tides and how to get a good drift through a rip. I didn't much care about the actual fishing. But I liked being on a boat with Paul at night. And I guess I could've been there last night, and I could've picked him up and thrown him overboard and then swam to shore and . . . "

I took both of her hands in mine. "Hey," I said softly.

"I know. I'm sorry, Brady."

"Just as long as you're telling me the truth."

She nodded. Tears brimmed in her eyes. "He's dead, isn't he?"

"I don't know. Let's talk to the police. Maybe they've learned something."

9

Olivia left her car in the Friendly's lot and rode with me into the business center of Newburyport. We parked in the municipal lot and headed for the police station. Newburyport, like most of the cities along the New England coastline, began as an old seafaring town because of its sheltered harbor. It was a fishing town and a trading town that grew and flourished inside the mouth of the Merrimack River. During the Industrial Revolution in the second half of the nineteenth century, factories were built along the riverbanks. Then, inevitably, the factories shut down and the merchant shipping industry faltered and Newburyport went through the predictable stages of decline.

During the past decade or two the city has been revitalized. The old factories have been converted into comtemporary office buildings and condominiums. The downtown area features brick-fronted shops that sell books and candles and chocolates and antiques. There are a dozen restaurants and taverns within a few blocks of each other, and all of them seem to be profitable.

Politically, Newburyport is a city. But it feels like a quaint old New England seaport town, just the way it's supposed to.

On this perfect Saturday morning in June, the twisting streets and the wide sidewalks were thronged with shoppers and tourists. Seagulls sailed overhead, and beyond the shops and restaurants the masts of schooners poked into the sky. The air tasted salty and clean.

"Where was Paul's house?" I asked Olivia as we crossed a brick-paved plaza.

"I don't know," she said. "Somewhere out on Plum Island."

"You've never been there?"

"No. He called it a shack. It's on some back road overlooking the marsh."

"He wouldn't let anybody borrow his boat?"

She laughed quickly. "Absolutely not."

"But he might've invited somebody along with him."

"Sure."

At the station, Olivia told the female desk cop that Lieutenant Kirschenbaum was expecting her, and a few minutes later a lanky, stoop-shouldered guy wearing a short-sleeved white shirt and baggy chino pants came out. "Mrs. Cizek?" he said.

"Yes. This is Mr. Coyne."

"Oh?" He had a thick mop of curly gray-blond hair. A pair of steel-rimmed glasses perched atop his head.

"He's my—our lawyer. Mine and Paul's."

Kirschenbaum looked at me and shrugged. "Sure, okay. You folks want to come on in here?"

He turned and slouched down a corridor, and we followed him into a small office. He folded himself into the swivel chair behind his desk, and Olivia and I took the straight-backed wooden chairs across from him.

Olivia put her forearms on the desk. "Do you know anything?"

"Nothing since we talked this morning," he said. "Someone radioed the Coast Guard that there was a boat adrift. That was around two in the morning. So they went out and towed it in. Nobody was aboard. They've got it at the Lifeboat Station on Water Street. There's a vehicle registered to Paul Cizek of Lynnfield parked at the public landing. It's got a boat trailer hooked to it." He poked at his hair, found his glasses, and placed them on the desk in front of him. "That's really all I can tell you. I was hoping you could shed some more light on it."

"You didn't find . . . ?"

He shook his head.

"I don't see how I can help you," she said.

"You two were, um, living apart."

She looked at him sharply. "Yes, we were. We separated at the end of March."

"Right," he said. He picked up his glasses and fitted them onto his ears, then rummaged around on his desk and found a manila folder. He opened it and bent to study the papers it held. Then he looked up at us. "He was renting the house at the end of Meadowridge Road, out on the island?"

She nodded. "That's right."

"He liked to fish," he said, still peering at the papers he was holding.

"He went out whenever he could. That's why when he moved out, he came up here. So he'd be near the ocean. He liked to go in the river and around Plum Island."

"And he fished at night?"

"Mostly at night, yes. He preferred to fish at night. He felt that's when the stripers bit the best. Anyway, he worked long hours during the day."

Kirschenbaum removed his glasses, folded them, and pointed them at Olivia. "He was pretty well known for defending some unsavory types."

"It's what he did."

"Yes. And he was very good at it, I understand. Was your husband suicidal, Mrs. Cizek?"

"Paul?" She frowned. "He was not happy. In fact, he's been quite depressed lately. But suicide?" She shook her head. "I don't think so. No. That wasn't Paul."

"Would you say he was a careful man?"

"What do you mean?"

"In his boat. Did he take risks?"

She shook her head. "I don't . . . "

"He never wore a life jacket," I said. "At least not when I was with him."

Kirschenbaum glanced at me, then turned back to Olivia. "There was a bad storm last night. We had big seas outside. Wind, heavy rain, lightning. Some pretty violent squalls. But he was out there in his boat."

"He had a lot of confidence in himself," she said. "He used to say that the fish bit best in the rain. He liked weather."

The cop turned to me. "Mr. Coyne, you were friends with Mr. Cizek, is that right?"

I nodded.

"Good friends?"

I shrugged. "Yes, I'd say we were good friends. We used to fish together. I was his family lawyer." I glanced at Olivia. She was peering at Kirschenbaum. "I did the Cizek's will and a few other legal odds and ends for them. Paul and I haven't been out fishing for a couple of years. We ran into each other now and then. Professionally, I mean. We threw business each other's way."

"You knew him pretty well, then?"

"I felt I knew him better a few years ago. Since he went private, we saw less of each other."

"What about recently?"

"I referred a client of mine to him, so I saw him several times this past fall and winter."

"That would be Falconer?"

"Yes. He defended Glen Falconer. Actually, Roger Falconer, Glen's father, is my client."

"And Mr. Cizek was successful in his defense of Mr. Falconer, as I remember."

I nodded.

"How did Cizek seem to you recently?"

"I haven't seen him since February. He was depressed. Confused."

Kirschenbaum arched his eyebrows.

"I recommended he get some counseling. I got some names for him, but I don't know if he ever followed up on it."

He turned to Olivia. "What about enemies, ma'am?"

She shrugged and looked at me.

"Lawyers make enemies," I said. "Paul had high-profile cases. He defended people who were accused of serious crimes, and he was often successful. There are always victims of serious crimes. He was threatened in court last winter. The husband of the woman who was killed by the drunk driver Paul defended."

Kirschenbaum nodded. "I remember hearing about that." He turned to Olivia. "Where were you last night, Mrs. Cizek?"

Olivia glanced at me, then turned to Kirschenbaum and smiled quickly. "After about eight o'clock, I don't have an alibi."

"Oh, I wasn't looking for an alibi," he said with a wave of his hand. "I was just wondering where you were."

"Home alone."

"When was the last time you talked to your husband?"

"A few days ago. Wednesday, I think it was. We talked on the phone for about an hour that evening. We were working out the terms of our separation."

"How did your husband seem?"

"Stressed out. Sad. Depressed."

"Did you argue?"

"No. We never argued. In all the time we've known each other, we haven't argued."

Kirschenbaum leaned forward. "Mrs. Cizek, I want to ask you a hard question."

She nodded. "All right."

"Was your husband involved with somebody else?"

"A woman, you mean?"

He spread his hands.

"I don't think so," she said.

"Then that's not what caused . . . ?"

"Our separation?" She shrugged. "No. Not as far as I know." She shook her head. "I don't know. Maybe. He'd grown awfully distant over the past couple of years."

"What about you?"

"Me?"

"Were you—"

"No. I wasn't involved with anybody. I was still involved with Paul."

Kirschenbaum glanced at his papers for a moment, then took off his glasses and stuck them on top of his head. "I guess you understand what we're looking at here," he said to Olivia.

"You think Paul's dead," she said.

He glanced at me, then nodded. "It's the logical assumption. The Coast Guard is searching for a body. The problem is, we don't know where he was when he—if he went over. The tide was running, there were heavy winds, we don't know how long the boat had been adrift before it was spotted. A few boats broke away from their moorings in the storm last night. But your husband trailered his, so that's out. He's not at his house. You haven't heard from him." He flapped his hands. "We try not to jump to conclusions, but . . . "

Olivia nodded. I could see her jaw muscles bunch and clench. "You'll keep me informed?" she said in a low voice.

"Of course," said Kirschenbaum. "And if you hear anything, you'll tell me."

"Yes."

"You too, Mr. Coyne."

"Sure," I said.

"You'll be available, then?" he said to Olivia.

"Don't leave town, right?" she said, trying to smile.

"I've got your number," he said.

Outside the police station, Olivia stopped, turned to me, and pressed her face against my chest. I put my arms around her and held her against me.

"I tried to keep it together in there," she mumbled.

"You did fine," I said.

"I don't know what to do."

"We can only wait."

"That's the hardest thing."

I patted her shoulders. "I know."

10

I fully agreed with Olivia. Waiting is hard. It's always better to do something, no matter what it is.

I drove her back to the Friendly's parking lot and gave her a hug. She climbed into her red Saab, and I waved to her as she headed home to Lynnfield. Then I turned around and drove back into Newburyport.

On my first try I went right past the Cashman Park boat ramp, the municipal launch area. I'd met Paul there a few times for fishing excursions, but that had been a couple of years earlier and at night. I remembered it was just before you cross Route 1 into town, so I turned around, drove back along the narrow street that paralleled the river, and found the entrance tucked alongside a big brick factory building.

The parking area was crowded with vehicles on this Saturday noon in June. Most of them had boat trailers attached. I found a slot near the entrance, wedged into it, and climbed out of my car.

I meandered down to the concrete ramp that slanted into the Merrimack. An elderly guy wearing baggy blue shorts and a plain white T-shirt was taking money from a young couple who were launching a small motorboat.

When they finished their transaction, I approached the man. He was wearing a cap that advertised Surfland Bait & Tackle. Tufts of white hair poked out from under it. "Excuse me," I said.

He turned to me, and I saw that his sun-browned face was patched with large, irregularly shaped freckles. "Hiya," he said. "You launching?"

"No. Can I ask you a couple questions?"

He shrugged. "About what?"

"Do you know Paul Cizek?"

He cocked his head and squinted at me. "Who're you?"

"I'm Paul's lawyer."

He nodded as if that made perfect sense. "Cops was already here. I told 'em everything."

"Did you see Paul last night?"

He smiled, and a maze of wrinkles spread over his face like a sudden breeze on a glassy pond. "Cops asked that. Told 'em I got off at seven. Mr. Cizek, he usually launches later, just around sunset. Night fisherman. He's got a season pass, see, so he don't need to do business with me. And usually he takes out before I get here in the morning. I bump into him once in a while. Usually, he's in and out when I'm not here." He shrugged. "I didn't see him last night. Nope."

"So you wouldn't know if he had anybody with him."

He shook his head. "Usually when I see him he's alone. Except for the fish. Often as not, he brings a keeper back with him. Good fisherman, Mr. Cizek. He can find 'em. Guess something happened to him, huh?"

I nodded. "The Coast Guard found his boat last night. He wasn't on it."

"Wish I could help you," he said. "Nice guy, Mr. Cizek. Friendly, you know? Treats a man like a man, if you understand me. Not like some of 'em." He jerked his shoulder at the parked cars. "I mean, I s'pose I'm just the guy they give their money to. But still . . ."

"Mr.—" I began.

"Randolph," he said.

"Mr. Randolph—"

"No, no," he said, shaking his head. "Randolph's my first name. They call me Dolph, mostly."

I held out my hand. "I'm Brady. That's my first name, too." We shook hands. "Dolph," I said, "I'm trying to figure out what happened last night."

"I sure don't know."

"What do you think?"

"Me?" He smiled. "Cops didn't ask me that. Guess they didn't figure I could think." He jabbed his forefinger at my shoulder. "Tell you what, though. They think Mr. Cizek went over in the storm. I don't buy it. Not him. Not in that Whaler of his. No, sir."

"Why not?"

"Mr. Cizek's a good sailor. Knows this river, knows the tides, knows how the winds work. He goes out last night, he knows where to go. Big seas like that, he's got his spots. Night like we had, he knows the bait gets blowed close to shore, in on the beaches, near the rocks. He fishes in weather all the time. Ain't gone over before, no reason he would last night." He paused. "Tell you what else. Say something did happen. What'd happen would be, he gets blowed onto the rocks, maybe, or onto some beach. See, that's where Mr. Cizek'd be. Where the bait is, which is where the fish are. Where'd they find that Whaler of his?"

"Adrift," I said. "Out past Plum Island."

Randolph shook his head. "Don't make sense. He wouldn't of been fishin' outside. He'd of been inside, workin' the rocks and jetties. Was it bunged up?"

"Huh?"

"You know. The boat. Was it bunged up? Like it got blowed against the rocks."

"I don't know."

"You might maybe want to find out."

I nodded. "Good idea."

"I don't buy it," he said again. "Not Mr. Cizek."

He pointed out Paul's car, a Jeep Cherokee with a trailer hitched behind it, and I went over and looked at it. But I didn't see anything that told me what had happened that night.

So I waved at Randolph, climbed back into my car, and drove through town and out Water Street to the Coast Guard station. I found a parking spot across the street. A long, double-wide driveway led past a hangar-shaped garage down to the water, and I followed it, half expecting to be halted by an armed sentry. But nobody seemed to notice me.

On the left was what I took to be the administration building, a low, rambling structure with a well-manicured lawn and flower gardens ablaze with marigolds and impatiens. Out back on a basketball court a gang of young men in shorts and T-shirts were playing volleyball. There were lots of shouts and curses and good-natured laughter, and I stopped to watch. They played with vast youthful energy and enthusiasm. One young fellow with a blond ponytail dove for a spectacular save, and I figured he'd have scabby knees for a month.

When he stood up, his teammates slapped his bottom, and I saw that he was a woman. In fact, several of the players were women.

None of them took notice of me, so I wandered down to the water. Half a dozen Coast Guard vessels of various sizes and configurations were moored there, along with a few other boats.

One was a Boston Whaler. I moved out onto the end of the short dock and read *Olivia* on her transom. From what I could see, she had not been bunged up at all.

I looked around, but still nobody seemed to be paying any attention to me. So I sat on the edge of the dock and slid aboard *Olivia*.

She was a sixteen- or seventeen-footer, with a center console, no cabin, shallow draft. A good boat to fish from, broad-beamed, high-sided, and open, but not made for the high seas. A tall antenna poked up from the console, and I remembered fly casting from the bow in the wind and snagging my line on it. Sure. *Olivia* had a radio, so if Paul had been in trouble, he'd have called for help. But Lieutenant Kirschenbaum hadn't mentioned any Mayday call from Paul, so I assumed he'd made none.

Whatever happened had happened suddenly and without warning.

I looked around the inside of the boat. Shipshape, the way Paul liked it. The rods with both level-wind and spinning reels were racked neatly in their holders along the gunwales. The lines were coiled and the bumpers stowed. I lifted the lid of the built-in bait box at the stern, but it was empty. So was the fish box beside it. I lifted the hatch in the bow and counted the life jackets. There were four, which was the number he always carried.

I went back to the console. I noticed that the key was in the ignition. The dry storage at its base was empty. It's where Paul always kept his tackle box.

I sat on the seat behind the wheel and lit a cigarette. No bait, no tackle box. It was puzzling.

"Can I help you, sir?"

I looked up. It was the ponytailed volleyball player.

"How can you do that without skinning your knees?" I said.

She frowned. She looked to be about Billy's age. My older son had just turned twenty-one. "Pardon me?" she said.

"The way you were diving on the court for the ball."

She smiled. "You've gotta know how to do it." She hesitated. "You're not supposed to be here. This isn't your boat, is it?"

"No. It belongs to a friend of mine."

"You better come up." She held her hand down to me. I took it and she helped me climb back onto the dock. "They brought her in last night some time," she said. "Found her adrift."

"I know. My friend was probably on it."

"Oh, geez," she said. "I thought it had just busted a mooring or something."

"No," I said. "It was launched from a trailer. I'm just trying to figure out what might've happened."

"One of the guys was talking about it," she said. "They got a call a little after midnight. Someone spotted her with nobody aboard. So they went out and brought her in. She was just the way she is now. Ignition and radio both off. No anchor over the side."

"And no bait and no tackle box."

She cocked her head. "So?"

"My friend used her for fishing. He's a bait fisherman. He wouldn't go out without some eels or bunker or whatever the bait of the hour might be. He always brought bait with him."

She shrugged. "Maybe he didn't last night. Maybe he was casting plugs or something. Maybe he was drift-fishing, so the engine was turned off, and he was leaning over or casting or something, you know, off balance, and a swell caught him and just flipped him out. He wouldn't've had a chance to use the radio if it happened like that."

"No tackle box, either," I said.

"It could've gone over, too. It was pretty choppy out there last night." She shook her head. "But, you know—"

At that moment, someone yelled, "Hey, Morrison! What in hell're you doing?"

The girl's cheeks reddened as she turned to face a man of about my age stalking rapidly toward us. He wore creased chino pants and a white polo shirt. When he got closer, I saw the Coast Guard insignia stitched on the shirt pocket.

"We were examining the craft, sir," she said.

"She was telling me I had to move away from it," I said.

He looked from Morrison to me, then back to her. Curly black hair matted his head and forearms and crawled out of his shirt at the throat. His shoulders and chest bulged. "Okay," he said after a moment. "Good work, Ensign. Dismissed."

"Yes, sir," she said, snapping him a quick salute. She started to leave, then turned to me. "I hope it works out okay with your friend," she said.

"Thank you. And you take care of your knees."

She grinned quickly, then headed back to the volleyball court.

"The police want us to keep people away from this boat," the man said to me.

"I didn't know," I said. "But that's what Ensign Morrison was telling me. She spoke very sternly to me."

He nodded. "I bet she did."

"This is Paul Cizek's boat," I said. "I'm his lawyer. He launched it from the municipal ramp last night sometime. It looks as if something happened to him."

"Looks that way," he said. "But I can't help you."

"I was wondering," I said. "Was there any bait in the bait box when you brought her in?"

He frowned. "Bait?"

"You know. Eels, menhaden, squid."

"I know what bait is," he said. "All I can tell you is that nobody's touched anything on that boat."

"I just thought if the bait box had bait in it . . . "

"Yeah," he said. "It'd stink up the place. But nobody cleaned it up, if that's what you were getting at. This is how she was when we found her. Look. I probably shouldn't have even told you that. It's a local police matter. You want to talk to anybody, talk to them."

I nodded. "Good advice. Thanks."

"I'll walk you out," he said, and I figured if I balked he'd carry me out.

"I think I can find my way," I said. "Thanks anyway."

When I got to the end of the driveway, I glanced back. He was standing there with his arms folded over his chest, watching me. I waved. He lifted one hand quickly, then turned away. I crossed the street and climbed into my car.

11

I went to The Grog, my favorite Newburyport hangout, and found an empty stool at the end of the bar. I ordered a draft beer and a cheeseburger, then sat there with my chin on my fist trying to imagine what might've happened to Paul.

I thought the obvious thoughts: A sudden gust of wind or a swell hitting the boat from the wrong angle had knocked him off balance and tumbled him overboard; he had gone voluntarily into the sea, a suicide; or, some enemy had managed to kill him and throw him to the ocean's scavengers.

I also considered the possibility that Paul had set it up, faking his death. Except the only people I'd ever heard of doing that were fugitives or life-insurance scammers, and Paul was neither of those. Anyway, he loved his boat too much to set it adrift in a storm.

The police evidently were leaning to the accident scenario, and for good reason. There are many more accidents at sea than suicides or murders or sham disappearances. The commonest things most commonly happen, they believe, and in the absence of evidence to the contrary, that is the theory they generally pursue.

I believe that, too. Except the absence of bait on *Olivia* made me doubt that Paul had ventured out to catch a striped bass, and if he hadn't gone fishing, there was no reason for him to have gone out in that storm at all.

Suicide? He'd been depressed, profoundly discontent with his work. His marriage was in the process of dissolving. Middle-aged angst. Midlife crisis. I understood the feelings. Most of my friends had them, and I certainly was not immune to them. But neither I nor any of my friends killed ourselves because we were starting to ask questions such as Is this all there is? and What's it all about, anyway?

That left murder. Paul Cizek, like most of us, had enemies, perhaps even people angry enough to want to kill him. I figured Lieutenant Kirschenbaum had probably considered that possibility, even if it wasn't the commonest thing. I had trouble imagining Paul Cizek being murdered. I had trouble imagining murder, period. It happened on the news. But it didn't happen to my friends.

When they found his body, they'd know. And if they never found his body, they never would know.

I ate my burger and drank my beer, then found the pay phone. Olivia answered in the middle of the first ring.

"It's Brady," I said.

"Oh, gee," she said. "Have you heard anything?"

"No. I—"

"When the phone rang, I was hoping . . . "

"I'm sorry. It's just me. I'm still here in Newburyport. You've had no news, either, then?"

"No. Nothing."

"Are you okay?"

She laughed quickly. "Okay? Well, no, I'm not okay at all. I'm having a lot of trouble with this, as a matter of fact. I'm sitting here staring at the telephone, trying to make it ring and for it to be Paul, telling me he's fine. And so far it isn't working." She hesitated. "You're in Newburyport?"

"Yes. I decided to poke around a little while I was here."

"Did you learn anything at all?"

I told her about my chat with Randolph and my visit to the Coast Guard station.

"What do you make of it?" she said. "He never went out without bait."

"It makes the accident scenario less likely, I guess," I said. "Otherwise, I don't know." I paused. "Olivia, did Paul have a lot of life insurance?"

"Oh, geez," she said. Then she laughed quickly. "You're thinking he—"

"It's a thought."

"He had a couple of small policies. Just enough to get himself buried, he liked to say. He figured he could take care of me better by investing."

"I just wondered," I said lamely.

She said nothing. Finally I said, "Are you there, Olivia?"

"I'm here," she said. "I was just thinking . . . "

"What?"

"That you're a nice man to—to care."

"Paul is my friend. So are you."

"You don't have to do this, Brady."

"It makes me feel better to be doing something."

"I wish *I* could do something."

"You guard that telephone. I'm sure you'll hear something soon."

"Are you?"

"Am I what?"

"Are you sure?"

"No, I guess not." I shifted the phone to my other ear, then said, "Do you know where his house is?"

"Paul's?"

"Yes."

"I've never been there, but he told me about it. It's on, um, Meadowridge Road, or Street, or something. On the island. When you cross the bridge, you go left, I remember him saying that, because if you turn right you go into the wildlife sanctuary. It's overlooking the marsh. He told me about all the ducks he could see from his windows. Why, Brady?"

"I thought I'd go out and take a look."

"You don't need to do this," she said softly.

"I'm right here. It'll make me feel useful."

"Well, that's nice. Let me know what you find, okay?"

"You can count on it."

So I got into my car and headed back out Water Street, past the Coast Guard station, and along the Merrimack River, and I kept following the river until I crossed the bridge and found myself on Plum Island. I turned left onto the narrow street. It was half covered with wind-blown sand, and it ran between the island's dunes on the right and the salt marsh bordering the river on the left. It was lined on both sides with closely packed summer cottages of every architectural description except "elegant." They looked cramped and run-down, the sorts of places that stay in families for generations of progressively accumulating neglect.

The yards were tiny and sandy, featuring tufts of marsh grass and plastic ride toys and clotheslines flapping with underwear and bathing suits and towels, and every hundred feet or so a little unpaved road bisected the street I was on, and along both sides of each side street were more ramshackle cottages.

I drove slowly, examining the road signs, and after about half a mile I spotted Meadowridge on the left. I pulled onto the sandy shoulder, turned off the ignition, and climbed out.

An insistent breeze blew directly down the street I had been traveling, and it tasted salty and peppered my bare arms and face with tiny grains of sand. I crossed quickly and started down Meadowridge. It was a short street—a couple of hundred feet long, at most—and I could see the marsh down at the end. Four cottages were lined up on each side, all of more or less similar design and set back precisely the same distance from the single-lane, packed-sand roadway.

An ancient yellow Volkswagen beetle was parked in the short driveway of the last cottage on the left. On the rear bumper was a sticker that read, JUST SAY YO.

I spotted a woman kneeling at a flower bed by the front steps. Her back was to me, so I approached to a distance from which I could speak to her without either startling her or invading her space. I cleared my throat, then said, "Excuse me?"

591

She turned her head, still kneeling. She looked like a teenager, although I have trouble judging the ages of young women. She wore dirty cotton gloves, and one hand held a trowel. She pointed the trowel at me and said, "Are you talking to me?"

"Yes. I'm sorry to bother you. I'm looking for Paul Cizek's house."

She sat back on her haunches and wiped her forehead with the back of her glove. She had blond hair held back with a rubber band, but wisps had gotten loose and she thrust out her lower lip and blew them away from her face. Then she frowned at me. "Who're you?"

"I'm a friend of Paul's."

"He's not home now."

"I know."

"Then—"

"Can you just tell me where he lives, Miss?"

She looked at me for a minute, then shook her head. "Sorry." She turned back and resumed troweling.

I took a few steps closer to her. "I know he lives on this street," I said. "I'm his lawyer."

"He's his own lawyer, far as I know," she mumbled without turning around.

"No. I'm his lawyer. We lawyers hire other lawyers to do our personal legal work for us. We say any lawyer who tries to do it himself has a fool for a lawyer. Lots of people say anyone who hires a lawyer has hired a fool."

I heard her chuckle, but she kept her back to me and didn't respond.

"Paul's boat was found adrift last night," I said. "He wasn't on it."

She turned. Her eyes bored into mine. They were green, almost the identical color of Alex's eyes. "What'd you say?" she said.

"Paul Cizek seems to be missing. The Coast Guard towed his boat in last night."

She stood up and came toward me. She was tall and lanky in her dirt-smeared T-shirt and snug running shorts. "You got some kind of identification, Mister?"

I fished a card from my wallet and held it out to her. She shucked off her gloves, tucked them into her armpit, took my card, and squinted at it. Then she looked up at me. "I still don't know what you want," she said.

I shrugged. "I don't honestly know myself. I've talked to the police, I've talked to the Coast Guard, and I've even talked to the guy at the boat launch. I'm just trying to figure out what happened to Paul. I thought I'd take a look at where he lived. I don't know what I expect to find, but—"

"He lives here."

"Here?"

"This is his place. I'm planting some flowers for him. It's kind of a surprise."

"Why?"

"He's—we're friends. I thought some petunias might cheer him up."

"Have you seen him today?"

"No. Listen. He's not missing."

"He's not?"

She smiled quickly. "Not Paul. There's a mistake. It's gotta be somebody else's boat they found. He'd never—"

"It's his boat," I said. "I saw it."

She stared at me. Then I saw the tears well up in her eyes. "Aw, shit," she said. "That bastard."

"Who?"

"Paul. That asshole. He did it, didn't he?"

"Did what?"

"He fucking killed himself." She made a fist and punched her thigh. "Son of a *bitch!*"

I reached out and touched her arm. "Can we talk?"

She narrowed her eyes. Tears streaked the dirt on her face. After a minute, she nodded. "Sure. We can talk. Come on."

I followed her onto the narrow deck that stretched across the back of the house. She lifted a flowerpot, removed a key, unlocked the door, then replaced the key. "Why don't you have a seat," she said, gesturing at a pair of wooden deck chairs. "I'll get us some iced tea. Okay?"

"That'd be fine," I said.

I sat in one of the chairs and lit a cigarette. Beyond a rim of low sand dunes lay a broad expanse of tall marsh grass. The tide was high, and little channels and creeks flowed through the marsh to the Merrimack half a mile away. A pair of black ducks skidded into a pothole in the grass, and seagulls wheeled in the breeze.

It struck me as a good place to sit and look and think, like my balcony over the harbor. I wondered how much time Paul had spent out here, sitting and looking and thinking.

The young woman came out a couple of minutes later carrying a pair of plastic glasses. "I'm Maddy Wilkins, by the way," she said. She handed me a glass. "I live a couple of streets down."

"Oh. I wondered . . . "

"If I was living with him?"

I nodded.

"I'm not, no. Not yet, anyway." She gestured at the glass I was holding. "Sun tea," she said. "I made it."

I took a sip. It tasted bitter.

"So you and Paul are—"

"Are what?"

I shrugged. "Lovers?"

She smiled. "That's a funny, old-fashioned word, isn't it?"

"Whatever."

"I don't see how that's any of your business," she said.

"He's married, you know."

"Yeah, I know that. So what? He's getting a divorce." She cocked her head. "I get it. You're his lawyer. The divorce, right?"

"They hadn't gotten that far, I guess. I wasn't representing him on it, anyway. I did other lawyer work for him. Him and his wife."

"So you know her, too, huh?"

"Yes."

She took the chair beside me. "Is he really missing?"

"Yes."

"They haven't—"

"They found his boat. Nobody knows what happened. You seem to think he might have taken his own life."

She hugged herself. "I don't know. He was always so sad. Except when he went fishing. Then he was a different man. But mostly he was just sad."

"Did he talk to you about it?"

"No, not really. He tried to act cheerful for me. But he wasn't very good at it. I'd come over, make supper for him, and we'd sit out on the deck and hold hands and watch the sun set over the marsh and all the ducks coming in, and he'd just stare into space, and . . . it was just *so* damn sad. I would've done anything to cheer him up. I tried every way I knew." She shook her head. "That's why I was planting those stupid petunias. Aw, shit." She tried to smile as the tears coursed down her cheeks. "My mother was right. If you don't love somebody, you can't get hurt. Damn it."

"Maddy," I said softly, "did he ever take you out on his boat?"

She nodded. "Sure. Boy, did he know how to find those fish."

"How did he catch them?"

"Eels, mostly. He'd either drift them or rig them and cast them. He loved eels. I never saw him fish any other way. He said later when the pogies started running he'd use them. But they haven't started yet."

"Did you see Paul yesterday?"

She shook her head. "I worked till eleven. I'm waitressing at Scandia. I'm in college, see, but we're done for the summer. So me and some girls've rented this place a couple streets down. Anyway, I came over when I got off, but he wasn't here. I figured he was fishing, even though it was wicked stormy."

"Did it surprise you that he'd go out in the storm?"

"Not at all. He went out in worse weather than that. I mean, I've been out with him in some pretty bad weather. We never had a problem. He'd stick close to land, and he was real careful. Always made me wear a life jacket."

"Did he wear one?"

She shook her head. "He said if you respected the sea and understood it, you'd never have a problem."

I sat there with Maddy Wilkins, sipping her bitter tea and trying to decide what else I might ask her. But I had run out of questions.

So I put down my half-empty glass, stood up, and said, "Thank you, Maddy."

She looked up and frowned. "For what?"

I shrugged. "For the tea. For the information. I hope you'll keep my card, and if you think of something or hear something you'll call me."

"Oh, sure. Okay."

She followed me off the deck and around to the front of Paul's little house. "Well," she said, "I might as well finish planting these petunias. For—for when he comes home."

"I'm sure he'll be cheered by them," I said.

We waved to each other and I started down Meadowridge Road to my parked car, and that's when I saw the big man with the black beard.

12

He was standing in the middle of the narrow sand road, about fifty feet from me, wearing blue jeans and a sleeveless muscle shirt and dark glasses. It looked as if he was staring at me from behind those glasses, but I couldn't see his eyes.

He looked familiar. I couldn't place him.

I started toward him, and he turned and walked briskly away, heading back to the main street.

Then I remembered. I had seen him with his fist shaking in the air and anger cut into his face. Thomas Gall. He had been shouting above the tumult in the courtroom, spitting threats at Glen Falconer and the judge and the jury. And at Paul Cizek.

"Hey," I called. "Hey, wait a minute."

He didn't turn. I started to jog after him as he disappeared around the corner.

When I got to the end of Meadowridge Road, I looked in the direction he had gone. A hundred yards or so down the street a dark pickup truck started up and pulled away from the side of the road, heading back toward the bridge that crossed the river into Newburyport.

I stood there watching the truck disappear down the street.

"Do you know that man?"

I turned. Maddy Wilkins was standing behind me.

"I know who he is," I said. "Did you recognize him?"

She tucked a long strand of blond hair behind her ear. "Sure. He's a friend of Paul's."

"A friend?"

"I guess so. I've seen him a few times. I came over one night and they were sitting out on Paul's deck."

"What were they doing?"

She shook her head. "I'd just gotten out of work—it must've been close to midnight—and I saw his lights on, so I thought I'd drop in and say hello. When I saw Paul had company, I turned around and left."

"You've seen him more than once, though, huh?"

"A couple times I noticed him sort of hanging around when Paul wasn't here. Kinda like he was doing today. I never talked to the man or anything." She frowned at me. "Is there some problem with him?"

"I don't know," I said. "Maybe."

I took Route 1A, the slow road, back toward Boston. It crossed tidal creeks and meandered past marshland and farmland and woods and passed through quiet little New England towns like Newbury and Rowley, with white Protestant churches and white eighteenth-century colonials perched on the rims of emerald village greens. I bore left on 133 in Ipswich and headed out toward Cape Ann, and in Essex I stopped at a seafood shanty and bought a quart of mussels and a couple of fresh tuna steaks. I picked up 128 in Gloucester and headed home.

It was nearly five in the afternoon when I got back to my apartment. I made room for the mussels and fish by removing a bottle of Samuel Adams from the refrigerator. Then Sam and I wandered into the living room. The red light on my answering machine indicated that three people had tried to call me—or that one person had tried three times, maybe.

Nope. Three people. The first was Alex, asking what our plan was. The second was Olivia, requesting that I call her.

The third was Gloria, my ex-wife. "Have you talked to Joseph?" her recorded voice said. "You better give me a call."

That sounded ominous, so I sat down, lit a cigarette, and dialed the Wellesley number that was still familiar more than a decade after it had been mine.

She answered after several rings. "Yes?" She sounded breathless. "Are you all right?" I said.

"Oh, Brady." I heard her let out a long breath. "Yes, I'm fine. I was just getting out of the shower."

"What's the matter with Joey?"

"Joseph?" She hesitated. "Oh. My message. Nothing's the matter. Did I say something was the matter?"

"Not exactly. You asked if I'd talked to him. It sounded like—"

"I didn't mean to upset you, Brady. Sometimes Joseph tells me things that he doesn't tell you, and sometimes it's vice versa, and sometimes he tells us both, and sometimes he gives each of us different stories. William mainly talks to you, I know. But with Joseph, you never can tell."

"I haven't talked to Joey in a while," I said.

"You don't know that he's coming home, then."

"No. When?"

"Tonight, actually."

"Well, great. It'll be terrific to see him."

"The thing is," said Gloria, "I'm picking him up at the airport tonight and he's got to be in Chatham tomorrow for his job."

"His job?"

"He's got a job at a restaurant. He starts tomorrow afternoon."

"Well, shit," I said. "He didn't tell me any of this. So I don't even get to see him."

"I guess the job was sort of a last-minute thing," she said. "Anyway, I wondered if you might like to meet him at the airport with me. You and Alex, I mean. We could have coffee or something."

"Absolutely. What time?"

"Eleven-twenty at United. He's spent the past week visiting with his brother, and he's coming in from Boise. I told him I'd meet him at the baggage claim."

"We'll be there," I said. "And Gloria?"

"Yes?"

"Thank you. You didn't have to do this."

"You'd have done the same if the situation were reversed," she said.

"I hope I would," I said.

After Gloria and I disconnected, I called the *Globe* and, at the command of the recorded voice, punched in Alex's extension.

"Alexandria Shaw," she said.

"Rearranging verbs?"

"Oh, hi, sweetie. No, right now I'm trying to lose a hundred words. Golden words, these. It seems uncuttable."

"I assume you're coming over afterwards."

"Absolutely. I propose a game of strip Trivial Pursuit on the living room floor."

"Wouldn't seem right," I said, "you being naked and me fully dressed."

"It hardly ever works out that way, if you've noticed."

"It's just that I hate to see a woman take off her clothes alone. I take off my clothes out of a sense of good fellowship. Anyway, before our contest of wits, we're going to the airport. Joey's flying in tonight."

"That's fine. Is he going to stay with you?"

"No. Gloria's going to be there, too. She's taking him down to the Cape tomorrow for his summer job. This'll be my only chance to see him."

Alex chuckled. "So I get to meet your son and your ex-wife all at the same time."

"You don't have to come. I mean, if you think it'll be awkward . . . "

"Don't you want me to?"

"I do. I hope you will."

"I'd like to. Let me clean things up here. I'll be there in an hour or so."

"I'll cook something."

"Good. I'm starving."

"Any buzz on Paul Cizek at the paper?"

"Not really. Can you talk about it?"

"Sure. When you get here."

Alex made kissing noises into the phone, and we disconnected. Then I called Olivia.

"Yes?" she answered.

"It's Brady."

"Oh, gee. Thanks for calling back. I just . . . I wanted to hear a friendly voice."

"No news, then?"

"Nothing. Not a word. I tried calling Lieutenant Kirschenbaum, but he wasn't there. Nobody would tell me anything."

"If they knew something, I think they'd tell you."

"I guess so. You haven't heard anything, either?"

"No." I hesitated, then said, "I went out to Paul's house and talked to somebody, but she didn't know anything."

"She?"

"Just one of Paul's neighbors," I said.

"Well," she said, "I guess we can only wait." She hesitated for a moment, then said, "Brady?"

"Yes?"

"You *are* my attorney here, aren't you?"

"I don't think you need an attorney, Olivia."

"I want to retain you."

"It's not necessary."

"I'd like you to help me figure out what happened, Brady. Help me deal with it. I'd feel better if it was businesslike."

"Fine, Olivia. If that's how you'd prefer it. I'll have Julie work up an agreement on Monday."

"Thank you," she said. "We'll stay in touch, okay?"

"Okay."

I hung up and wandered out onto my balcony with my bottle of beer. We were approaching the longest day of the year, and the sun's rays still beat down on the harbor from a high angle. A brisk breeze riffled the water, and gulls and terns were wheeling and cruising sideways, riding on air currents.

601

Olivia had hired herself an attorney. I wondered if there was anything she wasn't telling me.

I was at the kitchen sink scrubbing the sand and grit off the mussels with a stiff-bristled brush when I heard Alex's key in the door. A moment later her arms went around my waist and she was pressing herself against my back.

"Hey, babe," she whispered into my shoulder.

"Hey, yourself."

"Sorry I'm late. I needed to go over some things with Michael."

"Good old Michael."

She turned me around, held me by the hips, and leaned back so that her lower half was pressed against my lower half. She was grinning. "Are we jealous of Michael?"

"Not we," I said. "Me."

"Of Michael?"

"Sure. He commands meetings when you should be with me."

She went up on tiptoes and kissed me on the ear. "Actually," she said, "it was I who requested the meeting."

"While I slave over the kitchen sink."

"You're cute in your little apron." She wrapped her arms around my chest and tucked her head up under my chin. "What're you making?"

"Mussles steamed in wine and garlic, tuna steaks grilled on the hibachi with butter and lemon, baked new potatoes, tossed salad, a bottle of chilled Marques de Caceres Rioja." I stepped out of her embrace, took off my apron, and reached for her hand. "Come with me, woman."

She smiled. "Yes, sir."

I led her into the living room. "Sit," I commanded, and she sat on the sofa. I sat on the coffee table in front of her, lifted her feet onto my lap, and slid off her shoes. Then I set about massaging her feet, giving each toe the careful, individual attention it deserved.

Alex leaned back and closed her eyes. "Oh, my God," she groaned. "I think I'm gonna come."

I rubbed her ankles and kneaded the hard muscles of her calves.

Her skin was smooth and warm to my touch. "I like it best in the summer," I said, watching her face, "when you don't wear panty hose."

She opened her eyes and looked at me. "Brady?"

"Mmm?"

"Stop. Now."

"You don't like it?"

"I *love* it. Now stop. Right this minute."

"Oh, I get it."

She sat up, put her arms around my neck, and kissed me hard. "Are you really jealous of Michael?" she whispered.

"I'm jealous of every man, because I know what they're thinking when they see you."

"How do you know what they're thinking?"

"Because I know what *I'm* thinking when *I* see you."

"That's awfully sweet." She kissed me again, then pulled back. "Can we eat? I'm starved."

I tried to look hurt. "I was planning to work my way up past your knees and under your skirt."

"Just how far were you planning to go?"

"I hadn't really decided where I'd stop. I just wanted to relax you after your long Saturday at the office."

"Relax?"

"Isn't it relaxing?"

She smiled. "Hardly. Anyway, we shouldn't get into that yet. We might lose track of time and not make it to the airport."

I mixed a rum and tonic for Alex and forbade her from helping. I steamed the mussels and dumped them into a big bowl, and we ate them at the table by the sliding doors, shelling them and dipping them in their own broth, while the potatoes baked in the oven and the sky darkened over the harbor. Then I tossed the salad and grilled the tuna.

By the time we cleaned up the kitchen, the moon had risen and the stars had begun to wink. We sat out on the balcony with our coffee and watched the reflections play on the water.

"Tell me about your day," Alex said.

So I did, ending with my conversation with Olivia.

"She hired you?"

"Yes."

"What for?"

"I'm not sure. To help, she said. I think she just wants support. She's feeling alone and frightened."

"Should I be jealous?"

I reached for her hand and squeezed it. "Olivia is rather attractive, actually, in a reserved, British sort of way. I'd prefer it if you were jealous. It's only fair."

"Because you've got Michael to be jealous of."

"Exactly."

"Okay," she said. "You've got a deal."

"Is the paper running the story?"

"Sure. It's a pretty big story."

" 'Criminal Defender Paul Cizek Lost at Sea,' " I said. " 'Presumed Drowned.' "

"Something like that." She sighed. "From what you said, it sounds like there's more of a story there than that."

"Maybe there is."

"Any conflict if I look into it?"

"Not so far. Everything I told you up to Olivia's phone call this afternoon is fair game. But since I'm now officially her lawyer, I won't be able to tell you anything after today."

"Cizek was sleeping with that girl?"

"I wouldn't be surprised."

Alex nodded. "Nothing very unusual about that, I guess."

"Aside from the fact that Paul's about twice her age."

"What about this Thomas Gall?" she said.

I shrugged. "He threatened Paul in court, as you remember. He was there today. Maddy Wilkins said she'd seen him with Paul. I suppose an intrepid reporter might want to look into it."

"I'm only going to be intrepid for another couple of months, you know."

"I keep trying not to think about it."

"We'll work it out."

"Sure."

"My lease is up at the end of August. I told my landlord I'm not renewing it. I've got to start looking for a cheap place in the country. Will you help me?"

"Of course."

"Southern Vermont, maybe. Or Maine or New Hampshire. Massachusetts is just too expensive."

I stared out over the harbor.

Alex's hand touched my leg. "It's not exactly Montana, Brady."

"No," I said. "I'd never see you if you went to Montana."

"Unless you came with me. Then we'd see each other all the time, no matter where we were." She laid her head on my shoulder. "I want you to do what you want to do."

"Easier said than done."

"I just hate to see you stuck."

I thought of Paul Cizek. He'd felt stuck. A lot of men my age got stuck. Some of them stayed stuck all their lives. Some of them managed to get unstuck. And some of them tried to unstick themselves and failed to survive the process.

I spotted Gloria standing back from the crowd at the baggage claim area at the United terminal. I took Alex's hand. "Come on," I said to her.

Gloria saw us coming and smiled. I hugged her and she kissed my cheek.

"Gloria," I said, "this is Alex."

They shook hands. "I've read your stuff in the *Globe*," Gloria said. "You're very good."

"Thanks," said Alex. "Brady's showed me some of your photographs. I like them a lot."

The two of them smiled at each other, and the next thing I knew they were standing there chattering in soft voices, and I had the uncomfortable feeling that they were comparing notes on my various idiosyncrasies and shortcomings.

I kept looking for Joey, and when he appeared I didn't recognize him for an instant. His hair was longer and his tan was deeper than I'd ever seen. When he'd left for California a year earlier, he was a boy. Now he looked like an adult.

"Hey, Dad," he said. He held out his hand. I shook it. We hesitated, then I gave him a hug. "I was hoping you'd be here," he added.

"It was your mother's idea."

"I tried to call," he said. "Got your machine."

"You didn't leave a message."

"I was calling collect." He smiled. "I was at Billy's. I didn't want to stick him with the cost."

Joey gathered his bags and we found a coffee shop in the terminal. Joey told us about his year at Stanford and his visit with his brother in Idaho, and after ten or fifteen minutes he abruptly turned to Gloria and said, "We gotta get going. I told Debbie I'd be there by midnight."

"You have a date?" I said. "At midnight?"

"I haven't seen her in almost a year, Pop."

You haven't seen me for a year, either, I thought. But I just nodded. "That's a long time."

"Neither of us has been going out," he said. "You know how it is."

"I can imagine," I said.

The four of us walked to the parking garage. We stopped at Gloria's car. I shook hands with Joey. "Let me know when you have a day off," I said. "We'll come down and go fishing or something."

"That'd be great," he said.

Alex exchanged kisses with Joey and Gloria. I gave Gloria a hug. Then I took Alex's hand and we went looking for my car.

"Oh, I like her," said Alex as we prowled the aisles of parked cars. "Gloria?"

"Yes. I can see why you married her."

"Can you see why I divorced her?"

She squeezed my arm. "No. But I'm sure you had your reasons."

"We both did."

When we found my car and got in, Alex leaned toward me, put

her arms around my neck, and kissed my ear. "Are you all right?" she whispered.

"Me? Sure. Why?"

"Joey was pretty itchy to leave."

"I remember how it was."

"Kids grow up," she said.

"Yes," I said. "We all do, eventually."

13

The next morning Alex and I took the fat Sunday *Globe* and mugs of coffee out to the balcony. A few puffy white clouds floated in a clear blue sky. The breeze carved whitecaps on the blue water six stories below. White gulls wheeled in the sunlight. Another beautiful blue-and-white June day.

"You don't want to go lie on a beach or something, do you?" I said to Alex.

She was wearing jogging shorts and one of my big, baggy T-shirts. Her long, smooth legs were stretched out in front of her with her heels up on the railing. "God, no," she said. "All that sand and sweat, all those people with bad bodies in skimpy bathing suits throwing Frisbees and playing rap music on their boom boxes and making out on blankets. Are you kidding?"

"Actually, I was."

"You probably want to go fishing."

"Sure. I'd like to go fishing. But I'm not going to."

"You're thinking about Paul Cizek."

"Yes. And Olivia."

"You could worry about them while you're fishing, couldn't you?"

"I couldn't worry properly. The trout would keep interfering.

On the other hand, the worrying would interfere with the fishing. So I think I'll stick close to the phone."

We sipped coffee and kept swapping sections of the newspaper. After a while, Alex took our mugs in for refills, and when she came back she asked for the real estate section. She poked her glasses onto her nose and began studying it with a felt-tipped pen in her hand.

Precisely at noon, she took the real estate pages inside. I remained on the balcony. I could hear Alex talking on the phone. After a while, I wandered inside. She was seated at the kitchen table with the real estate ads spread out in front of her. She had marked them up with her pen, and she was writing notes on a yellow legal pad. The phone was wedged against her ear. She looked up at me, smiled quickly, then dropped her eyes and resumed her conversation.

I refilled my mug and went back out to the balcony.

She was really going to do it.

That evening, Alex and I drove out of the city to David's Bistro in Acton. It was a quiet, intimate little country place where there were no city noises or city people. We parked out back, and when we got out of the car, Alex started for the door but I held her arm. "Wait," I said. "Sniff the air."

She tipped up her head and snuffled loudly. Then she turned to me. "What?"

"A little trout stream flows not far from here. Nashoba Brook. It was one of the places I used to come to on opening day of the fishing season. A long time ago, when I was a kid. Can't you smell it?"

"I guess I don't know what a trout stream is supposed to smell like."

"It smells a lot like the absence of automobile exhaust and hot pavement and electricity," I said. "It smells of cold wet gravel and sun-warmed rocks and mayfly wings."

She sniffed again. "Okay," she said. "Sure. I got it now." She turned and put her arms around my neck. "I'm learning, huh?"

I kissed her forehead. "We're both learning," I said.

The pretty young hostess led us to our favorite corner table. She brought a bourbon old-fashioned for me and a gin and tonic for Alex. We declined appetizers. Alex went for the duckling and I ordered the pork tenderloin.

We touched glasses. "To mayfly wings," said Alex.

We sipped our drinks and Alex started telling me about her latest conversation with her agent, when she abruptly stopped and lifted her eyes. "Hello," she said.

I half turned. Glen Falconer was standing behind my shoulder. "Sorry to bother you," he said. "I saw you come in. Wanted to say hi."

He held out his hand and I took it. "Hi, Glen," I said.

Alex extended her hand toward him. "I'm Alex Shaw," she said.

He shook her hand. "I know," he said. "And I know you know me, too. You covered my trial."

Alex glanced up at Glen, then looked at me.

I frowned at her and mouthed the word "no," but she pretended not to notice. "Won't you sit with us for a minute?" she said.

"Well, sure," said Glen. "Thanks. Just for a minute." He pulled over a chair from an adjacent table and sat down. He had an empty highball glass in his hand. He craned his neck, caught a waitress's attention, and held up his glass. Then he turned to me. "I never thanked you," he said.

"For what?"

"For getting Paul Cizek for me. He saved my ass. Pardon me, Miss Shaw," he said to Alex.

"Brady talks that way all the time," she said.

"That Cizek," said Glen expansively. "Some lawyer. Did a number on dear old Dad, all right." He chuckled. "Did a number on everybody. Witnesses, jury, judge. Reporters, too." He glanced at Alex. "You know what I mean, Miss?"

Alex did not smile. "Sure. I know what you mean."

"I should have gone to prison," said Glen. "And I didn't. How 'bout that?"

"That makes you a lucky guy, I guess," I said. Glen, I realized, had already had a few drinks. His eyes glittered and his movements seemed slow and studied, as if he had to plan them out before making them.

"Anyhow," he continued, "I quit driving."

"Way to go," I said. "Congratulations."

He either ignored or didn't get my sarcasm. "Thanks. I feel good about it. I've got a bicycle, so I can drink all I want, and if I drive drunk, at least the only person I'll hurt will be myself for a while."

"For a while?" I said.

"Oh, I'll climb back behind the wheel one of these days. You can't keep a good man down, huh? But for now it's the bike. That's how I got here. On my bike."

"You pedaled here from Lincoln?" asked Alex.

"Yes, ma'am. Still living with my daddy, riding my bike around town."

"That's a long bike ride, isn't it?" she said. "All the way from Lincoln?"

"I haven't got anything else to do," he said. "I ride the bike everywhere. It passes the time."

The waitress sidled up to the table and placed a fresh highball in front of Glen. She hesitated, then said to me, "Shall I hold your salads for a few minutes?"

"No," I said. "We're starved."

"Another drink, Mr. Coyne? Miss Shaw?"

Alex shook her head. "We're fine, thanks," I said.

"I'll leave you two alone," said Glen. "I just wanted to say hello."

"Sure," I said. "Take it easy."

Glen picked up his drink and took a swallow. "I liked your editorial, by the way," he said to Alex.

"Editorial?" she said.

"The one you wrote the day after the trial. The one saying I should've been thrown in prison."

"That was unsigned," she said. "It represented the editorial position of the paper."

He nodded and smiled. "Sure. But you wrote it. It's okay. It was good. Maybe they *should* have found me guilty." He looked down at the table. "Sometimes I wish they had."

611

"You've got to live with it," I said.

"It's hard."

"The booze helps, huh?"

He looked up at me. "I can't quit drinking, Brady. So I quit driving cars. I figure if I kill myself, who cares? My life is ruined anyway."

"I think our salads are coming," I said.

Glen frowned at me. "Huh? Oh. Sorry. I'll get back to my table." He stood up, then reached hastily for his chair, which threatened to topple over. "Nice to see you folks. Sorry to interrupt your dinner. I'll just get back to my table now."

With studied precision, Glen turned his chair around and slid it back into its place at the next table. Then he picked up his high-ball and held it aloft. "Thank you both again," he said solemnly. "Thank you very much."

Alex and I watched him pick his way carefully across the dining room to a table against the far wall.

"He's eating alone," said Alex.

"Don't even think of it."

"Oh, I wasn't," she said. "Still, it's hard not to feel sorry for him."

"Don't," I said. "He doesn't deserve your sympathy. Did you hear him? *His* life is ruined? Like he didn't ruin the lives of that woman and her family?"

She smiled. "You're a hard man, Brady Coyne."

"He should've gone to prison. Did you hear him? He admits he can't quit drinking, and he's looking forward to climbing back behind the wheel."

"I know," she said. "You're right."

"I didn't hear anything like remorse out of him," I said. "Just self-pity. Anyway, he's drinking. He's all set. And one of these days he'll get into a car and smash into somebody else."

Our waitress brought our salads and ground some black pepper onto them. "Anything else, folks?"

"Let's have some wine," said Alex.

"Not me," I said.

"*We* are not drunks," she said.

I looked at her. "You're right. I'm sorry." I glanced at the card on the table listing David's recommended wines. "The sauvignon blanc?"

"Yes," said Alex.

After our waitress left, I reached for Alex's hand. "Did I misbehave?"

"No. You were rude to Glen, but he deserved it."

"I didn't embarrass you?"

"You never embarrass me."

"I embarrass myself sometimes."

"That's another thing I love about you," she said. "You're such a sensitive guy."

"Oh, shit," I mumbled. "Anything but that."

We ate our salads in silence, and then Alex patted her mouth with her napkin and said, "Brady?"

"Um?"

"We've got to talk about what we're going to do."

"What I'm going to do when you move, you mean."

She nodded. "Yes."

"Now?"

She cocked her head and smiled. "No. Not now. Let's just have a nice meal. Now I want you to tell me all about what it was like when you were a little boy on opening day of the fishing season."

"It always rained," I said.

A string quartet was playing on the PBS radio station as we drove back to the city, and we listened to it without talking. After a while, Alex murmured, "Brady?"

"Hm?"

"I don't mean to pressure you."

"You aren't, are you?"

"Not intentionally. Do you feel pressured?"

"Sometimes a man needs a nudge," I said.

"There's plenty of time," she said. "Just try to figure out what you really want."

"Easier said than done." After a minute, I said, "You know what I really want?"

She reached over and squeezed my leg. I heard her chuckle. "Yes," she said. "I think so."

14

I beat Julie to the office on Monday and had the coffee all brewed for her. We sat in my office while I recounted the events of the weekend—my late-night phone call from Olivia Cizek, the people I had talked to in Newburyport, my Thomas Gall sighting, my encounter with the drunken Glen Falconer.

When I told her that Alex and I had met Joey's plane, and that Gloria had been there, Julie's eyebrows went up. "How did it go?"

"Go?"

"You know. How'd Gloria react?"

"It was Gloria's idea," I said. "She reacted fine. They both did. Everybody did."

"Sometimes," said Julie, "I don't get it."

"Gloria and I have been divorced for a long time," I said gently.

She was shaking her head. "I know. Still . . . "

"Things change. You move on."

"I always thought—"

"That Gloria and I would get back together. I know. I used to think that sometimes. But we're not going to."

"You love Alex."

"Yes. I like Gloria. I care about her. I think she likes me, too.

We've become friends. But I love Alex, and I think Gloria approves."

Julie reached across my desk and put her hand on my cheek. "I do, too," she said. "You've been happy with Alex."

I thought of Alex moving to Vermont or Maine, and I wondered if I'd still be happy then. I decided not to discuss it with Julie. Not yet. I had to decide what I was going to do first.

I cleared my throat. "Not to change the subject," I said, "but I think we better get to work. First off, let's draw up a standard retainer contract for Olivia Cizek."

"That poor woman," said Julie.

I nodded.

"She must be feeling terribly guilty."

"Guilty?"

"The marriage failed. He left her. And now . . . "

"If she'd been a better wife it never would've happened," I said. "Is that what you mean?"

"It's what she'd think."

"It's not as if she abandoned him," I said. "It was the other way around. Why should she feel guilty?"

"It's how women are, Brady."

"Oh."

"Mr. and Mrs. Cizek already have an agreement with us, you know," she said. "Do you think a separate one with her is necessary?"

"Not really. But it's what she wants."

"Okay. Can do." Julie stood up and smoothed her skirt against the sides of her legs. "Check your In box, Brady." She started for the door, then turned. "I'm glad Gloria is okay," she said.

"She is," I said. "I promise."

Julie went out to her desk and I sat behind mine. My In box, as usual, was piled with papers that needed pushing.

So I pushed them around for a while. My mind kept wandering to Olivia and Paul. I called Olivia at home. Her machine invited me to leave a message. "It's Brady," I told it. "Monday morning. I'll try your office."

Olivia was unable to come to the phone, her secretary told me.

I left my name and number, emphasized that it was not urgent, and asked to have her return my call.

Then I called the Newburyport police. Lieutenant Kirschenbaum was on another line. I agreed to hold. I waited for the length of time it took me to smoke a cigarette before he growled, "Kirschenbaum."

"It's Brady Coyne, Lieutenant," I said. "I'm—"

"I remember you," he said. "The Cizek thing. What's up?"

"I wondered if you had any news."

"No."

"They haven't found Paul's body, then."

"I guess that would qualify as news, Mr. Coyne, don't you think?"

"I guess it would."

"That's why you called?"

"No," I said. "I wanted to share something with you."

"Sharing is good. One of those virtues you learn in kindergarten. Some guy made millions on a book about all the good stuff you learn in kindergarten. Share away, Mr. Coyne."

I told him about my conversation with Dolph at the boat ramp, my examination of Paul's boat at the Coast Guard station, and my visit with Maddy Wilkins at Paul's cottage on Plum Island. "And when I left," I said, "Thomas Gall was standing there outside the house. When I called to him, he walked away, got in his truck, and drove off. You know who Thomas Gall is, don't you?"

"Refresh my memory."

"This past winter Paul Cizek defended the man who killed Gall's wife in an auto accident. The jury came back with a 'not guilty' verdict. At the end of the trial, Gall threatened Paul. He yelled, 'I'll get you,' or something to that effect."

"So you think he got him, huh?"

"I don't know what to think. The girl said he'd been there before. So he knew where Paul was staying. If anybody had a motive—"

"We don't even know if Cizek's dead, Mr. Coyne. All we know is that his boat was adrift in the storm."

"He wasn't fishing. There was no bait aboard. So why was he out there?" I paused, then said, "According to his wife, he was not heavily insured, by the way."

Kirschenbaum chuckled. "Yeah, I thought of that."

"I thought you might have. I suppose you could check on the insurance, but—"

"Look," said Kirschenbaum, "I appreciate your help, I really do. I'll keep this Gall in mind. But, you know, we law enforcement people pretty much limit our work to solving crimes and apprehending criminals, and so far we don't seem to have a crime here. All we've got is a boat, you know?"

"Sure. I know that."

"But you're trying to make a murder case out of this."

"No, I'm not. I'd rather Paul was alive. But it doesn't look like he is."

I heard Kirschenbaum sigh. "No, it doesn't look that way, and I really don't mean to be short with you. I'm glad you told me about this Gall character and the insurance thing. Anything else, don't hesitate to call. Okay?"

"Okay."

"And if we learn anything, I'll pass it along to Mrs. Cizek."

"Since I'm her lawyer," I said, "it might be better if you pass it along to me."

"Because if it's bad news, you should be the one to break it to her. You being more sensitive and caring than me."

"Exactly," I said.

Olivia returned my call around noontime. "Have you heard something?" she said.

"No. Nothing. You?"

I heard her sigh. "No."

"I'm glad you're working," I said.

"It gives me something to do." She hesitated. "Brady?"

"Yes?"

"I think it would be better if you didn't call unless you had something to tell me. I mean, I appreciate your concern, but when

I saw that message from you, my heart started pounding and I felt like I had to throw up. Right now I'm figuring that no news is— well, at least no news is not bad news. I was so grateful to be able to come to work today. The weekend was hard. This gives me other things to think about. Do you understand?"

"Sure," I said. "No problem. I do understand."

"You're awfully sweet. And I do want to put this on a businesslike basis."

"I'm having Julie draw up a contract. We'll send it out to you this afternoon. And we'll do business when and if there's business to be done."

"Good," she said. "I'll sign it and write you a check and get it back to you."

"It's not necessary, you know."

"I'm more comfortable with it this way."

I ushered the day's last client out of my office on Wednesday afternoon. It was four o'clock, which, if I didn't dillydally, would give me just enough time to zip home, change my clothes, gather up some gear, and drive out to the Squannacook River in Townsend, where the trout would be feeding on mayflies. An attractive plan, I thought. I would do it. I owed myself one.

About then Julie tapped on the door, pushed it open, and stuck her head into my office. Her eyebrows were arched in her "May I come in?" expression. I crooked my finger at her, and she came in.

She closed the door behind her and stood in front of my desk. "Brady," she said, "there's a man here who wants to see you."

"He doesn't have an appointment?"

"No."

"You never let anyone see me without an appointment," I said. "I was actually thinking of going fishing."

"He's been waiting all afternoon. I told him you'd see him when you were done."

I slumped back in my chair. "He must be awfully persuasive. Or desperate. What's he want?"

"I don't know. He's desperate, I think. He came in, said he

needed to see you, and when I told him he could make an appointment, he just sat down and said he'd wait. I told him you were tied up all afternoon, and he said that was okay. He's been sitting there jiggling his knee and flipping through your old *Field & Streams*."

"You're telling me I should see him."

She nodded.

"Even though he doesn't have an appointment and he's not one of our clients."

She shrugged.

"The whole damn trout season is passing me by."

"He seems like a nice, quiet man with big problems."

"Fine. Okay. I'll see him." I shook my finger at her. "But don't you ever again accuse me of being a softie when I make house calls or forget to record all my billable time," I said, in what I thought was a convincing growl.

Julie grinned, came around the desk, and planted a wet kiss on my cheek. "You're a nice man," she said.

"I'm a sucker, is what I am," I said.

She went out, and a minute later she came back, followed by a short, round man with a high forehead and gray hair and dark eyes. He wore khaki pants and a green linen sport jacket, blue-and-white striped shirt, no tie, and a shy smile.

"Mr. Coyne," said Julie, "this is Mr. Vaccaro."

I stared at the man for a moment, then nodded. The last time I'd seen him, he'd been wearing a camel-hair topcoat in Skeeter's Infield, and he'd been talking to Paul Cizek. "We've met," I said to Julie. "Thanks."

She frowned for an instant, then shrugged and left the office, closing the door behind her.

I settled back in my chair. "What can I do for you, Mr. Vaccaro?"

"I need a lawyer."

"Who referred you to me?"

"No one. At least, not exactly. See, Mr. Cizek is my regular lawyer. Paul Cizek?"

I nodded. "Go ahead."

"Well, Mr. Cizek defended me. Almost two years ago, it was. And now—"

"I know all about you," I said.

He looked at me without expression.

"You work for the Russo family," I said. "Vinny Russo pays you to kill people. You shoot them in the eye. You're famous for that. You murdered an old man in a North End restaurant."

He shrugged. "They found me innocent."

"They found you not guilty," I said, "which is a lot different. Look, Mr. Vaccaro. I don't know what your problem is, but I'm not a criminal lawyer. I can't help you."

"You mean you don't want to help me," he said.

I nodded. "Yes, that's right."

"Mr. Cizek is missing," he said. "I need him."

I didn't say anything.

Vaccaro leaned forward. "You're looking for him. So am I. We can help each other."

"What makes you think I'm looking for him?"

He sat back in his chair and shrugged.

I lit a cigarette and looked at him through the smoke. "Why did you come here, Mr. Vaccaro?"

"I want Mr. Cizek. Look, can I tell you about it?"

I shrugged. "You've already ruined my fishing plans. Go ahead."

"Okay." He took a deep breath. "Okay," he said again. "Yeah, the cops had me by the nuts for poppin' that old guy in Natalie's. What they wanted was for me to give them Vinny Russo. You know, testify against him. They knew I coulda done it. I give them Uncle Vinny, they let me go. You know, move me someplace, give me a new name and some money. I told 'em no fuckin' way. I know how those deals work. The Russos'd find me in a month. I'd be a dead man. I told 'em to go fuck themselves. I'm better off going on trial. I figured they'd put me away. But Uncle Vinny got Mr. Cizek to defend me and he got me off."

"So what's your problem?"

He narrowed his eyes. "Now I think that prick Russo's gonna have me hit. I stood up for the son of a bitch, and now he decides he don't trust me. I wanna go back to the feds and give 'em Vinny and every other fuckin' Russo in Boston."

"Good idea," I said. "Do it. It's your civic responsibility."

He didn't smile. "It ain't that easy, Mr. Coyne."

"I don't want to hear this," I said. "You should go find yourself a lawyer who can help you."

"There's only one lawyer I trust. I gotta have Mr. Cizek. So you gotta find him for me. You find him and tell him I need him."

"As far as I know," I said, "Paul Cizek went overboard Friday night. They haven't found his body, but—"

"He's alive," said Vaccaro.

"What makes you think so?"

He shrugged. "He's gotta be alive. I need him."

"Well, I tell you what," I said. "If I see him, I'll give him your message. How's that?"

"Don't fuck with me, Mr. Coyne," he said softly. "I give you respect. You shouldn't disrespect me."

"Frankly, Mr. Vaccaro," I said, "I don't see any reason why I should respect you, and I don't think there's anything left for us to discuss."

"You kicking me out?" he said.

"I think you said what you had to say. Your appointment is over."

He stared at me for a moment, then shrugged. He reached into his jacket pocket and withdrew a roll of bills. He removed several of them one at a time and made a stack on my desk.

I pushed it away. "I don't want your money."

"You better take it."

"I'm not your lawyer. I don't want you for a client."

"You don't get it," he said. "You gotta be my lawyer."

"No, I don't. My clients are all people who I want to help. People I like and care about. I'm the one who decides who my clients are."

He smiled. "Yeah, that's pretty good, Mr. Coyne. I like that." His smile abruptly vanished. He leaned forward and peered at me with his hard little black eyes. "I know how it works, and so do you. I told you all this. I told you I was ready to give Uncle Vinny to the feds. That's important information. If it got out, it'd be bad for me. I can't have that happen. If you're my lawyer, you can't tell anyone else. If you're my lawyer, I can trust you. So you better take the money, Mr. Coyne, see?"

"Are you threatening me, Mr. Vaccaro?" I said quietly.

He waved his hand. "I'm just trying to hire a lawyer."

"And if I refuse to be hired?"

He leaned back, spread his hands, and smiled. "Please," he said. "Take the money."

I picked up the stack of bills from my desk. I counted them. There were twenty fifties. I took three of them and pushed the rest away. "Okay," I said. "That covers the time you've been here. So you can trust me. Now your appointment is over."

"Now you can't tell anybody what I told you."

"That's right."

He pushed the money back toward me. "Take more than that," he said.

"This is my regular fee."

"Go ahead. I've got plenty of money."

"So do I," I said.

He shrugged, picked up the stack of bills, and shoved it into his jacket pocket. "You tell Mr. Cizek I need him."

"I don't expect to see Paul Cizek."

"But if you do?"

"I'll tell him," I said.

"Good," he said. He stood up and held out his hand to me.

I did not shake it.

15

Julie stared at me. "He's a *what*?"

"A hit man," I said. "A murderer. An assassin for hire."

"But he seemed—"

"Like a nice, quiet man."

"Well, he did."

"Desperate, I think you said."

Julie nodded.

"He's desperate, all right. And quiet. But he's not nice."

She dropped into the armchair in my office and began hugging herself and shaking her head. "You mean he really—"

"Eddie Vaccaro makes his living by shooting people he doesn't even know," I said. "He does it without emotion. It's his profession. He uses a twenty-two automatic pistol. He usually puts the first one in their eye and another behind their ear."

"And I made you see him," she said.

I shrugged. "It's okay. I won't see him again."

"I'm sorry, Brady."

I patted her arm. "Don't worry about it." I decided not to tell her that *I* was worried about it. I didn't like having killers share their life-and-death secrets with me.

"So what did he want?" she said.

"He wants Paul Cizek. He said he's in trouble and needs a lawyer. Apparently Paul is the only one he trusts."

"Why come to you?"

"I don't know," I said. "He thinks I'm looking for Paul."

"Why would he think that?"

"I don't know," I said. "I don't even know if Vaccaro was telling me the truth."

Julie frowned. "If he was lying—"

"Let's not think about it," I said quickly. "It's time to go home."

Of course, I did think about it. I thought about it while I walked home from the office, and I thought about it while I sat on my balcony sipping Rebel Yell on the rocks, and I thought about it while I stared up into the darkness with Alex sleeping beside me that night.

If Vaccaro had been lying about the reason he wanted to find Paul Cizek, it meant he wanted him for something else.

If he'd been lying about the fact that he didn't know where Paul was, it meant he *did* know what had happened to him.

I decided I might as well assume Vaccaro had been telling me the truth. I figured being lied to by a Mafia hit man was bad news by definition.

And if Eddie Vaccaro had been telling me the truth, of course, it meant that he hadn't killed Paul.

And I fell asleep hoping that I'd done the right thing, accepting his money. I don't think I'd have fallen asleep at all if I had refused it. Anybody who killed people for money wouldn't hesitate to kill them for their silence.

Olivia called shortly after I arrived at the office on Friday morning. "I wonder if you can give me a hand," she said.

"I'll try," I said. "What's up?"

"The Coast Guard called. They want Paul's boat moved. I told them I'd arrange to come get it."

"When?"

"It's got to be this weekend. They said they'd have to dispose of it if it wasn't gone by Sunday."

"Can you get off this afternoon?"

"Let me check." A moment later she said, "I could meet you at that Friendly's ice cream place at four. Can you do that?"

"That'll work," I said. "We'll have to get Paul's car, because we need the trailer. Do you have a key?"

"To his car? No, I don't."

"There's probably a spare one at his cottage. We'll have to check there." I thought we could look around, and if we didn't find Paul's spare ignition key, Maddy Wilkins might help. I decided not to mention Maddy to Olivia unless it was necessary. "Okay," I said. "Friendly's at four. I'll be there."

"Brady," said Olivia, "you haven't heard anything, have you?"

I thought of my visit from Eddie Vaccaro. "No. We agreed not to keep calling each other unless we knew something. I've heard nothing."

"Me neither," she said.

Olivia was leaning against her red Saab with her face tilted up to the sun when I pulled into the lot at Friendly's. She was wearing sneakers and tight-fitting jeans and a plaid cotton shirt with the sleeves rolled up to her elbows, and she was sipping through a straw from a Friendly's cardboard drinking container, and for an instant I could picture her as a young, carefree college kid with nothing better to do than sip a soda and enjoy the sunshine. When she saw me, she waved, came over, and climbed in beside me.

"Another beautiful June afternoon," I said lamely.

"Yes, it is," she said. "Perfect."

I pulled out of the lot and headed into Newburyport. "How have you been?"

She laughed quickly. "I guess I've been numb. I have these— these moments. When it hits me. It's worst at night, when I'm home alone. I've been watching a lot of television. But mostly I just live my life. It's been a week. It seems like forever since I got that call. It was a week ago tonight."

I drove down High Street, onto Water Street, and out past the Coast Guard station, heading for Plum Island.

"How are we going to get into his place?" said Olivia.

"I know where the key's hidden."

She didn't ask how I knew, so I didn't have to mention Maddy.

And since Maddy's old yellow Volkswagen was not parked in Paul's yard when we got there, I still didn't have to mention her to Olivia. The newly planted petunias looked pink and perky in their little flower bed in the front yard. The key was still under the flower pot on the deck, and I used it to let us in.

Olivia looked around and smiled. "He wasn't much for picking up after himself," she said, and I didn't miss her use of the past tense. I figured that somewhere in her unconscious she'd already accepted the likelihood that Paul was dead.

There was a kitchen/dining room/living room area with a single picture window that overlooked the marsh. Beyond the living room were two closed doors—bedrooms, I assumed—and one open one, a bathroom. The decor was neo–K Mart—spindly chairs, a round pine table, matching pseudo-colonial sofa and armchair. Magazines and newspapers and shoes and socks littered the floor and furniture. Unopened mail was scattered across the top of the table. The kitchen sink was piled with pots and dishes.

"Where do we start?" said Olivia.

I shrugged. "We're all creatures of habit. Where did Paul usually keep his spare keys?"

"In his desk drawer." She looked around. "I don't see a desk in this place."

"There's probably a chest of drawers in his bedroom. Or maybe the spare bedroom has a desk in it." I gestured toward the closed doors. "Why don't you look around in there. I'll check out here."

Olivia headed for the bedrooms. I rummaged through the two drawers that bracketed the sink. One held a jumble of forks and knives and spoons and spatulas and can openers. There were screwdrivers and pliers and a hammer and an assortment of other junk in the other one. No keys. Nothing on the windowsill or on top of the refrigerator.

I sat at the kitchen table. A bunch of limp daisies drooped in a water glass. From Maddy, I guessed. I picked up a stack of mail and glanced through it. Mostly junk stuff addressed to "Occupant." I figured Paul hadn't gotten around to having his address permanently changed.

There were a few bills—electricity, water, telephone—a bank statement, some catalogs, a couple of *Newsweek* magazines.

No mysterious letters. Nothing to indicate what might've happened to him.

From one of the bedrooms, Olivia called, "Got it." She came out holding up a key. "This has to be it," she said.

"Good," I said. "Let's go do it."

She stood in the living room and nudged a balled-up sweatshirt with her toe. "This is spooky," she said.

"Being here?"

She nodded. "I mean, I *know* these clothes." She waved her hand at the shoes and T-shirts and socks scattered on the floor. "I've picked them up a hundred times. I've picked up his pants and shirts, washed them, folded them, hung them up . . . "

I went to her and touched her arm. "Olivia."

She looked up at me and smiled quickly. "I'm okay, Brady." She took a long look around the inside of the cottage, shook her head, and went outside.

We drove to the boat ramp. Paul's car was still parked there, and the key opened the door and fit into the ignition. Olivia got in and followed me to the Coast Guard station. We drove directly down to the dock, and by the time we had climbed out of the cars, a young guy had hurried down to join us.

"Something I can help you with, sir?" he said to me.

"We came to get the Whaler," I said, pointing at Paul's boat.

"Why don't you just hang on for a second." He turned and jogged back to the brick building, and a few minutes later the officer whom I'd seen on my previous visit strode down to us.

"Mr. Coyne," he said. "You've come for the boat."

I nodded. "This is Mrs. Cizek. The Whaler belongs to her husband."

He nodded to her and mumbled, "Ma'am." He turned to me. "No news, huh?"

I shook my head.

"Well, the Newburyport police tell us they're done with the boat, and we don't have any space for it, so I'm glad you can take it."

"Want me to back down?" said Olivia.

I laughed. "I'd be relieved. I'm not very good at backing trailers down boat ramps. I tend to bump into things."

"I've done it plenty of times," she said, and she proceeded to do it expertly.

A half hour later we had parked boat, trailer, and car in the side yard of Paul's cottage. Olivia insisted on returning the car key to where she had found it. Then we drove back to the Friendly's lot in my car.

Olivia suggested we have coffee, but I declined. It was Alex's turn to cook dinner, and I didn't want to be late, even if it turned out to be lentil soup.

16

Alex was out on the balcony when I got home. She was wearing
a pair of my boxer shorts and her own "Walk for Hunger" T-shirt.
She was tilted back in one of the aluminum chairs with her legs up
on the railing and her eyes closed.

I eased up her T-shirt to expose some smooth skin and kissed her
belly. Her fingers moved in my hair. "Mmm," she said. "Nice.
What was that for?"

"Does it have to be *for* something?"

"It's better if it isn't," she said.

"It's because I don't smell lentil soup."

She grabbed a handful of my hair, pulled my head up, and
clamped both arms around my neck. She put her mouth on my ear
and whispered, "Hungry?"

"How do you mean that?"

She kissed my mouth, then sat up. "For now, I'm talking about
dinner. Go grab yourself a beer and then stay out of my kitchen.
I'll call you to the table."

"You're awfully sexy when you're bossy," I said. "And you're
particularly sexy in my boxer shorts." I snapped her a salute. "I will
obey, sir."

I changed into my jeans and took a beer onto the balcony, where

I watched the setting sun splash colors on the cloud bank that was building on the horizon. Thoughts of Eddie Vaccaro and Paul Cizek flitted in and out of my consciousness. I willed myself not to focus on them, and had good success at it.

An hour or so later Alex called, "Come and get it." I went to the table.

Grilled lamb chops, boiled potatoes doused with melted butter and sprinkled with parsley, stir-fried snow peas, avocado on beds of Bibb lettuce, a sweet German wine. "You're an amazing woman," I said to Alex. "Do you make your own clothes, too?"

"No, I steal them from men," she said. "Tomorrow's Saturday. Are you going fishing tomorrow?"

"I'd like to. I'm going to call Charlie."

I did, and he was eager. We debated our options and decided on the Farmington River in Connecticut. We always found rising trout on the Farmington. I told him I'd pick him up at eight.

At six in the morning, when I woke up, an easterly wind was driving hard raindrops against the windows. They sounded like buckshot rattling on the glass. I stood there sipping my coffee and staring down through the sliding doors at the gray, churning surface of the harbor.

I felt Alex's hand on the back of my neck. Then her arms went around my chest and I felt her breasts pressing against my back. "It's a pretty lousy day," she murmured.

"Too lousy for trout fishing."

"I thought rain was good for fishing."

"No. That's a fallacy. This kind of rain ruins trout fishing. The Farmington will be high and muddy and the trout will be sulking on the bottom. Besides, it's no fun getting soaked."

"Macho-type men like confronting the elements, don't they? Isn't getting wet and freezing your ass off what it's all about?"

"No. Enjoying a pleasant June day and catching trout on dry flies is what it's all about."

"I'm sorry," she said. "I guess you'll go tomorrow, huh?"

"No," I said. "Tomorrow is Sunday, our only day together. Charlie and I can go fishing next Saturday."

631

"You can go tomorrow, Brady. I understand."

I turned around and hugged her. "It's not a sacrifice, you know, spending a day with you."

She looked up at me. "Mean it?"

I kissed her. "Yes."

She took my hand. "Since it's raining and you can't go fishing," she said, "you might as well come back to bed."

"I already had a mug of coffee. I'll never get back to sleep."

"Exactly," she said.

Sunday, of course, dawned clear and sunny. It would've been a perfect day for trout fishing.

"Why don't you go?" said Alex as we spread marmalade on English muffins at the table.

"I want to be with you."

"You deserve a nice fishing trip."

"One of these days, maybe I'll have one," I said. "Anyway, I also deserve a nice day with you."

"Well," she said, "we're going for a drive. You can bring your stuff, maybe stop somewhere along the way."

"Where are we going?"

"Maine."

"Is this a real estate excursion?"

She nodded.

"I thought you were interested in Vermont."

"I was. I've made a lot of calls. Vermont's too expensive. There are places in Maine I can afford. I found a nice real estate lady who's got several places for me to look at."

"How far up?"

"Not far. Maybe three hours from here."

"I don't know any good trout rivers in southern Maine."

She reached across the table and touched my hand. "Brady, I mean it," she said. "I wish you'd go fishing."

"I mean it, too," I said. "I want to go to Maine with you. I want to help you find a nice place to live."

★ ★ ★

Alex hugged my arm. "Oh, Brady," she said. "This is it. Don't you think?"

It was just the third place we'd looked at, a modest post-and-beam home that sat on a dirt road in Garrison, Maine, due west of Portland near the New Hampshire border. The entire first floor was a single open room with a wooden spiral staircase leading to the upstairs. A big picture window overlooked a valley and low rolling hills beyond. There was a wood stove at one end and a big fieldstone fireplace at the other. A fairly modern kitchen extended across half of the back wall. The double windows over the sink looked out into the woods.

Upstairs there were three decent-sized bedrooms and a bath. The place hadn't been lived in for a year, and the monthly rent had been reduced a few times. Now it was half what Alex was paying for her two-bedroom apartment on Marlborough Street in Boston.

The real estate agent, a gray-haired woman named Alice, said that the town kept the dirt road plowed in the winter, and a local man would keep her supplied with firewood and perform a variety of handyman chores.

"I think it's perfect," I said to Alex.

"But—"

"But nothing. It's perfect. Grab it."

She did. We drove back to the real estate office, where Alex signed a one-year renewable lease and wrote a check for two months' rent. The place would be hers on the first of September.

I bought us each a Pepsi at a Maine backroad mom-and-pop store on the way home. We leaned against the side of the car outside the store. I held up my Pepsi can. "To your new home," I said.

She gave me a small smile, then touched her can to mine.

"You're thinking it could be *our* new home?" I said.

She shrugged. "Something like that. Yes."

I nodded. "I guess it could. It's a nice place. I like it."

"I will never pressure you," she said. "You see the place. You know what it is. You know I'm going to be living there. Now you've got to decide what to do."

"Yes, I do. I don't have a choice. If I don't decide, that will be a decision, too."

"I'll love you no matter what you do," she said.

Yes, I thought. But it would never be quite the same.

We didn't talk much on the way home. I wanted to be more enthusiastic for Alex. I just couldn't fake it. And I suspected she was struggling to dampen her own enthusiasm out of deference to my feelings.

We stopped at a little Italian restaurant in Burlington for supper. The pasta was good and we split a carafe of the house wine. Alex chatted about her book and a couple of stories she was working on, trying very hard to avoid the subject we were both thinking about. I nodded and smiled in the right places, but after a while our conversation petered out.

It was dark when we got back to the city. I pulled into my parking slot beside Alex's car. "I think I'll go home now," said Alex.

"Oh?"

She tried to give me a bright smile. "I've got a busy day tomorrow."

"Sure. And you probably have laundry to do. Wash your hair, pay your bills, make some phone calls—"

She grabbed my arm. "Listen to me."

"I'm sorry," I said. "I was being childish."

"So was I," she said. "I wasn't saying what I meant. Let me try again."

I touched her face. "Okay."

"I just think . . . if I stayed tonight we'd feel—tension. I really don't want to influence your thinking. I'm not sure I know how to act right now. I'm excited by my new place. I'm sad because it's making a problem for you. Do you see?"

"I think so." I smiled. "Is this our first fight?" I tried to make it come out like a joke, but it didn't sound like one, even to my ears.

Alex shrugged. "We're—having a conflict. I'm sorry. I don't want to fight or argue or do anything but be happy with you. I don't want to be apart from you, but I'm going to be living in Maine, for the next two years. I really want to share my life with you. I want you to want that, too."

"It's not that I don't want to share my life with you," I said.

She looked at me for a moment, then nodded. "I believe you."

"You won't stay with me tonight?"

She shook her head. "No. I don't think I should. Not tonight. It'll be easier for you if I'm not around."

"Maybe you're right," I said.

She put her arms around my neck and gave me a long, hungry kiss. When she pulled back, her eyes were glistening.

When I got up to my apartment, I sloshed some Rebel Yell into a glass, added three ice cubes, and went out on the balcony. I sat there in the dark for a long time, sipping my drink and smoking cigarettes and watching the play of lights over the harbor.

After awhile I went to bed.

My pillow smelled like Alex's hair. I stared up at the ceiling. It took a while, but eventually I fell asleep.

The next morning I noticed that the light on my answering machine was blinking. I had forgotten to check it when I got home after my day of house-hunting with Alex.

I pressed the button. The machine whirred. Then a voice said, "Mr. Coyne, this is Brenda Falconer. Glen's wife. It's Sunday, around three in the afternoon. Something has happened. The Senator wants you to call him at home."

17

I poured a mug of coffee, lit a cigarette, and dialed Roger Falconer's number in Lincoln. After several rings, a woman's voice said, "Yes?"

"May I speak with Roger?"

"Who's calling?"

"It's Brady Coyne. Is this Brenda?"

"Yes. I'm sorry. I was sleeping. I had a late night." She paused, and I heard rustling noises that suggested she was sitting up in bed. "Thanks for calling back. The Senator's not here. I know he's eager to talk to you."

"Your message said something had happened."

"Oh, geez. You don't know."

"Know what?"

"Glen's in the hospital."

"What happened?"

"We're not sure. It was a bicycle accident. He's—he's in bad shape."

"How bad?"

"He's been unconscious since they found him. That was Sunday morning. He's got a fractured skull, broken pelvis, internal injuries."

"He was on his bike?"

I heard a short, ironic laugh. "Yes. He was apparently driving drunk again, only this time he didn't kill anybody except maybe himself. Since his last, um, accident, he's stopped driving automobiles. He's too weak to quit drinking, so he quit driving. He pedals around the back roads of Lincoln and Concord and Sudbury to the houses of people who will give him booze, and to bars and restaurants, and he gets plastered and brags about staying out of prison and talks about driving automobiles again pretty soon, and then he wobbles home. Saturday night he didn't make it. Some joggers found him in the morning, lying in the weeds beside the road near the river at Nine Acre Corner. They figure he'd been there for several hours, bleeding and his brain swelling." She blew out a breath. "I'm sorry to rattle on like this. It's been pretty stressful around here lately."

"Where is he?" I said.

"Emerson Hospital. His father spent the night there. He'd like to see you."

"Why does he want to see me?"

"I don't know, Mr. Coyne. I think he just needs comforting, and there's nobody else to give it to him."

I inferred that either Roger's daughter-in-law lacked the inclination to offer him comfort, or he lacked the inclination to accept it from her. "Okay," I said. "I'll be there in an hour."

I called the office and left a message on the machine, telling Julie that something had come up and I'd probably not get in much before noontime. Then I showered, got dressed, and took a mug of coffee down to my car.

I pulled into the visitors' lot at Emerson Hospital in Concord a little after eight. The woman at the desk said Glen Falconer was in the intensive care unit and told me how to find it.

Roger was sprawled on a chair in the waiting room. His legs were stretched out in front of him and his arms were folded across his chest and his head was thrown back. He was wearing a wrinkled seersucker suit. His necktie was pulled loose around his neck, and he looked more like someone who'd just crawled in from a bench on the Common than a man people called "Senator" out of respect for his power and wealth. His mouth was open and his eyes were closed and white whiskers sprouted on his jaw, and for the first time in my memory he looked older than his years rather than younger.

I sat in the chair beside him and poked his arm. "Hey, Roger," I said in a loud whisper.

He mumbled something, took a quick breath, and sat up. "What?" He looked at me. "Oh. Brady. What happened? What time is it?"

"You want some coffee or something?"

"Huh? Oh. No. Did you hear anything?"

"I just got here. Brenda called. It's Monday morning, around eight."

"I must've gone to sleep. They don't tell you anything around here."

"I'm sure if there was any news, they'd tell you."

"He didn't die, I guess."

"I think we should get some coffee and breakfast. What do you say?"

"I should be here."

"I'll tell them we'll be in the cafeteria. If there's any news, they'll find us. How's that?"

He shrugged. "Sure. Okay."

So I found a nurse and told her where we'd be, and then I took Roger's arm and steered him down the elevator to the cafeteria. I sat him at a table and then got coffee, juice, and muffins for both of us.

"I've been here since yesterday morning," he told me as he spread butter on his muffin. "They treat me like . . . " He shook his head.

"They probably treat you the same way they treat everybody else," I said. "Their job is to take care of the sick people."

He looked up at me and nodded. "He's going to have brain damage, even if he lives. He may stay unconscious for a long time. Maybe forever. They'll try to keep him alive with machines. They think his kidneys might be lacerated or something."

638

I touched his arm. "I'm sorry."

He picked up his muffin, looked at it, and then put it down. "I've been thinking about it," he said. "I think he wanted this to happen. I think that's why he kept getting drunk and riding his bike around at night. He wanted something to happen to him, the way something happened to that woman he hit." He sighed. "My son isn't much, I know. He's never accomplished anything, and he's a drunk. But, as your friend Cizek was so quick to tell everybody who'd listen, it wasn't Glen's fault."

"It wasn't?"

"No. It was mine."

"I bumped into Glen at a restaurant last week," I said. "He didn't seem particularly remorseful."

Roger nodded. "It's hard to be objective about one's own son. But I love him."

"What *did* happen, do they know?"

Roger shook his head. "I haven't talked to anybody. The police called and said he was here, so I came over, and I've been here ever since. The only people I've talked to have been doctors and nurses. The best they've been able to tell me is that he hasn't died yet."

We finished our skimpy breakfasts, and Roger wanted to go back to the ICU. I convinced him we'd do just as well waiting in the cafeteria for awhile, so I went back and joined the line to get us more coffee.

When I returned to the table, a black-haired fortyish man in a business suit was sitting with Roger. They both looked up at me, as if I'd interrupted something. I slid Roger's cup of coffee in front of him, then sat down.

"This is Brady Coyne," said Roger to the other guy. "He's my attorney."

"Dick Carlson," said the man, extending his hand. "Concord police."

"Lieutenant Carlson's a detective," said Roger.

I shook Carlson's hand.

"Start over," said Roger to Carlson. "I want Brady to hear it."

Carlson nodded, then turned to me. He had sharp gray eyes and a mouth that seemed too small for his face. "Basically," he said, "it looks like a hit and run. We think a car traveling at a high rate of speed ran into him head-on and kept going. There's no other way to explain it. The, um, the extent of the injuries. The bike is completely mangled. Somebody on a bike'd have to be going about sixty and run into a brick wall for that kind of thing to happen."

"Head-on?" I said.

Carlson nodded. "Looks that way."

"He couldn't have just run into a tree or something?" said Roger.

Carlson shook his head. "There wasn't any tree. Just thick weeds. Oh, he'd have hurt himself if he took a tumble. Maybe broken an arm or something. But not a fractured skull."

"So what are you thinking?" I said.

He shrugged. "Kids out late driving too fast, maybe they've had too many beers, they come around the corner and there's this guy riding a bike, weaving down the middle of the road. They hit him, he goes flying, they panic and keep going." He shrugged again.

"Any way to verify that?"

"The state police lab has the bike. Maybe they'll find traces of automobile paint or something on it."

"What can we do?" said Roger.

"I don't know, sir," said Carlson. "Pray for your son, I guess. I just wanted you to know what was going on. We'll find 'em sooner or later. There'll be dents and scrapes on their car. If it was kids, their old man'll see it or someone's conscience will get to them. You can't keep something like that quiet for very long." He glanced at his wristwatch, then stood up. "I've gotta go. I'll keep in touch with you."

He shook hands with Roger, then with me, and started for the door.

"I'll be right back," I said to Roger, and I hurried after Carlson. I caught up with him in the corridor. "Excuse me, Lieutenant," I said.

He turned. "Sure. What is it?"

"I have an idea of who might've run down Glen Falconer."

"Oh?"

"Yes."

"You're thinking it wasn't an accident."

"Do you have a minute?"

"Sure. Go ahead."

I told him about Glen's trial and how Thomas Gall had threatened to "get" him and everyone else who he seemed to feel was responsible for the "not guilty" verdict. I told him how Paul Cizek had disappeared from his boat, and how I had seen Gall at Paul's house on Plum Island the next day. I told him that I believed Thomas Gall was carrying out his threat. I told him that Lieutenant Kirschenbaum of the Newburyport police was investigating Paul's disappearance.

Carlson leaned against the wall and listened, his eyes focused on my face. When I finished my story, he pulled a notebook from his jacket pocket. "Spell 'Gall' and 'Cizek' and 'Kirschenbaum' for me," he said.

I spelled the names for him, and he scribbled in his notebook. Then he looked up at me and said, "Falconer kills Gall's wife with a car, so Gall kills Falconer with a car. That's what you're thinking."

"Yes."

"An eye-for-an-eye sort of thing."

I nodded.

"Interesting," he said.

I shrugged. "It fits, doesn't it?"

"Easy enough," he said thoughtfully, "getting someone to take a look at this Gall's car. And I suppose somebody could check on where he was Saturday night."

"And where he was the night Paul Cizek went off his boat," I added.

"They didn't find a body, though, huh?"

"No. Not yet."

"It's been what?"

"A week ago Friday night."

Carlson shook his head. "Over a week, no body."

"I know. Anything could've happened."

"No body, no homicide," he said.

"At this point, they don't even know if there was a crime."

"Well," he said, "it sure looks like there's a crime here."

And if Glen Falconer died, I thought, it would be a homicide. Just as it had been when the woman Glen hit died.

It seemed too ironic to be a coincidence.

A half hour later Roger and I returned to the ICU. Brenda Falconer was seated in the waiting room with a magazine spread open on her lap. She was wearing a short blue skirt and a white blouse and high heels, and her hair was done up in an intricate bun, and she smiled quickly when she saw us.

I went to her and she held out her hand. I took it and said, "How are you doing?"

"Fine," she said, as if it had been a dumb question.

Roger sat two chairs away from her, folded his arms, and put his chin on his chest. Neither of them had acknowledged the other.

I stood there looking from one to the other, then said, "Well, I'll leave you folks to enjoy each other's company. I've got to run to the office. Let me know if there's any news, okay?"

"Sure," said Roger without looking up.

Brenda glanced sideways at him, then looked at me and nodded. "Thank you for coming," she said.

"You're welcome," I said.

18

I called Kirschenbaum at the Newburyport police station as soon as I got back to the office, and when I told him what had happened to Glen Falconer and how I thought Thomas Gall was making good on his threat to get revenge for the death of his wife, the lieutenant said, "Accidents *do* happen, Mr. Coyne."

"It's not hard to make something look like an accident."

"It's harder than you think, actually. Automobiles hit people on bicycles all the time. And we've investigated the Cizek thing pretty thoroughly, believe it or not. Now, I can't tell you whether he went overboard accidentally or on purpose. But we can't find a stitch of evidence that someone pushed him."

"If you had his body . . . "

"That could tell us a lot, sure."

"Isn't it unusual that his body hasn't washed up somewhere?"

"Well, yes, kinda."

"So don't you think *not* finding his body is a kind of evidence?"

He chuckled. "I get your drift, Mr. Coyne. Like the dog that didn't bark in one of those Sherlock Holmes stories. Sure. But that's a big ocean out there, and it's full of scavengers with sharp teeth, and tides and currents do funny things. I'll tell you the truth. I wish we had his body. But without it, and in the absence of evidence to the contrary, I'm pretty much inclined to believe Mr. Cizek had an accident. Accidents happen all the time."

"And murders don't?"

"Murders that leave no clues? Murders that are cleverly made to look exactly like accidents?" He laughed quickly. "Hardly ever."

"You released Paul's boat. Does that mean you've closed the case?"

"Mr. Coyne," said Kirschenbaum, "there was never any case to close. At least, not a police case. Without a crime, there's no case. We examined the boat. Looking for clues, like responsible policemen. The Coast Guard wanted to get rid of it, and it had nothing more to tell us."

"And the fact that Glen Falconer—"

"I'm trying to be patient with you," he said. "On account of you're a lawyer, and you're sincere, and you're really not too much of a pain in the ass. But I don't know what you want me to do."

"Somebody should talk to Thomas Gall."

"Sure. And every other individual who might've had harsh words with Cizek. You're right. One of 'em might've murdered him. And if we had evidence that there was a murder, we'd most likely interrogate every last one of them."

"Glen Falconer got run down, don't forget."

I heard him sigh. "I'll talk to somebody in Concord if it'll make you happy."

"Carlson," I said. "He's the Concord detective. Dick Carlson. I gave your name to him."

"I'm sure I speak for both Detective Carlson and myself," he said, "when I say thank you, Mr. Coyne, for all your help."

After I hung up, I lit a cigarette. I swiveled around to gaze out the window at the steel and glass and concrete of Copley Square. When I finished the cigarette, I picked up the phone. I pecked out half of Alex's number at the *Globe* before I replaced the receiver. I wanted to talk with her. I wanted to tell her what had happened to Glen. There might be a story there for her. It would interest her. We could discuss the implications. She could tell me whether I was crazy to think Thomas Gall was involved.

No. That's not why I wanted to call her. I really wanted to hear her say that she'd changed her mind. She'd canceled her lease on the post-and-beam home in Garrison, Maine. She'd decided not to take a leave of absence from the paper. She'd thought about it, and she'd decided she wanted things to stay the same. She liked it just the way it was. She liked how we took turns making dinner and how we played Trivial Pursuit, and although we kept our separate apartments, we slept together most nights and woke up together almost every day, and it was too perfect to change.

She wouldn't say that. If I called her, she'd be friendly and warm and she'd listen to my story about Glen and cluck sympathetically when I told her that the police were patronizing me, and we wouldn't talk about what was going to happen with us.

Alex wasn't going to change her mind, of course, and it was selfish of me even to wish that she might. If there was any mind-changing to be done, I'd have to do it.

I didn't know how much I could change.

I didn't talk to Alex all day. I wanted to call her, but I didn't. Even more, I wanted her to call me. But she didn't.

I knew she wouldn't be there when I got back to my apartment after work, and she wasn't. I heated up a can of Dinty Moore beef stew and ate it on the balcony.

I watched *Jeopardy* and tried to shout out answers before the contestants could. But I was slow and I felt stupid. Alex would've gotten most of them right.

At eight o'clock I snapped off the TV, went down to my car, and drove to Plum Island. I wanted to talk with Maddy Wilkins again. It was something to do. Better than spending a quiet evening alone in my apartment.

By the time I crossed the bridge to the island, the sun had set and the moon had risen. I turned left, crept down the narrow street, and then turned onto Meadowridge. I parked beside Paul's Cherokee, which was where Olivia and I had left it in the driveway.

The full moon lit the yard and the marsh out back, but the house was dark, and I felt a stab of disappointment. I realized I had been vaguely hoping that Paul would be there, and that he'd greet me at the door and offer me a beer, and we'd sit on his deck gazing out over the marsh and laugh at the big misunderstanding, and afterward I'd go home and call Alex and tell her all about it, and she'd laugh, too, and everything would be all right.

But, of course, everything wasn't all right. Paul was not there and Alex was moving to Maine.

I walked back to the street that ran the length of the island. Maddy had said she lived a couple of streets down, and I thought I recalled her waving her hand to the left. So I took a left. Short, sandy roadways similar to the one Paul lived on bisected this main street. The moonlight turned the sand white, and I walked down each of the little roads, and near the end of the third one I spotted an old yellow Volkswagen pulled up beside a cottage almost identical to Paul's. When I moved closer, I saw the bumper sticker that said, JUST SAY YO.

The house was ablaze with lights, and the bass throb of rock music thumped out of the open windows. I walked up to the front. A young couple were seated side by side on the steps. She had one arm slung across his shoulders. Both of them were holding beer cans, and they looked up when they saw me.

"Lookin' for Karen?" said the boy.

"Maddy," I said. "Maddy Wilkins."

He half turned his head and yelled through the screen of the front door, "Hey, Maddy! There's a guy here for you."

"Thanks," I said.

"No prob," he said.

After a couple of minutes, I said, "Um, maybe she didn't hear you? The music and all?"

"Why'n't you go on in," said the girl. "Maddy's in there somewhere."

I nodded. They edged over and I squeezed past them, pulled open the screen door, and went inside. The interior of the place was like Paul's, except that it pulsated with rock music I didn't recognize, and about a dozen young people were sprawled on the furniture and sitting cross-legged on the floor. Some were drinking beer and some held bottles of designer water. Their legs and fingers jiggled and twitched to the beat of the music, and not a single one of them was smoking dope.

Maddy was sitting on the floor leaning her back against a chair. The bearded young man in the chair was absentmindedly stroking her hair as he talked with the two girls sitting on the sofa across from him. It reminded me of the way Roger Falconer dangled his hand down to pet Abe and Ike, his retrievers.

I went over, and Maddy looked up. She frowned for an instant, then widened her eyes and smiled. "Oh, hi," she said.

"Hi, Maddy."

"Hey, want a beer or something?"

I shook my head. "I wondered if we could talk for a minute."

"Oh, geez, sure." She scrambled to her feet, came over, and took my hand. "Come on. It's too noisy in here."

She led me outside. We walked away from the music. She was still holding my hand.

"I remember you, but I forget your name," she said. "I'm pretty bad with names. I'm sorry."

"Brady," I said. "Brady Coyne. I'm—"

"I know. Paul's friend. Is that why you're here? You know something about Paul?"

I shook my head. "I'm afraid I don't. It's been over a week. I was hoping—"

"That I'd heard something?" She shrugged. "I haven't. It makes me furious, you know?"

"What does?"

"That he'd do that."

"You think—"

"That he killed himself? Yeah. That's what I think. He was a sad guy. Always moping around. I kept trying to cheer him up. You know, flowers and stuff. Some guys like flowers. But he was too far gone, I guess. I'd try to talk to him about making plans, doing stuff. You know, get him to think about the future? He'd just say, like, well, I'm not going to be here much longer. You know—"

"He said that?"

"What?"

"That he wasn't going to be here much longer?"

She nodded. "He said it more than once."

"As if he were going somewhere?"

She shook her head. "Well, that's what I thought. But it's pretty obvious what he really meant."

"That he was planning on taking his own life."

She squeezed my hand, then let go of it, hooked her arm through mine, and hugged it against her. "It's so sad," she said. "I go over every day to water the petunias. In this sandy soil, they need a lot of water. I keep thinking I should straighten up the place so it'll be nice for him when he gets back. But I know that's dumb. I mean, he's not coming back."

She continued holding my arm. I could feel her soft breast pressing against it. I gently pulled away. "Maddy, remember the man we saw in the street that day?"

"Sure. The big guy with the black beard."

"That's the one. You told me you'd seen him before."

"Yes. He was with Paul. They were sitting on his deck talking one night."

"You didn't hear what they were talking about?"

She shook her head. "When I saw that Paul had company, I just left. I mean, how was I to know who that man was? It might've been embarrassing if I'd walked up to them and sat on Paul's lap and gave him a big fat kiss, you know?"

"Is that what you usually did?"

"Sit on his lap and give him a kiss?" She smiled. "Sure. Geez." She cocked her head at me. "You're not, like, old-fashioned, are you?"

"Me?" I shrugged. "Sometimes I guess I am. I try not to judge things."

She shook her head. "I wish I knew what happened. The hardest thing is not knowing."

Olivia had said the same thing, I recalled. "So you don't know what they were talking about that night?" I said.

"Paul and that man?" She shook her head. "It looked like Paul was doing all the talking. I think he was angry."

"Paul was angry?"

"Yes. By the way he was sitting. Sort of tense and leaning forward. I didn't hear what he was saying, but I remember the tone of his voice, too. Like he was really giving it to him."

I took out my cigarette pack and held it to Maddy. She shook her head.

I lit one. "Have you seen him again?"

"That man with the beard, you mean?"

"Yes, him."

"No. Not since that morning when you were here."

We stood there in the moonlight. After a minute, Maddy said, "Why?"

"Huh?"

"Why did you come here tonight? Why are you asking me these things? Is something going on?"

"No, not really. It's just puzzling. He was my friend. Anyway, I just needed to get out of the house."

"Problems with the wife, huh?"

"Something like that," I said.

"Well," she said, "you should come on in and party with us. Cheer you up."

"That's very kind," I said. "But I don't think so."

"It'd be okay, you know. I mean, you being, um, older and all."

"Thanks, Maddy. Maybe another time. I've got to get going now."

She leaned against me, tilted up her face, and kissed my ear. "What is it with you older guys, anyway?"

"What do you mean?"

"You're all so sad."

"We are, aren't we?"

Maddy and I said good-bye, and I walked back through the moonlight to Paul's house. I found the key under the flower pot on the deck and went inside.

I turned on the light and looked around. Nothing had changed since I'd been there with Olivia a couple of days earlier. Dirty clothes still littered the floor. Magazines and newspapers were still strewn around the furniture. Mail was scattered over the top of the kitchen table.

It was the dwelling of a man with minimally developed nesting instincts. The cheap furniture probably came with the place. No paintings or photographs hung on the wall, no CD's or records crammed any shelves. There was no television or audio system. The few meals Paul ate here, I guessed, he either took out to the deck or gobbled over the sink. He obviously didn't sit at the table.

According to Maddy Wilkins, Paul had said he wasn't going to be around much longer. She thought he meant that he planned to kill himself.

People who intend to die soon don't bother building comfortable homes for themselves.

On the other hand, I'd lived in my apartment on the harbor for many years, and the spare bedroom was still full of unopened boxes and assorted junk. I tended to leave socks and newspapers strewn around the floor, just like Paul.

A calendar hung on the kitchen wall. The month of June featured black-and-white cows in a green pasture. Compliments of Skibbee and Fosburg Realtors.

I turned the pages back. Paul was not, evidently, a man who noted his appointments on wall calendars.

I started looking in one of the bedrooms. There was a single bare twin bed in the first one. On it were piled several fishing rods, a few tackle boxes, and a pair of rubber chest-high waders. Sweats and flannel shirts and foul-weather gear hung in the closet. Otherwise, the room was empty.

The medicine cabinet in the bathroom held razor blades, shaving cream, underarm deodorant, toothpaste, Rolaids, aspirin.

The second bedroom was evidently the one Paul used. There was a rumpled twin bed with the blankets thrown back. An alarm clock and a lamp and a paperback copy of *The Great Gatsby* sat on the bedside table. It had one drawer, which contained a bottle of aspirin, some coins, and the spare key to his car. It also contained a tube of KY lubricating jelly and a package of condoms. The tube had been squeezed several times and the condom package was almost empty.

I wondered what Olivia had thought, seeing that tube of "personal lubricant" and those condoms in there when she was looking for the car key, and again when she'd returned it to the drawer. Lieutenant Kirschenbaum had asked her if Paul was involved with another woman. Olivia, I recalled, had replied that she didn't know. But maybe she did. Maybe she'd known all along. Or suspected. Or didn't care.

Three medium-weight business suits, a couple of linen sport jackets, and several dress shirts hung in his closet, reminding me that Paul had been commuting to his office from this place. I rummaged through his clothes and found a sheer, lace-trimmed nightgown hanging among them. It was pretty apparent that Maddy—or somebody—had done more than sit on Paul's lap and kiss him. It didn't shock me.

I went back to the kitchen, sat at the table, and thumbed through Paul's mail, which, I inferred, Maddy brought in every day. No warning letters from would-be assassins, no ransom demands from kidnappers, no threats from blackmailers or clients or jealous boyfriends. Nothing personal whatsoever. No clues. Just junk mail and catalogs and magazines and bills.

I thumbed through the mail. There were two telephone bills and two bank statements, which I shoved into my hip pocket. Then I stood up, shut off the light, and went outside.

I was tucking the key back under the flower pot when something crashed against the side of my head.

19

I staggered forward and went down on one knee. Before I could shake the cotton batting out of my head, he was on me. A forearm clamped around my throat and bent me backward. I grabbed at it with both hands, gagging for air. It felt like a steel band crushing my larynx. White lights began to explode in my head.

Then, abruptly, he shoved me down and my throat was free.

I lifted myself onto my hands and knees, sucking in long gulps of air.

"Why're you doing this to me?" It was a low, harsh voice.

I turned. Thomas Gall was squatting there. In the moonlight his eyes glittered. His face was a shadow behind his bushy black beard.

I pushed myself up and slumped into one of the deck chairs. I rubbed my throat. "What are you talking about?" I said.

"If you don't leave me alone," he said, "I'll kill you."

"Mr. Gall," I said, "I've never even met you. I don't know what you're talking about."

But as I said it, I realized that I *did* know what he was talking about. I had mentioned him to both the Newburyport and the Concord police. I guessed that somebody, in turn, had mentioned me to him. I didn't figure he was clever enough to figure it out by himself.

I fumbled a cigarette from my shirt pocket and got it lit. I noticed that my hands were a little shaky, and the smoke felt harsh in my throat.

Gall stood up. He was a big man, taller than me and considerably bulkier. He held his arms away from his sides as if he had too many muscles to let them dangle straight down. He glared at me for a minute, then said, "Just get off my case, that's all. Okay? Get it? 'Cause I mean it. I'll kill you. I got nothin' to lose."

"I'm sorry about—"

He raised his fist. "Don't," he said quickly. "I don't wanna hear it. I don't wanna listen to you. You stay away from here, and you mind your own business, that's all. Understand?"

I nodded.

"I mean it," he said.

"I believe you."

He bent over and put his face close to mine, and in the moonlight I saw tears welling up in his eyes. He grabbed a handful of my hair. His mouth was twisting as if he were trying to speak. But no words came out. The tears began to overflow and dribble down into his beard.

Abruptly he let go of my hair. He straightened and held his hands up, palms outward, as if he were fighting against the temptation to hit me again. He stared down at me, then, without another word, turned and walked away. A minute later I heard the sound of an engine starting up, and I listened until it faded into silence.

I sat there on Paul Cizek's moonlit deck and finished my cigarette. Then I got into my car and headed back to Boston.

I didn't know whether to feel sorry for Gall or to fear him. Both, I decided. The man had lost his wife in a senseless, random way, and the person responsible for it had gone free. Grief combined with betrayal could make a man crazy.

When I got home, I found my apartment as empty as Paul's little cottage on Plum Island had been. The red light on my answering machine glowed steadily. No messages. Alex was not there, and she had not called me all day, and by comparison, my encounter with Thomas Gall somehow seemed trivial.

Since Alex had started spending a lot of time at my place, I'd tried to confine my littering of dirty clothes to the floor of my bedroom. The top of my kitchen table was generally cleared off now, because Alex liked to set places when we ate at it. I still left magazines and newspapers strewn on the coffee table and sofa. Alex did the same thing in her apartment on Marlborough Street.

I wondered what kind of a nest she'd build for herself in Garrison, Maine.

It was around ten-thirty. The same full moon that had lit up the sand on Plum Island shone down over the harbor. Alex would not be asleep yet. She had come over at ten or ten-thirty in the evening plenty of times. She loved to sit out on the balcony and watch the moon reflecting off the water.

It had only been yesterday that we'd driven up to Maine. It felt like it had been a very long time.

I was being stubborn and childish, waiting for her to call me.

I poured some Rebel Yell into a glass, dumped in some ice cubes, sat at the table, and dialed her number.

It rang several times before she answered.

"Did I wake you up?" I said.

"Oh, hi. No. I'm awake."

"How was your day?"

"Fine. Busy. You know?"

"Sure," I said. "Me, too."

I heard her chuckle.

"What?" I said.

"I didn't say anything."

"You laughed."

"Nothing, really."

"Is something funny?"

"If I laughed," she said, "it was not a laugh of humor. It was a small, wry laugh. The way one laughs at the ironies of life and the ways people try to deal with them."

"Listen," I said.

"What?"

I felt myself shaking my head. "Nothing."

We were silent for a moment. Then Alex said, "I'm sorry for making you sad."

"It's my problem."

"Yes, I guess it is. But when you're sad, I'm sad." I heard her take a long breath and let it out. "I can't *not* do this, Brady. If I didn't do this because I didn't want to make you sad, I'd always regret it. And I'd resent it. I'd resent you. Do you understand?"

"I want you to do it," I said. "It's not what you're doing. I'm happy for you. It's just me. I went to Paul Cizek's place tonight."

"Oh Brady . . . "

"No, listen. Back in the winter, he told me he was feeling discontented, unfulfilled. He didn't like the people he had to defend. I guess his marriage wasn't working. So what did he do? He left. He got himself a new place, a new life."

"And then—"

"I know. And then something happened. But my point is, he just did it. He made a change. I've got a lot more incentive than Paul had. To change my life, I mean. I've got you. So what's the matter with me?"

"It's hard, Brady. I think there's something wrong with people who do it easily."

"There's a beautiful full moon tonight," I said. "It's like daylight out there. You should see it on the water."

She chuckled softly. "I'm not coming over."

"I know."

"On September first I'm moving to Maine. I want you to always be in my life. So I need to know what you're going to do. That's all. When you figure it out, whatever it is, tell me. We'll take it from there."

"That's fair, I guess."

Neither of us spoke for a long minute. Then Alex said, "I'm sorry about the moon on the water. I bet it's pretty."

"It is," I said. "It would look a lot prettier to me if . . . "

"I know," she said quietly.

"Well, good night, Alex."

"Good night, Brady." She hesitated. "I'm glad you called."

"Me, too," I said.

I held the phone at my ear for a long moment after she disconnected. Then I hung up.

In a week it would be July. Then I'd have two months to decide what to do, to make my choice.

Or I could not decide. But that would be a choice, too.

Alex had already made her choice.

I got up and sloshed a little more Rebel Yell into my glass. I stood at the sliding doors and watched the moonlight dance on the water.

Then I went back to the table, lit a cigarette, and took Paul's phone bills and bank statements from my pocket.

Tearing them open felt vaguely criminal.

The first bank statement covered the period from April 15 to May 14. I recalled that Paul had moved to Plum Island sometime in March or early April.

There were just six canceled checks. One was for $476.27 to a bank in Virginia. A credit card payment, I guessed. To Skibbee and Fosburg Realtors, $1,200. Two months' rent, probably. One each for gas, electricity, and telephone.

The last check was made out to cash for $40,000. It was dated April 29.

Forty grand in cash. It left a balance of a little over $2,000 in his account.

There were five canceled checks in the second bank statement. One month's rent, $600; $329.40 for the credit card; the three utilities.

The monthly phone bills, for some reason, covered the period from the twelfth to the eleventh. The first one, from April 12 to May 11, itemized no calls. Nothing collect, no long distance, no credit card.

The second phone bill showed a cluster of long-distance calls between the fifteenth and twentieth of May. All to the 603 area code. New Hampshire.

One of the numbers had been called three times on three consecutive days. The rest had been called just once.

I wondered who lived at that number, and I wondered if that person had collected forty thousand dollars in cash from Paul Cizek, and if so, I wondered what it was for.

The next morning after Julie and I had reviewed the day's schedule, I gave her Paul's phone bill. "See if you can find out who lives at these numbers," I told her.

"Why?"

"Excuse me?"

"What's the point?"

"I don't know. I guess I want to know what happened to Paul."

"You think the answer is at one of these places?" she said, tapping her fingernail on the phone bill.

"Maybe. He apparently talked to several people in New Hampshire. Maybe he mentioned something to them. He took forty thousand dollars out of his checking account in April, then he made all these calls in May. He called one number three times in three days. Maybe he was paying somebody off or something. I don't know what I think right now."

"How do you want me to handle it?"

"Call the numbers. Talk to whoever answers. Don't mention Paul. See if you can get their names. Improvise."

"You mean lie."

"Sure. Lie. Make something up. Maybe you could be selling something. Lightbulbs. Newspaper subscriptions. Investments."

Julie grinned. "Sounds like fun. We haven't got anything pressing until eleven. We'll do it now. I'll go into your office. You stay out here and play receptionist."

"I can handle that."

She shrugged. "Maybe. It's not as easy as it looks."

She went into my office. I sat at her desk. I called Roger Falconer's number in Lincoln. His answering machine invited me to leave a message. I declined. Then I called Emerson Hospital. They connected me to the ICU. I identified myself as Glen's attorney, and a pleasant nurse told me that there was no change in his condition.

About an hour later, the phone rang and a button began blinking on the console on Julie's desk. I picked up the phone, depressed the button, and said, "Yes? Hello?"

"Geez," said Julie. "You're supposed to say, 'Brady Coyne, Attorney. May I help you?'"

"I'll never get it right," I said. "I'm just no good at this receptionist stuff. I guess I should go back to being a lawyer."

"Well, I'm awfully good at lying and wangling information out of strangers," she said. "Why don't you come in here?"

I went in. She had her feet up on my desk and a big grin on her face. I sat in the client chair across from her. "What've you got?" I said.

She touched the phone bill with the tip of a pencil. "I figured this number, the one he called three times in three days, might be the important one. But he called the other ones first, so that's what I did. I called them in the same sequence he did. There are six of them. He called four of them one day, two the next. Guess what?"

"Come on, kid. I don't know."

"All right. I checked the calendar. The first four calls were all made on a Sunday afternoon. See, it gives the date and time."

"And?"

"And the other two were the following morning. And guess what else?"

"Julie—"

"Okay. They're all real estate places."

I remembered how Alex had pored over the real estate classifieds in the Sunday *Globe*. I imagined Paul Cizek doing the same thing. "Peculiar," I said. "He'd already rented the place on Plum Island. What's he calling real estate firms for?"

"Well, I don't know," she said. "But I did find out that all these places are in Keene, New Hampshire. Except this number, the one he called three times. That's in Jefferson."

I nodded. "Okay."

"He made the first call that Tuesday. Then one on Wednesday and the last one on Thursday."

"Did you call it?"

"Of course. I said to myself, I bet this is also a real estate firm. Guess what?"

"Julie, for Christ sake, stop asking me to guess."

"I'm not asking you to guess. I'm just building the suspense."

"Consider it built. What'd you find out?"

"It's *not* a real estate firm."

I shrugged. "I don't get it."

"But it *is* a woman with a place to rent. And guess what?"

"Listen—"

"Sorry," she said. "The place has been rented."

"Could you find out when it was rented?"

"Yep."

"Sometime shortly after Paul Cizek called for the third time?"

"Bingo," she said with a snap of her fingers. "It's a summer place on a little lake. Very isolated. It's the only place on this lake. Comes with a rowboat, no outboard motor. Not winterized. She rents it monthly or for the season. May through September. Sleeps four comfortably. A couple of rollaway cots so you can squeeze in six. A nice little place for a couple or a small family to get away from it all. There's bass in the lake and a little swimming beach. Just four-fifty a month or two thousand for the whole season. That sounds pretty cheap to me."

"You learned all that?"

"Yes, I did."

"You're amazing."

"I know. I even found out where the place is located. Jefferson, New Hampshire, is about a half hour northeast of Keene. I told her that it sounded like just what we were looking for and we might want to rent it, but she said it was taken for the entire season, so I said we might be interested for next year, and she said why didn't we take a drive up there, check it out, and then we could call her back. She gave me directions. She said she didn't think the man who was staying there now would mind."

"A man is staying there now?"

"That's what she said."

"Jesus," I whispered.

20

Keene is tucked in the southwest corner of New Hampshire about equidistant from the borders of Vermont and Massachusetts. I'd been through it a few times, always on my way somewhere else, and I remembered it as a pretty little community, which, at around twenty thousand people, made it one of the most populous in the state. I figured the state college there inflated the population figure. When I checked the road map, I saw that no significant highway passed very close to Keene.

I located Jefferson an inch or so northeast of Keene. No red line on the map passed through it.

I left the office at four on Wednesday, went back to my apartment, changed into comfortable clothes, and joined the daily exodus from Boston at around a quarter of five. I slid a tape of Beethoven's Eroica Symphony into my cassette. It kept me company through all the traffic on Storrow Drive and Route 2 and ended around the time I reached the rotary in Concord. The Emperor Concerto took me from there to Keene, and I thanked Beethoven for the diversion.

The directions Julie had taken from the woman on the telephone were precise, and twenty minutes later I found the dirt driveway on the right, four-tenths of a mile past the barn with the rusty tin roof. It was marked by a slab of wood nailed to a pine tree with GALLAGHER hand-painted on it.

I turned onto the roadway, stopped, and got out of the car. The driveway sloped downhill through a meadow for a couple hundred yards, then disappeared into a pine grove. I could see the late-afternoon sunlight glinting off a ribbon of water beyond the pines.

I keep binoculars in the trunk of my car. I fetched them, then rested my elbows on the hood and scanned the place. I saw the outline of a cottage through the trees. Nothing else. No sign of movement or life.

I got back into my car and followed the rutted roadway down to the bottom of the hill. The cottage was tucked into the pines on the right. Vertical, unpainted cedar sides, a brace of big rectangular windows facing the pond, a brick chimney at one end, and an open porch across the front. An old Chevy pickup truck had been backed in behind it.

I pulled up next to the truck, got out, and stretched my legs. Nobody came out of the cottage to greet me, so I mounted the two steps onto the porch and knocked on the screen door. After a minute or so, I cupped my hands around my eyes and peered in through the screen, but I saw no sign of life.

"Anybody home?" I called.

After another minute, I decided nobody was home.

I wandered down to the pond and stood at the little sand beach. It was no more than fifteen feet wide, and about five feet into the water the sand stopped and the muck bottom began. A minimal swimming beach.

The sun was sinking toward the hills on the far side of the pond. It ricocheted off the water into my eyes. I used my hand as a visor and scanned the pond. I saw the silhouette of somebody in a rowboat coming around a point on the left, moving slowly toward me parallel to the shore. A long wake trailed out behind the boat on the glassy water.

I went back to the cottage. There were two sturdy rocking chairs on the porch, and I sat in one of them. The rhythmic clank of oarlocks echoed across the pond. Somewhere a crow cawed, and a chorus of bullfrogs grumped at each other. Swallows swooped over the water. Their wings ticked the surface here and there, leaving rings like rising trout.

The sound of the oarlocks grew louder, and then the rowboat appeared from around the corner. The bow crunched on the sand beach. Paul Cizek shipped his oars and climbed out. He stood there for a moment, shading his eyes, looking in my direction. Then he walked up to the cottage. He nodded at me. "Brady," he said. "It's you."

"Hello, Paul."

"So you found me."

"I guess I did."

He shook his head and smiled. He showed me the fly rod he was holding. "I've been doing it your way," he said. "Some nice large-mouths in here." He leaned the rod against the wall. "Towards evening when it gets shady along the shore, they come to the surface for popping bugs. It's really a lot of fun."

He had bare feet and a half-grown reddish beard with gray streaks around his chin. He wore a pair of denim overalls over a black T-shirt. From behind his beard, he was grinning at me. "Come on in. Let's have a beer."

I got up and followed him inside. The description of the place the woman had given Julie over the phone had been generous. It was a single room with a ladder leading up to half a loft. A galley kitchen at one end, a woodstove at the other. A round table and four wooden chairs sat in front of a window with a view of the pond, and three raggedy sofas—convertibles, I assumed—occupied the rest of it. It was far less messy than the place on Plum Island. I figured Paul hadn't brought enough stuff with him to make a serious mess of it.

"Nice," I said.

Paul bent to the refrigerator, then turned and handed me a can of Budweiser. "We can sit on the porch," he said.

We went back out and sat in the rockers. The sun had sunk behind the trees, and the surface of the pond lay flat and dark.

"You don't seem surprised to see me," I said, watching the birds dart over the water.

"I heard your car coming down the hill. Sound travels clearly over the water. I knew it was somebody."

"I rather thought you'd be amazed at my canny detective work," I said.

"I give you more credit than that, Brady. You've done many cannier things than track me down. After it was too late, I realized I'd left my mail on the table. I figured the longer my body didn't turn up, the greater the chance that somebody would start snooping. I didn't think it would be the police. In the absence of a crime, they'd have no reason. It wouldn't be Olivia's style. But I know you."

"I'm the snoopy type."

"Yup. You like to know things."

"Well," I said, "now I know."

"If it had to be anybody," he said, "I'm glad it was you. So what are you going to do about it?"

"Do? I don't even know what I know. All I know is, you're here. You didn't fall off your boat." I turned to him. "But you tried to make it look that way."

He shrugged.

"Olivia's a wreck, you know."

"I figured she would be. She'll get over it."

"She'll be relieved—"

"No," he said. "You can't tell her."

"That's not fair."

"Trust me, Brady. It's fair."

"You'll have to convince me of that, my friend."

"It's really simple. This was the only way I could make a clean break. I tried the Plum Island solution. It didn't work. I couldn't get away from anybody or anything. Old man Tarlin had me involved in a bunch of cases that I couldn't gracefully pull out of. Olivia was hurt and confused. I realized there was no half measure. I had to find a way to start over again." He sighed. "I told you last winter, Brady. I was heading for a crack-up. Since I've been here, I'm a new man. Paul Cizek is dead. I guess this makes no sense to you."

"Actually, it does make sense," I said. "I've been thinking of making some changes myself. But I doubt if I'd fake my own death to accomplish it."

"Don't knock it unless you've tried it."

"You've hurt a lot of people," I said quietly. "There has to be a better way."

"You think it's a cop-out, huh?"

I nodded. "I guess I do."

"Well," he said, "it's what I'm doing, and I can't help what other people think." He hesitated, then said, "Are the police investigating my—my disappearance?"

"No, I don't think so. Not actively, anyway. You're missing at sea, as far as they're concerned. Some day your body may wash up somewhere."

"Good," he said. "That's good."

"But I've got to tell Olivia, Paul. She's hurting."

He shook his head. "No way. If she knows, she'll be hurt and confused for the rest of her life. I expect now she's grieving. Fine. She'll get over that. I'm dead. Out of her life. It's done, and it's final, and she'll move on."

"I'd be irresponsible not to tell her."

"You'd violate my trust if you told her. You're my lawyer."

"I'm her lawyer, too."

"Since when do you tell one client's secrets to another client?"

"You put me in a tough spot," I said.

"No. You put yourself in a tough spot by coming up here. As your client, I forbid you from telling anybody what you found out today."

"Shit, Paul."

"Think about it."

"I guess I'll have to."

"All you've got to do is forget it and leave me alone. It's really simple. Consider me dead. Don't screw things up for me."

"It may be simple," I said, "but it's not easy."

"It *is* easy. Just don't do anything."

I thought of Alex. She was moving to Maine. I had to decide whether to go with her. "You're wrong about that," I said to Paul. "Choosing to do nothing is still a choice. Not telling Olivia would be very hard. It would be lying."

"It would be preserving our confidential secret. That's different."

"How about another beer?" I said.

"Sure." He got up and went inside, and a moment later he returned. He handed me another Bud. "I generally go to bed when the sun sets," he said. "I read for awhile. I go to sleep easy, and I sleep soundly, and I wake up with the birds. I put on some coffee and go for a swim, and then I come back and have a mug or two on the porch and watch the sun come up. I'm doing a little writing. Some of my old cases have given me short story ideas. I don't think they're very good yet. But I'm practicing. I row around the pond every afternoon. I practice my fly casting, or sometimes I just drift and dangle a worm over the side and catch enough perch and bluegills for a meal. I chop wood. I walk through the woods. Once a week or so I take the truck to the store and get some groceries. Nobody sends me mail. I pay for everything with cash. There's no telephone or computer or television. Just a little radio that gets a PBS station." He shrugged. "I'm trying to cut my life closer to the bone, that's all."

"Simplify, simplify," I said.

"Thoreau," he said. "Sure. Old Mister Midlife Crisis himself. I've been reading *Walden* as I sit here listening to the birds and smelling the pines and trying to stop frittering away my life in details. Henry showed us the way."

"Hole up in a cabin in the woods."

"Why not? That's what he did. He made a convincing case for it."

"Well," I said, "I do know some things about quiet desperation. I just don't see how you can run away from it. But if you can carry it off, good luck to you."

"I *can* carry it off, Brady. You're the only one who can spoil it for me."

"I'll think about it," I said. I gazed at the pond for a few minutes, then said, "Maybe you can answer a question for me."

"Maybe," said Paul.

"Is it Thomas Gall you're running from?"

"Gall?"

"Don't pretend you don't know the name."

"Oh, I wasn't." He sipped from his beer. I thought he wasn't going to answer me, but after a long silence, he said, "How'd you find out about Gall?"

"I didn't find out anything, really. Just that he'd visited you on Plum Island."

"He did," he said. "We got some things straightened out."

"The man threatened to get you."

"Well, as you can see, he didn't."

"He threatened me, too," I said.

Paul turned to me. "Huh?"

"A couple nights ago. At your place, when I found your telephone bills."

"He was there?"

I nodded.

"What'd he do?"

"He hit me. He grabbed me by the throat. He said if I didn't leave him alone he'd kill me." I shrugged. "That's all."

Paul chuckled.

"That's funny?" I said.

"No, not really. I was just thinking. You probably figured Gall had dumped me off my boat. You thought he was a desperate murderer. But, as you can see, he didn't do anything to me. Don't be afraid of Gall. He's all ripped up inside. But I don't think he's gonna kill anyone."

"He might've already," I said.

"Huh?"

"Glen Falconer's in the hospital."

"Falconer? What happened?"

"Hit and run. He was riding a bicycle."

"A bicycle?"

"Yes. He'd given up driving cars because he couldn't give up drinking. Someone ran him down last Saturday night. He's in bad shape."

"He was driving his bike while he was drunk?"

"I guess so."

Paul snorted. "That's pretty fucking funny."

"You think so?"

"Sure. In an ironic sort of way. Another vehicular homicide, DUI. Except now the drunk's the victim. And he's riding a bike."

"Irony isn't always funny," I said.

"Valid point," said Paul. "So you think it was Gall?"

"It makes sense, doesn't it?"

"Maybe it does," he said. "Still, I wouldn't worry about Gall. He's a mess. Anyone would be in his situation. If he ran down Falconer—well, I can see that. But he won't hurt you."

"I'm vastly comforted," I said.

We sat in silence. The darkness that had filled the woods was seeping out into the clearing in front of the cottage. After awhile, Paul got up and went inside. He turned on a lamp. Its light filtered out the windows onto the porch. It cast shadows around the cottage and made the sky look black.

From behind the screen door, he said, "Another beer?"

"No. I've got to drive home."

"Why not stay for supper? I'll fry up some potatoes, open a can of beans."

"I've got to get going. Thanks anyway."

Paul came back out and sat beside me. We were silent for a few minutes, then he said, "What're you thinking, Brady?"

I shrugged. "Nothing, really. I guess I'm just glad to know you're alive."

"Yeah, I'm alive."

I turned to him. "How are you really, Paul?"

"I'm healing." He smiled. "It's slow. I'm working on it. Good days and not-so-good days. It was good to see you, Brady."

"It was good to see you, too," I said.

"Don't come back, though, okay?"

"I wasn't planning to."

"Nothing personal."

"I understand."

I got up and went to my car. Paul followed.

"I almost forgot," I said. "I've got a message for you."

"You can't." He grinned. "I'm dead."

"Eddie Vaccaro says he needs you."

"Vaccaro?" He hissed out a quick breath. "I'm not what that son of a bitch needs."

"He thinks the Russo family's got a contract on him. He wants to go into the witness protection program."

"Did you advise him to go to the feds?"

"Of course. But he wants you. You're the only one he trusts."

Paul laughed quickly. "I hope Russo gets him."

"He thinks pretty highly of you."

"It's hardly mutual. It was defending guys like Eddie Vaccaro that made me fall out of my boat." He hesitated for a moment, then said, "Vaccaro went to you, huh?"

"Yes. He showed up in my office last week."

"Fuck him," said Paul softly. "You absolutely must not tell him anything."

"I won't," I said. "But I want to tell you, Eddie Vaccaro is a very scary guy. He made me take a fee so he'd be a legitimate client and I'd have to protect his confidentiality. I think he would've shot me in the eye if I'd refused."

"Yeah," said Paul. "He probably would've."

21

Charlie was waiting at our regular table at Marie's when I got there a little after noon on Friday. He was sipping coffee and peering through his reading glasses at some legal-looking papers, and when I pulled out the chair across from him and sat down, he looked up and said, "Where've you been?"

I looked at my watch. "I'm five minutes late."

He nodded. "Exactly. You're late."

"Shit, Charlie."

"Do the math, Coyne. Five minutes is a measurable percentage of your lifetime. You shouldn't waste it."

Charlie McDevitt is the chief prosecutor for the Boston office of the Department of Justice. He's also my old Yale law school roommate, fishing and golfing partner, and best friend. We help each other out from time to time in exchange for a lunch at Marie's. Usually it's Charlie who helps me and I'm the one who pays for the best non–North End Italian food in Boston.

But this time he'd invited me to lunch. I assumed he wanted something.

"Sorry I kept you waiting," I said. "But you're usually not so damned crabby about it. What's up?"

He took off his glasses, folded them, and tucked them into the inside pocket of his suit jacket. He slid the papers into his briefcase, which sat on the floor beside his chair. Then he put his elbows onto the table, rested his chin on his clasped hands, and looked at me. "Eddie Vaccaro," he said.

"What about him?"

"Exactly. What about him?"

"Is that what this is about?" I said. "Here I am, thinking my old pal wants to buy me lunch, talk fishing, reminisce about our days in New Haven, tell a few jokes, and what it really is, he wants to play quiz games with me."

"A week ago Wednesday," said Charlie, "at one-thirty-seven P.M., Edward R. Vaccaro, a killer in the employ of Vincent Russo, who, as you probably know, the Feebs have been trying to nail for years, entered a certain one-man law office in Copley Square. He emerged at four-forty-two. As you undoubtedly also know, a couple years ago this Vaccaro, who makes a pretty decent living by shooting people in the eye with a twenty-two-caliber automatic pistol, refused to testify against Russo, even when given the opportunity to exchange an almost certain life term in a federal penitentiary for immunity from prosecution and life membership in the witness protection program. He went to trial and, *mirabile dictu,* a clever Boston defense attorney managed to outmaneuver a contingent of federal prosecuting attorneys. Vaccaro went free. No testimony. No Vincent Russo."

"Charlie—"

"Very embarrassing," he said. "It looked like a lock. We assumed somewhere in the course of the trial, Vaccaro and his smart lawyer would see the light and come across for us."

"Paul Cizek," I said, "being the smart lawyer."

"And your client, right?"

I shrugged. "You know better, Charlie."

"Sure, okay. Client privilege."

"You don't have to tell me about Vaccaro," I said. "I know who he is."

"I'm sure you do," said Charlie. "You probably also know why he spent over three hours in your office nine days ago."

"I do," I said. "How'd you know he was there?"

"How do you think?"

"Oh, sure," I said. "He's being followed."

"Yes. And the reports come to me. And when I read that he appears to be lining up a new attorney, I figure something's afoot. And I want to know what it is. So when this new attorney happens to be the one guy who—"

"Charlie," I said. "Please don't."

"Vaccaro's a cold-blooded killer," said Charlie. "And Vinny Russo's not exactly your Mr. Rogers, either. He gets kids hooked on drugs. He pays money to have people murdered. He lures young girls into prostitution. He—"

"You don't have to tell me this," I said.

"How do you think it looks?" he said. "Vaccaro hires Cizek, refuses our deal, and Cizek gets him off. Then Cizek, who's your client, turns up missing, probably dead. And then Vaccaro shows up in your office? And it just happens that you are my best friend?"

"I don't know what you're thinking," I said, "but whatever it is, it's wrong."

Charlie sat back and shook his head slowly. "I'm sure it is, Brady. I don't like what I'm thinking. I want you to straighten me out."

"I wish I could."

"Meaning what?"

"I met with Vaccaro for about twenty minutes. I will not meet with him again. But for reasons that you should be able to infer, I can't tell you what we talked about."

"You accepted a fee from Eddie Vaccaro?" Charlie shook his head.

"Charlie, shit—"

He held up his hand. "I can imagine how it was, Brady. He's a frightening man. I don't blame you."

"Believe me, Charlie—"

"Forget it," he said. He cocked his head and peered at me. "This has something to do with Paul Cizek's death, doesn't it?"

"Tell you what," I said. "Let's order lunch. Then I'll tell you something. How's that?"

"You'll actually tell me something? Wow."

"Don't, Charlie. You know you can trust me."

He nodded. "I always thought I could." He looked around, lifted his hand, and a moment later one of the BU undergraduates who Marie hires to wait tables came over.

Her name was Ellie, and she wore a gold stud in her nose and a gold cross around her neck. She told us she was a physics major with a minor in music and an ambition to go to law school. Charlie told her the law was a fine profession, and I didn't contradict him.

Charlie ordered the cannelloni, and I settled on the antipasto for one.

After Ellie left, I said, "I can tell you that Vaccaro wanted me to deliver a message to Paul Cizek. I can't tell you what that message was."

"Wait a minute," said Charlie. "Didn't Vaccaro know that Cizek had died?"

"He didn't seem to believe that Paul was dead."

"And that's why he went to you? Because he thought Cizek was still alive?"

"Seemed peculiar to me," I said. "At the time."

Charlie sat back and stared at me for a moment. Then he nodded. "At the time," he repeated. "You've learned something since then."

"I wish I could talk about it."

Charlie began nodding. "Cizek isn't dead, is he?"

"If I'd known what was on your mind today," I said, "I'd have refused to meet with you."

"Paul Cizek is alive, and that's another secret you can't share."

"Let's talk about fishing."

"He's your client," said Charlie. "So you can't tell his wife, and you can't tell his law firm, and you can't tell me."

"We should try to get to the Farmington this weekend," I said.

"Or maybe head out to the Deerfield. We haven't been trout fishing all spring."

Charlie smiled and nodded. "Sunday. Let's do it."

"We'll talk baseball and mayflies. I've got some woman problems I'd like to tell you about. We'll play blues tapes in the car. All professional subjects strictly verboten."

"Agreed," he said. "On Sunday we'll avoid sensitive legal topics. But—"

He looked up as Ellie delivered our lunches. After she left, he took a bite of his cannelloni, smiled, and mumbled, "Mmm."

I speared an anchovy from my antipasto. "Can we change the subject?"

"I'd sure love to know why Eddie Vaccaro wants to see Paul Cizek," he said.

"I think it's a moot question."

"Why? If Cizek's alive—"

"I didn't say he was alive."

Charlie took another mouthful of cannelloni. "A week or so ago," he mumbled, "we arrested a guy at Logan Airport because he had a homemade bomb in his carry-on luggage. Crude thing. Couple sticks of dynamite, wires, battery. Probably wouldn't have even worked. Still, a terrorist is a terrorist. Big federal offense, of course, taking bombs onto airplanes. We read him his rights, and he refused counsel. Turns out he works in a bookstore in Salem. Bachelor. Lifelong Republican. A deacon in the Episcopal church."

"Classic terrorist profile," I said.

He smiled. "I talked to him. He didn't seem to understand that he'd done anything wrong. Claimed he had no intention of detonating it, or using it as a threat to hijack the plane, or anything like that. Said he just felt better having it with him. I said, 'How could having a bomb on an airplane make you feel better?' He said he hated to fly. He had this terrible phobia that a terrorist would blow up the plane. I said, 'If you're so afraid of bombs, how come you tried to bring one aboard?' And this guy looks at me with these innocent, puppy-dog eyes and tells me, he says, 'I called up the airlines and I asked them what were the odds of there being a bomb on the plane. About a million to one, they said. So I thought about that,' he says, 'and then I asked what the odds were of there being two bombs on the same plane. Infinite, was the answer. There'd simply never be two separate bombs on the same plane. It wouldn't happen.' "

"Charlie, wait a minute," I said.

He lifted his hand. "Listen. The guy is looking at me. 'Now do you see?' he says. And I admit that I don't. So he says, 'It's simple. If *I* bring a bomb aboard, I'm safe.' " He spread his palms and grinned.

"That's a pretty funny story," I said. "What's your point?"

"Does there have to be a point?"

"There usually is," I said. "So what're you trying to tell me?"

Charlie shrugged.

"If you think too much, you twist simple things around until they seem complicated. Is that it?"

"That would work," he said.

"I'm not going to tell you what Eddie Vaccaro and I talked about."

"I know. You already said that."

"Justice may be simple to you," I said.

"Basically, it *is* simple. It's making sure that people who commit crimes are punished."

"No," I said, "it's much more complicated than that."

"Lawyers are the ones who make it complicated. The law is simple."

"So why don't you just talk to Vaccaro?" I said. "Ask him what we talked about? It seems to me that would be the simple thing to do."

"Yeah," said Charlie. "We'd like to."

"So . . . ?"

"But last night our guys lost him."

"He gave them the slip?"

Charlie nodded.

"Well," I said, "here's something I can tell you. I don't know where he is."

"Yeah, but Paul Cizek might know."

"I can't help you there," I said. "Sorry."

"Yeah," said Charlie. "Me, too."

22

Charlie and I agreed to meet in the parking lot of the Papa-Razzi restaurant on Route 2 in Concord at seven on Sunday morning. We still called it "the place where the Howard Johnson's used to be," although the old HoJo's with the orange tile roof had been gone for several years. We'd leave my car there and take Charlie's four-wheel-drive van, and we'd be on the banks of the Deerfield River by nine. In June there are insects on the water, and trout feeding on them, all day long. Sulfur-colored mayflies, tan caddisflies, a few stoneflies. We'd fish till dark. We'd make a day of it.

We would discuss no business. When Charlie and I played golf we sometimes discussed cases or clients or judges or legal theory. But we had agreed a long time ago that trout fishing is too important, and requires too much concentration, to corrupt with business conversation.

When I got back to my apartment that Friday evening, I heated a can of beans and ate them directly from the pot at the kitchen table while I flipped through the current issue of *American Angler*. Then I wandered around the place, assembling my trout-fishing gear. We weren't going until Sunday, but I wanted to have it all ready. It took me a couple of hours to find everything and to decide what to bring with me and to pile it all neatly beside the door.

Then I sprawled on the sofa and turned on the television. My old black-and-white Hitachi gets only five channels, two with considerable fuzziness, and on this Friday evening in the middle of June I found three sitcoms, an old John Wayne movie, and, on Channel 2, a show on home repair. I left it on Channel 2. A man in a beard was demonstrating the art of laying hardwood floors.

Even when I lived in a suburban house with Gloria and my two young sons, I had never contemplated laying a hardwood floor.

I was, of course, trying very hard not to think about Alex, and the fact that she wasn't with me, and that this was the first Friday evening in almost a year that we hadn't been together, and that I was facing the first weekend in that amount of time without her.

Trying not to think about her, of course, didn't work. I might as well have hung a big sign on the wall that said: DON'T THINK ABOUT ALEX.

I held out until a little past ten. Then I switched off the TV, poured two fingers of Rebel Yell over some ice cubes, lit a cigarette, took a deep breath, and called her.

She answered on the first ring with a cautious "Hello?"

"It's me."

"Oh, geez," she said. "I was going to call you."

"You were?"

"It's Friday. You're there and I'm here. It doesn't feel right."

"No," I said. "It doesn't."

"I was screwing up my courage," she said.

"If I'd known that, I'd have waited. I was very nervous, calling you."

"Nervous?"

"I was afraid you wouldn't want to talk to me," I said.

"Oh, Brady . . . "

"You know what I think?" I said after a moment.

"I wish I did," she said softly.

"I think that not seeing you is confusing me. It's not helping me to clarify things. Not seeing you makes me feel as if the only important thing is being with you, that nothing in my life matters except that. It makes me want to just chuck it all and go to Maine with you. It makes me want to ignore all the other variables. Not seeing you makes this big hole in me where you belong, and it hurts, and it needs filling, and the simplest thing would be just to go with you. Except it's not simple."

"I know," she said.

"I could think more clearly if that hole weren't there."

"Do you think so?"

"Yes."

"I do want you with me, you know."

"Sure," I said. "I know that."

"You have talked a lot about changing your life. You know, the Montana dream. Simplifying. Focusing on important things."

"I have talked about those things, I know."

"I think you've been serious about it."

"I think I have, too. But I'm not sure. I've got to figure it out."

"My moving is forcing you to do that."

"If you weren't moving," I said, "I might never do anything. I might just glide along the same way, year after year, until I was too old to do anything. It's good that you're moving. It's forcing me to think."

"Well," she said, "do you think you'd like to have company?"

"Now?"

"Is it too late?"

"Hell, no."

"I'll be there in an hour."

Her cheek rested on my shoulder and her fingers played on my chest. Her bare leg pressed against mine. I stroked her hair in the dark.

"If I kissed you ever so gently," she whispered, "you wouldn't think I was trying to manipulate you or influence any decisions you had to make, would you?"

"No. That would be small-minded and foolish of me."

I felt her mouth move on me.

"Or," she murmured, "if I touched you—there, like that—you wouldn't misconstrue my motives?"

"No. Definitely not."

"Or—mmm—if I did this . . . ?"

"Jesus, no, Alex. Of course not."

When I woke up, Alex was gone, and the hole in my stomach had returned. She had brewed a pot of coffee, and a note was propped against it. It read: "Call me. A. XXOO."

Alex worked on Saturdays. She got up at seven, while I was still asleep, showered, and slipped out without waking me up. She spent all day Saturday in her little cubicle at the *Globe,* hunched over her word processor, polishing her Sunday feature. Every Saturday.

Come September, she wouldn't be doing that anymore.

Eight or nine more Saturdays. Then things would change.

Around noon I called the Falconer house in Lincoln and found Roger at home. Glen's condition had deteriorated. He'd been unconscious for nearly a week. There had been some encouraging signs on Thursday. He'd moved one hand and mumbled. Then his coma had deepened. Now there were indications of kidney distress. I asked if there was anything I could do. No, Roger said. There didn't appear to be anything anyone could do. Brenda was there. She was a comfort, he said.

As far as he knew, the Concord police had made no progress in finding the hit-and-run driver, Roger said. They'd promised to tell him if and when they did.

I called Alex at one, when, I knew, she generally took a break. Her recording invited me to deposit a message in her voice mailbox.

"It is I," I said. "If you're—"

"Mmm," her unrecorded voice mumbled. "H'lo."

"Pastrami on rye?"

"Corned beef on wheat, actually," she said. "With a big fat dill pickle."

"How's tonight?"

"Sure. Let's go out and celebrate."

"Celebrate what?" I said.

"Independence Day."

"That's not for another week."

"Our independence, I mean."

"Independence from what?"

"Convention. Expectation. The humdrum and the mundane. The slings and the arrows. The tumult and the shouting. The agony and the ecstasy."

"Oh," I said. "That stuff."

We ate in one of the upstairs dining rooms at the Union Oyster House. We had Bloody Marys and Alex ordered baked finnan haddie and I had oyster stew, all in the two-hundred-year-old tradition of the Oyster House.

I wanted to tell her all about Glen Falconer's bicycle accident and my visit from Eddie Vaccaro and my confrontation with Thomas Gall. A lot had happened in the week we'd been apart. I wanted to brag about how I'd tracked down Paul Cizek, and how I'd found him emulating Thoreau on a little New Hampshire pond, trying to live deliberately, to front only the essential facts, to suck out all the marrow of life, to drive life into a corner and reduce it to its lowest terms.

I also wanted Alex to know that I didn't envy Paul. Beneath his brave talk of simplicity, I sensed that he had not really escaped the quiet desperation that had sent him fleeing in the first place.

I couldn't tell Alex about Paul Cizek, of course. She was a reporter, and I was a lawyer bound by law and ethic to protect my client's secrets. Anyway, if we'd talked about Paul, we'd have ended up talking about me, and my own quiet desperation, and how a little post-and-beam home on a dirt road in Maine could work the same as a cabin on a pond.

Simplify, simplify.

Sure. Easier said than done.

★　★　★

Sunday morning at six o'clock it was my turn to slip out of bed while Alex was still sleeping, brew a pot of coffee, and prop a note against it. "Love you," it said unoriginally. I added several X's and O's.

It was a glorious Sunday in June, and Charlie and I fished from a little after nine in the morning until dark, and all the way to the Deerfield and back, and during our frequent time-outs, when we sat on streamside boulders to listen to the river and watch the trout feed on insects, we did not once violate our sacred agreement to avoid all topics relating to the business of the law.

We fooled some trout, and some trout fooled us. Neither of us fell in. A perfect day of fishing. We stopped for burgers and beer at a roadside pub in Charlemont.

During the long ride home in the dark I talked about Alex, how she was moving to Maine at the end of the summer, and how I was afraid I'd lose her, and how tempting it was to go with her.

All Charlie said was "Change is hard, Brady. Either way, it's hard."

I dropped him at his car in Concord and it was nearly midnight when I pulled into the parking garage under my building.

I sat behind the wheel for a moment. It was late and I was tired, that healthy fatigue that comes from a long day of wading in a cold river and fly casting in the sunshine and fresh air. The yellow fluorescent lights of the garage cast odd shadows on the concrete pillars and the rows of parked vehicles, and through the half-opened car window I heard the soft echoes of water dripping somewhere.

I sighed, got out of the car, retrieved my fishing gear from the backseat, and headed for the elevator. I was reaching to push the button when I felt something hard ram into the back of my neck.

"Don't turn around," came a raspy voice I didn't recognize from behind me.

"You got it," I said.

"Drop your stuff."

I let my rod case and waders and fishing vest drop to the floor.

"Okay. Over there. In the corner."

He shifted the gun barrel to my back and used it to prod and steer me around the side of the elevator shaft into the dark corner beside a parked minivan.

An arm went around my chest, pulling me back against a man who I sensed was bigger and bulkier than I. The gun barrel left my back for a moment. Then it was pressed against the corner of my right eye.

"Jesus Christ," I mumbled.

"Shut up," came the voice, so close to my ear I could smell the tobacco and garlic on his breath. The pressure of the gun barrel made my eye ache.

"You're not Vaccaro," I said.

"Nah. I don't shoot guys in the eye like that weasel. I shoot 'em in the back of the head. Civilized, you know?"

"Can you move the gun, then?"

He chuckled. "Sure. Whatever you say." The gun left my eye and jabbed into the base of my spine. "That better?"

"Yes. Thank you."

"Where's Vaccaro?"

"Is that what this is?"

"My uncle needs to talk to him."

"I don't know where he is. I hardly know him. I—"

The gun barrel rammed into my side. "Don't bullshit me, pally. He was in your office the other day."

"Yes. But that was the only time, and he didn't tell me where he was going. I have no idea where he is."

"So what did he say?"

"He just said he was looking for his lawyer. Not me. A friend of mine. He thought I might know where he was. But I didn't."

"That's it?"

"That's it."

"What else?"

"Nothing."

The man hugging me against him was silent for a moment. Then he said, "Uncle tells me to bump you, that's what I do. Right? This time he says ask you questions polite. So I do that. I do what my uncle says. You telling me the truth, no problem. Okay?"

"Okay."

"Uncle finds out you're lying . . . "

"I hear you," I said.

"We got an eye on you," he said. His arm moved away and then the pressure from the gun barrel in my back was gone. "You stay right here for awhile. Got it?"

"Yes."

"Five minutes."

"All right."

I heard his feet moving on the concrete floor, and I listened until the echoes faded and died. I took a deep breath, hesitated, then turned. The parking garage was quiet and eerie and empty. I went to the elevator, gathered up my fishing gear, and rode up to my sixth-floor apartment.

I flicked on the lights and dropped my gear onto the floor. "Alex?" I called.

There was no answer. I went into the bedroom. She wasn't there. I sat on the edge of my bed, and that's when I noticed that my hands were trembling. I fumbled a cigarette, got it lit, and dialed Charlie's number on the phone by the bed.

It rang five or six times before he answered.

"It's Brady," I said.

"Christ, I just spent a whole day with you. I just got into bed. I'm pooped."

"Charlie . . ."

He hesitated, then said, "What is it? What's this I hear in your voice?"

"I just had a gun stuck into my eye by someone who was looking for Eddie Vaccaro."

"Oh, man . . ."

"He said—"

"Vinny Russo," said Charlie.

"He didn't say. He mentioned his uncle."

"That'd be Vinny." Charlie paused. "You met one of Russo's thugs. Look, Brady, you don't know where Vaccaro is. Hell, nobody knows where he is. They're just checking out all their possibilities. Okay?"

"I didn't like it at all," I said.

"No. But I don't think you need to worry."

"Ever had a gun stuck in your eye?"

"No. Listen, Brady. They've got no reason to hurt you. They don't hurt people for no reason. Understand? That's not how they operate."

"I lied to him," I said. "I didn't tell him that Vaccaro wanted to turn himself in to you."

Charlie chuckled. "You didn't even tell me that."

"I'm telling you now."

"We already knew that, Brady. I'd guess Russo knows it, too. It's no secret. That's why everyone's looking for him."

"So . . ."

"So you've probably got nothing to worry about."

"Probably? Shit, Charlie."

"Don't worry. Nothing's going to happen. Go to sleep."

"Fat chance," I said.

Eventually I did get to sleep. It took a while. When I woke up, the sun was shining and the fear I'd felt down there in the gloomy, midnight shadows of the parking garage had faded. Only a tender bruise near the base of my spine reminded me of my encounter with Vinny Russo's hired thug.

I spent Monday in court and ran into my old friend Judge Chester Popowski in the lobby afterward. When I told him about my adventure in the parking garage, Pops insisted on buying me a drink. He echoed Charlie's advice. I had nothing to worry about, he said, and he made me believe it. By the time we parted it was too late to go back to the office. It was another beautiful June-almost-July afternoon, so I walked all the way home from East Cambridge to my apartment on the harbor.

I found myself glancing back over my shoulder from time to time. Nobody seemed to be following me.

I got there around six. Alex was on the balcony munching an apple. Her shoes were off and her bare feet were propped up on the railing and she'd hiked her skirt up over her knees. Her glasses were perched on top of her head and her face was tilted to the sky and her eyes were closed. I kissed the side of her neck.

Without turning or opening her eyes, she reached up and touched the side of my face. "You're all sweaty," she said.

"I walked all the way from the courthouse."

"Good for you. Gonna join me?"

"Let me change and get an apple of my own."

I did, and when I sat beside her and propped my own heels on the railing next to hers, she reached for my hand and said, "I drove up there yesterday."

"To the—your place in Maine?"

"Yes."

"Why?"

She took her hand away and ran it through her hair. "I just wanted to see it. To see that it was real. To see if it was the way I remembered."

"And?"

"I love it. It's perfect. And it makes me sad."

"Alex—"

She turned, leaned toward me, and kissed my mouth. "Let's not talk about it," she said. "We've already said everything." She stood up and threw her apple core out into space. We watched it arc down to the water. The splash it made on impact was barely visible from my balcony.

She rubbed her hands together, then smoothed her skirt against the fronts of her thighs. "I bought salmon steaks and fresh peas and baby potatoes," she said. "You stay here and relax. I'm cooking."

Darkness was seeping into the apartment and Alex and I were patting our stomachs and sipping coffee at the table when the phone rang. I didn't move.

"Aren't you going to answer it?" she said.

"No. I'm too comfortable. Let the machine get it."

After the third ring, the answering machine in the corner of the living room clicked on, invited the caller to leave a message, and then beeped.

"Oh, Brady," came Olivia Cizek's voice. "Oh, Jesus. You've got to be there. Please answer."

I got up quickly and picked up the wall phone. "I'm here," I said. "What's up?"

"It's Paul . . . "

"Yes."

"He—I talked to him. He wants to see us."

"Us?"

"Yes. You and me."

"When?"

"Now. Tonight."

"I can't do it tonight, Olivia. I've got company."

"I know you talked to him," she said. Her breath seemed to catch in her throat, and I guessed that she was crying. "He told me everything. I—he's frightened. He sounds—I don't know. Desperate. I don't—"

"All right," I said. "I'll pick you up. I'll be there in half an hour."

"Please hurry," she said.

I hung up the phone. Alex was sitting with her elbows on the table and her chin propped up on her fists, staring out the window. I went over and stood beside her. "I've got to go out," I said.

She nodded without looking at me.

I squeezed her shoulder. "It's Olivia Cizek," I said. "It has to do with Paul. I'll explain later. I'm sorry."

She pressed her cheek against my hip. "It's okay. Go take care of business."

"Will you be here when I get back?"

"I don't know."

23

The traffic was light, and I pulled up in front of Olivia Cizek's house on their suburban side street in Lynnfield a little after nine-thirty. Before I could set the emergency brake, the passenger door opened and she slid in.

"Let's go," she said.

I pulled away from the curb. "Can you tell me what's going on?"

"What's going on is Paul's alive after all and he's somewhere in New Hampshire and he's in some kind of trouble. He said you knew how to get there."

"Yes. I found him. I couldn't—"

"I know. He told me. He made you promise not to tell me."

"I'm sorry."

"It's all right. Please. Just hurry."

Olivia sat there staring straight ahead. I drove fast. I tried to start a couple of conversations, but she made it clear she didn't want to talk. After a while I slid a tape of Bach's first two Brandenburg Concertos into the player.

An hour and a half later I passed the barn with the rusty tin roof. I found the "Gallagher" sign and turned onto the long dirt driveway that wound its way down to the pond.

The two big windows on the front of Paul's cabin threw a pair of pale yellow parallelograms onto the pine needles. Otherwise the darkness was complete in the thick grove of pines. I pulled up in front, and before I could turn off the ignition Olivia had opened the door, jumped out, and run over to the cabin.

I got out of the car just in time to hear her scream.

She was kneeling on the ground with her head bowed as if she were throwing up. Her fingers were clawing at the pine needles. Her breath came in long, gagging shudders.

I started toward her. "Olivia," I said. "What—?"

She stood, ran to me, and threw her arms around me. "It's him," she said. "It's—oh, God."

I looked over her shoulder and saw Paul.

He was sprawled on the ground in the shadow of the porch, face-down, with one arm reaching into one of those yellow rectangles of light. The pine needles all around his body were wet and shiny with blood.

I held Olivia tight. She lifted her head, looked blankly at me for a moment, then buried her face against my chest. Her fingers dug into my back. Her shoulders heaved.

As my eyes adjusted to the darkness, I could see that Paul's side from neck to waist was drenched with blood. He was wearing the same overalls and T-shirt he'd had on the day I'd visited him, and his feet were bare, and his body looked shrunken in his clothes.

"He's dead," she whispered. "Oh, Jesus. Somebody killed him. He's dead." She was shuddering against me, and I held her close.

And then I realized that whoever had done this to Paul could still be around, lurking in the shadows, fully prepared to do to me and Olivia what he had done to Paul. "We've got to get away from here," I said.

"But what about . . . ?"

"We can't help him. Come on. Let's go."

"Shouldn't we cover him or something?"

"We've got to leave him that way. For the police."

She nodded. "Yes, of course."

I put an arm around her waist and helped her stumble back to the car. I opened the passenger door and guided her inside. Then

I went around the other side and slid behind the wheel.

I turned around and headed back up the dirt road. Olivia huddled against the door, hugging herself.

I drove back the way we'd come. I remembered a little mom-and-pop store at a crossroads a couple of miles before we'd come to the barn with the tin roof. There had been a pair of gas pumps out front and a Coke machine beside the door and hand-printed signs advertising live bait and cold beer. I thought I recalled seeing a phone booth.

The phone booth was there. I pulled up beside it and got out, leaving the motor running and the headlights on. I told the officer that I was reporting what I thought was a murder. I started to try to give directions, but when I mentioned the "Gallagher" sign he said he knew where the Gallagher cottage was. He asked me my name and told me to meet him at the top of the driveway.

I got back into the car. "The police are coming," I told Olivia.

I headed back to Paul's place.

"I thought he was dead," Olivia whispered. "Then he called. And he wasn't dead after all. And now . . . "

I couldn't think of anything to say to her.

I turned onto the driveway and stopped. A minute or so later a police cruiser with its blue light flashing pulled up beside me. The window went down and a cop leaned out. "Follow us," he said.

We drove down to the cottage. Two uniformed officers got out. One of them went to the cottage and played a flashlight over Paul's body while the other one came over to my car. Olivia and I were sitting inside with the windows open, and he rested a forearm on the roof, bent down, and asked if we were okay. We both nodded.

"You folks wait right here," he said.

After a minute, the one with the flashlight went back to the cruiser. I could hear him speaking into the two-way radio, and I heard the crackling voice of a dispatcher. Then he came over to join us. "They're on their way," he said, and he joined his partner in leaning against my car to wait.

A few minutes later I heard sirens in the distance. Their wail grew steadily louder, and then a line of headlights appeared on the hillside, weaving its way down through the trees to us.

First came another cruiser, followed by a rescue wagon and two unmarked vehicles. Three EMTs hopped out of the wagon and jogged over to Paul's body. A man in a sport jacket opened the passenger door and said, "If you'll come with me, please, Miss." He took Olivia's elbow and led her to his sedan. A guy wearing a suit with no necktie introduced himself to me as Lieutenant Capshaw. I accepted his invitation to follow him over to his car. We sat in the front seat. He kept the door open, and the dome light illuminated the inside of the car and made the outside seem darker. I related the events of the evening, beginning with Olivia's phone call to me and ending with my phone call to the police.

When he asked me if I could think of anybody who might be inclined to kill Paul Cizek, I said, "Yes. Several people."

I told him about Thomas Gall, who had threatened Paul in court and who I had seen twice at Paul's place on Plum Island.

I told him about Eddie Vaccaro, who was looking for Paul and who certainly was capable of blowing away a man who crossed him. Or maybe one of Vinny Russo's gunmen, trying to use Paul to find Vaccaro.

I even mentioned Roger Falconer. The old man might have found a way to blame Paul for what had happened to Glen. Anyway, Roger hated Paul.

Capshaw kept nodding and taking notes, and when I paused, he said, "How would any of these people find him? He was hiding out up here, wasn't he?"

"Paul might've contacted one of them," I said. "Anyway, *I* found him. I guess someone else could, too." I hesitated. "Shit," I said. "Somebody could've followed me up here the other day. I could have led Paul's killer to him. This could be all my fault."

Capshaw nodded. "So it could," he said. Then he turned to me. "You didn't do it, did you?"

"Me?"

"You and her." He jerked his head in the direction of the other sedan, where Olivia was having her own conversation with a police officer. "The wife. You and the wife."

"No," I said. "We didn't do it."

He shrugged. "I was just asking. Better to confess up front, you know?"

"Sure," I said.

"You two weren't—you know, having an affair?"

"No."

"What about her?"

"What do you mean?"

"Think she did it?"

"Lieutenant," I said, "for one thing, I am Olivia's attorney, so if I did think she did it, I wouldn't tell you."

He looked at me for a minute. "What's the other thing?"

"The other thing is, I don't think she did it."

"She could've, you know," he said. "She could've come up here, blasted him, driven home, called you, and brought you up here to witness her grief when she saw the body."

"That's interesting," I said.

He shrugged.

"If she's a suspect," I said, "I should be with her."

"If or when she's a suspect, you will be, Mr. Coyne." He paused. "Unless you are, too, of course."

They were photographing Paul's body where he lay on his belly. The flashes lit up the pine grove like summer lightning. Then they zipped Paul up in a black body bag and loaded him into the wagon.

They took Olivia and me to the police station in separate vehicles. They assured me someone would be following along behind in my car.

Capshaw took me into his cubicle, gave me coffee in a Styrofoam cup, and questioned me all over again, this time with a tape recorder. He asked me the same questions and I gave him the same answers. Then he thanked me and led me out into what resembled a small hospital waiting room, with plastic chairs and a stack of frayed magazines on a table. I smoked a cigarette and drank coffee and ignored the magazines.

After a few minutes, Olivia came out with her interrogator. She

691

stood in front of me, rubbing her hands together as if they were cold. "They want me to identify his body," she said.

"Jesus," I said. "You shouldn't have to—"

"It's okay," she said. "It's got to be done."

It was a fifteen-minute drive to the little country hospital. Olivia and I sat in the back of a police cruiser. The two officers who had been the first to arrive at Paul's cabin sat in front. Neither of them spoke for the entire ride, either to each other or to us.

They led us inside. I waited with one of them in the lobby while the other took Olivia to an elevator.

I asked the cop if it would be okay for me to go outside for a cigarette. He shrugged and followed me out. We leaned against the building.

"Rough one," he muttered.

"It's her husband," I said.

"Don't know how they can expect her to look at him. I never seen such a mess. Looked like both barrels of buckshot from about ten feet. The whole side of his head was blown away. Shit."

I turned to look at him. He was staring down at the ground, shaking his head slowly back and forth.

We were still standing there when Olivia came out. She was holding onto the policeman's arm. She looked blankly at me, then gave me a small nod. "We can go home now," she said quietly.

It was after three in the morning, and the New Hampshire back roads were empty. Now and then we passed a house where a single downstairs window glowed orange, and I imagined a farmer or a milkman or a fisherman sitting at his kitchen table drinking coffee and getting ready for his day.

I had turned off the tape deck. Olivia said nothing, and I didn't try to talk, either. After a while, her breathing became slow and rhythmical and I figured she was sleeping.

About the time I turned onto Route 2 heading east, Olivia cleared her throat, and in the darkness she said, "The wedding ring and the watch. I gave him the watch on our fifth anniversary. The ring's inscribed with our initials and the date we got married. I had the watch inscribed, too. It says, 'Stand by your man.' It was a joke. They had taken the ring and the watch off him, and they asked me if there was any way I could positively identify them. I told them what the inscriptions said. And then they asked me if I'd be willing to look at his body, and I told them I'd try. They had put a towel or something over his face and chest and said I didn't have to look if I didn't want to, and I didn't. I couldn't. But they'd removed his clothes, and I told them I didn't need the ring or the watch. I slept beside that body for almost ten years."

"I'm terribly sorry, Olivia" was all I could think of to say.

"No, it's all right, Brady." I felt her hand touch mine on the steering wheel. "It's not your fault."

"Maybe if I'd told you—"

"Shh," she said. "He made you promise not to. You did the right thing."

"I might've believed suicide. He seemed very depressed when I saw him. Struggling with it. Looking for answers. Hiding out in a cabin in the woods."

"Yes. He'd been depressed for a long time."

"He quoted Thoreau to me," I said. "The reason Thoreau went to Walden was to get away from everything and sort things out. His brother had unexpectedly died. Thoreau was probably pretty depressed, too, although you don't get that in his writing."

"Nobody murdered Thoreau," said Olivia.

24

The sky was turning silver when I pulled into Olivia's driveway, and when I turned off the engine I could hear the mingled twitters, chirps, and squawks of several different species of suburban birds greeting the new day. They were dissonant and arrhythmic, like an orchestra warming up, but beautiful and comforting, too.

Olivia sat beside me looking at her house.

"Is there somebody who can stay with you?" I said to her.

She nodded. "Oh, sure."

"Look . . ."

She turned to me. "I'll be okay, Brady. I accepted the fact that he was dead once. I guess I can do it again."

"If there's anything I can do . . ."

"I know. Thank you." She leaned to me and kissed my cheek. Then she opened the car door, slid out, and closed it softly behind her. She walked up the path to her front door and went inside without looking back at me.

By the time I got to my apartment, the sun had risen above the harbor and was streaming through the glass doors. I slid them open and sprawled in one of the aluminum chairs on the balcony. I closed my eyes and felt the warmth of the sunlight and the salty cool of the sea breeze wash over my face. My eyes burned and my head ached and my stomach sloshed with acid and adrenaline, and I couldn't figure out whether to make coffee or go to bed.

Bed, I decided. I prepared a pot of coffee and set the timer for eleven. Then I called the office, and when the machine answered I told Julie that I'd had an all-nighter, that I'd explain when I saw her, that I'd try to be in by noontime, and that she'd have to reschedule anything I had for the morning.

Then I went into my bedroom. The shades were drawn, and it was cool and dark in there. I shucked off all of my clothes and crawled in naked.

And only then did it occur to me that Alex was not there. She had decided not to stay. She hadn't even left me a note with *X*'s and *O*'s on it propped against the coffee pot.

I lay awake longer than I'd expected to, trapped in that fuzzy place between consciousness and sleep. I thought that if Alex had been there in my bed, all warm-skinned and languid and mumbling, and if I could have held her against me with my chest against her back and my belly pressed tight against her bottom and my arm around her hip and her breast in my hand and her hair in my face, then maybe those pictures of Paul's dead body lying facedown on the pine needles would have stopped flashing in my brain and I'd have fallen asleep much more easily.

It was nearly one in the afternoon by the time I got to the office. Julie looked up at me, grinned, and said, "You look like roadkill."

"Compared to my usual bright-eyed, incredibly handsome self, you mean," I said, trying to smile and doing a poor job of it.

"No. Compared to anybody." She cocked her head and looked at me. "What happened? Wanna tell me about it?"

I nodded.

"Another all-night orgy?"

"You flatter me," I said. "I haven't had an all-night orgy since college." I sighed. "No, this was not a fun night."

I sat beside her desk and started to tell her about it. When I got to the place where Olivia found Paul's body lying on the pine needles, Julie murmured, "Oh, that poor woman," and I remembered the tube of KY lubricant and the half-empty package of condoms beside Paul's bed in the Plum Island cottage. I thought of telling Julie that Paul had apparently been screwing Maddy Wilkins. But I didn't see what difference that made. Paul was still dead and Olivia still mourned him. So I left that part out, and about halfway through my recitation, she slapped her forehead and said, "That reminds me. Lieutenant Horowitz called. He said it was important. I almost told him he could get you at home. You better call him."

"I didn't finish my story."

"It's an awful story," she said. "I'm not sure I want to hear the rest of it."

"I want to tell it to you. But I guess I better call Horowitz first."

I went into my office and dialed Horowitz's number at the state police headquarters at 1010 Commonwealth Avenue.

"Horowitz," he growled when the switchboard connected us.

"Coyne," I said.

"Our colleagues in the Live-Free-or-Die state ask us to pick up a couple guys they want to interrogate, and when I inquire as to what the fuck it's all about, they mention a homicide and damned if your name doesn't pop up. So maybe you can shed some light on it for me."

"Thomas Gall?" I said.

"Yup. And Eddie Vaccaro."

"So did you pick them up?"

"We got Gall. Haven't tracked down Vaccaro yet. I guess we're not the only ones trying. The feds are looking for him, too. But we're doing the neighborly thing. It's New Hampshire's problem, and they've got no obligation to explain it all to us. Still, Paul Cizek used to be a helluva prosecutor, and then he became a big pain in the ass as a defender. But he was always an okay guy, and more or less a friend of mine, and when my friends get murdered it kinda bothers me, and when I'm asked to pick up people who might've done it, I get curious. So talk to me."

I told Horowitz everything. I began back in November when I

persuaded Paul Cizek to take Glen Falconer's case, and I told him how Paul had seemed depressed and confused when he'd miraculously gotten Glen off, and how Thomas Gall had threatened everybody connected with Glen's shocking not-guilty verdict, including the jury and the judge and, of course, Paul Cizek, the defense attorney, and Glen himself. I told him how soon thereafter Paul had left his wife and moved to Plum Island and then, a few months later, disappeared, and how I'd run into Gall when I went to Paul's place, and how Maddy Wilkins had told me that she'd seen Paul and Gall together. I told Horowitz how I'd tracked Paul down in New Hampshire, where he'd seemed edgy and still a little depressed and, in retrospect, frightened. I told Horowitz about my unsettling visit from Eddie Vaccaro and my subsequent, and even more unsettling, encounter with Vinny Russo's thug, and I told him how Glen Falconer was run down by a hit-and-run driver, and how Paul had been killed, and that I thought it added up to Thomas Gall avenging the death of his wife and the injustice that had been done in court.

When I finished talking, Horowitz was quiet for a moment. Then he said, "Yeah, okay. Makes sense." Then he hung up.

I held the dead telephone in front of me. "You're welcome," I said to it.

Sometime in the middle of the afternoon I called Alex's number at the *Globe*. Her recorded voice invited me to leave a message.

"It's me," I said. "If you're upset, I want to explain. I didn't get back until about six this morning, and there's no logical reason why you should have waited all night for me, and I don't blame you for leaving. But I was sad that you weren't there. It's important for me to know what you were thinking and why you didn't leave me a note. A note with an *X* and an *O* on the bottom would've reassured me, and I probably would've gotten to sleep quicker. As it was I lay there with a million random thoughts colliding in my head, thoughts about you all mixed in with thoughts about Paul Cizek, who, as you probably know by now, we found murdered in New Hampshire, and I don't know why I'm rambling on like this except I am feeling especially lonely, which death always tends to do to me, especially the death of a friend." I took a deep breath. "I love you. Call me, okay?"

I waited at the office until after six, but Alex didn't call. Maybe she's going to surprise me, I thought. She'll be waiting at my place when I get there. She'll have her feet up on the rail of the balcony with her skirt bunched up around her waist. Or maybe she'll be curled in the corner of my sofa, wearing my baggy sweatpants and watching the evening news. She'll be eating an apple or sipping from a bottle of beer, and there'll be a pot of lentil soup simmering on the stove.

But she wasn't there. The red light on my answering machine glowed steadily. She hadn't called, either.

Around eleven the next morning, Julie buzzed me. "Mr. McDevitt on line two," she said.

I pushed the blinking button. "What's up, Charlie?"

"Eddie Vaccaro," he said.

"What about him?"

"My guys found him."

"Well, good. The state police are looking for him, too."

"They already know," he said. "He was propped up in the backseat of a ninety-three Buick Skylark in the parking garage at Logan. There was one bullet hole in his left eye and another behind his right ear."

"Oh, shit," I said.

"Shit, indeed," said Charlie.

25

On Wednesday morning I sat in a conference room in the federal office building in Government Center with Charlie and two of his fellow prosecutors, one male and one female, and talked into a tape recorder. I told them what Eddie Vaccaro had told me as well as I could remember it—that he believed his boss, Vincent Russo, had a contract out on him, that the hit man was terrified that he was going to get hit himself, that he was prepared to give testimony against Russo in exchange for immunity and a slot in the witness protection program, and that he trusted only Paul Cizek to negotiate it for him. I told them what I had told Vaccaro—that I didn't know where Paul was, that as far as I knew he'd gone overboard and drowned, and that he should retain another lawyer.

I told them about having a gun stuck in my eye in my parking garage.

I told Charlie and his friends that a week after my session with Vaccaro I had found Paul Cizek living in a cabin on a pond in New Hampshire and that I told Paul that Vaccaro was looking for him.

A few days later Paul Cizek was murdered. "And now Vaccaro's dead," I said.

"Cizek was murdered Monday, right?" said Charlie.

"Yes," I said.

"Okay," said Charlie. "That's it." He gestured to the young man and young woman who had been sitting with us. "Leave us alone for a few minutes."

After they turned off the tape recorder and left the office, Charlie leaned toward me. "They found Vaccaro's body early yesterday morning," he said. "Tuesday. The ME tells us he'd been dead between twenty-four and thirty-six hours."

"That would be—"

"Sunday night sometime."

"About the time I got a gun in my eye in my parking garage."

Charlie nodded.

"Which means—"

"It means Vaccaro died before Cizek, for one thing," he said. "So he couldn't've killed him."

"It also means he might've been dead when that gorilla was asking me where he was."

"Yep," said Charlie.

Vaccaro's body, said Charlie, had been noticed by a young couple returning from a vacation in Portugal. The Buick Skylark was parked beside their Honda in a dark corner of the third level of the airport parking garage.

Cause of death had been one of the two .22-caliber hollow-point slugs fired from close range into his brain—one through the left eye, the other through his skull, just behind his right ear.

"That was Vaccaro's trademark, of course," Charlie told me. "The left eye and behind the right ear. The eye was always the first one. When Vaccaro killed a man, it was always with a message from Vinny Russo, the man who paid him. Eddie wanted his victims to see exactly what was happening to them. Make sure they got Vinny's message. So he gave them a bullet in the eye. Whoever hit Vaccaro was obviously delivering a message, too."

The Skylark was registered to Vaccaro's wife, whose name was Marie and who lived in Malden. The steering wheel, door handles, dashboard, and vinyl upholstery had been wiped free of fingerprints, although the technicians had found some partials on the frame that matched Vaccaro's and some smudges that might've belonged to somebody else.

There were bloodstains on the backseat where the body had been lying, but they found no skull fragments or brain tissue in the car, suggesting that the actual shooting had happened somewhere else.

They found no murder weapon, no note, no matchbook or cigar butt or lost wallet in the car. No clues at all, obvious or microscopic.

"The absence of clues," said Charlie, "being an important clue, of course."

"A professional hit," I said.

"So it appears."

"That's what he was afraid of," I said, "and that's what happened."

"And there goes Vinny Russo," said Charlie. "Down the tubes. And now we've got to try to find the guy who hit Vaccaro, and we'll offer him immunity, and see if we can't get him to give us Vincent Russo. Uncle Vinny knows this, of course. So he'll hire someone to hit the hit man before we catch up with him, and so it goes, round and round. Next time a professional killer shows up in your office, why not have Julie give me a call, huh?"

"I doubt if it'll happen again," I said.

Alex wasn't there when I got home that afternoon. I hadn't expected she would be. I changed into jeans and sat on my balcony. I smoked and stared at the sky. I thought of Eddie Vaccaro and Glen Falconer—one dead, the other close to it. And I thought of Paul, of course. He was dead, too.

I thought of Vinny Russo sending his henchmen out to find and kill a man who might've already been dead.

My mind kept switching back to Alex. I contemplated the ephemeral nature of youth and happiness and love and life itself.

Images of Alex kept transforming into Olivia and Maddy Wilkins. Paul had apparently been screwing Maddy. If so, Olivia must have suspected. She couldn't have missed seeing the evidence in the drawer of Paul's bedside table when she retrieved his car key and again when she put it back.

Where did Thomas Gall fit into this equation? A sad, grieving, perhaps desperate man. But a murderer?

Eddie Vaccaro, of course, was a murderer. But he died first. So he couldn't have killed Paul.

The pink afterglow of the sunset still tinged the sky over the Plum Island marsh as I pulled in behind the yellow Volkswagen with the JUST SAY YO bumper sticker.

I mounted the steps of Maddy's cottage. The inside door was open, and amplified guitar music came at me through the screen door. Jimi Hendrix, if I wasn't mistaken. I rapped on the door frame and called, "Maddy? Are you there?"

A minute later she appeared on the other side of the screen door. She was holding a can of Diet Coke. She wore a plain blue T-shirt and pink shorts. She squinted at me through the screen. "Hello?" she said uncertainly.

"It's Brady Coyne," I said. "Paul Cizek's lawyer?"

"Oh, sure." She pushed the screen door open. "Come on in."

"I need to talk to you," I said. "Can you come outside?"

She glanced over her shoulder, then turned back to me and said, "I guess so. Want a Coke or something?"

"No, thank you."

She came out and we sat on the front steps. "What's up?" she said.

"I want to ask you a couple of things, Maddy. It's very important that you tell me the truth."

"Oh, wow," she said. "Like a cross-examination, huh?"

"Yes. It's actually possible that the questions I ask you could be asked of you in court, under oath."

"I haven't done anything wrong."

I flapped my hands and shrugged.

"Are you trying to scare me?"

"No. I just want you to tell me the truth."

She hugged herself. "You *are* scaring me. What's going on?"

"I'll explain," I said. "First, I want you to remember everything you can about the man with the black beard who we saw the first day I was here. You know who I mean?"

She nodded. "I already told you everything. He was at Paul's place a couple of times. I saw them one night talking out on his deck." She shrugged.

"Did you hear what they were saying?"

She shrugged. "I don't know. I don't remember."

"It could be very important. Please try."

She squeezed her eyes shut for a moment. Then she opened them and looked at me. "Well . . . "

"Yes?"

"I wasn't spying on them."

"I know, Maddy. I'm not accusing you of that. What did you hear?"

"I didn't realize that other man was there when I went over. I didn't mean to sneak around, but I was barefoot, and it was dark, and I guess they didn't know I was there. I heard voices out on his deck, so I went around the side of the house, and when I saw that Paul was with somebody I stopped so they wouldn't see me. Paul was . . . he said something like 'Play it my way' to that man. And the man kind of nodded, and Paul said, 'Trust me.' "

"Are you sure that's what he said? 'Play it my way'?"

She nodded. "Maybe not those exact words. But something like that, because I remember wondering what they were planning to do. I do remember him saying 'trust me.' It struck me as pretty strange."

"What else, Maddy? Did either of them say anything else?"

She looked at me and shook her head. "Nothing. I left. It was obviously a private conversation."

"Did Paul ever mention that man to you?"

"No. Never."

"And you didn't say anything to him about seeing them to-gether?"

"Oh, no."

"Can you remember anything else?"

703

"Not really. I hung around by the end of Paul's street, waiting for the man to leave, and after awhile the two of them came out and walked to where the man's truck was parked. They shook hands and then the man drove off and Paul went back to his place."

"They shook hands."

"Uh-huh."

I paused to light a cigarette. Then I said, "Okay, Maddy. Just one more question, okay?"

"I still don't understand—"

"I'll explain, I promise. First, I want you to tell me about you and Paul."

"What about us?"

"Were you lovers? Were you sleeping with him?"

She let out a long breath that could have been either a laugh or a sigh. "Is that a crime?" she asked softly.

"No," I said. "But lying about it might be."

She was shaking her head. "I liked to pretend," she whispered. "I had such a wicked crush on him. I told my friends that I was sleeping with him, that he loved me, that he'd promised to marry me as soon as he got his divorce. Half the time I believed it myself. He was so nice to me, it was easy to think he really loved me. I wanted to take care of him. I wanted to hold him and kiss him and make him happy. He was so sad and tense all the time. I *knew* I could make him feel better." She turned to me, and I could see tears glittering in her eyes. "You know what I mean?"

I nodded. "I know about love, yes," I said. "Are you saying that you and Paul never slept together?"

"Not even close," she said softly. "He treated me like a daughter, not a lover. He took me on his boat a couple of times. He let me cook for him. He liked to talk to me about my future and my career and stuff like that. One time he kissed me on the top of my head. That was the closest we ever came. I mean, he already had someone anyway. It was stupid of me to—"

"Someone else?"

"Sure."

"Another woman, you mean?"

She nodded. "She was there a lot. Whenever I saw her car there I'd get this twisted-up feeling in my stomach."

"Did you ever see this woman?"

"Oh, yeah." She smiled quickly. "I—I kinda spied on them a couple times."

"What did she look like?"

"She dressed rich. You can tell expensive stuff, even if it's just a skirt and a blouse or something. She seemed very sophisticated, and she was beautiful. Tall, thin, blond. It made me sad, you know? Next to her, who was I? I knew I could never compete with a classy lady like that."

"Her car was parked there, you said?"

"Yes."

"Do you remember what the car looked like?"

"Sure. It was a really neat little white sports car. A two-seater. A Mercedes convertible."

26

"Maddy," I said, "I've got to use your telephone."

"Sure, but—"

"I've got to make a call. It's important."

She shrugged. "Okay. Come on in."

Jimi Hendrix had stopped singing, and a young woman was sprawled on the sofa eating yogurt from a cardboard container and reading a magazine. Maddy pointed to the telephone on the wall in the kitchen, then stood there watching me.

"I need privacy, Maddy," I said.

"Huh? Oh, sure." She went over and sat with her friend on the sofa.

I glanced at my watch. It was a little after nine. I pecked out the number for Horowitz's office at state police headquarters. Horowitz wasn't there. I asked to be patched through to him and apparently managed to make a convincing case for it.

I waited a few minutes, and then Horowitz said, "This better be damn good, Coyne."

"I think it is," I said. "Or pretty bad, depending on how you look at it."

"I don't need any fucking riddles. What do you want?"

"I want you to tell your counterparts in New Hampshire to fingerprint Paul Cizek's body."

"Why?"

"To identify it, of course."

"Yeah, why else?" He paused. "Wait a minute. That body's already been ID'd, hasn't it?"

"Mrs. Cizek identified it, yes."

"Then—?"

"Lieutenant," I said, "I could be wrong. If I am, I'm sorry. But if I'm right, then that body doesn't belong to Paul Cizek."

"I thought you saw it."

"I saw a body," I said. "It was facedown."

"You mean you never . . . ?"

"No."

He was silent for a moment. "No shit?"

"No shit."

"I think you better explain, Coyne."

"If I'm right, I will. If I'm wrong, you'll be too mad at me to care."

"You got that right, pal," he said. "Okay. I'll get back to you."

After Horowitz and I disconnected, I dialed Roger Falconer's number in Lincoln. Brenda answered.

"It's Brady Coyne," I said. "I need to talk to you."

"Okay. Go ahead."

"I think it would be better in person."

She hesitated. "When?"

"As soon as possible. It'll take me at least an hour to get there. Make it ten-thirty."

"What's this all about, anyway?"

"You and Paul Cizek."

She was silent for a moment. Then she said, "Yes. All right." She paused. "I don't think you should come here."

"I agree. You tell me where."

"How about the Colonial Inn in Concord? Meet me on the front porch."

"I'm on my way," I said.

Brenda was sitting in one of the rockers on the front porch of the Colonial Inn, gazing out over the village green. She was wearing tight-fitting jeans and a sweatshirt with a picture of Wile E. Coyote on the front of it, and she was smoking a cigarette.

I'd never seen her in jeans, and I'd never seen her smoking, and I'd never have pegged her as a Wile E. fan.

I realized I barely knew her.

I took the rocker beside her. "I wanted to talk to you before the police did."

"I haven't committed any crime," she said quietly.

"No," I said, "but several crimes have been committed, and I suspect you can shed some light on them."

"I don't see how." She flipped her cigarette away, then turned to me. "Sure, I was sleeping with Paul. Frankly, I don't much care who knows it. Roger might be upset, but Glen's beyond understanding or caring. Actually, Glen's been beyond understanding or caring for years."

"I'm certainly not judging you," I said.

She angled her head and stared at me for a moment. Then she nodded. "Okay. Good. Then I don't know what you want. It's a simple story, see? Glen's a drunk, and drunks don't seem to have much interest in other people. They love their booze, not their wives, and you can forget sex, because drunks don't, um, function. Paul Cizek was a sexy guy, and he wasn't a drunk. He was separated from his wife. We hit it off. We were attracted to each other. Very attracted." She spread her hands. "Then he disappeared, and that was that."

"You never heard from him after that?"

"I assumed he fell off his boat and drowned."

"He didn't. He faked it. He was living in New Hampshire."

Both of her hands went to her mouth. "That bastard," she whispered.

"Did you ever talk to him about Glen?"

She nodded. "Sure. He talked about Olivia and I talked about Glen. I guess that's what adulterers mainly talk about. Their spouses."

"Did you tell him how Glen had given up driving cars and was riding bicycles around the back roads at night?"

"Sure. We laughed about it."

"Did Paul seem unusually interested in it? Did he ask questions about it?"

She narrowed her eyes. "Oh, Jesus," she said. "I know what you're thinking."

I waited, and a moment later she said, "Paul asked me a lot of questions about Glen. He wanted to know when he went out on his bike, the roads he took, the places he went to. It seemed like—you know, pillow talk." She fumbled in her bag and came out with a cigarette. I took out my Zippo and lit it for her. She took a long drag and exhaled it out there on the porch of the Colonial Inn. The pale glow of streetlights illuminated the trees growing on Concord's village green. From behind us, inside the inn, came muffled laughter. "He was using me," she said softly. "Using me to get Glen."

"I guess he could've done it without you," I said.

"But I helped."

"For Paul," I said, "I think his relationship with you probably started as a way to get back at Glen. Paul hated the people he defended, hated what they did, hated the fact that they went free, hated himself for every not-guilty verdict he got. Having an affair with you gave him a measure of revenge against Glen."

She was nodding as I spoke. "I guess I was getting some revenge against Glen, too," she said. She laughed quickly. "It's pretty ironic. I was attracted to Glen because he was so weak and dependent and needy. It took me a long time to figure that out, but I did. I thought about leaving him. But I couldn't make myself do it. Because—well, because he was so weak, dependent, and needy. Then Paul Cizek came along, and at first he seemed to be Glen's opposite. He seemed strong and independent and self-sufficient, living out there by himself on Plum Island. But when I got to know him, you know what?"

I nodded.

"Paul turned out to be weak, dependent, and needy, too," she said. "And part of me felt liberated when I heard he drowned. Just the way I feel liberated now that Glen's probably going to die, God help me."

Horowitz called me at my office the next afternoon. "You got some explaining to do, Coyne," he said.

"It's not Paul, is it?"

"No."

"Who is it, then?"

"They haven't figured that out yet. But whoever it is—"

"I know," I said. "Whoever it is, it's Paul Cizek who murdered him."

"Not only that—"

"Right," I said. "His wife was part of it."

"We tried to find her," said Horowitz. "Her Saab is in her garage, but she's not home and she's not at her office."

"She's gone," I said. "And so is Paul."

"We're looking for them," he said. "Now. Explain."

"Here's how I figure it," I said. "After Paul got Glen Falconer off, he separated from his wife and moved to Plum Island, where he began an affair with Glen's wife, and—"

"Whoa," said Horowitz. "What'd you say?"

"Paul was having an affair with Brenda Falconer," I said. "And that gave him the idea of killing Glen. Or maybe he had the idea first, and that's why he began the affair. Either way, he faked his own death and disappeared. He was presumed dead. So no one would suspect him when Glen was run down. When I tracked down Paul, I told him that Eddie Vaccaro was looking for him. That gave him another idea."

"You think Cizek's the one who did Falconer, then?"

"Yes. And Vaccaro, too."

Horowitz paused for a moment. "Pretty good," he said. "He kills a few people. One of 'em he dresses up in his own clothes, and he arranges for his wife to ID the body—"

"He had to," I said. "Because the first time he tried to fake his own death, I tracked him down. This time he made sure I was there to see firsthand that he was dead."

"And you bought it," he said.

"Yes," I said. "I did. But I never really looked at him. All I could think of was that whoever blasted Paul could still be lurking around, and we should get the hell out of there and call the police. And Olivia . . . "

"Sure," he said. "She reacted like it was him. And then she ID'd him for the cops. Who'd think to doubt the bereaved wife?"

"Exactly," I said. "Especially if the family lawyer is there to more or less corroborate it. Hell, he was there at the cottage, where we expected to find him. According to Olivia, he'd called saying he was scared, needed help, come fast. In the dark it looked enough like Paul. Dressed like him, same size, lying there on his belly in all that blood . . . "

"Don't beat up on yourself," said Horowitz. "They fooled the cops, too."

"Paul put his ring and watch on the guy," I said. "That was to make Olivia's ID work. And he dressed him in his clothes before he shot him. That was for my benefit. Those New Hampshire police probably never laid eyes on the real Paul Cizek. It wouldn't matter if they eventually realized they'd made a mistake. The Cizeks would be long gone by then."

"As it appears they are," said Horowitz with a sigh. "How'd you figure this out?"

"I didn't exactly figure it out," I said. "Not really. But there were things that didn't fit. Like Thomas Gall, the obvious suspect. I bumped into him once. He was upset, all right. He hit me. But I ended up feeling sorry for the guy. He just didn't seem like a vicious killer. And it turns out that Gall and Cizek had gotten together a couple of times on Plum Island, had a beer. A neighbor of Paul's overheard them talking. It sounded like the two of them were scheming something. I figure Paul told Gall that he was going to take care of Glen Falconer. Glen would be the one Gall hated the most, so that'd satisfy him. He wouldn't need to kill Paul to get the vengeance he wanted."

"So if it wasn't Gall . . . "

"I thought of Eddie Vaccaro, of course," I said. "Turns out he died before Cizek. And that raised the question of who killed Vaccaro. Russo, logically. Except I know for a fact that Russo was still looking for Vaccaro around the time the ME says he was already dead. So not only did Vaccaro not kill Paul Cizek, but . . . "

"I getcha," said Horowitz.

"I was thinking of Olivia, too," I continued. "You always suspect the spouse, and people fool you, but Olivia loved Paul. I'm sure of that. Even if she knew he was shacking up with Brenda Falconer, I couldn't see her as a killer. Anyway, I thought, if it wasn't any of them, who could it be? Which led me to conclude that it wasn't anybody. Paul's not dead. He's not a murder victim at all. On the contrary."

"In which case," said Horowitz, "that body belongs to somebody else. Which is where this conversation started. And the question is, who?"

"Like I told you," I said, "I don't know. But I'd check the whereabouts of some of Paul Cizek's old clients."

"Victor Benton," Horowitz told me on the phone the next morning. "Turns out he's been missing since Monday. The fingerprints matched."

"Victor Benton," I repeated. "The day-care guy who Paul Cizek defended."

"Child molester, kiddie porn. A vile son of a bitch. Nobody thought Cizek could get him off. But he did."

"And then he killed him," I said. "He killed Eddie Vaccaro, too. Paul was doing justice. Killing the bad guys, making up for the fact that he'd defended them successfully." I took a breath. "I forgot to mention before. There's an old pickup truck parked beside that cottage in New Hampshire. You should have your forensics guys check it."

"The vehicle that ran down Falconer, you think?"

"I'd be surprised if it's not."

I heard Horowitz chuckle.

"This is funny?" I said.

"Not hardly." I heard him blow a quick breath into the phone. "We found a Chevy station wagon parked in the outdoor lot by the international terminal at Logan. It was registered to Victor Benton."

"That's the car Paul and Olivia used, you think?"

"Sure. He must've convinced Benton to go visit him in New Hampshire, where he murdered him. Then he scooted in Benton's car. You and her went up there and found Benton's body dressed in Cizek's clothes, wearing Cizek's jewelry, established that it was Cizek, and you drove her home, the grieving widow. Then after you left, he came by in Benton's car, picked her up, and they drove to the airport. Thing is, none of the airlines have any record of either of them taking a flight."

"Fake passports, huh?"

"Probably. Or maybe they didn't go overseas at all."

After I got home and out of my office clothes that evening, I called Alex. When she answered the phone, I said, "I've got a story for you."

"Don't, Brady," she said. "Please."

"Don't what?"

"Don't say what you don't mean."

"Okay," I said. "What I mean is, I miss you terribly and I want to fix things. But I do have a story for you."

I heard her sigh. "I had to leave the other night. I just felt . . . I don't know. Like it was never going to work. I'm sorry."

"Love is never having to say—"

She laughed. "I think I'm gonna puke."

"We've got to try to make it work," I said.

"I know." She hesitated. "So do you want me to come over?"

"More than anything."

"Shall I bring some lentil soup?"

"I love lentil soup."

"Brady—"

"Okay. I'll say what I mean. I don't particularly like lentil soup. But I love you."

"Do you really have a story for me?"

"I've got a story, all right."

27

Brenda Falconer called me on the last Wednesday in July to tell me that Glen had finally died. "His organs were shutting down, one by one," she told me. "Roger and I had already pretty much agreed that he should be taken off life-support. Yesterday his heart stopped and they couldn't get it started again."

"I'm sorry" was all I could think of to say.

Alex and I attended the memorial service at Ste. Anne's Episcopal church in Lincoln on the following Saturday. It was a small, private gathering. I saw none of Roger's old political or business cronies. We sang "A Mighty Fortress Is Our God" and "Onward Christian Soldiers," and the priest read some Scripture and gave a short homily on the subject of dying young and unexpectedly.

There were no eulogies for Glen.

Roger and Brenda sat alone in the front pew, and when the service ended, Roger leaned heavily on her as she helped him up the aisle. In the month or so since I'd last seen him, Roger appeared to have aged twenty years.

Alex and I met them outside. Brenda caught my eye. She lifted her eyebrows, a question and a request, and I nodded. I saw no purpose in mentioning Paul Cizek's name.

Roger's eyes were red and watery, and from the way he mumbled I suspected that he was taking tranquilizers. I didn't mention the fact that the police had examined the pickup truck beside Paul Cizek's cottage in New Hampshire and found traces of paint that matched the bicycle Glen had been riding when he was hit. I didn't know if the police had talked with him about it. If they hadn't, it certainly wasn't up to me.

Brenda said she was going to stay on in the big house in Lincoln to look after Roger, at least for awhile. If she saw that as penance for what she might've perceived as her sins, it was understandable. She'd told me she was attracted to weak, needy, and dependent men. Roger now appeared to qualify admirably.

I reminded her that Glen's estate would need settling. I told her to call the office within the next couple of weeks and we'd get going on it.

While Brenda and I talked, Roger leaned on her arm and stared at the ground. Once in awhile he looked up at her and nodded vacantly. She called him "Roger" with what appeared to be genuine affection, and he called her "dear," and it occurred to me that at least one good thing had resulted from Glen's death.

There was no return address on the envelope, but it was postmarked from Key West. I sat at my kitchen table and tore it open. At the top of the first page of the letter, Olivia Cizek had written, "Somewhere in Florida, sometime in August." Her handwriting was small and precise.

Dear Brady,

An explanation is overdue, I know. Or an apology. I lied to a lot of people. But lying to you was the worst. You were very kind to me.

I'm feeling guilty enough. But I want you to know that I had nothing to do with what Paul did, right up to that night when we went to his place in New Hampshire. He did not tell me he was going to fake his death on his boat. He certainly didn't tell me he planned to murder three men.

When he called that night, I thought he was a ghost. I guess I was so stunned I would have agreed to do anything. He made it sound simple. There would be a dead man at his cottage. You, dear Brady, knew how to get there. All I had to do was get you to take me up there. I'd say the body was Paul. After that we'd be together again.

It didn't seem wrong when he explained it. I didn't ask any questions. Like I said, I was so surprised and dazed I couldn't really think. I just called you, and you know what happened after that.

You must think I'm quite a liar, or a great actress. I'm not. Not really. All the emotions I felt that night were real. The whole thing was crazy. I guess *I* was a little crazy—first hearing Paul's voice, then hearing his plan, and then, dear God, seeing that body. I was in a daze the whole night. The lies just came out the way Paul had given them to me.

I knew he'd gone over the edge, of course. But I denied it to myself. And even after it was over, I kept trying to deny it. He killed evil men. That's what he said. They deserved to die, to pay for their crimes, and I tried to convince myself that it was okay, that he had made justice happen.

But it didn't work. I know what he did—and what I helped him to do—is wrong. I'm glad I know that. It means I'm not crazy.

I knew he was having an affair with somebody, although I tried to deny it. He told me it was with the wife of that drunken driver he defended. He saw it as a kind of revenge, or retribution, as if that made it okay. I can forgive the affair. But I can't forgive him for doing it out of malice instead of love.

Anyway, Brady, now I've left him. I don't know where he is. Wandering around the Caribbean in his sailboat, I guess. He's a man without a country and without a family and without a career, and even though I know he's done horrible things, I feel sorry for him. But I can't be with him.

I'm staying with friends for now. They know everything. I'm afraid they'll get in trouble if I'm found here, so I guess I'll have to move on pretty soon. Some day I know I'll have to face up to my part of it. I won't be able to live this way much longer. I'll need a lawyer, so you can expect to hear from me again.

But I'm not quite ready. Not yet.

I hope you can forgive me.

She had signed it, "Very fondly, Olivia."

I called Horowitz, and he came by my office the following afternoon to pick up Olivia's letter. He read it, smiled, and said, "Oh, well."

"Now what happens?" I said.

"Oh, I'll turn this over to the feds. We'll see."

"He could get away with it?"

"He's roaming around the Caribbean on a sailboat? I guess he could."

"What about Olivia?"

"Everyone'd like to get her story. Be good if she'd turn herself in. She might not even be prosecuted. Not under the circumstances. It wouldn't take a Paul Cizek to get a jury crying over her story. Hell, even you could get her off."

"Thanks, pal," I said. I shook my head. "It's not right, though. Paul murdered three men. And he betrayed a lot of others."

"Like you."

"Yes," I said. "Like me."

Horowitz shrugged. "The feds've got their priorities. Nobody's exactly clamoring for blood in this case. I'd guess that unless Cizek does something stupid, sooner or later everybody'll forget about it. Nobody's mourning the deaths of a hit man, a child molester, and a drunk driver."

"Doesn't that piss you off?"

"It doesn't matter if it pisses me off, Coyne. That's the thing that guys like Cizek need to remember. Do the job. That's all. Feelings just get in the way." He jabbed my shoulder with his forefinger. "You too. You should remember that."

I nodded. "I guess you're right."

At 8:00 A.M. on the day before Labor Day, Joey and a gang of his old high-school friends backed a rented Ryder truck up to Alex's Marlborough Street apartment. They had her stuff loaded onto the truck by eleven, and by six that afternoon it had all been unloaded into her new place in Garrison, Maine.

We ate takeout pizza and drank sodas on Alex's deck, and then the boys piled into the truck and headed back for Boston.

Alex and I lingered on the deck. We sipped the housewarming champagne I'd brought and propped our heels up on the railing and watched the color fade from the western sky.

"Your balcony faces east," she said quietly. "You can watch the sun come up. My deck faces west. I see it set. What do you make of that?"

"It's probably profoundly significant," I said. "But damned if I know why."

"One of these days," she said a minute or two later, "we're going to have to figure it out."

"The significance of east and west?"

"No. What we're gonna do."

I reached for her hand. "I can't just chuck it all," I said.

She gave my hand a squeeze.

"I've got my clients, my friends, my routines. It's usually not stimulating. But it's my life."

"I understand," she murmured.

"And once in a while I get a—a case. Like Paul Cizek. And it's stimulating as hell."

"That's okay, Brady," said Alex.

I turned to face her. "I didn't want to tell you until I'd worked it out," I said. "I'll be closing my office on Fridays, beginning in October. It'll mean working a little harder the rest of the week, at least for awhile. But most of the time I should be able to drive up on Thursday evenings. It's only two and a half hours."

"So we'll have long weekends together?"

"Things might come up," I said. "But, yes. That's my goal. Thursday night through Sunday. If that's okay."

"And if I have to write in the mornings sometimes, that's okay with you?"

"There are lots of streams and ponds around here to explore," I said, "and you'll have firewood that needs splitting and various domestic chores that will require the attention of a handy person such as I. I'll try to stay out of your way."

"It's not exactly starting over again in Montana," she murmured.

"Maybe some people can do this sort of thing all at once," I said. "Paul Cizek tried. He couldn't make it work. Even Thoreau, when he lived at Walden, kept going home to visit his mother in Concord. I just don't think it's that easy, leaving everything behind. Anyway, I know me. I have to feel my way along."

She leaned toward me and kissed me under the ear. "So how does it feel so far?" she whispered.

"It feels like a commitment," I said.

"Scary, huh?"

"No," I said. "Actually, it feels just right."